PETALS ON THE RIVER

PETALS
ON THE
RIVER

KATHLEEN E.
WOODIWISS

DOUBLEDAY DIRECT LARGE PRINT EDITION

AVON BOOKS ◆ NEW YORK

AVON BOOKS
A division of
The Hearst Corporation
1350 Avenue of the Americas
New York, New York 10019

Printed in the U.S.A.

ISBN: 1-56865-537-1

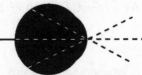

**This Large Print Book carries the
Seal of Approval of N.A.V.H.**

To my grandson, Seth Alexander Woodiwiss, who was the inspiration for the young boy in this book. Seth is so engaging and delightful to be around, I couldn't help but want to convey those kind of characteristics in Andrew.
I hope I was successful.

CHAPTER 1

Newportes Newes, Virginia
April 25, 1747

The *London Pride* chafed against the quay as the currents of a rising nor'easter slowly rocked the vessel on her cables. Close above her mastheads, errant clouds tumbled in darkening portent of an advancing storm. Gulls swooped in and out of the ship's rigging, lending their raucous cries to the rattle of chains as a double file of thin, ragged convicts stumbled up from the companionway and shuffled in unison across the weathered planking. The men, hobbled by leg irons and bound to each other by no more than a fathom's length of chain, were prodded into line for the bosun's inspection. The women were individually shackled and could move at their own pace toward the forward hatch where they had been told to wait.

Farther aft, a common swabber paused in his labors to observe the latter group. After casting a cautious glance toward the quarterdeck, he grew bold at the continued absence of Captain Fitch and his bovine wife and hastily stowed his mop and bucket before ambling across the deck. Strutting like a well-preened rooster around the shabby women, he provoked a near-solid bulwark of embittered glares with his leering grin and brash manner. The singular exception was a dark-eyed, raven-haired harlot who had been convicted of lifting the purses of the men she had bedded and of seriously wounding a goodly number in the process. She alone offered a promising smile to the tar.

"I ain't seen the bogtrotter 'round in nigh a week, Mr. Potts," the strumpet remarked coarsely, tossing a triumphant smirk toward her glowering companions. "Ye don't suppose the li'l beggar's gone an' caught her death in the cable tier, now do ye? 'Twould be a right fittin' comeuppance for biffin' me in the nose."

A small wisp of a woman with limp brown hair pushed her way out of the cluster of women and gave the harlot a crisp retort. "Ye can twist that lyin' tongue all ye want, Morrisa 'Atcher, but the lot o' us know m'liedy give ye no more'n ye deserved. The way ye jabbed her in the ribs when she weren't lookin', ye should've been the one what spent time in the chain locker! If 'tweren't for yer li'l lapdoggie here"—she indicated Potts with scathing abhorrence— "bendin' Mrs. Fitch's ear, m'liedy might've been allowed ta have her say."

Setting his beefy arms akimbo, Potts faced the small, feisty woman. "An' ye, Annie Carver, might've done us all a heap o' good fillin' our sheets with wind from yer ever-flappin' tongue. Ain't no question 'bout it, we'd have run ahead soarin' free on that gale."

The sound of dragging chains drifted up from the hold, claiming the swabber's attention. His small, beady eyes took on a sadistic gleam. "Well, blimey! I thinks I hear m'liedy comin' now." Chortling to himself, he lumbered toward the companionway and hunkered down to squint into the shadows below. "Eh, bogtrotter? Be it yer own bloomin' self comin' up from 'em lower chambers?"

Shemaine O'Hearn lifted seething green eyes toward the broad silhouette looming over the opening. For daring to defend herself against this oaf's shipboard doxy, she had spent the last four days isolated in a dank pit in the forward depths of the ship. There she had been forced to scrap with rats and roaches for every morsel of bread that had been tossed to her. If not for her sorely depleted strength, she might have clawed her way up the stairs and raked the tar's ugly visage with ragged nails, but heavy sarcasm was the most she could muster energy for. "And what other poor wretch would this smelly toad have come to fetch, if not me, Mr. Potts?" she asked, jerking her head to indicate the squat, little man who limped along beside her. "I was sure you had persuaded Mrs. Fitch to reserve those quarters for me alone."

Potts heaved an exaggerated sigh of displeasure, making much of her disparagement. "There ye go, Sh'maine, insultin' me friends again."

Her escort reached out and viciously pinched her arm for a second time since freeing her from the cable tier. Freddy was every bit as mean as Potts and needed no coaxing to take his spite out on anyone who couldn't fight back. "Watch yer manners, ye highfalutin tootie!"

"I will, Freddy," she gritted, snatching her arm away from his grubby fingers, "the very day the lot of you learn some."

Potts's gruff voice resonated through the companionway. "Ye'd better get up here an' be quick 'bout it, Sh'maine, or I'll have ta teach ye 'nother lesson."

The girl scoffed at the ogre's rapidly diminishing leverage. "Captain Fitch may have something to say about your heavy-handed ways if he intends to sell me today."

"The cap'n may have his say, al'right," Potts allowed, bestowing a cocky grin upon her as she struggled to make an ascent hindered by weighty iron anklets and chains. "But ever'body knows his missus has the final say on this here voyage."

Since being hauled in shackles aboard the bark, Shemaine had become convinced that no other place on earth was more akin to the pits of hell than an English prison ship bound for the colonies. And surely, no other person had done as much to advance that belief as Gertrude Turnbull Fitch, wife of its captain and only offspring of J. Horace Turnbull, solitary owner of the *London Pride* and a small fleet of other merchant ships.

With such a formidable reminder as Gertrude Fitch goading her to be wary, Shemaine paused to readjust a makeshift kerchief over her head. During several outings on deck, her fiery red tresses had incensed the dour-faced virago, causing Gertrude to berate the whole Irish race as a crass, slow-witted lot and to demean Shemaine as a filthy little bogtrotter, a derogatory appellation many an Englishman was wont to lay on the Irish.

"Don't ye dare dawdle now," Potts taunted. His pig eyes gleamed overbright, attesting to his penchant for cruelty as he eagerly watched for any infraction that he could pounce on.

"I'm coming! I'm coming!" Shemaine muttered testily, emerging from the passageway. The injustices she had suffered during the three-month voyage swept through her mind in bitter recall, sparking her resentment anew until she longed to spit a token of her rancor in the huge lummox's face. But experience had been a harsh taskmaster since her arrest in London, brutally convincing her that a coolheaded compliance was the only way a prisoner could ever hope to survive in an English court of law or on one of their hell ships.

Averse to revealing any hint of her waning strength, Shemaine managed to drag her encumbered limbs forward with a modicum of dignity. The scourging wind buffeted her, and she braced her bare feet slightly apart to steady herself and straightened her spine with tenacious resolve. The fresh air was a luxury that had become much too rare of late, and she lifted her head to slowly savor the salt-tinged essence of the coastal waters.

Potts's eyes narrowed as he noted the girl's stance. It seemed much too proud and undaunted to suit him. "Puttin' on airs 'gain, are ye? Like some high-flown doxy from court." Sweeping a hand downward to indicate her tattered garments, he brayed in loud amusement, "Beggars' court in Whitefriars, I'd be a-thinkin'!"

Shemaine had no difficulty imagining how pathetic she looked in soiled rags and iron fetters. Though her green velvet riding habit had once drawn envious stares from many overly pampered daughters of wealthy aristocrats (those same who had pettishly bemoaned her betrothal to the most handsome and possibly the richest bachelor in all of London), her present plight might have caused those same ladies to laugh in haughty pleasure.

Shemaine's forlorn sigh was certainly more heartfelt than feigned. Having known only a life of comfort and ease before her arrest, she had been thrust without cause into a vile prison where the pitifully destitute found naught but hatred, oppression and utter despair. " 'Tis indeed a dreadful inconvenience when a gentle-born lady must go abroad without her servants and couturier," she rejoined in satirical retrospect. "The attendants I've dealt with of late have no true ken of loyal service and cannot understand the simplest functions of a pursuivant."

Though unable to determine where an insult may have been rooted in her words, Potts was nevertheless distrustful. Her genteel way of speaking could make a bloke

feel out of sorts with his own tongue, especially one who had run away from home at
an early age after his widowed mother had
tried to curtail his roaming with ruffians.

Closing a massive fist around the chain
dangling between her shackled wrists, Potts
hauled Shemaine abruptly forward until her
entire vision was filled with the broad, be-
whiskered face of her tormentor and a red,
cyclopean eye. Even after enduring so many
hardships and abuse, the girl still refused to
yield him that very thing he craved most, an
undeniable feeling of superiority. "Ye mew-
lin' Irish bitch!" he snarled, cruelly yanking
her fetters. "Ye think ye're better'n me, don't
ye? Ye an' yer high-minded ways! Well,
ye're wrong, ye bog-Irish dung. Ye ain't
good enuff ta lick spittle from me boots."

Shemaine gagged at the rank stench of
the sailor's breath and could not help wincing as the iron bracelets bit cruelly into her
wrists. Almost from the first moment she laid
eyes on Jacob Potts, she had felt a sharp
aversion to the man. By mandate of the captain, the women's section had been restricted to all but the most trusted members
of the crew, but Potts had ignored the edict
and, with the pompous arrogance of a sultan

perusing his private harem, had paced outside their cell, tempting the more comely
ones with stolen food, fresh rainwater, and
other necessities until, in desperation, some
had given in to his perverted demands.
Their shame and humiliation had been ag-
onizingly shared by their cellmates, for no
one could escape the realization of what the
cad was forcing his victims to do. For those
who had turned away in disgust, Potts had
proven very vocal in his lecherous demands,
painting an obscene image even in the
minds of the most innocent among them.

A deep enmity had grown apace with the
swabber's clandestine visits, and except for
Morrisa Hatcher, who had worked her
wicked wiles upon him, Potts had soon been
shunned by all. But the harlot had served
her own purposes, exceeding his expectations, ensnaring him in a guileful web until
suddenly it was Potts doing Morrisa's bidding and appeasing her every whim.

*Persecuting her most dedicated chal-
lenger*, Shemaine mused with hostility.
Throwing caution aside, she dared to needle
the man. "If only *Mrs. Fitch* knew what
you've been getting as a reward for telling
your lies against me."

Potts's temper exploded. The little twit would relish setting that hag against him! "Ye'll not be tellin' her, wench! Or ye'll be gettin' more o' this!"

Laying back a brawny arm, Potts let it fly, catching Shemaine's shoulder just as she sought to duck and sending her reeling clumsily over her chains. His desire for revenge was hardly sated. He wanted to see her cringing before him in absolute terror. Spitefully he swept a canvas-shod toe outward to snare the links trailing from the leg irons, yanking her off her feet.

An indignant yelp of pain escaped Shemaine's lips as she sprawled backward against the deck's planking. In actuality the moored ship swayed only slightly against the quay, but for Shemaine, dazed and weak, the creak of timbers seemed to increase apace with the strengthening gusts and the heaving swells that passed beneath the hull until it seemed as if the deck had come alive. Casting a wary glance aloft to where the masts and spars spun in a dizzying blur against the whimsical countenance of a darkly brooding sky, she shuddered as her stomach convulsed at the strangely conflicting motions. Leery of heaving up what little she had eaten, she rolled over and lowered a clammy brow in the crook of her arm as she waited for her queasiness to ebb.

The bosun had turned from his inspection of the male convicts in time to witness the incident and, snatching up his cane, stalked forward irately. "Here now, Potts!" he barked. "Leave that wench be!"

"But, Mistah 'Arper!" Potts protested. "I was only tryin' ta protect meself afore this here adder sank her fangs inta me hide."

James Harper blew out a loud snort of derision. "Aye, Mr. Potts! And the sun sets in the east!"

"I gots witnesses, I do!" Seeking support for his fabrication, Potts glanced around for Morrisa.

"I'll hear no more lies from you or your lickspittle mate!" Harper retorted, raising the cane threateningly to lend emphasis to his words. A symbol of his authority, the stick had been used on many occasions to smarten dimwits and laggards. "Now listen well, you worthless swabby! I've had enough of your buffoonery! If the captain can't sell that prisoner for what she's worth, you'll be getting the best of this stick. Now help her up, damn you, and be gentle about it or you'll have a proper knot on your noggin."

Large hands slipped underneath Shemaine before she had fully regained her reason, but reality came washing hotly over her as the greedy hands cupped her soft breasts. With an outraged shriek totally unbecoming a lady, she rolled and kicked out sharply with a bare foot. Her haphazard aim was momentarily calamitous for the heavily endowed Potts. His pained yowl coincided with his backward, splaying fall, and as Shemaine scrambled to her feet, she had the satisfaction of seeing the fellow writhing in agony on the deck.

Prudence dictated that she remove herself swiftly out of sight and reach of the boor, and Shemaine saw a chance to accomplish that objective as some of the women hurriedly beckoned to her. Slipping quickly through their midst, she settled on the hatch cover as they closed ranks around her, concealing her from casual notice. Drawing her legs to her chest and pressing her face to her knees, she made herself as inconspicuous as possible.

Potts staggered to his feet and glared about him, consumed by a vengeful quest to vent his wrath upon the girl. Like an injured bull preparing to charge, he swung his straw-thatched head from side to side as his eyes flicked about in search of her. Through the drab, mundane hues of the women's tattered garments, he caught sight of a long red tress fluttering like a brightly hued pennant on a buffeting breeze. Curling his lips back from gnashing black-stained teeth, he growled and plowed toward Shemaine with evil intent.

"Potts!" James Harper bellowed sharply. He stalked forward several paces, for it seemed he would have to carry out his threat and beat the hulking loggerhead into submission. "You lay a hand on that wench and I'll see you flogged until your back is stripped of its hide! That much I promise you!"

The bosun's shout greeted Captain Fitch as the latter climbed to the quarterdeck behind his wife. Even as the call boy blew his whistle and announced, "Captain on the bridge!" Everette Fitch paused beside the rail to observe Potts's unfaltering advance on the main deck. Then his gaze swept outward, searching for the intended recipient of the sailor's assault until he spied the young beauty who had once rebuked him for what she and the other prisoners had regarded a deplorable injustice to one of their number. She had successfully claimed his notice with her scolding that day, but she had also, in her fervor to argue for another's rights as a human being, unwittingly kindled his lusts. From that moment on, Captain Fitch had found himself driven by a fierce yearning to enjoy all the delights Shemaine O'Hearn could offer a man. If not for Gertrude's stout stamina and iron-clad stomach resisting the doses of laudanum he had surreptitiously mixed in her wine, the girl would have surely paid the price demanded by his passion. His failure had only made him more desirous of having her, and Fitch had promised himself that upon their arrival in port he would covertly claim the wench for his own and ensconce her in a haven totally removed from his domineering wife. To disguise his infatuation, he had deemed it prudent to modify the punishments heaped upon Shemaine by his wife only when it became apparent that her life would be in jeopardy, but after Harper's warnings, it seemed reasonable to add his own thundering threat as a further deterrent.

"Cast that swabby in irons if he will not obey!" Fitch bellowed. Then he lowered his voice to a caustic rumble. "And should the blighter damage the wench, stripe his back with a score of lashes for every bruise she bears."

The stern warning finally penetrated the tar's thick skull, and Potts stumbled to a halt. Glowering at Shemaine, who had braced herself for flight, he ground out a garbled oath. "Mark me words well, bogtrotter. Be it a fortnight or even a year from now, I'll make ye rue the day ye laid me low, that ye will."

Shemaine kept her expression carefully passive, lest the slightest twitch push the man beyond the brink of control. She had escaped injury this time, but once she left the ship, if her new master couldn't defend her against this churlish lout, she would likely be found and severely punished.

"*Potts!*" James Harper shouted, commanding the sailor's attention.

Potts faced his superior, making no attempt to present a guise of respect. "Aye, Mistah 'Arper? What be ye wants now?"

The seaman's surly tone ignited Harper's temper, and he lashed out with a cutting retort. "A hanging from the yardarm for insubordination if I had my way!" He gestured angrily with his cane. "Now, you useless grog-sucker, get below! You've earned a three-day stint cleaning the mudhook's chains!"

"Come on now, Mistah 'Arper," Potts cajoled, waggling his head from side to side. "Here we be, 'bouts ta be given shore leave, an' I gots an itch in me crotch ta finds meself a doxy or two ta scratch meself 'pon."

"You'll stroll no further than the limits of the cable locker for the next five days," Harper rumbled, seething with rage. "*Now*, Potts, have you anything further to complain about?"

The pig eyes narrowed with almost tangible hostility, but the swabber had no choice but to obey or see his sentence lengthened by several more days. "Nary a thing, Mistah 'Arper."

"Good! Then report to the cable tier at once." Scowling darkly, James Harper briefly marked the huge swabber's progress, then signaled another seaman to follow and lock Potts in the forward compartment. Curtly dismissing the tar from mind, Harper faced the bosun's mate and lent his consideration to the matter at hand.

"The male prisoners've been accounted for, sir," the younger man announced as he handed over the list. Then he added for Harper's ears alone, "Minus the thirty-one what died en route."

" 'Tis an uncommon loss the *London Pride* has suffered, Mr. Blake," Harper muttered.

"Aye, sir, an' seein's as how ye begged the cap'n not ta let his missus limit the prisoners' rations afore we left, I figures ye gots good reason ta fret. Another week at sea an' there wouldna've been enough o' them poor devils alive ta pay for the crew's vittles, much less our wages."

Harper's jaw tensed as he recalled the numerous times he had been required to order the convicts' bodies hurled overboard, all because the ship's owner, J. Horace Turnbull, had grown suspicious of the *Pride*'s accounting from previous voyages and had insisted his daughter accompany her husband on this particular crossing to make a proper evaluation. Having given Gertrude unprecedented authority to examine the ship's ledgers, the old shipping baron had further instructed her to curb whatever costs she might consider superfluous, a mandate which had reaped dire consequences.

"One must imagine that when Mr. Turnbull gave his daughter leave to use her own judgments, he had no idea he'd be losing more on this voyage than in the last five years we've been delivering prisoners to the colonies. In her eagerness to save her father a few shillings, Mrs. Fitch has mindlessly managed to murder no less than a fourth of the prisoners. *That* should shorten the old man's profits by several hundred pounds, at least."

"If Mr. Turnbull thought there was thievin' goin' on afore this here voyage," Roger Blake mumbled grimly, "ye can bet he'll be thinkin' it for certain this time."

"And will no doubt send his precious daughter on the following voyage to take another accounting." Harper frowned at the gloomy prospect.

"Was Mr. Turnbull right, sir? Be there a thief among us?"

James Harper heaved a laborious sigh. "Whatever the truth, Mr. Blake, I prefer to keep my suspicions to myself." He shrugged as he added, "Still, if I were to discover the identity of the culprit, I'd be loath to ferret him out for Mrs. Fitch. She's made it evident she suspects us all of swindling her father."

"Aye, ta be sure, sir," Roger Blake heartily agreed. Mrs. Fitch definitely had a way of making an honest seaman feel less than worthy of respect and trust. Even the captain wasn't excluded from her criticism. She had, however, seemed peculiarly inclined to lend an attentive ear to the babble of Jacob Potts, although that vile tar had the distinction of being despised by their small company of officers and a goodly share of his shipmates.

Casting a glance toward the bridge, Roger Blake mentally laid odds that he would find the older couple locked in another verbal fray and smiled ruefully as he won his bet. The portly pair were at it again, and he knew by experience that Mrs. Fitch would not desist until she had gotten her way. Thankful that he was not encumbered with the likes of that great white whale for a wife, Roger returned to his duties.

Shemaine was able to enjoy a vague sense of relief after the banishment of Potts, but it was not long before the murmuring voices of the other women began to intrude into her awareness. Their fretting comments and morbid speculations on what further hardships they would experience under the authority of their new masters began to trickle down into her consciousness, heightening her dread with a pungent taste of grim reality. Despite the adversities she had been forced to endure since leaving England, she had sought to bolster her courage by clinging to a frail fragment of hope that, by some miracle, her parents or even her fiancé would find out where she had been taken and arrive in time to save her from the fate of being sold as an indentured servant. But as yet, no beloved face had appeared and only a few moments remained before that humiliating event was set to begin.

Shemaine ran her slender fingers beneath the iron band that encircled her wrist in an effort to ease the constant chafing. It was cruel irony that she was even there, but after sipping the bitter draught of English justice firsthand she had ceased to believe that she was the only prisoner aboard the *Pride* who had been unjustly condemned. Others had received equally harsh sentences for nothing more dastardly than stealing a loaf of bread or expressing a political view, which some of the young Irish hotbloods were wont to do. In spite of the frailty of their crimes and the sheer absurdity of their convictions, their departure as unsavory rabble from the shores of England had been expedited by pompous, bewigged magistrates who had enjoined the gaol keepers to offer royal pardons to any and every felon who would agree to a term of indentured labor in the colonies. The alternatives had made such proposals seem magnanimous. It was either bound servitude beyond the shores of England or a choice between two extremes: a hanging at Triple Tree for more grievous crimes or, for lesser offenses, the probability of rape, murder, or mutilation in the foul pits of Newgate Prison, a place where absolutely no attempt was made to distinguish between or to separate prisoners by gender, age, or severity of offenses.

It was impossible for Shemaine to forget the trauma of being snatched from her family's stable and, like the foulest offender, hauled into a court of law by an ugly slip of a man who had identified himself only as Ned, the thieftaker. A short stint in Newgate had taught her the futility of tearful supplications and desperately spoken promises of reward to anyone who would travel to her father's warehouses in Scotland and take her parents news of her arrest. It had been absurd to think that anyone would believe her guarantee of a weighty purse when she had been confronted by no kinder visage than the stony faces of criminals, gaolers, and their helpless victims.

Later, after she had come aboard the *London Pride* and witnessed firsthand the travails of others, she had lost all hope of ever finding a sympathetic benefactor. She had seen suckling babes torn from the breasts of desperately pleading mothers, like Annie Carver, who had not foreseen the possibility of her infant being snatched from her arms and sold to a passing stranger. Mere children, with haunted eyes and runnels of unchecked tears streaking down their thin filthy faces, had been left behind on the docks while they watched their only kin led across the gangplank in chains. Other youngsters, convicted of fretfully feeble crimes, had been shackled alongside hardened whoremongers and thieves. The only two to board the *Pride* had not survived.

Such sights had been an outrageous affront to Shemaine's sensibilities and carefully nurtured upbringing. She had not even imagined the like of such barbarism until she had seen and experienced it for herself. *En masse* they had been treated like common vermin, something detestable that had to be spewed forth from the shores of England to make the country fit and clean for a more genteel class of people, no doubt that same breed of aristocrat who had hired a thief-taker to seize her and to concoct a crime that would see her condemned to seven years in prison, just to prevent her from spoiling her fiancé's sterling heritage with her own Irish-blended blood.

Of late, Shemaine's memories of her past bliss had grown dim and strangely distant, as if she had but dreamed the princely Maurice du Mercer had asked her to marry him. After all, Maurice was a titled Englishman and could have chosen from a vast assortment of young maidens of the same noble standing as he, whereas she could claim no loftier status than being the solitary offspring of a marriage between a hotheaded Irish merchant and a gracious English lady.

"Impudent little peasant," countesses had been inclined to whisper whenever Maurice had swept her around in a promenade. Yet the wealth of her father probably would have staggered the wits of self-exalted aristocrats who were so eager to boast of their highly esteemed titles but in truth could lay claim to very little of actual monetary worth. Maurice, on the other hand, had not only been heir to the vast fortunes, estates, and title of his late father, the Marquess of Merlonridge, Phillip du Mercer, he was also the grandson of Edith du Mercer, a most formidable matron and protectress of a lineage well fortified with impeccable credentials.

Still, if the copious bribe which had been offered to her by the elder had not been motivated by bigotry, Shemaine pondered bitterly, why was she here aboard this convict ship and why had she suffered all the degradation of a condemned criminal after her refusal to leave Maurice and England behind her forever? Had she but agreed to the Grand Dame's terms, it seemed unlikely she would have come to this precise end.

Tears came to blur Shemaine's vision as waves of anguish washed over her, almost drowning her in a sea of despair, for if Edith du Mercer had indeed connived to have her whisked away from England, then the woman's schemes had been fully realized.

Not only was Shemaine a continent away from home and family, she was about to be cast into bondage and divested of her last shred of hope for deliverance from a way of life for which she was ill prepared. If she did not die of remorse, she would, in all probability, succumb to some other dreaded malady prevalent in the colonies or, if Potts found her, the mayhem he intended.

A thin arm slipped about Shemaine's shoulder, snatching her abruptly from her doleful reflections. With a start of surprise she glanced around to find Annie Carver watching her curiously.

"A fittin' justice for ol' Potts, eh, m'liedy?" the young woman ventured with a tentative smile as she sought a reason for her friend's tears. "Ye can bet he won't be gettin' a chance ta do any more o' Morrisa's foul deeds afore we leaves the ship."

Shemaine was far from convinced that she had seen the last of Potts. "I'd feel considerably more at ease if Mr. Harper would keep that beast locked away in the cable tier until the *London Pride* sails back to England," she confided glumly. "Morrisa knows just what it takes to get her bullyboy vexed with me, and she'll not rest until I've been severely punished for defying her these months at sea."

Annie mentally agreed. Prior to coming face-to-face with Shemaine aboard the ship, Morrisa had successfully coerced her cell-mates into giving her the best and greater portion of what little food had been doled out to them. She had fully expected Shemaine to comply as well, for it had been evident that the girl had lived a sheltered, pampered life far above their own. Yet in spite of the harlot's threats, Shemaine had stood her ground, resisting Morrisa's every effort to see her broken or brought down. Shemaine had eventually talked the rest of the women into revolting against the strumpet, deep-ening a virulent hatred. "Aye, ye managed ta set Morrisa awry from yer first encounter. She's been in a fair ta frothin' snit ever since."

The strife the harlot had caused She-maine had convinced her of one thing. "Mor-risa would like nothing better than to carve me up with that little knife of hers. Or better yet to get Potts to do her dirty work for her. She seems to enjoy giving orders, but she prefers others to reap the blame and rec-ompense."

Annie's gaze slipped beyond Shemaine and grew noticeably chilled. "Speakin' o' the witch, look 'oo's comin'."

Shemaine followed Annie's pointed stare and released a bleak sigh when she saw Morrisa's hip-swinging approach. "The devil's own, no less."

The dark-eyed harlot simpered smugly as she halted beside Shemaine. "Didn't like yer stay in the cable tier, eh dearie? Well, I can't says I blame ye none, though I knows nary 'nother what deserves 'em chambers more."

"Oh, I knows one al'right." Annie cut her eyes meaningfully toward the strumpet.

Lifting her lip in a cynical sneer, Morrisa bestowed a full measure of contempt upon the tiny woman. "Why, if'n it ain't the dour li'l crab scootin' 'round on her belly after her liedyship again, like she was hopin' for a handout in good looks. Well, dearie, ye're wastin' yer time with this here bog-Irish scum. Sh'maine ain't gots none ta spare."

"I knows me friends," Annie stated in a flat tone. "An' I knows me foes, an' 'tis sure ye ain't no friend o' mine. Truth be, I'd sooner be caught a-molderin' in a bogtrotter's grave than cavortin' with the likes o' some lecher's tart."

Morrisa's brown eyes flared at the slur, and she hauled back an arm to strike, but she froze in sudden wariness. In contests of brawn she had already discovered that Annie Carver could best any woman twice her size, and a swollen lip or a bruised eye could dissuade a buyer from taking a chance on a bondslave who might prove unruly. Though the urge was great, Morrisa could not bring herself to complete the stroke. Petulantly she lowered her arm and shrugged her shoulders, setting her thinly clad breasts briefly a-jiggle. By the wealth of curves she exhibited, it was not hard to determine that she had suffered no lack of victuals during the long voyage. "Too bad ol' Potts got carped by the bosun. The bugger might've resented ye callin' me names."

Shemaine sighed heavily, making much of her lamentation. "Poor, blind Potts. If he only knew how much you truly hated him. Why, he'd squash you like a bothersome gnat."

Morrisa smirked contentedly. "He wouldn't believe ye, dearie, even if ye told him. Ye sees, Sh'maine, I knows how ta handle ol' Potts. 'Sides, he may be useful ta me in these here colonies. The bloke's even been talkin' 'bout jumpin' ship an' stayin' on with me instead o' sailin' back ta England. Wouldn't the two o' ye be surprised if'n he did?"

Shemaine mentally shivered at the thought. Indeed, she could almost hear the banshees whispering her name. Despite the prickling dread that crawled up her nape, she made a point of growing thoughtful and voiced a possible solution to such a problem. "Perhaps I should warn the one who buys you that he'll likely get his throat slit by you or your lackey on a leash. I'm sure your master would be able to keep you adequately fettered and out of trouble, at least for a while. Besides, when Potts ceases to be of use to you, you'll find another buffoon to fetch and carry for you. I doubt that you have it in you to remain loyal to any man longer than it takes for him to hand over your fee."

Morrisa's haughty smirk twisted into an enraged grimace. "Ye don't know when ye're well off, do ye, Sh'maine! Anyone else would've learned by now, but not ye! I has ta pound it inta yer ugly noggin!"

Morrisa lunged at Shemaine with fingers curled into claws, having every intention of gouging those green eyes from their sockets, but the bosun's shout rang out for a second time, foiling another fight.

"Start anything, ladies," James Harper warned, using the title loosely, "and I'll have the both of you keelhauled 'til your tempers cool!"

Morrisa's glower conveyed her unabated fury, but the bosun was a man of his word, and such a dreadful threat from him gave her cause to reconsider. Her fingers finally relaxed, and with a flippant toss of her raven mane, she sauntered off, dragging her chains behind her.

The keening cry of a sea eagle pierced the blustering breezes, drawing Shemaine's gaze to the turbulent clouds churning overhead. Beneath their dark and looming shroud, frightened gulls wheeled on black-tipped wings and dove close to the water in an effort to escape their nemesis, but the erne seemed indifferent to the smaller birds as he casually rode the currents on wide-spread wings. Mesmerized by his free-spirited flight, Shemaine could almost envision herself mounting to the air on similar wings to escape the ordeal of what the coming moments or even the next seven years would bring. But harsh reality was only a heartbeat away. Chained by iron fetters and forever bound to earth, she could only watch in helpless dismay as the eagle soared beyond her restricted view. His freedom to wander hither and yon brutally mocked the constraints that she and the other prisoners had been subjected to since being convicted in an English court of law.

Annie sighed wistfully beside her. "I'll be happy ta leave the ship, m'liedy, but I'd be gladder still ta be bought by some kindly folk what gots a wee one or two for me ta tend."

"Perhaps you will be, Annie." Seeking encouragement for her friend, Shemaine climbed atop the hatch cover and stretched her own slight frame upward until she could see over the railing. Her gaze flitted over the colonials waiting on the quay for the shipboard sale to begin. To be sure, she was not greatly heartened by what she saw. The chance of Annie being purchased by a young family seemed ridiculously farfetched when she considered the potential buyers. Gray-haired men with pallid skin and short, plump wives; landowners with bald pates; and spinsterish-looking women with thin, hatchet faces seemed the primary choices.

Only one man stood apart from the rest in both distance and appearance. He was definitely young enough to lend some hope for the gratification of Annie's aspirations, yet his sharply brooding scowl was formidable. The other settlers eyed him furtively, as if afraid of meeting his stoic gaze, which did little to ease Shemaine's own speculations about the man. Yet, for all of the others' diffidence, he seemed to be the main reason for their incessant chatter.

James Harper approached the women and took a ring of keys from his belt as his gaze flitted over them. Gertrude Fitch had not allowed the female prisoners to come on deck and bathe in sight of the men in preparation of the sale. Instead, she had sent down a scant bar of soap and two buckets of water which they had immediately fought over and wasted. Three months at sea had taken its toll, for they looked no better than the poorest beggars of London. The odds of getting a fair price for any of them seemed remote, which of course would serve Turnbull's meddling daughter her proper due for not supplying ample rations and being so rigidly opposed to the crew viewing a naked breast, buttock, or two. When the women were all so scrawny and starved looking, a skeptical eyebrow was probably the most a glimpse would have raised.

"All right, ladies! Look lively now!" Harper bade, attempting a cheery tone. "Come now, and let us set you free. We can't let these colonial bumpkins see you in irons, now can we? 'Tisn't the end of the world, I'll warrant, but the beginning of a whole new life for all of you."

"Says 'oo?" an aging crone squawked.

Morrisa chortled and strode forward to challenge the bosun. "Why, Jamie, me boy, do ye think 'em irons matter a wit ta these here pilgrims? I heared it said more'n a few o' 'em blighters were sent o'er in chains just like the rest o' us poor buggers."

James Harper deliberately ignored the strumpet as he handed Roger Blake a single key and indicated the leg irons. "Loose their garters, mate, while I get their brace-lets. . . ."

On the quarterdeck, Captain Fitch wiped his glistening brow with a rumpled handker-chief as he stepped to the rail. Having finally acquiesced to the demands of his domi-neering wife, he called down to the bosun. "Mr. Harper, would you be kind enough to come up to the bridge." Fitch's frustration roiled like bitter acid in his stomach, for he could only wonder how his plans for a tryst were to succeed when his wife would be scrutinizing the sale of convicts with her usual tenacity. At the moment he wasn't the least bit desirous of masking her dictates with subtlety. "Mrs. Fitch wishes to make it clear to all concerned that she's to be given every opportunity to oversee the transactions completed here today."

"Aye, Captain," Harper responded, wondering just when Mrs. Fitch would take it upon herself to don her husband's breeches and assume full control of the ship. He greatly resented her intrusion into the normal protocol of the bark, but then, it was neither his vessel nor his command. "Right away, sir."

Harper faced the prisoners again. "Step in line, ladies, and let Mr. Blake strike those chains from you."

In dutiful respect to his captain, Harper handed the keys over to the bosun's mate and climbed to the bridge, leaving the younger man to carry out the inspection of the female prisoners, a task Harper did not especially envy. It made him uncomfortable to treat them like dumb animals being readied for sale. Some seemed as young and innocent as his own dear sweet sister.

Approaching the couple, Harper nodded crisply to his superior and then met the snobbish stare Gertrude fixed upon him. "Good day, madam."

"Mr. Harper!" Her voice was normally loud and even more so when she was determined to take charge of a situation, which apparently was now. "As you know, I have a direct interest in the proceedings aboard this vessel, and I wish to be kept apprised of every offer that is made before a sale of a convict is finalized. 'Twill enable me to keep a better record for my father. Do you understand?"

Since her sire owned the *Pride*, how could anyone on the ship ignore her behest? Captain Fitch had certainly seemed unable to. "As you wish, madam."

"There is another matter which greatly disturbs me, Mr. Harper," she informed him brusquely. "I don't approve of you locking Jacob Potts in the cable tier. The man has been beneficial in keeping me abreast of the prisoners' activities and willful violations of my orders. You'll rescind your directive at once and set the man at liberty."

Harper's jaw tensed, and it was with a hard-won guise of control that he presented his arguments against her edict. "Your pardon, madam. The man was deliberately insubordinate, and if I'm forced to negate his punishment, I'll no longer have any influence over the crew. 'Twould be folly to do so, madam."

Captain Fitch struggled to master his own ire. The fact that his wife had lent credence to the prattle of a common swabber was further cause to be offended by her presence aboard the *Pride*. An experienced officer would have considered the source and been suspicious of the tar's motives. "Gertrude, the bosun is right—"

"Nevertheless, Mr. Harper," she interrupted rudely, pointedly ignoring her husband. "You'll cancel your order or I'll see that Captain Fitch dismisses you from this ship forthwith!"

"Gertrude!" Fitch was appalled by her threat and hastened to dissuade her without causing an out-and-out rift with her father. "You cannot expect me to dismiss a man for doing his duty!"

"I expect you to remember who owns this ship!" Gertrude snapped.

"How can I forget when you constantly remind me?" her husband shot back.

"You forget yourself, Everette," Gertrude rumbled in a low, assertive tone as he scowled back at her. "I hope I won't have to make mention of this occasion to Papa."

James Harper resented the woman's manipulation of power but was hardly in a position to complain. Vowing never to sail on another ship with her, he drew himself up with all the dignity of a merchant seaman and forced himself to verbalize his words carefully, finding it difficult to speak in anything less than a roar. "Madam, I've always taken my orders directly from the captain. If he charges me to set Potts at liberty, then I'll have no other choice but to do so."

Knowing that he dumped the full weight of responsibility on his superior, Harper faced the older man and waited for the necessary dictum, which Fitch seemed reluctant to issue.

"Go about your business, Mr. Harper," Fitch finally urged. "We will confer on this matter at a more convenient time."

"Everette Fitch!" Gertrude's ponderous

bosom tested the restraints of her bodice as she puffed up like an outraged walrus. "Do you mean to say that you're going to let Mr. Harper get away with ignoring my wishes? If you will not make him do what I say, then perhaps Papa will have to remind you just where your loyalties should be fixed. He'll be arriving in New York on the *Black Prince* ere we leave port, and I'm sure he'll have something to say about your behavior today."

Captain Fitch managed to hide his annoyance behind a polite but stilted manner. He had learned by experience that to rile Gertrude was to invite the wrath of her father, who had never demonstrated compassion toward anyone, least of all to those who provoked him or his daughter. If not for the fact that Turnbull was sole owner of the *London Pride*, Fitch would have halted Gertrude's intrusions at the very start of the voyage, but he had been unable to forget who controlled the purse strings. It was one of the pitfalls of marrying for wealth, of which he had been able to enjoy very little. Except for the moneys he had managed to pilfer here and there, the greater bulk of Turnbull's wealth had remained inaccessible to him, and that goaded him unmercifully, for Horace Turnbull was rich beyond belief.

"Your pardon, Gertrude. I thought it prudent to wait and handle this matter after most of the crew have left the ship so they won't be aware of Potts's release."

Like an oversized cat, Gertrude snuggled her head back into the folds of her neck and smiled serenely, content that she would get her way. Jacob Potts had kept her abreast of the quick-tempered antics of a certain Irish chit who had foolishly upbraided her and her husband as if they were naught but wayward children. Shemaine's criticism had been initiated by the flogging of Annie Carver which had taken place shortly after their departure from England. It was the least the lackluster mouse had deserved for trying to kill herself after the loss of her babe, but Shemaine O'Hearn had deserved much more for daring to confront them about their treatment of the guttersnipe in front of the crew and the other convicts. Thereafter, Gertrude had yearned to see the girl's lifeless body dropped into the depths of the sea and, in that quest, had sought to exact the ultimate revenge. But no amount of arguing could sway Everette or get him to agree to anything more stringent than four days of isolation and limited rations for the Irish tart. Though he had also been the recipient of Shemaine's railing criticism that day, he had merely shrugged off the incident, saying that none of it had been his doing anyway and the blame lay solely on the one who had started it all by issuing orders for Annie's baby to be taken from her and sold.

Bracing a hand on the rail, Gertrude gazed down upon the one whom she had twice condemned to a secluded stay in the chain locker. A frayed, dingy kerchief covered the fiery tresses, but even as crude as the headpiece was, it failed to detract from the winsome beauty of the oval face and the large, emerald eyes that slanted upward beneath delicately sweeping brows. Glimpsing a hint of a water sprite or even a fairy queen in Shemaine's fragile beauty and thin willowy form, Gertrude yielded to her own shrewish nature.

"Look who's been let out of the murky depths," she heckled, drawing the younger woman's gaze swiftly upward. "Why, you've been down there so long, your toes must be webbed! And how quaint! You've made some adjustments to your appearance. But do you not ken, Shemaine? A red-haired witch is hard to disguise."

If anyone was a witch, Shemaine mentally scoffed, then surely it was this overstuffed grouse who, with her wickedly vindictive ways, had pecked away at the lives of the prisoners. Snatching the kerchief from her head, Shemaine threw caution literally to the wind and let the bright strands of hair whip out around her in riotous confusion, silently challenging the older woman, whose face slowly contorted with murderous hatred.

"You're a vile witch, Shemaine O'Hearn," Gertrude hissed through gnashing teeth. "I pity the fool who'll buy you!"

Of a sudden, the scudding breezes strengthened and swept across the deck, snatching Shemaine from a morass of morbid uncertainty as she met Gertrude's blazing glower. It dawned on her that she had much to be grateful for, for she had proven herself capable of existing under the most intolerable conditions, many of which this woman had purposely created. Yet, for all of the abuse and venomous reproofs she had endured, Shemaine knew, without a doubt, that she was still wonderfully, desperately alive! And that achievement was truly a thing to be thankful for!

"And a very good day to you, Mrs. Fitch," she called, lending a cheeriness to her Irish-infected greeting despite her aversion to the termagant. "Did I not tell you I'd survive the pit again, and here I am for yourself to see!"

Gertrude's lips tightened in a sneer. "More's the pity, Shemaine. More's the pity. But then, you may not be so lucky in the next seven years."

CHAPTER 2

The call boy blew his whistle, giving the signal for the waiting crowd of colonials to come aboard. Though most of the men had come to the ship intending to acquire field hands, they strolled leisurely past the female convicts as if seriously disposed toward making a purchase, at least until they reached Morrisa, who had settled in a provocative stance near the mizzenmast. They stared agog at her overt display and seemed unable to turn away. Their wives and other townswomen passed her by, lifting their noses in obvious disdain, and devoted their consideration to more practical possibilities. A short, balding man gaped in slack-jawed awe at the harlot's generous proportions, but when he made an attempt to question her, Morrisa waved him away in annoyance.

"Go 'way, li'l toad," she snapped. "I'm lookin' for a real man ta buy me."

The man's face darkened to a mottled red as he glowered at her, but Morrisa drew her lips back in distaste and made a hissing sound as if she were a snake frightening off a predator. Highly offended, he stumbled back a few steps and straightened his coat with an angry jerk.

"They drown witches here, ye know!" he warned direly. Then he sniffed in sharp disfavor and stalked off to join another handful of men who were scrutinizing Shemaine and some of the younger women.

It was almost more than Shemaine could bear to have the settlers sizing her up like so much merchandise. For this one and that, she had to stand and submit to a careful inspection of her teeth, hands, and arms. Her polite answers elicited approving nods from the women, but the warming glint in the men's eyes conveyed a more lurid imagination. The idea that she could be purchased merely to appease a prurient appetite was completely appalling, and she breathed a desperate plea that she would soon be bought by a kindly mistress who might patiently instruct her on the duties of a household servant.

"You women there!" James Harper called from the rail. "Step over here at once and give this man your attention!" He jerked a thumb to indicate a tall, dark-haired colonial who stood beside him. "His name is Gage Thornton, and he's here in search of a nursemaid to care for his two-year-old son."

A flurry of conjectures arose from the townspeople, and they gawked at the man as if he had suddenly grown two heads. Though Shemaine recognized him as the one who had kept to himself on the wharf, and the only one of the lot whom she had deemed young enough to offer some hope of fulfilling Annie's wishes, she could not fathom the reason for the amount of attention he was receiving.

Shemaine gave the tiny woman a gentle shove to encourage her. "Hurry, Annie! This may be your only chance!"

Annie was eager to comply and wasted no time in her attempt to be at the vanguard of those who surged forward. It was apparent from the enthusiasm of the other females that they, too, wanted the position Mr. Thornton offered. Young and old alike shoved and clawed their way toward him, for without a doubt the duties of nursemaid were greatly desired above those of a scullery maid, a field hand or the like.

"Remember you are ladies," Harper cautioned, wondering if he would soon have to quell the ruckus.

Shemaine was the only woman who refrained from joining the melee, but a deepening curiosity began to take root as she regarded the man. His sleeves were rolled up past his elbows, as if he had left some important task behind to make his way to the ship, yet his tense frown and rigid jaw strongly hinted of his distaste for the errand he was on, especially since it seemed likely he would be caught in the midst of an eye-gouging fray. Grimy fingers clung to the homespun shirt and hide breeches that covered the man's frame, while some women, with admiring oos and ahhs, were bold enough to stroke the torpid bulge casually defined by the clinging deerskin.

"Ladies!" Harper chided testily. "Hands off the buyer, please!"

"Awwh, mate," a snaggletoothed doxy grumbled in exaggerated disappointment. "He's the finest bloke we've seen in a goodly time, that he is! 'Sides, we can't sees where a li'l lovin' fondle would hurt the bloke none. Saints alive! We needs it more'n him!"

Three months sharing the same cell with these women had not been nearly enough time to dull Shemaine's sense of propriety. Acutely embarrassed for her gender, she also sensed the colonial's annoyance as he briefly lifted his gaze skyward. If he had sudden regrets about coming aboard the *London Pride* or, by chance, was silently pleading for intervention from above, it was much too late for either. Among her companions he remained the center of attention, and with good reason, Shemaine had to admit.

In a face that was intensely handsome and tanned golden by the sun, his eyes gleamed like warm brown crystals shot through with shards of amber. Shadowed by brooding, well-defined brows, they were darkly lashed and wonderfully translucent. His nose was thin and sculptured with a subtle, aristocratic curve that any noble Grecian might have envied. His cheekbones would have been equally coveted, for they were leanly fleshed and pleasantly prominent. Devoid of a beard, the jaw and chin were crisply wrought beneath bronzed skin. It was entirely a man's face and no less the torso beneath it.

He stood nearly a head taller than the stockier Mr. Harper, and though he was neither massively built nor one of great overwhelming brawn, his wide shoulders were sleekly buttressed by a tautly muscled chest that tapered to a trim waist and narrow hips. If the iron-thewed arms were any indication, then the rest of him had to be as hard as tempered steel.

The settler's expression grew pained as his eyes slowly scanned the women who stood around him. When Morrisa elbowed her way toward him, rudely displacing another with a sharp nudge of her hip, his dark eyebrows came together with the intensity of a thunderclap. He didn't seem the least bit intrigued by the transparency of her sagging blouse, only annoyed by her impertinence.

"Ain't ye a handsome bloke," the strumpet

cooed. Coyly tracing a finger along his fore-arm, she smiled up at him. "Me name's Mor-risa Hatcher, gov'na, an' I'd be o'erwhelmed with delight ta tend yer chit."

Gage Thornton was now convinced that he had come on a fool's errand. Only a short time ago he had been resolved to ignore the inevitable brashness of the female prisoners on the slim chance that among them he might find one who would meet his qualifi-cations, but he was quickly losing patience with this whole preposterous idea of his. How could he, even in his wildest imagina-tion, have ever hoped to obtain from such an unlikely source so rare an acquisition as he had mentally conjured? Perhaps his des-peration had surpassed even the degree he had realized it had reached. He was deter-mined to accept nothing less than his ideal, but it was becoming increasingly apparent that the kind of woman he was looking for wasn't to be found aboard a convict ship.

"I have different qualifications in mind than the ones you generously display, Miss Hatcher. I'm afraid you do not suit my pur-poses."

Morrisa nodded knowingly as she jeered, "Afraid o' yer wife, are ye?"

Gage felt his vitals slowly twist with indignation. This woman had no idea, of course, what he had gone through since Victoria's death, and certainly no stormy retort would enlighten her. "Your pardon," he replied succinctly. "My wife was killed in an accident a year ago. Were she alive today, I assure you I wouldn't be on this damn fool errand."

Timidly Annie stepped forward to tug at the man's sleeve. "Me name's Annie Carver, sir. Me own babe was sold soon after I boarded the ship, so 'tis me earnest wish ta have a wee one ta care for. I can promise ye I'd cherish yer son as me very own, sir." She blushed in sudden confusion and wrung her hands as she added, "That is, if ye'd be o' a mind ta lay out the coins ta buy me."

Gage's indomitable gaze softened somewhat as he looked down at the small, plain-faced woman, but her garbled speech bespoke her lack of schooling. "I was hoping to find a woman who could teach my son to read and write in years to come. Is it possible that you can instruct him?"

"Blimey no, gov'na!" Annie gasped, confounded by the requirement. Deeply disappointed, she was about to turn away when a sudden thought struck. Facing him again with an eager smile, she informed him, "But I knows one what can! She's a liedy, ta be sure, sir."

"A lady?" Gage was clearly dubious now that he had seen the greater share of women. "Here on a convict ship?"

"Aye, sir!" Annie's answer was emphatic. "M'liedy knows readin' an' writin' an' can even do sums in her head. I seen her do it, sir."

"Ninety years old, no doubt," Gage scoffed. He couldn't waste his funds on a woman who would probably fall dead five minutes after leaving the ship. Old arguments surfaced to cast his expectations into the realm of the absurd, stripping away his confidence and nullifying his hopes. Certainly no gentle-bred woman would have committed such a grievous crime to warrant being sent to the colonies on a convict ship, unless of course she had been thrown into debtor's prison. Even then, he had grave doubts that he could afford her. He had other commitments which negated his ability to pay off such encumbrances.

A smug smile twitched at the corners of

Annie's lips. "Nay, sir! A young liedy! An' a comely one at that, sir."

"Where is this marvel?" Gage asked blandly. He was afraid Annie didn't fully comprehend the meaning of the word *lady*, for he had neither seen nor heard any similarities since boarding the *Pride*.

Turning, Annie motioned for her companions to move aside as she searched for her friend. When a path had opened, she thrust out a thin arm to point to a lone figure sitting on the hatch cover. "That's 'er, gov'na! Shemaine O'Hearn, she be!"

Shemaine became instantly aware of the attention she had gained and the strength of those startlingly beautiful brown eyes as they settled on her in amazement. She could entertain no uncertainty about whether or not she had piqued the stranger's interest, for he was totally engrossed in looking her over.

Gage Thornton had worked too hard for everything he now owned to be fooled into believing his goal could be met so painlessly. This young woman was uncommonly fetching, a possible prize to be sure, but he was leery of some hidden flaw.

He leaned aside to question Annie. "A

lady, you say?" At her affirmative nod, he asked the obvious. "But why is she here? What offense did she commit that justified her being sent to these shores on a prison ship?"

Annie lowered her voice to a whisper. "A thieftaker snatched m'liedy whilst her parents were away an' wouldn't let her go an' fetch people what knew her, so ye see, sir, there weren't none ta say the bloke nay when he swore she were the one what stole another liedy's jewels."

Gage was hardly convinced, but his reservations were not enough to diminish his interest. Even with her cheeks smudged with grime and her hair wildly snarled about her thin shoulders and down her back, Shemaine's beauty was unmistakable. Her face seemed delicately wrought, as if some artist had painted an image of a dream and brought it to life with an enchanted kiss. Her breeding, he strongly suspected, was thoroughly Irish, for no other race seemed quite so naturally favored with combinations of flaming red hair, sparkling green eyes and creamy fair skin. Despite the rags that adorned her, her graceful bearing gave undeniable evidence of her refinement, for she held herself with a regal air, her chin slightly elevated, her eyes meeting his directly, as if she suffered no qualms about being his equal.

Gage marveled at the unusual tumult inside of him and could only wonder what excited him more, the discovery of a girl who seemed to fulfill his every requirement for a nursemaid or the other, unspoken purpose which he had not dared hope to satisfy. If he did acquire her, his future intentions would probably astound friend and foe alike. But then, it wouldn't be the first time he had gone against proper decorum to carve out a definite direction for his life.

Mentally Gage hauled back on the reins of his racing thoughts and, assuming a casualness he did not particularly feel, pointed the girl out to the bosun. "Mr. Harper, I'd like to make inquiries about that prisoner over there."

James Harper craned his neck to see which of the women had interested the man, just as an aging crone stepped in front of Shemaine. Harper bade the elder forward, mentally questioning the man's taste and good sense, but Gage negated the summons with an impatient slash of a hand.

Stepping to a place where he could command Shemaine's attention directly, he bade her to come forward with a single beckoning motion.

Conscious of those sparkling brown orbs feeding on her every movement, Shemaine rose from the hatch and slipped through the press of women whose troubled frowns openly conveyed their envy and dejection. Her progress went unhindered, however, until Morrisa blocked her path.

"If'n I were ye, dearie, I'd be a mite cautious o' goin' off with this here Thornton gent. Ye sees, Sh'maine, I ain't seen such a handsome bloke in all me born days, an' I wants him for meself. An' if'n ye keeps me from havin' him, I'll not be takin' it too kindly. For sure, I'll be wantin' ta slice ye up good an' proper."

Shemaine was amazed that Morrisa still sought to intimidate her. It seemed by now that even a half-wit would have realized she was too obstinate to be moved by threats. "And if I were you, Morrisa," she gritted back through a tight smile, "I'd consider the mayhem the man might heap upon your hide if you manage to harm a servant of his, especially one he's paid good money for."

"I'll come after ye, Sh'maine, mark me words. An' when I finds ye, I'll make ye sorry ye didn't heeds me warnin'. This here bloke won't wants ye after I gets through with ye."

The visual daggers that pierced the strumpet belied the softness of Shemaine's words. "I hope you'll not be too surprised, Morrisa, if I let Mr. Thornton know you've threatened to do me harm."

Morrisa snarled in exasperation as Shemaine brushed past her. Her failed attempts to see the bogtrotter killed or, at the very least, seriously maimed were even more grievous now, when it was evident the redhead had attracted the best of the lot. A scarred face would have certainly discouraged the handsome bloke from wanting the chit.

James Harper hadn't bothered to glance up as Shemaine halted beside them. He had grown impatient with all the fuss over the settler and, like Potts, was anxious to conclude the sale so he could enjoy his liberty on shore, for he had a fair thirst building for a large tankard of ale. Checking the lists, he questioned brusquely, "Your name?"

"Shemaine O'Hearn."

His head snapped up in surprise at the

velvety reply. The name conjured up different images of a slender, red-haired beauty he had both glimpsed from afar and ardently admired at close range. If there was one prisoner he was loath to see sold to another man, it was this girl who had aroused the hopes and imagination of many a sailor aboard the *London Pride*. Even Captain Fitch had been smitten, and only the most discreet members of the crew knew his wife would soon have valid reasons to be envious of the maid. Ere long, her husband would settle the girl in a nearby house and make her his mistress. It was not an arrangement Harper enjoyed making for his superior, but he simply had no choice in the matter.

He spoke in a hushed tone to the stranger. "I fear you'd not be content with this one, sir," he advised, having been instructed by Captain Fitch to discourage all serious buyers. "She has a sharp tongue which can lay a man open with a deft stroke. Ask the captain and his missus if you doubt what I say."

Having overheard the warning, Shemaine fixed Harper with an incredulous stare, wondering why he should be so callous as to distort the details of that specific day when he had assembled the prisoners on deck to witness the scourging of Annie Carver. They had been forced to watch the cat-o-nine rip open the small woman's back and were warned as the whip fell that similar infractions would result in like discipline. Their confused and questioning murmurs had turned rapidly to muttering indignation, for they had known only too well what had caused Annie's attempt to kill herself. One by one they had faced the quarterdeck where the captain had stood. Shemaine vividly recalled the contempt that had risen like sour gall in her throat when her own gaze had settled on the captain standing stoically beside his gloating wife. With as much passion as her Irish father had ever thought of venting, she had climbed atop the hatch cover and harshly berated the couple for their barbarous treatment of Annie.

Now, with considerably less venom than she had exhibited three months before, Shemaine questioned the bosun. "Will you give me no chance to explain, Mr. Harper?"

"Did I not tell the truth?" he queried, growing distressed because in the process of obeying orders he could turn her completely against him. He was no more partial to the idea of letting her go off with this man than he was to the captain's claiming her, but what could he do?

"You accused me rightly, sir," Shemaine admitted brittlely, lifting her chin as she met his troubled stare. "But there was much more to the incident than you infer. Mrs. Fitch's crimes against a grieving mother were tantamount to whipping a widow for mourning the death of her husband. Her only interest in keeping Annie alive was purely mercenary, but you, sir . . . could you not understand Annie's depth of despair when she tried to take her own life? Or are you so completely bereft of compassion that you cannot comprehend the sorrow of a young mother when she is robbed of her child? Or did you, indeed, see the need for her to be further punished by a flogging?"

"I could not disobey my superiors," Harper argued. "Nor was it my place to debate the matter with them."

"So, by your silence you consented to the whipping," Shemaine chided softly. "How chivalrous you are."

Harper blushed profusely, realizing her arguments had uprooted him from his firm stance. Her persuasive reasoning would no doubt sway the colonist in her favor. In hopes of dashing any idea of a gallant spirit, he sought to justify his claims. " 'Twas certainly not your place to accuse the captain or his wife and encourage the other prisoners to revolt!"

"Revolt?" Shemaine laughed in rampant disbelief. "They merely voiced their objections. Believe me, sir, revolt was not within their capability, not when they were half starved and weighed down with so much iron they could hardly move!"

"The bosun's right, gov'na," Morrisa interrupted, shouldering others aside. "That Irish tart gots a spitefully mean temper, she does. Laid me low more'n a few times, she did, without me e'er knowin' what set her off."

"Ye liar!" Annie shrieked. Catching hold of Morrisa's arm, she swung her around and then let go, sending the harlot reeling haphazardly into the churning body of women.

There had been times during the voyage when Annie's temper had completely amazed Shemaine, and the present moment was no exception. The woman had seemed like such a retiring little mouse at the onset of the voyage, but since that fateful day of her whipping, Annie had grown bolder, as if she had made a silent pledge to herself to reap vengeance on those who had abused her and to repay Shemaine for everything she had suffered after coming to her defense. To be sure, Annie had demonstrated her gratitude far more than Shemaine had ever expected from anyone or, for that matter, had ever thought her deed warranted.

It was Annie who returned to shake a dirty finger beneath the noble nose of Gage Thornton. "Whipped by order o' the cap'n's missus, I was, but m'liedy called her a mean an' heartless shrew—"

"Aye! An' Sh'maine had the lot o' us agreein' with her!" the snaggletoothed crone interjected. "Even chained, we were set ta break the bilboes an' waylay the crew 'til the cap'n agreed ta stop the floggin'."

Annie persisted in her defense. "An' we were bent on protestin' m'liedy's stay in the cable locker, too, but Sh'maine told us ta take care o' our own hides. She vowed ta show Mrs. Fitch the true cut o' her jib an' said she'd come out no worse for wear. . . ."

Shemaine groaned inwardly, convinced that her friend was far too vocal about her fleeting moment of folly. She had lost her temper, nothing more.

" 'Twas only the cap'n reducin' her stay ta four days 'stead o' four weeks what saved her skin," Annie added.

In all actuality, Annie's discourse had had little effect on Gage Thornton. He had made up his mind some moments earlier, during the argument between Harper and the girl. In protesting the bosun's accusations, she had readily confirmed her intelligence and schooling. Gage was delighted that she met his requirements so completely. The fact that she did allowed him to avoid a conflict within himself, for he really didn't want to deal with the dilemma of wanting her irregardless her merits.

Still, he could not let himself appear overeager when he had to lay out a significant sum of money. He had to be careful with the coins he had earned, at least until he finished building the ship he had designed and could find a buyer for it. Though he had every intention of becoming a rich man someday, he was by no means one yet. Having been denied any right to his father's fortune because of a rift that had sprung up between them, he had come to the colonies a veritable pauper. It had only been by a like amount of wit and grit that he had managed to succeed as well as he had. In truth, if he could somehow manage to give up his dream of building ships, the furniture that he and his four employees made in his cabinet shop would provide him with a goodly income, but there lay the crux of the difficulty. How could one give up a lifelong ambition?

"You don't mind if I have a closer look at the girl, do you, Mr. Harper?" Gage raised an eyebrow in cynical wonder, half expecting the bosun to deny his request.

Harper scowled sharply. The man's persistence grated on his temper. " 'Twill do you no good."

"Why not?" Gage asked curtly. "If I'm willing to take a chance on the girl's disposition, what else might prevent me from buying her?"

At the seaman's taciturn frown and rigid shrug, Gage pointedly dismissed him and moved beyond Annie to where Shemaine stood. She was not the cleanest creature he had ever seen or, for that matter, even smelled, but the fiery lights that flashed in those dark green orbs amused him. And that meant a great deal to him. If truth be known, he had almost forgotten how to laugh since the death of his wife.

"The girl looks half starved," Gage commented, giving Harper a challenging stare. He had heard rumors of privation aboard convict ships, and though their captains were wont to disavow such tales as gross exaggerations, the deplorable condition of the felons aboard this vessel seemed to bear out such unfavorable reports.

Harper ground his teeth in growing vexation. No matter how strenuously he had objected to the scarcity of victuals for the prisoners, the fact that *this* settler made reference to the starvation only served to heighten his irritation, for he was sure this interloper was trying to instigate a quarrel. " 'Tis no concern of yours what the girl's present state may be, Mr. Thornton. I've told you before, I cannot sell her to you."

"She'll fatten up right nicely, gov'na," Annie encouraged Gage impetuously as she came to Shemaine's side. "If'n ye be o' a mind ta give her a few good vittles, it won't take her no time at all."

"Hush, Annie!" The emerald eyes flashed an angry reproof. "I'm not a sow you're selling."

"Can you cook?" Gage asked.

Annie bobbed her head and hastily replied in her friend's stead. "O' course, she can, gov'na!"

"Will you not shush?" Shemaine whispered furiously. "You're bound to get me into trouble!"

Gage was certain he understood the drift of the admonition, but questioned Shemaine to be sure. "What did you say?"

Annie waved away his inquiry. "Oh, na' a thin', gov'na. M'liedy was just clearin' her throat, that she was! 'Tis all these here spores in the air, ye know."

"Annie!" The name came out sounding like steam hissing from a boiling kettle, and perhaps that description could have been directly applied to Shemaine. She was not very appreciative of being discussed as if she were a piglet being offered for sale.

Stepping slowly and purposefully around Shemaine, Gage contemplated her from every angle. Even a large cabin could get uncomfortably cramped when it served as home to two people who couldn't abide each other. Of late, he had become increasingly aware of the difficulty in coping with a woman, namely one Roxanne Corbin, who tried to smother him with her presence and attention. If not for his desperate need for a nursemaid to care for his son while he worked, he would never have considered taking Roxanne on in the first place, and now she expected far more from him than he was willing to give. In Shemaine's case, however, he thought he might enjoy having her underfoot and discovering every minute detail about her.

Pausing beside her, Gage reached out and slid his fingers curiously over the delicate bones of her wrist. The contact seemed far too bold and intimate to Shemaine. Had he branded her, she would have felt no less disturbed, for his touch seemed like a warm flame slowly licking upward along her skin.

"Please don't!" she begged breathlessly, pulling away. When he looked so sleek, hale, and hearty, what merit could he possibly find in a frail and filthy reed?

"I didn't mean to startle you, Shemaine," Gage apologized. "I only wanted to look at your hands. . . . May I?"

Shemaine didn't like being the recipient of such close attention, especially when she felt so utterly unclean. Grudgingly she lifted her hands, resenting her lack of an option.

She was just thankful he hadn't asked to see her teeth!

Gage examined the slender fingers with care, finding them grimy yet finely made. He stroked a thumb across the fragile bones in the back of her hands and, turning them over, inspected the palms that were as soft as any well-born lady's.

"You seem ill prepared for work, Shemaine," he observed in amazement.

Beneath his searching gaze, Shemaine felt a blush stealing into her cheeks. "I'm not afraid of work, sir," she said carefully, aware that her next words might greatly reduce the possibility of being purchased. "I'm just not well acquainted with it, that's all."

"I see," Gage responded in bemusement. Perhaps what Annie had told him was actually true, that Shemaine O'Hearn really had been brought up as a lady. Only the very wealthy could afford to coddle their offspring with servants, which seemed the only plausible explanation for her soft hands and lack of skills. "I sincerely hope you have a talent for learning on your own, Shemaine. I can ill afford a tutor for you, nor do I have the time or the ability to instruct you myself."

"I learn very quickly, sir," she averred

hastily. "If there are books to be had that give detailed instructions on the duties of a housekeeper, then I can teach myself."

"I will earnestly have to look for one."

" 'Twould help," she answered gingerly.

"Do you even know how to cook?" Gage posed the inquiry again, trying to subdue his sudden concern. He fervently hoped they wouldn't have to starve before she familiarized herself with some of the basics.

"I'm clever with a needle, sir," Shemaine hedged cautiously, not wanting to divulge what she was basically uncertain about. Her mother had thought it prudent for a young lady to be taught all the skills of a wife, and their cook had fervently agreed, but Shemaine had not been the most attentive of students and could make no guarantees as to the extent of her memory.

Accepting her reply as a negative response, Gage heaved a dismal sigh. He wasn't at all excited about the prospect of having to endure a novice's cooking, but even Roxanne's skills in that area could not compel him to veer from the course he was quickly laying out for himself. He knew by the very act of coming here today that he was seriously testing the winds of fate, but his desire to have Shemaine was beginning to far outweigh all other considerations.

"You seem very young," he remarked, not wanting to dwell on her inexperience.

"Not so young, sir," she readily rejoined, though at the moment she felt ancient. "I was ten and eight this past month."

"Young enough!" Gage scoffed. "Unless, of course, you think a score, ten, and three is ancient."

Shemaine was bemused by his statement. "What's so significant about a score, ten, and three, sir?"

" 'Tis my age," Gage informed her bluntly.

Oh! Shemaine's lips formed the word, though her voice failed to give utterance to the syllable. Embarrassed by her blunder, she avoided meeting his gaze for fear he might detect her astonishment. She hadn't really thought him to be that old!

An uneasy silence passed between them, and finally in fretful confusion, Shemaine raised her eyes to meet the ones that stared back at her. She fully expected him to tell her that he would have to seek elsewhere for a servant, but his eyes delved deeply into hers and seemed intent upon searching out her innermost secrets.

"Now," Gage breathed, as if speaking to himself, "all I have to do is convince Mr. Harper to sell you to me."

Shemaine's heart fluttered in genuine relief. Though she had desired earlier to be bought by a woman, there was something about this man that made her confident of his integrity. Perhaps it was the angry look that had sharply creased his brow when he had broached the subject of the prisoners being starved. She just hoped her lack of skills would not bring that particular disaster to bear upon his small family.

Gage returned to the bosun and offered a sum with a casual indifference that was well feigned. "I'll give you fifteen pounds for the girl."

James Harper felt his hackles rise. Perhaps it was his own jealousy that had raised its inflated green head like a wary serpent when the man had looked the girl over, but he was beginning to suspect the colonial wanted her, not as a nursemaid for his son, but as a mistress for himself. "The captain gave me strict orders about the girl, Mr. Thornton! She's not to be sold."

"Twenty pounds then," Gage said a bit more testily. He removed a leather purse from a larger pouch that was slung from a shoulder by a rawhide strap and worn on the opposite hip. Carefully he counted out the coins and offered them to the bosun. "That should be enough to suit your captain."

"I tell you, the girl is not to be sold!" Harper insisted, growing irate. He refused to even acknowledge the outstretched hand.

"Dammit, man!" Gage snapped. Realizing his heightening intention to buy Shemaine whatever the cost, he asked incredulously, "You bring your prison ship into port and flaunt the cargo for every man to see, then you say you have no intention of selling the best part of it?" He laughed with trenchant skepticism. "Come now, Mr. Harper, is this a game? If it is, I have no time to play. Now tell me, how much do you want for the girl?"

"What's going on here?" Captain Fitch demanded sharply as he joined the pair.

"Sir, this *pilgrim*," Harper derided as he indicated Gage with an angry jerk of his head, "is insisting that he be allowed to purchase Shemaine O'Hearn. His last offer was twenty pounds. He wants to know what you'll take for her."

Brushing back his frock coat from his ponderous belly, Captain Fitch hooked his thumbs in the pockets of his waistcoat and rocked back on his heels as he smirked at the tall stranger. "I fear you haven't nearly enough coins in your possession to buy the wench, sir. She's already spoken for."

Shemaine caught her breath in surprise and quickly closed the distance between them. "By whom, sir?"

Peering obliquely past the large prow of his nose, Everette Fitch lifted dark, wispy brows as he regarded the maiden. His sly smile lit his gray eyes with a glowing ardor that was unmistakable, bringing an outraged blush to Shemaine's cheeks as the realization dawned. Somehow the captain had contrived to have her for his own, even if he had to hide her beneath the very nose of his wife.

"Sir, I beg you!" Shemaine came threateningly close to tears as she considered the repulsive prospect. Becoming this man's plaything would be more horrible than anything she had yet imagined. "Please, Captain Fitch, I don't wish to arouse your wife's ire more than it has been." Indeed, a flogging would scarcely appease the woman's desire for retribution if she ever learned of her husband's intentions. "Let Mr. Thornton buy me. He's a widower, sir, and has a youngling that needs tending."

Recognizing the heavily weighted footfalls of his wife as she approached from behind, Everette stiffened and clasped his hands behind his back in perturbation. Throughout the voyage Gertrude had made it her business to dispatch her broad shape swiftly to his side whenever she sensed some monetary matter was being discussed. She was a needling, meddling, critical old jade, and he was anxious to experience a maid far more youthful, delectable and sweet.

"Everette, you're needed on the bridge to sign papers of indenture," Gertrude stated, snubbing her nose at James Harper.

"I'll be along in a moment, dearest," Everette said, trying to urge her back to the area of the ship from whence she had come. "Just as soon as I tend to the business here at hand."

Gage grasped the situation immediately and, after purposefully doubling the amount of coins in his purse to draw the woman's attention, spoke to her discreetly. "I was told the maid, Shemaine O'Hearn, cannot be purchased for any amount of coin that I have in my possession. Perhaps, madam, you'd care to count them for yourself."

Gertrude peered askance at the tall man as he pressed the purse into her hand. Then she cast a suspicious glare toward her husband as she judged the weight of the moneybag. She promptly made a more accurate accounting of the amount it contained.

Shemaine quaked in fearful apprehension. She was certain that if Gertrude Fitch suspected how desperately she wanted to be sold to Gage Thornton, the possibility would be promptly nullified.

Gertrude came to her own conclusions and, upon returning the coins to the bag, jerked the rawhide strings closed with a finality that doomed her husband's scheme. As much as she had yearned to see Shemaine dead and buried, she could not lightly dismiss a generous sum such as this. "Sign her papers, Everette," she instructed officiously. "We'll not likely gain a sum greater than forty pounds from another buyer."

Captain Fitch opened his mouth to protest but paused as he met the colonial's sardonic stare. He suddenly realized that if he wanted to continue commanding a ship, he had no choice but to sign the girl's papers of indenture and give her to the man. He handed the document over with a grumbling complaint. "I don't know what I'll tell the other gentleman when he comes to fetch the wench."

"I'm sure you'll think of something," Gage responded aridly. Allowing a spartan smile to touch his lips, he rolled the parchment and tucked it into the flat pouch at his side.

He glanced down at Shemaine. "Are you ready?"

She was anxious to be gone before Captain Fitch could think of a reason to delay them. Looking around for Annie, she found the woman timidly answering the inquiries of the short man Morrisa had rejected. She raised a hand in a gesture of farewell and hurriedly blinked back the moisture that blurred her own vision as Annie responded with an indistinct nod and a teary-eyed gaze. Facing her new master again, Shemaine sought to steel her emotions. "I have no other possessions than the clothes on my back, sir, poor as they are. I'm ready to leave whenever you are."

"Then let us be on our way," Gage urged. Meeting the cold-eyed glower of James Harper above her head, he added, "I have no further business here, and there seems to be a storm brewing all around us."

Shemaine lifted her gaze to the darkening sky looming close above their heads, but when she glanced around at the angry faces of the men who stood nearby, she realized the colonial's statement only partially pertained to the weather. Following in his wake, she allowed him to lead her away from those who watched them.

CHAPTER 3

For a man who had, of late, found frugality crucial to the furtherance of his ambitions, Gage Thornton realized he had just managed to suppress every miserly instinct he was capable of mustering in his determination to have Shemaine O'Hearn. No one could have guessed from his apparent eagerness to offer such a sizable purse that he would now have to postpone the purchase of much-needed building supplies for his ship until he could collect payment for several pieces of furniture he had recently finished for wealthy patrons living in Williamsburg. It was a delay he would not normally have entertained. Yet here he was, the owner of this bondswoman, and he could not have been more delighted had he spent the last year methodically planning and saving for the event. It was a rarity indeed to have one of his goals attained without first expending a grievous amount of planning, hard work, and careful scrimping toward its acquisition.

As for Shemaine, she had settled her mind on the fact that her papers of indenture were now owned by the colonial, Gage Thornton. For the next seven years of her life, she would be subject to his authority. She would keep his house, care for his child, and do all that was reasonably expected of a servant. Much remained to be seen, but for the moment at least her situation did not seem terribly offensive. In fact, she was relieved that it had turned out as well as it had. It seemed doubtful she would have cause to remember her departure from the *London Pride* with any import, except that it was equivalent to being given a reprieve from hell.

Gage stepped from the gangplank to the cobblestone quay and casually turned to offer assistance to his newly procured chattel, prompting Shemaine to flick a wary glance over the lean hand that was extended toward her. It had a recently scrubbed appearance that made her painfully conscious of just how utterly grubby her own hands were. Yet the man had inspected her palms only a few moments ago and had to be fully aware of just what he would be touching. Abashed by the sharp contrast, she reluctantly accepted his hand and found it deeply callused from hard work, his fingers thin and strong. Yet, surprisingly, his skin felt smooth beneath the soft texture of her own, as if conditioned by some strange oil or ointment.

No sooner had Shemaine stepped to the quay than she was struck with thoughts of retreating to the wooden gangplank. The frigidity of the stones beneath her bare feet made her anxious for something warmer upon which to stand, and if that was not enough to make her falter, the breezes that whipped through an invisible channel between the ships anchored against the wharf and the nearby warehouses seemed especially wicked. She was ill prepared for the inclement weather and those blustering blasts that sliced with brutal vengeance through her garments. No comfortable haven seemed attainable, and she could only shiver and clench her teeth against their chilling breath. Even her frantic efforts to subdue her recalcitrant skirts proved futile, for the frayed hem buffeted her slender calves and, now and then, swirled chaotically aloft, as if it had assumed a puckish life of its own and took mischievous delight in thwarting her.

Gage had always been a man to admire a finely turned ankle and did not deny himself the opportunity to appease that propensity now. It had, after all, been a considerable passage of time since he had been able to indulge himself with a worthy glimpse. Yet he was not exactly sure which held his attention more intently, the shapeliness of the slender calves or the telltale red weals that had been caused by a lengthy chafing of iron shackles. Dark bruises marred the flesh of her lower leg, hinting of a more recent injury. Beneath his stare, the slender toes curled inwardly, making him mindful of the girl's growing discomfiture. Reluctantly he lifted his eyes to meet the guarded green gaze.

"Have you no shoes?" he asked, sincerely hoping he wouldn't have to lay out another portion of his meager wealth to buy her a pair. The idea caused him to frown as he mentally debated how he might manage such a purchase.

Shemaine smoothed back the snarled strands of hair that were flying across her face as she peered up at her new master. His scowl was ominous enough to make her turn tail and run. "I'm sorry, Mr. Thornton," she murmured, hating the uncontrollable quaver in her voice. "My boots were stolen from me at Newgate shortly after my arrest." She reminded herself that she had done nothing deserving of her seizure or this shame which had been forced upon her. But the truth did not ease her humiliation, nor did the proximity of several older couples who had just arrived on the dock. In spite of their gaping curiosity and the battering wind that cut through her like an icy saber, she explained haltingly. "I can assure you, sir . . . the boots were a loss I sorely regretted. They were unique and very fine. . . . It cost my father a fair sum to have my initials etched in a pair of tiny gold pendants and for the cobbler to find a way to attach them to each boot at the ankles. At the time, it seemed wiser by far to hand them over without protest. Each of the two women who demanded them outweighed me twice over, and they were in such a frenzy to trade them for gin . . . I was convinced my life would be in jeopardy if I did not comply. Their theft made me grateful my riding habit had been torn and soiled during my capture. Otherwise, they'd have seen some profit in selling my clothes, too, and I'd be standing here now less than fully clothed."

Those amber-flecked orbs of lucent brown swept her from crown to toe, giving little indication of the colonial's thoughts. "A pity, for sure."

"Sir?" Shemaine was confused by the precise drift of his meaning and felt a prickling of apprehension as she questioned him. "Is it the loss of my boots you bemoan or the fact that I'm fully clothed?"

His smile was far too fleeting to convey any warmth. "Why, the loss of your boots, of course."

Shemaine wondered suddenly what sort of man had purchased her. Beneath that darkly stoic and inaccessible demeanor he now presented, would she find a disreputable rake? Was she destined to be used by Gage Thornton in the same way Captain

Fitch had intended? Or was there a waggish sense of humor that was wont to defy his conveniently assumed reticence? He seemed well acquainted with what he wanted out of life, indeed had already proven his dedication to the attainment of his goals, showing little concern for what others might think or say about him. He had certainly given no heed to the tongues that had started clacking soon after the bosun had announced his reason for being aboard the ship. Nor did he seem the least bit disturbed by the rudely inquisitive stares they were presently being subjected to. Apparently he was a man well accustomed to being talked about.

Reaching out a hand, Gage lightly flicked the back of his fingers over Shemaine's sleeve where it had been torn away from her bodice. "Unless rags have become the fashion, my girl, I'm inclined to disagree with you about being fully clothed."

Excruciatingly aware of her ragtag appearance, Shemaine dragged the rent together over her bare shoulder. " 'Tis a poor, drab servant you've bought for yourself, Mr. Thornton."

The brown eyes snared hers again and

probed deeply, seeming to reach into her very soul. They conveyed no warmth beyond the color, yet there was no coldness in them either. "Considering where I went to find one, Shemaine, I count myself fortunate to have come away with such a rare prize."

Her expression became one of confused wonder. "Have you no regrets about laying out so costly a purse for the likes of me, Mr. Thornton?"

Gage lightly scoffed at the idea. "I came here today with a definite purpose in mind, and I'm not one to lament my actions until they've been proven irreversibly foolish." He lifted a curious brow and presented a question of his own. "Knowing yourself as well as you do, Shemaine O'Hearn, would you be thinking I've wasted my wages?"

"I truly hope not, sir." Her voice was small and uncertain. "It all depends on what you want most from me. 'Tis no boast when I say that I'm capable of teaching your son to wield a quill with a goodly amount of skill, to do sums in his head, and to read with the best in years to come, but 'tis a sorry fact that you might have acquired a more capable housekeeper, nursemaid or cook by buying Annie or one of the other women."

Gage finally glanced toward the group of onlookers, setting them to nervous flight with nothing more than a thoughtful scowl. Of a sudden, they seemed in an anxious dither to cross the gangplank and board the ship. He gave little consideration to their undignified haste as he looked at her again. "You made your lack of skills quite clear ere I bought you, Shemaine. I cannot claim I've been defrauded. There'll be no taking you back."

Shemaine felt her heart grow light with relief. " 'Tis good to know that, sir."

Gage gestured casually to her riding habit, having noticed several tars watching the girl from afar. " 'Tis plain we'll have to do something about your clothing. I don't appreciate the stares you attract, nor would I have you shamed by my lack of generosity."

Once again Shemaine tried to read the inscrutable frown that occupied his sunbronzed brow as he slowly perused her, but the man himself seemed carefully reserved and enigmatic. Knowing only too well that her appearance could cause even the staunch-hearted to cringe in chagrin, she offered hesitantly, "If you'd prefer not to be seen with me, Mr. Thornton, I can follow several paces behind you so no one will know we're together."

Gage served quick death to her suggestion. "I didn't lay out forty pounds for you, girl, just to have you snatched behind my back. You have no understanding of this area, else you'd know there are not a lot of women to choose from, especially those worthy of being called pretty. There are, however, enough trappers and backwoodsmen wandering around to give a virtuous maid serious cause to worry. Any number of them would be willing to commit mayhem to get themselves a woman to take back to their camps. You'd be a fine catch for a man like that, especially during the winter months."

Shemaine was hardly appreciative of his scolding and explained brittlely. "I only meant to save you some embarrassment, sir."

"I know what you thought, Shemaine, but you were wrong. Even half-starved and filthy dirty, you're the comeliest maid the people of this hamlet have seen in some months."

Shemaine wasn't one to be easily taken in by a few charitable compliments. "Your flattery would surely turn a simple maid's head about on her shoulders, Mr. Thornton. Were I one, I'd probably be overwhelmed with gratitude, but I'm fully cognizant of just how wretched I look."

At her blatant rejection of his praise, Gage displayed a bit of exasperation of his own as he sighed. "In time, girl, you'll learn that I speak the plain truth. I don't hold with lying."

"And in time, sir," Shemaine was quick to rejoin in stilted tones, "you'll learn I'm not a mere girl."

Gage noted the deepening blush in his bondswoman's cheeks as she stood in rigid poise, as if bracing herself for his reprimand. Leaning toward her slightly, he commanded her full attention. Staring directly into those widened eyes, he breathed his answer. "Believe me, Shemaine, I know that now."

His emphatic admission disarmed Shemaine completely and opened up a plethora of questions in her mind. Of a sudden, she was not at all sure the colonial had been thinking solely of his son when he had laid out his purse for her. If he had told her outright that he had closely appraised her womanly curves for what enjoyment they could give to him, especially her bosom, which was probably the only curve she hadn't entirely forfeited through her lengthy ordeal, he could not have made her more uneasy.

Yet, when Shemaine considered how obstinate she could be, she deemed it advantageous to offer some insight into her own failings if she wanted to get along with the man or even held out hopes of staying with him long enough to win his approval. If she angered him unduly, there was absolutely no guarantee that he *had* to keep her. He could just as well sell her to the next stranger willing to pay his price. For her own preservation, it seemed imperative that she demonstrate a willingness to be submissive. And if any lecherous schemes were being entertained by the colonial, then those would have to be addressed once they became apparent. It was neither wise nor fair to judge a man prior to his offense.

"I've had little experience being a servant, Mr. Thornton," Shemaine murmured carefully. "You'll no doubt find me quite outspoken at times. Perhaps even impertinent."

His gaze never wavered from her face. "I'd rather have you speak your mind, Shemaine, than see you intimidated by my presence."

Equally surprised by his answer, she conceded, "I have many faults, sir, and one of them is my temper. I fear in that respect I'm very much like my father."

Gage countered with a warning of his own. "I'm sure you'll get to know my moods in time, Shemaine, and occasionally think me an ornery beast. But you needn't be afraid of me. I won't beat you."

Her responding smile was genuine. "I'm relieved to hear that, sir."

"Then come," he urged, taking her arm. Peering up at the threatening clouds looming overhead, he briefly mused on the prospects of a storm being unleashed upon them. "We'll get drenched in earnest if we stand here much longer."

Gage drew her with him as he made his way along the quay, passing people and stepping around wooden crates as if he had urgent duties elsewhere. His walk was brisk, his strides long. He was not a man who wasted time or dallied overmuch at doing nothing. His strength and energy were valuable assets, and he used them to good advantage. In his haste to get home before the rain started, he gave little heed to his servant's lack of vigor and lagging steps.

Shemaine's long fast in the cable tier had

left her feeling far too faint and weak to allow her to keep up with her new master. Even before they reached the end of the wharf, her legs had turned to fragile stilts that wobbled unsteadily beneath her and threatened to give way entirely. Perceiving the impending danger as her vision began to blur, and shapes and structures reeled woozily around her, Shemaine staggered to a faltering halt and begged weakly for her master to give her pause. Gaining her release, she stumbled away and clasped a nearby post for support. She closed her eyes and waited for her strength and wits to return, hoping fervently that they would.

Gage took note of the shaking hand the girl pressed over her mouth and the lack of color in her face and knew this was no feigned attack of the vapors. Half expecting her to collapse, he stepped beside her. "Are you ill?"

Not wishing to upset her equilibrium more than it was, Shemaine raised her gaze cautiously and was surprised to find him so near. Her stomach was so empty she wanted to retch, and it was a difficult moment before she managed to subdue the urge. "Give me a moment to catch my breath," she pleaded in a strained whisper. "Then I'll be better. 'Tis but a passing weakness, I'm sure."

Some understanding began to dawn on Gage as he considered her more closely. Her sunken cheeks and the all-too-obvious trembling of her slender hands indicated a frailty associated with a lengthy fast. "When was the last time you had anything to eat?"

Though the frigid breezes continued to sap her energy and drag her down into a mental stupor, Shemaine struggled desperately to remain coherent. "I was given several crusts of bread and a bucket of stale water during the four days I was locked away in the cable tier. . . ." She swayed dizzily, feeling an invading debility sapping the last vestige of her strength, but when he reached out and steadied her with a hand beneath her arm, she staggered back abruptly, feebly brushing away his grasp, and willed herself to stand alone. "In truth, sir . . ." She swallowed, fighting another wave of nausea, and continued with difficulty. "I'm so famished . . . I'm nigh to swooning."

Gage promptly hailed a passing vendor and went off to meet the man. After purchasing several wheat cakes, he returned and offered one to his bondslave. "Perhaps this will help."

Shemaine accepted the cake eagerly and, tearing it apart, greedily devoured the pieces, nearly choking as she stuffed them in her mouth. Mortified by her lack of manners, she refused to lift her gaze to the man whose tall, broad-shouldered frame sheltered her from the casual glances of those who traversed the main thoroughfare of the town. She swallowed the last crumbs and took a ragged breath, meeting his probing stare hesitantly. "I was considerably more fortunate than some of the other prisoners, sir. They died from the sparse fare. Thirty-one in all, to be exact."

Gage recalled the broad shapes of Captain Fitch and his wife and grew incensed at the thought of them wallowing in gluttony while their victims died of starvation. "I've heard tales of deprivation suffered aboard convict ships like the *London Pride,*" he reflected. "I sailed here as a passenger aboard a merchant vessel some years ago and have counted myself far luckier than most who have crossed the seas to get here."

Self-consciously Shemaine folded her arms across her midriff as her stomach began to rumble. "I'm grateful to be alive, sir, though at times I really had my doubts that I would survive."

Gage handed her another cake and waited patiently as she consumed it, this time with a little more dignity. She finished the last of them and immediately began to long for something to drink. Her new master seemed to read her mind as he motioned for the elderly vendor to bring a cup of cider to her.

Shemaine's initial hunger and thirst had been sated before she realized they were attracting the attention of nearly everyone who passed along the lane. Some of the villagers had paused nearby to stare in slack-jawed wonder. A few seemed wary of looking at all and tried to hide the fact. Others were nosy enough to step around to where they could get a better view. A handful of British soldiers, standing some distance off, laughed at remarks being made by several in their number as they eyed her openly.

It was not difficult for Shemaine to imagine what people were thinking or even saying. Lacking shoes and with the stiff breezes snatching her tattered skirts and unkempt hair, she could believe she looked as wild as some red-haired heathen. But she noticed that whenever any of the townspeople caught sight of her, their natural reaction was to glance at her escort to see what sort of person might be with her. Facial expressions registering varying degrees of astonishment became almost predictable the very moment the onlookers recognized Gage Thornton. Just as the other couples who had fled aboard the *London Pride*, they seemed suddenly intent on making good their escape before they fell under his grim stare.

Gage nodded a curt greeting to several male acquaintances, but they seemed almost flustered to have been caught gawking. Without giving him more than a disturbed glance, they hurried on their way. Finding no tangible reason to challenge them, Gage settled a curious gaze upon Shemaine. He was hardly surprised by the stares she received from the men. They'd have to have been blind not to see the girl's beauty behind all the grime. She was as delicately boned as his dead wife, but that was where the similarity ended. Compared to Victoria, Shemaine was almost vividly hued, shorter by several degrees and generally smaller, except that she had more of a bosom than his wife had been endowed with.

"Shemaine O'Hearn," he murmured thoughtfully, hardly realizing that he had spoken until she glanced up inquiringly.

"Sir?"

Gage could think of no credible excuse for staring at her so intently and harkened back to his earlier conjecture. "Irish, eh?"

The emerald eyes flashed with sudden indignation. *So!* Shemaine mentally jeered, *Gage Thornton will be like all the rest of the Englishmen who detest the Irish!* Raising her chin to an imperial level, she replied with emphatic crispness, "Aye, sir! The name is O'Hearn! Shemaine Patrice O'Hearn! Daughter of Shemus Patrick and Camille O'Hearn! Half Irish I am, to be sure, sir, and half English, if it matters a wit to you colonials!"

The dark brows jutted upward in curious surprise. However innocent his remark had been, Gage realized he had ignited that passionate spirit which the girl had warned him about. "There's no crime in being one or the other, Shemaine, or even both," he replied, seeking to allay her suspicions and resentment. "But tell me this, if you would. Annie said you are a lady, and though I've seen evidence of that fact, I cannot help but wonder how you came to be aboard a prison ship."

Shemaine's anger dwindled rapidly as she gleaned some evidence of his tolerance, but she was slow to answer. It seemed she had tried a thousand times to convince Ned, the thieftaker, the glum-faced magistrate, and the gaoler of her innocence, but none had lent credence to her tearful supplications. Perhaps they had been motivated by a hefty bribe, just as she had oft suspected. Whatever their reasons, she had grave doubts this stranger would believe her either.

"I didn't kill anyone, Mr. Thornton, if that's what you're worried about."

Gage responded with a dubious chuckle. "I never imagined you had, Shemaine."

His gaze was indomitable, and it was apparent that he awaited her answer and would not be satisfied with a feeble excuse. Heaving a sigh, Shemaine mentally braced herself for the ordeal of explaining and plunged reluctantly into the mire of her predicament. " 'Twas nigh to eight months ago when I had the pleasure, or perhaps one might say the misfortune, of becoming engaged to the Marquess du Mercer of London. His grandmother, Edith du Mercer, was not as receptive to my lack of aristocratic breeding as Maurice had proven to be. 'Twas Edith, I suspect, or at least someone in her service whom she could trust to be discreet, who hired a thieftaker to snatch me from my parents' home while they were away. Only servants and an aunt were looking after me at the time, a fact Edith knew well. It seemed to me a desperate bid to destroy the likelihood of her grandson taking me to wife. Maurice can be very adamant when he settles his mind on a matter, and Edith may have been unable to dissuade him. After my arrest, I was accused of thievery and sentenced to prison. It didn't seem feasible, after all my failed attempts to bribe someone to take word of my arrest to my parents or to my aunt, that my kin would discover my whereabouts by some other means. Even if I had had the coins in hand to entice the gaolers or turnkeys to carry news to my family, I seriously doubted that any of them would have ventured farther than the nearest alehouse. Rather than face the threat of being ravished or perhaps even murdered in Newgate, I signed my name to the long list of prisoners agreeing to be sold as indentured servants here in the colonies."

Gage had no trouble believing she could associate with aristocrats. Though a keen ear could recognize an Irish lilt to her words, she was articulate beyond his expectations and, in spite of her fiery temper, well mannered. As far as her being innocent of any crimes, he would have to accept her explanation as fact until he found out otherwise. " 'Twould seem your ill fortune has led to my gain, Shemaine. Though I can sympathize with you for what you've been through, perhaps you can understand if I cannot pretend to be saddened that you're here."

Shemaine felt his unyielding stare and inquired timidly, "Is it meet that I should know something about you, Mr. Thornton?"

Lifting his head, Gage gazed off into the distance for a moment before responding. "I'm a shipbuilder by preference, a cabinetmaker out of necessity. I've a workshop and a cabin a short distance from here on the James River. At present, I'm involved in building a ship of my own design, but the brigantine is still several months from completion. Once she's finished and sold, I intend to devote my energies entirely to building another, with the hope that someday I may become a major shipbuilder. Until then, I must pay for the labor and supplies with what I earn making furniture."

Shemaine could not imagine a man of limited resources being so adamant about buying her. "I was certain you had wealth to spare, Mr. Thornton."

Gage had definitely amazed himself in that respect. "You seem completely suited to my purposes, Shemaine. Had I searched every ship that came into port I cannot imagine finding another like you." Pausing a moment, he frowned and grew noticeably somber as he began to relate his own reason for coming to the colonies. "I was forced to leave London myself more than nine years past. I had a falling-out with my father because of my refusal to marry a young woman who claimed that I had compromised her innocence and gotten her with child. She was the daughter of an old acquaintance of his, and I'm sure 'twas out of loyalty to his friend that my father sought to force me into a marriage with her. I think he was afraid our name would be besmirched if I didn't placate Christine's demands that we be married posthaste, but I would not be bound by wedlock to the little liar, nor would I give my name to some other man's brat. I never really knew whether it was only a ruse to get me to marry her or if Christine was truly with child. She was pretty enough to attract more than enough suitors to her stoop, even without her sire's wealth. Because of my refusal to comply, my father cast me out of our home. So you see, Shemaine, we have both been set adrift by the wiles of conniving women. 'Twould no doubt sorely prick the tempers of those two shrews if we were to thrive in this wild land."

"You have a better chance of doing that than I have, Mr. Thornton," Shemaine replied glumly. "My only reprieve would be if my father somehow found out where I had been taken and sailed here to buy me back, but that seems farfetched, considering my past efforts. He would never dream of making inquiries at Newgate, and I have no more wealth now to bribe a messenger to bear a letter to England than I had in Newgate. Besides, any missive I manage to send would take months before it reached my family . . . if it ever did . . . and many more months ere they could possibly reach the colonies. If I'm found at all, it won't be within this present year, I'll warrant."

Gage spent a long moment in silent thought, understanding how thrilled the girl would be if her father were to find her and fetch her back to England, but he also knew the disappointment he would suffer if he had to begin his search again. Having survived an abrupt detachment from home and family himself, he sought to calm her fears about her future. "Sometimes, Shemaine, when we're forced to go beyond the protective walls of the homes we grew up in, we have an opportunity to become instrumental in determining our own fate. For years, I dreamed of constructing a ship of my own design in England, but my father needed my skills building the massive ships that he had always produced. It has been my belief all these many years that he did not under-stand my designs or trust me well enough because of my youth to let me create them from scratch. Having apprenticed for several years under a very talented cabinetmaker, I was better at the finish work than any of the other men my father employed, but when he thrust me away in anger and refused to even consider that I was the one who was an innocent victim, I found myself free to follow my own desires and ambitions."

Shemaine only knew how much she longed to see her parents and to be safe in their care again. "What you say may well be true, sir, but I have no greater ambition than to be rescued by my father and to go home again."

"We'll see how you feel seven years from now," Gage rejoined, not unkindly.

His statement drew a disconcerted glance from Shemaine, for he seemed to insinuate that nothing short of death would halt her years of service to him. She could only wonder what would happen if her father did manage to locate her. No provisions had been written in the laws of England that would force a master to sell a bondslave against his or her will. Her master's claim on her superseded all others? Even her betrothal contract was mullified by his ownership of her. She only wondered if this man could find it in his heart to sell her to her parent? Or would she be required to stay with him against her will?

Sensing a lingering presence nearby, Gage glanced around to find a thin, aging matron leaning forward in an avid quest to hear as much of their conversation as the buffeting wind would allow. Beneath his perusal, she straightened, only slightly abashed that she had been caught eavesdropping. She gave him a crisp nod of recognition.

"Well, Gage Thornton, what brings you into Newportes Newes today?"

Gage was well aware of the woman's strong penchant for gossip. Indeed, she was probably hoping he would oblige her and answer her simple question in ample detail. But he was hardly one to placate the meddlesome busybody and kept his own greeting politely reserved. "Good day, Mrs. Pettycomb."

The matron nodded curtly toward the girl. "And who might this stranger be?"

Though Gage sensed Shemaine's reluctance to be introduced, he took her arm and pulled her gently around to face the elder whose speculative stare had come nigh to boring a hole through her slender back. "May I present Mistress Shemaine O'Hearn from England?"

Alma Pettycomb's small, dark eyes descended to the bare feet visible beneath the swirling hem. Almost as quickly her sparse brows jutted sharply upward above the tiny, wire-rimmed eyeglasses perched on her thin, hawkish nose. Coming to her own conclusions, Alma clasped a blue-veined hand to her flat bosom, completely flabbergasted by this latest event in the life of the cabinet-maker. He was forever causing a stir among the villagers. Any normal man, for example, would have grieved no longer than a few months after the passing of his spouse. Times were hard here in the colonies, and men were expected to take new wives to relieve the burden of caring for their young. Many a father in the hamlet had foreseen Gage coming to court their cherished darlings and would have bestowed great favor upon him, but he had kept to himself, obviously preferring his state of widowerhood to marriage with any of the local girls. He had further daunted their expectations by hiring the smithy's daughter to care for his son.

"Gage Thornton! What in the world have you gone and done?" the matron gasped. "Can it be that you've bought yourself a bondswoman from that awful convict ship? Have you taken leave of your senses?"

"I don't think so, madam," Gage replied with detached coolness. "In fact, I've done exactly what I've been meaning to do for some time now."

A fierce blast of air flattened the brim of Alma's cloth bonnet over her wrinkled brow, but with an impatient upward thrust of her hand she brushed it back into place and gave him a blatantly suspicious stare. "Do you mean to say that you've actually been contemplating the purchase of an indentured servant, even before the *London Pride* sailed into harbor? Why, such a foolhardy deed gives me cause to think you've gone daft."

The muscles twitched in Gage's lean cheeks, attesting to his irritation, but his voice was as unfaltering as his gaze. "Be that as it may, madam. I've done what I've done and do not intend to make amends to anyone."

Mrs. Pettycomb raised her thin nose and squinted at him closely through her narrow spectacles. "Not even the smithy's daughter?" she prodded. "Surely, if there is one in this hamlet you owe an explanation and apology to, it's Roxanne Corbin. That poor, dear girl dotes on you as if you were some kind of god."

Gage remained totally unrepentant. "It has been on my mind of late that I've been intruding far too much on Roxanne's goodwill and should allow her to live her own life without imposing the care of my son upon her any longer. Her father has always required her to tend the chores at their home before coming to mine, and now that Hugh has been laid up with a broken leg, Roxanne won't be able to come at all, at least for a while. With no one to look after Andrew while I work, I saw the need to search for someone else." Though he had said as much to Roxanne, she had begged him to ask his neighbors to help out for a time, but he would never have laid more work on others who had just as much to do as he did. Besides, he would never have tolerated Andrew being away from home that much. "Roxanne knew of my need for a nursemaid better than anyone, Mrs. Pettycomb, so it's not as if this will be any surprise to her."

Pointedly rejecting his statement, Alma faced into the wind until he had finished speaking. Then she turned back sharply and shook a chiding finger beneath his nose. "You know very well, Gage Thornton, that Roxanne Corbin has never considered the care of your son an imposition. She loves Andrew as her very own. You'd be wise to realize just how good she's been to him, how he'd benefit from having her as his mother. In fact, you ought to bear in mind the problems you'll have to face taking a convict into your home. I've certainly never approved of those prison ships bringing the dregs of society to our shores. This girl could be a murderer for all you know! Indeed! You could be doing this hamlet a great disservice by harboring such a woman under your roof."

Gage was hardly pleased by Alma's harsh rebuff of Shemaine. The girl stood beside him in stony silence, but in the few short moments he had known Shemaine, he had learned to read the depth of her vexation by the unyielding rigidity of her back. He was tempted to tell the old crone to mind her own business, but he knew his wrath would only augment the gorgon's resentment of Shemaine. Quietly but firmly he reasserted his position. "I'm quite taken with my selection, Mrs. Pettycomb, and I intend to keep her."

"Aye! I can see where you may have cause to be," Alma rejoined snidely, and looked toward Shemaine with open disdain. She seemed to fight an inner battle with herself for a moment, as if she wanted to say more. When she continued, it was evident she had yielded to the temptation, for she unleashed a storm of criticism upon the man that was blacker than the menacing clouds overhead. "There are many in this hamlet who think you're a fool, Gage Thornton, and buying a female convict just about proves it! You've wasted nearly every coin you've managed to earn building that ridiculous boat of yours when everybody knows it will never leave the James!"

It was not the first time that Alma Pettycomb had defied proper decorum by passing judgment on the citizenry living in the area. And Gage Thornton was not the first by any means. Though she had taken special delight in closely observing him whenever he came into the hamlet, his reticence had often frustrated her and aroused her suspicions. A man as uncommunicative as he had proven to be usually had something to hide, she had concluded. Now here he was again, setting convention completely aside by taking this vile creature into his home, and he didn't seem the least bit contrite about doing so. In Alma's mind, he needed a good dressing-down.

Gage was by no means surprised by the woman's lack of finesse. In the nine years he had lived in the area, he had been forced to listen to many of her comments, either by way of her own lips or from others'. Frequently she was wont to express views on matters which did not directly pertain to her and was just as generous with her advice. He would never forget the afternoon he laid Victoria in the coffin he had built for her and brought her into town in the back of his wagon. It hadn't taken long for news of her death to spread or for Alma Pettycomb to set herself at the forefront of those demanding to be told the circumstances surrounding his wife's deadly fall from the unfinished prow of his ship and just what part he might have played in it, going so far as to suggest that he could have thrown Victoria off in a fit of temper. After all, just a month prior to that occasion he had thrashed a man soundly in their village without any apparent reason.

Roxanne had been anxious to explain that he could not have murdered Victoria and still been able to reach the spot where he had been when she first caught sight of him only moments after Victoria's fall. But there were those who had voiced skepticism, implying that the Smithy's daughter had been hopelessly infatuated with him for years and would say or do anything to see him exonerated, no matter how guilty he may have been.

When asked directly, Gage had neither confirmed nor denied Roxanne's story, but had simply explained that he had taken his son back to the cabin to wash him up and could not say what had really happened between the time he left Victoria on the ship and the moment Roxanne arrived by canoe. Having found no hard, fast proof to incriminate him in his wife's death, the British officials of the governing body of the area had concluded that they could not blandly ignore his alibi, no matter how enamored Roxanne may have been with him.

"My ship is a seafaring vessel, Mrs. Pettycomb," Gage informed her stiffly. "And I assure you, she will sail far beyond the tidewaters of this area. 'Twill only be a matter of time 'til she proves her worth."

Alma Pettycomb was hardly convinced. "That remains to be seen, doesn't it?"

Though a stranger to them both, Shemaine was certain the woman had to be nearly witless not to notice the turbulence brewing behind the exterior aloofness of the man. Knowing only too well how her own father would have reacted, she was rather amazed by her master's rigid control. Had Shemus O'Hearn been the recipient of such vicious chiding, Mrs. Pettycomb would have quickly fallen back before the onslaught of his verbal outrage. In sharp contrast, Gage Thornton kept tight rein on his temper, though he stood his ground like an impenetrable bastion and was intensely loyal to his own ambitions and ideals.

"I cannot expect you to understand, madam." Gage had never lent much value to Alma Pettycomb's opinions and was not motivated to do so now. "It takes someone far more knowledgeable about sailing ships to grasp the importance of my design and to perceive the brigantine's potential for greater speed ere the day of its launching."

Alma was not one to admit there was anything on this particular side of the continent that she didn't know a great deal about. In truth, she lacked understanding about a lot of things outside of her own realm of interests, at the forefront of which was sailing ships. Still, she avoided being challenged with pertinent questions by directing the subject elsewhere. "When you're unwilling to listen to reason, Gage Thornton, there's certainly no purpose in continuing this discussion about your boat. Waste all your time and money on your foolish endeavors, if you wish. What I'm mostly concerned about is Roxanne. She'll be terribly distressed by this recent purchase. Indeed, you can hardly expect her to entertain a marriage proposal while you have this . . . this *creature* living under the same roof with you."

Gage was no more grateful for the busybody's meddling advice than he had been her reproofs. "I fear you've been seriously misinformed if you think there is anything between Roxanne and me, Mrs. Pettycomb."

Alma elevated a thin brow as she cast a haughty glance toward Shemaine. "Certainly not since you've purchased this bondswoman."

Gage grew emphatic in his denial. "I beg

your pardon, madam, but there has *never* been anything between us."

"Are you disavowing any knowledge of the trousseau Roxanne has been embroidering . . . with *your initials*?"

Gage was momentarily dumbfounded by her statement. Roxanne had been making overtures ever since their first encounter nine years ago, when he had needed the blacksmith services of her father. More recently she had been strongly hinting that a match between them would be desirable, but he had been extremely careful not to give her any encouragement.

"I never once broached the subject of marriage with Roxanne or abetted any notion that there could possibly be anything between us."

Alma deliberately made a point of dismissing his denials. "You might as well know your claims will fall on deaf ears, Gage. Since there are no other marriageable men living in this area with the initials GHT, we've all assumed Roxanne is embroidering monograms that stand for Gage Harrison Thornton."

"Then you're mistaken, one and all," Gage replied brusquely.

Mrs. Pettycomb gazed at him in amplified disbelief. "Perhaps Roxanne has reason to believe you'll marry her because you've never gone out of your way to discourage her," the matron harped. " 'Tis plain to all that she has dreamt of becoming your wife for some time now, even before Victoria arrived here in Newportes Newes and captured your attention. If you can't see that Roxanne is taken with you and has been for some time, then everybody else around here can. You should have told her outright there was no hope instead of leading her on all these many years."

Having grown immensely tired of the busybody and her pettish accusations, Gage brought the discussion to an abrupt end. "I haven't time to debate this matter with you any longer, Mrs. Pettycomb. I'm sorry, but I must get back to my cabin and my son."

Alma pressed on, ignoring his curt rebuff. "If you were wise, Gage Thornton, you'd take my advice and forget this inanity of yours. Taking this"—briefly directing a contemptuous sneer upon Shemaine, she sniffed arrogantly and forced herself to be more charitable than she wanted to be— "*chit* home with you is bound to cause speculation as to your real reasons for buying her—"

"I must hurry," Gage insisted, cutting through her incessant chatter.

"Hurry! Hurry! Hurry!" the woman fussed. "That's all you do! You have no time to stop and think things through, Gage! Otherwise, you'd recognize when a woman has set her sights on you. You work relentlessly, never stopping. Why do you even bother?"

"For Andrew, Mrs. Pettycomb," Gage answered succinctly as a light smattering of raindrops began to fall upon them. "For my son."

Dismissing the elder, Gage took Shemaine's arm and led her away. As he did so, he inclined his head toward an area near the river. "My canoe is over there, only a short distance away. Do you think you can walk that far?"

"I'll do my best, sir," Shemaine replied with an indistinct nod.

As if to make a mockery of her statement, the gusts strengthened sharply, forcing Shemaine to retreat before their onslaught. Blinking against the heavy droplets that had begun to pelt them, she sought to put one foot before the other, but it seemed a useless endeavor, for the rising gale seemed to hold her prisoner.

Gage halted abruptly and turned to face her, causing Shemaine to cringe inwardly beneath his frown. She knew she was slow and clumsy, having little strength to rely upon, and fully expected to be reprimanded for impeding their progress. For a moment the tall, broad-shouldered form provided her shelter from the rain. Then, without a word, the man bent and picked her up in his arms.

"Mr. Thornton! What are you doing? Put me down!" Shemaine gasped, outraged that he had taken it upon himself to handle her with such familiarity. No man except her own father had ever been presumptuous enough to carry her, and even then she had been very young. It unsettled her to be clasped to her master's hardened frame, for his physical prowess made her painfully aware of just how thin and frail she had become. In the rain his clean manly scent was far more elusive, but it was enough to fill her head and fluster her even more, for she felt filthy to a fault. Faintly she added, "P-people will stare, Mr. Thornton."

Gage scoffed, rejecting her concern, and cast a quick glance over his shoulder to find

Alma Pettycomb doing just that despite the rapidly wilting bonnet that was crumpling down over her brow. "If any harping ol' biddy wants to stand in a downpour and gawk at us, then I'm inclined to let her!" he muttered. "As for me, I intend to get home as soon as possible, and I can't wait around for you to get your land legs back under you."

Gage sprinted across the thoroughfare of the hamlet, motivating Shemaine to throw her arms around his neck and hang on for dear life. They were proceeding at a pace far too swift for her peace of mind, and she could only guess what she would suffer if he slipped in the mud and she went flying. The bruises caused by Potts would probably seem insignificant in comparison.

His new bondslave was certainly no great burden to carry, Gage Thornton decided as he dashed toward the river's edge, for she seemed as light as thistledown in his arms. He was also struck by how soft and womanly she felt against him as she clasped her arms tightly about his neck. He likened himself to a teetotaler besotted by the intoxicating pressure of her rounded bosom. The pleasure he derived from the experience gave him cause to wonder if he had been a widower for so long that he had forgotten just how delicious it was to hold a young, beautiful woman within his grasp.

Gage entered the woods where a line of trees along the riverbank formed a sheltering canopy above their heads. There he came to a halt and stood his bondslave on her feet. Dragging a canoe from a nearby thicket, he nosed it into the water and silently directed Shemaine to the far end. The slender craft seemed far too flimsy to suit her, and though she obeyed her master's directive, she settled herself gingerly where he had indicated. Cautiously she looked around at the wide river beyond them and then cringed in sudden worry. Aware of the nervous fluttering in her stomach, she turned back, not wanting to face the possibility of being launched into that swirling expanse.

Taking a place at the opposite end, Gage braced the end of the paddle against the river's edge and shoved them away from shore. The current caught the canoe, making it wallow slightly, and Shemaine's heart leapt with fright. After all she had been through, it would be sheer travesty indeed if she were drowned only moments after leaving the *London Pride.*

Gage tossed a small tarp to her. "That should help keep you warm."

Grateful for the protection from the rain and the watery view surrounding them, Shemaine spread the tarp over her head and huddled beneath its folds. Despite the raindrops that slashed into her face, she fastened her gaze upon the land beyond the riverbanks, searching for signs of life and habitation. Just beyond the hamlet, the countryside seemed flat and low, in some areas a grassy marshland inhabited by waterfowl and reptiles, but in other places there were thickets so dense they seemed impenetrable to anything but the smallest of animals. Shemaine was immediately impressed by the beauty of the wilderness, yet a little frightened of it, too, for she had no idea what to expect from this land or if she would be able to survive in it.

Occasionally through the downpour she saw where a cabin and outbuildings were nestled in the trees or where others were in the process of being built. In a larger clearing she saw a much grander house being erected and was amazed at the spunk of the people who, having no guarantees of safety and security so far from civilization, would make such a commitment to the future.

The canoe glided with ease through the swiftly flowing current as Gage repeatedly dipped the wooden blade in the rain-pocked waters, stroking leisurely on one side and then the other, marking a course close to the riverbank where lofty, wide-spreading branches afforded them protection from the storm. Farther down the river, a profusion of pink and white petals, stripped from a snarled thicket of fruit trees growing near the shore, floated on the surface of the river beneath the shelter of their limbs. Others were being swept into the main channel, where they swirled chaotically in the current for a time before being drawn into the depths. Feeling as vulnerable as those tiny flower petals, Shemaine dismally mused on the similarities between her life and their short voyage on the river. Against her will, she had sailed across an ocean and was now being borne along to some strange destiny beyond her ken. Only time would reveal the outcome, if she would be swept under a darkly brooding morass of adversity or if she would remain afloat until she came to the end of her indentureship.

They finally came within sight of a sandy inlet where a partially finished ship rested in bracing stocks near the river's edge. No one had to tell Shemaine that here was where Gage Thornton endeavored to build his dream. As they drew near, the ship seemed to loom above them like a sleek-framed edifice, much larger by far than Shemaine had dared to imagine. This would truly be a sailing vessel for the high seas, she thought in awe, realizing just how dedicated and enterprising the man who had designed her really was.

A large cabin stood on higher ground beyond the ship. Its sharply pitched roof seemed to thrust upward into the belly of a gray, turbulent haze that roiled close above the tall pines and deciduous trees surrounding the cabin. Their branches swayed to and fro with the strong winds that blustered through them and seemed to answer with a plaintive wail, as if bemoaning the fact that they had been disturbed.

Gage drove the canoe into the shallows near the bank. There he jumped to shore and dragged the craft from the river. The pelting raindrops continued to slash down upon them with a vengeance as he lifted Shemaine in his arms and raced toward the cabin. Carrying her easily, he leapt up the front steps, strode across the covered porch and lifted the latch as he nudged the heavy-timbered door open with a shoulder. Once inside, he kicked the portal closed behind him and, withdrawing the arm he had clasped beneath her knees, allowed Shemaine to regain her footing. Leaving her, he pulled a towel from a rack near the door and proceeded to dry his face and arms and blot some of the moisture from his clothing as he moved about the spacious cabin, lighting several lanterns to chase away the gloominess of the interior.

"I'll open the shutters after the winds die down," Gage stated, drawing Shemaine's attention to the small-paned windows spaced at neat intervals in the cypress-paneled walls. Except for those that were protected beneath the overhanging roofs of the front and back porches, the rest of the windows were darkened by wooden shutters that had been closed and bolted from outside. "I put in the glass only a couple of months before my wife died, and it was no cheap or easy task. When there's a storm brewing, I usually close the shutters so there's no chance of the windows getting broken, mainly to save myself the trouble of repairing them."

Shemaine was impressed by the charm and comfort of the interior. "It's nice and cozy in here with the lanterns."

A loft had been built beneath the steeply pitched ceiling, partially forming a second story which, from a gracefully turned balustrade, overlooked the great room. Lending support to the loft on the main floor was an interior wall set back some distance from the end of the overhang. On the left, a massive stone fireplace had been built to provide a cooking area in the kitchen. Immediately to the right of the hearth and directly opposite the front entrance was a door that led to a wide corridor, at the end of which was a window and a back portal. On the far right of the interior wall, a second door stood ajar, revealing a neatly arranged storeroom. Adjoining that same wall was another partition which ran from front to back, behind which a spacious bedroom could be seen through an open doorway to the right of the entrance.

It was apparent that a gifted artisan had

crafted the furnishings, for they were as fine and elegant as any piece her own parents owned in England. Of most worthy note was a tall secretary standing against the parlor wall near the bedroom door. The piece had been painstakingly adorned with carved shells, gracefully curving drawers and burl-grained doors. A leather-tooled desktop had been folded down to display tiny compart-ments, drawers, and narrow cubicles where a collection of bric-a-brac had been nestled. Majestically crowning the piece were a pair of spiraled finials on each end and, in the middle, an elaborately carved shell, no doubt the handiwork of her new master.

Shemaine turned slowly about in amaze-ment. The costly appointments were a lux-ury she had not expected to see in the colonies. In fact, they were so much in evi-dence, she could not take them all in with a mere glance. A settee and two large, wing-backed chairs, upholstered in a Scottish plaid, were part of a small grouping that had been arranged within close proximity of the secretary.

In the kitchen, a wooden sink, a worktable and a tall cupboard lined the interior wall to the left of the hearth. A butter churn, crocks and other equipment abounded in this area, where, only a few steps away, a pair of high-backed wooden benches faced each other across a trestle table. A child's high chair had been placed conveniently at one end. A short distance away, a rocking chair stood near the fireplace where one could sit and enjoy its warmth or view the back corridor.

The stone hearth had an opening almost as large as Shemaine was tall. It was equipped with hooks and racks where iron kettles and skillets could be heated above the main fire. An iron oven stood to one side and could be readily moved about within the fireplace to make it more accessible to the heat. The massive chimney was solidly con-structed, no doubt lending substantial sup-port to the structure as it rose upward through the loft and the peaked roof.

"Did you build this cabin and all these things yourself?" Shemaine asked, turning to Gage in amazement.

"Aye, I built a small cabin for myself soon after arriving, but when I married Victoria, I enlarged it and started making the furniture for her." His eyes flicked about the room, touching familiar nooks and crannies. "She was the one who made the place into a home for us. She was as clever with a needle as any woman I've ever known." He indicated the settee and chairs. "She had me trade a table to a Scotsman for the plaid. After I attached the legs and arms to the frames, she stuffed the three pieces with horsehair, covered them with sailcloth and then the woolen."

"You must miss her terribly," Shemaine surmised, detecting a strange texture in his voice.

"Aye, I think of her a lot when I'm not busy," he acknowledged, returning the towel to a peg near the front door. "But you'll hear rumors to the contrary when you venture into the village. Alma Pettycomb and other scandalmongers in the hamlet doubt that I can love anything but the ship I'm building."

"I don't think I'll be lending too much credence to what Mrs. Pettycomb has to say about anyone or anything," Shemaine stated with firm conviction. She had already settled her mind on the fact that the woman was hardly worth knowing, much less listening to. "If you made all these furnishings for your wife, then I, for one, can believe you loved her very much."

A quickly vanishing smile was Gage's

only response before he moved to the hearth. There he stirred up the glowing embers and laid several pieces of wood on top.

As he fed the fire, Shemaine realized she had seen no one else in the cabin. "But where is your son?"

Gage swung a large kettle of water over the newly kindled flames and, turning to face her, casually motioned in a westerly direction. "I left him with a neighbor who lives up the river a piece. If not for the fact that Hannah Fields has a husband and seven children of her own to care for, I might have hired her on to cook and clean for us. But of course, I wanted someone who could instruct my son beyond the limits of her ability. Hannah is a good woman and a hard worker, and Andrew is always delighted when he has a chance to play with Malcolm and Duncan, her youngest two. I'm sure once you meet her, you'll find her very kindly and not given to gossip and the like."

" 'Twould be nice to find someone willing to teach me the duties of a servant, but I don't suppose Mrs. Fields has much time to do that with such a large family," Shemaine surmised with a tentative smile.

Although Gage tried to dismiss the girl's

shortcomings as something that could be easily dealt with, it was a simple fact that a man who worked hard all day could get mighty hungry for palatable food even in the presence of such a comely woman. "As soon as the storm lets up, I'll be leaving to fetch Andrew. While I'm at the Fields's cottage, I'll ask Hannah if she can come over one day soon and show you a few things about cooking. She'll probably be more than willing to visit with you. Except for her younger two, her other sons are older and have to help their father. She has two daughters, between ten and two and a pair of years more, but they're more concerned with neighbor boys than with matters that interest women. They prefer to stay at home just in case any should happen by." A grin briefly flicked across Gage's lips as he added, "Their father keeps as close a watch, and by the size of his gun, I can understand how he might discourage the lads from visiting unannounced."

Shemaine smiled. "Is it permissible to have a look around the cabin while you're gone?"

"Aye, but you'd better bathe and dress first so you can be assured of some privacy.

There are clothes in a trunk in the bedroom that can be altered to fit you. I'll get them now."

Curious to see what he would have her don, Shemaine followed him into the bedroom and found it spacious and comfortably furnished with a huge four-poster, a chest of drawers, an armoire and other handsome pieces. There was even a large bear rug on the floor beside the bed.

Part of the original room had been partitioned off to make a small bedroom for his son. No doors existed between the two rooms, only a wide passageway where a piece of sailcloth had been hung, but apparently it was rarely used, for the folds, which had settled into it over time, had become quite distinct, almost crisp. The child's room held a rocking chair, a chest-on-chest, an infant's crib and a trundle bed, all handsomely made pieces and all, no doubt, the handiwork of her master.

Gage lifted the curved lid of a trunk that stood at the foot of the four-poster in the larger room and swept a hand to indicate the contents. "These things belonged to my wife. She was tall and slender, and her feet and hands were rather long and thin, so you'll probably need to shorten the gowns and stuff a bit of cloth in the toes of the shoes until I can afford to buy you another pair, but you're welcome to use whatever you'd like."

Shemaine was overwhelmed by his generosity. "You'd have me wear your wife's clothes?"

Gage had no need to imagine the depth of her astonishment. It was blatant on her smudged face. His answer was rather laconic. "Better these clothes than that rag you're wearing."

A deep flush of color crept into Shemaine's cheeks as she dragged the torn sleeve over her shoulder again. "Your charity astounds me, Mr. Thornton. I would think you'd be reluctant to let a stranger wear something that once belonged to your wife."

"The clothes will serve your needs better than my memories," he answered curtly. "And right now I can ill afford to buy a bolt of cloth for you to make yourself a gown. I paid more for you than I had intended, and I must recoup my funds ere I can buy supplies for the ship."

"I'm not ungrateful, Mr. Thornton," Shemaine hastened to assure him. "I really hadn't expected to be given anything but a bit of food and perhaps a place to rest."

"The boy and I sleep here in these two rooms," Gage announced bluntly. "You may have the loft for your bedroom." Bidding her to follow, he led the way back across the great room and, passing through the door-way nearest the kitchen, entered the corri-dor that led to the back porch. On the wall to the right a large drafting desk resided be-neath a tall, shallow cupboard. On the left, a stairway provided access to the loft.

Gage raised a hand toward the stairs, in-viting her to precede him. He couldn't help but watch the way she moved as she climbed, for she had a graceful elegance about her that even the tattered garments could not disguise. Upon reaching the upper level, he stood aside as she strolled about the room. Silently she paused beside the narrow bed, glanced around at the other sparse furnishings and the small fireplace opening in the chimney, and then moved to the rail to look down upon the parlor below. Returning to the cot, she brushed her fin-gers thoughtfully across the top of a rough-hewn table that stood beside it.

"It's rather cramped up here, I know,"

Gage conceded after a moment, "but it's the best I can offer in the way of a separate room for you. Later this afternoon I'll stretch a rope above the balustrade and hang some sailing sheets across it for privacy."

" 'Tis far more than I ever expected, Mr. Thornton." Moved by his kindness, Shemaine tried to curb any outward display of emotion, but against her will it crept into her voice as she continued. "Compared to the cell I shared with the other women on the ship, it seems like a grand, lavish chamber. 'Tis comforting to know that I'll be able to enjoy privacy in something better than the cable tier."

Amazed by her trembling voice, Gage looked at her closely and noticed the teary brightness in the translucent eyes, but she stepped away in awkward silence. Not wishing to embarrass her, he went to the stairs and descended to the lower corridor.

"This is where I started making furniture," he explained after she had joined him there. "The first piece was a curio cabinet for a wealthy matron who assured me that if she liked the piece well enough when I finished it, she'd buy it from me. Since then, I've made quite a few items of furniture for her.

Presently I'm working on this breakfront which she ordered a few weeks ago."

He swept a hand toward the tilted top of the drafting desk, where several drawings of the piece in various stages of construction lay strewn. His talent for creating furniture apparently extended to his drawings as well, for they were as fine and precisely detailed as any finished piece of furniture would be.

Shemaine's eyes roamed upward to the shallow cabinet that hung on the wall above the desk. A diverse collection of ledgers, rolled parchments and sketches, perhaps similar to those which lay on the desktop, were stashed into the small drawers, cubbyholes and shelves of the piece, filling it near to overflowing and attesting to the extent of work her master did at the small desk.

"With all of the orders I've been getting the last few years, I've had to move the cabinet shop outside. It's now located in a large shed at the far end of the path that leads from the back porch. Two of my men have worked for me almost from the very beginning. They were complete novices when they first started, unable to tell the difference between a plank of maple and one of oak.

Even using a saw correctly seemed beyond their comprehension. I dared not trust them with major tasks. But throughout the years both Ramsey Tate and Sly Tucker have progressed far beyond my expectations. I now consider them two of the finest cabinetmakers in the area. Recently I began schooling two new apprentices, a young German and another fellow from Yorktown, but they haven't advanced much further than the saw yet. Normally, at this time of day, I'm working in the shop with them or else helping the old shipwright and his son, but I gave the lot of them the afternoon off so they could tend to some pressing matters of their own while I went to see what the *London Pride* had brought into Newportes Newes."

" 'Tis plain to see you're a very talented man, Mr. Thornton," Shemaine said with sincerity. "I know naught of building ships or the like, but I can recognize a handsome piece of furniture when I see it. If what you have here in this cabin is a fair indication of the quality of furniture you make for people in this area, then your customers will surely miss your craft if you decide to give up the trade entirely."

A brief twitch at the corner of his lips substituted for a smile before Gage raised his head to listen. The gentle pitter-patter of raindrops on the roof indicated the easing of the turbulent downpour and buffeting winds. "It sounds like the storm has slackened. I'd better leave while I can. It might start up again."

"But where should I bathe?" Shemaine queried, unfamiliar with the proper procedure of preparing a bath in a cabin. In her father's house, her baths had been prepared by servants.

"There's water heating over the fire for you already, and there's a well outside at the far end of the back porch from which you can draw more water if you need it. You'll find a washtub hanging in the storeroom. For the time being, it will have to suffice for any baths you and the boy take and any laundry that you do indoors. One of these days, when I have some time, I intend to turn the storeroom into a bathing chamber, but until then, we'll all have to make do with what's available. As long as the weather is tolerable, I bathe in the stream that runs through the inlet. You might have noticed it near the growth of trees on the way up to the cabin. There's not a great deal of privacy to offer a woman, only what the trees may provide, but if you're of such a mind, I'm sure my men and I would enjoy the view."

"I'll bathe inside, thank you," Shemaine replied pertly, feeling a warmth creep into her cheeks.

Once again Gage accepted her reply with a faint smile. "Hannah usually likes me to visit a while, so you should have plenty of time to bathe and dress while I'm gone. But it also depends on the weather." He faced her with a question. "Are you afraid to stay here alone?"

Shemaine smiled a lot easier than he seemed able to do. "Tonight I think I'll be happy to have some privacy. As you can probably imagine, there was a serious scarcity of it aboard the *London Pride*."

"The front door can be bolted from the inside once I'm gone," he informed her. "I'd advise you to take the precaution, just in case some stranger spies the cabin and comes searching for food or valuables and finds you here alone. I'd hate for you to be stolen away before I've even had a chance to see your face washed." Another meager glimpse of a smile hinted at his humor. "When I return, I'll knock three times to let you know it's safe to open the door. Otherwise, don't show yourself at the windows. Before the week is out, I'll try to get around to teaching you how to shoot a musket. I'm not gone that often, but when I am, you'll feel safer knowing how to use it. You can never predict when you might see a bear or wildcat—"

"Or an Indian?" she interjected, having heard rumors about their ferocity on the voyage.

"Or occasionally an Indian," Gage admitted. "But for the most part, they've moved into the mountains or the valleys beyond the Alleghenies. It's gotten too crowded for them around here with all the English, Germans, and those tenacious Scotch-Irish settling in the area."

Shemaine followed him to the door, wondering if there was any need to tell him about Jacob Potts and his threats so soon after he had bought her. But he had seemed distracted since buying her, and she didn't want to give him any excuse for taking her back. *At a more convenient time*, she reasoned, *when it won't trouble him overmuch.*

Pausing at the door, Gage indicated the tall kitchen cupboard standing near the hearth. "There's bread and cheese in there if you get hungry before I return. Hannah usually packs some food for me to bring home when she knows Andrew and I are here alone. At least tonight you'll be well fed. I can make no guarantees for the morrow."

Opening the heavy portal, he stepped out onto the porch, glanced quickly around the area, and then pulled the door closed behind him. The floorboards creaked slightly as he crossed to the front steps. After his departure, a long moment of enjoyable silence ensued. Then, with a soft smile, Shemaine laid the heavy bolt in place across the door, for the first time in many months feeling a surge of hope for the future.

CHAPTER 4

A lengthy shampoo and a warm, leisurely bath did wonders for Shemaine's spirit. She marveled at the enormous change in herself as she dragged on a frayed chemise from the dead woman's trunk. Once she would have casually discarded the undergarment as a castoff, not worthy of being used for anything but a servant's dust cloth or a scrub rag. Wearing a riding habit relentlessly day in and day out for several months certainly had a way of making one feel immensely grateful for any apparel that was clean and reasonably intact. Though there were nicer shifts packed away in the chest, even a lace-trimmed one which had obviously been the woman's best, Shemaine refused to take her new master's benevolence for granted. In determining her future needs, she had also laid out a second chemise, a green gown, a pale blue one, two long white aprons, and a pair of black slippers, all of which had seen a lot of use.

Once she had bathed and washed her hair, Shemaine began to sense the importance of demonstrating her gratitude to Gage Thornton for having bought her, and what better way of accomplishing that feat, she decided, than proving herself an enterprising cook and efficient servant. Granted, it would take some time before she regained her strength and stamina, but she wrapped a towel about her wet head and then, garbed only in the chemise, set about testing her ability in the preparation of food.

A few years had passed since Bess Huxley, their family cook, had tried to stimulate her interest in culinary endeavors and teach her the basic techniques required for success. At the time, Shemaine had grudgingly performed the tasks, doing them over and over again until she had attained the perfection the woman had demanded, but she had loathed stirring sauces endlessly so they wouldn't scorch and beating egg whites until they peaked. She had been convinced that Bess's instructions were a wasted effort, for even at a younger age she could not imagine herself marrying a man without the means and properties to warrant a house full of servants.

So much for her expectations, Shemaine mentally jeered. Bess had warned her not to be so high-minded, for a mere girl could not predict what man would ask for her hand or, for that matter, to whom she would give her heart . . . *if* she were fortunate enough to be allowed a choice. Despite the cook's arduous drilling, Shemaine was sure there was much that she had forgotten about her training. Yet it was now necessary for her to prove her capability and, if she could, to recall everything that Bess Huxley strove so hard to teach her. There was nothing quite as motivating as desperation to make one acutely attentive to another's sage advice.

Shemaine busied herself making crumpets from memory. While serving out her time in the solitude of the cable tier, she had yearningly remembered the relaxed afternoon teas she had once enjoyed with her family. Those cherished memories came drifting back now with poignant clarity as she made the basic dough. After mixing it, she covered the bowl with a cloth and set it near the warmth of the hearth where the bread could rise while she resumed her toilette.

It seemed an endless drudgery combing the stubborn snarls out of her wet hair as she sat before the fire. The task took much longer than Shemaine had expected, and she became concerned about the time, for the afternoon seemed to be flitting rapidly away. In desperation she searched about for a pair of scissors to make short work of her hair, but she found nothing better than a butcher knife. The disaster that particular tool might wreak promptly dissuaded her.

While going through the articles stored in the trunk, she had found a brush with several long strands of blond hair twined about the bristles. Though her new master had given her leave to use whatever she had need of, Shemaine could not bring herself to destroy such a precious keepsake. She searched through the man's possessions instead, finding most of his clothes and underwear neatly stacked and separated in his armoire. The only exception was a clean bundle of wrinkled shirts that were of much finer quality than the homespun garment he was presently wearing. They had been stuffed in the very back of the cabinet and had been there so long they had taken on the scent of the wood. As pleasant as the smell was, Shemaine decided that one of her very first laundry duties would be to wash, starch and iron the shirts for her master. After that, whether or not they were worn would be entirely up to the man, but at least he'd have an option.

The rain began again in earnest, and not knowing whether the downpour would deter or hasten Mr. Thornton's return, Shemaine did not dare dawdle over her hair any longer. She finally located a brush in a drawer in the man's shaving stand and made use of it to smooth the rest of the tangles from her hair. The heavy tresses were still slightly damp when she plaited them and coiled the resulting two braids close against her nape. Then she quickly washed the brush, dried it, and put it back where she had found it, hoping her master wouldn't notice that it had been used in his absence.

Both gowns were too long, as Gage had

predicted, and snug across her breasts. It amazed Shemaine that a man could remember his wife with such unerring accuracy that he could correctly judge the sizes of other women just by his memory of her a full year after her passing. The bodices could not be let out, Shemaine discovered after examining the seams, and any alterations to the hems would have to wait until she had more time. She selected the green gown to wear only because it seemed a trifle shorter. After donning the shoes, she strapped on thin rawhide laces to hold the light leather slippers on her feet and then wound the cords up around her ankles and tied them in a knot. She wrinkled her nose in disgust at how red and marred her ankles had become from the constant chafing of the shackles. She could only imagine how much more irritated they would become from the leather strips.

Shemaine checked the dough and, much to her relief and delight, found that it had risen quite well despite being rushed. She added the next ingredients until the batter became the right consistency. Once again she set the mixture near the fireplace. Then she busied herself dusting and tidying the cabin.

Once the dough had risen sufficiently for a second time, Shemaine laid a griddle on a rack where it could be heated to the right temperature by the flames. Having every intention of presenting her new master with an opportunity to enjoy a light, leisurely afternoon repast, she set a pot of tea to steep near the hearth, hoping fervently that he would return in time to taste the crumpets and tea while both were still hot and fresh.

Though the lessons had been learned years ago, they had undoubtedly been indelibly etched upon Shemaine's memory through constant repetition, for the crumpets were an unblemished marvel. For the first time in her life, she was ecstatic over the results and wonderfully grateful that Bess Huxley had demanded excellence in whatever cooking assignment her student had undertaken. If only, Shemaine sighed forlornly, she could recall all of Bess's meticulous instructions with the same success.

A rapid ascent of the front steps alerted her to the presence of another, then three quick raps on the heavy door eased the prickling along her nape. Leaving several crumpets browning on the iron griddle, Shemaine ran to the portal, lifted the bolt and swung the door wide to admit the rain-drenched man.

For the length of his return journey and during his rapid flight to the cabin, Gage Thornton had sought to keep both his young son, whom he now carried, and a large basket of food, which he bore over an arm, protected beneath a tarp. He was still intent upon his mission even as he stepped into the cabin. He gave Shemaine little notice as she hastened back to the hearth, but shoved the door closed with a shoulder and dropped the basket on a rough-hewn table near the entrance before he swept away the sheltering cover from his son. When the boy saw a stranger in the house, he pressed back against his father's shoulder, immediately shy and reluctant to be parted from the security of his parent, but the aroma filling the cabin soon drew his amber-lit brown eyes to the hearth.

"Daddee . . . Andee . . . hungee."

The delicious smell had attracted Gage's curiosity as well, and after setting his son down beside him, he peered inquiringly toward the griddle as he tugged the tail of his soaked shirt out of his buckskin breeches. "What smells so good?"

"I remembered how to make crumpets," Shemaine announced with a smile that wavered between timidity and pride.

Whatever she had been about to add was stricken from her mind as Gage dragged the sodden garment over his head and dropped it into an oaken bucket near the door. The sight of his lean waist, wide muscular shoulders and taut chest rippling with thews was more than a little unsettling for a young woman who, during her few excursions on the deck of the *London Pride*, had been subjected to the sight of many potbellied and narrow-shouldered sailors who had been amply disposed toward strutting about shirtless in front of the women, as if they had imagined themselves admirable examples of manly prowess, worthy of impressing the most discriminating of the opposite gender.

In comparison, Gage Thornton had an extraordinarily fine physique, possibly the best Shemaine could remember ever viewing in her limited encounters with half-garbed men. Yet, for all of that, he seemed oblivious to his own exceptional appearance and the mental disarray it caused his bondswoman.

Shemaine couldn't recall ever seeing a man who, by simply shedding a shirt, could unnerve her. With that invading jitteriness came the realization that except for the child she was completely alone with a strange man for the very first time in her life. Any true lady would have been less awed by his anatomy and far more cautious of the man, for under the circumstances she was really quite vulnerable to the whims of her master.

Abashed by her own forwardness at openly admiring his lightly furred chest and broad shoulders, and equally reluctant to be caught gaping, Shemaine turned back to her cooking, adding with a decidedly shaky comment, "I thought you and Andrew might enjoy some crumpets with your afternoon tea."

"Let me get out of these wet clothes and I'll be right with you," Gage replied eagerly as he hastened to his bedroom. The one thing that had spoiled his complete satisfaction with his indentured servant was his concern over her inability to cook. Despite his efforts not to, he had continued to worry over the matter, wondering how his small family would survive on poorly prepared meals. It was a tremendous relief to realize the girl knew more than she had first let on. When she could cook something that wafted so tantalizingly through his senses it could make his mouth water, it spurred some hope that she would be capable of doing even more.

"Daddee!" Andrew squealed in sudden anxiety, realizing his father had left him. He shot a wide-eyed look of panic at Shemaine and ran into the bedroom screaming in terror.

Shemaine smiled as she heard Gage soothe the fears of his sobbing son.

"It's all right, Andy. Shemaine is going to be living with us and taking care of you while Daddy makes chests and tables—"

"An' big ship, too, Daddee?" the boy asked through his tears.

"And big ship, too, Andy."

Shemaine set the teapot down on the table, added a cup and saucer, two small plates, utensils, and fruit preserves that she had found in the cupboard. A moment later Gage came out of the bedroom carrying his son, having changed into a pair of dark brown hide breeches and a loose-sleeved, homespun shirt. Before her arrest, Shemaine had found herself more inclined to admire men dressed to the hilt in elegant attire. Maurice had been an exceptionally garbed individual, looking the most handsome in black silk frock coats, waistcoats and breeches to match. With hair and eyes of the same dark hue, the stark contrast between the black silk garments and the snowy white shirts and stocks he usually wore with them had been no less than dramatic. Indeed, dressed out for formal occasions, Maurice had been most effective in causing feminine hearts to race in avid admiration. Still, when her new master came nigh to halting her breath wearing such rough garb, Shemaine had to wonder if she would ever again be moved to awe by princely appareled lords in silk stockings.

Gage sat the boy in the high chair at the end of the table, tied a bib around his neck, and then settled himself on the bench to Andrew's left. Shemaine leaned across the table to place the plate of crumpets in the center, prompting Gage to glance up as he thanked her, but as the hanging lantern cast its light upon her face, he saw her clearly for the first time since his return.

If there was anything capable of disrupting that maddeningly cryptic reserve of his or those sparse smiles, Shemaine guessed the change in her appearance qualified. When their gazes had first met on the *London Pride*, she had been startled by the strength of those glittering brown eyes, but there was something entirely different about the slow, exacting way he looked her over now, as if he were seeing her for the first time as a woman instead of a possession. Shemaine held her breath in trepidation, wondering if the sight of her wearing Victoria's clothes would cause him to regret his kindness to her.

"You look different . . ." Gage murmured finally. "Very nice, in fact." *Indeed! Too beautiful for a man who's been without a woman for the last year*, he thought, dropping his gaze and fixing it with great determination on the crumpets. Almost mechanically he reached for one, sliced it apart and spread preserves on one of the halves for his son.

"Should I pour Andrew some tea?" Shemaine asked uncertainly, still unable to determine Gage's mood, for he seemed even more distant than he had before.

Avoiding the folly of looking her way, Gage pushed himself to his feet. It was a painful truth that abstinence had a way of sharpening a man's senses to an agonizing intensity when a winsome maid was so near at hand. "I've got some milk cooling in the well," he answered at last. "If you'd like, I'll show you where it's kept."

"Should I get the tarp?" she inquired, not wishing to get soaked and cold again. She hadn't ventured out to the well while he was gone, for she had been anxious to bathe and had only waited until the water in the kettle had gotten warm enough to use.

"No, there's no need. I built a roof over the back porch and extended it far enough over the well so we can stay dry even when it's raining."

Gage led her through the back corridor, lifted the bolt from the door, and swung it open for her. Stepping past him, Shemaine went out onto the porch and once again had a chance to marvel at the diligent man. It was becoming increasingly evident to her that Gage Thornton enjoyed creating things that were not only beautiful to behold but completely serviceable as well.

At the far end of the porch was the well he had mentioned, constructed of stone and wood. But that was not all that she took note of. Where the back steps ended, flat stones had been laid close together, forming a winding path that ranged far beyond the cabin. A variety of rain-drenched spring flowers and herbs, tucked in here and there among blooming shrubs and fruit trees, bordered both sides of the meandering lane. A short distance away, a lean-to filled to capacity with cords of wood buttressed a small smokehouse. Beside it, dirt had been piled to form a generous knoll, at the front of which was a door that obviously served as an opening to a root cellar. Farther on, in the midst of a chicken yard, a henhouse had been equipped with cubbyholes lined along the side in a neat row, allowing for easy removal of eggs from the nests. Nearby, a shed had been built to accommodate two fenced pastures, one for a pair of horses, the other for a cow and a nursing calf. At the far end of the walk was a large, tin-roofed structure nestled in among the trees.

"That's where the men and I make the furniture," Gage announced, waving a hand in the general direction. "There's a large shed behind it where we season some of the wood that we use for building the ship and making the furniture."

"Daddee!" Andrew called worriedly from the cabin.

"I'm coming, Andy," Gage answered promptly, and pulled a rope out of the well, drawing forth a jug of milk. He hooked a finger through the handle, swung the door open for Shemaine, and eyed her tightly garbed bosom as she turned away. The subtle swing of her skirts held his gaze as she swept through the back room.

Returning to the table, Gage set the jug down, but stood waiting beside the bench. It was a full moment before Shemaine realized he was expecting her to sit down. At her questioning glance, he swept a hand invitingly toward the bench nearest her.

"Here in this cabin, Shemaine, we all eat together. You'll be treated as one of the family in my house and by all of those who enter in."

Sliding onto the polished plank of the seat, Shemaine meekly clasped her hands together in her lap and whispered gratefully, "Thank you, Mr. Thornton."

"Gage . . . my name is Gage." He sat down across from her, but he still couldn't trust himself to look at her too long, for fear of kindling desires that he would be hard-pressed to subdue. He had never owned a bondslave before, much less a woman, and although he had heard of masters ignoring the injunctions that forbade the rape and abuse of their indentured servants, he preferred not to add his name to their number. "Everybody calls me that. You should, too. I don't like being called Mr. Thornton . . . except by my enemies."

Hating the tears that welled in her eyes, Shemaine managed a small, submissive nod as she struggled to keep them hidden. "If that is your wish . . . Gage."

He passed the plate of crumpets across the table. "Now eat, Shemaine. You're too thin to my way of thinking."

"Yes, sir."

Andrew had followed this dialogue with interest, glancing from one to the other. Then he leaned close to the table and peered up at Shemaine inquisitively as she sat with her head bowed. Feeling the youngster's stare, she hurriedly blinked at the moisture blurring her vision and bravely bestowed a smile upon him. Curiously he looked toward his father.

"Sheeaim cry, Daddee."

Helplessly Shemaine lifted her head and

met the probing gaze of the man as tiny rivulets flowed freely down her cheeks. Considering how resolutely she had defied Morrisa's and Gertrude's attempts to see her humiliated and destroyed, she could hardly believe that she could lose control of herself just because someone was showing a bit of kindness to her. "I'm sorry, Mr. Thorn—" She halted, fearing her composure would crumple altogether if she corrected herself and used the more familiar form of address. She struggled to explain. "I didn't . . . expect to be treated so well. 'Tis been nigh to four months or more since I've heard a kind word spoken to me or had a gentleman open a door for me or to even stand until I was seated. I'm greatly embarrassed by my crying, sir . . . but I just can't seem to help myself."

Gage reached into his pants pocket, withdrew a clean handkerchief, and passed it to her. Then he rose and stepped away as she dabbed at her eyes. Opening the cupboard, he took out a pair of small mugs, poured milk nigh to the brim of one and then splashed a smaller amount into the other. Upon his return to the table, he passed her the full mug with an exhortation. "Drink it down, Shemaine. You need the milk more than tea. 'Twill help calm you." He sliced open another crumpet, spread both sides with fruit preserves, and then placed them on a second plate, which he set before her. "Enjoy your crumpets, girl. They smell wonderful."

Shemaine laughed despite her tears and noticed a brief smile chase across Gage's lips as he stared back at her. For some reason, it lightened her heart and spirits to see that meager easing of his stern demeanor. Obediently she sipped from the mug, finding the milk cold and delicious, and then eagerly nibbled the crumpets. Andrew drank noisily from the other mug, which his father helped to hold. Afterward, Gage poured tea for himself and began to partake of the cakes. They ate in silence for a moment, each enjoying the sumptuous fare. Then, with casual deliberation, Gage set about to ease his bondslave's tension with a tale of a bear that had pestered him for a while a few years ago.

"Ol' One Ear was an incredibly mean critter, hated people intensely, no doubt because he had lost an ear to a trapper who had barely escaped with his life. He ventured onto my property several times without doing much harm, but one early frosty morning after leaving the privy, I surprised Ol' One Ear trying to get to a young calf that I had bought earlier in the spring. I guess he had planned to break his morning fast with it, and when I came out and interrupted him, it enraged him. It didn't take me long to realize that Ol' One Ear wanted revenge, at the very least a bite out of my hide. I had left my musket in the cabin, and he stood there in front of me, just daring me to make a move. I was basically defenseless, with nothing but my breeches on. Victoria heard all the racket the bear was making and came running out the back door with my loaded muzzle-loader. She was nearly full term with Andrew by then, but she didn't hesitate. The bear swung around to charge her, but she laid the stock against her shoulder and blew a hole right between his eyes." A smile flashed almost as swift as the blink of an eye. "That's how we got a bear rug for the bedroom floor. I tanned the skin and put it on Victoria's side of the bed. It kept her feet from getting chilled that next winter when she had to get up during the night to nurse Andrew."

Though Shemaine's eyes were still red, the tears had stopped, and the green orbs were warmly animated behind long, wetly spiked lashes. Bracing a thin elbow on the table, she dropped her chin into her palm and grinned back at him. "I think you'd better teach me how to fire a musket, Mr. Thornton, for your safety as well as mine."

"Hopefully before the week is out," Gage replied as a responding smile flitted across his lips.

When the light repast drew to an end, Shemaine rose and began to gather up the dishes while Gage washed Andrew's face and hands and took the boy up in his arms. The youngster yawned and laid his head upon his father's shoulder as Gage made his way into the bedroom. When he stepped out again, Gage closed the door gently behind himself. Taking the jug of milk from the table, he returned it to the well and then came back to the kitchen carrying a small crock.

"This is a salve I use on anything that needs softening or healing," he told his bondslave. "It also works on more serious wounds, but I use it mainly on calluses, scrapes, and the like." Taking off the lid, he

approached the wooden sink, where Shemaine was presently washing dishes, and
held out the crock for her to look inside. "I
was thinking it may help soothe some of
those red weals around your wrists and ankles."

Shemaine put away the last dish in the
cupboard and then peered down into the jar,
finding a translucent ointment with a dark
yellowish cast. One small whiff of it, however, made her wrinkle her nose in distaste.

"I know. The smell is enough to kill a
skunk," Gage quipped. "But it will do everything I said it would."

Trying not to shudder, Shemaine glanced
up at him. "What should I do with it?"

"Actually, it needs to be really rubbed into
the chafed skin. If you'd allow me, I think I'd
be able to work it in better."

Shemaine felt a warmth creep into her
cheeks at the idea of a man doing such a
service for a lady, and hastened to deny his
request. "Oh, I don't think that would be
proper, sir."

"Why not, may I ask?" Gage questioned
curtly. When he had no other purpose in
mind but to help her, he could find little sympathy for her views on propriety. "Your

wrists and ankles need attention, Shemaine, and putting this salve on them isn't going to jeopardize your virtue in the least. Believe me, girl, you'll know it if I ever set my mind on compromising your modesty, because I won't start with your wrists *or* your ankles." His eyes dipped to her tautly garbed bosom, as if pointedly denoting the place where he'd begin, and then just as quickly rose to meet her astonished stare.

Shemaine closed her mouth, realizing it had sagged open. It certainly didn't help her composure to feel a scalding heat creeping into her cheeks. Self-consciously she crossed her arms in front of her, wishing the gown wasn't so tight. Though her protest wasn't exactly the truth, she declared it as such. "I-I c-can assure you, Mr. Thornton, that concern for my virtue was the farthest thing from my mind!"

A brief twitch served as substitute for a skeptical smile. "Then you're far different than most of the young women I've come in contact with in this area. There are many who think a widower is in such dire straits that he's liable to throw up the nearest skirt and have his way with a maid, by force if need be." Gage noticed her cheeks were now flaming and wondered if she was offended by his rather crude statement or if his needling had touched upon the truth. "Believe me, Shemaine, I'm a little more selective than that."

"So am I, sir!" Shemaine raised her chin in an obstinate huff. "And if I'm permitted to object to being likened to the other women you've met here, I can promise you that I'm an individual, sir, not prone to falling prostrate at *any* man's feet. Believe me, I'll be quite content to live out my days of service to you as an unsullied spinster. And I'll keep my wrists and ankles to myself, *if* you don't mind!"

An angry quirk tightened the corners of Gage's mouth as he stretched out a hand and settled the jar in her grasp. "If you should decide otherwise, Shemaine, I'll be happy to accommodate you . . . without compromising your virginity."

Pivoting about-face, he strode from the room and went out through the back entrance, causing Shemaine to jump as the door slammed loudly behind him. Of a sudden, her anger fled, to be replaced by an overwhelming sense of dread and worry. She could have acted more wisely, she chided herself. She didn't have to make it so clear to the man that she was afraid of him touching her with those nice, lean, beautiful hands.

Andrew began to whimper in the next room, perhaps having been awakened by the banging of the door. Shemaine hurried to the bedroom door, pushed it carefully open, and looked in. The boy was curled on his side in the middle of the four-poster with a coverlet spread over him. His eyes were closed, but a frown puckered his little brows. The corners of his mouth were downturned as he issued a soft, dejected mewl. Tiptoeing to the bed, she leaned across and slowly stroked the boy's face as she began to sing an Irish lullaby. The frown faded almost instantly, and his breathing deepened. Then with a serene sigh, he sprawled on his back and drifted soundly off to sleep. Humming softly, Shemaine covered the boy again and then turned to leave.

Her heart leapt nearly out of her bosom when her eyes fell on the darkly garbed form framed in the doorway. Gage stood there in a relaxed mode with a shoulder braced against the jamb, looking for all the world as if he had been watching her for some time.

The idea brought the heat rushing back into her cheeks as she tried to recall her actions over the last several moments. Unable to imagine what had compelled him to observe her without making his presence known, she hurried to the portal, intending to leave him to the privacy of his bedroom, but to her dismay, he made no move to retreat.

Finding her path completely blocked by his tall, broad-shouldered frame, Shemaine lifted her eyes to his, totally aware of how puny her strength was compared to his. If he decided to exert his will upon her, she knew well enough how it would end. With thumping heart she waited until he backed around into the parlor, finally allowing her an avenue of escape. Relief flooded through her as she stepped through the door. Aware of his proximity, she would have slipped quickly away, but as she passed he caught her arm, sending a multitude of anxious emotions catapulting through her. Now that the son was asleep, Shemaine was instantly alert to the possibility that the father might consider the moment favorable for launching an assault upon her person, which would force her to defend herself by whatever meager means were at her disposal. Though his grip was gentle, it was tantamount to being snared by a dreaded gaoler who had power to take her life or to free her. Fearing the worst, she braced herself as she cautiously met his gaze.

"Did you want something of me, Mr. Thornton?"

Gage leaned behind her, causing her to stiffen apprehensively, but he only pulled the bedroom door gently closed. "I came back to apologize," he said quietly as he straightened. "I know that you've been through a lot, and that Captain Fitch had a yearning to buy you and make you his mistress behind his wife's back, but not all men are like that. I shouldn't have baited you as I did, Shemaine. I'm sorry."

Shemaine stared at him in amazement. *That's all he wanted to do? To apologize? Didn't he know he came nigh to frightening a full score of years off my life?*

Shemaine smiled with difficulty, somewhat embarrassed because she had panicked and, without provocation, imagined that he had wanted to bed down with her, as if he might have found her irresistible. As he had already indicated, the fact that he was a widower didn't necessarily mean that he was also a lecher. Besides, he had said he thought her much too thin.

As her heart eased its frantic beating and her reasoning slowly returned, Shemaine was able to comprehend more fully what he had actually said to her and was somewhat surprised by his keen perception. Captain Fitch had thought himself shrewd in his efforts to arrange a tryst, but here was a total stranger who had detected his plan right away. Perhaps Gertrude Fitch was not as astute as she had imagined herself to be.

Still struggling with a copious measure of chagrin, Shemaine lowered her gaze as she responded demurely to his apology. "It doesn't make me feel any better knowing you had probable cause to take offense at my childishness, Mr. Thornton. All I was concerned about was how inappropriate it was for an unmarried gentleman like yourself to tend a lady's wrists and ankles. I realize now that you only meant to help me."

And not to rape me! she added mutely, mentally chiding herself.

"I'd like to," Gage reassured her gently, snatching her gaze upward as his reply intruded on the very heels of her whimsical thought. By dint of will, Shemaine curbed her unruly fantasies and disciplined herself to be more attentive to what her master was saying, lest she fall prey to her own illusions. His voice was strong, yet cajoling. "I believe the salve will soothe away much of the redness."

"Then you may." With that calmly spoken commitment, Shemaine released her breath in a wavering sigh, braving a smile. "But do be careful about my ankles. Jacob Potts yanked me off my feet today, and I'm not sure which is more bruised, my backside or my ankles."

The barest hint of a grin defied that prevalently somber visage. "I'd be happy to massage both areas if you'd like."

No sooner had Shemaine managed to gain control of her wandering imagination than he dashed her efforts to smithereens. It was no wonder she found herself susceptible to thinking the worst! His unpredictable humor encouraged such imprudent speculations!

The green eyes fixed a blatantly suspicious stare upon the handsome man as she dared to test the precise depth of his mettle. "If I were to guess the origin of those brief glimpses I've seen of your humor, Mr.

Thornton, I'd be of a mind to swear that you were stolen away as a wee babe by the little people, who took great delight in training you to tease the warts off a toad."

Her farfetched conjecture drew a genuine chuckle from the man. "And here I was thinking it was the stone I had kissed at Lord Blarney's castle," he countered, and swept a hand to indicate the rocking chair in front of the hearth. "Sit there, Shemaine, and I'll rub this concoction into your skin."

"I don't know if I'll be able to stand myself when you're through," she mumbled through an exaggerated groan. "The stench is enough to turn my stomach." Suddenly suspicious of his motives, she peered at him sharply. "You're not trying to make a fool of me with that stuff, are you?"

His eyes sparkled tantalizingly. "I'd certainly be able to sniff you out if you decided to run away."

Shemaine turned promptly about, intending to make good her escape right then and there, but with an evanescent chuckle, Gage caught her wrist and tugged her back.

"Come, Shemaine. I'm only doing what the wee little people taught me to do so well.

Being as Irish as you are, do you not ken when a body is teasing you?"

She tossed her head in rampant distrust. "At various times I've been able to understand why the English hate the Irish so much, for surely they can pester the devil himself 'til he screams. In this case, however, I think the roles have been reversed."

The amber-flecked brown eyes gleamed back at her, reflecting the firelight as well as a warmth that burned from within. "Have no fear, Shemaine," he urged. "The ointment can be washed off after I've massaged it into your skin, but even before then, it begins to lose some of its odor."

Shemaine settled into the rocking chair and cautiously submitted herself to his care as he knelt before her. Allowing him to fold back her sleeves didn't seem terribly difficult for her to bear, but she was leery nevertheless as he dipped his thin fingers into the ointment and began to rub her slender wrists, spreading the salve. He worked it into the reddened skin with a slow, gentle, circling motion of his thumb until the odor actually began to fade, amazing Shemaine completely, for in its stead a far more subtle scent reached her nostrils as her master bent his head forward while concentrating on his task. It was a strange, pleasant blend of odors: the homespun cloth of his shirt, the leather pants he wore, the soap he had recently used to wash his hands, and a clean, masculine smell, all combining to form a warm, thoroughly intriguing essence that quickened her awareness of the man. Shemaine realized she was affected in ways she had never dreamt possible, for her womanly senses responded to his gentle touch, awakening like the unfolding petals of a flower.

"I wouldn't use the leather cords to hold your slippers on anymore, Shemaine, at least not until your ankles heel," Gage advised as he unwound the slender thongs from around her feet. "They might hamper the healing process."

He lifted a bare foot in his hand, quickening the pace of Shemaine's heart. Her eyes were wide with uncertainty as she met his gaze, but he seemed totally unconcerned as he dipped his fingers in the balm again.

"You'd better lift your hem," Gage cautioned. "Otherwise it may get stained."

Hesitantly Shemaine pulled her chemise

and gown up a modest degree, and though Gage waited, there was no further response. Arching a challenging brow, he peered at her again until she grudgingly dragged the hems a bit higher. Still dissatisfied with the limited area she had left him to work in, Gage sighed in frustration, rested her bare foot on his thigh and, with his clean hand, pushed her skirts up almost to her knee, drawing a startled gasp from her. Ignoring her nervous confusion, he took her foot in his hand again and began spreading the balm around her ankle. He massaged it in gradually, rubbing his thumb around in ever-encompassing circles, over the top of her arch, down to her toes, beneath the sole of her foot. Cupping her small heel in the palm of one hand, he gently kneaded the whole of the foot with the other. His deliberate, methodical strokes soon calmed her, and Shemaine found herself slowly relaxing in the rocking chair, leaning her head back against the curved top.

"You have a nice voice, Shemaine," Gage commented softly as he began to rub ointment over her other foot. "Victoria used to sing to Andrew, too. Even as a small babe, he seemed to listen intently before he drifted off to sleep, but there has been no one to sing to him since the accident. I'm not very capable in that area."

"You're so gifted in many other ways, I find myself in awe of your talents," Shemaine replied, lulled by his tender ministrations and the warming fire that framed his wide shoulders and fine, dark head. "If you didn't have any flaws, Mr. Thornton, you wouldn't be human."

"Oh, I'm human all right," Gage averred, caressing her small, dainty foot with his hands. His thumbs combined to work their magic, scrolling leisurely over, around and under. It crossed his mind that he hadn't seen anything about his bondslave yet that wasn't worth admiring, even her delicately boned feet.

"We're all human." Shemaine sighed. "None of us is perfect, and we should not expect perfection from those around us. Indeed, if we understood our own flaws better, we'd be more tolerant of the faults of others and be less inclined to take offense at the slightest provocation. If men could forgive with the same fervent spirit with which they wage war, I think we'd be able to live more at peace with each other. Still, there are those who are so evil they must not be tolerated."

Gage's hands moved up to massage her ankle. "Did you meet someone like that on the *London Pride*?"

Shemaine knew the time had come to tell him of her enemies. "There were several aboard the *London Pride*. Gertrude Fitch, the captain's wife, was one. Jacob Potts was another. But Morrisa Hatcher was the most clever of the three. She worked her wiles to incite the other two, promising her favors to Potts, who, in turn, seemed capable of motivating Mrs. Fitch to take action against the rest of us with his conniving lies. Anyone who didn't kowtow to him or Morrisa was susceptible to being punished, mainly because of some mandate Mrs. Fitch managed to wheedle or harass from her husband. Although Mrs. Fitch thought herself to be clever, she was actually the most gullible of the three. Potts at least knew what he'd be getting in exchange for doing Morrisa's mischief. It was a vicious cycle, but Morrisa was the one to benefit from it the most. She seemed far more dedicated in her desire to reap havoc on her adversaries, most especially me. But 'twas obvious all three harbored resentment toward me and wanted to see me dead."

Gage noticed that Shemaine seemed suddenly on edge, as if fearful of something beyond his ken. "And do you think they will continue to seek your death?"

"Although Mrs. Fitch might long to see my demise, she would not outwardly seek it here in the colonies. 'Tis one thing for her to reign supreme on a ship owned by her father, but quite another to answer to British authorities in a strange land. As for the other two, they will continue their quest as long as they are here," Shemaine avouched with certainty. " 'Tis what they have promised. Morrisa will send Potts to do the deed and then laugh in glee when he does."

"Is he a man I saw on the ship?" Gage questioned, rubbing her leg again.

"James Harper banished him to the cable tier just moments before you came aboard. He's a huge man, half again your size, with straw-colored hair, ruddy cheeks and a rather large, bulbous nose."

A twinge of his lips gave hint to Gage's amusement. "Your description leaves me wondering if Potts haunts your dreams at night. You've obviously memorized him quite well, Shemaine."

"I'd recognize him a fair distance off, to be sure."

"Hopefully, you'll have time to warn me if you see him coming."

"But you will teach me how to fire a musket fairly soon, won't you?" she pressed anxiously, knowing there would likely be days when he would be gone and she'd be left to defend herself if Potts came looking for her.

Gage raised a brow with blatant skepticism as he asked a pertinent question. "Do you really think you have it in you to kill a man, Shemaine?"

"If Mr. Potts finds me, I may have to," she reasoned. "He'll kill me if I can't defend myself."

"Usually when any of the men or I spot a boat coming to shore, one of us goes down to meet it, but I must confess there are times when we get too busy to even look through the windows of the cabinet shop. Just ring the bell by the front steps or scream your head off if you see Potts. I'm sure one of us will hear one or the other and come running."

"I don't think you understand what you or your men would be up against, Mr. Thornton," Shemaine answered carefully. "The man is a brute. A huge beast of a man! It would take two like you fighting together to best the monster."

"I can usually take care of myself or anything else that belongs to me," Gage assured her, but he made allowances for his inability to accurately perceive trouble before it happened or to see clearly into the future. "But just in case, I'll teach you how to fire a musket."

Shemaine sighed in relief, having obtained what she had wanted. Leaning forward, she watched as he rubbed a towel down her legs to remove the excess ointment. Then he sat back on his haunches, allowing her to lower her skirts, and began wiping his hands on the towel, seeming perfectly at ease on the floor.

Shemaine was amazed that she was already experiencing some relief from the rawness of the sores. "I do believe, Mr. Thornton, that among your many other talents, you're also a very fine physician. My ankles feel better already. Thank you very much."

Gage dipped his head slightly in acceptance of her gracious comment, but it was not so much what she said that enthralled him as it was the inflection she placed on certain words, especially his name, for her syllables sounded as magical and pleasing as the silvery tinkling of tiny bells on a breezy morn. Well aware that he had all but insisted she call him by his given name, he had to admit that when the more formal address came from her lips, it stirred his senses no small degree. Her pronunciations, as articulate as they were, had definitely been influenced by the brogue of Shemus O'Hearn.

"Your ankles should be looking better in a few days," he predicted. "In a month's time, the redness will likely be gone, and perhaps by then I'll be able to afford a pair of shoes."

"You needn't worry about buying me any shoes, Mr. Thornton," Shemaine replied softly. "I'm grateful to have the ones you gave me to wear. As you accurately surmised, they are a bit long, but 'twill not be hard for me to get used to them. I know well what it's like to go without, and I'm thankful to have a pair, whatever their condition or fit. Truthfully, 'tis far more comfortable to have my feet shod than feel every pebble or splinter I come upon."

"It took no great insight on my part to determine that Victoria's shoes would be too large for you," Gage pointed out. "Though fine-boned, my wife was nearly half a head taller than you."

"Andrew will be tall too, I think," Shemaine predicted, glancing down at his father's hands. Gage's fingers were long, slender, and rather squarish at the tips, as handsome as the man himself. "How can the boy not be when you're so tall yourself? I'm sure he'll be the very image of you when he grows up."

"Victoria said as much soon after Andrew was born," Gage recalled. "And perhaps that will be true, since she was so fair. Her hair was as pale as cornsilk and had a sheen that matched. I used to watch it blowing in the wind and was always amazed by the fact that the strands never seemed to get tangled."

Self-consciously Shemaine smoothed a wispy curl back from her face. Her hair was far from finely textured. It was so thick and rebellious, the heavy curls had to be restrained by braids or upswept creations that could test the patience of the most ingenious coiffeur. Her lady's maid in England had enjoyed the challenge of combing her hair into beautiful styles and bragging about the golden highlights in it. But the woman had brushed and tended her hair since her tenth birthday and naturally was a bit prejudiced. In lauding her own praises, Nola had often claimed that no aristocrat's pampered darling would ever be as exquisitely coifed as *her* Shemaine.

"I fear my hair is as ornery as it looks," Shemaine complained, wishing she had but a small measure of Nola's talent. "I came nigh to cutting it off this afternoon, just to be free of the snarls."

Gage watched an obstinate tendril readily rebound as soon as her hand dropped away. He wanted to reach out and rub the curl between his fingers just to feel its silky texture, but he checked the urge, guessing his bondslave would bolt like a frightened deer. He was already familiar with a variety of her qualms and considered it a rare accomplishment indeed to have massaged those shapely limbs as long as he had. "I like your hair, Shemaine, and I would not take it kindly if you were to cut it off."

Suddenly apprehensive of the areas where she might unwittingly offend him, Shemaine began to fret about what she had already done and decided it was far better to admit the truth than have him learn of her deed in some other fashion. "I hope you won't be too angry with me, Mr. Thornton . . ." she said in an anxious rush. "After using it, I was careful to wash it and put it back where I found it. . . ."

"It?" Gage's brow lifted warily. "What are you trying to tell me, Shemaine? What is *it*?"

"Your brush," she answered simply. "I had to use it to get the snarls out of my hair."

Behind an abbreviated smile, Gage breathed a sigh of relief. "Is that all? The way you acted, I was sure you had committed some grievous mayhem."

"You don't mind that I used it?" Shemaine asked in amazement. "You're not angry?"

"Should I be?" he questioned with a devilish gleam in his eyes. "Do you have something I'd rather not have?"

Laughing, Shemaine shook her head. "I'm not aware of any infestation, sir."

Gage rubbed his chin reflectively, squelching the desire to grin as he teased. "Perhaps you should be afraid of what I may have given you, Shemaine. You *did* say you washed the brush afterwards and not before, didn't you?"

Bracing her hands upon her knees, Shemaine settled an impishly quizzical glare upon him. "Are you sure you're English, Mr. Thornton?"

He responded with a casual shrug. "If I'm my father's son, then I'm from a long line of Englishmen. If not, my mother was ravished in her sleep, for she laid all the credit for my birth, looks, and stubbornness to William Thornton."

"Daddee?" Andrew called sleepily from the bedroom.

"Coming, Andy," Gage replied, and rose to his feet in one swift, effortless movement that fairly bedazzled Shemaine with his strength and manly grace. Striding across the parlor to the bedroom, Gage was unaware of the emerald eyes that followed him across the room. He disappeared within, and Shemaine leaned back in her chair to listen as his muted voice blended with his son's sleepy tones. Though the words Gage spoke were of no great import, his tone was gentle and comforting, warming Shemaine's heart perhaps as much as the boy's.

Evening descended upon the land, and with it came thickening mists that rolled up around the cabin, making it an island unto itself. Outside an owl could be heard hooting in a tree somewhere in the woods to the west. With the darkness, the interior of the cabin had grown quiet except for the crackling and hissing of the fire and the scratching of a quill on parchment as Gage made notations in a ledger in the back corridor. Engrossed in his accounting, he seemed oblivious to the woman whom he had purchased earlier that day, but whenever Shemaine glanced up from her sewing in the kitchen, she could see him through the open doorway. She sat in the rocking chair on the far right of the hearth, with a clear view of half the hallway. After sharing the food Hannah Fields had sent over for supper with the Thorntons, she had readied the morning fare for an early rising and tidied the kitchen. Later, Gage had put Andrew to bed in his small nook just off the main bedroom, and then had settled down to work at his drafting table while she hemmed the blue gown and the second chemise she had chosen for herself.

It had certainly not been her intention to compare her master with her fiancé, but as her fingers plied the needle through the cloth, Shemaine's mind drifted far afield and the inevitable happened. In many ways the two were similar. Both men had hair as black as a raven's wing. Gage Thornton kept his clipped short and close against his nape, whereas Maurice tied his thick locks in a neat queue behind his head, shunning both powder and wigs. If there was a difference in the height of the two men, then it was too minuscule to even notice. Both were tall, broad-shouldered, lean but muscular, complementing whatever garments they wore, whether it was the deerhide breeches and homespun shirts that Gage favored or Maurice's more elegant garb. Although her betrothed usually preferred the dignity of black silk over other colors and fabrics for more formal attire, it came to her mind that the Marquess, as handsome as he was, had looked no more impressive in his courtly finery than Gage Thornton in his more durable clothes. Her master's waist and hips were narrow enough to be envied by the most conceited dandy, and the long buckskin trousers were slim enough to cling to every muscular contour, readily revealing the taut sinews that flexed through his thighs, clearly evidencing the athletic vigor of the man.

Maurice du Mercer was certainly not without strength, Shemaine mentally argued in an effort to keep her comparisons clearly in perspective. He was, in fact, a formidable swordsman and an accomplished equestrian. He was adept at all the courtly dances and moved through them with as much grace as he rode a horse. Yet the difference in the two men could have been summed up simply by the contrast between their hands. Gage's fingers were lean and hard. In the grip of such a steely vise, the pale, beautiful, uncallused hands of the Marquess du Mercer might have been severely broken.

At one time, perhaps a century or two ago, Shemaine had been convinced that the handsomeness of her betrothed was unequaled. Certainly none could have denied the aristocratic refinement of Maurice's features and the beauty of his darkly lashed black eyes. Upon hearing of his marriage proposal, her mother, who had previously demonstrated a firm confidence in her daughter's good sense, had expressed concern that Maurice and Shemaine had been influenced by a strong physical attraction for one another rather than a deep, unswerving devotion.

Some time later Camille had again posed the conjecture that Shemaine had been swept off her feet by the grandeur of her fiance's appearance and his station in life. Shemus O'Hearn may have had a temper to battle, but he was usually wise enough to take his wife's counsel to heart. Together they had concurred and refrained from giving their consent, begging her suitor to understand that they only wanted Shemaine to be aware of the life she would be committing herself to as a marchioness. Understanding their concern, Maurice had ardently declared his love for their daughter and had promised that she would want for nothing. At least a month had passed before the O'Hearns had finally relented, acquiescing to Shemaine's quietly spoken assurances that no other man whom she had ever met or possibly would ever meet could measure up to the man she had come to know Maurice to be.

That was eight months ago in England!

And this was a different continent and a different time!

And much had happened since that balmy day in London when Maurice had asked her to be his bride. No longer was she a young lady of leisure, but a bondslave, bought and paid for by a colonial who scraped and worked to make something of himself and his aspirations!

Shemaine tried tenaciously to summon forth a clear image of her betrothed in her mind, and it was an uncommonly long moment before she realized the difficulty in conjuring a noble semblance of her fiancé stemmed basically from the fact that the sun-bronzed, hard-muscled and very vibrant Mr. Thornton was there in front of her where he could be closely observed each and every time she glanced up.

Gage closed his ledger, thrust the quill into the well and pushed his stool back from the desk. Taking up a candlestick, he touched the wick to a lighted taper and then snuffed the other candles in the room. Leaving the corridor, he approached the rocking chair as Shemaine hurriedly folded the chemise that she had been hemming.

"You'll need this to find your way up-stairs," he said, offering her the lighted can-dle. "There's a quilt in the chest near the bed if you have need of it. I strung a line across the balustrade and hung canvas over it while you were finishing up in the kitchen. All you need do is draw it closed."

Thanking him, Shemaine accepted the candlestick and watched in confusion as he picked up a nearby lantern, bade her good night, and made his way toward his bed-room. Refusing to embarrass herself by con-fessing her failure to provide herself with sleeping attire from Victoria's trunk earlier that afternoon, she gathered the garments she had mended and moved toward the kitchen door.

Gage reached the entrance of his bed-room before he remembered his servant's sparse clothing. He turned, drawing her at-tention as he spoke. "I'm sorry, Shemaine. I quite forgot to ask if you might need any-thing else from Victoria's trunk."

"A nightgown and robe would be nice, sir, if you don't mind," she admitted shyly. "I didn't think of them earlier."

"Then come and fetch them. There's no need for you to be timid." He beckoned to her before turning away and entering his bedroom.

By the time Shemaine followed, Gage had already lifted the trunk lid and was sorting through the contents. As she watched, he dug past a torn nightgown that lay near the top and delved deeper through the clothes, finally setting aside a gown which she had previously admired as the prettiest of the lot. He chose another for her, heedless of its better quality and dainty smocking, added the only robe to be found in the trunk, and handed the three garments to her.

"But these are much too fine for a servant to wear," Shemaine insisted, making no attempt to take them.

Gage pushed them toward her, forcing her to take them. "There's no sense in letting them go to waste, Shemaine."

"You can save them for your wife when you get married again," she argued, helplessly clasping the bundle to her.

As if considering her suggestion, Gage set his jaw thoughtfully askew as he slowly contemplated her. Seeming to come to a sudden decision, he gave a slight nod. "If I like the way you look in them, perhaps I'll take your advice and marry you."

Shemaine stared at him agog, incapable of forcing any words past her gaping lips. She was too astounded by his suggestion to even mutter a refusal.

With a devilishly smug look, Gage placed a forefinger beneath her small chin and slowly closed her mouth. "Don't look so shocked, Shemaine. It wouldn't be the first time a marriage of convenience has taken place here in the colonies, nor would it be the last. With such a shortage of available women, it's not an uncommon occurrence for a man to take a stranger to wife. If he's too shy, he'll likely find the maid snatched away by another before he can loosen his tongue to propose."

Shemaine finally found her voice and hastened to assure him, "I didn't mean to suggest that we should marry, Mr. Thornton . . . I mean . . . I certainly never thought of such a thing . . . I would never presume . . . I . . . couldn't . . . I was betrothed, you see. . . ." She stumbled to a sudden halt, realizing she was protesting far too much.

" 'Tis a late hour for us to be quibbling over such matters, Shemaine. Wear one of the nightgowns and go to bed. Rest yourself. Regain your strength. Hopefully, before too much time has elapsed, my men and I can deliver the furniture we've finished to our customers in Williamsburg. Whenever we go, whether a couple of weeks or even a month from now, I would like to take Andrew with me, but I'll need you to come with us to watch after him. The men and I will have to carry the pieces from the barge, load them on wagons and then take them into Williamsburg. I can't rightly do that and look after the boy, too. I'm sure you'll need all the strength you can muster to keep up with him the whole day long."

"I'll try to be fit whenever you decide to go, Mr. Thornton," she answered, retreating through the doorway.

Gage followed as far as the door and, lifting a forearm, braced it across the jamb as he caught her gaze and held it with unwavering brown eyes. "If you aren't aware of it, Shemaine O'Hearn, you speak with a very nice brogue. I hear it quite clearly when you address me by my proper name, and since you seem disinclined to use my given name, you may continue calling me Mr. Thornton with my wholehearted approval." A quick grin flashed, and his eyes gleamed teasingly. "Until that day we marry, of course."

"Warts off a toad," Shemaine mumbled petulantly as she turned crisply on a heel, but his laughter made her break into a smile as she dispatched herself with haste toward the back room.

In the silence of the cabin the hurried slip-slap of her slippers drifted back to the man, and for a long passage of time he listened to her movements upstairs, thankful there was something more pleasurable for him to hear than the haunting screams of his dead wife.

CHAPTER 5

It had long been the custom for the adult members in the Thornton household to begin stirring ere the sun showed its face above the treetops. Shemaine was unacquainted with predawn risings, for in England she had been allowed to slumber well past the daily appearance of the solar orb. She had been pampered to a goodly extent, being the only child. Nevertheless, she had been repeatedly cautioned by her mother and the old family cook that things would change drastically once she became mistress of her own house. On the *London Pride* she had slept whenever she could, but those tormented attempts had been anything but soothing. In contrast, her first night in the Thornton cabin had been both physically relaxing and mentally nurturing. Her awakening, however, came with the harsh reality that she could no longer lie abed until a leisurely hour. She was a bondswoman now and was therefore expected to function as one, serving instead of being served.

She had first been roused to a vague awareness of her surroundings when Gage's bedroom door had opened that morning, but when his footfalls progressed across the parlor and entered the back corridor, she came fully awake, expecting her new master to climb up the stairs and roust her out of bed. Then the subtle squeak of the porch door as it was opened and closed indicated his departure from the cabin, and the frantic beating of her heart eased to a steadier pace.

Shemaine was still a-tremble as she scrambled from the cot and struck sparks from a tinderbox to light a candle. Dragging the dead woman's robe over the nightgown she'd been given, she took up the taper and hastened from the loft. The tiny flame dipped and sputtered in the breeze she created in her brisk descent to the kitchen. Despite her state of dishabille, she lit a lantern, stirred up the fire in the hearth and started putting a meal together, having already decided that her morning toilette would have to wait until a later hour. As for now, she had work to do.

Having planned the morning fare the night before and set a batch of buns to rising away from the heat of the hearth, Shemaine had managed to avoid the folly of being ill prepared. Bess Huxley had once lauded the wisdom and importance of a woman being well organized in whatever task she set herself to and had tried to instill such motivations in her young student. But it was only now, when Shemaine felt pressed to prove her merits to the man who owned her, that the benefits of good, orderly timing were finally recognized and appreciated. The pleasure Shemaine derived at seeing the hot cross buns browning in the hearth oven, the smoked strips of venison sizzling on a griddle, and eggs thickening as she stirred them in a skillet above an open fire was totally different from the boredom she had once suffered when pressed to do such monotonous tasks. While still at home with her parents, she had considered any assignment in the kitchen a loathsome imposition and had done what had been required only to mollify Cook or to perhaps win a few days of reprieve from the tedium of her instructions.

The first rays of the morning sun streamed in through the windowpanes when Gage began folding back the shutters. By the time he finished his outside chores and returned to the cabin with a pail of fresh milk and a basket of eggs, the interior abounded with light and the delectable aromas of hot buns and venison. Upon passing Shemaine in the kitchen, Gage stared in amazement at the fare she was dishing up.

"You've made yourself out to be a liar, Shemaine," he observed, setting the bucket and basket down on the side table near where she worked. He could hardly take his eyes off the rolls, for he seriously doubted he had ever seen bread that looked so delicious. But then, it may have been his own hunger that befogged his memory.

His statement caused Shemaine immediate consternation. "How so, sir?"

"Well, 'tis apparent you know how to cook," Gage replied, sweeping a hand to indicate the food. "Perhaps even well enough to put Roxanne Corbin to shame. Why did you let me believe the converse?"

Intent upon learning the reason, Gage bestowed his full attention on her, but the thoughtful frown that had creased his brow gradually faded as those warm brown orbs slowly descended, sweeping downward from her untidy pigtails to the thin toes peaking from beneath her hem. Those small extremities curled awkwardly beneath his casual contemplation before he reversed his scrutiny. This time his eyes glided upward, pausing ever so briefly on the soft, rounded bosom that was obviously unfettered beneath her night garb.

Painfully conscious of her disarray, Shemaine laid an arm at an angle across her chest and dragged the lace-edged collar of the robe up close around her neck. Had the garments been transparent and her pale body completely vulnerable to his unswerving regard, she would have found no less cause to be disconcerted. His close attention made her jittery to a fault, for she had absolutely no assurance that he would continue treating her with polite deference. She was, after all, nothing more than a slave. She had no haven to which she could run and absolutely no one from whom she could obtain protection. Indeed, if she had correctly discerned the timidity of the hamlet's inhabitants when Gage Thornton had looked their way, then she could suppose they'd be far too cowardly to confront the man on her behalf. Others like Alma Pettycomb might have the nerve, but if similarly averse to convicts, they certainly wouldn't bother.

Gage finally dragged his gaze higher to meet hers, but Shemaine turned away to hide her vivid blush and quickly busied herself spooning eggs into a bowl. For all of her effort to appear unruffled, he might as well have been breathing down her neck. Every fiber of her being screamed of his nearness.

Trying to control the quaver in her voice, Shemaine hastened to answer him, hoping he would then move away. "When you questioned me about my abilities, sir, I wasn't at all sure what I would be able to remember. You see, my mother thought it essential that I be instructed by our cook, but I detested the lessons and saw no future in them. They kept me from what I really enjoyed doing."

Taking up the bowl and the platter of meat, Shemaine stepped to the table and leaned across to place the serving dishes conveniently near the two plates she had set out earlier for her master and his son. She had no need to take note of the direction of her master's gaze, for she could feel the weight of it roaming her back.

"And what was that, Shemaine?" Gage asked, intrigued by the way the nightgown and wrapper molded her trim buttocks. The degree of detail she unwittingly presented him was definitely worth admiring for as long as she afforded him the view.

"Riding, sir," Shemaine replied, feeling some chagrin over her passion for horses. Edith du Mercer had disdained the idea of a young woman racing recklessly across the countryside on the back of a headstrong stallion which many a man had proven incapable of handling. Shemus O'Hearn had taught her to ride at an early age, and the two of them had shared a great love for the sport. Maurice was the only one she had ever known who could ride as well as her sire. "My father owned some of the finest steeds in all of London. He put me on the back of a mare when I was only two, and my mother swore thereafter that that single event proved my undoing in years to come.

I suppose she was right in a way. 'Twas clear the thieftaker knew where to wait for me, for 'twas in the stable that he made his arrest."

"Are you suggesting that the thieftaker had been told of your penchant for horses by your fiancé's grandmother?" Gage queried, only slightly disappointed when she faced him. Her loosely garbed bosom was tempting enough to draw more than a few surreptitious glances. The soft peaks teased him with random appearances, stirring his imagination no small degree.

"Or at least by someone in her hire, sir," Shemaine replied. "That's what I've come to believe. I've had a lot of time to think it through since my arrest, and the clandestine way in which it was all done convinced me that someone wanted to keep my disappearance a secret, for no one was around when I was taken. The grooms had gone to feed grain to the mares in the field. If I'm wrong about what I've come to surmise, then I've done a great disservice to the lady by judging her unfairly."

"If you were found by your family, would your suspicions about this woman hinder you from marrying your fiancé? This . . . Maurice du Mercer?"

That particular issue had monopolized Shemaine's thoughts almost from the time of her arrest, and she was extremely weary of the mental debate. She certainly hadn't been able to arrive at any firm conclusions, but the need to do so didn't seem so crucial now, for she could not imagine a marquess taking to wife a convict. " 'Tis highly unlikely that my parents or even Maurice would ever think of searching for me here. Besides, I rather doubt that Maurice would be able to spare the time for such a quest. He has many affairs and properties in England that demand his constant attention, and I cannot imagine him lightly setting aside his obligations to come here."

"Not even to seek his betrothed?" Gage was rather amazed at her conclusion, for he couldn't conceive of any man forgetting a woman as winsome as she.

Shemaine resented having to explain and did so succinctly. "Maurice never had a shortage of titled ladies fawning over him before our engagement. I'm sure by now he's turned his thoughts and attentions elsewhere."

Gage studied her closely as he posed a question. "Then you've put that part of your life behind you?"

Unable to trust the stability of her composure, Shemaine gave him a jerky nod and busied herself putting butter and fruit preserves on the table, lest she fall prey to feelings of loss and regret.

Thoughtfully Gage reached across the space between them and took a bun from the breadbasket. Tearing off a piece, he mulled over her reply as he popped the morsel in his mouth and began to chew. After a moment the luscious flavor seized his full attention, and his eyes began to sparkle with hearty pleasure. It was a cold, hard fact that he hadn't tasted anything so delectable since leaving his father's house. Not even Victoria had been able to make such delicious bread.

"I shouldn't have limited my comparison to Roxanne Corbin, Shemaine. 'Tis no far-fetched compliment to say that you may be the best cook in the area."

Shemaine smoothed a wayward tendril back from her face as she peered up at him. "Does that mean you'll be keeping me, Mr. Thornton?"

Gage was surprised by her question. "Of course, Shemaine! I told you before that I wouldn't be taking you back. Didn't you believe me?"

"Some men say one thing, sir, and do something else entirely," she answered diffidently.

"I'm not one of those men."

His bedroom door creaked slowly open, and they glanced around as Andrew came padding barefoot across the floor. The boy looked so adorable in his little nightshirt and with his dark, curling hair rumpled and falling into his eyes that Shemaine wanted to go to him herself and gather him up in her arms, but she knew he was still leery of her. She was, after all, nothing more than a stranger.

Gage approached his son, and with a yawn Andrew trustingly raised his arms. His father swung him up high into the air, drawing a burst of giggles from the youngster before he was settled on a shoulder.

"We'll be back in a couple of moments, Shemaine," Gage said, approaching the back hall. "Andy has been trained to use a chamber pot, but he prefers to go outside to the privy. You'll have to go with him when I can't. He tries to act like a man, but 'tis best to be careful."

"Of course, Mr. Thornton." Shemaine turned away, fighting a blush. In England, she had occasionally passed through the countryside and, from her carriage windows, seen young children playing naked in the rain or in water-filled gullies. As brief as those occurrences had been, she had gained some insight into the anatomy of little boys. Still, she suspected she was not quite as knowledgeable about the opposite gender as her master might have supposed.

A short time later Gage returned to the washstand in the kitchen. There he elicited more giggles from his son as he made a game of washing their hands and the boy's face.

With the food now laid out for the family, Shemaine could foresee an easy escape to her room. She was reluctant to put a blight on their morning meal with her disheveled appearance and had every intention of leaving as Gage settled his son in the high chair. She passed behind them, heading for the rear corridor, but her master, sensing her intentions, reached out and caught her arm, bringing her abruptly about in some surprise.

With heart-thumping confusion, Shemaine searched the sun-bronzed visage for some hint of her master's mood, but the only thing she could be certain of at the moment was his height, for Gage Thornton stood more than a head taller than she. The quaver in her own voice made her realize just how fainthearted she had become, for she was as skittish of the man as his son had been of her. "Is there something else you wish, Mr. Thornton?"

"Aye, Shemaine, there is." His smile was brief enough to be terse. "I'd like you to stay and eat with us."

Self-consciously she folded her arms across her bosom, not at all sure what he could see. "I'm not decently dressed, sir."

"You look just fine," Gage assured her as his eyes touched her face and the curling wisps that coyly framed it. It had always amazed him how fetching Victoria had looked scurrying about the kitchen in her nightgown and bare feet. Since her death he had felt a strange, haunting vacancy in the kitchen, even when Roxanne had occupied it, but this girl, with her ratty pigtails and a dusting of flour on her saucy nose, filled that dark void with a feeling of warmth and life. Just for a few moments more he wanted to savor her presence, and hopefully that gnawing sense of emptiness would fade forever from his awareness.

"I don't think Andrew and I have ever shared a meal as appetizing as the one you've prepared for us this morning, Shemaine. Roxanne always had to cook breakfast for her father before coming out here. That left me with the task of putting together something for the boy and me. I can seriously attest that it was a poor attempt at best. And we certainly haven't been able to enjoy the presence of a beautiful lady at our table since Victoria was taken from us. I'd like you to stay with us, Shemaine, just the way you are. Will you?"

Shemaine was no less embarrassed now by his careful perusal of her face than she had been by his earlier inspection of her form, but she thought it wise not to complain. If he limited himself to looking, then she'd have to consider herself fortunate indeed. "If 'tis your wish, sir."

"Aye, 'tis," Gage whispered. Deliberately

he leaned forward to breathe in the fragrance of her hair. "You smell nice, too."

Unsettled by his close attention, Shemaine ran her fingers nervously through the long, feathery strands that had escaped at her temples, fervently wishing she could retreat to the safety of the loft. "I probably smell like bread—"

"Like any woman when she's been cooking in a kitchen," Gage murmured warmly. He swept a hand invitingly toward the bench where she had sat the night before. "After you, Shemaine."

Obediently she slid into the high-backed seat and accepted a cup of tea from him as Andrew cocked his head and looked at her curiously. Smiling in response, she reached for a piece of bread which she had rolled out and cut into the shape of a man for him earlier that morning.

"This is for you, Andrew," she said, offering it to him.

"Daddee!" he exclaimed excitedly, showing his father what she had given him. "Sheeaim cook man!"

Shemaine laughed and, reaching out a hand, ruffled the boy's hair. He chortled, wrinkling his nose at her and, with his little fingers, pried off an arm from the bread and stuffed it into his mouth. Her eyes glowed as she watched him chew the piece with relish. Then he looked up at his father again and giggled.

"Man yummy, Daddee!"

Gage chuckled as he spooned scrambled eggs seasoned with chives onto his own plate. "I know, Andy. I like the bread, too."

"Sheeaim make you man, Daddee?" Andrew asked, leaning forward to search his father's plate.

"No, Andy, Shemaine made the man especially for you, but she cooked a delicious breakfast for us both."

"Sheeaim nice, Daddee?"

"Shemaine *very* nice, Andy."

The emphasis Gage placed on the single word made Shemaine glance up in surprise, and for a brief moment she found her gaze ensnared as he probed the translucent depths of green. Then Andrew asked to be given eggs, and his father readily complied.

Shemaine's appetite was still far from adequate, and after only a few bites she grew uncomfortably queasy. She made a brave attempt to finish the small portions she had taken on her plate, but the threat of heaving

up what little she had eaten made her reconsider. Averting her gaze from the table,
she folded her hands in her lap as the other
two continued to eat. Since they were apparently enjoying the meal and were plainly
in no rush to conclude it, she could foresee
a lengthy delay before she would be able to
escape to the loft.

Gage Thornton was hardly oblivious to his
bondswoman. He had made a concerted effort not to peruse her any more than he had
already, despite the instincts that compelled
him to do so. If he had found it difficult to
keep his eyes from straying to her after he
had returned from Hannah Fields's, then it
was doubly hard this morning, when her
clothes were less confining. He was especially desirous of scanning her breasts.
Though ample enough to arouse any man's
lusting admiration, the fullness was youth-
fully proud, stirring within him a strong
yearning to stroke his hands over their softness and pluck them free of her garments.
But such an idea caused havoc within him,
for it made him painfully sensitive to the
hard-pressing needs that were in serious
want of being sated.

Despite his reluctance to let her go, Gage

could no longer ignore Shemaine's impatience to leave the table and finally peered up at her as she rose to pour him another cup of tea. The wary glance she cast him in return and her unmistakable incertitude made him realize that she was feeling as trapped as a caged sparrow. He had no choice but to relent. "Perhaps I've been unkind to insist you stay with us, Shemaine. If you'd like, you may go to your room and get dressed."

Relief flooded through Shemaine, bringing a wavering smile to her lips. "Thank you, sir. I do believe I made myself sick trying to eat so much."

"That's understandable, considering what you've been through," Gage replied, feeling some chagrin for having kept her. "Just let me know when you're feeling better. My men will be arriving within the hour, and I'll need to leave Andrew with you so I can start work."

"I won't be long, sir."

Shemaine was anxious to leave the torturous sight of food behind her, but after washing her face and body with cool water, she revived considerably. She laid out the blue gown, noticing that she had overlooked the fact that the lace trim on the rounded collar was loose in the back, but she didn't dare take time to mend it. After donning her clothes and combing her hair into a sedate coiffure, she took a moment to set the loft in order and drag aside the canvas sheets that had been hung above the balustrade.

Upon her return to the kitchen, Shemaine found Gage seated in the rocking chair near the hearth. He was reading to Andrew, who was listening intently as he reclined upon his father's chest. Reluctant to leave the security of the elder's arms, the boy refused to go to her or to acknowledge her efforts to draw him away until Shemaine created a playful diversion. Singing an Irish ditty she had learned as a child, she wrapped a cloth around her hand, marked a face on the back of it, defining the lips on her thumb and forefinger, and hid her sleeved arm behind Gage's. Moving the digits to make it seem as if her makeshift puppet could talk, she cajoled Andrew in a squeaky voice, winning his undivided attention. Soon he was chortling in glee and evoking chuckles from his father. Then she slowly withdrew the puppet from view, pulling it down behind the elder's arm. Eagerly Andrew leaned across his father's lap to search for it, and much to his delight and surprise, Shemaine popped it into view.

"Peekaboo! I see you!"

Amid the youngster's laughter, Shemaine failed to notice the man turning his head to catch the subtle scent of her hair as she leaned close. Neither was she cognizant of his gaze leisurely stroking a small ear and the neat braid she had coiled in a knot at the nape of her neck. Had she been inclined to lift her head, she might have glimpsed a hungry yearning in those amber-lit eyes that all but devoured her.

Finally Andrew agreed to come into her arms and seemed content to be there. Singing softly against the boy's cheek, Shemaine followed his father to the back porch. There she coaxed Andrew into waving farewell as Gage strode toward the steps.

"Bye, Daddee," Andrew called at her whispered urging, and then wrinkled his small nose above a wide grin when his father glanced around with a chuckle.

Coming back, Gage placed a lean knuckle beneath his son's chin and tilted the small face upward for a doting kiss on the forehead. "Be a good boy, Andy."

Andrew turned wide, inquisitive brown eyes to the woman who held him and then, very curiously, peered up at his father again. "Kiss Sheeaim, Daddee?"

"Oh, no, Andrew!" Shemaine gasped, and quickly shook her head, hoping the man wouldn't think she had given his son the idea. Gage willingly obliged and lifted her face as he settled his lips upon her gaping mouth, much to Andrew's giggling amusement. His kiss went far beyond the boundaries of a casual peck between strangers. Indeed, it was as warm and sultry as any Maurice had given her.

Shemaine stumbled back in confusion, amazed that such a brief meeting of lips could awaken so many strangely delectable stirrings within her young woman's body. With an odd quirk of a smile, Gage met her astonished stare and then touched a finger to his brow in a casual salute before he whirled and crossed the porch in swift, lengthy strides. His haste seemed to convey an indifference which, in contrast to the wealth of emotions Shemaine was struggling to subdue, was enough to scald not only her face but her pride as well.

She remembered only too well that Maurice had been prone to pursue her kisses with passionate fervor and, more than once, had to be urged to cool his ardor until after they were wed. After the formality of their engagement, he had implored her to give herself to him, promising to be careful with her and equally discreet so no one else would know. But with calm deliberation and a pragmatism that had equaled anything her mother had ever displayed, Shemaine had convinced him that it would be better for them to wait and enjoy the intimate delights of marriage on their wedding night rather than ignore the consequences she might reap if some fatal accident struck him down and she be found with child.

Gage left them with a wave of a hand and strode briskly down the lane toward his workshop. His men were already arriving on horseback, having come from their homes by the narrow, winding road through the woods. For most of the day, he and his employees would have to wrap and crate the finished furniture in preparation for the trip to Williamsburg. Though no firm date had been set aside for the delivery, there was less chance of damage being done to the pieces if they were packed now. Hopefully, before too much time elapsed, they would be making the trip upriver to deliver and collect payment for the completed items. Until then, the old shipwright, Flannery Morgan, and his son, Gillian, would have to work on the vessel by themselves, for the limited supplies did not allow enough progress to be made to warrant Gage's close supervision or assistance.

Shortly after padding and wrapping the pieces, the five men began the chore of crating them. Gage stepped outside with Ramsey Tate, a tall, broad-shouldered man of an age a year past two score, and began stacking rough-sawn planks together to carry inside. Their progress went unhindered until Gage happened to glance toward the cabin. Then he slowly straightened.

Curious to see what had ensnared his employer's attention, Ramsey followed the other's steadfast gaze until he spied a fiery-haired young woman drawing water from the well. He had no need for further enlightenment, for he could clearly see the reason for Gage's sudden preoccupation.

"That yer new bondswoman?" Though Ramsey offered the conjecture in the form of an inquiry, he could have saved his breath, for he already knew the answer.

Gage slowly nodded in distraction.

Ramsey shaded his eyes with a hand in an effort to see the woman better. "She looks mighty fetchin' from here."

"She is."

"She doesn't favor yer wife much, though, with all that red hair."

"Not a bit."

"Ye gonna keep her for a while?"

"As long as it takes."

Thoughtfully rolling a drooping end of his mustache between his fingers, Ramsey cocked a bushy brow in wonder as he contemplated his friend. "As long as it takes for what?"

The slender, feminine figure disappeared inside the cabin, and beneath the speculative stare of the older man, Gage returned his full attention to hefting one end of the stacked boards. When his cabinetmaker failed to do likewise, he barked an impatient question. "What's the matter with you, Ramsey? Wake up!"

Ramsey snorted as he squatted down to obey. "If'n ye ask me, I think ye've been bitten."

"What the hell are you talking about?"

"What do ye think?" Ramsey snapped back. "That li'l bitty redhead saunters out onto the porch, an' all of a sudden ye've lost yer bloomin' mind. I've never seen ye so wrought up before! Ye never stopped ta drool like a hungry hound when Roxanne came prancin' herself down here lookin' for ye."

"No, and you never will either," Gage muttered.

"So, what are ye goin' ta do 'bout her?"

Gage looked at the man as if he had taken leave of his senses. "Who? Roxanne?"

Ramsey rolled his eyes in disbelief and almost shouted his reply. "No, *dammit!* The redhead!"

Gage cocked a brow sharply as he fixed his gaze upon his employee. "I'll let you know that when I get good and ready," he rejoined gruffly. "Until then, you hairy ol' nail-driver, mind your own business."

Ramsey squawked in feigned outrage. "If'n ye don't mind me rufflin' yer feathers a mite by remindin' ye, *Mister* Thornton, ye *are* me whole bloomin' business! Not one of us is worth our salt without ye! An' if'n I've gots a mind ta worry 'bouts ye, I'm only lookin' out for me own frazzled hide an' me family's."

Gage waved away his comments. "You're not old enough to be my father, so stop acting like it. You've got enough sons to take care of as it is without adding me to your litter."

"Well, think of me as yer friend, then," Ramsey suggested with a sudden chortle. "An' whilst I'm at it, ye seem ta be needin' a bit of advice. Ye're a man what's in bad need of what only a woman can give ye, an' by that lustin' look in yer eye, ye won't be happy just sniffin' 'round the skirts of that li'l girlie, not when ye'd rather be twixt 'em."

Gage winced uncomfortably under the man's chiding. The fact that Ramsey had hit at the core of what was vexing him gave him cause to wonder just how transparent he had become. He had never been one to seek favors from hired strumpets, and he had tried to dismiss his growing need for a woman by devoting himself entirely to his work. The kiss he had given Shemaine had surprised him, perhaps more than it had the girl, for it had gone through him like a searing hot iron, instantly awakening his senses to the hunger roiling within him. Rather than embarrass himself by letting her see just how she had affected him, he had lit out like a scalded dog. Yet even now he outwardly disavowed his need for the logic that Ramsey offered him.

"Your counsel, my dear friend, is about as basic as a bull in a breeding pen, but I'm after something more than that."

Ramsey scoffed at his claims and cast a last wry glance toward the cabin. "Aye, I noticed."

Shemaine's talent for entertaining youngsters had never been realized before this day in history. In spite of her lack of experience with children, she managed to win Andrew's trust and arouse his eager curiosity with her gift of the bread man and her impromptu puppet. He was ready to make friends with her and willingly cooperated as she bathed him in the washtub and shampooed his hair. When she lathered up her hands and blew soap bubbles into the air, the boy chortled heartily, deriving great enjoyment from poking a finger at the ones that floated near and seeing them pop and vanish in a flick of an eye.

Shemaine was in the process of dressing him in the master bedroom when an insistent rapping came upon the front door of the cabin. After wrapping Andrew in a small blanket, she gathered him up in her arms and hastened to open the portal. A tall woman with harsh features and straw-colored hair drawn back tightly in a severe knot behind her nape stood at the threshold. In response to Shemaine's cautious nod of greeting, the stranger managed a stiff smile.

"I'm Roxanne Corbin. . . ." The gray eyes slipped downward, skimming over the slender form and the painfully familiar frayed gown. It was one that Victoria Thornton had worn more than any other while working in the garden or at some other untidy task which might have damaged her better gowns. To see a convict wearing the deceased woman's garb caused a festering resentment to sink its claws into Roxanne's heart as she met the curious green eyes. "And you must be the bondswoman, Shemaine O'Hearn."

Shemaine resettled Andrew in her arms and answered the other's supposition with another careful nod. "If you've come to see

Mr. Thornton, I believe he's working in his shop."

"Actually, I came to see you." There was a penetrating coldness in Roxanne's glower that caused its recipient to shiver. "To see just what kind of nursemaid Gage managed to buy from a prison ship."

Shemaine's face grew warm at the jeering repugnance heavily imbued in the other's tone. She wished in good manner that she could send the woman on her way and return to the bedroom with Andrew, for her weakened arms were growing increasingly strained from his weight. The risk of dropping him made her anxious, but she could think of no gracious way of inviting the visitor to leave.

Shemaine noticed, however, that for all of Mrs. Pettycomb's avowed claims that Andrew was fond of Roxanne, he barely glanced at his former nursemaid. He seemed far more interested in poking a finger in the rebellious wisps of hair that were wont to curl against her own temple.

Shemaine lifted Andrew higher in her grasp once again, summoning forth the last vestiges of strength she could claim. She was grateful when Andrew wrapped both arms around her neck and, for added security, locked his fingers in the cloth of her collar.

"Is there something you wish of me, Roxanne?" Shemaine questioned, trying to bring a quick conclusion to her predicament. "If not, I should get Andrew dressed now."

"Mistress Roxanne to you, girl," the blonde corrected haughtily. "If you don't learn anything else, you should at least be taught the proper way to address your betters."

"Mistress Roxanne, if you'd prefer," Shemaine replied rigidly.

The back door opened and closed, and manly footsteps progressed a short distance into the corridor. A shuffling of papers evidenced the fact that Gage had stopped at his desk and was searching through it.

Shemaine felt a surge of relief with his presence. "Mr. Thornton is here now," she readily announced to the woman. "Perhaps you'd care to visit with him."

Gage heard her voice but continued leafing through his receipts as he called out, "Is someone here, Shemaine?"

"You have a visitor, Mr. Thornton," Shemaine declared over her shoulder. In the next instant she found herself stumbling back from the portal as Roxanne pushed her way in.

Gage stepped to the kitchen door and then halted abruptly when he recognized his guest. Though he tried to conceal his annoyance, his brows gathered in a tense frown, for he knew what would be forthcoming. "I'm surprised to see you here, Roxanne. I thought you'd be taking care of your father."

The blonde lifted her chin in the guise of a suffering martyr. "I came to see what you had bought for yourself, Gage, *since* you had made no effort to inform me of your intentions. Mrs. Pettycomb, on the other hand, was most eager to bring me news of your new purchase. 'Twas so *gracious* of you to let me know that you had found someone to replace me and that my services would no longer be required."

"I told you before, Roxanne, that I would be needing someone and couldn't wait until your father got back on his feet," Gage countered, yearning to put Mrs. Pettycomb out of her meddling misery. "You must have been aware of that fact more than anybody. I'm sorry I didn't have time to stop by your place and tell you yesterday, but with the storm and all, I had to get back here. I was just making plans to come into town today and had intended to let you know while I was there." He paused, curbing a vexed sigh. He was sorry that she had been subjected to the gossip's insensitivity, but he had given Roxanne plenty of warning. She just hadn't wanted to listen. "I should have realized Mrs. Pettycomb would beat a path to your door in her eagerness to be the first to tell you the news. And for that, I must apologize—"

"Of all the women in this area," Roxanne interrupted, having dismissed much of what he had said, "why did you have to buy a convict to care for your son? And this one in particular?" Her voice became wheedling, almost pleading. "Aren't you afraid of what this creature might do to Andrew?"

Though his hackles rose at her questions, Gage managed to meet Roxanne's gaze with a tolerant stare. He was unwilling to hurt her with the truth, that he had made up his mind to be free of her long before the smithy had ever run afoul of a horse and gotten his leg broken. But he refused to be grilled about his motives for singling out

Shemaine as his choice. "I'm capable of making rational judgments as to the merits of the woman I engage as a nursemaid, Roxanne, and I'm confident that Shemaine is everything I was looking for."

Wondering what effect the conversation was having on the girl, Gage allowed his gaze to stray beyond Roxanne. Shemaine was clearly distressed, but the main reason seemed to stem from the fact that she was progressively losing her struggle to hold Andrew in her arms. Her whole body was shaking with her effort to keep a grip on him. Indeed, a fall seemed imminent.

Gage ran to help his bondslave, giving little thought to how quickly he would be rousing his visitor's jealous indignation. Shemaine was more than willing to yield her burden to more capable arms and leaned forward as her master slipped an arm between them to gather his son to him. The shock of that steely limb sliding against her breast sent a hot blush rushing into Shemaine's cheeks, and in painful embarrassment she sought to retreat and was brought immediately up short. To her chagrin, she found herself a prisoner of Andrew, whose fingers had become entangled in the torn lace of her collar. Urgently seeking to free herself, most of all from the man, Shemaine struggled blindly behind her neck to free the tiny digits.

"Here, let me," Gage urged, brushing one of her hands aside. "You're only making it worse."

Though excruciatingly conscious of her predicament, Shemaine stood submissively still, not wishing to compound her dilemma. With Andrew between them, Gage had to lean into her to see behind her neck as he sought to unravel the lace from his son's fingers. Totally conscious of him, Shemaine dared not lift her gaze to his handsome features, but kept it fixed unswervingly on Andrew, who patiently endured their attempts to separate him from Shemaine.

Gage could hardly ignore the intriguing pressure of the soft womanly bosom against his arm, but as delightful as it was to be snuggled close to Shemaine, he couldn't allow himself to be carried away, certainly not with Roxanne standing there watching them.

As she viewed the pair, Roxanne was confronted by familiar yearnings that had been far too frequently felt during the length of her infatuation with Gage Thornton. She longed with all of her heart to be where the bartered woman was at that precise moment, but she stood alone, for the most part forgotten. It wasn't the first time she had been overlooked when another woman was in the room. It was just a different time and a different face.

It had been a terrible assault on Roxanne's emotions to hear that she had been replaced by a convict in the Thornton household, but she had held out hopes that Alma Pettycomb had been deliberately brewing trouble when the matron claimed the chit was notably pretty, perhaps even more lovely than Victoria. Roxanne had been nettled, taking offense at what she perceived was nothing more than an unspoken insult. The gossipmonger *never* praised anyone unless she had intentions of making her listener feel slighted. Roxanne's heart had nearly failed her when she saw Shemaine for herself and realized that Alma hadn't exaggerated. The girl was exceptionally pretty, as difficult as it was for Roxanne to admit. And although it was the heart of the man she had desired more than the position, she now saw the danger of that, too, being stolen from her. The fear of losing Gage wasn't anything she hadn't experienced before, but it flogged Roxanne unmercifully, stirring up an old grudge that had sunk its cloven claws deep into her heart several years ago.

Roxanne could not bear watching them together a moment longer. Vowing to lend whatever assistance she could to bring this outrageous and disgusting farce to an end, she stalked forward with fury flaring in her eyes. Her frustration was supreme, and she saw the bondslave through a raging red haze.

Andrew's fingers were finally set free, and with a sigh of relief Shemaine stumbled back, still refusing to meet the man's gaze. Before her nerves had time to settle, however, the sound of rapidly advancing footsteps intruded into her awareness, and she glanced around to find herself the recipient of a glower so menacing it would have readily put to shame any that Morrisa had ever bestowed on her. Wary of being attacked, Shemaine fell back before the other's approach.

The blonde forged on like a fierce gale. "You conniving little bitch—"

"Roxanne!" Her caustic slur had brought Gage around in sharp surprise. Although years ago the woman had let him know in no uncertain terms how he had disappointed her by taking another to wife, she had never verbally attacked Victoria. But he would tolerate it no better now than he would have then. "I'll hear no insults in my house! Do you hear?"

His crisp tone sliced through Roxanne's fury, and as if in a stunned daze, she turned and stared at him in painful supplication. "Could you not see through the girl's ruse, Gage?" she asked in anguish. "Did you not see how she was throwing herself at you . . . letting you touch her . . . ?"

Shemaine's face flamed at the woman's accusation, and she opened her mouth to protest, but words failed her. How many times had she tried to deny her guilt before the magistrate's bench, only to be sentenced to prison? Explanations seemed no less futile now.

Gage was greatly disturbed by Roxanne's behavior. The color had faded from her cheeks and her eyelids fluttered unsteadily over a lusterless gaze, as if she balanced precariously on a pinnacle between sanity and madness. He had no way of predicting what she would do next, whether she would swoon or fly at his bondslave with claws bared.

Turning his back upon Shemaine, Gage set himself before her as a protective barrier as he faced his visitor. Once again he tried to explain, hoping he could bring Roxanne out of her trauma by a softly spoken rationale. "I thought you understood, Roxanne, that I couldn't wait until your father was on his feet again. I needed a nursemaid who would be more accountable to my dictates than to another's, someone who could teach Andrew to read and cipher in years to come. Shemaine has been well tutored and is capable of fulfilling those requirements, and I could not dismiss her abilities when I had such a need—"

"No need!" Roxanne snarled in denial, reclaiming her former wrath. "That's only your feeble excuse for getting rid of me." She could almost hear the villagers whispering and laughing behind her back, cruelly berating her for being so foolish as to think that Gage Thornton, of all people, would actually marry her. He had ignored maids far more comely than she and had taken to wife a young beauty none of them had been able to surpass. Fool she was to believe that *any* man would take her to wife, they would say. And more fool she for setting her hopes so inconceivably high that she would dare to imagine the cabinetmaker would ever court her. She was, after all, the smithy's daughter, the plain-faced offspring of that rough-featured, callous man whose wife, years ago, had deserted him and their daughter to run away with a traveling man. Just like then, there would be the pitying stares, the sadly shaking heads, and the long serpent tongues that would suddenly start hissing whenever she approached. "I'd have come back to work for you just as soon as the splint had come off Pa's leg. Hannah could have watched Andrew until then!"

Frightened by the woman's angry tone, Andrew began to whimper as he clung to his father. Turning aside, Gage tried to reassure him, but he could feel the boy trembling against him.

"You know what I say is true," Roxanne accused harshly, moving toward him.

Gage glared over his shoulder, bringing Roxanne up short with the penetrating chill of his gaze. "We'll have to discuss this matter at a later time, Roxanne," he muttered. "You're upsetting Andrew—"

"I'm upsetting him?" Roxanne railed, out-raged at his accusation. She was equally in-censed by his curtness. Jeeringly she thrust her chin outward to indicate Shemaine. "And what about that filthy little baggage you've bought for yourself? Your son has more cause to be frightened of her than of me! You don't know what she's done, Gage! She may be a murderess for all you know!"

Gage whirled to face the blonde with fire in his eyes, but when his actions caused An-drew to cry out in sudden alarm, he bit back the angry retort he had been about to make. Taking himself firmly in hand, he gave his sobbing son back to Shemaine and silently motioned her into his bedroom. He closed the door behind them and then, grasping Roxanne's elbow as gently as he could manage at the moment, ushered her out to the front porch, but he did not stop there. Escorting her down the steps at a rapid pace, he took her back along the path to-ward the riverbank, where he espied her fa-ther's dinghy pulled up on shore. It was only after he had put his ship behind him and was well out of earshot of the two men who were working there that he could finally trust himself to speak and not to roar.

"Roxanne, you and your father were among the first people I met after my arrival in Virginia," he began in tense but moderate tones. Dropping her arm, he faced her. "You brought baskets of food to me when I was building my cabin here, though I assured you at the time I didn't want you to go to the trouble. When Victoria arrived in the colonies with her parents, you were kind to them and befriended her." He paused at the sharp prodding of his conscience, for in all actuality it had been Victoria who had gone out of her way to take Roxanne under her wing, having felt a great empathy for the spinster. But he could not bring himself to callously remind the woman that she had virtually been without friends until Victoria had taken pity on her. "Months later, you consoled Victoria when her folks died. I know you think I betrayed you when I married her. You said as much, in fact. But you finally visited us, and for a time, it seemed that you had forgiven me. You came with some of the other women to help out the night Andrew was born. You were the one who assured me that everything would go well with Victoria . . . that she was too strong to die in childbirth. You were here many times after that, helping her care for Andrew. Shortly after she was killed, you pleaded with me to let you clean my house and look after Andrew, saying that being here would help you get over your grieving.

"During all of that time, Roxanne, I never knowingly encouraged you or gave you reason to hope or to expect anything more from our acquaintance than the friendship I had offered you. But you wanted something more, something I wasn't able to give. I know now that I must speak clearly of this matter so there will be no further cause for error. If you have *ever* imagined there could be anything more between us than a willingness to be friends, then you've been mistaken, Roxanne, and have simply presumed too much."

His stoic rebuff crushed the lifeblood from Roxanne's heart. All the love she had felt for him earlier now congealed into a seething hatred. "You presumed too much, Gage Thornton. If you think I'm going to keep still about Victoria . . ."

Gage felt a cold prickling along his nape and an uneasiness in his vitals. She had never outwardly threatened him since Victoria's death, but after his purchase of Shemaine, he had foreseen the likelihood. Cautiously he asked, "What do you mean?"

"I trusted you. . . ." Roxanne's voice cracked as she blurted out, "I loved you, and I just couldn't believe you could actually kill your own wife, but I was a fool to ignore the facts. I came here *after* Victoria was dead, *after* you had taken Andrew back to the cabin. No one else was around that day, remember? Your men had the day off. Wondering about it all, I recently went up to the ship's prow to see for myself, and I realized that it would have taken a strong man to throw Victoria over the rail to the rocks heaped below, rocks that you and your men had hauled in to fortify the bracing stocks so the spring rains wouldn't wash away the sand from beneath the supports. Unless your wife had reason to kill herself, then you are the only one who could have done it, Gage Thornton, because you were the only man around at the time. Perhaps you *did* kill her in a fit of temper as the townspeople have suggested, and you tried to make it look like an accident. Whatever the truth, I've no choice but to believe that when you saw me coming in the dinghy that day, you threw Victoria over the prow and then ran back to the cabin with Andrew to let *me* be the one to find her because you *knew* how I felt about you! You *knew* I would willingly accept anything you told me! But I'm smarter now, and I've come to believe that you killed Victoria that day, one way or the other!"

"That's a lie!" Gage barked. "I heard Victoria scream after I reached the cabin, and when I came running back, you were standing over her dead body! If I had thought for one instant that you had the strength to accomplish her murder, I'd have seen you arrested that very day. But as you say, it would've taken a strong man to carry Victoria up to the prow and hurl her down, and as yet, I haven't found anyone with reason enough to want to hurt her, much less kill her."

"You're the one who's lying, Gage Thornton. Not me. And I'm going to let everybody know it!"

He laughed scathingly at her threat. "Do you think anyone will believe you after you swore you heard Victoria scream and hurried up from the dinghy in time to see me running from the cabin? I was too far away to have come from the ship, you said. I sincerely doubt that your new story will have much effect on the townspeople, Roxanne. With Shemaine here, everyone will see through your spiteful jealousy and accept it for what it is."

"You murdered her!" Roxanne shrieked, hauling back an arm. With teeth gnashing and eyes blazing, she flung the flat of her hand across his cheek and felt the painful sting of the blow herself in her bruised and prickling palm. All the force of her pent-up fury could not be spent so easily, however. She wanted revenge to ease her seething rage.

For a brief moment, Gage stood as she had left him, with his eyes closed, his face averted, his clamped jaw tensed with rigid control. Gradually turning his head, he arched an eyebrow sharply and glared at her.

"Don't ever do that again, Roxanne," he warned. "If you do, you will see just what I'm capable of."

"Will you throw me from the prow of your ship as you did Victoria?" she taunted bitingly.

For no more than a passing moment, Gage stared at her, amazing Roxanne with the frigid coldness in those ordinarily warm brown eyes. Then, pivoting sharply about, he left her.

The bedroom door was still closed when Gage entered the cabin. He stood just inside the front portal for a long moment, listening to Shemaine singing a sprightly verse to his son, who giggled in delight as she punctuated each verse in a way Gage could only imagine was a gentle tickling or a clucking of his little chin. Raising a knuckle, he wiped a trickle of blood from the corner of his mouth and, with measured tread, crossed to his bedroom door. Lifting the latch, he pushed the portal inward to find Shemaine kneeling beside his bed. Andrew was now fully dressed and sitting on the edge of the bed within the circle of her arms. As he entered, the girl's eyes were drawn immediately to his burning cheek, and in some embarrassment she scrambled to her feet.

Gage tried to smile to put her at ease, but his attempt was sorely strained. "I've got to take the wagon into town this afternoon, Shemaine, and I'd like you and Andrew to go with me." He didn't dare leave them when Roxanne could come back and assault the girl. "One of my men brought word this morning that there's a widow visiting in the area who wants to meet with me about ordering a hutch. If she does, I'll have enough funds to pick up a few supplies for the ship and order you a pair of shoes."

Shemaine was astounded by his generosity. "I told you before, Mr. Thornton. I'm quite content wearing what you've already given me. I don't need another pair."

Gage finally managed a small quirk of a grin. "Unfortunately, the slip-slap of your slippers flapping at your heels is enough to drive a sane man mad. Now go, woman, and get yourself dressed. And be quick about it."

Shemaine's own smile was no less than dazzling. "Yes, sir."

Still, she paused at the door to kick off the slippers and, gathering them in her hand, tossed back a laughing glance as she ran from the room. Her effervescent spirit was contagious, and as Gage stepped into the parlor to mark her flight, he realized his mood was already pulling free of that dark morass that had so recently imprisoned it.

CHAPTER 6

Newportes Newes had been founded by an Irishman a hundred years earlier and had originally been settled by more of the same. Shemaine would have probably felt right at home in the hamlet had she known the inhabitants better, but after first coming in contact with Mrs. Pettycomb and Roxanne, she had good cause to be cautious. Then, too, she wasn't sure how the populace of the small hamlet would receive her once word got around that she was a convict from Newgate Prison. And in light of Mrs. Pettycomb's indiscretion, Shemaine could assume the news had already reached every ear.

A small, white-haired woman had just taken leave of the general store when Gage drew the wagon to a halt in front of it. He jumped down to tether the horse to a nearby hitching rail and, upon facing the elder, touched the brim of his hat politely.

"Good morning, Mrs. McGee."

"An' a right fair good mornin' ta ye, Gage Thornton," she bade cheerily, leaning on a cane as she approached him. "What brings ye ta our fair hamlet on this fine, bright day, an' yer bold, handsome self escortin' such a pretty young stranger an' yer wee, fine son?"

Gage embellished his own words with an impressive Irish brogue. "Ah, 'twould be rare indeed ta find in this whole wide world a colleen prettier than the widow Mary Margaret McGee."

"Ha!" The woman tossed her fine head in disbelief as Gage lifted Andrew down from the wagon, but her bright blue eyes twinkled with pleasure nevertheless. "Do ye expect a clever woman like meself ta believe yer winsome lies, ye good-lookin' devil?" she queried impertinently. "I'll not have ye be thinkin' I'm like all those other addlepated fillies who drool every time they espy ye comin' inta the hamlet. But 'tis good o' ye ta visit us so's I can see for meself what ye've done. I've been hearin' such wild rumors 'bout ye, I came nigh ta hitchin' up me shay an' drivin' out ta yer cabin just ta see if they be true." Her gaze settled on Shemaine, and as if deciding a matter in her mind, she slowly nodded. "Aye, the gossipmongers have done her justice. A bogtrotter, so I've heard from one sour soul who's been in the tavern sippin' whiskey for nearly half a day." She waved an elegant hand, casually indicating the establishment next door. Then her grin widened to show an unmarred set of small, white teeth. "Ta be sure, had the callused oaf been more me size, I'd have whittled him down with me cane for slanderin' such a noble race as the Irish an' callin' the lot o' us bogtrotters ... as if that clumsy codfish ne'er saw a marsh in all o' England!"

Shemaine's trepidation rapidly vanished at the irresistible humor of Mrs. McGee. The widow was certainly a pleasant surprise after her first two encounters with the citizens of the hamlet. The woman inspired some hope that there were others of a similarly delightful nature in the area.

Mary Margaret gestured imperiously, silently commanding Gage to lend assistance to the girl. "What? Have ye forgotten yer manners, fine sir? Or would ye be thinkin' since she's yer bondswoman she'd be havin' no need o' yer help ta get down from a wagon?"

Suffering a bit of chagrin beneath the woman's good-spirited needling, Gage faced the conveyance and, flicking his eyes briefly upward, beckoned Shemaine across the seat. As he slipped his hands about her slender waist and swept her to the boardwalk, Shemaine noticed that his face had taken on a ruddy hue beneath the bronze, as if he were abashed at the possibility that she might think him rude or uncouth. It did strange things to her heart to perceive that boyish quality in such a stalwart man. Obviously he cared about her impression of him.

"Madam, may I present Miss Shemaine O'Hearn to you," Gage announced, whisking his hat off with debonair flair. Even so, he had to drag his thoughts away from the realization of just how close his fingers had come to encircling the girl's waist. Even thin, she had more curves than a cabinetmaker could work into a serpentine scroll. He swept a hand gallantly to indicate the elder. "Shemaine, this grand lady is perhaps the most notable member of our small community, the undeniably dignified, sweet-tempered widow, Mrs. Mary Margaret McGee."

"Ah, go on with ye!" Mary Margaret chortled, and waved away his extravagant flattery with a graceful flourish of a fine-boned hand. Facing the younger woman, she smiled kindly and clasped Shemaine's thin hand in her own. " 'Tis a pleasure ta make yer acquaintance, dearie, an' if there be none other in this hamlet who has done so, may I say welcome ta ye."

"Your kindness is greatly appreciated, madam," Shemaine responded with genuine honesty.

Mary Margaret lifted an inquiring gaze to the tall man who now stood holding his son in his arms. "Would a fine gentleman like yerself be opposed ta an old widow takin' yer bondswoman off ta meet a few o' the inhabitants o' this hamlet?"

Gage cocked a wondering brow as he met the woman's stare. Then he scanned the street, spying several young bachelors who were much closer to the girl's age than he was. Though he was fond of the elder, he was certainly not blind to her romantic bent. She had already arranged at least three marriages between newly arrived members of the Irish race and long-established residents of the hamlet. He would not take it kindly if she encouraged some fellow to start pestering him about selling the girl. "I'll leave Shemaine to your care, Mary Margaret, but I beg you not to create mischief behind my back."

The woman displayed a fair bit of indignation. "Now what kind o' mischief would ye be thinkin' a helpless widow like meself might be capable o' doin', Gage Thornton?"

He remained implacable. "You have the subtle wiles of a matchmaker, Mary Margaret, and I'll not have you plucking some young swain's heartstrings to win sympathy for my bondswoman. In short, I won't be selling her to some infatuated Romeo so he can take her to wife. Do I make myself clear?"

Mary Margaret curbed a desire to smile in sweet contentment as she raised an elegant brow in feigned innocence. "What say ye, Mr. Thornton? Should I be thinkin' ye've cast yer sights on this one yerself?"

Gage struggled to remain unruffled beneath the woman's steadfast stare. "Think what you will, Mary Margaret, but if you would wish to remain my friend, have a care how you conduct yourself with my property."

The elder dipped her elegant head in acknowledgment. "Yer warning is well taken, sir. I shall take special care."

"Good!" With a curt nod, Gage left them and carried Andrew into the general store.

Smiling thoughtfully, Mary Margaret turned and, resting her dainty hands upon the handle of her cane, gave Shemaine a slow, exacting perusal. "Ye're a pretty thing, ta be sure," she stated at last. "No doubt, with ye gainin' a place in Mr. Thornton's household, ye'll soon be the envy o' every young maid an' spinster livin' in the area. I can only hope they don't get too green-eyed mean over ye hookin' the finest fish in the sea. They've been tryin' ta catch that fine, sleek grayling in their nets for nigh the whole year past. There's one in particular I should warn ye 'bout, but then, mayhap ye've already met her."

Carefully avoiding the curious stare the elder had settled upon her, Shemaine feigned naïveté. "I'm not exactly sure whom you mean, madam."

Mary Margaret regarded Shemaine with unyielding persistence until she regained that one's cautious attention. "I perceive, dearie, that ye're an intelligent girl, and there's no need for me to explain. Watch yerself with Roxanne," she advised. "She's been moonstruck over yer master for some time now, perhaps as long as eight or nine years, certainly well before he met an' married Victoria. Lately Roxanne has had everyone in the hamlet believin' that Gage intended ta marry her, what with the way she's been outfittin' her trousseau an' talkin' 'bout him as if he were her very own. If yer master doesn't wed her, she'll be blamin' ye for causin' the split. If he does, then ye'll likely be sold ta another before the nuptials are exchanged." Mary Margaret paused, wondering if she would see some indication of the other's dismay, and when the delicately refined features remained discreetly void of emotion, a tiny seed of respect began to germinate within her breast. Too many of the prettier fillies were rash and frivolous, spilling every secret without giving the slightest heed to the consequences. Mary Margaret heaved a reflective sigh. "But I can't rightly see that happenin' though, since he warned me against stirrin' up the hopes o' other men."

"So far, madam, I've found Mr. Thornton to be a kind and courteous gentleman," Shemaine stated carefully. "He's treated me far better than I ever expected to be and has made no improper advances or demands." Her declaration was made with prudent deliberation in an effort to snuff out any rumors that might have been going around. She knew people were bound to talk about them. Mrs. Pettycomb had boldly stated as much. But she hoped to remain unimpaired by such slanderous chatter long after she returned to England, though it be seven years from now.

The elder slowly nodded as if championing her cause and then, after a moment, pointed down the lane with her cane. "Let's walk a ways. I dare not take ye the full length o' town seein' as how his noble self is anxious ta keep ye a secret from all the other hot-blooded males who are lookin' for a mate. Ta be sure, there's been a serious shortage o' decent women in the hamlet, which has made the area a ripe haven for another sort entirely, but their kind usually hang around the men in the tavern an' leave the streets for the rest o' us, at least durin' the daylight hours."

Without comment Shemaine fell in beside the widow, and they progressed at a leisurely pace as Mary Margaret, with a flourish of a bony hand or a nod of her white head, drew her attention to several establishments located along the boardwalk. Shemaine took special note of the apothecary shop when Mrs. McGee described the owner, Sidney Pettycomb, as a fine, upstanding member of their community. Having met his wife, Shemaine could only reserve judgment of the man.

Several chattering matrons bustled out of the shop, oblivious to everything but what they were discussing until they espied the two who approached; then they nearly stumbled over each other in their haste to reenter. There was an immediate flurry of activity as each of them struggled for a favorable position behind the window, and much like a gaggle of excited geese, they stretched their long necks and bobbed their bonneted heads up and down in an effort to see Shemaine better.

"Don't be alarmed by those biddies, dearie," Mrs. McGee cautioned, tilting her head ever so slightly to indicate the group. "They're some o' Mrs. Pettycomb's cohorts. They've no doubt heard o' ye an' are eager ta dissect ye for themselves."

Shemaine glanced askance at the variety of faces pressed near the glass, but the group fell back almost in unison as Mrs. McGee waved and called out a cheery greeting.

"Good day, Agnus, Sarah . . . Mabel . . . Phobe . . . Josephine," she greeted, marking each of the women with her eyes as she named them. "Fine weather we're havin' today, is it not?"

If the matrons had hoped to remain inconspicuous behind the window, then the elderly woman made their failure obvious as she named them one by one. It brought an amused smile to Shemaine's lips, not only because of the sudden astonishment and discomfiture of the gossips but because of the delightfully puckish humor of Mary Margaret McGee.

Mrs. McGee grinned at her young companion. "I'd be a-thinkin' the lot o' them might've imagined themselves invisible behind the glass, like wee mice huddlin' in a corner."

Since none of them could have been considered tiny by any stretch of the imagination, the elder's comment seemed all the
more farfetched. Shemaine began to giggle
as she looked into the blue eyes that twinkled with mischievous mirth. The woman
was so delightful, Shemaine couldn't help
but feel safe and at ease in her company.

They continued on their way, but after
passing the only inn in the hamlet, they
paused, and the elder gestured toward the
end of town, where the blacksmith's shop
and house were located.

"Roxanne an' her father live over there,
but neither o' them is kindly favored toward
the company o' strangers. . . ." The delicate
brows shrugged upward briefly. "Or even
neighbors, for that matter. Hugh Corbin is
just as surly now as he used to be when he
had a young wife at his beck an' call, but
Leona deserted the family years ago ta run
off with a travelin' man, leaving Roxanne ta
learn firsthand what it means ta live alone
with an ornery brute of a father. One would
think she'd have grown up timid, bein' constantly under her pa's thumb, but I think
Roxanne has more'n her fair share o' Hugh
Corbin runnin' in her veins. If she doesn't

crack open his head one o' these days 'cause o' the way he orders her 'bout, 'twill be a wonder, for sure."

"I think she's to be pitied," Shemaine murmured quietly.

Mary Margaret looked at Shemaine in alarm. "Aaiiee, don't ye be givin' her none o' that ta her face or she'll be turnin' on ye like a wild banshee! Ta be sure, Roxanne will not take it kindly, ye pityin' her. 'Tis what drives her near mad now, thinkin' we're all feelin' sorry for her 'cause she's been a homely spinster for so long." A sad smile touched the elder's lips as she thoughtfully considered the red-haired beauty. "But ye've a keen eye an' a sympathetic heart, Shemaine O'Hearn. She *is* a wounded soul what needs pityin'. An' far be it that any o' us should condemn her, seein' as how she's had ta live with a grumpy ol' bear all these many years."

"Why do you suppose Mr. Corbin is like that?" Shemaine asked, thankful her own father had carefully nurtured his family with love and respect. Strangers and casual acquaintances had not always fared well in his presence, however, for his temper had a way of showing itself in a forceful way whenever he was pushed or prodded. A wise man it was who minded his manners around Shemus O'Hearn.

Mary Margaret chuckled. "Oh, dearie, if I knew that, I'd be a soothsayer. Still, 'tis been on me mind all these years that Hugh had his heart set firmly on sirin' a son an' ne'er forgave his wife for losin' the one what was born ta them early on in their marriage. Though Leona carried the babe full term, he came stillborn, ne'er drawin' a breath beyond his mother's womb. Or at least that's what we were told. Hugh made sure they kept ta themselves even then an' wouldn't allow the neighbors ta help. 'Twas four years later when Leona finally delivered another child, but Hugh didn't take kindly ta it bein' a girl. After Roxanne, there ne'er came another, an' shortly after the girl's fifth birthday, Leona was seen buyin' a fancy comb from a travelin' salesman. That stingy flint, Hugh, was overheard yelling and raising a loud ruckus 'bout how he'd ne'er given her coin ta make such a purchase though she took in washin' ta help out. The next afternoon, the rovin' man came 'round ta their place again, an' Leona slipped out o' the house an' was ne'er seen again. She was a pretty li'l thing, ta be sure, an' with the way Hugh treated her, no one could blame her much for following her heart. 'Tis truly a pity that Roxanne took her looks from her pa and not her ma."

Suddenly a harsh, fiendish shriek rent the serenity of the village, drawing the startled attention of both women toward the boardwalk in front of the tavern, where a grotesquely deformed hunchback was cowering in terror at the feet of a tall, burly, lank-haired man who was guffawing loudly as he pummeled the deformed man with a stout stick. With savage cruelty, the ruffian kicked his victim in the stomach and viciously maligned him, calling him every foul name that found its way to his tongue.

Months ago that same huge, hulking form which towered over the disfigured man had been etched with startling clarity in Shemaine's memory. Despite her outrage over his mistreatment of another human being, it was the sight of Jacob Potts that compelled her to tear herself away from Mrs. McGee. Catching up her skirts, she raced toward the tavern as if rage had set wings to her feet.

"Shemaine!" Mary Margaret cried in sudden alarm. "Have a care, child!"

Shemaine's ire reached its zenith as more blows rained down upon the hapless, shivering hunchback, and as she ran, she railed at the top of her lungs, "You filthy, blood-sucking swine! Leave that man be!"

Although the feminine screech reached a higher pitch than he could remember ever hearing on the *London Pride*, Jacob Potts knew without a doubt that it was the one he had been straining to hear amid the diverse jargon of the colonials. Now, at last, he would vent his revenge on the bogtrotter for all the times she had made him feel like a bumbling dullard. No bog-Irish tart had a right to be so uppity and high-minded. Still, the idea of slicing the girl's throat with a knife had been Morrisa's idea, not his. It was a command she had given nigh to three months ago. But that particular method was too swift and sure to sate his own desire for vengeance. He wanted Shemaine O'Hearn to die a slow, agonizing death.

Tossing away the stick, Potts set his arms akimbo as he observed the girl. His grin grew cocky and his pig eyes gleamed in malevolent pleasure as the prize for which he had been searching rapidly approached.

"Why, if'n it ain't the bog-Irish tart comin' ta stick her nose in me affairs again."

"You sorry excuse for a man!" Shemaine snarled through gnashing teeth. "I've had enough of you bullying poor innocents." Passing a barrel of long, wooden ax handles that had been placed in front of the general store, she snatched one out and, upon reaching Potts, swung it about with every measure of might she could muster, catching him across the ear and alongside the head. His loud yowl of pain promptly brought men and fancy-dressed women stumbling from the tavern to gawk at them in surprise. Though the ogre held a hand clasped over his bloodied ear and continued to howl in deafening anguish, Shemaine would not relent. Drawing back her makeshift club, she clasped it in both hands and whipped it around again with brutal determination, this time bashing the knuckles of the hand that Potts held over his bruised ear and scraping it upward across the top of his head. Had it been a knife, Shemaine might have accomplished a scalping right then and there, but the affront to his pride was too much for Potts to bear. With a roar of rage, he caught the stick in a meaty fist and, twisting it from

her grasp, tossed it aside. His eyes fairly
blazed with fury as he reached out and
seized Shemaine by the throat. Lifting her to
the tips of her toes, he hauled her abruptly
forward until his sour whiskey breath tainted
the air she struggled to breathe. His heavy
lips twisted in a gleeful smirk as she hung
helpless in his grasp.

"This time ye'll die, bitch!" he hissed as
his long, thick fingers slowly tightened
around the slender neck. "An' this time ye
can be assured Mistah 'Arper ain't here ta
save ye!"

Shemaine clawed at his tightening hands,
trying to pry them away from her throat, but
she could not free herself from his grasp.
Neither could she draw a breath. Though it
seemed a useless effort, she fought valiantly
on, seeking to break his stranglehold, but
her strength began to slowly ebb, and her
grip on his wrists slackened. The broad visage before her, the gaping faces of the people, even the sun in the sky became a dark,
indistinct blur. Vaguely she became aware
of someone, perhaps the hunchback, pushing through the crowd of onlookers. But the
man seemed so very far away that she
could not hope he would reach her in time

to loosen the steely vise around her throat and save her from death. Her arms sagged listlessly to her sides as she gave up her feeble attempts. It would be over very, very soon.

Gage had left the general store to see what the commotion was outside and had stepped near the crowd to peer over the shoulders and heads of those who buttressed the outer ring of onlookers. It was the sight of Shemaine hanging by her throat in the grasp of some brawny hulk of a beast that sent his temper soaring. With a savage curse he caught the nearest spectator by the scruff of the neck and threw him aside. Shoving others right and left, he pushed toward the core of the circle, scooping up the handle that Potts had thrown aside as he went. Reaching his goal, he drove the blunt end of the stick into the soft, protruding belly of the tar with enough force to double the man over with a loud grunt of pain, breaking the brute's tenacious grip on the girl and sending him stumbling backward.

Gage pivoted sharply to catch Shemaine as she crumpled forward. He promptly swept her up in his arms and searched her face, but she lay frighteningly limp within his grasp, having slipped into the netherworld of the unconscious. Her head lolled over his shoulder as he lifted her higher. After pushing and elbowing his way through the crowd, he almost ran with her toward the general store, where Andrew watched in trepidation from the door.

The sound of running feet and a warning scream from Mrs. McGee made Gage step deftly aside just as the great oaf lunged forward to tackle him from behind. Meeting nothing firmer than thin air, Potts sailed past with arms flailing. For good measure, Gage planted a boot firmly on the man's broad rear, sending him hurtling helplessly into the empty space beyond the boardwalk. Several feet away, Potts landed facedown in a large puddle of muck, which, in the preceding hours, had been liberally enriched with fresh manure from passing horses. Spewing out a mouthful of filth, he pushed himself to his hands and knees and struggled to rise. But his feet slipped and skidded on the slick bottom, and he pitched forward again, gulping more of the vile sludge. His second attempt was equally ineffectual and his third swiftly aborted. Loud, guffawing laughter soon accompanied his frustrated efforts to leave the muddy hole, and by the time he managed to extricate himself from the foul ooze, the crowd was in hilarious uproar. Heckling catcalls and cries of "Mudsucker!" liberally christened him as he trudged dripping and stinking down the street.

"Sheeaim hurt, Daddee?" Andrew asked worriedly after following his father into the store.

Gage laid Shemaine on a reclining leather chaise and knelt on one knee beside it. She had not yet roused from her oblivion, but she was breathing, and that gave him hope, small as it was. He glanced aside at his son, whose eyes were swimming with frightened tears, and tried to soothe the boy's tender heart. "Shemaine will be all right, Andy. Don't fret now."

Andrew sniffed and wiped at his tears as Mary Margaret and the storekeeper, Adam Foster, approached. The latter had scurried to pour water into a basin and now set it down on a small table beside the chaise. He stepped near Gage to look down at the girl, unconsciously blocking the boy's view.

"This is awful," Mr. Foster fussed in a dither. Vexed by the incident, he continued his ranting in short, incomplete statements.

"Attacking a woman in such a vile manner! Should be drawn and quartered!"

Mary Margaret sighed ruefully. "A pity the punishment isn't allowable here in the colonies."

Deterred from reaching Shemaine or his father, Andrew glanced aimlessly about the store until he detected a movement near the entrance. Peering intently into the shadows behind a collection of hoes, rakes and shovels that stood on end in a small barrel next to the door, he crept closer, thinking it might be a dog or a cat that had wandered into the store. Then his eyes began to adapt to the tenebrous gloom behind the equipment. They widened abruptly as he finally spied the darkly clad form crouching there in pensive silence. It was a ghastly being with short legs, long arms and shaggy tan hair hanging over a jutting brow. It was a truly monstrous sight for a young child to settle his gaze upon. Venting a terrified shriek, Andrew did an abrupt about-face and, tottering full tilt around the elders, threw himself against his father and clutched at him in desperation.

Gage lifted his son in his arms and glanced around to see what had given the boy such a fright. Then his eyes lit on the deformed man who had lumbered forward into view, and he understood the reason for the child's panic.

"What is it, Cain?" Gage asked kindly, rising to his feet. "What do you want?" He was puzzled by the hunchback's presence in the store, for Cain usually kept well away from strangers. He only came into the hamlet to barter with Mr. Foster or to have his mule shod by Hugh Corbin. Otherwise, the man was rarely seen.

Cain shuffled forward warily despite the impediment of malformed legs, arms and shoulders that had hung askew from birth, but he paused in indecision as Andrew strained away and began to scream again in fright. Quieting his son with words of reassurance, Gage set him down beside Mrs. McGee, who took Andrew's hand and led him to the back of the store to show him a jar of sweets.

Tilting his head askance, Cain peered from a badly distorted face as the taller man approached. It was the first time Gage could remember ever being able to draw near the hunchback without seeing him scurry away. Perhaps, more than anybody, Cain realized how hideously ugly he was and preferred hiding himself. His nose was large and queerly pugged, his eyes set at odd angles beneath heavily shagged brows. His teeth were sparse, and in a copious mouth that hung awkwardly agape, his tongue had a tendency to loll uncontrollably. Several jagged cuts and lacerated scrapes on his face still oozed blood, giving evidence of recent abuse.

"Did you want something, Cain?" Gage questioned the man again.

The hunchback lifted a large, hairy hand toward Shemaine, who had not yet revived. Then he gaped up at Gage again as he issued a garbled question. "Sha dawd?"

Gage frowned a moment, trying to decipher the muddled speech. Then comprehension finally dawned. "No, she's not dead. She just fainted. She should come around after a while."

Cain thrust his hand clumsily in the pocket of his thin, ragged coat and withdrew a pair of slippers which had fallen from Shemaine's feet while she hung senseless in Potts's grasp. "Har shaws."

"Thank you," Gage replied, frowning in bemusement as he accepted the shoes. It was rare indeed that Cain displayed such concern for another or went out of his way to return lost possessions, especially when it meant that he would have to show himself to any of the villagers. "I'll tell Shemaine that you brought them back. She'll be grateful."

"Shamawn?"

"She-maine O'Hearn," Gage pronounced carefully for the man's benefit, unable to understand what had aroused Cain's interest in the girl. In the nine years Gage had lived in the area, he had never heard the hunchback say as many words as he had managed to speak that day. A few villagers had expressed doubt that Cain could even talk, but that had been mainly the opinion of those who had kept their distance from the man, believing him demented.

As an infant, Cain had been left on the doorstep of a half-crazed old woman who had lived by herself in a crude hovel in the woods. Because of his deformities, the elder had dubbed him Cain, for she had averred the poor babe had been severely marked by a finger of God. Over the passage of years the previously feisty woman had become increasingly frail and finally succumbed before Cain's ninth year. Thereafter the child had

had to scrounge for his mere existence, but the hag had required Cain to work for his keep at an early age and had taught him how to trap, grub, and forage for food. He still lived in the woman's hut, keeping to himself for the most part, but when he had a need for essentials that he couldn't find in the woods, he would bring deerhides, rabbit fur and other pelts to trade with Mr. Foster. Even then, Cain took care to remain in the shadows and secret nooks where it was safe until the storekeeper gathered whatever supplies he had come in for.

On rare occasions, and at the persistent urging of the storekeeper, the hunchback would relent and bring in wooden birds that he had a talent for carving, allowing them to be sold. But according to Foster, Cain disliked parting with them because he considered the sculptures his friends, and although Foster had promised Cain a goodly sum to encourage him, none had been forthcoming for some years now.

With the possible exceptions of Mr. Foster, Mary Margaret, and Hugh and Roxanne Corbin, most of the townspeople were afraid of Cain and, if he happened near, were wont to shoo him away with brooms, sticks, rocks, or whatever else came readily to hand, but to Gage's knowledge the man had never done anyone any harm. Indeed, from what he had heard and seen with his own eyes, he was convinced that Cain had far more reason to be afraid of the villagers, for the young toughs were prone to use him as a whipping boy to prove their manhood—or, Gage mentally jeered, the lack of it.

A shadow fell across the doorway, and Gage glanced up to find Roxanne poised on the threshold in indecision. Though he was still stewing over her threats, he gave her a curt nod of recognition, deciding it was wiser by far not to antagonize her. At his stilted greeting, the hunchback shuffled awkwardly around to peer toward the portal.

"Cain didn't hurt her, did he?" Roxanne asked apprehensively, shifting her gaze toward the unconscious Shemaine.

"As far as I know, Cain had nothing to do with the incident," Gage replied stiffly. "The man who attacked her was a sailor from the *London Pride.* I'm not sure how it all started, but he seemed intent upon killing her."

Mary Margaret came forward with Andrew in tow. "I can tell ye what happened," she volunteered. "I saw it all with me own eyes."

Although the elder had halted within easy reach of Cain, Andrew was almost oblivious to his presence, for he now had a sucker to hold and admire until his parent gave him permission to eat it.

Gage was curious about the attack on Shemaine and directed his full attention upon the woman. "What did you see, Mary Margaret?"

The elder gestured toward the couch. "That dear, brave girl thrashed that odious sailor with a stick after she saw him beating Cain, an' she came nigh ta losin' her life for it, too, despite all those drunken souls who were standin' 'round watchin' it all happen. Were I a man, I'd have given those clods a cuff or two ta bring them out o' their sense-less stupor! Ta be sure, they were sailin' with six sheets ta the wind. Aye, an' 'tis sorry I am that the Irish are so fond o' talkin' an' sippin'. The more they tipple, the more they prattle."

"Shemaine will be all right, won't she?" Roxanne queried worriedly.

Mary Margaret was amazed at her con-cern. "Aye, she'll be as good as ever after a bit o' rest an' tender care."

Roxanne smiled rigidly, sweeping her

gaze toward Gage. "You be sure and let me know if there's anything I can do to help."

Gage couldn't imagine himself being so foolish. Still, he found himself amazed anew at her change of moods. To say that she was erratic at times might have been an understatement. It all depended on her perspective, how she saw things that personally affected her. "No need to concern yourself, Roxanne."

Nodding a silent farewell to him and then to the elder, Roxanne stepped back from the door. Then she lifted her hand and beckoned to Cain. "Come along now before you get into more trouble."

The hunchback cast a glance toward Shemaine, then obediently left the store and scuffled along the boardwalk with his cumbersome gait, moving in the general direction of the blacksmith shop.

"Poor soul." Mary Margaret sighed, stepping to the door to watch him go. "He's like a lost, mangled sheep searching for a shepherd to lead him. I think he'd be loyal to anyone who would befriend him."

"Do you find it unusual that Roxanne concerns herself over his welfare?" Gage inquired as he sat down on the couch beside

Shemaine. He dipped a cloth into the basin of cool water and began to bathe the girl's face as he awaited Mary Margaret's response.

The elder sighed and shook her head. "They're both lost sheep, at odds with this hamlet and, I think, the world."

Floating slowly upward through an eerie fog, Shemaine became increasingly aware of a painful constriction in her throat. She swallowed, and then winced at the agony it caused her. Rolling her head on the leather cushion beneath her head, she opened her eyes a mere slit and tried to focus on the cherubic face that was braced on two small fists near her own, but her eyelids scratched like dry parchment against the tender orbs, causing tears to start.

"Andrew?" she whispered raspingly. "Could you ask someone to fetch me a glass of water?"

"Daddee?" The boy glanced up to find his father already leaning forward with a tin cup in his hand.

"Here's some water, Shemaine," Gage said, slipping an arm beneath her shoulders and lifting her up. He was amazed once again at how light and fragile she felt against his arm. It was certainly a poignant reminder of just how long it had been since he had held a woman in his embrace. He pressed the cup to her lips and held it as she slowly sipped, as closely attentive to her as he had been to Andrew earlier that morning.

Mary Margaret came near and leaned on her cane as she contemplated Shemaine over the top of Andrew's head. She was relieved to see some color returning to the girl's cheeks, for she had begun to worry that some permanent damage had been done. "That was a very brave thing you did, me girl, takin' up for Cain, but I must say ye were also very foolish, considerin' the size o' that buffoon ye attacked."

"Cain?" Shemaine wheezed. Her brows gathered in confusion, for she was unable to remember anyone by that name. "Who . . . ?"

"The hunchback, dearie." The elder supplied the information with a pitying smile. "His adoptive mother thought the name suited him."

Gage set the cup aside and lowered his bondswoman back to the cushion. Reasonably assured that she hadn't been harmed beyond repair, he couldn't keep still any longer about her moment of folly. "Why didn't you call me and let me handle the matter, Shemaine? I wasn't so far away that I couldn't have heard you, had you done so." He leaned forward to command her attention with a stern frown. "I won't have you risking your life like that again, do you hear?"

Shemaine felt like a child being reproved by her father. It didn't make her feel any better knowing he was right. It was unsettling to realize just how foolhardy she had been and what the consequences might have been if she hadn't been snatched away. Potts could have killed her. Still, she was pricked by her own lack of consideration for Gage. He would have been hard-pressed to find the funds to buy another bondswoman. Indeed, he might have been left for some time without a nursemaid to tend his son.

"I'm sorry, Mr. Thornton. I fear I lost my head when I saw Potts beating that poor man," she apologized contritely. "I should have been more careful and considerate of the great sum you have invested in me. I shall strive to be more thoughtful in the future."

Gage was incensed at her faulty conjectures. "Do you honestly think the forty pounds I paid for you is worth more than your life?" he asked angrily. " 'Tis the foolishness of endangering yourself that I speak of. Who was that man, anyway? Don't tell me he's the one you warned me about."

"Aye, Jacob Potts, the sailor from the *London Pride*," Shemaine answered in a hoarse croak. "Before I left the ship, he vowed to kill me."

"He very nearly did!" Gage retorted tersely, exasperated with her because she had blindly ignored the man's threats and attacked him, in all probability provoking deeper grudges. For her own peace of mind, he hoped it wouldn't be too long before the tar put to sea again.

Shemaine was unable to remember anything beyond the shadowy haze that had swept over her and was curious to know how she had managed to be so lightly scathed after Potts's assault. "What made him stop?"

"Mr. Thornton saved ye, dearie," Mary Margaret answered in Gage's stead. She had listened attentively to his scolding and was pleased that he actually seemed to feel a genuine concern for the girl and not his own purse. Living so near the village, she had been privy to all the ugly rumors that had cast him as a cold, insensitive man, but she had reserved her opinion, preferring to see irrefutable proof before condemning him as many in the hamlet had relentlessly done. In spite of the gossip, she had grown rather fond of the cabinetmaker throughout the years, adopting him into her heart as she would a son, which she had never been fortunate to have. She found it difficult to imagine herself being such a poor judge of character that she would have come to admire a murderer. "Ye should've seen his handsome self plowin' through all those men ta get ta ye."

Gage tossed a perturbed scowl toward the woman. He was sure she saw prospects for matrimony in every unattached couple she crossed paths with, but he knew only too well the risks of the widow expressing such ideas about town. With Roxanne threatening to incriminate him, her hopeful chatter could well prove his undoing. "Don't make it out to be more than what it was, Mary Margaret."

The Irish woman smiled sweetly, taking his rebuke in stride. For as long as she could remember, Gage Thornton had been persistently reticent about himself and shrugged off praise as if it were the plague. He had once saved a four-year-old girl from drowning in the river, but when her parents and most of the townsfolk, who had witnessed his daring rescue from shore, had tried to cheer and clap him on the back, he had handed the child over to her mother with a strong admonition to watch the youngster in the future. Then he had strode through their midst, pausing only to pick up his musket and pack, which he had tossed aside before plunging into the river. After sliding his canoe into the water, he had taken his leave in the same aloof manner that people had come to expect of him.

The fact that he was disinclined to let the girl know that he had nearly uprooted the whole circle of men to get to her side made Mary Margaret wonder about his reasons. Was he embarrassed by his warrior spirit? Or was he averse to having others suspect that, like all the other men who might admire Shemaine and feel a strong attraction to her, he was perhaps one who found himself hopelessly smitten?

Mary Margaret smiled at the idea that the tall, rugged man was so vulnerable. It only affirmed that he was human, a trait that many in the hamlet had voiced doubts about. But such judgments had been made from a distance by those who snooped and spied from behind shaded windows, much like those plump hens in the apothecary shop, for none who really knew the man had ever spoken harshly of him.

Now Gage Thornton had a new enemy, Mary Margaret mused, thinking of the tar wallowing in the mudhole. But hopefully this one would be gone in a few weeks. " 'Tis sure I am that Mr. Potts will be seeking vindication now that he has been made the laughingstock o' the village. Indeed, he'll be ready ta kill us all if anyone happens ta call him 'Mudsucker' in his presence."

Gage's disposition softened a trifle, and a grin passed briefly across his lips. "After being laughed out of town, I doubt that Jacob Potts will ever want to show his face again in Newportes Newes."

Shemaine scoffed. "It has been my experience that Mr. Potts pays back double for any offense he has been subjected to. He'll not rest until he avenges himself."

"Then the two o' ye will likely be seein' the man again," Mary Margaret predicted somberly, "because ye both shamed him ta the core. Imagine! A little slip o' girl givin' that big hulk a proper threshin'! An' if that wasn't enough, her master bootin' him inta the muck. Potts's pride has suffered mightily under yer insults. He'll not be able ta live it down for years ta come."

Gage rose from the lounge and faced the elder, desiring to change the subject for Shemaine's sake. "I have business to take care of while I'm here in town. If it wouldn't be too much of an imposition, Mary Margaret, I'd like to leave Shemaine with you for a while so she can rest."

" 'Twill be a delight ta have her as a guest in me home," the elder avowed. "And I'd consider it an honor if ye'd let Andrew stay with me, too. He's such a good boy, I love ta have him around. I'll even cook us up a bit o' food, so ye needn't fret they'll go hungry afore ye get back."

"Your kindness is appreciated, madam." Gage glanced around in search of the storekeeper, who, at the moment, was nowhere in sight. "If you'll excuse me, I must find Mr. Foster and thank him before we take our leave."

Mrs. McGee casually indicated the rear of

the store. "I believe Adam was headin' toward the back the last time I saw him."

Gage completed his mission in short order and returned to escort the women outside. Once in the wagon, Shemaine took Andrew on her lap to make room for Mary Margaret on the seat beside her. Gage climbed in and, slapping the reins, set the mare in motion. They traversed the road through Newportes Newes and, a few moments later, halted in front of a small, quaint cottage located on the outskirts of the hamlet. Gathering Andrew in his arms, Gage accompanied the two women to the door, measuring his pace to the careful steps of his bondswoman, who refused his assistance. After seeing her settled, he took his leave in the wagon, pledging to return as soon as he could.

Three hours later, Gage finished loading supplies in the wagon, having been enlisted to make several dining pieces for a wealthy woman from Richmond. With the order, he had been able to recoup almost half of what he had spent for Shemaine's papers. It relieved the strain on his budget considerably, and he was confident that progress would again be made in a good, timely order on the ship.

He returned to the Widow McGee's cottage and was silently motioned into the interior by the elder. She laid a finger across her lips and pointed to a closed door down the hall.

"Shemaine laid down with Andrew ta put him ta sleep 'bout an hour ago," she whispered softly. "Since then, I haven't heard a peep from either o' them."

Gage stepped quietly to the portal and, after a light knock that gained no response, turned the handle and pushed the door slowly inward. The sight that greeted him warmed his heart as it had not been warmed in many months, and he crept forward carefully to bask in the wonder of the scene. Shemaine and Andrew were both sleeping soundly. Sharing the same pillow, they were cuddled spoon fashion in the middle of the bed with Andrew on his side with his back against the girl's chest. Her cheek rested against his curls and her arm lay over him, like a mother with her son.

"Would ye be carin' for a cup o' tea, Mr. Thornton?" Mary Margaret murmured quietly from nearby.

Gage glanced around, surprised to find the woman leaning against the doorjamb.

She smiled at him, and he inclined his head a slight degree, not at all sure that he should take the time, for he needed to get home soon and he still hadn't taken Shemaine to the cobbler to order a pair of shoes.

" 'Twould be an awful shame ta disturb such peace, do ye not think, Mr. Thornton?" the woman ventured, contemplating him covertly.

Gage's eyes were drawn back to the bed, to the sight of Shemaine lost in slumber. She looked immensely delicate and beautiful, like a small, bright flower in a shady spot of verdant green. Her soft, pink lips were slightly parted, as if she anticipated being kissed by a phantom lover. Her silken lashes, of a dark brown hue, rested on cheeks that had grown rosy in her sleep. Her round bosom rose and fell in languid repose against the small back of her sleeping companion, and at that moment, Gage almost envied his son.

"She must be exhausted to sleep so soundly," he mused in a hushed tone. "I cannot imagine she was able to get much rest on the voyage over here."

Mrs. McGee followed his unswerving stare and thoughtfully tilted her head as she, too, contemplated the girl. "She's a rare beauty, isn't she?"

Gage cocked a wondering brow as he cast a glance awry at the widow, for it was apparent what she was about. But he curbed the temptation to question her plans to make a match. "Do you have the tea already brewed, or should I awaken Shemaine and Andrew and be on my way?"

"Smooth yer ruffled plumes, me fine-feathered peacock," Mary Margaret gently chided, beckoning him to follow as she led the way back to the hearth. There she took up the teapot and thoughtfully poured a cup full. "If I'd have ye speak the words with the girl, 'tis only a desire o' me own ta see ye an' yer son with a good woman in the house."

"How can you say that Shemaine is good when you don't know anything about her?"

Mrs. McGee smiled and tapped a forefinger against her temple. "I've a bit o' wisdom up here in me noggin an' can see what's plainly in view before me eyes."

"And what is that, old woman?" Gage questioned as she handed him a cup of tea.

"Shemaine is as much o' a lady as any woman in this village. I can see it in the way she walks an' carries herself. She has the confident, refined elegance o' one who's been well tutored and instructed in the social graces. I can hear it when she talks, despite that wee bit o' an Irish brogue. She's well worth the hefty price ye paid for her, Mr. Thornton, if ye didn't know it."

"She's all of what you say, and more," Gage admitted. "Her talents are unlimited. Andrew is already becoming attached to her. Perhaps you saw his concern when he thought she had been hurt. She's very good with him, better than—" He paused suddenly, realizing he was being much too verbose about the girl.

"Roxanne?" Mary Margaret supplied the name in a gently questioning tone, not wishing to set the man at odds with her.

"Shemaine has a way about her," Gage said, preferring not to answer the elder's query. "She's very gifted."

"Oh, no doubt. No doubt." The elder paused to take a sip from her own cup and then settled in a rocking chair in front of the hearth. For a lengthy moment she stared into the flickering flames as she savored the brew. Then she tossed a quick furtive glance toward the tall man. "But I should warn ye 'bout the rumors that are already makin' their way 'bout town, many with the aid o' Mrs. Pettycomb, who, if she minded her own business as much as she did others', would be a blessed saint."

"I can imagine the rumors are not very pleasant," Gage muttered above his teacup. "They never are."

"When ye're as handsome as yerself, sir, ye're bound ta cause talk, but when ye've also got a girl as winsome as Shemaine O'Hearn livin' under the same roof with ye . . . well, such talk is almost ta be expected. Some folks are already callin' her foul names an' sayin' as how ye bought her for yerself ta sport with. Ta be sure, they'll be watchin' her belly ta see if it grows heavy with child."

The muscles tensed in Gage's cheeks as he stubbornly declared, "I bought Shemaine because she'll be able to teach Andrew how to read and write in years to come."

"Is that the only reason?" Mary Margaret inquired softly.

Gage looked at her in surprise, but for the life of him he couldn't make any denials to the elder's unspoken insinuation, for he'd be lying through his teeth.

"If I were a man as fine as yerself, ownin' a bondswoman as comely as Shemaine," Mary Margaret ventured, "I'd not allow any space for the rumors ta hatch. I'd marry the girl an' grin with pride when the ol' biddies see her belly growin'."

Her guest raised a brow in quizzical wonder. "You never give up, do you, Mary Margaret?"

"What in the world do ye mean?" She feigned innocence with a sweet smile.

"You know very well what I mean," Gage challenged. "The realms of the lower world would freeze over ere you'd cease your attempts to marry off couples. You have a very determined nature, madam."

The elder grinned back at him as she shrugged her thin shoulders. "What do ye expect? I'm Irish!"

Gage tossed a pleading glance upward. "Heaven protect this Englishman from all the Irishwomen in the world!"

CHAPTER 7

The cobbler's workshop was nigh the heart of Newportes Newes, and though the afternoon was swiftly aging, Gage refused to leave the hamlet without completing all the errands he had set out to do, the last being to order shoes for his bondswoman. He pulled the wagon to a halt in front of the cobbler's shop and lifted his son and then Shemaine down to the boardwalk. As he did so, he noticed that a number of people had stopped along the thoroughfare and were watching them in unabashed curiosity. Their interest seemed mainly centered on the girl, and after his recent chat with Mrs. McGee, it wasn't hard to surmise what most of them were thinking. Then, too, accounts of Shemaine's recent set-to with Potts might have been spreading through the village, and some people were no doubt interested in seeing how the girl had fared.

Several bachelors were edging closer for a better look as well. Though Gage couldn't imagine the pinch-faced Mrs. Pettycomb lauding the beauty of a convict, other residents of the community had witnessed his purchase of Shemaine and were far more apt to describe her in greater detail. It was conceivable that such talk had given rise to the curiosity of the young gallants. But then, considering the scarcity of available women, they would have looked with yearning at any fetching maid who might have ventured into the area.

Gage knew most of the men well enough, some certainly better than others. Two of the younger ones had even worked for him as apprentices for a time, but they had failed to come up to his expectations, and he had let them go. He was cognizant of the bachelors' lengthy struggles to find themselves wives. He had experienced many of the same frustrations himself ere he had married Victoria and again in more recent months, but their plight was of little consequence to him. Had any of them been of such a mind, they could have braved the bigoted opinions of the town biddies and gone to the *London Pride*, just as he had done. But they hadn't, and he'd be hanged before letting them skim off the best of the cream now. Shemaine was *his* possession, and short of her parents arriving to buy back her freedom, he had no intention of selling her, even at a huge profit. She was precisely the kind of bondswoman he had been hoping to find, perhaps even better and more beautiful than he had dared to envision, and that was enough reason to refuse any and all overtures.

"Why, if it isn't Mr. Thornton and Shemaine O'Hearn!" a woman jeered behind them.

The harsh feminine voice was only vaguely familiar to Gage, but Shemaine knew it too well. Its caustic tone evoked dark memories of long hours locked away in a cable tier and morbid scenes of lifeless bodies being dumped into the sea. Drawing in a deep breath to steady herself, Shemaine reluctantly responded in like manner as

Gage faced the woman whom she and the other convicts had derisively dubbed "Mrs. Captain Fitch."

"Madam." Gage briefly tipped his hat as he recognized Gertrude Fitch. Then, with an equally concise greeting, he acknowledged her glowering husband. "Captain Fitch."

Gertrude raked her gaze scathingly over the object of her hatred and felt a bitter disappointment as she took note of the much-improved appearance of the girl. Her lips twisted downward snidely as she made comment. "Life as a servant certainly seems to agree with you, Shemaine."

Gertrude Fitch had been motivated by spite to find out how the bogtrotter was faring as a bondslave. In fact, she had all but demanded that her husband escort her about the hamlet, on the chance that she would glean dreadful news of Shemaine's circumstances from various remarks townspeople were wont to make. But when she saw the colonial reach out and gently gather the girl's slender fingers in his own, Gertrude nearly choked on the bitter bile of animosity. Whether a gesture of reassurance, compassion, or (worse yet) tender affection, it conveyed sentiments that pierced her heart anew with hostility. When the man made it evident that Shemaine was under his protection, Gertrude could foresee nothing radically unfavorable happening to the girl.

A brief silence ensued as Gertrude glared at Shemaine, but Captain Fitch was totally unsympathetic with his wife's enmity toward the girl and tromped on her onerous taciturnity with a faint trace of scorn in his smirk. "This is the first time my wife has ever ventured beyond the shores of England. She was so curious about this blasted colony, she nigh threatened me with mayhem if I didn't show her about." Disguising his resentment with a humorless chuckle, he rocked back upon his heels as he cast an irksome glance down the thoroughfare. Knowing full well that Gertrude had been hoping to hear tales of Shemaine's adversity, he continued with his subtle innuendos. "I assured her there would probably be nothing worthwhile to see, but I suppose she was longing to find a wee bauble or even a bit of news to content her."

Everette Fitch settled his gaze fleetingly on Shemaine. With her hair combed and subdued in a braided knot behind her nape, the girl looked as prim and comely as he had once imagined she would under better circumstances. Considering the depth of Gertrude's hateful expectations, he could only surmise that by now his wife was seething with disappointment.

Gage was keenly perceptive of the glance Captain Fitch flicked over Shemaine and the torturous yearning burning within the gray eyes. He had also caught the significance of the man's words and answered him adroitly. "Aye, there *are* treasures to be found . . . but in their true form, they might not always appeal to the one who searches for them so diligently. But to others, they are highly prized. In fact, some men would chance everything to have them safely within their grasp."

The guileful insinuations riled Everette so thoroughly that he could hardly trust himself to meet the amber-flecked gaze, much less to speak. He was still incensed over losing Shemaine, but he was even more resentful of the fact that this impudent interloper had challenged his authority as ship's captain by cunningly petitioning Gertrude to consider his offer to buy Shemaine, as if the man had actually perceived that it was his wife who held the ultimate power. The fellow's success in plucking the girl from his grasp would have been a despicable blow to any man's pride, but for Everette Fitch, it was compounded by the suspicion that J. Horace Turnbull had deliberately arranged matters so that Gertrude would be the controlling entity in any situation, perhaps for no other purpose than to see his son-in-law thoroughly humiliated.

Gertrude was oblivious to what had really been bandied back and forth between the two men. During their exchange, she had swept her eyes over the mud-pocked thoroughfare and wooden buildings that lined the boardwalk and drawn her own conclusions. With a sneer she conveyed her distaste. "I've seen nothing in this settlement that would make me want to *ever* come back."

Gage managed a tolerant smile. "Newportes Newes is but a babe compared to London, madam. Still, there are other cities in this land that are becoming quite impressive even in their youth. Williamsburg, for instance. The governor's palace is representative of a more gracious way of life than you will see here in this port. As for myself, I enjoy living on the river, and I treasure the space and freedom of this area. The spirit of adventure thrives in this land and appeals to my heart."

Gertrude wasn't very appreciative of the tenets of a backwoods colonial, especially one whom she could only presume was low-born. "I'm sure you must be overwhelmed with excitement in this savage wilderness, sir, but I much prefer the civilized refinement of England to this small, filthy hamlet. Of course, only an enlightened Englishman would esteem his cultural heritage."

Her sneering tones worried Andrew. The child had heard about witches from his playmate, Malcolm Fields, and was afraid he was seeing one right now. Stumbling around, he hid his face against his father's buckskin-clad thighs, desperately wishing the ugly, gruff-voiced woman would go away.

Gage combed his fingers idly through his son's hair as he offered a reply. "I know London very well, madam. I grew up there and worked nearby building ships for my father. I've met aristocrats who thought themselves knowledgeable beyond the common man. Granted, some were, but more than not, I sensed the views they expressed originated from a narrow-minded prejudice."

Gertrude sniffed arrogantly. Such a clod needed to be set in his proper place, and what better way to accomplish that feat than to demean his ancestry. "You say your father is a shipbuilder, sir, but I wonder if anyone in England has ever heard of him. You'd not be living here in this backwoods settlement if he were all that successful. What may his name be?"

"William Medford Thornton," Gage answered, preferring to leave off the title of *lord*.

Gertrude shook her head, unable to recall anyone by that name, but she failed to consider that her own world was painfully narrow, her circle of friends even more so. In supercilious pride she posed another supposition. "I'm sure you've heard of *my* father. He's quite well-known among the best of circles. Almost everyone in the shipping trade knows J. Horace Turnbull."

Gage lifted a brow in amused wonder. "J. Horace Turnbull, did you say?"

"Then you *have* heard of him."

"Oh, indeed!" His reply was emphatic though somewhat cryptic.

Gertrude smiled smugly, pleased that she had proven her point. " 'Twould seem his fame has spread even here. But tell me, Mr. Thornton, how is that you know of my father?"

A dark brow twisted dubiously upward as Gage met her gaze. "I'm not sure that I should tell you, madam."

"Oh, you must!" she insisted. "I'll not have it any other way."

Gage glanced down at Shemaine, who had sidled close to him, as if unconsciously seeking safe refuge, like Andrew. His answer would probably be the only revenge the girl could ever savor. He squeezed the thin fingers reassuringly.

"Ten years ago or so my father sent me on a mission to find your father, madam," he said, once more bestowing his attention upon the matron. "Before the occurrence of that event, J. Horace Turnbull had taken possession of a ship he had ordered from my father and had left a chest of coins as payment in full. The contents were carefully counted before the agreement was sealed, but after your father sailed away on the ship, the chest was taken to a London bank. When it was opened, musket balls were all that it contained. At some place and point in time, your father had managed to switch two trunks that were exactly alike, except for their contents, a connivance which we later learned he had planned with Lendon Crocket, once one of our most trusted men."

Pausing as Gertrude gasped an outraged denial, Gage noticed that Captain Fitch seemed peculiarly elated by the tale. The woman's stuttering attempts to convince him of her father's integrity were slowly silenced as Gage continued. "Though Turnbull had assured Lendon Crocket that it would be the bankers who'd be held accountable and no one would ever know of the healthy bribe he had been given, it seemed his real purpose was to let our man take the blame. Mr. Crocket was wise enough to realize that he had been duped and told all, shortening by some degree a very lengthy sentence in Newgate.

"Though I was only a couple of years past a score of age at the time, my father sent me out on a ship manned with an extra crew with orders to hunt Turnbull down to the ends of the earth if need be. We found the vessel taking on supplies as near as Portsmouth and waited 'til the eve of the scheduled sailing, when most of the men were enjoying a last fling in the taverns. While they were doing so, we slipped aboard the ship, threw the rest of the crew over the side and sailed her back to the River Thames. My father sold the cargo and kept the profit as usury for what your father had tried to steal from him. Turnbull was enraged and tried to call it thievery, but he forgot about our man in Newgate, who was willing to testify in our behalf. Turnbull had enough wealth to buy his freedom and was released to carry on his shipping trade. Needless to say, it was the last time we ever built a ship for your father."

"I've never heard of anything so preposterous!" Gertrude squawked indignantly. "I don't understand your purpose, Mr. Thornton, but I *do* know your story is nothing more than a vicious, slanderous lie!"

Her eyes flared with unsurpassed fury as they settled on Shemaine. "You little trollop! Somehow you convinced your master to tell these lies against my father." Despite the frantic shaking of the fiery red head, Gertrude snarled in contempt, "What did Mr. Thornton require to see it done? A night's toss in bed?"

"That's enough!" Gage barked sharply. "Shemaine had nothing to do with this! You insisted on being told, and I obliged you, madam! If you're so set on accusing someone, then talk to your father the next time you see him! Perhaps he'll tell you the truth. But leave the girl out of this! She's done nothing!"

"*Ha!*" Gertrude scoffed. "She'd do anything to see me shamed!"

"You shame yourself, madam," Gage accused brusquely. "You abuse others out of malice and then judge them by your own despicable character. I assure you, madam, that whatever shame or slander you or your father reap in this world, you'll have brought it down upon your own heads. Now good day to you." Releasing Shemaine's fingers, he slid a hand beneath her elbow and gently guided her toward the door. Feeling her trembling, he wanted to pause long enough to quietly reassure her, but there was no privacy to be had, for the cobbler awaited them in his shop and, behind them, Mrs. Fitch still stewed.

Andrew cast a frightened glance toward the large woman as he trailed behind his parent. In his pair of years on earth, he had never seen anyone look so mean or turn such an ugly color. Tottering hurriedly through the doorway after his father, he tugged at the elder's breeches, winning Gage's immediate attention. Fearfully he pointed toward the matron with the liver-hued face. "Fat witch mad, Daddee?"

His son's anxious question did much to relieve the tension that had beset Gage since their arrival in the hamlet. Even as he looked back at Gertrude Fitch, he had diffi-culty subduing his mirth, and by the time he swung the portal shut behind them, he was guffawing out loud, amazing Shemaine, who stared at him in wonder.

"Whatever has taken hold of you, Mr. Thornton?" she asked, startled by his mirth. It was totally unlike the man, whose smiles were far too sparse and rarely glimpsed.

"Fat witch mad," Gage mimicked, and in-clined his head toward Gertrude, who still mouthed threats at them through the small, square panes of glass which made up the larger window that stretched across the front of the shop. "Would you say that's an un-derstatement?"

Shemaine felt a strange, burgeoning con-tentment rise up within her as she glanced toward the fuming woman. After all the abuse she had suffered at Gertrude's hands, she found it rather satisfying to have witnessed the puncturing of the shrew's overly inflated pride.

They'll both pay for this! Gertrude silently promised herself.

Whether her subconscious summoned forth an evil incantation or, more farfetched, providence yielded to her beck and call, a silky voice queried from behind her, "What're ye gonna do 'bout them two, Mrs. Fitch? Ye ain't gonna let Sh'maine's lover get away with callin' yer pa a thief, now are ye?"

Gertrude turned her bulk stiffly about to face the woman who posed such a question, and with a confident smile, Morrisa Hatcher sauntered from the doorway of the adjoining building, where she had deliberately tarried to hear the whole exchange. The last Gertrude had seen of Morrisa was when the harlot had strutted away from the ship with the bawdily garbed older woman who had bought her. In high spirits, Morrisa had thrown kisses to all the sailors who had called to her and had invited them to come visit her at the tavern.

"What does it matter to you, Morrisa?" Gertrude asked haughtily.

" 'Tain't none o' my concern, Mrs. Fitch, but it just seems ta me ye ought ta see 'bout silencin' all them lies they're tellin' 'bout yer pa," Morrisa replied with an indolent shrug. She had been displeased by Potts's recent failure to deal a death blow to her adversary and could now see a need for another monkey on her leash. Gertrude Fitch had served her well enough on the ship, albeit through Potts, but if handled right, the old crow could be a useful ally. According to what Gertrude had said while liberally lauding her father aboard ship, it would only be a matter of time before he docked somewhere north of Virginia. "If Lord Turnbull was right here today, I'd bet me last shift he'd set his mind on doin' somethin' 'bout them two."

Against the shrewd wiles of a skilled manipulator, Gertrude was as pliable as rain-soaked mud. Her pride swelled at the harlot's deliberate magnification of her parent's importance, and she deigned to consider her suggestion. Gertrude knew that within a fortnight or two her father would be sailing into the harbor of New York on the *Black Prince*, no less than the biggest and best of his merchant ships. Perhaps if she were to arrange for a message to be awaiting him when he arrived, he'd be willing to sail south and deal with this Thornton fellow. Once they faced the wrath of J. Horace Turnbull, the colonial and his bitch of a bondswoman would soon realize the insanity of telling their vindictive lies about him!

Gertrude conveyed her gratitude with a crisply cynical smile, the best she could manage for the slut. "You needn't fret yourself over such matters, Morrisa. I'm sure ere long they'll both reap their just recompense."

Morrisa emulated solicitude with a troubled frown. "Seein's as how Mr. Turnbull is so well-known an' admired, m'liedy, it just seems a bloomin' shame when a common yokel like that colonial can sully yer pa's good name." She smiled and waved coyly at Captain Fitch, making him bluster in red-faced discomfiture. Easing his plight only slightly, Morrisa took her departure of Gertrude with the same light fluttering of her fingers. "A right good evenin' ta ye both."

Gertrude jeered in distaste as she watched the fancy-garbed harlot saunter leisurely toward the tavern. Then she cast a glare toward her husband, who had carefully fixed his gaze on some insignificant spot in the opposite direction. The fact that Gertrude hadn't let him out of her sight since leaving England saved Everette the odious task of answering a lot of angry accusations. He had been as much her prisoner as had the convicts on the *London Pride*.

Once again lending her attention to the young woman in the cobbler's shop, Gertrude frowned menacingly and shook a fat finger as if chiding a naughty child. "You filthy little bogtrotter. I'll make you sorry yet."

Shemaine shrugged off the muffled threat and faced her master again. "I think you deliberately provoked the woman, Mr. Thornton, and I could kiss you for it."

Gage leaned forward slightly with a broader grin. "If that's a promise, Shemaine, I'll collect when we get home."

"Well, I really wasn't . . . I mean, I was only . . ." Shemaine was rather astonished at the colonial's ability to unnerve her, for she couldn't recall ever being flustered in Maurice's presence. And her betrothed was a *marquess*, for heaven's sakes!

Becoming aware of the cobbler waiting expectantly, Shemaine indicated the man in helpless confusion. "Shouldn't we order the shoes now so we can get back to your cabin before dark?"

Lifting a hand, Gage bade the man to draw near. "Miles, I've got a girl here who needs to be fitted for a pair of shoes. Can you accommodate us?"

The gray-haired man hurried forward eagerly. "Sure thing, Gage."

"Shemaine . . ." Gage politely made the introductions. ". . . Mr. Miles Becker. Miles . . . may I present Mistress Shemaine O'Hearn."

Miles Becker nodded a jerky greeting. "Miles, if you'd prefer, Miss O'Hearn," he offered with a fleeting smile. Motioning for her to take a seat in a chair, he settled on a stool in front of her and slipped one of the oversized shoes off. He admired the trimness of her stockinged foot for a moment before he raised his gaze to the greenest eyes he had ever seen. A seasoned bachelor, he was rather astounded by his suddenly racing pulse as he stared into those sparkling orbs. He didn't dare trust himself to speak as he measured her foot and traced an outline of it on a piece of wood. Yet he could not entirely ignore her effect on him. It was tantamount to the giddiness derived from strong libation, which he felt in great need of at the moment.

Gage's brows gathered slightly as he detected the shoemaker's sudden confusion, for it was not difficult to discern the reason for it. Being within close proximity to Shemaine O'Hearn certainly had its disadvantages, he realized. Indeed, if she was able to stagger the wits of a bachelor like Miles Becker with nothing more than an innocent stare, then no man would be safe from her beauty and guileless charm, least of all one who was ever near.

"What kind of shoe will you be wanting, Miss O'Hearn?" Miles inquired, his voice quavering. He cleared his throat nervously, hoping she wouldn't notice his discomposure.

"Something serviceable," Shemaine answered, marveling at the change in herself. Not so long ago she would have ordered the costliest silk or the softest leather for her slippers without suffering the slightest concern over how they would last. But that had been when she could rely upon her father to pay for all her clothing and accessories. Now she had to consider the limited resources of the man who owned her and refrain from being a burden. "They must wear well and not cost too much."

"I've got two styles that fit those requirements," Miles informed her as he stepped to his workbench. After sorting through a small, jumbled pile, he brought back two different kinds of shoes which he was sure would serve her well. "These are rather bulky and not much to look at, but they're extremely durable, miss."

Shemaine was somewhat distressed at the ugliness of both and wondered how she would be able to wear them for any measurable length of time without the stiff leather blistering her feet or their burdensome weight causing her legs to cramp. Unfortunately, she couldn't allow herself to worry about such minor details. She was a bondslave, she reminded herself, and indentured servants could ill afford to be choosy. "If it's all right with Mr. Thornton . . ."

Two pair of eyes lifted inquiringly to Gage, drawing his attention away from the girl. Chiding himself for being no less vulnerable to Shemaine's allure than Miles Becker, he took a shoe in each hand and examined them side by side, then tested the pliability and weight of each before handing them back with an admonition. "You're not shoeing a horse, Miles. The girl will need something lighter and more flexible than these cumbersome clogs."

"A better leather will cost you more money, Gage," the cobbler advised, "and may not last as long."

"Did I ask you to worry about the size of my purse?" Gage questioned testily. "Now let me see what else you have. I'll not see Shemaine hobbled by those clumsy things."

Miles complied, and they finally settled on a more suitable pair that was also better looking. Gage counted out coins for a deposit and then, with a nod of farewell to the cobbler, lifted Andrew in his arms and followed Shemaine outside.

Dusk had settled, and lamps had been lit in the tavern a short distance down the boardwalk. Boisterous laughter and a lively plucking of a stringed instrument drifted from its doors and flowed into the street beyond.

"Daddee . . . me . . . hungee. . . ."

"So am I, Andy," Gage replied, realizing he hadn't stopped long enough to eat anything since the morning meal. "Too hungry to wait until we get home to eat."

Glancing at Shemaine, he jerked his head toward the establishment. "It's not a proper tavern or a coffeehouse like some I've visited in the Carolinas. There's usually a lot of drinking and revelry going on inside, considerably more than a well-brought-up young lady might feel comfortable with. But in Newportes Newes, it just happens to be the best place to get a cooked meal outside of a private home. But if you'd rather not . . ."

Shemaine gave him a brief glimpse of a smile. After her confrontation with Potts, she hadn't felt like eating anything at Mrs. McGee's. "Actually, I'm starving, and as long as there's food inside, I wouldn't care if the place were an old barn."

"We'll probably meet up with more sailors from the *London Pride*," Gage warned. "It's a place that's often frequented by seamen *and* their ladies."

Undismayed by his information, Shemaine responded with a casual shrug of her shoulders. He was apparently trying to fortify her against the possibility that some unseemly event would take place on the premises, but she wondered if such an incident could be any worse than what the prisoners had been subjected to during the ocean crossing. Being caged with Morrisa for three months had been a very enlightening experience, one she wished never to repeat. "I think I could even tolerate another encounter with Mrs. Fitch if it meant having a meal."

Shifting Andrew to his outside arm, Gage slid a hand to the small of her back and rested it there as they walked along the boardwalk toward the tavern. Shemaine held herself in rigid reserve, acutely aware of the tall, handsome man strolling beside her and his lean hand lightly riding her waist.

A furtive movement in the recessed entrance of the general store made Gage halt in sudden apprehension. Delaying Shemaine with a hand on her arm, he silently bade her to wait and put Andrew down beside her. He crept forward cautiously, wondering if Jacob Potts had decided to come back and launch another assault. But when he reached the covered entry, Gage released a sigh of relief, for he saw only the hunchback crouching in the shadows.

Realizing that he had been found out, Cain shuffled from his cubbyhole and, leaning forward, peeked around the front of the store at Shemaine. In his hand he carried a wilted bouquet of wildflowers. Facing Gage, he held them up, but when the tall man refrained from taking them, Cain lifted a hand to indicate the girl.

"Floawers . . . faw . . . Shamawn. Plawse . . . gawve . . . haw . . . floawers."

"You give them to her," Gage urged, and motioned for his bondswoman to draw near. "It's all right, Shemaine. It's Cain. He'd like to give you something."

Shemaine reached down to take Andrew's hand, but he balked at the idea of going anywhere near the deformed man and shook his head vehemently. Despite her soft assurances, the boy would not be convinced and hung back in trepidation, making it absolutely clear he wanted nothing to do with Cain. Finally leaving him, Shemaine moved to the doorway where his father stood. At her approach, Cain retreated back into the shadows again, as if reluctant to let her see him up close, but her smile encouraged him, and as she waited, he stepped forward clumsily and handed her the bouquet.

"Thank you for the flowers, Cain. They're very lovely," she murmured kindly. On an impulse, she leaned forward and bestowed a kiss upon the man's cheek.

Cain stumbled back in astonishment and gaped up at her. Then, quite baffled, as if unable to believe what she had done, he gently touched the place where her lips had brushed.

Gage marveled at her benevolence. " 'Twould seem you've won his heart, Shemaine."

She had seen many heart-wrenching sights since her arrest and, in many cases, had been frustrated by her own helplessness. There was nothing like cruel incarceration to make one yearn for a kindly word or a charitable deed. The hateful insults and the mean-spirited persecution to which she had been repeatedly subjected during her confinement had instilled within Shemaine a deeper compassion for the pitiful and less fortunate. It was not hard for her to discern that this poor, unsightly man, ill-favored from birth, was most desperately in need of friendship and a little tenderness.

Shemaine clasped the nosegay to her bosom. "I shall treasure your gift, Cain," she gently pledged. "Thank you again for your kindness and also for the return of my shoes. I don't know many people here in the hamlet, so if you don't mind, I shall consider you a friend."

Not knowing what to answer, the misshapen man canted his head to peer up at Gage as if to glean a bit of understanding from one who knew this gentle-hearted creature. Gage could offer the hunchback nothing at all, for he was just as amazed by her compassion as the one upon whom she had bestowed it.

Bewildered and yet filled with a rare feeling of awe, Cain took his leave, shuffling away in the opposite direction from where the young child stood rooted in wide-eyed trepidation.

Gage took pity on his frightened son and, stepping near, swung him up in his arms. Andrew hugged his father's neck, extremely relieved that he was safe and the monster man had gone.

"Are you still hungry?" Gage asked softly, drawing back to look into his son's face. The child nodded eagerly and, with a sudden grin, tightened his arms around the elder. Gage smiled and embraced him in return. Glancing toward Shemaine, who seemed poignantly distracted by the flowers, he whispered in the boy's ear, "What about Shemaine?"

"Come . . . Sheeaim," Andrew called, extending an arm toward her. "Daddee . . . hungee."

Shemaine laughed as she glanced at the two grinning males. Heeding the irresistible summons, she approached them, but the familiarity of the sprightly tune flowing from the tavern seized hold of her Irish spirit, and with a soft cry of glee, she danced a fleet-footed jig toward them, much to Andrew's giggling delight and Gage's smiling pleasure.

When she fell in beside him, Gage resettled his hand at the small of her back. It was a nice, comfortable place for his hand to rest, and he really didn't care what lewd conjectures were being dispersed about the village in regards to his motivation for buying her. He enjoyed touching her, and that was enough justification for him.

"I'd better take you home soon," he remarked as his lips twitched with unquenchable humor. "Or I might find myself fighting off the town bachelors in droves. And I can assure you, my girl, it wouldn't be because they'd have a yearning to kill you like Potts tried to do. Indeed! They'd be trying to steal you from me!"

Shemaine could imagine the proud and elegant Edith du Mercer fainting from shock after witnessing her undignified cavorting. Mimicking the elder's condescending demeanor, she held out a hand as if laying it upon the carved silver handle of the tall walking stick the woman had never gone without and, lifting her chin, strolled forward imperiously. "I suppose you'd prefer me to act more refined and aloof, sir."

Gage's eyes glowed as he viewed her enchanting mime. "Andrew and I like you just the way you are."

Rising upon her toes, Shemaine twirled about to face him and then sank into a deep, graceful curtsy equal to those she had once executed at lavish balls. At their applause, she laughed and threw up her arms in girlish verve. "You may blame it on the Irish blood, Mr. Thornton. 'Tis strong-willed and usually gets the upper hand despite my very best efforts to control it. More often than not, it tempts me to play the jester."

Gage was captivated by her playful antics. "You bring a lightness to our hearts that we've not experienced for some time, Shemaine," he acknowledged with a lopsided grin. "You make our spirits soar."

Shemaine felt strangely exhilarated by his relaxed smile. Beaming, she bobbed a curtsy. "I'm delighted you're delighted, sir!"

At Gage's responding laughter, Andrew clapped his small hands, showing his own approval.

"Sheeaim funny, Daddee!"

"You're funny!" Shemaine accused, pressing her face close to the young one's. She snickered playfully and waggled her head from side to side. When she straightened, she gently tweaked the small nose, evoking more giggles.

Once they stepped beyond the tavern door, a loud din assailed their senses. Andrew wisely covered his ears. Shemaine cringed, wanting to do the same. Gage promptly suffered second thoughts about his ability to endure the noisy bedlam. The place was alive with imbibing sailors and loose women decked out in colorful garb. Shemaine saw Morrisa Hatcher sitting on a man's knee and leisurely sipping from a mug of ale as she watched him playing a game of chance. Her attire was as brazen as her profession, which apparently would continue under the supervision of her new owner. Thus far the woman had failed to notice them, and Shemaine sincerely hoped they would be able to find a secluded nook before she did. Hardly anyone in the tavern gave them heed, for the customers seemed too involved in their own adventures and endeavors to care what happened beyond their narrow world. While the patrons laid out coin for food and libations, frazzled tavern maids in drab garb rushed about with large platters of food or mugs balanced on trays. One serving wench passed near the door, and Andrew's eyes widened at the heavily laden trenchers she maneuvered through the crowd.

"Perhaps we can find a quieter corner in back," Gage suggested, taking Shemaine's hand in his and leading the way.

James Harper had quaffed a liberal amount of ale by the time he caught sight of the tall, dark-haired man and recognized him as the colonial who had bought Shemaine. With a sudden snarl contorting his visage, the bosun pushed through his companions in a concerted effort to block the other man's passage. Upon reaching Gage, he rose on his toes and leaned forward to gaze intently into the colonial's face. "I don't like you, Mr. Thornton," he sneered drunkenly as he sought to focus his gaze. He staggered back unsteadily, then caught himself. Assuming a more dignified mien, he straightened his coat with a jerk and stumbled a step closer. "In truth, I think you're the most obstinate, conniving scalawag ever born. 'Tis certain that Shemaine O'Hearn is far too good for the likes of you."

"I came in here to eat," Gage announced gruffly. "If you want a fight, I'll have to accommodate you another day. I've got my son and Shemaine with me now."

James Harper's brows arched to lofty heights as he searched beyond the colonial for the young woman he had become enamored with. He settled a bleary-eyed gaze upon her and began to leer with avid appreciation of her refreshing beauty. Spreading his arms, he plowed toward her as if he would take her into his embrace, but he came up short when Gage caught his lapel in one hand and yanked him around.

"Keep your distance, Mr. Harper," Gage growled in low tones. Though he held his son within the crook of his other arm, Gage stretched the stocky fellow to the very tips of his toes and held him in a steely vise. "She's mine now, not yours, and I'll break your bloody hands if you try touching her again. Do you understand me?"

"You don't frighten me," Harper mumbled above the white-knuckled fist clasping his coat. "You're only a cloddish colonial. . . ."

Gage gave the bosun a rough, angry shake, causing Harper's eyes to roll like loose marbles in their sockets. "I may be a cloddish colonial, but you're a fool if you don't think I can embarrass you in front of your shipmates. If you don't leave us alone, you'll be licking spittle from the spittoon ere I'm finished with you. Do you understand me now?" Lending emphasis to his threat, he lifted the man until his feet dangled above the floor.

Some sanity returned when James Harper tried to draw a breath and found that he couldn't. The other's fist was wedged tightly against his windpipe, preventing any passage of air to his lungs. Suddenly doubtful of his survival, Harper nodded briskly, and then, almost gently, he was lowered to his feet. The hard fist relaxed and dropped away. In the next brief moment the lean fingers were again clasping Shemaine's hand

and leading her through the spectators, who had halted what they were doing to gape at them.

Testing the condition of his throat, James Harper swallowed several times and gingerly stretched his neck to assure himself that nothing vital had been damaged or broken. Though he might have suffered some shortage of breath for a few moments, he felt amazingly clearheaded for a man who had partaken copiously of so much ale. He lurched toward a chair and slithered loose-jointedly into the seat. Thankful to be alive, he heaved a wavering sigh of relief, expelling fumes that reeked of strong ale.

A serving wench paused beside him and tilted her head aslant as she considered first the bosun and then the couple who were presently making their way toward the back of the tavern. "By rights, gov'na, ye should consider yerself fortunate," she informed the seaman. "That Thornton fella can be mighty mean when he wants ta be. Once I saw him thrash a man twice his size when the bloke tried ta accost his wife on the street outside this here tavern. O' course, Miz Thornton's dead now, an' some maybe wonder if'n Mr. Thornton didn't kill her himself, seein's as how he's so ornery an' all, but ta me own way o' thinkin', that would be a bloomin' shame 'cause he's so handsome an' all."

Harper had difficulty deciphering her words at precisely the time she said them. The dawning came with agonizing slowness several moments later, prompting him to finally lift his gaze and stare aghast at the dowdy woman.

The serving maid grew immediately worried at his stricken expression. "Ye needn't fret so fearful like, lovey." She patted his shoulder in a motherly fashion. "Mr. Thornton's forgotten ye by now. Ye're safe."

Morrisa Hatcher elbowed her way through the crowd, shoving the serving maid out of her path as she passed the bosun. James Harper's eyes wavered unsteadily as he observed the widely swinging, gyrating motion of her hips, but the harlot gave him no heed as she followed in the wake of her red-haired adversary. Halting at the table Gage had selected near the back, Morrisa struck a sensual pose and smoothed a hand over her voluptuous curves as she awaited his notice. Gage stood Andrew in a chair between himself and Shemaine, and then pulled another chair out for his bond-slave. Finally facing Morrisa, he acknowledged her presence with a stiff twitch of his lips, the best greeting he could offer the woman.

"Morrisa Hatcher, I believe."

"Right ye are, gov'na." The harlot flexed her arm in a sly movement that sent the sleeve of her magenta gown falling over her shoulder, leaving much of it bare. "I been watchin' for ye ta come in here, but I didn't knows ye'd be o' a mind ta bring yer son in with ye. A right handsome li'l boy he is, too." She considered the child thoughtfully for a moment before concluding, " 'Tain't hard ta see ye done yer manly duty by his ma. He's the spittin' image o' ye, al'right."

"Did you want something?" Gage asked impatiently, hardly in the mood to tolerate her mischief.

"Nothin' what could be called real important, gov'na." She shrugged, managing to lower her neckline over her bosom. "Just thought I'd invite ye ta come back an' stay a spell when ye ain't got yer kid or Sh'maine hangin' onta yer shirttails. If'n ye be o' a mind, I can service yer manly needs right good-like. I knows more'n Sh'maine 'bout what kind o' things can pleasure a bloke like yerself. I might could even teach ye a thing or two, if'n ye'd let me."

Shemaine's face flamed scarlet at Morrisa's bold solicitation. Quickly directing her attention to Andrew, whose nose barely reached the edge of the table now that he was sitting down, Shemaine jumped to her feet again and made use of a small nearby cask, which she turned on end and, as his father lifted up the boy, placed in the chair beneath Andrew.

After Andrew was resettled on the keg, Gage faced the harlot again and grew rather annoyed that she hadn't decided to leave of her own accord. He sighed in exasperation. "All I really want right now, Morrisa, is to be left alone with my son and Shemaine. I sincerely hope that's not too much to ask of you or anyone else here."

His reply drew an angry sneer from Morrisa. "Ye ain't a very friendly bloke, are ye?"

"No, I'm not," Gage admitted. "It seems everywhere I've gone today I've met someone from the *London Pride*, and the encounters have always ended in some kind of fray, so I beg you leave us in peace before I *really* lose my temper."

"Suit yerself, gov'na!" Morrisa snapped in a huff. "I was only tryin' ta offer me services . . . seein's as how ye've got a li'l know-nothin' under yer roof." Morrisa started to turn away, but paused as she glanced at Shemaine. Gratification had turned rapidly to frustration when the colonial had snatched the Irish twit from Potts's grasp. She yearned to deliver a death blow to her adversary even now, but while there were witnesses to mark her actions, she had to limit her efforts to a more acceptable form of torture. "I hears Annie's papers got bought up by that squeaky li'l mouse what came aboard the *Pride* yesterday ta look us over, Sh'maine. Him bein' single an' all, I 'spect Annie won't be havin' any babies ta look after. But as I figgers it, she'll be needin' shelter from that sour ol' carp afore too long. A li'l mouse like Samuel Myers can be meaner'n a big rat when ye gets right down ta the truth o' the matter."

"Are you finished?" Gage asked curtly, seeing through the harlot's vicious schemes. The distressed frown that Shemaine now wore was a fair indication of her deep concern for her friend.

"That's all, gov'na! Sees ye 'round sometime . . . maybe after ye gets tired o' M'liedy Prig here." With that, Morrisa tossed her dark mane over her shoulder and pranced off, exaggerating the sway of her hips as she went.

Shemaine leaned forward to claim her master's attention. "Mr. Thornton, do you really think Annie is in danger of being abused by the man who bought her? That Mr. Myers?"

Gage met his bondslave's troubled gaze. "I don't know, Shemaine, but if you'd like, I can make inquiries about the nature of the man from some of the townspeople who know him better."

"I'd be grateful, Mr. Thornton. Annie has been hurt in so many ways. I'd like to see her able to enjoy her work and be content with her life."

"I'll see what I can find out."

A serving wench came to their table and, in a bored tone, announced the fare. "We've got Burgoo and biscuits. Take 'em or leave 'em."

"We'll take 'em," Gage informed her, and

then gestured toward Andrew. "Not so much for the boy."

"Burgoo and biscuits?" Shemaine repeated in confusion after the woman had left. She had chewed on a few hard biscuits in the dank hole of the *London Pride*, but the word *burgoo* meant nothing to her.

Gage responded with a casual shrug. "Burgoo is a stew made with different meats and vegetables. Biscuits are a type of bread we eat here . . . definitely much better than the sea biscuits you might have tolerated on the voyage."

In a few short moments, separate dishes of the stew and a large platter of biscuits were placed before them. Shemaine copied Gage's lead as he buttered Andrew's bread, and then, at his urging, she sampled a bite. Much to her amazement, she found them delicious.

Gage smiled, noticing how brightly her eyes glowed when she was elated, and watched in anticipation as she carefully tasted the stew. "Good?"

Shemaine nodded eagerly. "Oh, yes!"

"Good, Daddee," Andrew agreed with a toothy grin.

Gage peered at the girl questioningly,

managing a crooked grin. "Then you'll forgive me for bringing you in here?"

Shemaine was amazed that a master would even concern himself about his slave's feelings. "There's nothing to forgive, Mr. Thornton. You're not responsible for other people's actions. You're no better able to dictate Morrisa or Mr. Harper's behavior than you can command the sun to go hither or yon and expect it to obey."

"I was, at the very least, tempting fate by bringing you in here. For some years now, the sailors have been inclined to gather here for odd and sundry reasons."

After being around Morrisa, Shemaine could well imagine what those reasons were. "You gave me a chance to decline, but I must tell you truly, sir, that I have seen and heard far worse on the *London Pride* than I've noticed going on here tonight. If I was at all naive about life before my arrest, then I can honestly say, Mr. Thornton, I've learned much through my ordeal, some of which I'd rather forget. I assure you I'm not made of spun sugar. I'll not shatter into a thousand pieces the very moment I'm faced with adversities. I'd not be sitting here now if I were so fragile. I'd have probably succumbed to Mrs. Fitch's abuse or Morrisa's spite long before the ship ever reached safe harbor."

" 'Tis good to know that, Shemaine," Gage murmured, "because this land is tough and sometimes rather austere. It's difficult for the weak to survive here. The hardships can overwhelm, even break, a strong-minded person if he's not prepared to meet the challenges of living in the wilderness. It certainly helps to be resilient."

"Growing up in the safety of my parents' home, I never once imagined there would come a day when I would have to face calamity," Shemaine mused aloud. "Before my arrest, I seemed destined to become a marchioness. Little did I suppose that I would soon be subjected to the hostility and brutality of others who had the power and authority to dictate my circumstances, or that I'd be cast adrift in a way of life with which I was unfamiliar. I've learned some harsh lessons since the thieftaker snatched me, Mr. Thornton, but I've come to realize that I'm not without substance or stamina. God willing, I'll see these seven years through to good advantage."

Gage permitted her a glimpse of a smile.

"I think I'm already seeing a change in you since yesterday."

Shemaine blushed, realizing she might have sounded a bit boastful of her own strengths and perseverance. "I understand, Mr. Thornton, that any benefit I might derive from my servitude to you will stem mainly from your forbearance with my shortcomings. I know there is much that I have yet to learn, but if you will be patient with me, I'll try to overcome my faults."

"You're much more of a blessing to Andrew and me than you realize, Shemaine," Gage said with a generous measure of honesty. "You're as refreshing as a spring shower after a harsh winter. Right now, I'm too busy appreciating your worth to notice whether or not you have any flaws."

Shemaine smiled, feeling pleasantly reassured. "If we're not too late arriving home, perhaps you and Andrew would like to have some custard pie before you retire. I made it for you both this morning."

A nearby lamp cast a golden aura over Gage's face, lending a luster of softly polished brass to his noble features. For Shemaine, it was like looking at a statue of a fabled god who had come to life. The same glow lightened his brown eyes to a rich, translucent amber, making her marvel at how beautiful they were. But it was the gentle radiance of his smile that infused her heart with a strange, stirring warmth.

CHAPTER 8

Night had descended by the time they left the tavern, but a mild breeze had sprung up from the south. Its fragrant warmth was intoxicating to Shemaine, who, not too many days ago, had almost despaired of ever savoring fresh air again. She accepted Gage's assistance in mounting to the seat of the wagon, and receiving his drowsy son from him, cuddled the boy on her lap as his father stepped away to free the horse's tether. But a muttered oath from Gage made her glance up in sudden worry.

"Is something the matter?"

"The mare has thrown a shoe." Gage

ground his teeth, knowing only too well what that would entail. He sighed pensively. "There's no escape from it, I fear. We'll have to pay a visit to the Corbins before we can leave for home."

Shemaine shuddered at the thought of having to face Roxanne again, but she said nothing, for Gage was apparently suffering similar qualms. "Should we get down so you can unhitch the wagon?"

"You can stay where you are for the moment. I'll lead the mare to the smithy's and unhitch the wagon once I get there."

Upon reaching the blacksmith's shop, at the far end of town, Gage helped Shemaine down and then handed Andrew back to her. He unharnessed the mare and led the animal to a covered lean-to where a glowing heat could still be seen radiating upward from a brick-hewn forge.

A large man with a ponderous belly hobbled out the front door of the log cabin with the aid of a makeshift crutch. Holding his broken, wood-splinted leg carefully aloft, he made his way to the edge of the porch and braced himself there on his good foot as he peered intently into the night-born shadows that surrounded the visitors. His gruff voice seemed to boom through the darkness. "Who's out there?"

"It's Gage Thornton, Mr. Corbin. My horse threw a shoe."

Hugh Corbin responded with a loud, angry snort. " 'Tis a poor late hour of the night for ye ta be makin' your way here with a horse that's lost a shoe. Any levelheaded man would be at home where he belongs, but ye're not such a man, are ye?"

"Are you able to help me or not?" Gage questioned gruffly, ignoring the insult.

"I guess I've no choice in the matter if I want ye out of here," Hugh retorted irascibly. "Let me fetch a lantern from the house."

Having recognized Gage's voice in the brief exchange, Roxanne stepped out the front door with a lantern that she had hurriedly lit. Her hair hung loose down her back, and she had hastened to don a wrapper over her nightgown.

"Get some clothes on!" Hugh barked at his daughter as he sought to take the lamp from her.

"I'm wearing clothes!" Roxanne snapped back, snatching the light beyond his reach. She quickly descended the steps and almost ran toward the blacksmith shop, making no effort to accommodate her father's hitching gait. In the lantern glow, her eyes seemed animated and full of joy until the aura of light spread beyond Gage to the slender form standing a short distance from him. Then the gray orbs took on a steely hardness. She had hoped that Shemaine would still be incapacitated after her ordeal and that Gage had reconsidered his options after her warning that morning and was there wanting to apologize. But Roxanne now realized such a notion was farfetched. The cabinetmaker was as stubborn as her father.

Sauntering close to the bondslave, Roxanne swept her with a malevolent perusal. "Well, Shemaine, I see you've recovered well enough. But then, perhaps you weren't really hurt after all. Perhaps it was just a ploy to extract a bit of sympathy from your master."

Shemaine smiled blandly. "Imagine what you will, Miss Corbin. I'm sure nothing I say will change your mind."

Raising her chin to a haughty level, Roxanne smirked. "You're right, of course. I'd never pay much heed to what a convict has to say."

Roxanne whirled away, and with the breezes billowing beneath her wrapper, it seemed as if she floated toward the man to whom she had once offered her heart and who, after the months of devoted service she had given him, had cruelly rejected her gift of love. In a hushed, hurt tone she confided, "I thought you had come to make amends, Gage, perhaps even to tell me that you'd be getting rid of your bondswoman. But I see you intend to be obstinate. True to your inclinations as always, aren't you?" She shook her head regretfully. "A pity . . . for your sake as well as your son's."

Sensing a threat in her words, Gage fixed her with a harsh scowl, but he remained mute, preferring not to get into another hassle with her or anyone else while Shemaine was near enough to hear. It seemed the whole day long he had been involved in one confrontation after another, and all he wanted at the moment was to go home and enjoy a nice, peaceful evening alone with his son and his bondslave.

Limping to the forge, Hugh rested on his crutch as he barked at Gage. "Stoke the embers and make yerself useful if ye want me ta shoe yer horse. I can't do it alone."

"I'm able to do it myself if you'd prefer," Gage offered. "All I need from you is the loan of your equipment."

"Ye'll pay the same no matter who does it," the elder informed him brusquely. "So don't think ye'll be using me as your dupe."

"I hadn't intended to," Gage rejoined tersely. With a slowly steeping resentment brewing inside of him, he began pumping the billows to push air into the forge.

The smithy pivoted about to settle a speculative stare upon Shemaine, pricking her mettle with his disparaging perusal. Turning stoically, she carried Andrew to a large tree stump some distance from the blacksmith shop and sat down upon it, hoping that she had gone far enough to be safely off the Corbin property, for she had already concluded that she liked the blacksmith no better than his daughter.

Cuddling the boy to her, Shemaine began to sing to him as she rocked back and forth. Gradually Andrew relaxed in her arms until his eyelids sagged. A sigh slipped from his parted lips, and he fell asleep, snuggled close against her soft breast.

Hugh fought an inner conflict with himself as he watched Shemaine gently nurturing the boy, but he was powerless to subdue the raging turmoil that roiled within his heart and mind. Tormenting impressions spewed upward from the murky depths of long-buried memories, vexing him sorely, and he turned on Gage, bedeviled by a darkly brooding envy. "Ye've bought yerself a fine-lookin' convict there," he jeered in scorching reproof. "No doubt, with ye ownin' her, ye'll be gettin' yer manly cravings appeased at the snap o' yer finger, so's I'm thinkin' ye'll be havin' second thoughts 'bout weddin' me girl."

Gage had been leaning over the forge, examining the horseshoe he had been heating, but at the man's words, he lifted his eyes to Roxanne. The woman grew unsettled beneath his sharply pointed stare and, turning away, busied herself suddenly by hanging the lantern on a nearby post. Gage's angry scowl reverted back to the smithy. "I'm afraid you're mistaken, Mr. Corbin, if you think I have *ever* asked your daughter to marry me. Since that is definitely not the case, I really don't see that I owe you any explanation about my reasons for buying Shemaine. In short, Mr. Corbin, it's none of your damn business."

"Ye arrogant libertine! I'll teach ye ta show proper respect for yer elders!" In a spitting rage, Hugh seized the small end of the crutch in his hand and, holding it like a club, hopped forward on one foot, intending to give the younger man a proper thrashing.

Slowly straightening to his full height, Gage raised a condescending brow as he regarded the elder. "If you mean to hit me with that, Mr. Corbin, be assured that I won't stand here and take it meekly. I'll finish anything you start, believe me."

The cold gaze piercing the lantern-lit gloom cooled Hugh's temper effectively. The memory of the pain he had suffered when the horse he had been shoeing sat on him and broke his leg was too fresh in his mind for him to willingly invite further injury. Finding no graceful way of retreating from a confrontation, he flung up a hand in a vivid display of temper and snarled, "Finish what ye're doin' and then get out of here. Me girl and me don't want ye and that filthy li'l slut around here, do ye hear!"

It took a fierce effort of will for Gage to curb the goading temptation to drive his fist into the man's face. All the reasons for refraining from such an assault were there before him, so obvious a simple dolt could recognize them. Hugh Corbin was twice as old as he was and, at the moment, lame. If he punched the elder, he'd be no better than Jacob Potts battering Cain. No matter how much he longed to at that precise moment, he just couldn't hit a crippled old man!

"Shemaine is *not* a slut, and I take great exception to you calling her that," Gage ground out. "My only regret right now is that I must finish shoeing the mare. Otherwise, I'd tell you to go to hell." He snorted in contempt as he thought about it. "But why should I waste my breath? As mean as you are, you're bound to go there anyway."

The air fairly crackled with tension as the two men glared at each other. Hugh wanted to launch an assault right then and there, but he just couldn't dismiss the dreadful prospect that he might come to further harm. For once, better judgment took precedence, though he still chafed beneath the harsh bit of fermenting animosities.

Hobbling around, Hugh returned to the porch with a halting gait and clumsily took a seat on the edge. From that vantage spot, he could keep watch until the shoeing was complete. Though he had never had a reason to believe that Gage Thornton would ever cheat him, Hugh trusted no man with his possessions. Once he received the coins due him, he would send the cabinetmaker on his way.

Leisurely Roxanne meandered back to a spot where she could see Gage more clearly. Leaning against a post, she scanned his downturned face above the glowing coals and was amazed that even now she yearned to look into that fine, handsome countenance and declare her love. It would take nothing more than a gentle smile from him to encourage her. But even as she admired his noble visage, Roxanne saw his brows gather in a harsh frown, as if he were annoyed by her close attention. The idea set spurs to her temper. "What are you going to do, Gage? Fight every man who insults your convict?"

"If I have to!" he retorted sharply without glancing up.

"You're a stubborn man, Gage Thornton, and right now, I think you're a fool. Shemaine doesn't deserve your protection."

Though her words incensed him, Gage refused to yield his gaze to her. "Your opinions really don't concern me, Roxanne. They never have."

His words assaulted her as brutally as any slap across the face, and Roxanne felt her temper soar at his blatant indifference. How many times throughout the nine years she had known him had she guilefully offered herself to him? And how many times had he failed to notice? Or had that been a deliberate ruse on his part? It had driven her nearly mad wanting him the way she had and then being politely dismissed each and every time, as if he were unable to think of her as his mistress . . . or his wife. She could not imagine him being so insensitive to his bondslave. Oh, no! He had other plans for the convict!

"You intend to take that trollop into your bed, don't you?" Roxanne demanded, her voice fraught with emotion. "That's been your desire from the first moment you saw her, to fornicate with that slut!"

"What if it has been?" Gage barked angrily, seeing no difference between father and daughter. Despite his qualms about pushing the woman closer to the crumbling precipice of an irrational jealousy, he deliberately whipped her ire into a slavering frenzy as he braced his palms on the brick buttressing the forge and leaned forward to fix her with a probing glare. "Tell me, Roxanne, is it really any of your business what I choose to do with Shemaine in the privacy of my cabin . . . or, for that matter, my bed?"

The corners of Roxanne's mouth twisted downward in an ugly grimace, and in the depths of her throat, a low gurgling growl was born. With all the fury of a woman scorned, it burst forth in a horrendous shriek. The hem of her robe swirled around her bare legs as she whirled and, like a wraith in the night, fled back to the cabin. Racing past her father, she stormed through the front portal. The resounding crash of the door slamming against the jamb made Hugh Corbin duck his head and grimace as if he fully expected the porch rafters to fall down upon him.

On the long ride home, Shemaine sat quietly on the wagon seat beside Gage, holding his sleeping son in her arms. The moon had risen above the trees and cast its silvery glow upon the land, enabling Shemaine to see the ominous scowl that drew the man's magnificent brows sharply together. She dared not ask what was troubling him. It went against all propriety for a bondslave to inquire into the personal thoughts, inner turmoil and feelings of her master, but she could not help but wonder what the Corbins had said that had caused his mood to turn so bleak. She had been aware of the quarrels that had arisen. Indeed, she would have had to have been completely inattentive to miss the threat that Hugh Corbin had made with his crutch or the rage that Roxanne had exhibited just before she had fled back to the cabin, but the wind had snatched away their words, sweeping them into oblivion. Still, Shemaine was of a mind to think, inasmuch as the first altercation had begun shortly after Hugh had eyed her, that the argument had started because of something he had said about her.

Even in the meager light of the lunar orb, Gage felt the museful stare of his indentured servant resting on him, but many miles were traversed before he could trust himself to glance her way. Finally doing so, he found himself staring into shining, moonlit eyes. "You are troubled, Shemaine?"

"I only sense your anger, Mr. Thornton," she murmured timidly, "and wonder what I

might do to soothe it. I perceive that somehow I am to blame."

"It's not your fault," Gage stated emphatically.

No, he thought pensively, the difficulty
had started soon after his arrival in Newportes Newes. It hadn't taken Roxanne long
after meeting him to develop an obsession
to become his wife. She had woven her wily
tricks to entrap him in a forced marriage,
feigning innocence as she brushed herself
against him in provocative ways, clearly
hoping to arouse his bachelor's starving
senses. Recognizing his own vulnerability
as a man with unsatisfied carnal needs, he
had been extremely cautious to ignore any
and all overtures, even at the cost of seeming thick-witted. After all, he had not fled England and pretty Christine just to dally with
a woman he couldn't bear to look at the
morning after. Judiciously he had busied
himself elsewhere.

When he had wed Victoria some years
later, Roxanne had shut herself up in her
father's house and grieved as if the end of
the world had come. At length, she had
emerged from her den of gloom. Even so,
she had treated him for a time with all the

contempt and hatred that a defiled maiden might have heaped upon an unprincipled roué who had callously thrown her aside after stripping away her innocence. Her bitterness after being spurned had eventually subsided, giving way to yearning looks, wavering smiles and, finally, subtle overtures, until he had come to dread and even abhor her visits. Victoria had failed to see through Roxanne's subterfuge. Nor had he cared to enlighten her. His wife had merely felt sorry for the spinster and, in her gentle way, had been the best friend Roxanne had ever had.

After his wife's death, Roxanne had once more proven herself determined to take over that intimate position in his life. By being immediately at hand at the time of Victoria's fatal fall, she had obviously thought she had been provided with some strange sort of leverage by which she could force him to the altar. Though unspoken, the threat had been there all along. She would tell the truth or even lie, but this time she meant to have him . . . or he would have nothing at all.

Having fully comprehended what he chanced by thwarting Roxanne's aspirations, he had gone to the *London Pride* literally to buy back his own freedom and to set the course of his life on a different bearing than she had mapped out for him. He had anticipated beforehand that Roxanne would have difficulty accepting his purchase of a bondslave. No doubt, in her mind, any woman he bought would be just another usurper, perhaps in the same way she had imagined Victoria had been. Sad to say, Roxanne had lived up to the precise letter of his expectations.

Hugh Corbin had been just as difficult, and Gage knew it was not beneath the man to use Shemaine's presence as an excuse to pick a quarrel with him. The smithy would have snatched at limp straws if they had provided him with such leverage. Hugh's hatred of him was clearly conveyed in every spitting word the man issued.

"In the eight or nine years I've known him," Gage reflected, glancing aside at Shemaine, "Hugh Corbin has been surly and contentious, but recently he has become almost intolerable, about as mean and ornery as Ol' One Ear. He's free with his insults and seems to go out of his way to provoke me, especially when I'm with my family . . . or, as I saw tonight . . . with you. Once, not very long ago, I caught him watching Andrew with a strange, haunted look in his eyes. It unnerved me considerably. I don't know what the man might be capable of . . . if he'd ever take his spite out on a young child, but his actions worried me. Several times in the past, Roxanne asked me to let her take Andrew home with her so he could stay the night, but I just couldn't bring myself to give my consent. I dared not trust her father."

"Mrs. McGee told me that Mr. Corbin had wanted a son of his own," Shemaine rejoined softly. "The only one he fathered arrived stillborn four years before Roxanne was born. Perhaps when he sees you with Andrew, Mr. Corbin is reminded of his own failure to sire a son. It might well be envy he feels toward you instead of hatred."

The brooding rage that had vexed Gage's mood for the last hour began to slowly dissipate as he considered her conjecture. From his past experiences with the smithy, he had to admit that her supposition had merit. Though he had met the cantankerous blacksmith and his then-nineteen-year-old daughter shortly after his arrival in the colonies, it had only been within the last couple of years that the man had displayed such a serious aversion to him.

Gage shook his head in wonder, berating himself for not having considered the idea before. It had taken a girl younger than a score of years to enlighten him to the possibility. He marveled at her insight. "You're very perceptive, Shemaine. Far more than I have been. I just couldn't understand why Hugh had taken such a dislike to me."

"Perhaps you were too close to the situation to recognize his jealousy for what it is," she suggested, glancing up at him. What she saw warmed her heart considerably. His expression had softened and his lips now bore the slightest hint of a smile. He turned to meet her gaze, and she held her breath as his eyes caressed her face. Then they swept downward to the small head cradled against her breast.

"Your arms must be getting tired." Gathering the reins in one hand, Gage lifted his free arm and laid it along the upper portion of the seat behind her, carefully avoiding the mistake of touching her and frightening her off to the far side. "Why don't you slide close to me and lay Andrew's head in my lap? 'Twill relieve the weight on your arm, and then you'd be more comfortable."

Shemaine was more than willing to ease

her cramping muscles, but when she sought to move, she realized she lacked the strength to lift the boy and herself at the same time so she could scoot across the seat. After several aborted attempts, she confessed in helpless defeat. "I'm sorry, Mr. Thornton, I don't seem able to."

Clamping the reins between his legs, Gage wrapped his right arm behind her waist and slid his left hand beneath her knees. It required no real effort on his part to resettle her snugly against his right side. His arm remained as a sturdy support behind her back as she withdrew her own arm from under the boy's shoulder and eased the small dark head into Gage's lap. A deep sigh escaped Andrew, but he never woke.

Gage glanced down at his sleeping son, seeing the small, upturned face bathed in soft moonlight. Long lashes rested in peaceful repose upon the boy's cheeks, but with his jaw slackened in sleep, his mouth soon fell agape. Shemaine reached across and very gently laid her hand alongside the boy's cheek, placing a thumb beneath the tiny chin and closing the small mouth. Immediately Andrew stirred, flopping over on his right side toward his father as he flung an arm across Shemaine's, entrapping her arm and the hand that was caught between his cheek and the elder's loins.

A shocked gasp was torn from Shemaine as she sought to extricate herself from the tightening wedge into which her hand had been caught. Though restrained no more than a fleeting moment, a grueling eternity might as well have passed before she managed to drag her hand free, in the course of which she heightened a multitude of sensations that had already been sharply stimulated in the man.

The hot blood had surged through Gage with swift and fiery intensity at the very instant of her hand's entrapment, making him achingly aware of his ravaging desire. Now, long moments after her hand had been safely clasped within her other, the ravenous flames still pulsed with excruciating vigor through his manly loins, searing holes in the thin wall of his restraint. With every fiber of his being, he was acutely aware of the elusive fragrance of his bondslave filling his head, that same which he had breathed in with intoxicating pleasure every time he had touched or drawn near her that day. It was the sweet *scent* of a woman, one which he had not even been cognizant of having craved until this very moment. Her soft bosom drew his sweeping perusal, and when he finally lifted his gaze to meet hers, he found himself staring into widened eyes filled with dismay. Even in the meager light, he thought he could detect her cheeks deepening to a vivid hue beneath his scrutiny.

"I'm . . . I'm sorry!" Shemaine's strangled whisper seemed to fill the night, attesting to her shame. Though she clutched the offending hand against her breast, she could still sense the branding heat of his maleness against the back of it, the unexpected firmness that had grown rapidly pronounced, leaving her breathlessly aware of the bold, mature difference between the man and his son. Despite the instincts that urged her to hold her silence and pretend it never happened, Shemaine implored his pardon, hoping to banish any notion that it might have been a deliberate act on her part. "I didn't mean to touch you, Mr. Thornton."

Facing the shadowed road once more, Gage made no comment, but clicked to the mare, urging her to a faster pace. It was nigh impossible for him to ignore the soft, womanly form beside him and, more difficult by far, the memory of her hand brushing deliciously hard against his manhood.

Settling into a regular routine would probably take time, Shemaine decided after the morning meal a week later, since her primary concern, as her master had pointed out, would be taking care of Andrew. Even so, between cooking and attending the needs of the boy, she found herself accomplishing far more than she had previously thought herself even remotely capable of.

Gage had received word from his primary customer in Williamsburg that delivery of the new furniture would have to be delayed for an indefinite time. The workmen were still trying to complete his house, and he could not accept the furnishings until the rooms were ready. In the meantime Gage had started work on the dining room pieces he had recently contracted for in Newportes Newes. In the evenings he drafted out the plans, drawing patterns for the arms and legs of the chairs and designing a new sideboard. During the daylight hours, he worked with his men on several other pieces, but frequently he could be found aboard the ship, helping Flannery with some of the more precise work.

Before leaving the cabin on this particular morn, Gage had announced that he would be working on the ship for most of the day. If she were of such a mind, he told Shemaine, she could bring Andrew and victuals enough for the shipwrights and the cabinetmakers around noon, and they could all enjoy a midday repast on the deck of the ship, as it promised to be a fine, sunny day.

"Ring the bell by the front steps when you're ready to come to the ship," Gage instructed after she had assured him that she would be able to do such a thing, "and I'll send someone to fetch the food."

Shemaine immediately accepted the challenge of preparing a tasty feast to satisfy the appetites of hardworking men. While roaming around the immediate area several days earlier, she had ventured into the root cellar which her master had dug into a hillock near the cabin. It was there that Shemaine and Andrew went to collect carrots, onions, and an assortment of other vegetables for the venison stew she would make. It would be her own version of a hearty Irish dish that Bess Huxley had often made for Shemaine's father. In no time it was simmering above the fire.

Shemaine had set bread dough to rising earlier that morning. After punching it down, she separated it into smaller loaves and placed them near the warmth of the hearth for a second rising. She peeled a goodly number of potatoes and put them in a kettle to boil. Then she proceeded to make a spice cake. While the latter was baking, Shemaine busied herself doing other tasks around the cabin.

The laundering techniques of a chore maid had been an integral part of the instructions that she had received while still under her mother's tutelage, if for no other reason than to learn firsthand how to manage a houseful of servants. Shemaine had no trouble recalling the advice that she had once been given. With Andrew's eager assistance, she stripped the sheets from the beds and washed them along with several linen towels, a few of the boy's garments and the shirts which she had found in Gage's armoire soon after her arrival. She hung the clothes outside where they could catch the breezes and the full light of the sun. While they dried, she aired the pillows, swept and damp-mopped the recently scrubbed floors, polished the furniture and generally cleaned the interior until it gleamed, all the while making a game of the chores to keep Andrew entertained. She even began to teach him a counting song and laughed with pleasure at his pronunciations. He was delighted with it all and giggled uproariously, trying hard to mimic her.

For the outing on the ship, Shemaine collected a goodly supply of utensils, tin plates and cups from the storeroom, added a tablecloth and napkins that she had found among the kitchen linens, and packed them all in a basket, along with the cake that she had frosted. She cut the bread, tied it in a clean cloth, and set part of it aside for Andrew to carry. A jug of cool cider was drawn up from the well, and the kettle of stew from the hearth was covered and placed with everything else at the edge of the front porch. Lastly she whipped and flavored the potatoes, spooned them into a dish with a lid, and wrapped a small quilt around it to keep them warm.

A few moments after Shemaine rang the bell hanging from the post near the front steps, a tall gangly young man sprinted up to the cabin to help carry the supplies and food back to the ship. As he halted pantingly on the steps, he tipped his hat politely and grinned, transforming his rather rugged face into a very likable one. Shemaine was sure he had the deepest blue eyes and the blackest hair she had ever seen, even in Ireland.

"Morn'n, miss," he bade cheerily. "I'm Gillian Morgan. The cap'n sent me ta fetch the vittles back ta the ship."

Shemaine's fleeting frown revealed her bemusement. "The captain?"

"Mr. Thornton, I mean, miss," Gillian readily explained. "Exceptin' he don't like ta be called that. But seein's as how Mr. Thornton is the master-builder what designed the ship and the man what pays our wages, not ta mention him bein' 'bout ten and three years older'n meself, me pa raised a fair ta middlin' fuss over the idea o' me callin' Mr. Thornton by his Christian name. So's me an' Pa dubbed him the cap'n."

"I see." Shemaine nodded and smiled. "Mr. Thornton did tell me that he has an aversion to people calling him by his proper name, but I can't bring myself to be so familiar with the man that I would feel right using anything else."

It was Gillian's turn to be confounded. "An aversion?"

"Loathing . . . or dislike," Shemaine explained, and cocked her head curiously. "Has Mr. Thornton ever explained why he doesn't like being addressed by his proper name?"

"Well, he just said that when he was still buildin' ships for his pa, he'd work alongside other men doin' the same job as them, but his pa always insisted they call him Mr. Thornton, 'cause he was the proprietor's son. The cap'n hated it, for sure."

Shemaine gestured to the covered kettle of stew and the quilt-bound bowl of potatoes. "We'd better get this food to the ship before it cools or Mr. Thornton will be hating us!"

"Aye! Chewin' our hides, he'll be," Gillian offered in chuckling agreement. "He definitely has a way o' lettin' us know when he's riled."

"He isn't mean, is he?" she questioned apprehensively.

"Nay, not mean, just particular 'bout the work we do for him. He expects the best we can give him. Ye'll do well ta do the same, miss."

Shemaine released a soft, fretful sigh. "I will surely try."

She hung the cloth that had been tied around a loaf of bread over Andrew's arm and took his other hand as she picked up the basket. Gillian loaded himself down with the kettle, bowl and jug, and then led the way as she followed more slowly with the child. When they came near, Gage came down the building slip to meet them and, lifting Andrew, took the basket from her and escorted her to the partially finished deck.

The four cabinetmakers and the older shipwright were already waiting on board with amiable eagerness to make her acquaintance, having hinted (and teased) loudly enough that it was about time that *Mister* Thornton stop his worrisome fretting over losing her to one of them and commit himself to making the introductions. Gillian took Andrew from his father and started wrestling and rolling about on the deck with the boy, evoking shrieks of giggling glee from the youngster as Gage finally performed the formality. Shemaine recognized Ramsey Tate as the man who had been helping her master outside the cabinet shop the day following her purchase. Sly Tucker, a large, rather portly man with reddish-blond hair and a bushy beard, was another full-fledged cabinetmaker. The two apprentices were close in age, perhaps no more than two or three years past a score of years. One was a German by the name of Erich Wernher, an even-featured young man with dark hair and eyes; and the other was Tom Whittaker, a handsome colonial with tan hair and gray eyes. Flannery Morgan was a grizzled old man with nigh as many wrinkles in his weathered face as the night sky had stars. Yet he had a sharp wit that could easily set the others to guffawing in loud mirth.

Each and every one of them showed Shemaine the proper respect due a lady, which she readily assumed was in deference to their employer. They rushed to lay planks across carpenter benches as she brought out a tablecloth and then, after the linen had been spread over the makeshift table, helped to lay out the plates and cups. Because he doubled as a circuit rider on rare occasions, Sly Tucker offered grace before the meal. Raves of delight and appreciation soon followed as the workers began to devour the stew they had piled on the potatoes and to wolf down the bread. The jug of cool cider was handed around several times to fill the tin cups, quenching the thirst of the men. By the time the spice cake was passed, some of them had begun to groan in mock agony.

For the first time since being bought by Gage Thornton, Shemaine found herself able to eat the portion of food she had taken on her plate, but the weight of it on her stomach made her drowsy. She yearned to take Andrew back to the cabin for his afternoon nap, but it was obvious, with Gillian near at hand, that the boy would not be willing to leave soon.

Gage had chosen to sit on a keg of nails at the end of the makeshift table, and when he finally pushed away his plate, he tilted the keg back slightly, leaning against the roughed-in structure of the rail. From that particular vantage point, he was able to consider his men and the enjoyment they had derived from the meal. He was sure at the moment that Shemaine could have been a warty old toad and his men would have admired her just the same for her talent with food.

Gage allowed his men a few moments of rest before they returned to their labors, for it was evident they needed it after such a hearty meal. The younger men were given the chore of collecting the dirty dishes, the empty kettle and the last bit of food, which they carried back to the cabin while Shemaine remained on deck with Andrew for a few moments longer. She wandered around with the boy, admiring the fine workmanship of the craft as Gage discussed the difficulties they were having with some improperly seasoned compass timber that Gillian had brought up from the shed.

" 'Em shakes'll be splittin' on us afore the week is out, Cap'n. We'll be havin' ta take 'em out soon an' replace 'em," Flannery Morgan advised his employer.

"Then do it if it must be done," Gage replied with simple logic. " 'Twould appear we've no other choice."

Andrew spied a gull soaring close over the forward part of the ship and ran ahead in hopes of catching it. Shemaine followed quickly behind, but as swift as a little mouse, the boy started climbing across boards in his eagerness to get close. The bird hovered temptingly above him, as if to tease the child. Struggling against her own lethargy, Shemaine scrambled after him, jumping over timbers and crossing braces as she made her ascent. She was amazed that such a little boy had so much energy and such skill at climbing, but just as abruptly, Andrew's interest was drawn elsewhere, and he began a rapid descent to the main deck, where a frog leaped across the planks. Pausing to catch her breath, Shemaine found herself well forward of the deck and, much intrigued by the view, stepped close to the precipice. Glancing down, she could see large rocks piled around the bracing stocks, but when she looked outward, the scenery was lush and beautiful around the cabin.

"Dammit, Shemaine!" a voice bellowed, nearly causing her to stumble from her lofty perch. *"Get down from there! Get down before you fall!"*

Shemaine realized that Gage was already racing toward her, and before she could adequately obey, he was beside her, catching her arm and snatching her away from the edge. After gaining the main deck, he caught her shoulders and gave her a harsh shake as he rebuked her angrily.

"Don't *ever* go up there again, do you hear! It's not safe! Just stay away!"

Shemaine nodded fearfully, shaken by his rage. "Y-yes . . . of c-course, Mr. Thornton," she stammered, fighting tears of pain. His fingers clasped her arms so tightly she suffered no uncertainty that she would later find herself bruised. Wincing, she sought to shrug free of his steely grasp. "Please, Mr. Thornton, you're hurting me."

As if startled by his own ferocity, Gage dropped his hands away and staggered back a step. "I'm sorry," he rasped in a hoarse whisper. "I didn't mean to . . ."

Turning crisply on a heel, he left her and strode briskly from the deck of the ship. Like statues of stone, Shemaine and his men watched him make a hasty descent of the building slip. Then, as if the banshees of hell continued to dog his heels, he stalked rapidly toward the cabinet shop, and a moment later the distant slamming of a door sounded like thunder in the silence created by his departure.

Shemaine turned to Gillian with a perplexed frown, shaken by the rage her master had displayed. "What did I do? Why was Mr. Thornton so angry with me?"

"Don't ye go frettin' yerself that the cap'n was vexed with ye, miss," the young man murmured, seeking to allay her fears. " 'Twas the sight of ye on the prow what frightened him. 'Twas where his wife had climbed afore she fell ta her death."

Shemaine clasped a hand over her mouth, smothering a groan of despair. How could she have blundered so badly?

"Why don't ye take Andy back ta the cabin now, miss?" Gillian suggested. "I'll bring whate'er is left."

Shemaine accepted his advice and led Andrew from the ship. She was grateful to find that the younger men had rinsed off the tin plates and cups in the river and had left them in the basket beside the door. It took only a few moments to wash them in soapy water, scald them, and clean the kitchen.

Bringing in the fresh-scented sheets and pillows from outside, Shemaine made the beds and finally lay down with Andrew on her own cot in the loft. She read to him until he fell asleep. With his small head resting on her shoulder, she lay for a long time staring at the ceiling as she recalled Gage's angry reaction when he had seen her on the prow of his ship. Though she could understand his sensitivity about the way his wife had met her death, in that brief passage of time, during which he had railed at her and shaken her, she had glimpsed a painful torment in those eyes that she had never noticed before. He was indubitably a man haunted by a dreadful memory, perhaps a deed he had done or failed to do, which had not yet faded into liberating forgetfulness. What was there about the accident that she had not been told? What terrible thing, beyond the death of a young wife and mother, had happened that day that had had the power to rend a man to the depths of his soul and leave him roiling in anguish?

Mulling over the many possibilities exhausted Shemaine mentally, for she could find no simple answers to her questions. With a troubled sigh, she laid an arm over Andrew and curled up beside him, submitting herself to the drowsiness that had crept stealthily over her.

Ramsey Tate approached the cabinet shop and preceded his entrance with a light rap. At a muttered call from within, he swung open the door and stepped inside, closing the portal quietly behind him. His employer stared broodingly out of a window with a sharp frown creasing his brow, and a stern glance in his direction did little to reassure Ramsey that his presence would be tolerated.

"Sly an' the other men are afraid ta come in here, thinkin' they'll disturb ye," the older man said uneasily. "They sent me in ta ask if'n ye be wantin' them ta return ta work."

Gage snorted irritably and tossed a darker glower toward his chief cabinetmaker. "What do you think?"

Ramsey flicked his bushy eyebrows briefly upward. "Aye, I told 'em as much, that ye'd be wantin' the work done as usual, no matter how gloomy an' sour yer mood might be. I need not tell ye how ye frightened yer woman. She was sure she had done somethin' ta offend ye 'til Gillian told her ye were just grievin' over yer wife."

Gage deliberately ignored the man's probing chatter about Shemaine. He knew better than anyone that he had alarmed the girl, but the sight of her leaning forward over the prow had seared his brain with harrowing visions of Victoria doing the same. In a fleeting moment reality had become entangled in a web of tormenting illusion as he suffered through another nightmarish reenactment of the death scene, those damnable paralyzing images that had persisted since his wife's death, snatching him up from the depths of sleep to send him prowling about his room like a caged animal. Only this time, it had been Shemaine hurtling helplessly to the rocks below while he had seen himself leaning over the prow, watching it all happen from above.

"My disposition has nothing to do with my expectations," Gage retorted at last. "I expect the men to finish the day out and give me a fair exchange for their wages. I've checked the way they've laid out the patterns on the wood for the new pieces, and I think there's much to be desired in the grains they've selected and designated for my inspection. I would have burled wood for the doors and matching grains for the drawers."

"Perhaps ye'd like ta show us what ye want," Ramsey suggested, not unkindly. He knew that neither he nor any of the other workmen could envision the finished product as well as the master woodwright. He also recognized that work could serve as a healing balm for what was tormenting Gage Thornton, at least until he decided to take himself a woman.

"Call the men in here," Gage bade sharply. "I'll show them what I want."

"An' the Morgans?" Ramsey queried uncertainly. "They'll be wantin' ta know if ye'll be goin' back ta work on the ship today."

"Flannery has to replace some planks," Gage stated curtly. "He'll not need me for that chore."

Wiping a hand across his eyes, Gage released a dismal sigh as the man left. By dint of will, he dragged his thoughts away from that nagging, frightfully deceptive scene of Shemaine falling to her death. He could only wonder about himself, if he would ever find release from the tumult that continued to rage within him, at times leaving him feeling sorely bruised and battered.

That evening the occupants of the cabin enjoyed a hearty soup for supper, and while the dishes were being washed, Gage read to Andrew and then put him to bed. When he returned to the kitchen, Gage found Shemaine awaiting him.

"I'm sorry if I disturbed you today on the ship, Mr. Thornton," she murmured softly. "I didn't realize how your wife had been killed."

A brief quirk at the edge of his mouth was

all the smile Gage could manage. "It just frightened me to see you so close to the edge and to think that Victoria may have gone up there in much the same way."

"I have nothing pressing to do at the moment, Mr. Thornton," she said quietly. "Perhaps you'd feel better if you were able to talk about it."

Her gentle suggestion seemed full of compassion, and he could not bring himself to offend her by refusing. "I wasn't there when . . . my wife . . . fell," he replied haltingly. "I had brought Andrew back here to the cabin to clean some tar off his fingers after he had gotten into the oakum on the ship. While I was here, I heard Victoria scream. She sounded frightened. Barely an instant later I heard other screams. I left Andy in his bed and ran to see what had happened. When I got back to the ship, I found Roxanne sobbing in hysterics over the dead body of my wife. She said she had just nudged her canoe into the shallows when she heard Victoria scream. When she reached the ship, she saw my wife lying on the rocks below the prow. The fall had broken Victoria's neck, and there was absolutely nothing I could do to revive her. I built a pine box to put her body in and took her into town to be buried in the church cemetery beside her parents."

He refrained from mentioning what he had been subjected to once he reached Newportes Newes. It certainly hadn't helped that in prior years he had set himself against certain inhabitants of the hamlet by daring to point out the foolishness of several laws they had pompously proposed for their area. Thereafter, they had looked upon him as an antagonist, and their vindictiveness had become apparent soon after Victoria's death. British authorities had concluded that their interrogation of him was nothing more than a mean-spirited inquisition and had further suggested that his wife could have climbed to the prow herself and merely slipped. While most of the townspeople had agreed, defaming gossip had continued to boil over the dark, odious caldron of hearsay and defamation.

"After the accident, I felt as if I had descended into a dark dungeon from which I would never emerge," Gage continued. "But grief has a way of easing with the passage of time. Caring for Andrew helped me over the hurdle."

"You have a delightful son, Mr. Thornton," Shemaine assured him gently. "Andrew would win anyone's heart."

"He's been a blessing to me in many ways." Gage sighed. An awkward moment of silence passed between them, then he inclined his head toward the back corridor. "If you'd like to take a bath now, Shemaine, you may. I don't intend to work at my desk tonight, so you'll have time to enjoy yourself at your leisure."

"Thank you, Mr. Thornton," she replied, smiling. "Going without a bath on the *London Pride* was rather torturous for me, to say the least. I appreciate being clean more than I ever gave heed to before. I'd like nothing better than to indulge myself in a lengthy soak."

"Then, by all means, do so," Gage encouraged. "I'll read for a while here in the kitchen, so I'll probably still be up when you finish."

Shemaine scurried about to prepare her bath, pouring three buckets of hot water into the tub and bringing two more in from the well. After Andrew's nap that afternoon she had read to him for a time on the back porch and then later, while she watched him play, had folded freshly laundered clothes. She had stacked everything in a basket, placing the towels on top, but in her haste to start supper and bathe Andrew before the meal, she had left the basket beside her chair on the back porch. While toting in the last pail of water, she carried in the wicker receptacle, leaving it atop Gage's stool before dumping the water into the tub.

A moment later Shemaine settled into the steamy water with a deep sigh of appreciation. It was not the fanciest of tubs or the gentlest of soaps, but she reveled in the bath as if attended by serving maids of the royal court. Indeed, she stayed in the tub so long her fingers and toes began to wrinkle and the water took on a decided chill. Only then did she consider leaving it.

Shemaine pushed herself to her feet and reached for a towel. Grabbing a corner, she swept it from the basket, noticing a strange weightiness to the linen. In the next instant, cold icy horror congealed within her, wrenching a startled gasp from her as a large snake plummeted to the floor. It promptly started hissing and twisting as it righted itself onto its stomach. The reptile's eyes fixed menacingly on her, and its tongue flicked excitably from its fanged mouth as it hissed a warning. Its knobby tail rose in agitation and began to shake, emitting an odd, rattling sound.

The snake's head shot forward, and with a frightened scream Shemaine rapidly retreated out the back side of the tub. She heard what sounded like a chair overturning in the kitchen and footsteps running to the portal. Gage shouted her name in an anxious tone, but she had no time to answer as the serpent lunged toward her again, wrenching another cry from her. Clutching the towel to her, Shemaine stumbled back against the desk just as the kitchen door was flung open.

The adder, tenacious in its zeal to catch her, had slithered around the tub and was near the door when this new menace appeared. The reptile turned abruptly, striking out as the man stepped through the portal, but Gage leapt back, out of harm's way, and raced to the storeroom. When he returned, he held a long, wicked-looking knife in his hand. The viper eyed him warily, seeking a chance to sink its fangs into him. Gage eluded another attack, and when the snake recoiled, he was ready. Stepping quickly forward, he brought the wide blade down, chopping through the snake's skull and pinning the partially severed head to the floor.

Shuddering, Shemaine clutched the now dampened towel to her as she observed the bizarre coiling of the reptilian body in the throes of death. Gage opened the back door, and then, scooping the flat side of the knife beneath the serpent's mangled head, clasped his other hand around the scaly body near the tail. Lifting the reptile from the floor, he carried it out beyond the back porch.

Shemaine sagged in weak relief against the desk, still a-tremble and unnerved. It was a long moment before the thought occurred to her that there might be another snake in the basket. She had no knowledge of whether reptiles grouped together. But surely another one would have made its presence known by now.

Shemaine's breath eased outward in a long sigh of relief as she recognized her disquiet. She was simply letting her imagination run wild. She was safe now, she reassured herself. Her master had killed the snake, and if any more were in the basket, then he would kill them, too.

Water splashed on the porch, making Shemaine realize that she had wasted a chance to escape with her modesty reasonably intact. Clutching the towel to her, she started to race toward the stairs, but when she heard footsteps approaching the open door, she froze in sudden dilemma. She could not leave her cubbyhole without exposing her nakedness to Gage. But if she stayed, the brevity and dampness of the towel would afford her little protection, for the linen only partially masked the front of her. Nervously Shemaine chewed a lip as she eyed the basket, on the far side of the tub. A second towel would provide her better covering, but could she grab one in time?

Gage stepped through the portal, ending her debate, and in desperation Shemaine wedged herself between the wall and the desk, clasping an arm over her breasts and laying the other aslant her abdomen. It was the best she could do. Even so, her fluttering heart would not be calmed.

A wealth of emotions swept over Gage as he noticed his bondslave seeking haven behind his desk. He was totally amazed that she hadn't yet taken flight. With a shoulder, he nudged the door closed behind him and

advanced with measured tread into the corridor, diligently lending his attention to drying
water spots off the knife with an oiled rag
that he kept for such purposes in a box near
the portal. Pausing beside his bondslave, he
stroked the cloth along the now gleaming
blade, conveying a casualness that he
strove hard to maintain.

"You were lucky, Shemaine," he announced. The faltering limits of his will were
sorely strained as he sought to keep himself
distracted. He knew well enough what the
sight of her scantily clad form would do to
him. Yet, for the life of him, he could not
abandon the tantalizing situation he now
found himself in. "The snake was poisonous. It could have killed you. Or at the very
least made you ill. Do you have any idea
how it got in here?"

Shemaine could not still the nervous
quaking that had seized her. She was too
exposed to feel anything but trepidation with
a man in the room. Indeed, her uneasiness
troubled her tongue as she offered an explanation. "The s-snake must have found its
way into the b-basket of clothes I left on the
porch this afternoon. I w-would assume it
curled inside the towel to s-sleep."

"You should be thankful it didn't try to strike while you were bringing in the basket."

Shemaine raised her gaze hesitantly to his, and Gage felt inclined to meet it. That simple act proved his undoing. Whatever noble intentions he had meant to manifest in her presence, no matter how scant they may have been, were hacked asunder as his male instincts rose up like some fierce, sword-wielding barbarian on a black charger. He was a man famished for want of a woman, and his hungering eyes devoured the delicious sights as if he contemplated his first meal after a lengthy fast. Heretofore he had cursed the scarcity of the linens, finding them limited in their usefulness for toweling a man's body dry, but tonight he was greatly appreciative of the fact that this one, in particular, was narrow enough to be extremely generous.

His gaze ranged eagerly downward from creamy shoulders to her ripe breasts, temptingly squeezed upward by an encompassing arm. The top of the towel was only partially visible above her silken limb, and its furrowed edges did little to hide the cleavage deepened by the pressure of confinement.

Indeed, from his height, he could see down into the makeshift bodice where the cloth slanted briefly away from the tantalizing fullness. His advantage allowed him a minute glimpse of a pale pink hue, making him anxious to view the whole of it.

Where her arms did not hinder his perusal, the dampened cloth revealed every curve and hollow as it clung cloyingly to the womanly terrain, liberally hinting of the sweet delights it veiled. Her whole side, from her right breast downward past the towel that ended at a shapely thigh, lay bare to his wandering gaze. In truth, her skin was as soft and fair as he had imagined it would be. And he was sure it would be just as delectable and sweet to taste.

His eyes smoldered darkly as they swept upward again, making Shemaine painfully aware of just how vulnerable she was. She could not quell her violent trembling or tame the unceasing frantic thudding of her heart. Indeed, the desire blazing in those brown orbs would have made a warrior maid feel threatened. Fully cognizant of her master's greater strength, she could entertain no hope of holding him off if he decided to throw her down and have his way with her.

The moment dragged on beyond endurance, doing much to provoke Shemaine's Irish temper. Her ire finally displayed itself in a blunt question as she vented her frustration with his brazen scrutiny. "Would you mind if I get some clothes on now, Mr. Thornton?" Shemaine gave him a copious serving of sarcasm as she prodded. "*If* perchance you *haven't* noticed, this towel leaves much to be desired as sufficient clothing."

"Your pardon, Shemaine," Gage apologized with a brief, amused twitch of his lips. "The sights are so lush and pleasurable, I nigh forgot that you might be distressed over your lack of attire. Please forgive me."

Shemaine raised her chin to a haughty level, wondering if he made light of his ogling because she had voiced no objection until now. Lest he feel encouraged by her tardiness, she cut keenly through to the heart of the matter. "Aye, I *am* distressed, Mr. Thornton, but 'tis what I see in your eyes that makes me fear what will come of this. If you do not intend to dishonor me, sir, I beg you leave now before you reconsider."

After another totally encompassing perusal, Gage inclined his head in a gesture of compliance and stepped to the interior door. Passing through the portal without pausing or glancing back, he closed it gently behind him. A moment later she heard what sounded like a chair being righted in the kitchen.

"Warts off a toad," Shemaine fussed, flinging away the treasonous towel. Saucily waggling her head, she mimicked her master's jaunty excuse in a hissing whisper. "I nigh forgot you might be distressed over your lack of attire, Shemaine. Ohhhh, Mr. Thornton! What deceptive wiles you practice!"

She snatched on her nightgown and slipped a robe over it, knotting the narrow sash firmly about her slender waist though she had grave doubts that any garment would be adequate defense against the lust that she had glimpsed in those lucent eyes. She was rather naive about the prurient appetites of the opposite gender, but she was perceptive enough to know that when a man looked at a woman the way Gage Thornton had just looked at her, he definitely had mating on the mind.

*   *   *

When Gage folded back the bedcovers and slipped between the sheets a short time later, the delightful air-freshened scent permeated his senses, making him aware of a definite change that his pillows and linens had undergone since his departure from bed that morning. Whatever Shemaine had done, it soon became apparent to him that Roxanne had been far too busy chasing after him to do the same. He found it immensely pleasurable to fluff the goose-down pillows beneath his head and inhale their sweet fragrance. Truly, after spending the whole of the afternoon in brooding contemplation, he realized he had become quite relaxed and was ready to taste the sweet succor of sleep, like a babe who had just been suckled. But then, he couldn't quite keep his mind from dwelling on the stirring vision of Shemaine's ripe breasts swelling upward above the towel or the delicious fantasy that any man might linger over, the thought of savoring their fullness with warm, wanton kisses.

CHAPTER 9

A lesson on loading and firing a muzzle-loader commenced shortly after supper four days later. Gage approached Shemaine soon after she had dried and put away the dishes. For the sake of caution, he bade Andrew to stay on the back porch and play with his blocks where they could keep a close eye on him, well away from the target which Gage proceeded to set up in the opposite direction. Before giving his bondswoman a weapon, Gage explained its proper loading and priming, then carefully demonstrated the procedure. He fired a shot and then watched closely as she readied the rifle for another one.

Prior to letting her shoot, Gage warned Shemaine that pulling the trigger would only be the first step in the lengthy process of firing a rifle. Once the hammer fell and hit the frizzen, the flint would touch off sparks to ignite the powder, which would then explode and launch the lead shot through the barrel. Altogether, it would seem like a full moment had passed before the flintlock fired, but of course it wouldn't take quite that long.

Gage suggested a convenient way for her to hold the firearm so the weight of it wouldn't tire her arms overmuch and, to critique her stance, stepped close behind her to adjust the weapon in her grasp. The warm pressure of his long body casually conforming to her back was enormously distracting to Shemaine, and in a few short moments the simple act of breathing became difficult. It was a turnabout, to be sure, to find herself coping with her own reaction to his proximity; an uncontrollable trembling being the least of it. She certainly could not judge the man too harshly for the blatant desire she had glimpsed in his eyes a few nights back when she now felt her own heart rush to a swifter pace each and every time the inside of his arm grazed her breast or his thighs brushed against her buttocks. Her skirts lent her no protection. Indeed, she would have required a sturdy suit of armor to shield herself from the searing contact of his male form. She could not imagine her tutor remaining oblivious to her chaotically thumping heart, but if by some chance he was, then she most definitely was not. It took great resolve for her not to bolt and run.

Despite her nervous agitation, the horrendous noise of the gunshots, and the jolt of the stock against her shoulder that slammed her back against the man, Shemaine managed to glean a goodly amount of knowledge about the proper handling of firearms. Though his nearness flustered her no small degree, Gage made shooting almost as much of a thrill as dancing at a ball. She was delighted with her ability as a novice to hit a stationary target and eagerly anticipated the day when she could fix her sights on a moving mark and shoot a hole through it as well. She suffered serious doubts about her ability to kill an animal or a man and fervently hoped the day would never come when her mettle would be tested in such a way, but she knew she would probably find herself of a different mind-set entirely if she ever had to face the threat of being beaten senseless or even killed by Jacob Potts.

" 'Twould seem, my girl, you're a natural at hitting the target," Gage boasted in her behalf the next day. "Now let's see what you can do with a moving target."

Gillian had volunteered to throw a tin plate high into the air for them, but Gage, having taken up a position close behind Shemaine, had slipped his arms around her to help her hold the weapon and to lead her through the procedure from the first sighting and finally the firing. Although Gage would allow her to actually aim the flintlock and pull the trigger, he was there to make sure none of the shots went wild. But he could feel her whole body trembling against him and, mistaking her trepidation, tried to soothe whatever fears she had.

"You're doing exceptionally well for a beginner, Shemaine, so just relax and let me show you how to swing through a target."

Well before the shot was made, Shemaine realized that it was nigh impossible for her to concentrate on sighting anything, for her thoughts were completely engrossed with the man, not the weapon in her grasp. Once the rifle went off, missing the plate by a lengthy margin, and the exploding shot had slammed her back against the stalwart form, a startled gasp was wrenched from her, and with good reason. It was definitely a shock to her womanly being to find her soft buttocks suddenly buttressing a rock-hard thigh. Had she sat upon hot coals, her reaction would have been no different, for she jerked away as if her backside had been scalded.

"That wasn't nearly as good as what you did yesterday, but we'll try again," Gage commented casually, leaning close over her shoulder so he could have some idea where she would be aiming the next time. He was not oblivious to her soft form within the circle of his arms, but he had made up his mind to crush his wayward thoughts, especially during her lessons. "No need to be nervous now, Shemaine. Just relax."

There is absolutely every reason to be nervous! Shemaine thought in a panic, feeling his chest pressing against her back and his arm casually encircling her as he held a hand beneath the barrel of the flintlock so its weight wouldn't drain her strength. Of a sudden, she felt suffocated, unable to breathe, and she knew she would have to escape ere she embarrassed herself completely.

Throwing off his arms, she left the flintlock in his grasp and bolted away with a breathless excuse. "I've got to knead my bread! I don't have time for any more lessons now."

"Shemaine, where are you go—? Come back here!" His mouth dropped open as she lifted her skirts and raced off toward the back porch. Totally bemused, he exchanged a glance with Gillian, who was just as mystified.

The younger man shrugged, contemplated the tin plate that was still intact and, lifting it for his employer's inspection, grinned as he stated the obvious. "Well, at least ye can still eat vittles from this one."

The next day Hannah Fields and her two younger sons came for a visit, much to the delight of Andrew. The three boys romped and played in the back yard while Shemaine and the older woman watched from the porch and got to know each other better.

"Yer master's li'l tyke is adorable," the portly, jolly-faced woman declared, smiling as her eyes followed Andrew about the yard. " 'Tis certain his father is bringin' him up good an' true."

"Have you known Mr. Thornton for long?" Shemaine queried, wanting to understand the man better. Though on the night of her confrontation with the snake she had glimpsed a sensual hunger in his eyes that had made her more than a little uneasy about being alone with him, since then Gage Thornton had treated her with all the consideration a gentleman might show a lady. She could not, of course, read his mind, and at sundry times, when she glanced up and caught him regarding her so intently, she couldn't help but wonder what he was thinking . . . or perhaps yearning for.

" 'Bout as long as yer master's lived here," Hannah answered with a chortle. "We settled here a couple o' years afore Gage came. His missus was a real lady, she was. Not so much high-minded or haughty like some are, ye understand, but kindly an' sweet-natured. I ne'er saw a woman what loved her mister as much as she did Mr. Thornton. Some say he didn't deserve her 'cause he didn't love nothin' but his ship, yet 'tis been much on me mind that whate'er work he did, he did as much for her as he did for himself."

"Mr. Thornton has certainly proven himself an ambitious and talented man," Shemaine observed, sweeping a hand to indicate the neat path meandering from the porch through the fruit trees and on out to the barns and buildings he had constructed. "I can see proof of his hard work everywhere I turn."

Hannah flicked her eyes toward Shemaine, wondering just what she had been told about her master. It seemed unlikely the girl would have been so casually resigned to her indentureship if she had heard any part of what Mrs. Pettycomb and her circle of bigoted friends were prone to say behind Gage Thornton's back. The gossips were eager to delve into malicious speculation and sometimes lent voice to such wild imaginings that few could withstand their attacks. Gage had done so. With stoic determination, he had continued working as usual, daring anybody else to face him with their tales. Whatever the truth about Victoria's fatal fall, Hannah had no intention of spreading the like of such talk herself. Wrongfully maligning an innocent man was a serious offense in her own mind, no matter how much Alma Pettycomb and others like her were wont to disregard the damage their long tongues could do.

"I came prepared ta teach ye what li'l I know 'bout cookin'," Hannah informed Shemaine with a twinkle of amusement in her eyes. "But yer master told me soon after I arrived that ye've been doin' well enough on yer own . . . so's I'm thinkin' ye maybe don't need me help."

"Actually, I would love to learn to make biscuits the way they make them at the tavern . . . that is, if you know how," Shemaine replied eagerly. "I had sea biscuits on the voyage over here, but they were nothing like the ones at the tavern. It took a strong stomach to tolerate those things, what with all the maggots and such that were oftentimes found in them."

"We can make a batch o' biscuits for the noon meal," the older woman suggested with a merry laugh. "I brought a basket o' food with me, thinkin' ye might be a bit tired o' yer own cookin'. The biscuits'll be a tasty addition ta the vittles."

"Perhaps we should bring the boys in to play in the cabin while we cook," Shemaine said worriedly. "Recently I had such a fright with a poisonous snake, I fret that another may be near."

"Those nasty things! They make me blood turn cold with fear! There's some they call rattlers, an' if'n ye've e'er heard one, ye know the reason why."

"I've heard one already, and it was too close for comfort," Shemaine replied with a shudder.

Hannah clapped her hands loudly together as she called to the youngsters. "Come in now, boys. An' Malcolm an' Duncan, I want ye ta mind yer manners in Mr. Thornton's nice, clean house. I wouldn't have Mistress Shemaine thinkin' I'm raisin' a pack o' wild hooligans upriver."

As boys are wont to do once they've been confined to small areas, they began to wrestle and play rough. Andrew got the worst of it, being the youngest, and Shemaine felt her own heart catch when he got knocked around in the scuffling. In seeking to protect him, she tried finesse in separating the three. The older ones were used to playing with each other and were far tougher than she deemed safe for Andrew, but he was brave despite the bruises he acquired and went back into the frisky fray with a cry of glee. The boisterous tussling, however, was sharply curtailed when Hannah finally blared an order at her sons, bringing them to swift and alert attention.

"I told ye boys ta mind yer manners, an' if'n ye don't, I'll be layin' ye both 'cross me knees an' paddlin' yer bare backsides good an' proper. An' ye know I mean what I say!"

From then on, the two boys could have been likened to little angels, except for the devilish gleams in their eyes. But they obviously understood their mother was serious with her threats, for they even consented to take a nap with Andrew while Hannah and Shemaine cleaned up the kitchen.

Before coming to visit, Hannah had prepared a meal for her own family and had left her daughters with the task of serving supper if she returned late, so when Gage encouraged his neighbor to stay and share the evening fare with them, Hannah readily accepted, welcoming the respite from her enormous duties as mother and wife. It was obvious she relished the food Shemaine had prepared, and when Gage encouraged her to indulge herself in a second helping, she readily complied. Afterward, Hannah pushed back from the table with a groan.

"I hope me boat don't sink on the way home, 'cause I'd ne'er be able ta swim ta shore. Me poor Charlie would ne'er forgive me for leavin' him with the task o' raisin' our brood by his lonesome."

Gage grinned. "Would you care to be escorted home?"

Hannah cast him a glance askance, her eyes glittering with puckish delight. "I should accept yer offer after all yer wicked attempts ta fatten me up," she chided jovially, then waved away the possibility. "If'n the boat starts sinkin' I'll just tie a rope 'round Malcolm an' Duncan an' let 'em swim home."

"Ma!" the boys cried in unison, and stared at their mother with mouths agape. At her resulting laughter, they made much of her threat as they poked bony fingers at each other.

"Malcolm's gonna be the first!"

"Nah, Ma! Throw Duncan out! I wanna see him swim home!"

"I'll throw ye both out!" Hannah warned as they began to wrestle and wallop each other.

Gage chuckled as the woman looked at

him in helpless appeal and, with waggish humor, proposed, "You could lassoo both of them now and save yourself the trouble later."

"Ye ain't suggestin' nothin' I ain't already thought o' meself," their mother declared, heaving an exasperated sigh. "The way they tear 'round with each other, 'twill be a wonder for sure if those boys survive 'til they're full grown."

"Imagine their future as valiant soldiers or something of that sort," Gage suggested with a grin. "They're getting all the experience they'll ever need right now."

"Ye can say that, sure enough! But there be times I'd like a li'l truce betwixt the battles so's I can learn a li'l strategy o' me own . . . like how ta knock their noggins together without gettin' me fingers smashed."

The woman's humor was too much for Shemaine to bear soberly. Having overheard their conversation as she readied Andrew's bath, she tried to squelch her giggles as she lifted a caldron of steaming water from the fireplace hook. Her mirth proved unruly, for it kept escaping in brief snatches as she rushed the kettle to the back corridor and soon became uncontrollably and highly infectious, making the rounds first to Andrew and then to Gage and Hannah, who had stepped near the front door. Many months had passed since the cabin had overflowed with such joyful sounds. For Gage, it was like a magic elixir warming his whole being.

Finally the chortles subsided, and Hannah, preparing to take her leave, waved a hand toward the front porch as she asked a favor. "If'n ye don't mind, Gage, I left a pair o' chairs for ye ta mend when ye've got some time ta spare. It needn't be right away, ye understand, but it'd be nice ta have 'em afore the year is out. The chairs don't look it at first peek, but the backs are nigh ta fallin' 'way from the seats. 'Tain't safe sittin' in 'em."

"I'll see what I can do, Hannah," Gage assured her. "But are you sure you won't be needing them before year's end?"

"We've got more'n enough chairs for our own family. 'Twill only be Christmas that we'll be needin' 'em for kinfolk. Charlie's brothers an' sisters'll be comin', an' there's so many, it'll be like an army invadin' us."

Gage chuckled at the idea of having so much time to repair them. "I might not get around to repairing them for a month or two, but I'll have them ready well before Christmas. If you need them sooner, just let me know. Until then, I'll keep them on the porch as a reminder."

Hannah cocked her head and paused to listen to the song that Shemaine was singing to Andrew in the back corridor, where she was bathing him. It was a bright and airy tune, definitely of Irish origin, and the voice was as sweet and pleasing as any Hannah had ever heard. The matron looked up at Gage and smiled. "If'n ye're not aware of it, Gage Thornton, yer bondswoman could teach me a thing or two, and it wouldn't be 'bout cookin' either. She's got a good head on her shoulders, that she does, not ta mention havin' a voice o' an angel. I'm thinkin' I ought ta come over an' sit in on some o' Andrew's readin' lessons once they start. I was ne'er much good at that sort o' thing."

"Shemaine is everything I had hoped to find and more," Gage admitted.

"And ye said she couldn't cook," Hannah chided affably, shaking her head.

Gage lifted his wide shoulders in a casual shrug. "I don't think Shemaine realizes yet just how talented she really is. She's a wonder when cooking food, but she mothers Andrew as if he were her very own. The boy is quite taken with her."

"Aye, I saw their affection for each other this mornin' when Shemaine was tryin' ta protect Andy from me boys. She didn't know quite how ta go 'bout it for fear o' woundin' me feelin's. I let the roughhousin' go on for a wee bit just ta see how she'd react, an' I can tell ye true, no mother hen e'er watched over one o' her biddies with as much concern as she showed for yer son."

"Shemaine seems naturally inclined to be a mother," Gage responded. "I think she has a special gift for bringing peace and assurance to the child, making him feel wanted, nurtured . . . and loved."

Hannah smiled in satisfaction as she discerned the change that had also taken place in the man. All the girl's attributes which he had claimed Andrew had benefited from had obviously touched him as well. He seemed far more relaxed and at peace with himself than she had seen him since that horrible day of Victoria's death. " 'Tis fortunate ye are ta have found Shemaine. Women like her are not usually ta be had for any size purse."

* * *

A distant mewling invaded Shemaine's slumber, but she was reluctant to be parted from her dreams. Once again she had experienced the thrill and exhilaration of racing across her father's countryside estate on the back of her stallion, Donegal. She had felt the wind whipping her hair, snatching at the hem of her habit, and had rejoiced in the freedom to ride in whatever direction caught her fancy.

Her revelry gradually dissipated as the whimpering continued and the bars of Newgate Prison closed around her. She was haunted once again by the cries and hopeless sobs of the destitute, the shuffling feet and restless pacing that were always accompanied by the clank of chains. The dreadful black despair of utter gloom swept over her, almost smothering the breath from her.

Shemaine came upright with a sharp gasp and, as her heart thumped frantically against the wall of her chest, she peered intently into the darkness around her, searching for the dour-faced inmates of Newgate and waiting in apprehension for the scraping feet to approach. By slow, agonizing degrees Shemaine managed to separate reality from the deluding dimensions of sleep and finally realized that what she was actually hearing was Andrew whimpering in his bedroom downstairs. She listened for several moments longer, expecting to hear some movement of the elder Thornton in response to the plaintive sobs, but the weeping grew louder and, it seemed, a bit more frightened. She could not imagine Gage sleeping through his son's tears, and she began to chafe. What if something had happened to his father? Or if the elder had gone to the privy and couldn't hear Andrew?

Feeling an urgency to comfort the boy, Shemaine tossed aside the covers and shrugged into her dressing robe as she hurriedly descended. The door of Gage's bedroom stood open, but the firelight from the kitchen hearth, combined with the moonlight streaming through the windows above the bed, provided enough illumination to assure her that her master was not in the parlor or his bedroom. Cautiously she crept through the elder's private quarters toward Andrew's small nook, half afraid that she had been mistaken and she would bump into the man before reaching the boy. But her fears proved groundless. There was no one but Andrew there.

The sobs were coming more harshly now, wrenching Shemaine's heart, and she quickly crossed to the child's trundle bed and gathered him up in her arms. Soothing him with a cradlesong, she paced about the room as she snuggled him close against her, kissed his tear-streaked cheek and smoothed his tousled hair. Gradually the frightened crying ceased and the child's breathing deepened, but when she sought to put him down again, a fearful gasp escaped him. Once again she held him close and retraced her steps from his bed to the much larger one in the master's bedroom, back and forth, over and over until she felt the tiny head begin to droop over her shoulder. She hushed her singing and, in slow stages, halted her pacing, wanting to make absolutely sure that the boy would stay asleep once she returned him to his bed.

Shemaine was admiring his handsome features in the meager light, swaying from side to side, when she became mindful of a presence in the larger room. It was not so much the sound of the man's entrance that alerted her as it was his shivering shudder as he stepped to the far side of the bed. She glanced up, intending to explain her reason for intruding into his private domain, but words failed her when she saw him standing naked in a shaft of moonlight. Tiny droplets of water gleamed like diamonds over his muscular torso and limbs, evidencing his recent dip in the stream outside. At present, he had a towel over his head and was vigorously rubbing his hair. Apparently he had not yet become aware of her.

Shemaine, however, was acutely conscious of him. She had never seen a naked man before, and the sight of that long, powerful form was rather shocking to her virginal senses. Yet at the same time she was completely enthralled with the beauty and bold, manly grace of it. As his clothes had revealed, his shoulders were incredibly wide and had no need of the padding that pompous lords usually demanded in their coats. His broad chest tapered sleekly to a tautly muscled waist and narrow hips. A thin line of hair traced downward from his lightly furred chest across his flat, hard belly, drawing her eyes irresistibly lower.

Her cheeks burning, her heart hammering wildly, Shemaine stood frozen, unable to drag her gaze away. For all of her mother's delicate, somewhat embarrassed descriptions of the male form and her gentle counseling about what to expect once she married Maurice, Shemaine realized that she had not expected quite so much . . . maturity!

Having no wish to draw attention to herself and thereby suffer the humiliation of having her master know that she had looked upon his male nudity and not fled like a flustered maid, Shemaine retreated very slowly, very quietly, stepping backward toward Andrew's small room. Even so, her racing thoughts could find no way of escape, not when she knew she would eventually have to pass near the man.

Suddenly Shemaine halted, aware of a change taking place in the manly loins. The male flesh was now becoming much more pronounced and obtrusive.

Her gaze flew upward, piercing the shafts of moonlight and shadowed spaces, until she met the silvery-lit orbs smiling at her from the far side of the bed. The towel lay about Gage's sturdy neck, and his arms hung relaxed at his sides. The black hair, wetly spiked and wildly tossed, gleamed in the gloom.

"I'm sorry," she strangled out, painfully aware that she had been apologizing much too often since her indentureship. "Andrew was crying, and I didn't know where you had gone!"

In the silence that followed, Shemaine pivoted crisply about on bare feet and lowered the boy into his bed. Feeling the heat of shame consume her, she closed her eyes, trembling in every part of her body as she struggled to gather her scattered wits. Despite her best efforts, a vision of what she had just seen was now forever lodged in her memory. It blazed before her mind's eye as clearly as if she still stared at the man.

Whirling, Shemaine kept her gaze carefully averted from that male nakedness as she fled to the open door and made her escape into the parlor. In her haste she stumbled on the stairs and gritted her teeth against the sudden pain throbbing in her bruised shin, but she did not pause. Flinging herself into her cot, she turned her face to the wall and yanked the covers up over her head, wishing fervently the world would dissolve around her.

CHAPTER 10

Shemaine faced the morning with a definite dread, reluctant to meet her master and suffer through the painful trauma of being within close proximity to him when both of them would find it difficult to think of anything except the night before, when he had caught her ogling his manly parts like some lewd strumpet. It had been embarrassing enough when she had found her hand caught against his loins, but what had happened during the night was even more humiliating. She yearned to lie abed until Gage went to his shop to work, but her duties as an indentured servant denied her the privilege of hiding out in her room like a spineless coward. She must make the best of their inevitable meeting, no matter how fervently she longed to vanish into thin air before that particular event came about.

When she made a cautious descent, Shemaine was relieved to find that Gage had already gone outside to attend his morning chores. It was not until she had breakfast laid out on the table and had found time to dress herself that he returned to the cabin with his usual offering of rations, a basket of eggs and a pail of milk. He glanced in appreciation at the food-laden table before setting the basket and pail on the counter beside her.

"It smells delicious, Shemaine." Since she had been there, Gage had come to anticipate the morning meal perhaps more than any other, for she seemed to excel in cooking tasty dishes that he had memories of eating in his father's home in England. "Can we eat now? I'm starving."

Timid about meeting his gaze, Shemaine focused her attention on pouring the contents of a small pan into a gravy boat. " 'Tis ready to be eaten as soon as I finish dishing up this sauce. Should I awaken Andrew?"

"Let him sleep. Poor little fellow, he had a hard night."

However innocent his remark had been, it seemed to Shemaine a painfully blunt reminder of her horrendous blunder. The spoon that she had been about to put into the sauce shot through her fingers as if it had stiff springs attached to it. As she watched in horrified dismay, it skittered across the edge of the counter before plummeting to the floor. She bent quickly to retrieve it, but nearly collided with Gage, whose reflexes were faster. He scooped up the ladle and, offering it back to her, clapped his heels together. She shot a nervous glance toward him as she took it, provoking his curiosity. He could not help but notice her scarlet cheeks and the incertitude visible in her eyes. Stepping close, he canted his head in an effort to draw her gaze upward, but she feigned a sudden need to find another spoon and refused to look at him.

Gage was determined. He took her small chin between his thumb and forefinger and turned her face toward the light until he could search the beautiful visage. "What ails you, Shemaine?" he asked gently. "Do you think I care a whit that you saw me naked last night? Or that you may have spent a fleeting moment looking at me and perhaps appeasing your maidenly curiosity about men? Good heavens, girl, I understand that you went in there not to seduce me, but to comfort my son, and I'm grateful for that. What I must do is apologize for startling you, but a man cannot always control how his body responds to a beautiful woman. I've not been with another since Victoria died. There was certainly no woman in the hamlet I wanted to bed down with, and seeing you in my room aroused longings I've struggled hard to suppress since becoming a widower. I'm a man, Shemaine, subject to all the feelings and flaws of my gender. As a man, I greatly admire your beauty and enjoy your presence in my home. Watching you pleases me. You're soft, alluring, gentle, and kind. You grace this cabin and our lives like a delicate flower that bestirs the senses with its fragrance and beauty. In the short time I've known you, I've come to realize I *do* desire you as a woman. Yet I would never force you, Shemaine . . . or knowingly hurt you. I want the best for you, so don't feel chagrined about what happened last night. As you may have surmised, I enjoyed you looking at me. It was most stimulating to find you in my room. Condemn me for that if you will, or simply accept me as a man who's very interested in you as a woman."

A soft, quavering sigh wafted from Shemaine's lips. "I didn't want to face you today," she admitted diffidently. "I thought I couldn't bear it."

"You needn't ever feel ashamed in my presence, Shemaine. I'll never chide you for having honest feelings or being human."

Still unsure of herself and even less certain of her situation, Shemaine inclined her head toward the table, murmuring quietly, "Your breakfast is getting cold, Mr. Thornton."

"After you, Miss O'Hearn," Gage replied, stepping back into a gallant bow and sweeping an arm before him invitingly.

"Daddee, where're you?" Andrew called from the bedroom before he came tottering drowsily into the parlor.

"There you are, Sleepyhead," Gage cried with a chuckle. Squatting down, he held his arms out wide for the boy.

Laughing, the youngster ran into his father's embrace and was swung high into the air. Then upon gathering the boy close,

Gage playfully nipped at his taut little stomach through the nightshirt, exaggerating a monstrous growl that evoked gleeful shrieks and giggles.

When Andrew was finally lowered into his high chair, he surveyed the food laid out before him and gave Shemaine a toothy grin. "Yummy! Yummy!"

Gage grinned at his bondslave. "I think that means 'Let's eat.' Shall we oblige him?"

Shemaine found herself once more enchanted by the pair and, despite her continuing reservations, showed her obeisance with a curtsy. "I'm here to obey, m'lord."

"Any claims to that title I left behind me in England," Gage remarked offhandedly.

Shemaine's brows gathered in confusion as she slowly straightened. Wondering what he had meant, she queried, "Is there a Lord Thornton?"

"My father, William, Earl of Thornhedge." Gage lifted his shoulders in a casual dismissal of the title's significance. "Not as impressive as a marquessate, but here in the colonies a title holds little importance to most of the populace, except for the British dignitaries."

He swept a hand to indicate the bench behind her, silently bidding Shemaine to take a seat. As she did so, he slipped into the bench opposite her. Once before he had told her the story about Ol' One Ear to put her at ease. This morning he recounted the tale of Sly Tucker trying to escape a bee while unloading supplies from the back of a wagon.

"Sly took a flying leap off the rear of it, but his toe got caught in a hole at the very end. He fell forward like a dead weight and sprawled flat on the ground, nearly breaking his nose. It was so badly bruised and skinned, everyone who saw him started laughing. Sly is usually rather gentle in nature, but the guffaws the incident provoked were loud enough to set him on edge. He mumbled many times afterwards that he would have been better off letting the bee sting him than contending with all the hilarity provoked by the sight of his swollen and bruised nose."

Shemaine found herself suddenly giggling at the story. Then she glanced up and found her master regarding her with warmly glowing eyes, as if satisfied that he had been able to draw her out of her timidity. Shemaine dipped her head in acknowledgment of his accomplishment. "Thank you, Mr. Thornton."

Gage feigned naïveté. "What did I do?"

"I think you know well enough," she countered. "I was terribly discomfited by what happened last night, but you made me laugh, and for a moment I forgot that dreadful incident."

He cocked his head at a contemplative angle. "What did you find so dreadful about it?"

Taken aback by his question, Shemaine had difficulty explaining all the emotions she had felt after realizing he had caught her ogling him. When she finally answered him, she could not keep her gaze from wavering beneath his steadfast stare, though she spoke with candor. "The fact that you might have thought me forward, Mr. Thornton."

Gage shrugged away the notion. "You're merely an innocent, curious about men. 'Tis natural for an untried maid to be inquisitive."

"You seem to know a lot about women, Mr. Thornton," she gently goaded.

His lips curved with amusement as his brown eyes challenged her. "Certainly more than you know about men, Miss O'Hearn."

Shemaine stared at him in shock, unable

to dispute his statement. "Aye," she sighed at length, lowering her gaze to her plate. "There is much I have to learn about men."

Gage smiled at her bowed head, for he could think of no finer delight than to be the one to instruct her.

Ramsey Tate knocked on the back door while they were still at the morning meal, and leaned in to inquire, "May I enter?"

"Aye, Ramsey, come on in," Gage bade, sliding down the bench to allow his friend to sit beside him. When Ramsey entered the kitchen, Gage couldn't help but notice the dark circles beneath the man's eyes, but he kept his inquiry simple. "Have you eaten?"

"Not anythin' what looked this good, I can assure ye," Ramsey said with a rueful chuckle, but he held up a hand to halt She-maine when she made to rise and fetch a plate. "Nay, miss, I'd better not. What I ate is sittin' like a hard lump on me belly. I cooked it meself an' been regrettin' it e'er since."

"You're here much earlier than usual," Gage stated. "Is anything the matter?"

"Me missus is in a bad way," Ramsey replied glumly. "I'm worried 'bout her, an' I'd like ta stay with her today in case she needs me."

Gage was immediately concerned. "Take as many days off as you need. Is there anything we can do?"

"Well, I'm not much on cookin'. If'n ye can manage ta send o'er 'nough vittles for Calley an' me youngest boy, Robbie, I'd appreciate it. I can make do meself with what I'm able ta put together, but I ne'er learnt meself ta cook, an' it don't seem right somehow ta make Calley suffer more'n she's doin' already. Me older boys've gone upriver ta work for their uncle 'til midsummer, so at present there's just us three at home."

Gage was cautious about offering Shemaine's services when he wasn't sure if what Calley had was contagious. If food had to be delivered, then he would do it himself, keeping his distance for the sake of Andrew and the girl. "What do you suppose is the matter?"

Ramsey released a halting sigh. "I told ye some time ago 'at Calley was gonna whelp 'nother kid in late spring, but we're now fearin' she might be close ta losin' the li'l fella. Accordin' ta her count, it's too early for the babe ta be comin'."

Gage's manner became resolute. "Calley should have a doctor's care. If you don't mind, I'll bring Shemaine and Andrew over when I come and then fetch Dr. Ferris from town. Do you have any objections?"

Ramsey blinked away a start of tears. "I'd be grateful, Gage."

"Go now, and see to Calley," Gage enjoined. "We'll be along as soon as we can."

"Thank ye kindly."

Some time later, Gage drew the wagon to a halt in front of the Tate cottage and escorted Andrew and Shemaine inside. Almost immediately Andrew and the three-year-old Robbie settled down on the kitchen floor to play with a set of wooden animals that Ramsey had made for his youngest son. Ramsey led Gage and Shemaine to the back of the house, where his stricken wife was ensconced in their bed. He went to her bedside and beckoned for their visitors to approach as he took his wife's hand and introduced the newcomer.

"Calley, this be Mr. Thornton's new bondswoman, Miss Shemaine. She's here ta cook a meal for ye an' li'l Robbie."

Gage stepped near. "Shemaine will watch

after you and the boys for a while until I return with a doctor. You'll be in good hands, Calley."

The woman nodded in answer and tried to smile as she shifted her gaze to the girl. "Pleasured ta make yer acquaintance, miss. I only wish it be under better circumstances."

Gage and Ramsey took their leave, and Shemaine began to fluff the woman's pillows and tidy the bed. Solicitously she asked, "Is there anything I can do for you?"

"Maybe keep me company for a while," Calley suggested with a tentative smile. "Ramsey gets in such a stew when one o' us gets sick, I'm almost relieved ta see him go ta work. His fidgetin' wears on me."

"No doubt he loves his family very much, and it makes him anxious when he sees one of you ailing," Shemaine gently surmised.

"Oh, I knows that ta be true, al'right," Calley declared with an abbreviated chuckle, but she stiffened suddenly as a spasm gripped her. Clenching her teeth, she silently endured the discomfort until the pain began to ebb. Then she looked up at Shemaine through a start of tears. "I was a-thinkin' this babe might be a girl. We've five sons already, an' I was sure, what with me carryin' this one so different, we'd be havin' ourselves a precious li'l girl this time."

Shemaine gripped the woman's slender hand. "Don't lose hope, Mrs. Tate. Perhaps the doctor will be able to help you."

Calley's lips trembled with anxiety. "I ne'er had any trouble afore, an' I'm frightened for me poor li'l babe."

Bracing her hands on the mattress, Shemaine leaned forward to claim the other's misty-eyed attention. "Then I'd say you've been very fortunate until now, Mrs. Tate. My own mother lost a baby after I was born and could not get with child again. So you see how tremendously blessed you've already been."

With eyes closed and her lips moving fervently in prayer, Calley writhed in silent agony upon the bed. "The way I'm feelin', miss, I fear I'll be losing it afore Dr. Ferris can get here."

Leaving her, Shemaine rushed to the kitchen. Gage had gone, and in his absence Ramsey was roaming about like a lost soul, not knowing what to do with himself. "You'd better get some water boiling just in case," she urged, putting to flight his confusion.

"And ready some rags and towels, but don't bring them to the bedroom until I call for them."

"Yes'm," Ramsey replied, and set himself to completing her directive.

Folding back her sleeves, Shemaine pushed through the bedroom door and mumbled a silent prayer of her own as she returned to the woman's bedside. "You know more about this kind of thing than I do, Mrs. Tate. I'm not squeamish. The voyage from England took away any girlish notions that I once might have had about being prudish, so if you're of a mind to trust me, I'll stay with you and do what needs to be done if such help is required before the doctor comes."

"I trust ye," Calley answered in a whisper. She began to twist again and claw at the sheets as she grieved over her impending misfortune, getting so worked up emotionally that she could not lie still.

"Relax if you can," Shemaine soothed, remembering how her friend Annie had helped one of their cellmates on the *London Pride* through childbirth. The baby had been badly malformed, perhaps because of the lack of nourishment his mother had been subjected to. He hadn't lived beyond a day, but Annie had coaxed the woman and brought her through her labor in good order. This was not the same kind of circumstance, Shemaine realized, but she grew resolved to help Calley in a similar fashion if she could. Except for her first experience of seeing a child born, she wasn't knowledgeable enough to be of much benefit otherwise. "Try to imagine the baby and how you might help her by remaining calm. Don't strain yourself or bear down to make her feel unwanted. Let her feel nurtured in the safe, warm haven of your body. Close your eyes and see how beautiful your daughter is. I think she will look like you, with hair like wheat and eyes the color of the sky. She'll be the treasured pride of her brothers. . . ."

With lashes tightly closed, Calley nodded eagerly as an image of the girl began to form in her mind. Her breathing slowed, as if by magic, and the tears faded, to be replaced by a smile. "Aye, she'll have a winsome face."

Shemaine leaned forward to whisper close to her ear. "Can you see yourself holding your daughter close to your breast and gently rocking her as you sing a lullaby?"

Calley heaved a blissful sigh. "Aye, she likes the singing."

"You're smiling, Mrs. Tate," Shemaine murmured. When the woman's eyes came open in surprise, she laughed softly. "And the pain has passed."

"Well, so it has!" Turning her head on the pillow, Calley looked at Shemaine through elated tears. "Can it be true? Can I talk meself into keeping this babe?"

"I don't know, Mrs. Tate," Shemaine answered honestly. "But 'twould seem to me that being hopeful and relaxed can be more advantageous to the both of you than being anxious and fretful."

"Call me Calley, mum," the woman earnestly implored. "I can tell ye're a real lady, just like Mr. Thornton is a proper gentleman. He needs a wife like ye."

"I'm only his bondswoman," Shemaine asserted. The last thing she wanted, especially after the previous night's ordeal, was to have this woman presume that her master intended to marry her and to make the mistake of saying something to him about it. She had apologized to Gage Thornton much too often of late.

"That'll change," Calley predicted, growing more confident. "Ramsey says it will. He said Mr. Thornton is already taken with ye."

"Mr. Thornton is taken with my cooking," Shemaine stated firmly. "Nothing more. Your husband is mistaken."

Calley was amazed by her insistence that nothing could come of their association. "Would ye not marry him if he asked ye?"

"I was engaged to be married before I came here . . ." Shemaine's words trailed to a halt, and she found herself unable to finish her statement. The memory of her betrothal seemed strangely detached from the reality of the present.

"England is a far piece off, mum, an' Mr. Thornton is here, right ready ta become a husband. Do ye not think he'd make a handsome one?"

"Certainly, he would, but I . . ." Again words failed Shemaine.

"The man ye were engaged ta in England, was he as handsome as Mr. Thornton?" Calley pressed.

"I don't know. . . ." Shemaine moaned, uneasy with such questions. By the standards of every eligible young lady in England, Maurice du Mercer had been considered the best-looking man in all of

London. Yet Gage Thornton would have caused as much confusion in the hearts of those same maidens as she was presently experiencing. It seemed somehow disloyal to imagine her former fiancé as less attractive. It also seemed silly to fret about the degree of handsomeness of one over the other. She was sure that if she *did* think that Gage Thornton was more appealing, it was only because he was near and Maurice so far away.

"Do ye still love your fiancé?"

"I thought I did once," Shemaine admitted lamely. "But that seems so long ago, and much has happened. I'm indentured to Mr. Thornton, and even if Maurice were to find me, I would not be free to marry him unless Mr. Thornton was willing to release me. Besides, Maurice may not even want me anymore, considering my arrest and all."

"Mr. Thornton wants ye, ta be sure."

"This discussion really seems pointless," Shemaine replied, hoping to squelch the disturbing conjectures. "No one can predict with any certainty what Mr. Thornton may be thinking. I am simply his bondslave, and unless he speaks for himself, I shall consider any discussion on the subject of marriage purely speculative."

"Aye, 'tain't right for us ta say what Mr. Thornton will do," Calley conceded. "There be plenty enough o' those what try ta guess at what he's up ta without us doin' the same."

Shemaine breathed a sigh of relief, having made her point. Gathering the woman's fingers in her own, she smiled down at her. "How are you feeling now?"

"A bit tired," Calley acknowledged, smiling easier. "But better."

"A little rest may do you and the baby good."

"Aye, I think I can rest now . . . and hope."

"Then I'll leave you so you can. If you should have need of me, I'll be in the kitchen."

With a relaxed sigh, Calley closed her eyes, and Shemaine slipped quietly from the room. Ramsey was waiting in front of the hearth, and the stricken look on his face made her hasten to allay his fears.

"Your wife is feeling much better now and will be able to rest for a while." The strain of the last hours was evident in his face, moving her to compassion. "I think 'twould do you good to get some sleep, too," she said kindly. "I'll call you if something happens."

Gage Thornton climbed down from his wagon and approached the physician's cottage. A small woman in a neighboring yard was pulling weeds that had overgrown an earlier year's garden, but when he strode up the walk, she straightened and squinted against the sun to watch him. When he tapped on the front door, she called to him.

"If ye've come ta see the doc, he's gone upriver a ways ta mend a broken leg. He won't be back for a spell. If'n ye can write, ye can leave a note sayin' where ye wants him ta go once he gets back. Doc Ferris said for me to say as much ta any what came. He also left a quill an' things on his porch for those what be o' such a mind."

Gage Thornton faced the drably garbed woman, wondering if he had ever met her before, for her voice sounded strangely familiar. As he walked across the lawn toward her, he noticed that the whole side of her jaw was darkly bruised and swollen. Even so, he keenly recalled the tiny woman who had encouraged him to buy Shemaine on the *London Pride.*

"Annie Carver?" The facial bruises looked even worse up close, and he couldn't help but inquire, "Good heavens, woman, what has happened to you?"

Dumbfounded, Annie lifted a dirt-crusted hand and shaded her eyes against the brightness of the solar orb as she tried to see him clearly. " 'Oo is it?"

"Gage Thornton. I bought Shemaine O'Hearn, remember?"

The woman hooted and slapped a hand against her leaner cheek. "Blimey, gov'na! Remember ye? How could I forget? It just took me a bit ta see ye clearly, what with the sun in me eyes an' all. How's Shemaine?" Her eyes filled with sudden apprehension. "She ain't hurt, is she? Be that why ye're wantin' the doc?"

"No, she's all right, Annie. Actually I came for a friend of mine. His wife is due to give birth in late spring, but she's having trouble now . . . may even lose the babe."

"I knows a thing or two about birthin' babies," Annie informed him shyly. "Me ma were a midwife afore she took ill an' died, but she taught me what ta do ta help a woman a wee bit. But me master, he'd ne'er let me go with ye."

"Did your master do that to you?" Gage asked gently, indicating her blackened cheek.

Embarrassed, Annie lifted her shoulders in a feeblehearted shrug. "I guess Mr. Myers thought I deserved a knock or two for burnin' his supper. He told me ta go out an' chop some wood 'cause his parlor was chilly. It took a mite longer'n I figgered." She peered at Gage quizzically. "What 'bout yerself, gov'na? Ye gettin' 'nough ta eat with Sh'maine cookin' for ye?"

"I'm happy to say she's an exceptional cook, Annie. I couldn't have found a better one had I ventured clear to London town."

Annie gave him a sober, sidelong stare. "Last night, this here Mrs. Pettycomb come o'er ta talk ta me master . . . Samuel Myers . . . 'bout how ye'd gone an' bought yerself a convict ta service yer manly cravings, an' how ye'd almost killed the bosun from the *London Pride* 'cause he tried ta take her away from ye."

Gage grew a bit irate over the unswerving verve of the old busybody in spreading her biased stories about the hamlet. "Mrs. Pettycomb usually enlarges upon everything she hears, Annie, so I wouldn't put much stock in what she says if I were you. She seems to enjoy deliberately distorting the facts to enliven her tales."

Annie was in hopes that he would explain further, but Gage remained reticent about his purposes for buying Shemaine, for he saw no reason for justifying himself to everybody who lent an ear to the lurid tales being told about him. If he ever made such an attempt, he'd never come to the end of it, especially since the matron and her circle of busybodies seemed inclined to prattle about him continuously.

The front door was snatched open, and Samuel Myers stalked out to the edge of his porch, where he stood with one arm behind his back. Glaring at them, he assumed the disposition of a red-faced dictator. "You lazy bitch!" he snarled at Annie. "I didn't buy your papers so you could talk to every no-account that passes my gate. Get back to your work before I lay my fist to your other cheek. And I warn you, if you know what's good for you, you'll stay busy while I'm gone, or I'll flay your blooming hide. I can't leave my shop every hour on the hour just to check on you. My customers will begin to fret and think I've left town."

Gage's brow grew sharply peaked as he peered across the yard at the man. For once, he had to agree with Morrisa Hatcher. The little man was as detestable as the meanest rat. The idea of leaving Annie in his care without making some attempt to help her just didn't seem right somehow. "Would you be of a mind to hire your bondswoman out for a fee, Mr. Myers?"

Samuel Myers was clearly bemused. He pushed his spectacles up higher on his broad nose and, with a dubious smirk, contemplated Gage more closely. "What's the matter, *Mister* Thornton? One wench *ain't* enough for you? You've got to have *two* in your bed?"

If it had been the man's intent to rile Gage, then he surely accomplished his purpose, for Gage could feel an intensifying animosity building within him as he returned a stony stare to the other's taunting jeer. Myers had evidently heard a great many rumors about him, whereas Gage knew only that the man he conversed with was a haberdasher of gentlemen's clothing. Considering the gossips' zeal to wag their tongues, it would not have surprised Gage if Samuel Myers considered him a dangerous man. As for that, the way Myers kept his right arm tucked carefully behind his back led Gage to believe that a pistol was cocked and held ready in the man's hand, for he just couldn't imagine the little weasel being so reckless otherwise, especially if he believed all the rumors that were being circulated about how dangerous the cabinetmaker was.

"I have an employee whose wife is dangerously close to having a miscarriage," Gage replied with measured care. It was not the threat of a pistol that made him cautious, but the realization that any show of hostility might spoil his chances to help Shemaine's friend. "Annie said she could possibly be of assistance to Mrs. Tate if she were able to go. If you'd allow her to leave with me, I'd be willing to pay you for her time. The doctor might be gone for a while, and right now there's no one else at the Tates' who knows what to do."

"You could just as well take your own bondswoman over there, *Mister* Thornton," Myers suggested, curling his lip in a sneer. "Unless, of course, you can't bring yourself to part with the wench that long. She's mighty fetching for an Irish bitch, and I'm wondering if she's as pleasing to look at in bed as out."

"You use the word *bitch* much too loosely, Mr. Myers, and presume upon a lady's character," Gage retorted, feeling his temper rising sharply. He paused a moment to regain control of himself before he spoke again. "The girl is already there doing what she can, but she doesn't know enough to be of much help to Mrs. Tate."

Samuel Myers was always willing to make a coin in one fashion or another, and he could think of no easier way to collect a goodly sum than to allow his bondslave to earn it for him. "How do I know I can trust you to bring Annie back?"

Gage realized he would have to offer a generous guarantee to even interest the man. "If you'd like, I can leave a deposit in your care equal to what you paid for her. All you need do is show me some evidence of what that amount may be and then sign a receipt promising to return it once I bring Annie back."

"She cost me fifteen pounds," the man stated with a caustic snort. "But 'twill cost you another five to lease her out."

age declined with a disdaining jeer.
u may keep the gown, Mr. Myers. I'm
e I've seen better in Mrs. Tate's rag bin."

Gage reclaimed his seat in the wagon a
w moments later and headed back toward
e Tates' cabin, accompanied by Annie,
who had garbed herself in the gown she had
worn during the voyage. It was still just as
ragged, but thankfully it had been washed.

Shemaine would be relieved to see her
friend, Gage knew, but as for himself, there
was much to think about. He would have to
figure out a way to recoup his losses, because he just couldn't feature himself returning a bondslave to a master who abused
women like Samuel Myers had proven himself capable of doing. Neither could he
imagine keeping Annie himself, for he was
completely content with Shemaine and
didn't want to invite another woman into his
home on a permanent basis. Although the
Tates needed Annie at the present time,
they couldn't afford to buy her when they
were saving nearly every farthing for their
sons' education. At present, he couldn't
think of what other options were open to
him, but hoped that he'd have some idea by

"Five pounds! Good heave. not keeping her for a year!"

" 'Twill be five pounds or noth Mr. Myers shrugged as he exagg. own needs. "I have important work to do here and must be compens. any delay her absence will cause me

Gage became a little more dema. himself. "For five pounds, I'll expect to her for at least two full weeks, nothing le.

Samuel Myers smirked. "I suppose I c. make do on my own for that long, but b warned, if you don't bring her back, all the money will be mine."

"All the money will be yours," Gage grumbled in agreement, feeling as if he'd just been swindled. "But I'll need that receipt just in case you might be of a mind to say that I've stolen her from you."

"You'll get your receipt," Mr. Myers retorted insolently, "but she'll leave here in the same clothes she came in."

Gage glanced around to see what Annie was wearing and promptly wondered why the clothier concerned himself about such an unworthy garment.

"Unless, of course," Myers prodded, "you're willing to pay for the gown, too."

the time her services were no longer needed by the Tates.

On the seat beside him, Annie chafed like an overanxious mother. "Did ye leave the doc a note so's he'd know where ta come when he returns?"

"I took care of that while you were changing clothes."

"An' ye put it in a place where he'll find it as soon as he returns?"

"Aye."

"In a safe place, where Mr. Myers can't find it?"

"I slipped the note beneath his door, and the door is locked," Gage answered, wearied by her relentless inquiries.

"What if he don't look down? The doc is gettin' on in years, ye know. He said he'd be two score an' five years come Friday next." It seemed an extremely ancient age to Annie, who had barely a score of years to her credit.

"Annie, stop your fretting," Gage urged impatiently. "You vex me with all your questions."

"I'm sorry, Mr. Thornton," she murmured contritely. "I just want ta make sure the doc'll be comin' so's yer friends won't be dependin' on me alone. I knows a lot 'bout birthin' babies, coolin' a fever, or tendin' wounds, but I'm thinkin' it might be better ta have someone there what's had some proper learnin'."

"Proper learning or not, Annie, you'll be staying with the Tates for a while to watch over Calley, so you may not be able to rely on the doctor being there when you need him the most. Ramsey works for me. He's also my friend, and I want you to do what you can for his wife, to make her comfortable and, if it's within your capability, to save the baby. His family means a lot to him. Do you understand?"

"Aye, gov'na," she answered meekly.

"They have a little boy you'll be taking care of until Calley is on her feet again," he said, glancing askance at her.

Annie's sudden elation was proof that she was now looking forward to staying with the family. Blissfully she sighed, "Oh, I'd like that."

Upon their arrival at the Tates', Gage went into the cottage to look for Shemaine and found her in the kitchen preparing the noon meal. He paused beside the hearth as she knelt to push a loaf of bread into the iron oven. "I brought a woman back with me who can help out here for a while, so you and Andy can come back home with me when I leave."

"Mr. Tate insisted that I cook enough for all of us," she explained, closing the oven door and rising to her feet. "He was quite emphatic about you staying to eat with him."

"We can stay that long if it means so much to him," Gage assured her.

Shemaine smiled gently. "I'm sure your presence will help distract him, Mr. Thornton. He's been beside himself since you left. He refused to sleep, though I told him Calley was feeling better. He's out chopping wood in the back yard right now just to keep himself from worrying. Perhaps if you'd spend some time with him before we leave, it would help him get through this."

"I'll do what I can, Shemaine," Gage replied. "In the meantime, why don't you show the woman into the bedroom and introduce her to Calley?"

Shemaine was somewhat bewildered by his directive, for she could only assume the woman would have to introduce herself, but when Gage stepped aside to reveal the one who had followed him in, Shemaine gave a glad cry and flung herself into the open arms of her friend.

"Oh, Annie! I was so worried about you!" she exclaimed with tears filling her eyes. She hugged the tiny woman and then stepped back to have a better look at her, but her joyful expression turned to one of gloom as she noticed Annie's face. Reaching out a hand, she touched the bruised cheek tenderly. "Is this something your master did, or did you perhaps walk into a wall?"

Annie waved away her concern. "Ne'er mind me face, m'liedy. Just let me look at ye!" Her eyes swept the slender form. Then she gathered Shemaine's thin hands in her own and laughed in pleasure. "Ye're lookin' grand! Simply grand!"

"Come into the bedroom and meet Calley," Shemaine urged, taking Annie's arm. "And then you can tell us how you came to be here."

"Oh, I'll tell ye right now. If 'tweren't for yer master layin' out twenty pounds for me, I'd ne'er be here at all."

Shemaine halted abruptly and, tugging on Annie's arm, pulled the tiny woman around to face her. "What do you mean, Annie? Did Mr. Thornton buy you?"

"Not exactly." Annie shrugged. "He paid out five pounds ta rent me, so ta speak, but if'n he don't take me back, then he'll be twenty pounds poorer." She shook her head in wonder, amazed by his ability to lay out such a large sum. "Yer Mr. Thornton must be rich or somethin'."

"He's not rich, Annie, just very, very wonderful, I'm thinking," Shemaine said with an elated smile.

Dr. Colby Ferris, a tall, gray-haired man with gaunt features and a perpetual stubble covering half his face, arrived before they finished the noon meal. Annie took her duties seriously and provided the physician with warm water and soap to wash his hands and clean linens with which to dry them before she would allow him in the woman's bedroom.

"Me ma said 'tweren't right for a midwife ta leave one house an' go ta 'nother where babies were bein' born without showin' proper respect ta the mothers by washin' yer hands."

The tall doctor settled a stern stare upon the small woman. "Young lady, do you know how many babes I've brought into this world?"

Annie settled her thin arms akimbo and stubbornly held her ground. "Prob'ly more'n I can count, but what hurt is it gonna do ta wash yer bloomin' hands after tendin' the sick or maybe touchin' the dead . . . or . . ." She searched mentally for another good reason and finally flung up a hand in frustration toward the window through which the mount he had arrived on could be seen. "Or ridin' a smelly ol' horse?"

Dr. Ferris seemed momentarily taken aback by the small woman's impertinence, but after a lengthy pause, he scrubbed a hand reflectively over his bristly chin and began to chuckle, much to the relief of those who had witnessed the confrontation. "I guess there'll be no harm done by washing my hands. What about my feet? Will you be inspecting them, too?"

Annie glanced down without thinking, and then clapped a hand over her mouth as she saw his dusty boots and realized that she had been a victim of his humor. Leaning her head back to meet his gaze, she gave him a wide grin, lending some charm to her plain face. "Wipin' 'em will be good enough for the time bein', I suppose, but ye'd best be mindin' yer manners, 'cause I'm gonna be meetin' ye at the door when ye come back . . . at least for a while."

A hoary brow shot up to a lofty level, as if the doctor had taken offense at her threat, but his next query had nothing to do with her demands. "What about that toad, Myers? Is he going to let you stay here without raising a ruckus?"

Annie Carver was astounded by the physician's obvious conclusion. "I came here with his consent, I did, so ye needn't be a-thinkin' I skedaddled. Mr. Thornton gots a paper ta proves it."

Dr. Colby Ferris scoffed. "It must have taken a goodly sum to get you out of that toad's clutches. Myers has never been overly generous with his possessions."

"Oh, it took a goodly sum, al'right," Annie agreed, and threw a thumb over her shoulder to indicate her benefactor. "Mr. Thornton had ta lay out twenty pounds, five ta rent me an' fifteen 'gainst the likelihood o' me not bein' returned."

"Are you saying that Myers actually signed a receipt to that effect?"

Annie nodded cautiously, not at all sure

why the doctor was so shocked. "That he did, gov'na."

Colby Ferris looked pointedly at Gage. "Then I'd advise you to keep the receipt safe, sir, because Myers isn't to be trusted. He'll cheat you if he can . . . or find some way to call you a thief."

"I don't know the man very well, except that I've come to dislike him in a very short span of time," Gage admitted. "You can be certain I'll be as careful as I can."

The doctor waved a hand toward Annie's battered face. "You know, of course, that Myers will do more of this to the girl if you take her back to him."

"Do you have any suggestions as to what I should do?" Gage was eager for a solution to his quandary. He briefly indicated Shemaine, who stood washing Andrew's face at the far end of the table. "I have a bondswoman already, and there's no room in my cabin for another."

The elder stroked his chin thoughtfully. "I've seen the girl working at Myers's place and know what she's capable of." He snorted as he digressed a bit. "Work that Myers should've been doing instead of laying such tasks on a little girl."

"Do you need an assistant?" Gage queried hopefully. "Annie says she's had some experience with midwifery and such. Perhaps you could use a servant to keep your house."

Dr. Ferris seemed to dismiss the notion as he tossed a glance toward Annie. "What? And see myself vexed into washing my hands every time I sneeze? Lord save me from such a fate."

"Ye needn't worry 'bout me!" Annie declared hotly, miffed by the doctor's casual rebuff. "I'll go back ta Mr. Myers when I'm done here. 'Twouldn't be the first time I've been knocked 'longside the head."

Stepping to the washstand, Dr. Ferris proceeded to scrub his hands and face until they were clean. Drying them on a towel, he offered Annie a grin. "Are you going to show me where Mrs. Tate is now? Or are you going to stand there like an outraged porcupine with your quills all bristled?"

"Mrs. Tate's doin' better since M'liedy Sh'maine had a talk with her. Maybe ye could buy Shemaine from Mr. Thornton an' take her on yer calls with ye," Annie suggested tartly.

Gage lowered an ominous scowl upon the

small woman. "I didn't lay out my hard-earned money for you, Annie, so you could sell Shemaine behind my back."

Annie grinned back at him. "Mighty touchy 'bout her, ain't ye? Maybe ye like her more'n a mite."

"I like Shemaine just fine," Gage stated emphatically. "And I'm not willing to sell her. Do I make myself clear?"

Ferris glanced at Annie, curbing a chuckle. "I guess that means I'd better look elsewhere for an assistant."

"That's the bloomin' truth if I e'er heard it," Annie agreed, cackling gleefully as she cast an eye toward Gage, who finally relented enough to smile.

"Come on, Doc," Annie urged, beckoning to him. "I'll show ye the missus."

She led the doctor to the back bedroom, and while Ramsey paced with renewed anxiety, Gage helped Shemaine clear the food and dishes from the table in spite of her repeated assurances that there was no need for him to do so. Several reasons prevented Gage from taking his leave before the doctor had completed his examination. He knew Shemaine wanted to hear the verdict, and Ramsey needed him there as a buffer against possible bad tidings. Then, there were his own concerns, for he realized he was not as distant to the matter as he might have supposed. The Tates were his friends, and he wanted to be there to offer support in whatever way proved beneficial.

The baby's condition could not be determined, Dr. Ferris announced solemnly when he returned to the parlor. Nor could he predict whether Calley would carry her child full term or if she would lose it in the weeks to come. It was imperative that she remain in bed if she held out any hope of giving birth to a healthy baby, and he instructed Annie to watch over the woman carefully, for it would be no easy task keeping a hard-working mother inactive. If there was anyone who could accomplish such a feat, he was sure it was Annie. After all, he needled with amusement, she had made him wash his hands.

The doctor wisely advised Ramsey Tate to return to his cabinetmaking, for his wife's sake as well as his own. It would only make Calley anxious if she saw her husband fearful, he reasoned. Working would not only serve to occupy Ramsey's time, but his thoughts as well, no doubt reducing his constant worry.

Before Dr. Ferris took his leave, he promised to make regular house calls to keep abreast of Calley's condition and, if a meal was furnished at such a time to ease his widowed state, he would count that as payment enough. Then he quipped that he hoped Annie was as good at cooking as she was at taking charge.

CHAPTER 11

Life as a bondslave could be easily tolerated when one had a master charitable and noble enough to expend a sizeable portion of his limited resources to help an employee and an abused bondswoman, Shemaine decided. She considered herself immensely fortunate to have been bought by such a man.

Soon after their return to the riverside cabin, Gage carried his sleeping son into the smaller bedroom. When he came back to the parlor, he found his bondswoman awaiting him with a soft smile lighting her face.

Entranced by the shining green eyes, Gage tilted his head at a curious angle.

"Did you want something, Shemaine?"

"Aye, Mr. Thornton," she murmured with an almost imperceptible nod. "I have a great desire to thank you for helping Annie. Working for the Tates will be a relief after what she has experienced with Mr. Myers."

The silkiness of her voice sent warm shivers racing through his senses, but Gage sought to drag free of the mind-numbing spell she cast, for he knew he could not let her build her hopes on what he had done when he had no intention of letting Annie come live with them.

"I have to tell you, Shemaine, that once Annie has served her usefulness at the Tates', I must sell her to get back what I laid out for her. She won't be coming here to live."

"I know that, Mr. Thornton," Shemaine assured him softly, "but I trust you mean to find her a far more worthy master than Mr. Myers has proven himself to be. Truly, in the short time I've been here, I've come to believe that you're a very honorable man. Indeed, sir, I can think of no other man whom I admire more at this very moment."

Gage struggled to keep himself from imagining more than she had actually meant to convey. The word *admire* could insinuate a whole plethora of connotations, all pleasing to be sure, but it would be foolish for him to presume too much. He was still her master, and she his bondslave.

Momentarily at a loss for words, he sidestepped around her, knowing if he stayed in the cabin one moment longer he'd be tempted to delve into another matter, one that required a more careful discussion than he presently had time for. "I'd better go out to the shop and see what progress the men have made in my absence."

Shemaine was perplexed by his hasty departure, but she laid it to his impatience to get back to work. She set herself to completing the chores which had been left undone earlier that morning. After putting the house in order, she heated several irons near the fire and began the task of pressing their clothes. It gave her a strange satisfaction to smooth her master's more costly garments beneath her hand and to exert great care in doing them justice. It was no mean accomplishment to imagine how handsome Gage Thornton would look in neatly pressed white shirts instead of the wrinkled home-spun ones he had been wearing. A fine frock coat and breeches would do much to complement them, but she suffered no uncertainty that it would be the man himself who would enhance the apparel. Her imagination seemed quite frivolous when she envisioned herself dancing the minuet with her richly garbed master as she and Maurice had done on numerous occasions. In her fantasy Gage was as graceful of step as he was courtly and attentive of manner, rivaling Maurice, who had been exceedingly well tutored in all the social graces. Each time Gage came near, she saw a promise in his eyes that made her breathless with anticipation.

It was just an illusion, Shemaine warned herself, and rarely was reality as enticing as one's fantasies. In an effort to redirect her thoughts to something less titillating, she sought to turn her reverie into a memory of an evening when she had entertained Maurice in her family's parlor. In guiding her imagination in a close semblance of accuracy, the figure of her fiancé was just as tall, his hair just as black, his smile just as engaging as her master's, but instead of amber-brown eyes, thickly lashed ebon eyes gleamed above her own. Maurice's lips were touched with a natural reddish hue, and as he lowered his head, they parted in eagerness of the kiss he would extract from hers.

But suddenly her dream went awry, and it was a sun-bronzed visage that loomed close above her own and her master's opening mouth seizing hers with ardent desire. Just as swiftly, an intoxicating ecstasy surged upward within her, evoking a strange craving in her womanly being that was unsettling at best. To be sure, the delectable warmth that swept through her breasts was no less devastating than the feelings elicited when Gage's arm had casually stroked her curves during shooting practice not so long ago.

Shemaine lifted a trembling hand and, in distraction, wiped at the sheen of perspiration now dampening her burning cheeks. The shock of her reaction completely shattered the fanciful notion that she was an impenetrable fortress of serene virtue. Where once she might have remained calm and collected in spite of Maurice's attempts to persuade her that they were as good as married, she was not at all sure she would stay so coolly detached if Gage Thornton ever employed a like amount of dedication to winning her favors. Her cheeks grew hot and her breath came in quickening snatches as she recalled his manly loins casually brushing her backside while he demonstrated the proper way to hold a muzzle-loader. Treading close on the heels of that memory came another bold reminder of his male nudity bathed in moonlight. With it came a burgeoning heat that flared upward, setting her senses aflame. The depth of her arousal shocked her unduly. Indeed, if she could be affected to such an extent by memories, then there was definitely a side of her that was not nearly as levelheaded and reserved as she once might have supposed.

Having now discovered a sensuality within herself that she had previously been ignorant of, Shemaine found it difficult to keep her thoughts well aligned to that which a virtuous maid might ponder. Her sudden propensity for wayward musings became even more apparent when Gage returned to the cabin later that afternoon. His very presence in the kitchen evoked an unfamiliar tumult within her, making her fearful of what he might discern if he looked into her flushed face or took note of her trembling fingers.

When he sprawled on the rug in the parlor to wrestle and play with Andrew, the distance between them gave her relief. Even so, as she grated carrots, her eyes were wont to covertly caress the manly torso. It shocked her unduly when she found herself closely eyeing the buckskin breeches that lay softly over his loins. The torpid fullness led her mind swiftly astray to visions of his long, nude body glistening with silvery droplets. The kindling warmth that swept through her in ever-strengthening surges affected her breathing until she became a bit ambiguous about her own reserve. In truth, if she were again faced with his intrusion into her bath and he looked at her with as much hunger as he had that night, she wondered if she would be quite so insistent upon him leaving her as she had been then.

The conversation was a trifle lacking at supper. Gage and Shemaine were keenly aware of each other, yet reluctant to reveal the extent of their preoccupation or their growing enthrallment. Across the width of the trestle table, their eyes surreptitiously drank their fill, stroking the face and form of the recipient of their attention. A brief contact of a hand or arm left their skins tingling, their senses stimulated. A murmured word or a direct gaze readily gained their undivided attention. Later, when they brushed against each other in passing, kindling fires were a delectable yet unquenchable torture for which neither could find a befitting assuagement.

Despite the assurances Gage had given his bondslave, he was relentlessly drawn toward reflections of that moment when he had finished toweling his hair and swept the linen around his neck. In the soft aura bathing the interior, he had noticed Shemaine right away, even as she backed stealthily toward Andrew's room. Her translucent eyes had glimmered, reflecting the silvery light streaming through the window and betraying the direction in which she stared. He had dared not move lest he frighten her beyond reason, but he had felt much like a man subjected to an exquisite seduction while bound to a stake. The interlude was so enticing, even in recall, that it roused all the painful yearnings he had been contending with, even while he struggled to emulate a leisured calm. In truth, he longed to create other such moments wherein he could instruct Shemaine further in the intimate secrets of a man's body.

After the meal, Gage found he had little patience to expend on his drawings. He had spent the remainder of the afternoon setting aright several mistakes made by his apprentices during his absence, and he was plagued with a desire to simply relax and do something other than work before he went to bed. In heightening frustration he closed his desk, announcing in a disgruntled tone that he had finished for the evening if Shemaine cared to take an early bath. He put Andrew to bed and returned to the parlor to find her carrying buckets of steaming water into the back room. Sitting down in the rocking chair near the hearth, he picked up a book to read, hoping it would soothe the inexplicable restlessness that roiled within him. Though he made a concerted effort to concentrate on the pages, the words in the volume could not hold his attention for any measurable length of time, not when his gaze was inclined to wander above the pages and follow Shemaine as she scurried back and forth between the hearth and the back corridor. After dumping the last pail of water, she came to stand beside his chair with a towel folded over her arm, drawing his bemused attention.

"What is it, Shemaine?"

"I thought since there's a bit of a nip in the air this evening, sir, that you might enjoy taking a bath indoors tonight," she explained in a nervous rush. "I've taken the liberty of preparing you one, if you're of such a mind."

A hot bath in a tub was a luxury Gage had not been able to indulge in very often since Victoria's death. He had been far too busy with work and other things, and his nightly dips in the pond had sufficed for cleanliness. Any sensible man would find the idea of a relaxing soak in a tub most appealing, and he considered himself such.

"And what of you, Shemaine?" he asked, hesitating. " 'Twill take time to heat more water. Will you have to wait until a later hour before you can take your bath?"

"There'll be enough hot water for me as soon as you're done, sir," she answered, drawing his attention to the large cauldron that she had brought in from outside and had placed above the fire. "I didn't think it fair that you should suffer in a cold stream while your bondslave enjoyed so many comforts indoors." Tilting her head at a contemplative angle, she inquired, "Might you be interested, sir?"

"Indeed!" Coming to his feet, Gage set aside the book and began loosening the laces at the neck of his buckskin shirt. "To be honest, I wasn't looking forward to taking a cold bath outside tonight."

"I didn't think you would be," Shemaine murmured softly with a smile. Handing him the towel, she swept a hand toward the back room and, mimicking the deportment of a prim chambermaid, bobbed a pert curtsy. "Everything is in readiness, m'lord."

His brown eyes glowed with warmth as he gazed down at her. "You spoil me, Shemaine."

Her lips curved upward even as she tried to hide a blush of pleasure. "Is it not gratifying to be spoiled once in a while, sir?"

"Your very presence spoils me to distraction, Shemaine," he replied with sudden candor.

Shemaine could only wonder if he now found her occupancy of the cabin an impediment to his work, for he had seemed almost angry when he had left his desk. It would be a decided turnabout in her experience with

men if she were to desire to be within proximity to one who wanted nothing to do with
her. Contritely she dropped her gaze to the
floor, her feelings smitten. "I'm sorry, sir."

Amusement tugged at the corners of
Gage's mouth as he contemplated the
bowed head. "So distracting, Shemaine," he
murmured, "I doubt that I shall ever observe
the subtle sway of another woman's skirts
as much I've watched yours tonight."

Shemaine's head snapped up in surprise,
and she stared at him with jaw aslack. His
bold gaze never wavered, and finally, in
some confusion, she breathed, "Warts off a
toad."

Gage's brow arched dubiously. "I think
you lay too much credit to my wit, Shemaine, and not the sobriety of my tongue."

With that, he left her and strode across
the room, pulling the buckskin shirt over his
head as he went. Shemaine turned, still a
bit overwhelmed by his acknowledgment,
but she soon realized her mistake in letting
her eyes follow him. The sight of those taut
muscles flexing and knotting beneath the
smooth, bronze skin of his back was immensely disquieting to a young woman

whose passions had just begun to emerge from her inner being.

Gage paused at the door and, half turning, relented to a lopsided grin. "I don't suppose you'd consider scrubbing my back."

Shemaine had difficulty subduing a grin of her own as she imagined the surprise he would suffer if she accepted his invitation. Knowing that he teased her, she shooed him away with a flick of a hand. "Be off with you, sir. I'll be having no more of your shenanigans now. You've addled me quite enough as it is."

Even after he had closed the door behind him, Shemaine could still hear his chuckling laughter in the quietness of the cabin. Smiling to herself, she began putting together the dry ingredients for a batch of biscuits that she intended making the next morning, but as she worked, fleeting images of her master in various stages of undress began to assail her senses once again. She grew flushed and warm, while in the depths of her being there again sprouted that strange, insatiable longing that grew apace with her mindful meanderings, as if her young body desperately hungered for fulfillment from that particular entity whose face and form haunted her imaginings.

When Gage came out to the kitchen again, he was clothed in nothing more than the buckskin breeches he had been wearing when he went in. His long, bony feet were bare, and his black hair gleamed wetly beneath the glow of the hanging lantern. He said no word to her but went directly to the hearth, dipped two pails into the kettle of water simmering over the fire and carried them to the back room, where he emptied them into the tub. Returning twice more to the fireplace, he refilled the buckets nigh to brimming each time and dumped them into the washtub as well. Finally he came to stand before Shemaine and, with a flourish of a hand, showed a leg in a gentlemanly bow, copying her earlier performance.

"Your bath awaits, my lady."

Shemaine settled her hands on her narrow waist and raised a skeptical brow. "So! 'Tis your grand self doing chores for a bondslave, eh?" she chided, but her eyes sparkled brightly, nearly mesmerizing him. "As if I couldn't empty the tub myself and fill it up again. A turnabout, to be sure, Mr. Thornton."

Gage gave her a crooked grin as his eyes swept her in a way that bestirred her senses, for he made no attempt to hide the desire smoldering in his eyes. "Have a care, Shemaine. The water may be a bit hot for a woman of such soft, fair skin, and if you scream, I will surely come running. But this time, be warned. I won't be in a mood to leave at your command."

Leaving her, he ambled leisurely across the parlor toward his bedroom, unaware of the green eyes that devoured every graceful movement of his slow, animal saunter. Realizing that she was allowing her fascination with the man to dominate her thoughts, Shemaine let her breath out in slow, halting degrees and turned away. Such lustful musings could well undermine her intent to remain unscathed for the entirety of her indentureship, especially when she was being so persistently besieged so early in her years of service.

For a time, the night passed in wakeful silence for the adult occupants of the cabin. They lay in their separate beds, staring through the moonlit shadows at their ceilings as they listened attentively to the sounds that drifted from the upper story or lower bedroom. A creaking of a bed, a cough, a sigh, a muttered curse attested to the disquiet with which each contended. It was a late hour, indeed, before Shemaine realized she lay in rigid repose upon her cot, completely alert to the restless tossing and turning of the man downstairs. Whenever she closed her eyes, she could envision him standing beside her bed, looking down at her with eyes glowing with desire, and then her arms would lift to welcome him with all the hunger and passion she was capable of exhibiting.

This will never do! Shemaine rebuked herself and, with tenacious resolve, took her wandering thoughts in tow. She folded a pillow over her ears to impede any intrusion into her concentration and began to mentally recite a mélange of poems that had become endeared to her throughout the years. By slow degrees, she lulled herself to a relaxed drowsiness and, with a final sigh, turned on her side to drift into the cradling arms of Morpheus.

In his lonely bed downstairs Gage could not quench the fires of lust that beset him and denied him sleep. His thoughts were filled with tormenting visions of his bondslave lying upon her narrow couch upstairs, her heavy braids coiling tantalizingly around her naked breasts and her arms out-stretched and beckoning to him. He saw her green eyes grow limpid with desire and her soft lips part to receive his kiss. He sensed in every fiber of his being the stirring excite-ment of his manhood pressing home and her slender limbs clasping him to her. But no satisfying release came to appease his passion, and he found himself more agitated than ever. It took a concerted effort to force his thoughts upon a different course, a far less appealing path to be sure, but one that eventually brought him tranquillity . . . and fi-nally restful slumber.

Desiring to set her mind to something less disturbing than the handsome face and phy-sique of her master, Shemaine began to ponder the two horses which her master kept in the paddock. Besides the mare that Gage had hitched to the wagon for their trip into Newportes Newes, there was also a rather nice-looking gelding in the corral. Shemaine could think of no better diversion for herself than teaching Andrew how to ride. She broached the subject shortly after

Gage completed his morning chores and came into the kitchen to eat.

"Can either of your horses be ridden?"

"They're both well broke to saddle and harness," Gage replied, lifting Andrew into his high chair. The morning meal awaited them, but he noticed that his bondslave seemed unusually absorbed with the subject of horses. "The gelding is a bit headstrong and needs a more experienced rider, but the mare is well behaved. Why do you ask?"

Shemaine explained in a rush before she lost her nerve. "I was wondering if you might allow me to give Andrew a riding lesson after my morning chores are done."

"I'm sure that can be arranged," Gage answered, sliding onto his bench as she finally settled across from him. "Just let me know when you're ready. I'll come down and saddle the mare for you. She'll be better behaved for Andrew."

"Oh, that won't be necessary," Shemaine hastened to assure him with a flitting smile. "My father required me to know how to saddle and bridle a horse at a very early age."

"Well, at least I can brush her down for

you," Gage insisted, spooning food onto Andrew's plate.

Shemaine folded her hands in her lap as she carefully rejected his help. "Your offer is most appreciated, Mr. Thornton, but I would hate to take you away from your work when I'm fully capable of doing it myself. Besides, Andrew will have to learn." It would be better by far if her master kept his distance and allowed her to cool her infatuation. That was the whole point of asking him to let her teach his son how to ride, to get her thoughts directed elsewhere. Shemaine glanced quickly away as she ventured to another request. "I was also wondering if you would mind if I rode with Andrew."

Gage was impressed by the clearness of her eyes in profile, for they looked like tiny, rounded caps of emerald glass afixed to the white. "Victoria's sidesaddle is in the tack room," he murmured in distraction. "You're welcome to use it, if you wish."

"Thank you, Mr. Thornton," she said, demurely yielding him her attention as she handed a basket of biscuits across the table, "but I think it would be better if Andrew and I rode together without a saddle. I'm sure yours would be much too big for him and would not allow me to sit at ease behind him."

Andrew had followed their conversation closely, and after a momentary silence in which the elders searched each other's gazes, he leaned forward to claim Shemaine's attention. "Sheeaim an' Andee gonna ride horsey?"

She nodded. "After I finish my morning chores."

"Andee help you," the boy eagerly volunteered.

It was mid-morning when Shemaine finally hoisted Andrew astride the mare and, after taking a place behind him, adjusted her full skirts to preserve her modesty. The boy was delighted and anxious to learn all that she could teach him. He proved most attentive, and soon he was reining the horse around the yard himself, albeit under her careful supervision.

As for Gage, the sawdust-covered windows of the cabinet shop greatly hindered his view, and wiping the panes with a dampened cloth, he realized, left them streaked with a thick, murky film. After noticing the pair in the back yard, his usual zeal and dedication to work declined sharply. Indeed, he seemed oblivious to his apprentices and the several questions they asked him. Gage had sensed in the kitchen that Shemaine really didn't want him anywhere around during the lessons, and though he tried to restrain himself, the sight of her riding in elegant form behind his son sharply piqued his interest, and he was soon motivated by a growing desire to watch her at closer range. Finally he gave up the struggle and, with a muttered excuse, left the shop, heedless that Sly and the others were nudging each other and exchanging meaningful winks.

The excitement and delight Andrew derived from directing the mare around the yard became immediately apparent to Gage, as did the equestrian skills of his bondslave. Indeed, she sat a horse as if she had been born to it.

"Come, Daddee, ride with us," the youngster urged eagerly, and motioned for his father to get on behind Shemaine. "Take us on the road. Please, Daddee!"

Chuckling at the charming summons, Gage approached them.

Shemaine nearly panicked at the thought

of being caught between the man and the boy. "I'll get down and let you take Andrew."

"No need," Gage assured her, stepping beside them. "The mare is able to bear our combined weight for a short ride."

"Oh, but I have things to do," Shemaine argued, unwilling to experience another heady encounter similar to that which she had endured during shooting practice.

Gage peered at her curiously. "But I thought you said you were going to tend your chores before coming out here."

Small, white teeth tugged nervously at a bottom lip as Shemaine met his pointed stare. She didn't want him to think she had lied, and yet no other excuse had seemed as viable. Her delay in answering concluded the matter for Gage, and with a quick movement, he swung up behind her. Settling against her rigid back, he reached around in front of them and took the reins from Andrew.

"Hold the boy," he instructed, curbing a chuckle as he sensed his bondslave's tension. "And try to relax, Shemaine. You're as stiff as a cypress plank."

She heard the laughter imbued in his tone and wanted to hotly declare her inability to comply. It would have been impossible for any woman to blandly ignore the sturdy thighs buttressing her buttocks. Indeed, she was nearly undone by the pressure of his work-hardened form against her back. Yet the protestations that raced through her frantic thoughts and tempted her tongue would have readily revealed what she was really afraid of.

Gage reined the mare around and touched his heel lightly to her flank to send the animal in a leisurely canter toward the lane. He rode easily and, Shemaine thought, well enough to hold his own in the company of equestrians with whom she was either acquainted or kin. But then, his performance and riding ability could have been better evaluated if she were not virtually sitting in his lap.

The lane twined lazily through the trees, turning this way and that beneath a lofty canopy of overhanging branches. A doe with her fawn darted across the road ahead of them, drawing an excited cry from Andrew. Almost as quickly, the deer disappeared into the woods on the far side. For a time, Gage kept the mare to a walk as he indulged himself with studying minute parts of the young woman he casually embraced. His gaze admiringly caressed a small ear and a pale, creamy nape where curling wisps escaped a braided knot, while her delicate fragrance bestirred his senses. His greatest delight, however, was being able to surround her with his arms and body.

A nervous glance cast quickly by Shemaine over her shoulder made Gage aware that she was sensitive to his close scrutiny, and he knew if he didn't soon relent, she'd be leaving them and walking home. Though she had not yet voiced an objection, she was nevertheless prone to twitch uncomfortably when his male form pressed too close. The temptation to do so was almost more than he could withstand.

Upon reaching a shallow stream (the same which fed the pond in front of the cabin), Gage forced his thoughts onto a different path and urged the steed into the brook at a fast trot, making Andrew and Shemaine squeal in surprise as the water sprayed upward from the flashing hooves. His chuckles clearly conveyed his mischievous delight.

When they reached the far bank, Andrew wanted more. "Do it 'gain, Daddee!"

"If you insist," Gage replied with a chuckle, turning the horse back into the creek and drawing more delighted shrieks from his companions.

"I'm going to be soaked if you don't stop!" Shemaine cried through her laughter.

" 'Tis a warm day," Gage reasoned with humor behind her.

"Aye, but the water is cold!" she protested, and then sucked in her breath as a new volley of droplets splashed her. She wiped wet runnels from her face and, for the sake of modesty, ignored those that trickled down into the deep crevice between her breasts.

Once they reached the horses' paddock near the cabin, Gage slid to the ground and lifted Andrew down. After sweeping Shemaine from the back of the steed, he stood her to her feet and stepped back with a grin before his eyes were lured downward by the wetness of her gown.

Following his descending gaze, Shemaine glanced down in some confusion and felt a hot blush suffuse her cheeks as she saw her soaked bodice molding her breasts, clearly defining the chilled tautness of her nipples. With a low mortified moan, she fled into the house, stumbling on the way and, in the process, losing her slippers. She dared not pause to retrieve them, but leapt barefooted up the porch steps, snatched open the back door and disappeared within.

Gage followed with Andrew at a much more dignified pace and scooped up her wet shoes as he went. He was standing near the hearth in the kitchen, trying to appease his son's unquenchable curiosity about a wide variety of subjects, when Shemaine finally came downstairs garbed in a fresh gown. Her dampened hair had been combed into a neat bun behind her nape, and the lace of her collar stood on end around her long, creamy throat. Her beauty bestirred his awe, and he was wont to appease his hungering eyes. Indeed, he couldn't seem to get enough of looking at her lately.

Hesitantly Shemaine reached out a hand. "My shoes."

Gage glanced down and realized he was still holding them in his hand. "They're damp."

"So are yours," she said, indicating his boots and the leggings of his buckskin breeches, which were thoroughly soaked to his knees and damp along the outer sides of his thighs and hips. Her skirts had obviously provided protection for other areas, which were dry. "You'd better get changed. I'll have food on the table before too long."

"After I tend the mare," he answered, and left through the back corridor.

Breathing a sigh of relief, Shemaine took Andrew into his bedroom to change his clothes. A few moments later the back door opened and closed, and then, after a short delay, the floor in the parlor creaked as silent footfalls advanced across it. To give warning of her presence in the boy's room, she began to sing a child's song, but she nearly stumbled over the words as Gage entered wearing only the breeches he had ridden in. The fluttering of her heart started anew as her eyes stealthily swept his wide shoulders and firmly muscled waist. Though she would have willingly admired the sights as long as he was there, she refused to allow herself to gawk at him like some mindless twit. She had to escape!

"Come, Andrew," Shemaine bade, taking his small hand in hers. "Let's go into the kitchen by the fire and finish dressing you while your father changes his clothes."

Before she could flee, Gage sauntered leisurely to his armoire, crossing her path and halting her progress altogether as he opened the doors of the cabinet. To Shemaine, it seemed a deliberate impediment, especially after she had just announced her intentions, but she could do naught but wait until he completed his search.

Gage tossed a shirt over his shoulder and sailed a pair of hide breeches onto the bed before he stepped back and closed the cabinet. Shaking out the folds of the shirt, he turned to face her. "Do you dance as well as you ride, Shemaine?"

The question startled her, and she nodded warily. Then she hurriedly shook her head as she realized he might think her boastful. "I mean, I have danced before . . . often, in fact."

"Perhaps you'd care to attend a soiree they're having in the village this coming Saturday. I haven't gone to one since Victoria was alive, but there's usually a lot of dancing and feasting. I would imagine nearly everyone in the hamlet will be there. The fees that are usually collected go to help the orphans in the area and the few women who care for them. So we'd be doing a good service by going. If you're willing, I'd like to."

"Oh no, I couldn't possibly!" Shemaine declared in an anxious rush. "Surely not when everyone knows I'm your bondslave and a . . . convict. 'Twould be improper to force my presence on the townspeople like that. Why, they'd likely be outraged if I went."

" 'Twould be nice to have a beautiful woman to dance with," he cajoled.

Her cheeks warmed with his compliment. "I just don't think it would be wise when circumstances are what they are, Mr. Thornton. Andrew and I will be fine here alone if you'd care to take another woman."

Gage's gaze snared hers. "I don't care to take anyone else, Shemaine, so if you insist upon staying home, so will I."

Confusion reigned in her thoughts as she struggled to find an appropriate answer. She didn't want to be the cause of him having to stay away. Neither could she imagine herself attending such an affair.

Her gaze lowered, and in a rather breathless tone, she asked to be excused. Gage stepped back against the armoire, giving her room to pass, but Shemaine could feel his eyes following her to the door. Escaping to the kitchen hearth, she dressed Andrew and then began to put the meal on the table, but try as she might, she could not banish the thought of dancing with her handsome master from her mind.

CHAPTER 12

When Shemaine retired to the loft the next evening, she was surprised to find a pale pink-and-white-striped muslin gown lying upon her cot. Its square-neck collar was adorned with pink ruching, but the garment was badly crushed and wrinkled from having been packed away in Victoria's trunk. Shemaine remembered having seen it near the bottom and had concluded at the time that it was one of the better gowns the woman had owned. A chemise, no less than Victoria's best, had also been left. It lay alongside a pair of white stockings and soft leather slippers. There were even ribbons to tie them on with.

A brief note written in handsome script and signed by Gage lay atop the garments. He urged her to address her attention to whatever alterations or washings the clothes would require before Saturday, for it would greatly please him to take her to the social. As for her concerns, he would not allow a few sour souls to affect any decisions made in his household. Her only reprieve would be if she came down with some serious malady for which a doctor would be required. In other words, he left her no option unless she was near death.

Shemaine mentally groaned at the idea of having to face the established matrons of the area, some of whom she had seen fleeing before her master's attention could come to bear upon them. She hoped fervently that they would prove equally as cautious about voicing their objections when his bondslave entered upon his arm.

Saturday came, and shortly after his afternoon nap, Andrew was taken over to the Fields's where he would stay the night. Just before Shemaine finished dressing, Gage called upstairs from the back door to announce that he was going out to harness the gelding. It seemed an admonition to hurry, and Shemaine's fingers fairly flew as she wound the ribbons around her ankles. In a few short moments she was all but racing down the path toward the corral.

At the sound of pattering footfalls on the stone steps, Gage tightened the last strap on the shaft of the chaise and straightened. What had been intended as a casual glance over the tall back of the gelding turned into a long, slow scrutiny that swept upward from small, white slippers to the pert lace cap adorning her upswept coiffure. It was a full moment before Gage realized his breath had nigh halted.

"Do I look acceptable?" Shemaine questioned worriedly, uneasy with his lengthy silence.

"Aye," he sighed, "like a ray of light to a blind man."

A fleeting smile answered him before he came around the back of the conveyance. Once he stepped into full view, Shemaine felt inclined to say something as lavish as his praise of her. She greatly admired the dashing figure he presented, for he was even more handsome in courtly garb than she had dared to imagine. The clothes were not nearly as costly as those Maurice usually wore, but this man, by his exceptional physique and good looks, made the garments seem far richer than their cost. The frock coat of deep burgundy complemented the taupe-colored waistcoat, breeches, and stockings, while the white shirt and stock she had ironed accentuated his bronzed skin.

Gage swept her a flamboyant bow, which gained a deep curtsy from his companion. "You smell as sweet as you look," he remarked, stepping near to savor her delectable scent. He was intrigued by every womanly detail of her and, upon closer inspection, noticed where the seams over her bosom had been let out and neatly resewn. His gaze passed in ample appreciation over the fullness before Shemaine turned with burning cheeks to face the conveyance. Catching hold of the dash, she lifted a foot on the metal rung and felt Gage's hands on her waist as he boosted her into the chaise. Sitting back against the seat, she swept up the tricorn that lay on the cushion beside her and brushed her fingers caressingly over the plain trim that finished the turned-up brim. It

was so like the man to shun elaborate decorations. But then, with his face and form, he needed none.

"Your hat, m'lord," she murmured, offering it to him with a smile as he climbed in beside her. Her green eyes glowed with admiration as she watched him slide it snugly into place, and she continued to marvel at his handsome profile as he unwound the reins from the dash and clicked to the gelding. In the narrow confines of the seat, there was not enough space to allow them to sit apart. Gage's shoulder overlapped hers, and just as unavoidably, the back of his arm brushed her bosom. Shemaine accepted the light strokes in silence, strangely pleasured by his casual touch, and wondered if her master even noticed. With an imperceptible sigh, she relaxed against the cushioned seat, having every intention of enjoying the ride.

The gelding was a high-headed, high-stepping animal who apparently enjoyed a fast trot. They were soon being whisked along the road toward Newportes Newes, and by their speed, it was easy to predict they would reach the hamlet well before the sun even thought of setting. If Shemaine

could surmise anything from the grin that flitted rather frequently across her master's lips, she could believe that Gage Thornton relished a brisk gait as well and was wont to encourage it. She found herself smiling with the exhilaration of the ride, and once they passed Sly Tucker and his wife in their horse-drawn chaise, laughed at the race that quickly ensued. It soon became apparent that the gelding had a competitive heart and wouldn't be outdone by another steed. Reaching out with his long legs, he left the Tuckers behind in short order.

Once they reached the hamlet, Gage left the gelding at the livery stable, where the animal would receive a cooling walk after his long jaunt into town and, afterward, water to quench his thirst, for it promised to be several hours before they embarked upon their journey home. From the livery, Gage escorted Shemaine along the boardwalk at a leisurely pace, drawing shocked and curious stares from nearly everyone who recognized them. A small group of British soldiers who approached from the opposite direction eyed Shemaine with close attention, but they remembered her companion only too well as the one who had booted the huge

tar into the road. They had deemed the oafish sailor much in need of a harsh comeuppance for hurting the girl, and out of respect for the man, they politely curtailed their admiration for his companion to nothing more than a casual glance or two.

Potts had been leaning against a post in front of the tavern, but when he saw Gage and Shemaine, he muttered something over his shoulder, bringing Morrisa promptly through the doors of the establishment. After a jeering perusal of Shemaine and a more admiring one for the tall man who strolled beside her, the harlot spoke to the swabber and jerked her head in their direction. As if bidden, Potts came sauntering purposefully across the street toward them.

The last thing Gage wanted right then and there was a fight, but it seemed unlikely that Potts would allow him to escape without some kind of fray, no matter how much Gage was loath to see his first evening out with Shemaine destroyed. He just hoped he'd still be on his feet when the conflict ended.

"I think he intends to box your ears," Shemaine murmured fearfully, casting a furtive glance toward her hulking adversary.

The four soldiers, who had been walking toward Gage, espied Morrisa. After a brief discussion, they veered from their course, making their way across the street toward her. As they neared Potts, one of them recognized him.

"Why, it's the *mudsucker!* Blimey, if it isn't!"

His companions had also witnessed the swabber's difficulty in leaving the muck after being booted into it and were just as eager to have a little fun with the callous ox.

One of the soldiers wrinkled his nose in feigned repugnance. "Eh, what's that awful stench?"

"Manure!" a fellow soldier roared in rampant hilarity. "Mudsucker ain't partial ta baths, don't ye know!"

"He must relish the stuff," another commented, " 'cause he sure ate enough o' it!"

Their bantering had brought the red-faced sailor to an abrupt halt in the middle of the street, and there Potts stood with massive hands clenched into white-knuckled fists as he seethed with violent rage. His pig eyes blazed at the four, two of whom nearly dwarfed him. "Cares ta see which o' ye buffoons can say that right up close ta me face?"

The soldiers grinned and glanced at each other. After briefly considering the tar's invitation, they allowed the smallest one to answer for them. "Aye, we'll meet ye 'round back o' the tavern where our cap'n won't see us."

The threatening altercation allowed Gage and Shemaine to pass virtually unnoticed—except for Morrisa, who glared after them. Unconcerned with how the harlot snarled and stewed, they continued on down the thoroughfare.

The meeting hall was the place where all public functions were held, for it was the largest building in the hamlet. Gage had said nearly everyone would be there, and Shemaine could almost guess that that was exactly the case as she recognized several amiable faces and many others who were not as pleasant. The Tates hadn't been able to come since Calley was still confined to her bed, but Gage's two apprentices and the shipwright, Gillian, were there. Sly Tucker and his wife arrived shortly after his employer, about the same time that Mary Margaret hastened across the hall with the aid of her cane. Other friends smiled and waved or called out a greeting. But Alma Pettycomb and her following gawked and hurriedly whispered to each other behind their fans as they rudely eyed the gown Shemaine was wearing. Roxanne sat at a table near the entrance, having been enlisted to take an accounting of those who entered and to charge the appropriate fee. Upon seeing Gage and his companion, she began to sulk in darkly brooding vexation.

Mary Margaret took Shemaine's hand and patted it affectionately as she warbled, "Oh, don't ye take the prize for beauty." The Irishwoman cast a sparkling glance toward Gage and grinned. "I'm also delighted ta see his handsome self lookin' so fetchin' in gentleman's attire."

Gillian was right behind her, asking Gage's permission to dance with Shemaine. "If'n ye don't mind, Cap'n."

Gage chafed at the idea that he wouldn't be the first to dance with Shemaine, but he gave her over to the younger man and watched with close attention as they faced each other in a contredanse.

"Well, Gage, I never expected to see you here," Roxanne commented from the table.

"I can only say you've shown your usual nerve."

After hanging his tricorn near the entrance, Gage approached her and counted out the toll. "Two for the meal and the dancing."

Roxanne took exception to his simple declaration and accepted his coins snippishly. "I can count, Gage! And I'm not blind! I can see you've brought your slave with you. But tell me this, if you would. If you bought her to take care of Andrew and to teach him, why is she here with you?"

"I asked her," Gage replied laconically.

"Why? Were you afraid some other woman would turn down your invitation if you asked her?" By supposing upon his reticence on that account, Roxanne sought to assuage the hurt gnawing at her heart by convincing herself that he hadn't asked her solely because he had assumed she'd reject him outright. After her threats, was it not reasonable to imagine that he'd be aloof with her?

Gage felt a need to be plainspoken with the woman. She had imagined far too much as it was. "I didn't care to bring anyone but Shemaine."

Roxanne's gray eyes flared with fiery indignation at his frankness. No matter how many times she had told herself that Gage *just had* to feel some tiny bit of tenderness toward her, her searching heart was always rebuffed. Perhaps the time had come for her to stop lying to herself and to cease making excuses for his cool reserve. "I'm sure Mrs. Pettycomb will delight herself by spreading tales of your latest effrontery about the village. Gage Thornton bringing his bondslave to an event intended for freemen. That should perk up everybody's ears."

"I have no doubt it will." With a tense smile, Gage turned and strolled back to Mrs. McGee.

The widow grinned as she folded her slender hands upon the head of her cane. "I see, fine sir, that ye've come ta enliven me drab life with yer winsome face an' yer devilish ways."

"I'm glad to be of service, madam," Gage said debonairly, clicking his leather heels and tilting his head in a clipped, precise nod that sufficed as a bow.

The elder briefly marked Roxanne with a glance as the younger woman accepted the required fee from several newcomers. "I also saw the torment o' wantin' ye in the eyes o' that poor soul ye just left."

Gage sighed pensively. "I can't live my life trying to avoid Roxanne, Mary Margaret."

"Nay, nor do I expect ye ta do anythin' less than what you're doin' now. Ye've as much right ta be here as Roxanne."

Gage made no reply as his gaze found Shemaine. She was being escorted through the steps of the contredanse by the younger man and seemed in a vivacious mood, having lost her fear of attending. He saw several bachelors closely perusing her, but he intended to be at her side well before any of them could interfere.

"Yer mind is fixed on yer bondslave," Mary Margaret ventured with a smile.

The brown eyes twinkled with amusement as Gage flicked a glance askance at the widow. "Aye, I'm impatiently awaiting my turn. Is that what you want to hear, old woman?"

She nodded pertly, noticing a welcomed change in the man. While Roxanne worked for him, he had seemed tense, but he now appeared at ease and happy. "Aye, that will do for starters."

When the dance ended, Shemaine saw

Gage moving through the crowd toward her. Their gazes melded in warm communication, and when he took her hand and led her into the reel, she could not subdue the nervous fluttering in her breast no matter how many times she silently reminded herself that he was just a man.

Stepping back into a line of women facing men, Shemaine sank into a deep curtsy before him, and he, in turn, bowed before her. The other couples moved out as their time came and sashayed down the line while the rest of them clapped. Then it was their turn. Of a sudden, it was as if her fantasy had become reality, for her handsome escort seemed to have eyes for no one else but her as he swept her toward the far end.

"People are staring at us," Shemaine whispered as they moved together. Indeed, there were many who had stepped to the sidelines to openly view them, including Roxanne, who had left her reception duties long enough to do so.

"They have good cause," Gage breathed, leaning near his bondslave. "You're the comeliest maid here."

"They're observing both of us," Shemaine corrected in passing. "Do you suppose

they're expecting us to do something outrageous?"

"Perhaps we should," Gage suggested,
curbing a grin. Briefly considering several
possibilities, he nodded after coming to a
decision. "A kiss might suffice."

"Oh, sir, you wouldn't!" Shemaine hissed
in a whisper.

A chuckle accompanied the sudden roguish gleam in his eye. "Wouldn't I?"

Having no doubt that Gage Thornton
would do whatever he pleased, Shemaine
made to turn away, but he caught an arm
around her waist, temporarily imprisoning
her close against his side. A sudden murmur
in the crowd affirmed the constant vigil
maintained by their audience.

"Stay with me or I shall kiss you here and
now," he threatened, squeezing her waist.

Shemaine nodded readily, wishing to
avoid the tumult which would certainly be
created if he did such a thing. "Mary Margaret was right, sir!"

"In what way, my sweet?"

Her soft lips curved in a fetching smile.
"You *are* a devil!"

Gage threw his head back and laughed,

raising the eyebrows of many who had not heard the like from him in some time.

When the dance ended, Shemaine was inclined to let her fingers linger in his as they made their way across the hall. The gentle pressure of his grip assured her that it suited him to hold her hand. They were so intent upon each other as they exchanged smiles and murmured comments on the music, they failed to see Roxanne scowling at them as they passed in front.

The evening continued pleasurably for each of them. They shared most of the dances, yet the two apprentices and Gillian were always eager to ask their employer's permission for a spin about the floor with her. Except for the gossipmongers and those resentful of Gage Thornton, the townspeople seemed to tolerate Shemaine's presence. They could do nothing less with her stalwart protector near at hand.

It was much later when Gage leaned near his bondslave to ask, "Are you hungry, Shemaine? We can eat now if you wish."

"Mmm, I'm starving!"

A grin accompanied his reply. "Then come, my sweet slave, and I shall find us a spot where we may indulge our appetites."

Gage straightened and motioned for his friends to join them at a far table. They were quick to respond and, after fetching food which Sly graced, they entered a lively repartee about the wit of the Irish, which Gillian and Mary Margaret had started some moments earlier. Laughter made the rounds as they ate, but silence descended like a sledgehammer driving nails when a caustic male voice intruded.

"Humph! Bringing a convict to mingle with the good folk of this community. Some men don't care how they abuse their neighbors."

Gage turned sharply to find Samuel Myers sneering at him past the profiles of the hawk-nosed Alma Pettycomb and other women of her sort who had gathered nearby to observe the couple. The clothier obviously thought himself safe from reprisal with such formidable witnesses near at hand, but with an angry snarl Gage pushed himself back from the table, setting the women to flight. He would have stood up to confront the man, but both Shemaine and Sly were quick to intercede before he could rise from his chair, the girl by a gentle hand on his arm and the cabinetmaker by a rumbling entreaty.

"Forget the li'l pipsqueak, Gage," Sly urged, loud enough for the clothier to hear. "He's not worth yer bother."

"Why, you cloddish oaf! Who do you think you're calling a pipsqueak?" Myers demanded, stalking with stiff-legged outrage toward Sly's chair.

Gillian snickered in sudden delight. "Show 'im, Sly!"

The apprentices made no effort to restrain their mirth as the hulking cabinetmaker pushed himself leisurely to his feet. Myers's gaze was drawn slowly upward until he had to lean his head far back to even meet the chiding gaze of the other. Myers's jaw slackened abruptly, and he gulped hard as he considered the breadth and height of his antagonist. Faced with such overwhelming strength, he could find no more caustic comments to make.

"Me name's Sly Tucker, if'n ye're curious," the cabinetmaker informed him bluntly.

"Yes, well, I won't bother you any longer," Myers replied in anxious haste. "I'm sorry to have disturbed you."

Gage chuckled as his friend resettled himself in his chair. "You do seem to have a calming influence on some men, Sly. Remind me to take you with me if I ever go to war. The enemy would see you coming and likely turn tail and run, saving me a lot of trouble."

The relaxed camaraderie resumed, as did the dancing. Mrs. Pettycomb never ceased her chattering, nor Roxanne her scowling and stewing, but for Shemaine and Gage, the affair ended on an enjoyable note as they finished the last dance together. After bidding adieu to their friends, Gage drew his bondslave's arm through his and escorted her back toward the livery, ignoring those who gaped and sneered after them.

They passed the tavern in time to see Freddy serving as a human crutch for Potts, who appeared to have some difficulty walking upright as he staggered through the doors. The swabber held an arm clutched across his midsection and was groaning aloud as if in great pain. A makeshift bandage had been wrapped around his brow, and another swathed his knuckles. From the poor condition he was in, it was clear that he had come out much the worse for wear in his private set-to with the British soldiers.

Moments later at the livery, Gage was

harnessing the gelding to the chaise when shuffling footfalls drew their attention to the deeper shadows running alongside the barn. As Gage stepped around to peer into the darkness, Cain emerged with his cumbersome gait. The hunchback looked cautiously at the man and held out his hand to reveal a wooden image of a graceful heron, as if to convey his reason for wanting to approach Shemaine. Gage gave his softly muted consent and watched as the cripple made his way to her.

"Shamawn tawk bawrd . . . gawft faw maw frawn," Cain mumbled, holding out the bird.

Gage was able to interpret the garbled words more quickly now and offered an explanation to Shemaine, who seemed confounded by what the hunchback had said to her. "I think Cain would like you to take the bird as a gift because you're his friend."

"Cawn mawk bawrd faw Shamawn."

"He made it for you," Gage informed her.

"Oh, Cain, it's beautiful," Shemaine murmured with a feeling of awe. Though hideously deformed himself, the man had obviously been impressed by the beauty of the bird and had painstakingly translated it into a wooden likeness. "You have a rare talent, Cain, and I'm honored by your gift. 'Tis a lovely memento of our friendship. Thank you."

Shemaine moved forward, and Cain, with a look of wonder on his distorted face, received another gentle kiss upon his brow. Briefly she wrapped her arms around him, giving him an affectionate hug, and then stood back with a tender smile. Once again Cain seemed astonished by her deeds and, as if again unable to believe what he had just received, touched the place where her lips had brushed and hugged himself as he offered a crooked smile that showed his sparse and crooked teeth. Then he mumbled a farewell, turned and left, shuffling back into the shadows from whence he had come.

Gage stepped beside Shemaine to look at the gift. He, too, was amazed at her compassion. "I think you've earned a friend for life, my sweet."

"Oh, sir, Cain is so lonely and pitiful," she replied with heartfelt empathy. "It makes me sad to think of what that poor soul has been through, being an outcast. Whatever I've suffered because of my arrest seems so insignificant in comparison to what he has had to endure all his life. Indeed, I must be grateful for all that I've been blessed with."

"You've made his life better because of your kindness, Shemaine," Gage pointed out quietly. "Cain would not want you to be sad. That's not why he worked so diligently to carve your gift. It was to give you back some bit of the pleasure you've given him by your simple display of affection."

Shemaine smiled at his gentle reassurances and allowed him to assist her into the chaise. Soon they were on the road again, making good time as they sped home. Shemaine reflected upon Cain's sculpture, studying it as much as she could by moonlight, but she was tired after such a long day, and the rhythmic clip-clop of the horse's hooves and the gentle sway of the lightly sprung chaise lulled her to sleep. Her head bobbed forward several times, jerking her momentarily awake, until a hand came up and gently pressed it down upon a sturdy shoulder. What remained of the ride passed into oblivion for Shemaine, and even when Gage halted the gelding near the corral some time later, she slept on, undisturbed.

Gage tied the reins around the dash before he leaned back in the seat and considered his slumbering companion. Her head still rested on his shoulder, and she was cuddled close against his side as if she sought his warmth. A soft breast seemed to brand him through his sleeve, and it was all he could do to keep his hand from encompassing that tempting fullness. Her nearness had filled his senses with a delicate essence of violets from the first moment he had sat beside her earlier that afternoon. In all, it had been a delightful experience to court her throughout the evening. It was just as pleasurable to watch her sleeping and, albeit by moonlight, to closely scrutinize every minute detail about her.

Gage swept an arm behind her, shifting her forward slightly until he could lay it close about her shoulders. A sigh escaped her parted lips, caressing his face as he leaned near. It seemed only natural to touch the softness of her mouth with his own and awaken her with a kiss.

Shemaine was dreaming of a chivalrous knight, and answering his kiss seemed in full accord with her own desires, for the mouth moving over her own was warm and stirring, evoking an excitement that was uncommonly real even for one of her dreams. The face above her own seemed dark and featureless, yet she added details that had become familiar to her dreams, a thin nose and a crisply chiseled countenance that was marvelous to behold.

The visage receded, and with a disappointed sigh Shemaine struggled upward through hazy shadows. Her mind seemed strangely detached, and inexplicably there remained in her mouth a heady taste, somewhat similar to that which she had smelled on her master's breath shortly after he had quaffed a glass of ale with his employees. She licked her lips, savoring the flavor, and yearned for the knight's kisses to return. The last had been the best of all!

Reality would no longer be denied. As it came winging slowly back, Shemaine stared through the shadows into the face of the one who regarded her, feeling a lingering confusion. Was he the man in her fantasy? Or was she still dreaming? Then she saw a smile trace across the handsome lips, and a soft murmur assured her that she was awake.

"I thought I'd have to carry you upstairs."

"Are we home?" she queried, glancing slowly around.

"Aye, safe and sound."

Shemaine realized his arm lay around her, but she made no effort to pull away. It offered her warmth and comfort, but most of all, she enjoyed having it there. "How long have I been asleep?"

The upward movement of Gage's shoulder caught a shaft of moonlight that was otherwise limited to the area beyond the chaise's leather top. "Shortly after we left Newportes Newes. You seemed destined to sleep the night through."

"I was dreaming," she sighed.

Gage dropped an arm across his knee as he leaned forward to search out her features in the shadows. "What were you dreaming about, my sweet?"

Shemaine turned her face aside, unwilling to answer him. If she *had* dreamed it all, then she certainly didn't want him to know about her flights of fancy. If she *hadn't*, then it was perhaps best that she remain ignorant of all that had transpired between them. "We'd better go into the house now." She rubbed her arms, feeling a sudden chill as a breeze penetrated her sleeve. "I'm cold."

Gage stepped lightly to the ground and doffed his coat as he came around to her side. As she turned on the seat to face him, he plucked the heron from her lap and, with a smile, handed it to her. After lifting her down, he draped the oversized garment over her shoulders and took her free hand to escort her into the cabin. Pausing in the back corridor to light a pair of tapers, he placed a candlestand on the stairs as she stood drowsily admiring the wooden sculpture.

"I'll have to tend the gelding," he murmured, stepping near to indulge himself in her sweet scent.

"Does he have a name?" Shemaine asked, smothering a yawn as she glanced up.

Gage grinned down at her as he slipped his coat from her shoulders and laid it across the tall stool near his desk. "Sooner."

"Sooner?" she repeated, a little bemused. "That's an odd name for a horse."

"Aye, but he gets to where we're going sooner than the mare."

She smiled sleepily at his wit. "And the mare?"

"Later."

"Sooner? And Later?"

He nodded briefly.

"Thank goodness you didn't name your offspring using such logic."

Humor tugged at the corners of his mouth. "Victoria wouldn't let me."

"Well, I wouldn't either if I were your wife," Shemaine replied, muffling another yawn.

Gage's eyes danced, commanding her full attention. "We'll discuss it more at length after you've given birth to our first."

The last dregs of sleep vanished abruptly as Shemaine's head snapped up. She stared at him in astonishment, having no idea whether he was teasing her again or else predicting a drastic change in their relationship. She decided not to waste time with questions. Indeed, it seemed prudent to beat a hasty retreat.

Gage observed her flight to the stairs. "Coward!"

Shemaine halted instantly with a foot on the bottom step. Glancing back at him, she elevated an eyebrow. "Sir? Are you calling me a coward?"

"Aye." Gage folded his arms across his chest and challenged her with a direct stare.

Shemaine faced him, a bit stymied by his

slur. "Sir, I would like to know why you choose to call me a coward. To my knowledge, I've done nothing deserving of that insult."

His wide shoulders lifted briefly. "You obviously assume the worst, Shemaine, and rather than ask questions, you race upstairs as if your petticoats were on fire."

A rush of color brightened her cheeks. "It didn't seem advisable to delve into your meaning, sir. After all, we are quite alone, and I *am* your bondslave."

"And I'm a widower," he needled. "In dire straits."

Shemaine's blush deepened as she recalled his comments about the ladies of the village and their expectations of a widower. Lowering her gaze to the wooden heron she held, she gently prodded, "You've already admitted that you desire me, sir. Should I think otherwise now that we're alone?"

"I also said I wouldn't force you, Shemaine," he reminded her softly.

She lifted her head and probed his smiling stare, not knowing what to answer.

"But there is one thing I would desire," Gage rasped in a whisper.

Shemaine held her breath, wondering what would follow.

"The evening was so delightful, I'd like to end it with a kiss. . . ."

"A kiss?" Shemaine marveled at the sudden thrill that swept through her and the chaotic beating of her heart. She could only wonder if kissing him in actuality was as delectable as it had seemed in her imagination.

Gage paced forward carefully, as if stalking a wary dove. "Is it too much to ask?"

Fearful that her voice would betray the fermenting excitement within her, Shemaine shook her head.

"You're not frightened, are you?"

"No," she managed, trying to calm her jitters as he stepped near. Lifting her face, she waited in anticipation.

Gage smiled. She seemed so willing, he thought he should warn her about his intentions. "This will be no simple peck, my sweet, but a kiss between a man and a woman."

Strokes of lightning sizzled along her nerves, dazzling Shemaine with the intensity of her excitement. Despite the thundering beat of her pulse, she managed a brief nod. "I understand, Mr. Thornton."

Suddenly his arms were around her, snatching her close against him. Her breath escaped her, and for one startled moment Shemaine stared up at him, totally conscious of his unyielding, muscular body. In the next instant, his mouth came down like a plummeting fireball, scalding her lips and forcing them apart in frenzied passion. The suddenness of his ardor overwhelmed her and yet, at the same time, thoroughly excited her. Turning slowly, he pressed her back over his arm as he continued to kiss her with a consuming fervor that left her breathless and a bit faint. His mouth was insistent, relentless, slanting across hers as a fiery torch plundered the warm, honeyed depths with ravenous greed. Her breasts throbbed against his chest, their nipples drawing tight with a yearning excitement, and Shemaine knew if he had touched them at that moment, she would have cried out from the sheer pleasure of it. His purposeful persuasion sapped the strength from her limbs and evoked sharp cravings that spread upward like molten lava from her loins. Of a sudden, she found herself answering his kiss, turning her face to drink in the sultry delights more fully as her arms slipped upward and locked in a fierce embrace around his neck. She felt her small tongue being drawn inward by some force beyond her own and soon it was caressing his and being caressed. The temptation to yield herself to whatever he desired of her was great. His encompassing arms supported her, and now with her eager response, he would no doubt proceed with his manly bent, claiming all that she had to give. And then, what would she be afterward? A plaything for his entertainment and perhaps, in time, a castoff? Like a garment when it has served out its usefulness and been relegated to the rag bin?

Shemaine found the idea of rejection totally offensive to her nature. Gage had said he would not force her. So it was up to her to put an end to this madness!

She wedged an arm down between them and pushed against his chest as she turned her face aside. Twisting from his grasp, she stumbled away and then turned to stare at him in wide-eyed amazement with a trembling hand clutched over lips that still throbbed. She recognized a burning hunger in his eyes that was perhaps no different from her own. Even now she was besieged by an overwhelming desire to surrender to that compelling plea. Yet she found a tiny fragment of logic to cling to. It was the realization that if she gave herself to him, she would be fulfilling all the vicious conjectures that were making their way around to nearly every ear in the hamlet. She swore she would *not* give the gossips the satisfaction of seeing her belly grow fat with child.

Whirling, Shemaine fled to the stairs and snatched up the candleholder that had been left for her there. She nearly snuffed the flame in her swift flight upstairs, but she knew if she stayed one moment longer in the same room with Gage Thornton, she would be the one to lead him to *her* bed.

In her absence, Gage leaned his head far back upon his shoulders and stared at the shadowed ceiling, his self-control sorely strained. His loins throbbed with his lusting need, and with every fiber of his being, he wanted to leap up the stairs and take her down upon her cot. It was the only way he'd be able to relieve the ache that rapidly intensified at the root of his manly being. But he could not! Would not! He wanted far more from Shemaine O'Hearn than the mere easing of one night's passion.

With a heavy sigh, he turned and walked out onto the porch. What he needed at the moment was a frigid dousing to cool his brain and his body.

Shemaine stood near her cot, listening to the sounds of Gage's departure from the cabin. She thumped a small fist against her chest, hoping to chase away the pang that bloomed there. She was still panting as if she had run a fierce race, but it was only the emotion of tearing herself away from that stirring individual to whom she longed to give herself.

In an effort to calm the quaking within her, Shemaine let her breath out in halting degrees and began to undress, not even caring to pull the canvas sheets closed across the balustrade. Her clothes were cast aside as she paced restlessly about, and by rote she withdrew a nightgown from the cabinet, yet she felt no desire to don it or to slip into bed. The soft aura of the candle bathed her naked body in its warm light, and she gazed down at herself as one totally removed from the outer shell of her being. Would Gage still think her thin? She gazed down at her delicately hued breasts, remembering how he had perused her curves just before their trip into the hamlet. Curiously she cupped their fullness and rubbed her palms over their soft peaks, trying to imagine how it would feel to have his hands come upon her in a similar fashion. Moments earlier she had been alert to the warm throbbing of her nipples as he held her against him, but now that blissful feeling was absent. There was only the unquenchable yearning to have him touch her, to caress her until she moaned with sensual delight. But her arms were empty . . . and so was the cabin.

Heaving a shaky sigh, Shemaine dragged the nightgown over her head and smoothed it down over a body that would not be calmed. She was restless and could find no comfort in the haven that had served her well since the day Gage had brought her home. Having listened intently for the sound of his return, she knew he had not yet come inside. In all probability he was still tending the gelding and would be out there for a while. She could not guess how much time had elapsed since they had parted, but it seemed like a century or two. If he only knew how much she wanted him back with her, he'd forget the steed and come running. Then the evening would pass much too swiftly.

Feeling in desperate need of the calming coolness of the night-borne breezes, Shemaine cautiously made a descent to the lower level. Except for the single candle burning in the back corridor, the rest of the house was dark except for places near the windows where the moon shone in. Shadows seemed impenetrable between the dull shafts of light, yet she knew every stick of furniture, every obstacle between her and the front door.

The gentle zephyrs wafted across the wide expanse of the covered porch as she went to lean against the rail and gazed out upon the bejeweled night. Crickets and tree frogs filled the glade with sound, and in a tree beyond the pond an owl hooted softly. Patches of mottled light moved in undulating motion on the ground beneath several trees as the moonlight streamed through gently swaying branches that were still sparsely leafed.

A muted sound, like a soft splashing, drew her attention to the pond, and she peered intently into the darkness enshrouding it. As she watched, a long arm emerged from the shadows, rising gracefully upward, forward, and then downward as it cleaved the water. Another arm followed, and she realized it was a man swimming toward shore. He pushed himself upright in the shallows. There he began soaping and washing himself down. No one had to tell her that it was Gage. Very few men could lay claim to such an exceptional physique.

Once before Shemaine had watched her naked master. They had been in a shadowed room after he had come in from his nightly bath, and upon her discovery, she had fled in painful embarrassment. This time, she had no intention of giving away her presence. She knew she must enter before he made his way to the cabin, but until then she would observe him much as she had that night. Only now it was different. Her desire for him had replaced her maidenly curiosity.

The moonlight was favorable, casting her in dark shadows beneath the porch roof while it bathed him with its soft radiance, adorning his long, naked body in glistening raiment. She felt her own body glowing with sensual warmth as her eyes fed upon his nakedness. The sights were there for the taking, and she devoured them all in a womanly awakening, all the while yearning to make her presence known, to slip out of her gown and join him there at the pond.

Gage climbed out of the water and reached for a towel that he had left on a rock near the stream. Briefly he toweled himself and then laid the linen around his neck. He came forward, scooping up his clothes from the place where he had left them. Quietly Shemaine turned and slipped inside the cabin, opening and closing the door without a sound. She was in the loft when she heard the floor creak in the back corridor. Her heart began to race with anticipation at the thought of him coming upstairs. Then the glow which had partially lit the now-darkened loft began to move, and she realized that Gage had only returned to the back hall to fetch the second candle he had earlier lit. Her legs trembled beneath her as she sank upon the cot in roweling disappointment.

CHAPTER 13

The cabin had grown unusually quiet with Andrew taking an afternoon nap and his father working in the cabinet shop with his men. A thrice of days had passed since their last trip into the hamlet, and after finishing her mending, Shemaine tiptoed into the boy's room to check on him. He was sleeping soundly, cuddled against the cloth rabbit she had made for him. His breathing was heavy and relaxed, and it did not seem likely that he would bestir himself any time soon.

Carrying a small basket of laundry to the stream in front of the cabin, Shemaine knelt beside a rock at the edge of the brook and began scrubbing the soiled knees of Andrew's britches. The trilling of songbirds was a joyous and melodious celebration of spring, and with a sigh of pleasure, she sat back upon her heels and scanned the treetops, curious to discover what strange and marvelous birds inhabited this clime and filled the day with such a sweet symphony of song. Their warbling melded with the gentle burbling of the brook, as if conducted by a master musician. Small birds flitted from branch to bush or flew across the open spaces from one tree to the next, while overhead more determined flocks of ducks and geese steadily winged their way northward across the sky. Snowy egrets languidly traversed the heights as well or stalked about the river's edge in search of food.

Inhaling a deep breath of fragrant air, Shemaine drank in the serenity of the lush glade. Far beyond the wide-spreading boughs of pine and newly greening oak, fluffy white clouds sailed across an azure sky much like lofty ships at sea. On the opposite side of the stream from her, a young stag cautiously approached from the thicket, but upon spying her, he turned and, flagging his tail, bounded off in the direction from whence he had come.

Into this paradise, the muffled whinny of a horse intruded, provoking Shemaine's curiosity, for the neigh drifted from the depths of the verdant forest instead of the corral behind the cabin. She peered intently into the leafy shadows until her eyes began to adjust to the gloom. Another nicker reached her ears, drawing her gaze directly toward the sound. Some distance off, she saw a saddled chestnut steed of rather questionable quality tethered to the branch of a tree. A feeling of unease began to creep up her spine as she searched for its rider. Her tension changed abruptly to alarm when she espied a large man in a light-colored shirt and dark breeches creeping through the trees toward her. For a young woman who had spent several months dreading the sight of that hulking form, it was nigh impossible for Shemaine to mistake Jacob Potts.

With a startled gasp, Shemaine pushed herself upright, bringing Potts to a sudden halt with her movement. His intent changed abruptly, becoming immediately more threatening. Bracing his legs apart, he extended his arms straight out in front of him and cupped his huge hands around the butt of a flintlock pistol, taking careful aim. It was frighteningly obvious to Shemaine what the man had come to do. He would kill her if he could!

Shemaine was painfully aware of her vulnerability, for she had absolutely nothing at hand with which to defend herself. Her only hope was to flee to safety before he fired. She started to whirl, but before she could lift a foot to make the turn, the explosion of gunpowder rent the peaceful cooing and twittering of birds, sending them flying helter-skelter from the trees and brush. In the very next instant a shot zinged past, slicing open a layer of flesh across her ribs as it went. Shemaine screamed at the pain inflicted upon her and clasped a hand over her left side, feeling an oozing warmth dribbling through her fingers. Frantically she scrambled up toward the cabin, throwing a frightened glance over her shoulder. Potts was busy reloading, but she knew he would soon follow in a zealous quest to catch her before she could make good her escape.

A shout drew Shemaine's attention to the area in front of the cabinet shop, and she felt a surge of relief when she saw Gage and all four of his men sprinting out of the structure with muzzleloaders in hand. In the opposite direction the Morgans were racing down the building slip with weapons of their own. Apparently they had all heard the shot, her scream, or both, and perceived that something was amiss.

Potts glanced around to see the handful of men racing toward him through the woods and promptly decided it was time to leave. He bolted through the trees and, upon nearing the chestnut, dragged the reins free from the branch. Hauling himself astride, he turned the animal about to face Shemaine and shook a brawny fist as he bellowed at her. *" 'Tain't over yet, bogtrotter! Not 'til ye're dead!"*

Potts whipped the steed about and slammed his heels into the chestnut flanks, sending the horse racing recklessly through the trees. Realizing the tar would be out of range soon, Gage skidded to a halt and brought the muzzleloader to his shoulder. The density of the trees hindered him from taking a clear shot, and he was well aware that he would waste his attempt if he did not time the horizontal movement of the weapon to the rate of Potts's speed. Swinging the rifle from a point behind his target, he squeezed the trigger as the bore passed in an imaginary line through Potts. Continuing the lead, Gage moved the sights well ahead of the tar to a spot between two trees. The tar had not yet reached that particular site when the gun finally discharged. A deafening roar reverberated throughout the glade as the lead shot zinged through the trees, meeting its mark just as Potts passed between the pair of oaks. A loud roar of pain evidenced the sailor's wounding, and he slumped forward in the saddle as a large, dark blotch bloomed on the side of his shirt. The horse, confused by the shifting weight, slowed his gait, but Potts, now fearing the marksmanship of the colonial, pummeled the beast with booted heels, cursing savagely as he drove the animal to a faster pace.

Ramsey stumbled to a halt beside his employer as Gage received a loaded Jaeger from his German apprentice and took aim again, but the darkening shadows and the thickness of the forest obscured the rapidly diminishing target.

"He's gone," Gage muttered in frustration, lowering the rifle.

"But you vounded him, Mr. Thornton!" Erich Wernher boasted. "None of zhe rest of us could have done as well!"

Gage heaved a regretful sigh. "Aye, but wounding Jacob Potts is not nearly as beneficial to our existence as killing him."

"I think yer woman is hurt," Ramsey announced, directing Gage's attention to where Shemaine stood clutching a hand tightly to her bleeding midriff.

Tossing the rifle back to the German, Gage sprinted swiftly across the space between them, now wishing he had killed Potts.

Shemaine stepped stiltedly toward him, trying not to wince as he came near. "I'm all right," she managed rigidly. " 'Tis merely a flesh wound."

Gage was not so certain. Blood had already soaked the side of her bodice and was beginning to darken her skirt near the waist. Gently lifting her in his arms, he spoke in concern, "We'll see what damage has been done once I get you to the cabin."

Shemaine winced in pain as Gage carried her up the path. To keep from crying out, she gritted her teeth as she clutched an arm tightly about his neck. Then she recalled the task that she had been performing before she noticed the horse's whinny and issued a soft, fretful groan, drawing Gage's anxious regard until she confided in some embarrassment. "I'm sorry, Mr. Thornton. I'm afraid I left the washing by the stream."

"Forget the clothes!" Gage bade her gruffly. "They can float away for all I care."

Unlatching the front door, he shoved it wide with a shoulder and carried her through the cabin to the back corridor, where he set her gently on her feet. Turning her around so her injury faced the light, he went down on one knee beside her and plucked at the blood-soaked cloth. The gown was still intact except for two small rents where the lead ball had gone completely through her bodice, but he was hindered from seeing the wound or the source of the bleeding. Taking hold of the fabric, he would have ripped it apart, but Shemaine stumbled away, immediately incensed that he should consider such a thing.

"I do not intend to stand here like a helpless twit and let you tear off my clothes, Mr. Thornton. I'm sure the gown can be washed and easily mended as it is, and I will not see such a serviceable garment ruined beyond repair."

Gaze sighed in vexation. "There are other gowns in Victoria's trunk, Shemaine, and I give you leave to take what you like of them."

Though he reached toward her again, Shemaine stepped beyond his grasp, stubbornly shaking her head. "I'll not impose upon your generosity, Mr. Thornton. You've given me far too much as it is."

"Take the gown off, if you must!" Gage urged testily. "But I'll not rest 'til I've seen to your wound."

"And that I will allow you to do, sir, but only in a manner I will feel comfortable with." Shemaine peered up at him as she softly suggested, "If I may have a loan of an old shirt, perhaps one that opens down the front, then I'll be able to accommodate you more readily."

With a frustrated growl, Gage left her and, after a moment, returned from his bedroom with a homespun shirt. "You can put this on while I get some water from the well."

Shemaine accepted the garment from him and waited as he took the pitcher from the washstand and strode out the back door, closing it behind him. Unfastening her bodice and chemise, she slipped them from her shoulders and then gritted her teeth against the pain as she pulled the cloth away from the wound. She cast an anxious glance over her shoulder to reassure herself that Gage was nowhere in sight as she lowered the garments to her waist. Ever so carefully, she slipped into the shirt, fastened it between her breasts, and rolled up the long sleeves to free her hands. While she waited for her master's return, she found an old sheet in the storeroom and began making bandages.

A quick rap of knuckles against the back door preceded Gage's entrance, and Shemaine waited self-consciously as he poured water into the washbasin and fetched more from the hearth to heat it. When he returned to her side and pulled the shirt up from her ribs, she turned her face away, blushing as she folded her arms carefully around her bosom. Without such precautions, the shirt would have allowed a liberal view of everything beneath it, for it was like a tent enveloping her.

Wetting a cloth, Gage gently swabbed and cleansed the bloody gash until he was able to determine the extent of her injury. He was relieved to see that it wasn't as severe as he had first thought, only a laceration across a rib, deep enough to cause profuse bleeding, but hardly life-threatening. The only hazard would be if it became infected, but he intended to prevent such a likelihood by the use of the malodorous balm.

"It's not serious," he announced with relief, "but 'twill require a tight bandage to stem the bleeding."

Gingerly Shemaine pointed toward the strips of cloth she had wound into neat rolls, trying not to show how much his careful ministering had hurt her. "Will those suffice?"

"Aye, they'll do nicely. Now lift up the end of the shirt and hold it out of my way," he instructed. "I'll have to wrap the bandages around your waist to keep them snug, and I can't do that fumbling blind beneath the shirt."

Gage left Shemaine to consider his directive as he went to fetch the noisome salve. When he returned, the ends of the shirttail had been gathered together and were neatly knotted between her breasts, leaving her midsection bare. He couldn't help but admire the results, for the soft homespun cloth molded her bosom to perfection, hinting of the soft nipples and the youthful firmness of the full curves. Her waist was incredibly narrow, and though he could still count nearly every rib she had, her silken flesh stirred his admiration in ways similar to what he had felt the night the snake invaded. Except for her recent injury, her skin was just as delectable as it had seemed that evening.

"You'll have a slight scar after this to remember Potts by," Gage warned, placing his tall stool beside her and setting the container of emollient on top of it. "But it shouldn't pucker. Once the redness fades, you'll hardly notice it."

"Do you have to put that ointment on me?" Shemaine wrinkled her nose in distaste as he opened the crock. "It smells awful."

"Aye, but 'twill help heal the wound and prevent infection," he argued, glancing up at her profile in time to see the comical face she made to exaggerate her aversion. Her protestations were as winsome as those of a young child trying to cajole her parent. Though he leaned near that visage, she stared straight ahead, silently admonishing him by refusing to acknowledge his proximity. "And I'd prefer not to take any chances with such a valuable possession. You suit me well, Shemaine O'Hearn, and I'd rather not lose you. 'Twould be impossible to find another bondswoman as beautiful and talented as you are."

"You're only being generous because I've been hurt," Shemaine complained glumly, then caught her breath in a sharp gasp as he began to wash the torn flesh again. Feeling suddenly light-headed and nauseous, she swayed on her feet.

Gage hurriedly slipped an arm around in front of her as she slumped forward, and secured his hold on her with a hand on her far hip. The pressure of her scantily clad bosom against the inside of his arm was unsettling to his manly senses, so much so that he dared not move a muscle lest she fly away again like she had that night after his kiss. Huskily he asked, "Are you all right?"

Weakly shaking her head, Shemaine gave the only answer she could as she continued to cling to him. She felt as listless as a rag doll, and it was a lengthy moment before her lethargy began to ebb. Gathering strength by slow degrees, she managed to push herself upright, but she was nevertheless grateful that he kept an arm wrapped around her, lending her support.

"I'm sorry. I really don't know what caused me to feel so faint," Shemaine whispered in chagrin, and met his gaze shyly. His face was so close, she could have stolen a kiss with very little effort. A strange thought indeed at such a time!

Managing to convey a casualness he did not necessarily feel, Gage suggested, "You should lie down and rest after I dress the wound."

"But what about the washing? And the cooking? And Andrew? He'll be awake soon."

"My men will have to do without me for the rest of the afternoon." Gage offered her a subdued grin. "I intend to be at your beck and call 'til sunrise."

Shemaine elevated a lovely brow above a teasing smile as she searched his face. "So, you mean to do chores like any common servant, eh? Have you no ken, sir? 'Tis I who should be at your beck and call."

The brown eyes sparkled with teasing warmth. "And if I were to call, Shemaine O'Hearn, would you truly come to me?"

"Of course, sir!" she replied with a small

dip of her head. "You bought me, and I must obey."

"But what if you were free of bondage, Shemaine?" Gage pressed. "Would you still come at my call?"

Shemaine found the brush of his breath against her face especially pleasing. Still, she stared fixedly at the desk as she sought to emulate a crisp detachment. "But I'm not free, sir, and will not be for seven years yet."

"Seven years." Gage sighed as his eyes stroked her face. " 'Tis a long time for a man and a woman to live together under the same roof and not be wed or close kin."

Cocking a brow, Shemaine eyed him curiously at very close range, wondering what he was getting at. If he meant to proposition her for her favors, then his timing was poor indeed. "I'll be bleeding to death, Mr. Thornton, if you waste any more time talking," she reminded him dryly. She was disturbed by his close attention, for she had not been able to forget his passionate kiss and its weakening effect on her. Indeed, her cot had become a place of torture of late, for she did little else but toss and turn as she sought relief from that burning desire that nearly consumed her. Feigning an impudence she did not necessarily feel, She-maine inclined her head toward the salve he had left on top of the stool. "I hope you're having second thoughts about using that awful concoction. 'Twill certainly be all right with me if you ha—"

"I haven't," Gage interrupted. Stepping back, he spread the odorous dressing over her ribs, causing her to suck in her breath sharply. Taking up a bandage, he leaned forward and slipped his arms about her as he wrapped it snugly around her midriff. "Keep this on until morning, and then I'll change it for a clean one."

Shemaine rolled her eyes, looking up at him askance as she grumbled, "With more of that loathsome salve, I suppose."

"I'll use less in the morning if you abhor it so much." Gage ripped the bandage slightly and then knotted it so it wouldn't tear back any farther. It was certainly no unpleasant task to embrace his bondslave as he wound another strip around her waist and tied it off. Indeed, he was rather disappointed there were no more bandages left to apply.

"Potts will be more adamant about killing us now," Shemaine gritted through a wince as she tried to accustom herself to the tight bandages. "He'll seize upon his wounding as an affront to his pride and will hound us 'til he catches us unawares. After his fight with the soldiers, you can believe he'll be in a mood to annihilate us all."

"Aye, and perhaps I'll be more fortunate the next time and put a permanent end to his visits," Gage rejoined gruffly. "I can understand now why you were so anxious about the man. He certainly seems intent upon doing you harm. Believe me, my sweet, we'll get back to those shooting lessons as soon as you're able."

"This afternoon will not be soon enough," Shemaine replied gloomily. She would never feel free again to roam the glade until Potts was either gone or dead.

Gage already knew what he must do, for the tar had left him no other choice. "If Potts is still in Newportes Newes, then I'll find him and have it out with him. If he doesn't take my warning seriously, I'll have to kill him."

"Morrisa will know where he is," Shemaine replied, stepping gingerly away. "From the way Potts was hanging around the tavern, I doubt that much has changed since he did her bidding on the *London Pride.* In fact, it wouldn't be at all out of character if Morrisa had encouraged him to come out here and kill me. 'Tis what she has threatened all along."

"Why does she bear you such a grudge?"

Shemaine's brows gathered in a perplexed frown. It was something she couldn't rightly answer. "I'm not sure I can lay the blame to anything specific, Mr. Thornton. True, I thwarted her efforts to rule over the women by encouraging Annie and the others to stand firm against her, but unless she's demented, I can't imagine that my refusal to submit to her dictates would be reason enough for her to want to see me dead."

"Perhaps she's jealous."

"Oh, she wanted you, all right," Shemaine readily acknowledged, subduing another grimace. "She vowed to cut me up if I left the ship with you."

"Morrisa obviously considers herself a handsome woman and is intent upon having her pick among the men. She may resent being outdone by another woman."

"I can't quite lay a finger to it, but I think there's another purpose behind her motives. 'Tis only a suspicion, but I've been wondering about her ever since she came aboard the *London Pride*."

"Why is that?"

"Morrisa had never laid eyes on me before she was brought down to our cell in the hold. She had been at Newgate but in another section. After looking the women over, she asked which one of us was Shemaine O'Hearn. I didn't care to identify myself at the time, and the other women played ignorant. Morrisa dubbed me 'Bogtrotter' and didn't ask again. Later, she and I got into a fray because she demanded the food I'd been given. She pulled a knife on me, and I threw a pail of water in her face. The bosun came down to settle the squabble and called me by name. I rather gathered from the way Morrisa smirked that she had already figured out my name. She had certainly done everything she could to rouse the ire of Gertrude Fitch and Jacob Potts against me."

"Who might have told her about you?"

"I can't imagine why anyone would have talked to her about me. We were all strangers. Except for the gaoler and the bosun when they were taking account of the prisoners, there was only one other who ever asked me to identify myself outright and that was a turnkey at Newgate. The first time he came to my cell was shortly after I signed on to come to the colonies."

"Did he ever try to harm you?"

"I'm not totally sure about that. I just know he watched me a lot."

"Perhaps he admired your beauty," Gage suggested, having seen her effect on some men.

Shemaine scoffed. "I really don't think I was a particular favorite of his. Shortly before they came to take us to the *London Pride*, I was caught in the midst of a row between some of the prisoners, and I very nearly got my head bashed open when one of the toughs started beating it against a stone wall. The turnkey witnessed the whole thing but never tried to stop it. It was only when the gaoler heard the commotion and came to investigate that I was able to gain my release.

"Then, several nights later when everyone was sleeping, a noise awakened me, and when I opened my eyes, I saw the turnkey creeping toward the corner where I lay. He had a short rope in his hands, and the way he held it made me think he meant to strangle someone, whether me or a prisoner nearby I cannot say. The only way he could get to us was by stepping over the convicts sleeping on the floor of the cell. When he trod on a woman's hand, her outraged shrieks brought the gaoler at a run. The turnkey gave him some lame excuse about seeing a rat. It seemed a feeble story to me. It certainly made the gaoler laugh. He jeered something about a fool trying to hang a rodent and told the turnkey to get out. The next day, I was taken to the ship, and I never saw the turnkey again."

"Could the turnkey have been acquainted with the thieftaker?"

Shemaine lifted her shoulders in an attempt to shrug but immediately regretted the motion. She walked stiffly to his stool instead and braced a hand against it for support.

"Perhaps I'd better carry you upstairs so you can rest now," Gage suggested. "You also might consider wearing a nightgown for the rest of the day. 'Twould be more comfortable for you."

" 'Tis unsuitable to wear nightclothes so early in the afternoon," Shemaine argued. "It's barely half past three o'clock, and your men are still here."

"They'll be leaving soon," Gage countered, "and if anyone else should come, I'll just have to explain that you've been wounded and need your rest."

"Likely story, they'll say," Shemaine scoffed, and tossed her head. "From what I've heard from Annie, I'm sure some of the townspeople would be expecting to see me in my nightgown, but not because I've been hurt. Their imagination is far more indecent. I'm sure Mrs. Pettycomb has done her best to besmirch our reputations, especially after you took me to the soiree and had the audacity to dance with me while everybody watched."

"I've heard some of the talk," Gage conceded. "Mary Margaret thought we should do something to silence it."

Shemaine's soft brows slanted upward, conveying her skepticism. "And did Mary Margaret perhaps advise you just how we might go about accomplishing that deed, sir?"

His eyes flicked briefly upward to meet hers. "She said we should thwart the gossips by getting married."

Shemaine was aghast that such a well-intentioned woman had so little diplomacy. "Well, that may be suitable for Mary Margaret to suggest, seeing as how she's always seeking to make a match between couples, but did she take into consideration that you might not want to take a condemned convict to wife? I find it most disconcerting that she could even recommend such a solution to you. The impropriety of the woman! Truly, sir, I would be mortified to have you imagine that I may have put her up to suggesting such a thing. Why, the idea is so farfetched, it's ludicrous."

Gage lifted his shoulders in a casual shrug. "Actually, Mary Margaret wasn't the first to conceive of the idea."

Shemaine was dumbstruck, unable to imagine another who would be so bold. "Well, I don't think Roxanne would have made such a suggestion, not when she's made it apparent that she wants you for herself."

"Nay, 'twould hardly be Roxanne," he affirmed with a chuckle.

"Calley, then," she stated with conviction.

"Not Calley either."

Shemaine looked at him in growing confusion. "Might I ask who took such liberty, sir?"

The door of the bedroom opened, and

Andrew came out to the parlor dragging a rocking horse behind him. Gage went immediately to his son's assistance before any damage could be done to the furniture. He lifted the boy into the padded buckskin saddle as Shemaine stepped to the door of the kitchen to watch.

Rocking back and forth, Andrew was soon lost in childish delight as he mimicked the cries of a teamster he had once heard. "Geeyup yair! Yah! Yah! Fastah, ya' mules!"

Shemaine and Gage dissolved into laughter as they watched the boy, whose curls were still wildly tousled from his lengthy nap. For the moment, Andrew seemed oblivious to either of them.

"Another example of your many talents, Mr. Thornton?" Shemaine queried, indicating the wooden horse.

Gage dipped his head in a brief affirmation as he came back to her, but he was frustrated by the noise his son was making. Lifting a hand, he motioned for Shemaine to follow him into the back room again. As she did so, he put aside the crock of ointment and lifted her gently onto the stool. For a brief moment, he searched her face, recognizing her bewilderment, and sought to put her at ease.

"I told you when you first came here, Shemaine, that I'd be making a trip upriver to Williamsburg. Thus far, I've been detained from doing so, but yesterday I received word that my customer's house is complete and he'd like his furniture now. If you're feeling strong enough two weeks from tomorrow, I'd very much like to take you and Andrew with me when my men and I make the delivery."

"I'm sure by then I'll be able to go with you and look after Andrew, Mr. Thornton."

"While we're there, I'd like to take care of another matter of great importance to me . . . if you're willing. . . ."

"If I'm willing?" Her eyebrows gathered. "What is there that I must consent to, Mr. Thornton?"

"I need to discuss this matter with you tonight, and I pray you will give me an answer posthaste, for I'll not rest until I know one way or the other."

Outwardly Shemaine seemed composed, but inwardly she quaked. She had noticed that Gage had started pacing restlessly about the narrow corridor, and she could only imagine that whatever he wanted to discuss, it was of a serious nature. Perhaps he was having second thoughts about keeping her. Potts's attempt to kill her might have convinced him of the danger her presence posed to his small family. Carefully she asked, "What matter do you wish to speak with me about, Mr. Thornton?"

Gage stepped back in front of her, earnestly desiring to make certain truths known to her. "I wasn't necessarily teasing when I told you once that I'd consider taking you to wife. Even before I ventured to the *London Pride*, I had given careful consideration to the idea of marrying again. I needed a nursemaid for Andrew, but I wanted a wife for myself almost as much. As I've told you before, there's a serious dearth of young, marriageable women in the area. The ones who are here are eager to wed, as Roxanne has clearly demonstrated, but none has appealed to me. When I went to the ship, I never thought I'd be fortunate enough to find a woman who'd even suffice as a nursemaid . . . much less a wife. But I was wrong, Shemaine. You are much more than I had hoped to find."

Shemaine stared at him, completely astounded by his revelation. "You want to marry me?" Her mind raced, trying to understand his reasoning. Surely he had taken the consequences of marrying one with a tarnished reputation into consideration. She could believe that he might have wanted to bed her because she was handy, but marriage had seemed out of the question despite his wont to tease her. "Why in the world would you want to do that, Mr. Thornton, when the very sight of me leaves honest people wondering what grievous crime I committed in England? Surely they've wondered about my incarceration and have made much of my indentureship to you. You saw how Samuel Myers behaved when he saw me at the dance. I was brought to this country in chains, sir, and if you take me to wife, you'll be a marked man. The husband of a convict, they'll hiss behind your back. No doubt Mrs. Pettycomb has done her best to tell everyone in the hamlet that I'm not worthy of being received by any respectable family, and I seriously suspect it would do me little good to explain to her or the other gossipmongers that I did nothing deserving of my arrest. How could you even consider inviting that kind of criticism upon yourself?"

Gage was just as incredulous. "Do you

honestly think I care one whit about what that woman may say or think? Alma Pettycomb is so pure in her own eyes, she's unable to see how utterly mean and malicious she really is. She feeds on the flesh of innocents, and I'm sure that one day she'll reap dire consequences for wagging that long, serpent tongue of hers. Believe me, Shemaine, she isn't worth your slightest concern. Nor should she hinder or influence any decision you might make. It should be done of your own free will without intimidation. The matter of our marriage is entirely between you and me, no one else."

Taking her small hand between his, Gage searched her green eyes for some hint of a denial, but he found none. "Shemaine O'Hearn, I would be greatly honored if you would accept my proposal of marriage and become my wife."

"You'd have no qualms about taking a convict to wife?" she inquired in amazement. It was almost as if she were waking from a long sleep, for the full realization of what he wanted was just now beginning to hasten the beat of her heart. "You wouldn't regret our marriage after the fact?"

"I would be taking you to wife, Shemaine,

and that's all that matters to me," Gage declared. "Here in the colonies you'll find that rumors grow stale very quickly. Such epithets as 'convict,' 'rogue,' and 'thief' are short-lived unless there are frequent repetitions of offenses to remind people of one's dastardly bent. Once wed, we'll be like every other married couple around here."

"Is that the way we'll be?" Shemaine inquired timidly. For all of her wanton imaginings, when it came to presenting herself as a bride, she could only worry about her thinness and lack of desirability. "Will we share ourselves as other couples do?"

Now it was Gage's turn to grow troubled and perplexed. "What are you asking, Shemaine? That I be something less than a husband to you?"

A crimson blush stained her cheeks. "I shouldn't expect that of you, Mr. Thornton, but I'm dreadfully thin and . . . and not very pleasant to look at without . . ."

"Your clothes?" Gage finished for her, sensing her reluctance to continue. His eyes dropped briefly to her softly clad bosom, then returned to caress her face. He could only wonder how she was able to imagine herself as unappealing when he was certain she was the most beautiful woman he had ever seen. "If you were to insist upon abstinence in our union, Shemaine, 'twould be better for us not to wed at all, for I could not endure seeing you near . . . wanting you . . . and not being intimate with you. I'm a man, Shemaine, not a monk. I desire you as much as any man can desire a woman. I think you must know that by now. If you're bothered at all about being thin or weak, believe me when I say that it just doesn't matter that much to me. I *want* you just the way you are! And if you should still feel frail when we're married, be assured that my strength is enough for the two of us. I would take care not to hurt you and would nurture any tenderness you might feel. So I entreat you, my dear Shemaine, to consider me as a suitor desirous of becoming your husband in every sense of the word."

"You do overwhelm a girl, Mr. Thornton," Shemaine breathed, hardly able to keep her thoughts from imagining his wonderfully contoured body in sharp contrast to her thin form. The images of them lying together in bed began to rush upon her and were far more sensual than she would have cared to admit. Now that she had *admired* a naked man for herself, her mother's rather embarrassed explanations about what went on between a husband and a wife were enlarged upon and elucidated in her mind.

Gage raised a hand and gently brushed his knuckles against her flushed cheek. "Will you be my wife, Shemaine?"

Shemaine remembered the pomp that had surrounded the occasion when Maurice du Mercer had voiced such a question, but for the life of her, she could not recall her heart thumping quite so wildly within her chest as it did after this man's simple but stirring proposal. She considered what it would mean being married to a colonial and committing herself to staying with him long after the seven years on her original indentureship. She still yearned to see her family, but for reasons that were both clear and ambiguous, she could no longer feature herself returning to England and marrying an affluent husband there. It seemed more appropriate for her to stay and make a home with the man who had awakened the passion within her. If she did not love him at this time, she certainly desired him, and she could not continue living in the same house with him without seeking fulfillment as a woman. It was far better to marry than to try to bridle her cravings for the next seven years.

Slowly Shemaine responded with a consenting nod. "Aye, Mr. Thornton, I will be your wife . . . in every sense of the word."

Gage became eager and lighthearted. "We can be married in Williamsburg," he said softly. "By then, your side will be on the mend, and we can return by evening and spend our wedding night here in the cabin."

Despite her efforts to appear calm, her voice quavered. "Whatever you think best, Mr. Thornton."

Lifting her chin, Gage settled a gently caressing kiss upon her lips, as if afraid he'd hurt her with anything more passionate. When he drew back, he explored her face with shining eyes as he whispered, "Shouldn't you think about calling me Gage now? After all, I'll soon be your husband."

"Gage." His name came in a tremulous sigh as he lowered his lips to hers again, but this time his mouth slanted across hers in a devouring search, quickening her pulse until she felt the stirring of ardor in her woman's body once more. His tongue slipped between her lips with provocative boldness, claiming the warm cavern with a possessive voracity that set her senses to flight and awakening a memory of an evening not so long ago. Of a sudden, she was eager for the weeks to pass.

"Daddee, Andee go preevee!" Andrew cried suddenly, breaking them apart with the effectiveness of a bucket of cold water. Racing into the corridor, the boy danced up and down in an anxious dither. Gage swept him up and was out the back door in a flash, leaving Shemaine fairly dazed with awe. Having previously been aroused by an ardent kiss from his lips and having found this recent one gentler but no less stirring, she was convinced that there was much more sensual zeal in Gage Thornton than even her dreams had portrayed. Indeed, she found herself growing increasingly exhilarated by the idea of being intimate with the man.

Was she dreaming again? Was this really happening to her? Would she soon be sharing a bed with Gage Thornton? Or would he return from taking Andrew to the privy and say that he had only been teasing her? Warts off a toad, more or less?

CHAPTER 14

Gage left his canoe by the river and entered the hamlet of Newportes Newes with a definite purpose in mind. He went first to the *London Pride*, but at his terse inquiry, the bosun's mate informed him that Jacob Potts was at liberty and wasn't expected to return to the ship until the following week. When Gage pushed through the doors of the tavern several moments later, he overheard Morrisa being chided by her new owner, an older and rather portly woman wearing a tawdry red gown and a frizzy white wig which sat slightly askew atop her head.

"The gent's paid good money ta have ye,

an' ye'll accommodate him," the elder insisted, pounding a fist upon the table. "An' I'll be hearin' no more o' yer carpin' 'bout him bein' a li'l weasel or that he's low-down mean like the other girls told ye. I've heard meself Sam Myers ain't got much in his breeches ta speak o', an' he likes ta prove himself a man in other ways. But as long as he's willin' ta pay the higher fees I charge him for lettin' me girls go over ta his place ta service his needs, ye'll tolerate his cuffs an' his dirty li'l tricks an' mind yer manners whilst ye're doin' it. Do ye hear?"

"Aye, I hear ye, Freida," Morrisa mumbled, but she was hardly amenable to the idea. There were ways of dealing with odious little rattails like Samuel Myers. Why, with a simple flick of a blade, Jacob Potts could put that blooming toad out of his misery. That is, if her li'l lapdoggie ever got on his feet again and came out of hiding.

It seemed lately that Potts couldn't do *anything* right where the bogtrotter was concerned, Morrisa mentally jeered. Hadn't she sent him out to challenge Gage on the street the night of the dance? But what did Potts do? He got himself beat up good and proper, that's what! Then, after venturing onto the colonial's land, he came back with a big hole in his side and was now laid out like an ailing walrus. Freddy had taken him a fair distance away, where he could be treated by a doctor and where he'd be out of harm's way in case the colonial came looking for him. But for the time being, the swabber was utterly useless to her.

Freida leaned forward to claim Morrisa's attention with a dark scowl. "I've been makin' some good money since I brought me girls inta this here area, an' I ain't wantin' no li'l snitch like Myers callin' foul an' sayin' he's been cheated. He just might scare off some o' our customers if'n he did. I bought ye off that prison ship so's ye could help me business along, not ta set me at odds with the gents. An' if'n ye don't make double o' what I paid for ye within the first year, ye can bet I'll be takin' it out o' yer hide."

Morrisa sulked in mutinous discontent as she turned away from the harping crone, but her expression changed to one of wonder when she espied Gage Thornton coming through the door. She was anxious to hear how Shemaine had fared after being wounded, and he was certainly her best source for getting that information. Hopefully the li'l beggar had taken a fever and would soon die like she should have done long ago.

Growing smug in her confidence that she could wreak revenge on her adversary, Morrisa offered a sultry-eyed smile to Gage as she ran a hand invitingly over her voluptuous form. "Well, gov'na, I sees ye've changed yer mind 'bout me offer, eh? I knew 'twould only be a matter o' time afore ye tired o' Sh'maine." Her eyes slowly dropped to her lap as she voiced a probing conjecture. "Sh'maine must've made ye real mad for ye ta leave her so sudden like, though. I didn't expect ye for a couple o' weeks or so yet. Makes me wonder what she's done ta ye."

Leaning back in her chair, Freida gave the tall, handsome stranger a lengthy scrutiny. It was rare to see such a good-looking gent seeking favors from a harlot. Usually such men got their needs met without laying out a single coin. Her heavily rouged lips twisted in a lopsided leer as she sized him up with a keen eye. "Ye're a right fine one, ye are," she observed coarsely. "Too fine ta me way o' thinkin'. I'll be havin' ta keep me eyes open just ta see what me girls give away ta ye, seein's as how they might be wantin' ta treat ye for the pleasure o' it. Aye, I'll be takin' a close accountin' after they've been with ye just ta make sure they've collected their normal fees."

Gage ignored the madam's comments and divesting perusal as he settled his gaze upon Morrisa. "I'm looking for Jacob Potts. Have you seen him?"

Morrisa lifted her shoulders in an indolent shrug as she closely examined her nails. "Whate'er would ye be wantin' ol' Potts for?"

Gage mentally laid odds that Morrisa knew exactly where the tar was and why he sought him. "I'd like to ask him a few questions."

The harlot gave him a sidelong stare above a calculating smile. "Don't tell me the bogtrotter's been complainin' 'bout Potts again, makin' ye feel sorry for her. How is she, anyway?"

Gage's gaze never wavered from her. "She's fine."

"Fine?" Morrisa seemed momentarily befuddled. "Ye mean she . . . she ain't . . . she didn't send ye in here after Potts?"

"Actually, I came of my own accord to see how Potts was doing after I wounded him."

As if taken by surprise, Morrisa slumped in her chair and her red lips pursed in an expressive "Oh." An accomplished actress, she pretended confusion as she posed a query. "Why in the world would ye shoot poor ol' Potts?"

Gage raised a curious brow, noting that her voice had sounded unnaturally tense. "Who said I shot him?"

Morrisa frowned sharply, a bit flustered by his response. The colonial was no ignoramus! So why was she being so careless around him? "Why, ye did," she insisted. "I heared ye say so meself!"

"I said I *wounded* him," Gage corrected. "I said nothing about shooting him."

Morrisa turned aside with a carefully blasé shrug. "How else could a bloke get hisself wounded if'n 'tain't by gettin' shot?"

Gage smiled blandly. "A knife could do as much harm, and I've heard that Potts is especially partial to knives, as you are. Perhaps you already know that Potts went out to my place to kill Shemaine and that I shot him during his attempt to escape. Perhaps you were even the one who sent him. You would like to see Shemaine dead, wouldn't you, Morrisa?"

The strumpet grew outwardly miffed and inwardly nervous. "I don't know what ye're talkin' 'bout, Gage Thornton! An' I don't know where Potts is, either! I'm not the swabber's keeper! The last time I seen him, he was a-thinkin' o' maybe goin' off ta Hampton or someplace like that. So ye'll just have ta go an' search for him yerself, *Mister* Thornton!"

Gage was only inclined to believe that Potts had left the area. "If he should come to visit you, Morrisa, you'd better tell him that if I ever catch him on my property again, I'll kill him without stopping to ask why he's there. You will tell him that, won't you?"

Morrisa slanted an icy glare toward him. "I'll tell him, but if'n ye knew Potts at all, ye'd be mindful o' just how ornery he can be. Yer warnin' ain't gonna make much difference ta the bloke. Ye see, when ol' Potts gets his head set on doin' mischief, he ain't too keen 'bout changin' his mind for nobody."

"Then, too, you might not want to give him the message for reasons of your own," Gage needled. "Such a warning might deter Potts from fulfilling your behest. Who can really say how he'd react? He just might be inclined to take heed of my warning rather than chance his life being snuffed out. But whether you tell him or not, Morrisa, just be assured of one thing. If Shemaine is killed or harmed in any way because of his actions, I'll come looking not only for Potts but for you as well. And I may well kill you both."

With that, Gage stepped back, gave each woman a crisp nod of farewell, and took his leave of the tavern.

Freida leaned forward in her chair as she fixed a squint upon her newest acquisition. "What did ye say that bloke's name was?"

Morrisa jeered after his departing figure. "Gage Thornton! Maybe the meanest man I e'er come 'cross in me whole bloomin' life!"

"Well, dearie, if'n ye knows what's good for ye, ye'd better take his advice," the procuress warned. "I've heard a lot 'bout that there bloke since I come here, an' 'tain't entirely all good. Some say he got vexed with his wife one day an' threw her off the ship what he's a-buildin' near his cabin upriver. An' from what I hear, there's a spinster what lives down the road a piece what may've seen him do it, but she's too bloomin' scared ta open her mouth 'cause o' what he might do ta her if'n she talks."

"Ye don't say now," Morrisa replied with

a complacent grin. "I wonder if'n Sh'maine knows 'bout that."

"The bloke ain't very talkative 'bout himself, so's I hear. Most likely he'll keep his deeds ta himself, but if'n the rumors be true, ye can bet this Sh'maine ain't as well off as one might suppose. The bloke might kill her just like he kilt his wife."

Morrisa smirked. "An' I could collect me reward without liftin' a finger."

Freida looked at her narrowly. "What reward be ye talkin' 'bout?"

The harlot waved away her question with a backward sweep of a hand. " 'Tain't nothin'. Just somethin' I was promised by a turnkey when the lot o' us was leavin' Newgate an' bein' carted off ta the ship. But there ain't no way o' knowin' for sure if what he said be true 'til I can send back proof the deed be done. An' I ain't been able ta do that yet."

"Do ye mean ye were promised payment ta kill another prisoner?"

Morrisa looked astounded at the woman's suggestion. "Do I look like I could kill anybody?"

Freida chortled and laid her fleshy arms upon the table as she leaned forward to look directly into Morrisa's gaze. "From what I hear, dearie, ye came mighty close ta slittin' a few manly gullets afore yer arrest, but I won't be havin' that kind o' trouble here! I have ways o' dealin' with unruly bawds, an' I swears ta ye, girlie, ye've met yer match in me. Anything ye've done, I've done ye one better, so's ye'd best heed me warnin'. Do ye ken?"

Morrisa spread her arms in a guise of innocence. "I ain't meanin' ta do a bloomin' thing but what ye tell me, Freida."

"That's good!" The madam nodded slowly as she leaned back in her chair. " 'Cause if'n ye don't mind yer manners with me, I'll make ye regret it like ye've never done nothin' before. Ye don't know what misery is 'til I gives ye some. An' I can assure ye, if'n ye vex me long an' hard enough, ye won't be walkin' away from a grave."

Morrisa felt a shiver go up her spine at the penetrating coldness in Freida's eyes. For the first time in her life, Morrisa understood exactly what it felt like to be on the nasty end of a turnabout and to have her life threatened by another woman.

* * *

Gage entered the goldsmith's shop and bought a wedding band, having determined the appropriate size by tying a piece of heavy twine around Shemaine's finger and slipping it off. He considered the elderly proprietor a gentleman of principles and felt no need to urge him to hold his tongue, for the man would be as closemouthed about his customers' affairs as he was his own. From there, Gage went to the cobbler's shop and found Mary Margaret waiting for Miles, who had gone to the back of his shop to fetch a pair of shoes which he had repaired for the elder.

"I didn't think I'd be layin' me sights 'pon yer handsome face for at least a fortnight or so after all the ruckus ye caused by bringin' Shemaine in for the dance," Mary Margaret warbled. "Ye set the town awhirl, ye did. Pity the poor windbags, they've barely stopped chatterin' long enough ta catch their breath." Her blue eyes twinkled with pleasure as she drew an honest chuckle from the man. "Ahhh, 'tis good ta see that life is treatin' ye well again, Gage Thornton. 'Tis been nigh ta a year since I heard ye laugh with such mirth."

" 'Tis your fair face, Mary Margaret

McGee, that has made my day," Gage responded with debonair flair.

The woman's thin shoulders shook with dubious amusement. "Aye, an' I love all Englishman like yerself, sir," she quipped. Then she nodded pertly as she accused, "Ta be sure, ye've been gifted with the silver tongue o' the Irish ta tell a lie so beautifully. But tell me, sir, what be ye doin' here in our fair-ta-middlin' town?"

"I came for the pair of shoes I had ordered for Shemaine, but if you have a moment or two to spare, madam, I shall have need of your services."

"My services?" Mary Margaret was momentarily taken aback. "And what assistance would a grand gentleman like yerself be wantin' from an ol' lady like meself?"

"Your advice will suffice for now," Gage answered with a grin.

Mary Margaret looked him over suspiciously as she sought to quell the irrepressible quiver at the corners of her lips. "I thought ye didn't care for my counsel."

"I guess that isn't necessarily true since I'll be taking it fairly soon. In fact, if you find yourself free two weeks from today, you may come with us to Williamsburg to see the deed done."

The elder was thoroughly confused. "I'll accept the invitation, ye handsome rogue, but ta be sure, I have no ken what ye're talkin' about."

"Then, if you cannot use your imagination, old woman, it may well be a surprise. I'll have Ramsey Tate fetch you from your cottage Friday two weeks from today, in the morning about six."

"And what advice would ye be needin' from this ol' woman, may I ask?"

"I intend to buy Shemaine cloth for a new gown, and I have no idea what she may require to finish it."

"Shoes from the cobbler? Cloth for a new gown?" Though Mary Margaret's thin lips barely curved, her eyes glowed brightly. "What gift will you be wantin' ta give the girl next, Mr. Thornton?"

Gage stared through the small panes of the window, seeming to ponder her question. "Perhaps a brush and comb of her own, a bit of toilet water and some nice scented soap."

"For a bondslave, Mr. Thornton?"

Gage pivoted on his heels and looked

down at the elder with a puckish gleam in his amber-flecked brown eyes. "For a wife, Mrs. McGee."

A hoot of glee escaped Mary Margaret before she clapped a hand over her mouth to silence the outburst. Even so, she danced a rather lame jig with the help of her cane, and then, reclaiming some degree of dignity, peered up at him. "I suppose ye'll be countin' on me ta keep this news ta meself ere the vows are spoken."

"Aye, madam. 'Twill be news for only my closest friends to savor 'til then."

Mary Margaret nodded in agreement with his judicious decision. " 'Tis wise, o' course, not ta befuddle Mrs. Pettycomb overmuch. She might squawk or have a seizure from the wonder o' it. She's clearly expectin' Shemaine ta start showin' her condition ere three months pass . . . but, o' course, without benefit o' a weddin' ring." She chortled in mirth at the idea of the matron's astonishment. "Ahh, 'twould be delightful ta be a wee little mouse in her house when she hears the news. 'Twill pop her eyes out for sure."

"You're ruthless through and through, madam," Gage accused with a chuckle. "May

I never find you in the ranks of my enemies. 'Twould be my ill fortune, to be sure."

"Aye, 'twould," she concurred cheerily.

Leaning on her cane, Mary Margaret approached the doorway leading to the back of the store and called down the corridor. "Mr. Becker, ye might want ta fetch Shemaine O'Hearn's shoes whilst ye're back there. Mr. Thornton is here ta fetch them. An' would ye mind hurryin' yerself along? Mr. Thornton an' I have some important things ta do today."

At first, two weeks from Friday had seemed so far away that Shemaine had foreseen no difficulty in accomplishing everything she had planned to do before that particular day arrived. She had asked Gage if she could alter one of Victoria's gowns which she considered especially lovely. Instead, with a boyish grin that Andrew emulated so well, he had presented her with a bolt of fine cloth for a fashionable gown, lace with which to trim it, and enough soft, delicate batiste to make a new chemise and a nightgown. Shemaine was delighted with his gifts but, at the same time, a bit fretful because of them. Her normal chores usually kept her busy for most of the day, and she could not imagine how she'd ever find time to finish all of the garments before her wedding day. Gage soon solved her dilemma by conveying Mary Margaret's offer of help, which she eagerly accepted. It helped tremendously when Ramsey volunteered to pick up the woman at her cottage for the next two weeks and bring her out with him when he came to work.

Finally the designated Friday arrived, and a heavy barge, outfitted with a large rudder and an odd collection of sails and manned by a crusty old mariner who had given up sea voyages for a quieter life, nudged up against the new loading dock that Gage and his men had built the previous week. The crated furniture was carried on first to avoid damage to the pieces, but driving the team of horses aboard proved difficult, for they were skittish about the craft and even more so about pulling the wagon across the noisy planks that served as a bridge. Gage finally had to get down from the seat and lead them on. The wedding party was the last to go aboard, and did so conveying a small assortment of valises, clothes, and other paraphernalia.

An early morning fog hung over the marshes along the river and seemed to roll up around the barge as it made its way westward. At their approach, egrets, herons, and other birds took flight, while a flock of pigeons winged its way across the skies above grassy sloughs. In other areas oaks, scrub cedar and pine masked the tidal shores.

After the island of Jamestown came in sight, the captain turned the barge into the inlet, and it was here they began to unload. Once the wagon was driven onto dry land, one of the larger crates was hefted into the bed. Gage took three of his men along with him to deliver the breakfront to a wealthy widow while Erich Wernher stayed with the women aboard the river craft. Another three trips saw the rest of the furniture transported to the new owner's recently finished home in Williamsburg. There, the pieces were painstakingly unpacked, inspected and dispatched with infinite care to a place of residency inside the dwelling.

Before they left, the man surprised Gage by giving him a generous bonus for the excellent quality he had achieved in his designs and in the workmanship. Since his efforts and talent had amounted to at least sixty percent of the total undertaking, Gage considered it only fair that he keep fifty percent of the gift and portion off the rest, dividing forty percent evenly between Ramsey and Sly Tucker and distributing the remaining ten in equal shares to the two apprentices.

After restacking the dismantled crates in the wagon, Gage and his men took their leave and headed back toward the barge. But upon nearing the edge of town, Gage drew the team to a halt beside a fenced garden where an old woman in a cloth bonnet was carefully tilling the soil with a hoe. He jumped down and, sweeping off his hat, approached the fence near the spot where she labored.

"Your pardon, madam, but seeing as this is my wedding day, I wonder if you might allow me to buy a bouquet of flowers for my bride from your beautiful garden."

The woman flicked a keen gaze over him, thoughtfully sizing him up. "And what has been your delay in coming to the altar, sir? You're no untried youth, I vow."

Gage smiled in amusement at her perception. "Nay, madam, I've been a widower for the last year now. I have a young son two years of age."

Her bright eyes glittered with unquenchable humor. "And your bride? Is she a widow, too? Or have you stolen some wee young thing from her mother?"

"A maid of eight and ten, as beautiful as yourself, madam."

The elder swept a hand toward the gate. "Come into my garden, sir, and I'll cut you a bouquet myself . . . not for your smooth tongue, I trow, but for your child bride. Aye, I was wed to a widower, too, at a very young age, and I gave birth to five sons and saw them all grown ere my John was taken from me, but to be sure, 'twas no dreaded weakness or illness that claimed my husband, but a stout tree that fell upon him while he was cutting it down. It took revenge and sent him to the grave."

"I'm sorry, madam."

"Don't be," the widow urged with a smile. "We had a good life together, my John and I."

Upon clipping the freshest flowers from her garden, the woman presented them to Gage and graciously bestowed her blessing. "May you and your young bride ride the fickle tides of life with grace and dignity, sir, and may you have plenty of sons and daughters to bring you joy throughout the years to come and, in your doddering old age, a wealth of grandchildren to lighten your hearts with pride at what you've reaped. Now go, and may God watch over you both through your marriage and may you grow to love each other more with each passing day."

Strangely moved by her blessing, Gage thanked her and opened his purse to pay her for the flowers, but the woman waved her hand in denial.

"Nay, sir. The flowers are my wedding gift to you. Give them to your bride and watch her smile. Then urge her to press them in a book. They'll give you both memories for a lifetime."

Gage approached the barge by foot after climbing down from the wagon. Shemaine had not seen him whisk the bouquet behind his back, but from the gleam in his eyes, she was wont to believe he was up to some mischief. Facing him as he came toward her across the gangplank, she settled her arms akimbo, subduing her amusement behind a suspicious perusal.

"Ye can bet he's up ta no good," Mary Margaret ventured with a warbling chuckle. "He looks like the fox what swallowed the chick."

"Aye," Shemaine agreed warmly. "He does, at that."

Her eyes fed upon his every movement until he halted before her. Then her heart quickened with the thrill of his presence.

"For my bride," Gage announced, sweeping the flowers from behind his back and presenting them with a well-executed bow.

"Oh, Gage!" Shemaine cried, gathering them to her breast. "They're lovely!"

"A gift from an old woman I met along the way. She also sent her blessings for our marriage."

"A dear soul, to be sure," she crooned, admiring the colorful blossoms.

Gage was anxious to proceed with the forthcoming events. "Now, my sweet, if you'll indicate what things you want to take along with you, I'd like to be on our way. I've rented a room for an hour at the Wetherburn Tavern so we'll have a place to ready ourselves before going to the church."

Shemaine swept a hand toward her valise and her sheet-covered wedding gown, which lay across it. "All I will need is there."

Gage picked up both their satchels and his clothes as she folded her gown over her free arm. He called to his son, who was watching fish swimming near the barge. "Andrew, will you take Mrs. McGee's hand and escort her to the wagon?" Gage smiled at the wide grin of pleasure that spread across his son's face and his eagerness to comply. Gage knew the task would seem like man's work to the boy. "We'll follow you."

Erich stepped alongside his employer. "Is zhere somethin' I can help vith?"

Gage gave the baggage over willingly and was grateful that he could now lend assistance to his bride. "Allow me, my sweet," he urged, taking her gown and laying it over his own clothes. After a brief adjustment, he presented his arm. "If you'll do me the honor, my lady, I'll attend you to your carriage."

Giving him a radiant smile, Shemaine looped her arm through his and hugged it close to her bosom. As the others proceeded them, they lagged back long enough

for Gage to steal a soft kiss from his bride.
When he raised his head, she sighed with
pleasure and smiled up at him in warm communication as she felt the muscles in his
arm tighten against her breast.

"Tonight you'll be mine, my love," he
breathed in sweet promise.

Williamsburg was a costly gem in comparison to the small hamlet of Newportes
Newes. Shemaine decided that fact after
Gage took them on a wagon tour of the city.
From the Duke of Gloucester Street, she
saw a sizeable palace sitting at the far end
of carefully maintained grounds that were
liberally bedecked with flowers and sculptured shrubs. At least a dozen shops lined
the street. An octagonal brick magazine and
a guardhouse were located a short distance
away. In all, it was a young but beautiful city.

Mary Margaret helped Shemaine dress in
the room at the inn. When she emerged,
Gage turned eagerly to devour her beauty.
His bride was radiant in a pale green polo-
naise adorned with a white shawl collar that
draped her shoulders. Several rows of lace
trimmed the edges of the collar and the mid-
length sleeves. More of the ruffled lace had
been gathered inside the neckline, accen-

tuating her long, graceful neck, and a pert white lace cap, artfully trimmed with green ribbon, covered the upswept knot of fiery hair. A lace handkerchief had been tied about the stems of the flowers, bunching them together, and the resulting bouquet lay over her arm.

Going to her, Gage took her hand in his and brought it to his lips for a kiss. "You're beautiful, my sweet."

Ramsey winked at his fellow cabinetmakers and cast an eye toward the clock. "Ye'd better hurry, Gage, or ye'll be missin' yer own weddin'."

Gage tossed a grin over his shoulder. "Never fear, you grizzled ol' nail-driver. I won't be letting any snails pass beneath my feet."

A chorus of chuckles came from his men. More than any others, they had seen the moody depths into which Gage Thornton had sunk after Victoria's death—and now, in sharp contrast, they witnessed the heights of joy to which he was soaring. The four cabinetmakers settled in to wait once more, but Gage was as good as his word. After bathing away the residue of sweat from his body, he garbed himself in a white shirt and stock, a handsomely tailored dark blue frock coat, and a waistcoat and breeches of a lighter gray hue, all of which he had worn at his first wedding several years prior.

The sight of her groom in gentlemanly apparel made Shemaine recall her mother's concerns after Maurice proposed. The elder had fretted that her daughter was being lured to the altar by his splendid face. That was not entirely true in this case, Shemaine decided in waggish reflection, for she was just as fascinated by her master's exceptional physique.

The Bruton Parish Church was just west of the palace grounds. It was there the small wedding party gathered for the ceremony. At one hour past noon, the rector quietly united Gage Harrison Thornton and Shemaine Patrice O'Hearn in holy matrimony. Mary Margaret and the four men took up positions on either side of the couple while Andrew stood close beside his father. Proudly wearing the wedding ring on his thumb, the boy faced the altar in anticipation of that moment when it would be needed. He was pleased that he had been included in the service, and when asked to provide the ring, he held the tiny digit aloft with a toothy grin.

The pronouncement that the couple had been joined into one was sealed with a kiss, and though it was brief and gentle, Gage's eyes glowed warmly into Shemaine's, assuring her that it was but a small sampling of the passion that would be forthcoming. Taking her hand, he pulled her arm through his, and together they turned to receive the good wishes of their friends.

"A handsome couple, ye be." Mary Margaret sniffed, dabbing at the moisture in her eyes.

"Ye're a lucky man," Ramsey declared, grinning broadly. "But then, I think ye knew that the first time ye saw her."

"Aye, I did," Gage admitted, thinking back on that moment when he had first espied Shemaine sitting on the ship's hatch cover. He had hardly been able to believe she was real and not some vision he had conjured in his mind, but he distinctly recalled having been startled by the sudden clarity of his thoughts almost as soon as he laid eyes on her.

Andrew was somewhat baffled by all the well-wishing, but his father lifted him up in his arms and presented him to his new mother, hoping to help him understand.

"We'll be a family now, Andy, and you'll have a mother, just like Malcolm and Duncan do."

"Sheeaim my mommee?" the boy asked curiously, looking at his parent intently.

"Aye," Gage replied with a nod. "She's your mommy now, just like I'm your daddy."

Andrew waggled his head from side to side and began to chant in childish glee. "Mommee and Daddee! Mommee and Daddee! Mommee and Daddee!"

"I think he likes the sound o' it," Mary Margaret surmised with a chuckle.

"Me hungee," Andrew announced, turning the subject to more important matters.

"You're always hungry," Gage teased, playfully tweaking the tiny nose.

"Me hungee," Shemaine chimed in near her husband's shoulder.

The bridegroom settled a brief but provocative kiss upon her lips. "Will that do, my sweet?"

Wrapping her arms around her new husband and son, Shemaine rose on tiptoes to bestow an affectionate kiss upon Andrew's rosy cheek and then pressed a much warmer one upon Gage's smiling mouth. Even so, she denied that it would be a fair exchange as she gave him a sparkling smile. "As sweet as your kisses are, my dear husband, I must insist that Andrew and I be given something more substantial lest we faint from starvation."

Gage laughed and raised an arm to attract Ramsey's attention. "My family demands nourishment. Will you bring our carriage about, my good man?"

"At yer service, m'lord," his friend replied with a chortle, and sweeping them a bow, he went out to bring the wagon around.

At the Wetherburn Tavern, they enjoyed a hearty repast replete with a liberal amount of toasting and sipping. But as time progressed Gage became increasingly anxious to be home and laughingly bade his guests to return to their conveyance so they could be driven back to the barge ere the day was well spent. It was Gage, the only truly sober one among the men, who finally collected his guests and his family and ushered them back to the craft.

A brief stop was made on the way downriver from Williamsburg to deliver Andrew to the Fields's cottage. There the boy could play with Malcolm and Duncan to his heart's content, allowing his father and new mother to enjoy being alone together in the privacy of their home. After hearing of Gage's plans to marry Shemaine, Hannah had insisted that Andrew stay with her family for several days. His father had willingly acceded. As they were preparing to leave, Hannah smilingly presented the newly espoused couple with a basket of food to enjoy later that evening, knowing the preparation of a meal would likely be considered an intrusion.

"So's ye won't be havin' ta get out o' bed ta eat, I'm thinkin'," Ramsey murmured near the bridegroom's ear after Gage had thanked the woman for her wedding present. Lifting his gaze to the rough-hewn beams of the ceiling, the older man rocked back on his heels. "I've also been thinkin' o' maybe comin' ta do some work in the mornin', just ta catch up with a few things whilst there's no one in the shop."

With a roguishly baleful gleam in his eyes, Gage fixed his gaze upon his favorite cabinetmaker and quietly hissed a warning. "If I see any hint of your ugly face anywhere around my place for the next several days, I'll be doing a little target practice on your ornery hide. If you haven't caught on, my oafish friend, I plan to have Shemaine entirely to myself for the whole of these few days, and I'd not take it kindly if some simple dolt like yourself took a fancy to come out and visit us. Need I explain myself further?"

Ramsey scrubbed a hand reflectively down his mouth several times, managing to smother a grin as he smoothed his bushy mustache. "I guess I can recognize a threat when I hear it."

"Then perhaps there's some hope for you after all, old man," Gage retorted with a chuckle.

Saying his farewells, Gage gave Andrew a loving hug followed by a kiss. "Be a good boy, Andy, and mind Mrs. Fields," he entreated. "I'll come back to get you come Monday morning."

When Gage turned away to speak with Hannah, Shemaine bent down and enfolded the boy in her embrace, exaggerating a lengthy grunt of pleasure as she did so. "I'll miss you, Andy."

Giggling, Andrew responded in kind, and then ran to join his friends, proudly boasting, "Sheeaim my mommee now! My daddee said!"

Grinning, Hannah glanced up at Gage. "I

think your son is as happy to have a mother as you are to have a wife."

"I nearly despaired of finding a woman who could fulfill the requirements of both positions, but Shemaine has proven herself more than capable," Gage replied with a full measure of pride. As his wife came near, he reached out an arm to pull her close against his side and smiled down into her shining green eyes. "I don't know how it could be possible that I could be so fortunate, Hannah, but Shemaine is everything I had been yearning for."

Shemaine reached up a hand and, with the back of her knuckles, gently stroked her bridegroom's cheek. "Even if the choice were presented to me at this moment, I don't think I could leave what I've come to treasure."

Marveling at her words, Gage had no name for the soft, strange emotion that he saw in her luminous gaze, except that it was very close to what he had often seen in Victoria's blue eyes in the blissful hush of sated desires.

CHAPTER 15

When the wedding party arrived at the Thornton cabin, Gage swept his bride into his arms and, leaving his men to assist Mary Margaret, sprinted up to the cabin well ahead of everyone else. For one tantalizing moment before their guests arrived, he clasped his bride to him and kissed her with all the passion he had been holding in check since the night of the dance. His mouth moved demandingly until her soft lips parted with an ardor that matched his own. Then footsteps came across the porch, and Gage recognized Ramsey's overloud remarks on the beauty of the night, no doubt meant to warn him of their approach, and the couple parted shakily to welcome the others as the door was swept open. After much well-wishing and the presentation of handmade gifts by the men, the wedding guests soon dispersed to their various destinations, leaving the couple completely alone.

"Come here, wife," Gage murmured huskily, pulling his bride close again. Taking care not to brush his hand against her healing wound, he slipped an arm about her waist and drew her snugly against him, pressing her soft feminine form against his muscular body. In the warm glow of the lantern light, his eyes leisurely drank their fill, savoring the intoxicating beauty of her face. Ever so slowly he lowered his mouth upon hers and caressed her eagerly parting lips with a long, languid kiss. It was bold and astonishingly thorough in its possession, yet provocative and persuasive in its gentleness. Shemaine's reserve was rapidly stripped away, and with mounting passion she answered him, holding nothing back. Her small tongue was lured to play chase with his, and as his hand wandered with bold familiarity over her hip, she leaned into him, feeling her breasts tingle against the hard contours of his chest.

Gage finally raised his head, and his hungering gaze feasted upon her delicate features. "Do you have any inkling how often I yearned to take you in my arms and kiss you until you begged me to stop? My desire for you began in earnest that first night when I saw you standing beside my kitchen table, freshly washed and gowned. I realized then I wouldn't be able to keep my hands off of you for the full seven years of your indentured service. I only bided my time until I gleaned some chance of you accepting my proposal of marriage."

"Would you like to know a secret, Mr. Thornton?" Shemaine whispered with a winsome smile. "When you stepped through the doorway that very same night and pulled your wet shirt over your head, I think that must have been the moment Maurice du Mercer began to fade into the shadows of oblivion."

Gage cocked his head in wonderment, thoroughly amazed. "Was it now?"

"If you didn't know it, sir, you're quite a handsome man for a woman to feast her eyes upon, even with all your clothes on," she murmured warmly.

"Right now, you're one step ahead of me."

It was Shemaine's turn to cant her head and stare up at him in confusion. "How so, sir?"

"I haven't yet seen you completely naked, and that I'm most anxious to do, madam."

"Oh, but when you killed the snake, I had nothing on beneath the towel," she argued.

"I noticed," Gage assured her with a grin. "The towel was not as wet as I would have preferred, but I relished the way it teased me with a glimpse of this . . ." He stroked the back of a finger lightly over a nipple, indicating the place and, in the process, sending waves of scintillating delight flaring through her senses and causing her breath to halt at the thrill of his touch. " 'Tis no lie that I wanted to make love to you that night and many times afterwards."

Shemaine remembered the hunger she had seen in his gaze and recalled how after her first lesson with the flintlock she had trembled with her own yearning needs every time he had touched her. "I'm glad you couldn't read my mind."

"Why is that, my sweet?"

"You would have been shocked by what I was thinking."

"Then 'tis well you couldn't read mine, madam, for you'd have thought me a lascivious rogue."

Shemaine giggled as she snuggled her head beneath his chin. "Do you want to eat now? Hannah outdid herself cooking for us."

"I'm hungry for you, wife." Sliding his hands down the length of her back to her buttocks, Gage pressed her tightly to him, making her aware of his hotly flaming passion. "My needs prod me sore, and I would be about consummating our marriage ere the hour is out. Beyond that time, I'd be hard-pressed to endure the wait."

At his boldness, a sultry excitement blazed in her body. "I made a new nightgown for our wedding night. Will you allow me time to prepare myself for you?"

"Be quick about it," Gage urged softly.

"I will," she promised. Rising on her toes, she lifted her mouth to meet his and felt thoroughly inflamed by his fervor as he kissed her with fiery passion. Drawing away with a rapturous sigh, she slipped away from him and hurried to his bedroom door. There she paused to smile back at him. "You will come when I call?"

His grin would have convinced her by itself, but his verbal answer set aside any idea of a delay. "Aye, madam. Nothing short of this earth crumbling could deter me from reaching your side."

Leaving the door ajar behind her, Shemaine entered the room and marveled at the preparations that had been made for them. Candles had been lit on either side of the bed, and the sheets and bedcovers had been folded down invitingly to display sunbleached linens adorned with Irish lace, no doubt a gift from a certain widow. Shemaine's new nightgown had been carefully laid out on one side, and with an excited gasp, she realized that it had also been embellished around the collar and cuffs with smaller bands of the same intricate needlework.

"Oh, Mary Margaret," she crooned softly in awe. "How very talented you are."

Hearing an indistinct murmur, Gage stepped close to the door. "Shemaine? Are you all right?"

"Aye, husband," Shemaine laughingly reassured him. "I was just admiring Mary Margaret's lacework on the new bed linens she gave us, but please don't come in yet. You can see everything in a moment."

Gage paced restlessly about the parlor, trying to bide his time. Readying himself for his bride as much as he dared without running the chance of startling her, he doffed his frock coat, laid aside his waistcoat, and then stripped away the stock, freeing the opening of his shirt. He prowled the interior again, and several moments later found himself searching through a little-used cabinet for a bottle of Madeira that had been stored there. Finding the flask tucked behind several other brews, he drew it out, broke the wax seal, and poured a small sampling into a cup. He tasted it and deemed it worthy enough to share with his young bride.

At last Shemaine called to him from his bedroom. "You may come in now, Gage."

"Aye, love . . . be right there," he replied, and hastened to find a pair of heavy crystal goblets which Victoria had once foreseen as the first acquisitions of a collection she had hoped to complete. He splashed the dark wine into the bottom of each and, pushing open the bedroom door with a shoulder, carried them into the bedroom. Pausing just beyond the threshold, he smiled as his gaze settled on his bride. Shemaine was sitting up in his bed with her back braced against a lace-edged pillow that cushioned the headboard. Gowned in a soft, gossamer creation trimmed with tiny tucks and delicate lace, she was a stirringly beautiful example of what every bridegroom held hopes of viewing on his wedding night.

Gage recalled his burning desire to have his way with her, especially after she had accepted his proposal. Yet in spite of the anguish he had suffered being around her and wanting her with every fiber in his being, he had been reluctant to take her virginity while she was still his bondslave. He hadn't wanted her to feel as if she must yield to his demands. As his gaze caressed her now, he was gratified that he hadn't pressed her unduly. The wait had been worth all of his fleshly cravings. She was his bride, his lovely one, and tonight would be forever marked in their memory as the one in which they came together as man and wife.

"Mary Margaret gave us these for a wedding present." Shemaine swept a hand about to indicate the lace-trimmed sheets and pillowcases. "She made the lace by hand."

Moving around to the side of the bed where Shemaine sat, Gage passed her a goblet with a token kiss. Then, as she sampled the contents of the glass, he ran a hand admiringly over the dainty threadwork, remembering Mary Margaret's haste to shoo him out of his own bedroom that morning before they left for Williamsburg, and then, only a little while ago, her smiling reticence and her quick flight to the bedroom while Ramsey and the other men presented their own handsome, wood-crafted gifts.

"That lady is a blooming marvel in more ways than I'd ever dare to count," Gage quipped with a grin.

Shemaine lightly brushed her fingers across the lace of her collar, drawing his regard. "Mary Margaret trimmed my nightgown, too."

Gage's eyes glowed above a smile as his gaze devoured her in a sweeping glance. Setting aside his goblet, he sat down beside her and lifted a lighted taper aloft to closely inspect the minutely detailed edging.

" 'Tis beautiful," he breathed, but his eyes were drawn irresistibly downward to the tan-

talizing fullness of her bosom. In the candlelight the translucent cloth was barely a milky
haze over the delicate pink and creamy perfection of her breasts. Victoria's thinness
had extended to her bosom, and except for
the months she had nursed Andrew, she
had been rather self-conscious about the
smallness of her breasts, even though she
had never been less than womanly to him.
Now here he was admiring ample curves
that made him tremble with anticipation.

Shemaine felt suffocated by the heat of his
perusal, but she waited in silence as his eyes
slowly swept her meagerly clad bosom and
the heavy single braid she had intertwined
with ribbon. The thick brush of black lashes
veiled his beautiful eyes from her, forbidding
her visual access into those translucent
depths, and though she searched his noble
visage, she had no way of knowing what to
expect. She could only wonder if this
stranger, to whom she was now married,
would turn suddenly savage in his quest to
fulfill his desires.

Gathering her fingers and lifting them to
his mouth, Gage met her wide-eyed stare as
he lightly nibbled the slender knuckles. Then
he smiled with incredible warmth, and it was

like all of paradise opening before Shemaine. Her breath slipped from her in a
softly fluttering sigh of awe.

"Aye, my sweet, the gown is beautiful," he
breathed, "but not nearly as lovely as the
one who wears it."

Gage returned the candlestand to the table and, leaning near his young wife, bent
his head aslant to caress her mouth with his
own. The kiss was warm and heady, no less
intoxicating than the Madeira, a leisured
meeting of parting lips and questing
tongues, the eagerness of one yielding to
the bold intrusion of the other. A faint sigh
wafted from Shemaine's lips as his kisses
blazed a trail along her throat, brushing past
the delicate lace collar and continuing downward until his mouth claimed the soft peak
of her breast. She caught her breath at the
sudden jolt of pleasure that leapt through
her. The sultry wetness penetrated the delicate fabric of her nightgown, torching the
sensitive pinnacle until a breathless moan
escaped her lips. Her head fell back upon
the pillow as her senses basked in pure
bliss, and for a moment she wondered if she
would be able to bear it all without dissolving
in ecstasy.

"Oh, don't stop," she begged in a plaintive whisper as her husband drew back. Her whole body quaked with what he had started. Lifting her head, she searched his chiseled face, silently pleading for him to continue.

The brown eyes delved into hers as he leaned over her. " 'Tis only a brief delay to allow me to disrobe, my love," he murmured huskily. Clasping a hand over a breast, he stroked a thumb across the dampened cloth molding the peak. "I must pace myself carefully lest I cheat you of your wifely pleasure."

"Oh, sir, I daresay you haven't been cheating me," Shemaine assured him in a voice that quavered with emotion. "Feel my heart, how it quakes beneath your touch." She caressed the back of his hand lightly with her fingertips as he pressed the fullness more firmly to feel the swiftly thumping rhythm beneath. "You see? You make me anxious for more of what you have to teach."

"Never have I had a more willing student," Gage breathed, turning his palm toward hers and threading his fingers through hers. Lifting her hand to his lips, he pressed another kiss upon the back of it and then rose to his feet, making no effort to turn aside as her gaze was drawn irresistibly downward. Almost as quickly the green orbs flew upward to meet his smiling regard. "Aye, madam, I'm anxious, too."

Gage moved around the end of the bed and approached a chair that stood against the far wall. Turning aside slightly to spare her the full shock of his arousal, he stripped to his breeches. Peeling that garment downward, he clasped a knee and, with his other hand, dragged the narrow legging free as his young bride eyed him furtively. Muscles flexed tautly in his buttocks and thighs as he balanced on one foot. Shifting his weight to his right leg, he raised his left knee to pull the breeches free, allowing other manly parts to come boldly into view. Shemaine felt a scalding hotness rushing into her cheeks as she viewed the fullness thrusting outward from under his thigh. Unable to drag her gaze away, she sat as one frozen by shock. The moonlight by which she had twice observed him had been rather deceptive, revealing his body as something incredibly beautiful. It was all of that, to be sure, but it was immensely threatening as well. At the moment nothing seemed quite as intimidating as that bold blade of passion.

Gage turned back to the bed in all of his naked glory, and Shemaine quickly averted her gaze, fixing it nervously upon the armoire until he slipped into bed. Tactfully keeping the lace-edged linen over his hips, Gage slid close beside her and propped a pillow behind his back as he leaned against the headboard. He noticed the trembling of her hands and, taking one, threaded his fingers through hers. With a free hand he turned her face to his until he could search those wide, hesitant green eyes.

"Are you afraid, Shemaine?"

"A little," she confessed in a barely audible whisper.

"It seems but a fleeting discomfort, my sweet," Gage said gently. "A sacrifice for a bride, to be sure, but a small one compared to the pleasure that's to be had beyond the rending of her virginity. And I promise you, dearest wife, I will give you as much enjoyment as I'm able."

When her bridegroom seemed so concerned with her fear, Shemaine could not believe he would be anything but considerate of her. Though the smile she offered him still wavered unsteadily, it was from the heart. " 'Twas nothing more than a fleeting moment of panic, Mr. Thornton."

"Aye, Mrs. Thornton," Gage replied, comforted by the tender gaze she bestowed upon him. "Now, madam, I would like to propose a toast to our marriage." Reaching across her, he claimed his goblet and waited until she had lifted her own glass. Then he smiled into her searching eyes. "May it be all that we both want it to be, and after a long life together, may we look back in peaceful contentment, knowing we've been amply blessed with a large family."

"Hear! Hear!" Shemaine agreed, her cheerfulness restored. Looping her arm through his, she tentatively took a sip. The wine was a bit stronger than she was used to, and she had to clear her throat before she could beg a blessing of her own. "And may we find at the end of our lives that we've enjoyed a deep love that has bound us together in a caring, nurturing unity."

"Amen!"

They dissolved into laughter and leaned their heads together to sip from their glasses again. A brief meeting of their lips promptly dissolved their amusement and swiftly ushered them toward emotions far more sensual. Gage took their goblets and set them aside. Then he raised an arm and laid it around his wife's shoulders, gathering her close for another kiss. It was an enticing exchange of lip and tongue, breathless sighs blended with the flavor of Madeira, and a leisured exploration of two hearts and minds in one accord. When Gage lifted his head, his warmly flecked eyes delved glowingly into hers as he plucked open the buttons of her gown. They were tiny and difficult, but he was tenacious.

He swept the garment open, pushing it around one creamy mound and then another until the swelling ripeness of her bosom thrust forward impudently. Shemaine watched him with bated breath as he indulged his senses, searing her skin with the heat of his gaze and making her shiver with ecstasy as he stroked a thumb across a soft, pliant peak.

In some awe Gage feasted his gaze on the lustrous orbs, amazed at their perfection. They were creamy satin adorned with delicate pink rosebuds, incredibly soft to the touch. Beneath his roaming hand, they seemed even more daintily hued.

"I'm besotted with such rich fare laid bare before me," Gage whispered. "You're more beautiful than I imagined."

He leaned down to lightly caress a pink crest with a licking torch, snatching her breath for one ecstatic moment. Then he straightened, and Shemaine's disappointment reached its zenith. She watched him worriedly until she realized he had only paused to readjust their positions. He pulled her lower in the bed, and a soft mewl escaped her lips as his mouth returned to take full possession, devouring the hills and valleys with ravenous greed. Her fingers slipped through the hair at the back of his nape as she arched her back, thrusting the creamy mounds upward against the wet, fiery brand that caressed her nipples with slow, undulating strokes. His teasing tongue sent sparks flaring upward until she was nearly overwhelmed by the ever-rushing excitement washing over her. It was difficult to catch her breath with such pleasure billowing over her, arousing her to a heightening fervor that made her loins hungry for appeasement.

The sheet was dragged away from her silken limbs, and a lengthy caress of a slender thigh swept her gown upward. Even as his mouth worked its wiles upon her breasts, his hand slipped between her thighs with purposeful intent, quickening her breath and evoking soft blissful moans of pleasure with his rousing enchantment.

When he drew away, Shemaine followed eagerly, lifting her face to claim another passionate kiss. Gage held nothing back, seizing her mouth much like a starving man who had just been served a feast. A sigh slipped from her lips when the kiss ended, but the effects lingered like a strong intoxicant, leaving her in a delicious trance. She was only vaguely aware that her gown was being pulled up over her body and lifted free of her arms and head. Then she was swept flat upon the bed, and when her husband pulled her close, she could feel every muscular curve and bulge of his naked body. The experience was immensely arousing. No longer did she fear the warm, alien hardness that she had glimpsed and now felt against her.

Gage was aware of the strengthening tremors quaking through his own body as he struggled to pace himself and forestall the driving urges that raged within him. His hard-won restraint was sorely tested, but when he felt the timid brush of his wife's hand against his thigh and her slender fingers searching out the manly hardness, he was brought up short by the sweet, brutal intensity of his hunger.

"Ah, love, you've lit fires that must now be quenched," he rasped, closing his steely fingers around hers. It was exquisite torture, but he could not endure it for long. He was far too close to ecstasy to trust himself. "My needs roil in merry pain, madam, yet I would seek to give you pleasure ere my release."

Sweeping her beneath him, Gage kissed her with all the zeal of a lusting suitor as his manhood probed within the sweet moistness of her. Penetration came with a clean, swift thrust, startling a gasp from his bride. Yet he held himself in rigid reserve upon the threshold of rapture, soothing her pain and fears, kissing her mouth and fondling her soft breasts until by gradual degrees he could feel her warmth yielding to his intrusion, becoming more pliant and, then, increasingly hungry for what was coming.

It was a ritual of lovers, mesmerizing movements that made Shemaine's breath come in quickening gasps and her heart race to a swifter rhythm, nearly matching the thunderous roar of her husband's. Like silk, her limbs twined about his narrow hips, catching him close against her as her fingertips dug into the muscular ridges of his back. Responding to the guiding hands beneath her buttocks, she rose upward to meet the surging strokes of his body. Of a sudden, she felt driven by some strange, heightening urgency that she had been hitherto ignorant of. Gage knew it well enough and sought it with fervor and zeal, and it came for them both in a stunning array of splintering brightness that pulsed in an ever-increasing crescendo through the fibers of their beings, lifting them on soaring wings to a rapturous exultation and ultimately into a dazzling pinnacle beyond the realm of reality, into a place of such pure bliss that it left them spellbound as they floated like soft thistledown back to earth and their own bed.

Shemaine clasped a trembling hand to her brow and gazed up in amazement at her smiling husband. His eyes glowed with a luster that she had never seen before. "Oh, Mr. Thornton, you *do* overwhelm a girl."

"And you, my beautiful Shemaine, have amazed this erstwhile widower far beyond my expectations," he averred. "I cannot, in truth, lay the merit to my lengthy abstinence. Were I to search out the cause for such exquisite delight, I'd lay it to your eagerness to pleasure me and be satisfied in return."

Shemaine was a bit concerned about her own behavior. "You are displeased with my boldness?"

"Indeed no, madam!" Gage laughed at the absurdity of the idea. "I was gratified beyond belief to discover that you are a very passionate woman, so gratified I would like another taste! But you are tender, and I promised I'd be careful of you."

Shemaine twined her silken arms about his neck, enjoying the thrilling pressure of his manly body upon her own. "Strange, I don't feel tender."

"Perhaps we should explore this matter further," Gage suggested, contemplating the idea. Still, there were other things he wanted to show her. "But 'twill have to wait until a later moment, my sweet. Right now, I have a surprise for you. Your wedding present awaits in another room."

"My wedding present?" Shemaine was clearly astounded. "But I have nothing for you."

"How can you say that, dear wife, when you have just given me what I've been yearning for ever since I brought you home with me?" He kissed her with renewed ardor, making her aware of his passion. "There now, you see how much I want you? But I'm just as eager to show you your gift."

Gage withdrew from her and, rolling to the edge of the bed, came to his feet. Striding to the door in naked grandeur, he paused there to look back at his wife, who had been intent upon observing him until he glanced around. Shyly she dragged the sheet up to cover her nakedness as he grinned invitingly. "Are you coming?"

Eagerly Shemaine nodded and left the bed, wrapping the top sheet around her and tucking the tail of it between her breasts. As she came forward, Gage's gaze wandered back to the bed. Glancing over her shoulder to see what had caught his attention, Shemaine saw the red stains marring the whiteness of the sheet. Her cheeks brightened with a blush, but her husband laid an arm around her creamy shoulders and pulled her close against his side, saying nothing, only smiling.

As Gage led her into the parlor, Shemaine

couldn't resist a glance askance at his manly torso. Though her husband seemed completely at ease with his lack of attire, she was still timid about openly appeasing her curiosity. Like so many other parents with their daughters, her own had preferred to shelter her, keeping her for the most part ignorant and in the dark about men. Yet their reticence had in no wise prevented Shemaine from being curious. She was eager to gain all the wifely knowledge she could about her husband, for no one had to tell her that Gage Thornton was truly a fine specimen of the male gender.

Gage smiled as he glanced down and caught her ogling him. "Can I interest you in taking a bath with me, my dear?"

"You jest, of course." Considering the limited space in the washtub, Shemaine was sure he was teasing her. "We'll certainly need a larger tub if we're ever to share one together."

"Do you not think such a thing would make a fitting wedding present?" he asked, leaning down to brush his lips against her brow.

Placing a hand on his chest, Shemaine leaned her head back to look up into his face as he straightened. "What would make a fitting wedding present?"

Gage swept a hand toward the closed door of the storeroom. "After you, madam."

A slight frown of confusion lingered on her face as she picked up a tallow lantern and led the way toward the back. Pushing open the door of the storeroom, Shemaine gasped in surprise as she saw a lavish bathtub, easily large enough for two, in the middle of the room. A folding screen stood behind it, and as her eyes swept about the small room, she realized that it no longer resembled a storage area but was a bathing chamber outfitted with a washstand, a dressing table with its own chair, Gage's shaving stand, and a chamber chair barely visible beyond a screen. There was even a tall stool near the washstand, no doubt to aid Andrew in reaching it.

Gage followed her through the doorway and, taking the lantern from her, lit several other candles to chase away the darkness. "I had the Morgans working in here while we were gone today. Do you like the changes they made?"

"Oh, yes, Gage!" Whirling, Shemaine flung her arms about his neck, giving him an exuberant hug, and then leaned back in his arms to express her pleasure in eager tones. "Thank you for being so thoughtful!"

Gage smiled down at her. "I've noticed how much you relish your baths and thought of the pleasure I would derive from sharing them with you when I have the time. The tub is too heavy for you to move on your own, even when it's empty, so I determined that it needed to be drained where it stood. I had Flannery Morgan bore a hole at one end of it, fashion copper sheathing into a funnel beneath the hole and extend more of the sheathing under the floor so the water could run away from the house. All you need do, madam, is pull the cork out of the hole in the tub and watch it drain."

Shemaine marveled at the cleverness of his plan. "You're ingenious, Mr. Thornton!"

His brows flicked upward as he dismissed her compliment. "I was motivated to a great degree by my own desires. You're a very tempting bride, Shemaine, and I wanted to share with you all the comforts and pleasures I could possibly imagine."

A smile coyly curved her soft lips. "No one need tell me how vivid your imagination is, sir. There is ample proof of that everywhere I turn."

A slow grin accompanied his reply. "It always helps to be inspired by such beauty as yours, my sweet."

"Now you'll be able to enjoy the comfort of bathing indoors," she pointed out happily.

Gage reached up to pluck the corner of the sheet from the enticing valley between her breasts. "Bathing in the stream isn't so bad when it's shared by two who are enamored of each other. On the morrow I'll show you some of the delights to be had there." Sweeping his hands downward over her round breasts and slender waist, he watched her eyes grow dark and limpid as he hastened the descent of the sheet. It caught on her hips, where it lay bunched in folds.

"Shall we add the water now?" she asked breathlessly.

"Get the soap and the towels," Gage bade huskily, leaning near to nibble at her ear. "I'll get the water." But he made no effort to leave as his hands continued their stroking caresses downward, loosening the sheet in the process.

Shemaine caught the falling linen and,

swirling it around behind her, held it out-spread like giant wings as she willingly sub-mitted herself to the magical seduction of his hands. They moved with knowledgeable boldness over her body and were complete in their possession, exploring, fondling, and searching out the hidden places. The ec-stasy he elicited made her catch her breath in quick snatches and then slowly release it in blissful sighs. Like a moth warmed by a flame, she followed irresistibly as he stepped slowly backward toward the high stool. Upon reaching it, he sat upon the edge. Her eyes glazed with passion as he lifted her astride him and resettled her onto the full warmth of him. The sheet fluttered to the floor unheeded as she arched her back over his encompassing arms, thrusting her breasts forward to meet his hot, greedy kisses and the blazing heat of his tongue. His hand slipped downward to clasp her but-tocks, urging her response in the sensual rites of love and passion. She stroked against him with increasing intensity until a surging rapture began to wash over her, wrenching breathless gasps from her. Gage's own breathing grew harsh and rag-ged as his passion raged in a zealous quest to be sated. Once again they were forged together in a rhapsodic bliss, and it was a very long moment before reality came sweeping back.

In the aftermath of their lovemaking, Shemaine snuggled within her husband's encompassing arms, unwilling to break away. Gage held her close, caressing her mouth with his own or closing her eyelids with gentle kisses as he luxuriated in the silky softness of her breasts against his chest and the gratifying feel of her warmth encompassing his manhood.

Soon after they parted, Gage wrapped Shemaine in the sheet until it resembled an enveloping cocoon. She sat on the high stool with a foot balanced on a rung, another drawn up on the seat, and a knee tucked beneath her chin. Gage paused briefly at the washstand for a quick cleansing and then started carrying in buckets of water for their bath. Her husband seemed totally uninhibited about his nakedness, and it was so tempting for Shemaine to watch him. She yearned to appease her own curiosity and found her knowledge of the male form increasing by leaps and bounds as she observed him. Still, whenever he came her way, she cast her gaze elsewhere, unwilling to let him know of her wanton interest in his manly habits and parts.

Finally the bath was ready, and Gage returned to the stool where his young wife perched. "Your bath is ready, m'lady," he said, taking her hand and drawing her up from the stool. "And your husband is eager to share it with you."

Shemaine paused to readjust the sheet, but Gage caught her hand, halting her.

"You're far too comely to be kept under a tarp, madam. Besides, I want to look at you. Do you want to look at me?"

Despite the vivid blush that swept downward nigh to her breasts, Shemaine nodded in quick answer. "Aye! I want to very much."

"Then I give you leave to look at me to your heart's content," Gage invited warmly. Taking her hand, he stroked it down his firm torso. "It pleasures me to have you do so."

"And it pleasures me to do so," Shemaine breathed, feeling the drumbeat of her own heart as he instructed her in the art of fondling, as much to her awe and delight as his.

His whisper was ragged and strained. "You see, madam? I'm naught but potter's clay in your hands."

"No potter's clay, I trow," she sighed in admiration, "but a mighty oak."

"Then come, little bird, and perch upon my branch," he coaxed, pressing his lips against her temple.

"What about our bath?"

"We will enjoy it to the utmost, madam, for 'twill be there that the mighty oak will be felled by a little bird."

CHAPTER 16

The jubilant trilling of birds nesting in the tall pine near the bedroom window awakened the newly wedded couple, rousing them to a delectable awareness of each other and the dawning of a new day. As her husband stirred against her back, Shemaine smiled sleepily, enjoying the feel of his hard, masculine form against her own. She lay on her side, nestled in the cradle of his naked body with his thighs tucked close beneath her own. After no more than a few moments of wear, her new nightgown had been discarded and draped over the same chair where his clothes had been left the night before. Only the bed linens covered them, and underneath, their bodies were as warm as their thoughts.

"As much as I desire to stay here and have my way with you once more, my sweet," Gage breathed close against her ear, "I must leave this sweet haven and attend the morning chores."

Shemaine snuggled back against him, reluctant to have him go. "We didn't get much sleep."

"Aye, we spent too much time dallying in the tub, but what does sleep matter when we enjoyed such bliss? I can still see your wet, lovely body in the candlelight, the glistening hills and the shadowed valleys, tempting me to touch and to taste."

Even now the memory of his passionate fervor drew her breath out in a halting sigh. She had been no less intrigued by the sight of him. The tiny flames had bathed his glistening frame with a golden aura, highlighting the knotted sinews over his lean ribs and the long, flexing cords in his shoulders, thighs and arms, leaving her much in awe of his manly physique. "Never has a wedding gift been put to such amorous use, I think, and never again will I make the mistake of thinking that a couples' bed is the only place where children are conceived."

"If we're alone together, madam, any moment is ripe, any place convenient for making love, whether it's fully clothed or as bare as the day we came into the world. It doesn't matter. When two are willing, there's always a way."

"I shall endeavor to look for such opportunities to challenge your statement, sir," she teased, finding the idea of such a venture totally intriguing.

"Don't be surprised if they come upon you unexpectedly," Gage warmly advised, pressing himself against her buttocks to illustrate his statement.

Shemaine lifted a bare foot and stroked it along his hard calf. "As long as I can hear your footsteps, you'll find me waiting in anticipation."

His hand slid over the tantalizing curve of her hip and wandered downward along the side of her thigh as he leaned forward to caress her cheek with the gentle brush of his lips. "Will you wait for me here until I get back?"

Shemaine cast him a look of surprise over her shoulder. "Would you not rather have me cook you the morning meal? We hardly touched the food that Hannah sent home with us. She'll be disappointed to learn how little we ate of it."

Gage chuckled softly. "I'm sure Hannah would understand if we were to tell her, but I see no need of that, madam, do you?"

A sigh of delight slipped from her as his mouth slid down her throat and across her shoulder. " 'Twould only make Hannah wonder what we were doing."

His laughing breath warmed her skin. "Considering the number of children she has given birth to, I'm sure she'll be able to guess."

Shemaine wondered if all couples were as active on their wedding night as they had been, but she immediately remembered that a few of her friends in England, after becoming brides, had voiced their aversion "to everything that went on in a marriage bed." She, on the other hand, had been immensely thrilled and pleasured by Gage's passion. " 'Tis best to be discreet," she reasoned. "We wouldn't want anyone to think we spent the whole night in a private orgy."

"Ahh, but we did, madam," Gage replied, his voice imbued with humor.

Smiling, Shemaine nestled in cozy contentment against him. "I know, Gage, but no one else need know that. They'd really be inclined to think you married a wanton."

Her husband sighed, as if in rueful reflection. "It seems there's no help for it. Truth has a way of coming out."

Shemaine gasped in a feigned display of temper. "Oh, you cad! You English rogue! You use me and then abuse me! What a contemptible knave you are!"

Laughing in glee, she would have scrambled from the bed, but Gage flung out an arm and pulled her back. For a moment, they wrestled in playful abandon until he threw a thigh over her thrashing limbs. Spreading her arms out wide, he pinned her wrists to the mattress and rose above her.

"Did I not tell you how much I relish having a beautiful wanton in my bed?" he whispered, plying her soft mouth with sultry kisses.

"If I'm a wanton, sir," she rejoined, readily adjusting herself to accommodate his encroaching weight, "then you're the one who has made me insatiable for the delights to be had between a husband and a wife." She spoke partly in jest, but mostly in truth, for he had aroused her ardor provocatively, sweeping her to heights of unimaginable ecstasy, making her eager for more of his attention.

Gage braced on his elbows above her, and his brown eyes burned with a consuming fire as they caressed her face. "Think of what we can learn together, my sweet."

"You mean there is still that which you do not know?" Shemaine asked in amazement.

Gage was amused and yet a bit staggered by the idea that his bride thought him completely knowledgeable about women. "There is much I have to learn, my sweet, especially about you. If we're fortunate enough to live out our lives together, then I'm sure you'll come to read me like an old book that you've memorized over the years. I hope you won't become too bored with me."

Shemaine scoffed in light-hearted skepticism. "Hardly that, Mr. Thornton! Truly, I fear the reverse may prove true."

"Never!"

"The morning sun is rising," she reminded him softly.

"Aye, I know, and I suppose I must let you go, but only if you promise not to get dressed," Gage bargained. "That first morning you were here, when you were scurrying around in the kitchen, trying to cook us a meal, I have memorized the way you looked then, all soft and unfettered beneath your nightclothes. I tell you truly, madam, my senses were besotted with the way your garments clung to your backside and breasts. Your nipples seemed eager for attention, and I was even more eager to give it."

Shemaine moaned, recalling her own disquiet that morning. "So that's why you were looking at me so hard."

Gage slid his hands from her wrists inward along her arms and then downward over her breasts. "You were so alluring, I wanted to have my way with you then and there." He grinned as he added, "And many times thereafter."

Shemaine lifted a hand and threaded slender fingers through his black, rumpled hair. "If I had known what awaited me, I would have been eager to wed soon after we left the *London Pride.* You do have a way about you, Mr. Thornton. Truly, when I think of what I've been missing, I wonder if

I should feel envious of all the women you've made love to over the years."

A dark brow twisted upward dubiously. "What do you think me, madam? A rapacious libertine? Have I not assured you that I've been selective with the women I bed down with?" Lifting himself off her, he snuggled alongside and braced up on an elbow to grin down at her. "Besides, when I first started searching for a mate, you were not old enough to catch my eye. Why, you're no more than a babe now."

"Do I look like a babe?" Shemaine queried, feigning a pout. Stretching sensuously for his consideration, she won his unswerving attention.

"Nay, madam, and that's a plain fact." The amber-lit brown eyes blazed with fiery warmth as he watched her pale body writhe invitingly upon the bed. "Has anyone ever told you how perfectly beautiful you are without your clothes? Especially this delectable portion here." He was caressing her breasts and was struck by the sharp contrast between their fairness and his sun-bronzed hand. The morning light streaming in through the pine boughs outside the window gave the luscious globes the look of alabaster. The lure of such perfection was irresistible, and he leaned down to savor the delectable sweetness of a pale peak, branding her with the white-hot heat of his mouth and halting her breath with the warm caress of his tongue.

"If you continue along this path, sir," she whispered tremblingly, "be assured that I'll be unwilling to let you go until you finish what you start."

Gage was also having second thoughts about leaving and would have proceeded with his manly bent except that his wife's stomach growled, making him cognizant of her lengthy fast. "I suppose you're hungry for food."

"I'm famished," Shemaine admitted, and then giggled as he growled in mock anger and threatened to take a playful nip out of her breast. "I can't help it! You're a slave driver."

"Slave driver, eh?" His laughing breath brushed her ear. "And here I thought I was being lenient with you. Should I show you what demands I'd make if you were not still tender?"

"Oh, yes!"

Her enthusiasm made him laugh with

hearty mirth. Thus far, he had found no hindrance to his incessant demands. Nor would he, it seemed. "I will, my sweet, but you'll need nourishment to give you strength. So, my little bird, it must be *after* you're fed. Now get you up, wife, and cook a meal fit for your husband."

Shemaine gasped in surprise as he whipped the covers back, leaving them without a stitch. Laughing, she scrambled across the mattress, only to find him moving quickly after her. As she came to her feet, she realized he was already rising behind her. Catching hold of the corner post, she sought to swing herself around it, but she could not escape his reaching arm and was promptly swept backward to that wonderfully exciting form.

"You shan't escape me, vixen," Gage rasped near her ear as his hands moved over her body in slow, provocative caresses. He turned her, and his descending mouth snared hers as he clasped her tightly to him. Shemaine answered him with quickening passion, eagerly pressing her soft curves to the steely hardness of his, but it soon became evident to them both that if they did not desist posthaste, the chores would never get done. Reluctantly Gage set her from him.

"Alas, I must milk the poor cow ere she bursts." Yet his hands came up to leisurely stroke her bosom while his eyes caressed and admired the tempting roundness. "Though I'd much rather stay here and milk the sweet nectar from these pale breasts."

Sitting back upon the bed, Gage pulled her close between his thighs and hungrily mouthed the luscious fullness until Shemaine's strength waned. She melted against him with no more resistance than a rag doll. His own driving need began to goad Gage, and he gave up trying to resist, becoming more purposeful as he pulled her silken thighs across his.

"Did you always ride sidesaddle when you raced your stallion across the fields?" he whispered huskily.

Somewhat confused, Shemaine searched his face. "Not always."

Gage's lips curved with seductive enticement. "I know you've ridden astride. Does it pleasure you to do so?"

A glimmer of understanding dawned, provoking a responding smile from Shemaine's lips. "Aye, when I have a fine stallion beneath me."

"What think you of me, madam?"

"The very best, I trow," she sighed, sweeping her hands admiringly over his chest as he leaned back upon the bed. He moved effortlessly, carrying their weight to the center of the bed, and smiled up at her with glowing eyes as he joined himself to her.

"Ride to your heart's content, my lady fair."

No other stallion had ever served her as well as this muscular, bronzed-skin Hercules who raced beneath her. Sweeping her ever onward, he drew her breath out in panting gasps with his thrilling boldness, surging upward to meet her and touching her in ways that made her shiver with delight. Scintillating excitement washed over her, as if she raced through the breakers crashing upon a beach. She could almost feel the wind swirling through her hair, the salt spray snatching her breath and misting her naked body with tiny droplets as her hips stroked with quickening intensity the sleek, sturdy loins rising up beneath her own. The ride became more dedicated until the billowing spasms swept over them, bathing them in joyful rapture and sweeping them out into a sea of ecstasy.

Time ceased to be as they drifted ever so slowly back to shore, where they lay locked together in sweet repose. It was some moments later when Gage finally left his bride. Curled languidly upon the bed, Shemaine watched with curious interest and pleasure as her husband took buckskin britches from the armoire and yanked them on. He fastened them, pulled on a pair of soft hide boots, and then came back to the bed. Smiling down into her glowing green eyes, he spread a sheet over her lovely body.

"You were right, my sweet."

A slight twisting of her brow conveyed her confusion.

"You do ride well."

The corners of Shemaine's lips turned upward enticingly. "I had an excellent steed, the finest I've ever ridden."

Gage dipped his head in acknowledgment of her compliment and then asked, "Would you care for a dip in the stream after we eat?"

His wife shivered at the thought. "Too cold."

"I'll keep you warm," Gage coaxed.

Shemaine raised a wondering brow at him, realizing he was serious. "The sun is up. Anybody who happened by could see us."

"I warned my men to stay away. They wouldn't dare intrude upon us."

"And Potts? What of him?"

"Until his wound heals, 'tis unlikely he'll have the endurance to come this far from the hamlet, even if he's there." Gage canted his head and gave her a beguiling smile. "I can teach you some things we haven't done yet."

Shemaine pursed her lips in a coy pout. " 'Tis unfair the way you bribe me."

"Aye, I know," he replied with a chuckle.

"Go get your chores done, my handsome husband," she urged with sudden enthusiasm. "And be quick about it. As for me, I'll see what I can cook up for us in a hurry."

His laughter accompanied his exit, and Shemaine found herself smiling dreamily at the ceiling as she recalled the night of passion they had shared together. She was now convinced that Gage Thornton was far more clever at making love than he was at building furniture, and that profession, to be sure, he excelled at.

The moments passed swiftly as they completed their separate tasks, and an hour aged into two while they broke the morning fast together. Seated on the same bench, they shared their food as willingly as they shared each other, feeding and being fed, kissing and caressing, fondling and stroking as if they couldn't get enough of each other.

Shemaine was garbed in nothing more than a dressing gown when she followed Gage across the front porch and accepted his helping hand in descending the stairs. At the water's edge, she was timid about discarding the robe and exposing herself to the uncertainty of her surroundings, but after watching Gage strip to the buff and plunge into the water, she finally relented.

"Oh, it's cold!" she complained, wading through the shallows.

"Refreshing and invigorating!" Gage corrected with a chuckle, feasting his gaze upon her soft curves as he ran his fingers through his wet hair.

"Chilling and frigid!" Shemaine insisted,

shivering as the water came up around her thighs.

"Come, love, I'll warm you." Spreading his arms invitingly, her husband beckoned to her with a luminous smile. "Only a little bit more and you'll be in my embrace."

Shemaine gritted her teeth and forced herself through the deepening stream until Gage reached out and pulled her to him. Drawing her arms around his neck, he smiled and folded his own about her.

"You're warm," Shemaine murmured in admiration.

"Aye, just looking at you does that to me," Gage admitted, lightly caressing her parted lips with his own. Her nipples were cold and hard and seemed to bore twin holes in his chest as he clasped her close against him.

"I like the way you look at me," Shemaine whispered beneath his kisses. "And I like what I see when I look at you. I enjoy watching you dress, too. I've never seen a man clothe himself before today."

"You'll grow tired of looking when I'm old and feeble."

"Doubtful," she sighed with a smile.

"At least you're no longer afraid of looking at me."

"I never was." Shemaine waited for his response and laughed softly when he drew back with a skeptical brow elevated. "I was only fearful of you catching me at it."

Enlightenment dawned, wrenching a grin from Gage. "You may look at me to your heart's content, madam. I'm yours, to have and to hold."

"To have and to hold," she repeated softly, slipping her hands upward over his hard chest and then around behind him to his firm buttocks. "Such a delectable thought, to know that you're mine and I can freely touch you whenever I want. You have such gratifying places to caress and fondle."

"No less than you, madam," Gage muttered against her throat as he reciprocated in kind.

Shemaine turned her face toward his cheek and brushed the tanned skin with her lips. "Do what you promised before you went out to gather the eggs," she breathed. "Teach me something new."

Lifting her against him, he slipped a hand between them to make them one, drawing a trembling sigh from her.

"Do you like that?" he rasped, resettling his hands beneath her buttocks as she twined her limbs about him to secure their bond.

"Oh, yes!" She was breathless with bliss. "I like everything you do to me."

"Disgusting!"

The word shattered their passion instantly, breaking them apart in acute surprise. Almost in unison they looked around to find Roxanne standing in rigid disdain at the edge of the glade. Mortified that another had intruded into their intimacy, Shemaine folded her arms over her bosom and collapsed against Gage as he drew her back to him.

"What in the hell are you doing here, Roxanne?" he barked. The realization struck him that she looked as wild and savage as a fair-haired witch. She had not taken time to comb her hair, and with the breezes, the snarled strands seemed to fly about her face and shoulders as if charged by her own fury.

Roxanne glared at them, conveying the venom that roiled within her. With a defiant toss of her head, she sneered at Gage. "I heard this morning that you had married your bitch of a bondswoman! But I had to come see the truth for myself, because I had difficulty believing you could be so foolish."

"Why? Because I didn't marry *you*?" Gage asked caustically.

"No!" the woman shot back. "Because you were foolish enough to take another wife after you were almost hanged for killing your first one!"

Shemaine's startled gasp wrenched a chuckling smirk from Roxanne, but Gage's roar of denial came swiftly to negate her claim.

"That's a bloody lie, Roxanne, and you know it!"

The blonde bestowed her pitying gaze upon Shemaine. "He'll kill you, too, just like he killed Victoria. . . . When your husband grows vexed with you, that's when he'll do it."

"I will tolerate no more of your vindictive accusations!" Gage bellowed. "You know better than anybody that I didn't kill Victoria, but you came out here to deliberately frighten Shemaine with your malicious lies!"

Shemaine's mind whirled in sudden confusion, and she shivered against her husband, wondering if the woman's allegations had any merit. But then, why would Roxanne be so eager to have Gage for her own if she thought him capable of murder? If the woman truly believed what she said, wouldn't she be afraid to come near him? After all, if he had killed before, he could do so again. What would prevent him from flying into a rage and snuffing out another life, just as he had Victoria's? Yet Roxanne had been thoroughly committed to winning him for herself.

Bracing up her chin, Shemaine glared back at Roxanne, refusing to give their adversary the satisfaction of seeing her draw away from Gage. "I don't believe you, Roxanne. My husband wouldn't kill anyone!"

"Wouldn't he?" Roxanne simpered smugly as she strolled to the edge of the pool. The stream-fed pond was clear enough to allow her to see a vague blur of their pale bodies as they clung together. The sight cut her heart to the quick, deepening her hatred for them both. It was what she had feared the first time she had laid eyes upon Shemaine. What man could resist such beauty? Certainly not Gage, she mentally jeered. He had always had an eye for beauty! Victoria had once been proof of that. Now this hussy who had lured him into marriage with her liquid eyes and sultry ways verified the fact again that Gage Thornton would never have considered taking a plain-faced woman to wife. But she meant to have her revenge upon them both! Gage couldn't toss her aside a second time and not feel the brunt of her rancor. "Everyone around here knows what a vicious temper Gage has, and Victoria fell prey to it."

It was Gage's turn to scoff harshly. "Do you think anyone will listen to your lies after you argued so vehemently that I was innocent of any wrongdoing? Besides, if you were *really* convinced of the readiness of the townspeople to believe your change of story, why didn't you tell them differently after you came out here the last time? But as far as I know, you said nothing. I don't think you expect anything to come of this! All you want to do is frighten Shemaine."

"Do you honestly think I'm going to keep quiet for another season or two while you bed your filthy little convict?" the blonde countered sharply. "Do you expect me to wait around until you grow tired of her like you did Victoria?" Roxanne drew her lip up in a bitter sneer. *"Never!* In fact, the thing you really should be concerned about right now is what you'll have to do to save your family once it gets out that you killed Victoria. I warned you that you wouldn't be able to hide behind my skirts anymore, and now I'll be telling everyone what really happened."

"Aye! Do that!" Gage challenged sharply. "Tell them what part you played in my wife's death, because you were there when she fell! I wasn't!"

"Victoria was dead when I got here!" Roxanne protested.

Gage jeered. "I doubt that seriously!"

"Are you saying that I was able to lift your wife over the prow and throw her down? Am I so strong?" she derided. "And are you so desperate to lay the blame on another that you're willing to toss all reason aside and claim that I could have actually overpowered Victoria? Don't you think she would have fought me tooth and nail to keep me from throwing her off the prow?"

"Perhaps you were able to surprise her," Gage suggested brusquely. "Perhaps you pushed her from behind."

"Come now, Gage," Roxanne chided. "Be logical. You know well enough that Victoria would have seen me coming up the building slip. In fact, she probably would have come down to meet me. We were friends! Or have you forgotten?"

"I don't know how you could have managed such a feat, Roxanne," Gage acknowledged. "All I know is that you were driven by an unreasonable jealousy from the first day I started courting Victoria. And now you're being goaded by envy once again. Your unreasonable jealousy attests to the fact that you're the only one who had a motive for killing Victoria."

Roxanne jeered scathingly. "What vile rage took hold of you that day that made you murder the mother of your child, and Andrew barely weaned?"

Shemaine promptly decided she had had enough of the shrew's assertions. Perhaps her own knowledge of love and jealousy were seriously limited, but she could not believe any woman of rational temperament would continue to chase after a man whom she seriously suspected of murder. Roxanne, however, had made it obvious just how desperately she had wanted Gage and had been in such a turmoil after he had gone to the *London Pride* that she had been on the verge of losing control. Apparently she hadn't been so terrified of him that she feared rousing the temper that she now claimed was so vicious.

Slipping a hand behind Gage's neck, Shemaine pulled his head down and, ignoring his surprise, placed a loving kiss upon his lips.

"I'm cold, and I'm tired of listening to this woman's inane prattle," she announced loudly for Roxanne's benefit. "I'm going back to the cabin to take a warm bath. If you'd care to join me, perhaps we'll have some privacy there and can finish what we started before we were so *rudely* interrupted."

Gage felt his jaw sagging in astonishment. Of all the reactions he had expected from his bride, he had never anticipated a fierce, unswerving loyalty in the face of Roxanne's malicious allegations. He watched in awe as Shemaine turned and slowly waded out of the pool, making no effort to cover her nakedness as she emerged from the water. Climbing on the rock where she had left her robe, his wife picked it up, laid it with deliberate care over her arm, and then turned to face him in all the glory of her naked beauty. It was a bold, proud statement she made to the other woman as she smiled at him invitingly.

"Coming, my love?"

Gage felt his heart soar, and in a voice fraught with emotion, he answered, "Aye, love, as soon as our visitor leaves . . . unless you'd rather I come now. . . ."

"Nay, husband," Shemaine replied emphatically. "I would not share even a glimpse of what is mine with another woman. Come when you can. I'll be waiting for you."

Though Gage could not resist admiring her nakedness as she strolled up the trail to the cabin, he cast a glance askance at Roxanne and felt jubilation rise up within him when he found her gaping in slack-jawed astonishment at his wife's departing form.

"Would you mind leaving now?" he invited sharply, folding his hands deliberately over his manhood. He couldn't be sure just what Roxanne was able to see through the water, but he'd be damned before allowing her even an obscure glimpse of what Shemaine had claimed as hers. "I'm cold, and my wife is waiting for me."

Roxanne faced him with gnashing teeth. "You haven't heard the last of this, Gage

Thornton! You'll be sorry you tossed me aside and married that bitch!"

"I don't think so," Gage said with a calm assurance that had settled over him only a few moments ago, after his wife had declared her trust in him. "In fact, the more I'm around Shemaine, the more I believe I've found an exceptional woman. Indeed, if I could accurately discern the feelings I have for her right now, I'd say that I have come to love her very much."

"Aaarrrghh!" Roxanne's snarl of rage seemed to fill every hollow and rill around them with deafening sound, startling shrieks and squawks from nesting birds and sending them flying chaotically into the air. Amid the confusion of their darting flights, Roxanne whirled and scrambled back toward the riverbank from whence she had come.

Gage waited until he heard the oars bump against her father's boat before he waded to shore. After donning his breeches, he picked up his boots and meandered barefoot up the trail to the cabin and quietly made his entrance. Shemaine had garbed herself in a robe, which she clutched closed at her throat with one hand as she hastened toward the new bathing chamber with a bucket of hot water. She cast him a shivering smile of greeting.

"If y-you help me carry the w-water," she said through chattering teeth, "we'll be able t-to get w-warm sooner."

"I'll get the water," Gage said, tossing aside his boots. "You'd better stand by the fire until I fill the tub for us."

His wife halted and looked at him as if he had taken leave of his senses. "A-aren't y-you c-cold, too?"

A smile curved his lips. "I'm used to it." He shrugged. "Perhaps you're not as cold, Shemaine, as you are upset."

"Roxanne upset me, all right!" Shemaine affirmed testily. "The gall of that woman, thinking I'd believe her!" Her anger dwindled rapidly, replaced by a painful chagrin. Her face threatened to crumple as tears brightened her eyes. She made an earnest effort to bolster her mettle, but as her husband stepped near and took her in his arms, she began to weep in embarrassment against his chest. "I disgraced myself! And I disgraced you, Gage! I allowed that woman to provoke me until I dismissed everything I had been taught about common decency and propriety! The way I flaunted my nakedness before you both, I'm sure Roxanne has no doubts about me being a trollop now!"

"Whoa!" Gage chuckled. Pulling away from her, he searched her teary eyes. "What are you more upset about, Shemaine? The accusations Roxanne made against me? Or the fact that you pranced up here stark naked?"

New tears sprang forth at his candid question, and in renewed agony Shemaine muttered a question. "Did I embarrass you terribly?"

"Good heavens, woman! Banish the thought!" Gage urged with hearty laughter. "I nearly hooted with glee!" He clasped his wife to him again and rested his cheek against the top of her head. "Shemaine, do you not realize what pleasure it gave me when you declared your trust in me? It was like heaven opening up and shining down upon me. Truly, my love, I felt much like an emperor being restored to his kingdom after years in exile and prison. The joy I experienced was beyond measure. I could not have imagined that you would remain unaffected by Roxanne's malevolent charges. The experience left me overwhelmed . . . and a bit amazed at your confidence in me."

Shemaine was perplexed by his reaction to her shameless display, but after reaping the dire fruits of a thieftaker's allegations and finding no one who had cared enough about compassion and human decency to consider that she might have been innocent, she could well understand another's fervent desire to be believed and trusted. In some surprise she realized she was no longer shaking. Snuggling against her husband, she giggled.

"I *was* terribly wicked, wasn't I?"

Gage chuckled and held her wonderfully close to his heart. "Absolutely depraved, my love."

CHAPTER 17

The return of Andrew resettled the Thorntons into the comfortable niche of a genuine family, and although the boy found it strange that Shemaine was now ensconced in his father's bedroom, he willingly accepted her as a replacement for the mother whom he barely remembered. Indistinct memories of a loving face and long, pale hair through which he had once twined his fingers as his mother rocked and sang to him occasionally flitted through his child's mind. Another, more troubling, memory of his father leaving him sobbing in his bed and, after a terrifying space of time, returning to the cabin with the limp, battered form of that beautiful lady in his arms haunted his dreams. Even after so long a time a recurring vision of her lying on the larger bed with a trickle of blood running from the corner of her pale lips could wrench him awake and leave him sobbing and yearning to be reassured that all was well.

His new mother sang to him, too, and when he woke from a nightmare, she would hold and comfort him. She would even take him into bed with her. It was her shoulder upon which his head rested as she sang him a lullaby and his father's arm under which the two of them snuggled until he drifted to sleep again. Then, some time later, he would rouse long enough to be aware that he was being carried back to his own bed by his father. There he would pass the remainder of the night in peaceful contentment.

In the ensuing days, Andrew's room became officially separated from his parents'. A wall with a door was built into the large opening between the two rooms, and another door was added on the adjacent wall, allowing direct access from his bedroom to the parlor and the main living area. The division lessened the chances of Andrew being disturbed by the noises and murmuring voices that drifted from the master bedroom, while it allowed his father and new mother more privacy.

The new door did not totally negate the possibility of interruption. That fact was made evident when Andrew awoke during the night with an urgent need to go to the privy and, after swinging wide the door between, ran into the master bedroom. The boy did not understand his father's mad scramble to roll to the far side of the bed away from Shemaine or their frantic snatching for bedcovers. He heard a muted groan as his father fell back upon his pillow, and he wondered if his stomach was hurting. Their sudden amusement was just as confusing. He only knew his need was great, and as he halted near the bed and peered through the moonlit shadows into Shemaine's smiling face, he could hardly restrain himself.

From then on, a small chamber pot was placed in Andrew's room each night before he went to bed. With its initial presence came his father's encouragement to use it whenever he had a need during the night. A latch was soon affixed to the opposite side of the door which connected the two rooms, alleviating the likelihood of the couple being intruded upon without prior warning or the child being startled by seeing something he shouldn't.

From Newportes Newes drifted rumors that Roxanne was carrying through with her threats, but as yet, none of the inhabitants had deigned to give the spinster an attentive ear, though she earnestly sought to convince everyone of Gage's responsibility for Victoria's death. The majority of the townspeople were of the opinion that after being rejected for a second time by a man whom she had adored for nigh on to ten years, Roxanne had been inflamed by spite rather than by any new discovery or revelation. Then, too, speculations as to the real reason for Victoria Thornton's death had become rather hackneyed, especially after Mrs. Pettycomb had spent the better part of the last year voicing her own theories, trying to implicate Gage Thornton and blacken his name. But even the hawk-nosed matron did not dare repeat Roxanne's recent assertions with her usual verve for fear of being reproached by those who had declared that no one in their right mind would believe the spinster.

Though several weeks passed, no official came out from town to make an arrest. Gage cautiously breathed a sigh of relief, as did his wife, and their lives began to take on a new significance. To their amazement visitors from the hamlet began to bring small gifts as token offerings of friendship to Shemaine, as if to declare their acceptance of her and their desire to get acquainted. It was mainly through the persistence of Calley Tate (by way of callers coming to her bedside), Hannah Fields, and Mary Margaret McGee that a change in attitudes was beginning to take place. The three women fervently lauded the praises of their new friend, declaring to everyone who would listen that Shemaine was a genteel lady who had been wrongly convicted.

Life was not altogether idyllic, however, for Shemaine began to suspect that Jacob Potts had recovered from his wound and was back in the area. She could hardly walk outside without sensing that she was being spied upon by someone hiding deep within the wooded copse. Gage searched the forest time and again, but he could find only some freshly broken twigs and recent disturbances of the rotting leaves that covered the forest floor. A deer or some other animal could have done as much. Even so, Shemaine could not escape a feeling of foreboding, and for the sake of caution, she began toting a flintlock with her whenever she went outside. Whether she went to play outside with Andrew, to wash clothes or to do some other chore, she was intent upon being prepared for the worst. If her apprehensions proved to be nothing more than an overly active imagination, then she had lost nothing, but if Potts was really out there somewhere, she wanted to stop him before he harmed one of them. After Gage gave her further instructions on the use of the firearm, her accuracy improved to the degree that she began to feel quite tenacious about using the weapon if circumstances warranted it.

Gage kept up a constant vigil even though his young wife remained unaware of the depth of his concern. Every morning and afternoon, he or one of his workmen would either ride in a wide sweep through the woods or tread more stealthily on foot to see what they could find or even surprise. None of them were experienced trackers, and they only noticed what was apparent, which was very little. If Potts was hiding in the trees, then he was being extremely cautious about it.

After bidding his men to keep a protective eye on his family, Gage ventured into New-portes Newes to question Morrisa again. But the harlot had been ordered to go down to the docks with some of the other strumpets and meet the large ship that was just coming into port. The *London Pride* would be setting sail soon, now that her cargo holds were full, and the girls were expected to find new customers among the incoming male passengers and crew. If their earnings diminished, Freida had threatened, they would soon find their victuals limited to the bare necessities. Except for a curt retort denying the whereabouts of Potts, Morrisa refused to be delayed unless Gage could promise her a full evening's entertainment upstairs with her fee paid in advance, for she could not chance arousing the madam's ire.

"That li'l pipsqueak Myers complained ta Freida 'bout me, an' now I'm havin' ta drum up twice as many gents ta placate the shrew. 'Tain't 'cause I'm fond o' bein' at her beck an' call, ye understand. I'd just as soon stay here with ye an' give ye me services free, just ta show ye how much better I can pleasure ye than that li'l bogtrotter ye married. But if'n I cheat Freida out o' what she thinks is due her, she's threatenin' to sell me ta one o' them mountain men what comes in here. Do ye ken how mean an' nasty those brutes are? Why, one took a bite o' me so hard he drew blood. Made me scream, he did!"

"You should be used to such behavior after being with Potts," Gage remarked without a trace of sympathy.

Morrisa squawked in outrage and swept up a heavy pewter mug from a nearby table. She hauled back an arm to send it flying, but the unperturbed smile on Gage's lips made her pause in sudden wariness.

"Freida is watching," he warned with a full measure of satisfaction. The harlot's rage rapidly dwindled as he raised a hand to direct her attention to the stairs, where the madam stood like a well-fortified fortress. With her pale, flabby arms folded in front of her and her slippered toe tapping an irritated staccato on the step, Freida readily conveyed the fact that Morrisa would forfeit more than a few victuals if she aroused the ire of another customer.

Morrisa carefully lowered the tankard to the table as Freida strode down the stairs and came forward. Gage had no wish to hear the stern rebuke that promised to be forthcoming, and he took his leave of the tavern, almost colliding with Mrs. Pettycomb, who was hurrying along the boardwalk in front.

"Well, if it isn't Gage Thornton!" the matron declared in surprise. She readjusted the wire-rimmed spectacles on her thin, hawkish nose in an effort to see every minute detail as her small, dark eyes swept over him. Any man who wed a convict could well expect recompense in some form or another if he didn't defer to his wife's whims, but much to Alma's disappointment, Gage had no blackened eyes or bruised jaw. Curiously Alma peered through the open door of the tavern and probed the interior until her gaze settled on Morrisa. Her thin eyebrows lifted sharply, and with a smug smile, she returned her attention to the tall man. "Out visiting, Gage?"

The brown eyes chilled to a penetrating coldness at her erroneous conjecture.

"Merely taking care of business, Mrs. Pettycomb."

"Oh, of course." Alma smirked. "I'm sure that's what all the men say when they've been caught sporting with loose women."

Gage snorted, irritated by her assumption. "That's hardly the case, Mrs. Pettycomb, but think what you will!"

Alma pursed her thin lips in complacent haughtiness, but in the very next instant, she had to step hastily aside as Morrisa stormed out of the tavern. The harlot seemed oblivious to the flustered matron as she glowered at the man.

"If'n ye weren't so caught on that bogtrotter ye married, Gage Thornton, ye'd see how good it could be betwixt the two o' us. But no! Ye've got ta be a proper husband ta M'liedy Sh'maine. Well, I hope ye'll be satisfied with the bundle o' brats ye'll be gettin from her, 'cause that's all she'll be givin' ye. She don't know anythin' more'n that! As for me, I'm goin' ta see what gents'll be arrivin' at the docks. Maybe I'll catch me a looker this time."

Stalking past him, Morrisa made her way across the thoroughfare as Alma, much agog, stared after her. The matron snapped her mouth closed as Gage turned away.

"Going to meet the ship, too, Gage?" she prodded, unwilling to relent. "It should be of some interest to you, being an English ship, but I'll warrant this one is far too fine to be carrying a cargo of convicts."

Glancing back over his shoulder, Gage gave her an enigmatic smile. "I have no reason to go to the docks, madam. As Morrisa has rightly determined, I have all that I want at home, and I can think of absolutely no one who might be aboard the vessel who would be of interest to me. Now, good day to you."

With that, Gage strode off toward the riverbank, where he had left his canoe. His curt riposte left Mrs. Pettycomb feeling much like an old hen whose feathers had just been singed. Bristling with indignation, she glared after him, yearning to unleash her ire full in his face. But it was safer by far to go behind the man's back with her little tales and seek her revenge through ignominious means.

After making her own way to the docks, Alma Pettycomb approached the newly arrived vessel and stood nearby, closely perusing the passengers as they disembarked.

She noticed Morrisa wandering off on the arm of a fairly young man, but she gave no further heed to the harlot as a tall, gray-haired man of notable appearance was escorted down the gangplank by the captain. The clothes of the older gentleman tastefully attested to his wealth, yet he was quite handsome and needed no costly raiment to attract attention. For a short time he and the sea captain stood conversing on the quay, and Alma Pettycomb found herself greatly intrigued by the respectful esteem exhibited by the captain. Anxious to hear their discussion, she moved within close proximity of the two.

"If you should require assistance in any way, my lord, I'll be happy to do what I can to expedite your search," the captain of the vessel offered graciously. "I wish I knew more than what I've already told you, but I'm afraid I saw no more of my passenger after he left my ship that day."

"Hopefully the information you've given me is still useful despite the years that have passed since you first dropped anchor in these waters. If providence is with me, then 'twill be only a matter of time before I find the one I'm seeking."

The captain beckoned to a sailor who was making his way down the gangplank with a large leather chest on his shoulder. "Judd, you're to stay with his lordship and assist him with his trunk until he has no further need of you, then you may return to the ship for shore leave."

"Aye, Cap'n."

The two men parted, and his lordship waited a moment until the tar had joined him, then he turned to make his way toward the hamlet. Immediately he found himself confronting the pinch-faced Mrs. Pettycomb, who had approached so close that she was in danger of being trodden upon.

"I beg your pardon," the man apologized, and stepped aside to pass around her.

"'Tis your pardon I must beg, sir," the gossipmonger responded, eager to hold him there until she gained knowledge of the man and his search. "My name is Alma Pettycomb, and I couldn't help overhearing your conversation with the captain. I was wondering if I might be of some assistance to you. I know this area well and have a wide knowledge of the people living hereabouts. I understand you're looking for someone. Perhaps I might know of him." She waited expectantly, but her question gained no immediate response.

His lordship looked at her cautiously. Perhaps it might have been his imagination, but when he had taken note of her shadow being cast beside his own, it had almost seemed as if the matron had been leaning forward in an effort to hear his conversation with the captain. But then, a busybody was probably the best one to ask, for they usually knew more about everybody's business than anyone else. "Have you knowledge of a man named Thornton living in the area? He left England almost ten years ago and the ship on which he sailed docked here at Newportes Newes."

Alma Pettycomb could only wonder why a lord of the realm would be seeking a lowly commoner, especially one as cantankerous as the cabinetmaker. "There's a Gage Thornton who lives upriver a ways," she informed the stranger, puffed up by her own consequence. "Would he be the one you're looking for?"

His lordship smiled suddenly, as if in great relief. "Aye, that's the one."

The woman couldn't resist asking for more information than she was entitled to.

"Your pardon again, my lord, but I'm curious to know what Gage Thornton may have done that would cause a gentleman like yourself to pursue him all the way from England. And after so many years have passed."

His lordship's eyes chilled suddenly to a cold, amber-brown. "He has done nothing that I know of, madam. Why would you assume that he has?"

"Well, he's certainly done enough here to make the good citizens of this hamlet fear for their lives," Alma readily rejoined. "They say he murdered his first wife, yet he walks around as if he owns the world. Now he has taken to wife a convict, and there's no one who'll dare say what crimes she committed in England. I warned him the day he bought her that he was doing this town a disservice."

"Where may I find this Mr. Thornton?"

The curtness of the question failed to discourage Alma, and she hastened to give directions, as well as the names of several men who would be willing to take him upriver for a fee. His lordship politely expressed his gratitude and beckoned for the sailor to follow him, but Alma made the gentleman pause again.

"May I have the pleasure of knowing your lordship's name?"

The nobleman gave her a sparse smile, somewhat reminiscent of one she had received earlier in the same hour. "Lord William Thornton, Earl of Thornhedge."

Mrs. Pettycomb's jaw sagged briefly before she brought a trembling hand slowly upward to cover her gaping mouth. In a stunned daze she asked, "Any relation to Gage Thornton?"

"He is my son, madam." With that, his lordship moved past the astounded woman and strode toward the river as Judd followed. In a few moments he was on his way upriver and waving farewell to the sailor.

The rap of knuckles on the front door awakened Andrew and Shemaine from an afternoon nap, and though the boy hurriedly wriggled off his father's bed and ran toward the portal, Shemaine scurried after him in sudden fear. She could not believe Potts would be bold enough to come right up to their cabin, especially after being wounded, but she couldn't take any chances.

"Don't open the door, Andrew, until I see who it is," she bade in an anxious tone.

The boy halted obediently and then waited as she went to the front window and looked out, but the man who stood on the porch was a total stranger to Shemaine, someone she could not remember even catching a glimpse of in Newportes Newes. He had a proud look about him and bore himself with a dignity that was unmistakable.

Joining Andrew at the portal, Shemaine lifted the latch and allowed the child to swing open the door. The man's attention was first drawn to the boy, and Shemaine could not help but take note of his surprise and the subtle softening of his visage. Then, after a moment, the amber-brown eyes rose to look at her in stony detachment. A gasp of surprise came from her lips, and it was all that Shemaine could do to meet that stoic regard and not retreat, for there was no doubt in her mind that there stood Gage's father. The resemblance was too close for her to mistake.

"Is Mr. Thornton here?" he asked in a cool tone.

"I'm sure he must be by now," she answered, somewhat flustered. "One of the men said he went into Newportes Newes earlier, but if you'd like to come inside and wait with the boy, my lord, I'll run to the cabinet shop and see if he has returned."

Amazed at her perception, William stepped inside where he could look at her more closely. Noting the delicately refined features and the wedding band on the third finger of her left hand, he arched a brow at her. "You know who I am?"

Shemaine laid her hands on the boy's shoulders. "I believe you're Andrew's grandfather . . . and my husband's father."

William's lips tightened slightly as he sought to hide his irritation. The gossipmonger was right! Not only had Gage gotten into some kind of trouble over his first wife, but he had given his name to a convicted felon. Still, the girl was far more observant and obviously a lot smarter than he had expected a common criminal to be.

"Does it disturb you that your son and I are married?" Shemaine asked quietly.

His inquiry was far more blunt. "Are you the convict Mrs. Pettycomb told me about?"

Shemaine lifted her chin in defiance. "Would it matter to you that I was unjustly condemned?"

"It might, if there was a way of proving your innocence, but the colonies are a long way from England, and I would presume there is no one here who can confirm what you say," William answered crisply. "No father would fancy his son taking a criminal to wife, and I am no different."

"Fancy it or not, my lord, the deed is done," she murmured. "And there'll be no undoing the vows unless you would have your son set me aside with an annulment. I'll tell you truly, though, 'tis gone too far for that."

"My son has already proven he has a mind of his own," William stated tersely, and then heaved a sigh as he remembered his last altercation with Gage. It had taken several years before the truth had come out, but he had been struck by the loneliness of his loss from the first. "It wouldn't matter what I may advise, Gage will do what he thinks best, and I'm sure he would be reluctant to give up a young woman as winsome as you despite the crimes you may have committed in the past."

Aware of the antagonism sprouting between them, Shemaine felt her heart grow cold with dread. This man had set his mind to the fact that she was a felon, and nothing short of proving her integrity would content him. It was the same kind of trap in which she had found herself after being arrested by Ned, the thieftaker. Though she had been innocent of all that little man had claimed, no magistrate had been willing to believe her.

"Will you stay with Andrew while I go out to see if Gage is here?" As his lordship nodded, Shemaine swept her hand to indicate the settee. "You may sit down if you'd like. I won't be long."

Andrew balked at the idea of being left with a stranger and let out a shriek of fear when Shemaine started toward the door. He ran after her, and though she sought to console him, the boy clung to her in desperation. William was closely attentive to her soothing words as she caressed the boy's cheek and took his small hand in his.

"I'm sorry, my lord," she apologized. "Andrew doesn't care to stay with you right now. After he gets to know you better, he'll be more willing to make friends."

"I understand."

As they left the cabin, William leaned back on the settee and looked around at the interior. Recognizing excellence when he saw it, he was overwhelmed at the high quality of workmanship in every item of furniture his eyes touched upon. After he had been put ashore with his trunk and had enlisted Gillian's aid in carrying the chest to the porch, he had paused near the building slip to admire the half-finished vessel and to question the old man, Flannery, about his son's design. The two shipwrights had been eager to show him through the vessel and had been just as quick to laud the praises of their employer. His heart had swelled with pride as he took everything in and finally began to comprehend what Gage had once tried to talk him into building in England. After nearly ten years' estrangement from his son, looking at what Gage had created was almost as enlightening as finally being able to understand why his son had left the family home and England.

Three years short a day from the time Gage had left, Christine had succumbed to a bout of pneumonia (or a broken heart, as she had raspingly maintained). On her deathbed, she had tearfully confessed to her father that she had been so enamored of Gage that she had sought to entrap him in marriage by claiming he had gotten her with child. She had died a virgin, having sullied her own name, but, according to her, she had deemed her attempt well worth the price, for she had never wanted another man as much as she had wanted Gage Thornton.

After her funeral, her father had beseeched William to forgive his family for bringing about the alienation of his son, but in his long and frustrating search, William had come to realize that it had probably been his own prideful stubbornness that had brought about the rift. He had been so determined to force his son to obey him that he had been unwilling to entertain the possibility that Gage might have been an innocent pawn in the lady's game.

The back door opened again, and William rose to his feet in anxious haste as Gage strode down the corridor toward the parlor. It was the father rather than the son who quickly traversed the space between them and, through welling tears, gazed upon the younger. It was an older, more mature face the father saw, but with its bronze skin and leanly chiseled features, it was even more handsome than before. In it, William saw a strong duplication of his own, except for his advancing years and the yearning regret that had exacted a harsh toll, leaving deep creases across his brow and a poignant sadness in the lines around his mouth.

"I nearly gave up all hope of finding you," William managed to choke out through a gathering thickness in his throat. His stoic demeanor began to waver, and he clasped Gage's shoulders and shook him gently as if in a desperate effort to make him understand how deeply he had been missed. "I've searched for you all these many years without success and have sent men to the far reaches of the world in a hopeless quest to find you. It was only through a chance meeting that I happened upon the man who had captained the ship on which you had sailed. My dear son, can you ever forgive me for driving you away from our home?"

Gage was astounded at the emotion visible in his father's face. He had never thought he would see the elder so vulnerable and humble. It was a side of William Thornton that he had never seen before. His mother had died after his twelfth birthday, and the pain of her loss had seemed to harden his father, turning him into a tough disciplinarian. Now here the elder stood, almost sobbing with joy over their reunion.

The change was so great, Gage felt at odds with himself and a bit cautious about how he should react. He wanted to wrap his arms about his sire and clasp him firmly to his breast in a hearty embrace, but he felt strange and clumsy doing so until his father responded in kind.

"My son! My son!" William wept against his shoulder.

The back door creaked open, and Andrew came running in. He halted abruptly when he saw the stranger still in the parlor. The two men turned to the boy, and Andrew noticed a strange wetness in his father's eyes.

"Daddee, yu cry?" he asked in amazement.

In some embarrassment, Gage brushed a hand across his face before he lifted his son in his arms and presented him to his grandfather. "Andy, this is *my* father, *my* daddy . . . and your grandfather, your *grandpa*."

"Gran'pa?" Andrew looked at the elder curiously. Malcolm and Duncan had a grandpa who frequently visited them, but his father had never told him before now that he had one, too.

William held out his arms to take the boy, but Andrew pressed back against his father's shoulder and shook his head.

"Where's Mommy?" Gage queried, realizing that Shemaine had not come in with Andrew.

The boy waved his arm, pointing toward the back. "Mommee Sheeaim on porch."

Gage put his son down and, with gentle firmness, bade him to stay. "Wait here with your grandfather, Andy. I'm just going out to the porch. I'll be right back."

Gage stepped out the rear door and glanced down the lane toward the workshop before he realized that Shemaine was huddled in a knot in a chair at the far end of the porch. Her knees were drawn up close beneath her chin and her arms were folded around her legs, holding them to her chest. As he approached, she cast him a shy glance that clearly bespoke of her trepidation. He squatted on his haunches beside her and peered up at her for a long moment, noting the wetness in the silken lashes. Reaching out, he claimed a slender hand and drew the trembling fingers to his lips for a kiss. "Why didn't you come in with Andrew?"

Shemaine shrugged diffidently and cast her gaze away. "I thought you and your father would need some time to be alone together."

"Why are you so troubled, then?"

Cautiously Shemaine withdrew from him and entwined her fingers together as she rested both hands upon her knees. "Mrs. Pettycomb told your father I was a convict."

Gage muttered a curse and silently vowed to wring the scrawny neck of that meddlesome busybody. But more importantly he had to know what his father had said or done to hurt his wife. "Did he say anything to you?"

"No," she lied, and shook her head, refusing to cause another fissure between Gage and his father, especially so soon after they had been reunited.

Gage was not at all convinced. "He must have said something."

"Nothing!" Shemaine insisted, her voice faltering.

"You don't lie very well, Shemaine," her husband gently chided. "Now tell me, love, what did my father say to you?"

Shemaine remained stoically mute, and Gage knew it was useless to persist. "Come inside," he urged, rising to his feet. "I want to present you as my wife."

Shemaine realized the futility of resisting as he reclaimed her hand. Rising from the chair, she brushed at the wetness in her eyes and smoothed the hair at her temples, ignoring the long braid that trailed down her back. Her husband regarded her swift attempts to make herself more presentable and smiled as he slipped his arms about her and pulled her close.

"You're beautiful just the way you are, my sweet," he breathed as he lowered his mouth to hers. His kiss was gentle and loving, causing Shemaine to realize just how deeply she had come to love him in the time they had been together. How could she live if William Thornton managed to separate them?

Her arms crept around his lean waist in a fierce embrace, and she answered his kiss with all of her heart, soul and mind. Finally Gage lifted his head and gazed down at her with glowing eyes. "We'll finish this later in bed, but if we delay much longer now, Andrew will come looking for us."

"We'd better go in, then," Shemaine murmured. "He doesn't like to be left with strangers."

As soon as they opened the back door, Andrew came racing back to the corridor to meet them. His father swung him up in his arms, smoothing away the worried frown on the boy's brow, and together the three went in to face his lordship.

"Father, this is my new wife, Shemaine," Gage announced rather stiffly. Wrapping an arm around her shoulders as if to affirm his possession of her, he went on to explain. "Andrew's mother died in an accident about a year ago and left me a widower. Before Shemaine came here, she was betrothed to the Marquess du Mercer in London. While there, she was seized from her parents' home and, by devious methods, convicted of thievery and shipped here on the *London Pride.*"

William remembered seeing the ship when they came into port. He had recognized it as being one among many vessels belonging to their adversary, J. Horace Turnbull. He also knew the Du Mercers and, just before leaving England, had heard some scandal about Maurice's betrothed fleeing London before a marriage could take place, which some said had positively delighted his grandmother. "Then you and Shemaine haven't been married very long?"

Gage felt the rigidity of his own smile. "Long enough to have become appreciative of our union."

William stiffened as he noted the firmness in his son's tone. Obviously the little hussy had wasted no time in complaining to Gage about his displeasure over their marriage. No wonder she looked so embarrassed now. "So, she told you that I didn't appreciate you taking a convict to wife, eh?"

Gage's jaw tensed until the tendons flexed in his cheeks. "Shemaine never said a word about that, Father, but because you've never shown such hesitancy before, I thought you might voice your opinion about her." With each word he uttered, his ire sharpened. "From now on I will insist that when you have anything to say about our marriage that you say it to me instead of Shemaine. I don't *appreciate* you upsetting my wife, and I will not stand for it, *do you hear!*"

Beginning to quake, Andrew hid his face in the bend of his arm as he rested it upon his father's shoulder. Sensing his son's distress, Gage laid a consoling hand upon Andrew's back, knowing he must curb his temper, if only for the child's sake.

"I'm sorry, Father," he apologized arduously. "We seem to be at odds even now. And as yet, I've not learned to hold my tongue."

"Perhaps it would be best if I leave," William replied, his voice strained. He turned and would have made his way to the door, but Shemaine left Gage's side and hurried to lay a hand upon the elder's arm.

"Don't go, my lord, please," she begged. "I don't want to be the cause of another breach between the two of you. Stay and have supper with us, and if you would consent to share our home for a while, there's a small bedroom upstairs where you might have a bit of privacy." Bravely she brushed trembling fingers over the thin, blue-veined hand as she softly cajoled, "You must stay for Andrew's sake. You're the only grandparent he has."

William looked at her through the tears that had come despite his attempt to force them back. "It has taken me so long to find my son, I hate to leave without getting to know his family better."

Shemaine's heart went out to the lonely man and with a gently coaxing smile, she urged, "Then stay, my lord, and be a part of our family."

William gently patted the back of her hand as she continued to stroke his. "Thank you, Shemaine. I would enjoy that."

Slipping her arm through his, Shemaine drew him back to Gage. "For Andrew's sake, there will be no more outbursts," she pleaded, looking directly at her husband as she took his arm. "You may have nurtured hurts from years long past, my love, but without forgiveness, how can any of us forget the injuries that have been done and release the weight on our hearts?"

Gage recognized her wisdom, but a long moment passed before he could meet his father's worried gaze and ask, "Would you like to look over the ship I'm building?"

Relief flooded through William. "Aye, and I'm interested in seeing your cabinet shop, too." He swept his hand about to indicate the interior pieces. "Furnishings like these are only seen in the best houses in England. You ought to be very proud of your accomplishments, Gage."

Andrew raised his head and looked

around at his grandfather, then he peered inquiringly into his father's face. "Can I come too, Daddee?"

Gage's lips twisted upward. "You can help me show your grandfather around."

Andrew wrinkled his nose and copied his father's grin. "Gran'pa goin' to help yu build ship, Daddee?"

"He might, if he can learn to take orders like the rest of the men I hire," Gage teased, causing his father to choke on an intake of air. He clapped the elder on the back to help him regain his breath, but couldn't resist repeating some of the same requirements his father had once demanded of him. "But you'll have to start as an apprentice until you've proven your worth."

William had difficulty deciding whether to cough, groan or laugh. "Blast you, Gage, if you're not going to take your revenge on me yet!"

The younger man chuckled as his tension eased. "Aye, I might."

In the front bedroom later that evening, Shemaine dragged her nightgown up over her head and tossed it onto the bed before slipping between the sheets and into the waiting arms of her husband. Gage smiled with a mixture of amusement and delight as she cuddled against him.

"Most women don their nightgown before getting into bed, my sweet, but you do just the opposite."

Shemaine nipped playfully at his chest, drawing a surprised start and a laughing "Ouch!" from him. Then she giggled contentedly. "Most women don't have a man like you waiting for them in their beds, my love." She swept a hand over his naked body and cooed in admiration at what she found. "If they did, they wouldn't waste time garbing themselves in a gown. They'd be waiting in their beds with open arms."

Gage twisted his head on the pillow, slanting his gaze down upon his wife's smiling face. "Then why was I the one waiting for you, madam?"

Lifting a thigh across his, Shemaine wiggled closer until her soft curves and tempting crevices were warmly cleaving to his muscular torso. "Because I had some chores to do in the kitchen after my bath. You didn't want me to go around stark naked with your father in the house, now did you?"

"No, madam. Such sights I reserve for my own pleasure," Gage breathed, clasping her knee and pulling it higher. His hand slid caressingly along the underside of her thigh, moving toward her buttock. "I refuse to share them with anyone."

Shemaine's breath halted blissfully as his hand veered, searching out the softness of her womanhood. "Do you think your father will be able to hear us from upstairs?"

"Hopefully not, but I'm not going to let fear of that intrude into our pleasure, my love. I've been waiting anxiously all afternoon to collect on what you promised on the back porch."

Rising up on his chest, she frowned down at him in confusion. "What did I promise?"

His hand swept upward behind her head and pressed her face near until her lips hovered close above his. " 'Twas what your kiss promised, my love, and I'm always eager to reap the fruits of such provocative invitations."

Her laughing eyes gleamed brightly in the soft candlelight. "You see an invitation in the simplest twitch of my skirt, sir," she teased. "Indeed, I'm beginning to think you've but one thing continually on your mind, and that is basically and unequivocally mating."

Gage grinned up at her. "Now you know me through and through, madam."

CHAPTER 18

William Thornton was not at all sure he enjoyed being awakened by a noisy twittering of birds before the sun showed its face above the horizon. Even so, he was roused to full awareness by a cacophony of shrieks, warbles and strange hissing that went on in the trees beyond the cabin. It became evident to him that he could not go back to sleep with such a racket going on, and he decided to venture outside and begin to explore this strange wilderness.

After pulling on a pair of breeches, he bundled the tail of his nightshirt into the top of them and then yanked on a pair of boots.

He found his way downstairs, unlatched the door and stepped out onto the front porch. An owl passing across his line of vision flapped its wings almost leisurely in comparison to the smaller bird that gave chase close behind it, no doubt seeking retribution for some unknown offense. An early morning raid to steal eggs or hatchlings from a nest might have been the reason for part of the noisy clamor.

For a moment, William savored the warm, blossom-scented air and the moonlit scenery around him, then he crossed to the steps and made his way down the path toward the river. Daylight would be breaking in less than an hour, and he could imagine that the heady sights of a dawning sun coming up on this verdant glade would be better seen from the deck of a ship than from the confines of a cabin. Desiring to indulge himself in a view that promised to be breathtaking, he sauntered down toward the vessel, but as he neared it, he realized that a smaller craft had been pulled ashore alongside and several men were moving furtively to and fro between the two vessels. Stepping behind a tree, William chose to remain hidden until he could determine the intent of the visitors.

William's hackles rose in apprehension as he saw a huge hulk of a man making his way up the building slip with a wooden keg on his shoulder. Its heavy weight was made obvious by the way in which the fellow heaved it over into the arms of another who met him at the top of the slip. As William continued to watch, the man returned to the boat to fetch another keg. Then a large, portly man stepped from the small boat and made his way along the river's edge toward the ship with the aid of a long staff or, more precisely, a soldier's pike, which he loosely clasped near the head. William had seen that particular pike-assisted stride before, and though the other's shape had widened throughout the years, he was almost certain it was the same man. His suspicions were promptly confirmed as he heard the man declare to a tar who walked beside him, "Six kegs of gunpowder should splinter every plank aboard her. 'Twill be just revenge for what those Thorntons once stole from me."

William stealthily retreated and quickly made his way back to the cabin. Taking care that he did not alert the miscreants, he pushed the front portal open carefully and hastened to the door of the first bedroom. A

quick rap of knuckles on the planks announced his presence as he burst into the
moonlit room. He had given the couple no
time to respond, and his son bolted upright
with a start, drawing a gasp from Shemaine,
who had been nestled against him.

"Gage, you must hurry!" William bade in
an urgent whisper. "There are men down by
the river, and I think they're planning on
blowing up your ship. If my memory serves
me true, 'tis none other than Horace Turnbull down there directing them."

Throwing back the covers with a muttered
curse, Gage leapt from the bed and, in two
long strides, reached the chair where he had
left his clothes the night before. He thrust
first one leg and then the other into a pair of
buckskin trousers, clothing his naked loins
as he asked, "How many men are with
him?"

"I caught sight of at least six, but I'm sure
there are more." Out of the corner of his
eye, William saw Shemaine reach for the
nightgown that lay atop the covers. Dragging it beneath the bed linens, she swept the
covers over her head. From her movements,
he could only assume that she was hastily

trying to don the garment beneath the make-shift tent.

"Too many for the two of us to finish off with flintlocks," Gage muttered, snatching on hide boots.

"I can help," Shemaine offered, uncovering her head again but clasping the bed linens close beneath her chin.

"You stay put!" Gage barked sternly, turning to her. "It's too dangerous. I'd rather let them blow the damn ship than lose you!"

"But, Gage, you taught me how to shoot!" she argued, trying to fasten the gown at her throat. "And you know I usually hit what I aim at now!"

William interceded in the couple's dispute. "To win the day, Gage, we'll need every weapon at our disposal. If Shemaine can stay behind a tree and fire at the brigands, then she may be able to keep them pinned down for a moment or two while we board the ship."

Gage bent a worried frown upon his wife as he shoved a pair of pistols into the waist of his breeches. "I guess you can help, but only if you promise to stay back a ways where they can't see you."

Shemaine had no time to respond as William urged, "Hurry, Gage!"

William ran from the room, and his son followed close behind as Shemaine jumped from their bed and snatched up her robe. Gage grabbed up another pair of muzzle-loaders from a parlor cabinet, tossed one to his father, and then slapped a pistol into his hand. They hurriedly loaded the weapons and left.

Beyond the front door, Gage quickly took the lead and sprinted on ahead. A moment later the door was pushed slowly open again, and Shemaine crept out with a flint-lock pistol. She flitted through the shadows toward the nearest tree and paused there as she watched Gage and his father go on ahead.

The sky was beginning to lighten in the east, allowing Gage to view the activity around the ship. As he neared the building slip, one of the miscreants espied him and shouted a warning. Grabbing a pistol from his belt, the man took a shot at Gage, bringing his accomplices' attention to bear upon the father and son. The lead ball zinged harmlessly past, and Gage promptly repaid the fellow by firing the rifle, sending the brigand sprawling backward with a large hole in his chest.

Gage had no time to reload and tossed the rifle aside. He snatched the pistols from his trousers just as his father raised the rifle and sent another fellow to his doom, halting that one before he could fire his pistol at Gage. William ran forward, scooping up the man's weapon, and immediately made use of it as another culprit settled the sights of a flintlock upon him. The ruffian was jerked abruptly backward as the lead ball hit him squarely in the chest. As the man collapsed, two smaller rapscallions rushed forward to tackle William. He swept a pistol across the face of one, sending the man reeling away, and confronted the other with a sharp jab of a fist against a stubbled chin. Stumbling back, the rogue waited a moment for his spinning world to stop turning and then ran forward again for more of the same punishment.

Gage was already leaping up the building slip. Firing at the first two men he met, he shot one in the face and the other in the throat. As a towering, bulky giant came lumbering toward him across the deck, Gage snatched up a wooden cudgel and swung the club with brutal force against the man's bald pate. The huge hulk staggered back several steps with a stunned look, but after a sharp shake of his head, he reclaimed what senses he had and settled a menacing glower upon his adversary. With a loud snarl of rage, he rushed forward with an ungainly gait and, as the club was raised for another blow, he swept it away with a roar and an angry swipe of his hand.

Gage ducked as the giant thrust a broad fist toward his face, causing his weighty opponent to totter off balance. The oaf quickly recovered, and Gage feinted forward, trying to snatch up the cudgel from the deck. But the brute, realizing what his opponent was after, seized it within his own grasp. Gage promptly retreated, but he was brought up short by the stack of powder kegs that had been heaped all together. His adversary stole the advantage and, leaping forward, swung the cudgel with a backward stroke of his arm. A sudden brilliant flash of pain flared through Gage's head as the bat forcefully scraped his head, and he stumbled away in a dazed stupor.

The giant chortled in glee, seeing the smaller man at his mercy, and threw aside

the club. Cracking his knuckles in anticipation, he stalked forward menacingly.

William gained the top of the building slip
just in time to see a brawny fist driving into
his son's face. Gage sprawled back upon
the casks and, after a moment, sluggishly
pushed himself upright on an elbow, but the
giant was already moving in for the kill.

William raised the sights of his pistol toward the man and began to squeeze the
trigger, but before he could complete the
motion, the roar of another flintlock echoed
in resounding waves across the ship. Ever
so slowly, the huge brigand's knees buck-
led, twisting oddly beneath him as his body
began to collapse. Blood glistened wetly in
the rosy shades of the coming dawn as it
oozed from a large hole in his head and cas-
caded down over his ear. William turned in
wonder, curious to know who had brought
about the culprit's demise.

Shemaine stood at the top of the building
slip with a smoking flintlock still clutched in
her hands. Even in the meager light William
could see that she was shaking uncontrollably, having now killed a man.

A cry of rage brought their attention to
bear upon the portly man scrambling up

from the companionway. Upon reaching the deck, Horace Turnbull halted and wheezed air into his lungs as he surveyed the carnage in the dawning light. In his hand he still clasped the pike, a weapon he had learned to use as a foot soldier at a much younger age. A broken leg had seen him cashiered from the ranks, but by then he had already acquired a skill and a fondness for the lance. It had become a keepsake of sorts, for he had started acquiring his wealth by both devious and slightly more honest methods soon after his leg had mended. He still carried the weapon on missions such as these, for he had never learned proficiency with black-powder firearms, and he never knew who might seek revenge.

Horace Turnbull's eyes flared brightly as he fixed his gaze upon the one who had sailed away from Portsmouth with his cargo long years ago. The man sat on a cask with his head cradled in a hand, completely vulnerable to his whim and unaware of the danger he was in.

Turnbull hauled back the pike and took aim. "Look now, Lord Thornton," he bellowed, having recognized his lordship right off. "See how I will now exact vengeance on you both . . . for your son, death. For you, the agony of his loss, for 'twas you who sent him to pirate my cargo!"

"Turnbull, nooo!" William railed, but it was too late.

The lance was already flying forward.

Shemaine screamed, but there was absolutely nothing she could do but watch in paralyzed horror. William, however, was not willing to give his son up to the grave so soon after he had found him. With strength born of desperation, he leapt forward, throwing himself in front of Gage. The pike sank deep into his back, wrenching a startled gasp from him. Then, almost stiltedly, he staggered about to face Turnbull and lifted his arm, painfully taking aim with the pistol he had not yet fired.

The wealthy shipping baron gaped into the bore of the flintlock and his eyes nearly bulged out of his head as he stared into the face of death. Raising his gaze to William, he shook his head frantically. "No . . . please! You mustn't!" he blubbered, and began to bargain pleadingly, "I'll give you all my wealth. . . ."

The pistol barked in an ear-numbing explosion, projecting the small leaden ball through the air. A second later it seemed to bore a third eye between Turnbull's brows. Like a stiff statue, the man toppled backward into the companionway, where he lay with head slanting downward on the stairs, his eyes open but unseeing.

Shemaine ran to William as his legs began to give way beneath him. Bracing him up with her own body, she eased him to the top of a cask near the one Gage sat on. Blood flowed from the wound in William's back, turning his white nightshirt ominously dark in the meager light. Shemaine pressed a hand upon his shoulder and, grasping the wooden shaft, tried to pull it out, but her efforts proved futile, for it refused to come free.

The sound of running footfalls came from the building slip, bringing Shemaine around with a start, but her breath eased out in a long sigh of relief when she saw Gillian. In increasing apprehension the young man had taken account of the bodies scattered around the ship as he hurried to the slip. Now he also saw one on the deck and another in the companionway. He looked at Shemaine, totally astounded.

"What happened?"

"Never mind that now, Gillian," she replied anxiously. "Help me get Gage and his father down to the cabin. They've both been hurt, his lordship seriously."

The situation demanded action. Gillian could see that for himself. He ran back to the rail and looked toward the small craft that he and his father had just pulled ashore. Spying the elder in the tree-shrouded gloom, he yelled down to him. "Hurry, Pa! The Thorntons are wounded!"

Flannery Morgan was far more nimble and quick-footed than one might have thought. In less than a moment he was on the deck, helping his son with William Thornton. Flannery was against pulling out the pike without a doctor present, but to relieve the pain of its weight upon the wound, he sawed off the shaft as Gillian held it firm, leaving just enough to be firmly grasped. Between the two of them, they carried the elder Thornton to the cabin loft and then returned for their captain.

Gage had fallen into a deep, traumatized sleep in his wife's arms. He could not be roused, deepening Shemaine's fear, and she hurried along beside the two shipwrights as they bore her husband to the front bedroom. She asked their assistance in removing Gage's boots and the shirt which had gotten bloodied from the open wound in his scalp. Promptly she set to work cleaning the injury, and then she ran upstairs to see how she might help William. Her anxiety for both men brought tears to her eyes as she worked to cut away the nightshirt from the elder, who, even in his agony, tried to lend her assistance.

"Rest yourself if you can, my lord," she urged, sniffing and wiping at the blinding tears with the sleeve of her robe.

"How's Gage?" William rasped through his pain.

"I don't know," she answered in a choked voice. "He's unconscious."

"He must live!"

Shemaine's face threatened to crumple with pent-up emotion, but she promptly sucked in a breath, willing herself not to break down. "You both must live!"

Upon Erich Wernher's arrival for work several moments earlier, he had been sent out on the back of Sooner to fetch Dr. Ferris. He was the best rider they had, and it was up to him to bring the physician back post-haste. When the doctor came racing up on the back of his own capable steed about an hour later, he was whisked directly upstairs, where he examined the elder Thornton, who lay fully awake on his side. Colby Ferris immediately sent Gillian down to search the kitchen for a strong brew to fortify his lordship against the discomfort he was presently suffering, as well as the agony which would be forthcoming once the extraction of the lance commenced. Thus far the elder Thornton had remained alert to everything happening around him, but Colby was of the belief that his lordship would be better off unconscious. In a few short moments Gillian returned with a jug of brew that his own father normally kept aboard the ship for his customary tipple before heading home each evening.

"Watch over his lordship until I can see how his son is doing downstairs," Colby instructed the young man. "Encourage him to drink as much as he can . . . *even* if you have to sip along with him. Just be sure there's enough left to flush the wound before and after."

Gillian scanned the long form of the Englishman as he lay on his side facing the wall. With part of the pike still imbedded in his lordship's back, he could only imagine the agony the elder had to be suffering and would have to endure if he tried to push himself upright. "But how will his lordship drink it dow. . . ."

William looked around with a painful grimace and beckoned to be given the jug. Then, with Colby's and Gillian's help, he braced himself up on an elbow as they stuffed pillows beneath him. Satisfied that his patient was willing, the doctor left the Irishman the unusual task of getting an English lord thoroughly intoxicated.

Leaving them, Colby went downstairs to examine the injury on Gage's head. By now the rent had stopped bleeding, but there was a large knot on the skull beneath it. At the moment Colby couldn't make a firm evaluation of his patient's condition. "Your husband may come out of it just fine . . ." he told Shemaine. "And then again, he may not. Just keep a cool, wet compress on the wound and watch him closely. I'll have to stitch his scalp together once I finish tending his father. Your husband has obviously suffered a concussion and, for a time, may drift in and out of a stupor. It all depends on how much pressure is building beneath the skull."

Shemaine felt her legs begin to give way beneath her as a debilitating coldness swept through her, but she gritted her teeth in sudden determination and refused to yield to the pervading fear. This was her husband, and he needed her! She could not allow herself to faint!

All the commotion in the house had served to awaken Andrew, and Shemaine took a few moments to feed and dress the boy before she washed and garbed herself. Then the two of them carried the rocking chair from his small bedroom into the larger one, where they could look after Gage. Cuddling Andrew against her, Shemaine rocked and sang to him, and together they waited and prayed that all would be well with the husband and father they both loved. After a time, Andrew slipped from her lap and crawled up onto the bed to snuggle against his parent. Shemaine followed and, wrapping her arm around the boy, rested a hand against her husband's chest and took comfort in his strong, sturdy heartbeat.

When Colby Ferris went to the loft to see how Gillian was faring with William, he found

his lordship clearheaded and fully conscious. Gillian, however, had begun to slur
his words, not having acquired much stamina against the brew. Deeming the young
shipwright in need of some fresh air and
himself in want of two strong men to hold
down his lordship, Colby sent him to fetch
Ramsey Tate and Sly Tucker, who were
helping Flannery load the dead men in a
wagon for their final trip to Newportes
Newes.

Except for cleansing the wound, the whiskey was not as beneficial as Colby had
hoped, for his lordship remained fully cognizant during the whole painful process of
removing the pike from his back. No major
organs had been damaged, but the puncture
was deep nevertheless. Cleaning the open
wound with the fiery liquid would have undone a lesser man, but William, who was
forced to remain on his stomach throughout
the ordeal, clenched his teeth and buried his
face in the pillows to still any sound. The
tremors that shook his tensed body were
vivid proof of the effort he made not to cry
out. It was only at the very last, when the
large gap in his shoulder was being sewn up,
that his lordship finally yielded up his con-

sciousness, leaving the doctor astounded at the older man's fortitude and obstinate will.

When Colby went downstairs again, he found Andrew and Shemaine curled up close together on the bed beside Gage. They were both sleeping, but Gage had awakened and was scrutinizing his wife and son as if they were rare treasures.

"How do you feel?" Colby asked softly after stitching the gash.

"Like I've been hit in the head with the fat end of a mallet."

"You can be glad you're alive."

A frown gathered Gage's brow, but he soon repented of any facial expressions. "Was I hit that hard?"

"Not that I know of." Colby swept a hand briefly toward Shemaine. "According to your father, your wife shot and killed the man who was trying to kill you." He paused to let that fact sink in and saw a look of wonder pass over the other man's face. "*And* according to Shemaine, your father deliberately threw himself in front of you to take the lance that was meant for you."

Startled, Gage looked at the physician. Fearing the worst, it was a long moment before he could trust himself to speak. "Is he dead?"

"No, his lordship should mend fairly well unless the wound becomes tainted, but Flannery's jug of whiskey should have cauterized it completely. I've never tasted anything stronger in my life, but it seemed to have little effect on his lordship. Frankly, I'm amazed by his stamina and tolerance for pain. He never once fainted or cried out despite the agony we put him through. Your father and wife must love you very much, Mr. Thornton."

Swept with a feeling of wonderment as he considered the doctor's statement, Gage was only vaguely aware of his own reply, which had become almost second nature to him whenever he was addressed by his proper name. "My name is Gage."

"Rest as much as you can, Gage," Colby instructed. "You'll be better off if you do and will be back on your feet much faster for it."

Gage recalled the last time he had seen the doctor. "How is Calley doing anyway? Ramsey keeps telling me she's much better, but I still worry about her. She should be nearing her time pretty soon, shouldn't she?"

"Calley is doing remarkably well, and yes, she should be delivering any day now. Annie is keeping a close eye on her and is just as anxious as the mother for the baby to be born."

"Ramsey wants to keep Annie on for his wife's sake," Gage informed him, "but Calley says they can't afford her. She wants at least one of their five sons to go to William and Mary and is saving every farthing she can to make sure that will happen. If left to her, all of them will be tutored there."

Dr. Ferris scrubbed a booted toe across the cypress floor. "Actually, I've been thinking about buying Annie from you. . . ."

Surprised, Gage looked at the man. "I thought you said—"

"Never mind what I said. Annie would be an excellent assistant, and lately I've been thinking I'd like to marry again. I'm still young enough to have children. My wife couldn't have any, and she died childless. A child of her own is what Annie wants, and I think I'm able to give her that. She may not love me now, but perhaps in the future. . . ."

"Have you asked her yet?"

"No, I couldn't, not with you owning her. Myers has been complaining to me about how you said you were going to bring her back but never have. He thinks you should give him more money for tricking him."

Gage snorted. "He's been paid far too well as it is."

"I figured as much, but I thought you should know. He's not above making trouble whenever he can. He and Roxanne Corbin got into a row because Mrs. Pettycomb repeated a remark that he had made about Roxanne's expectations being too far-fetched if she actually believed that any man would marry a horse-faced spinster. Roxanne came over and confronted him right on his front porch, called him a spineless little toad because he hadn't dared say what he thought to her face. Well, he repeated the insult for her benefit, and Roxanne just about gouged his eyes out before he began to pound on her. I ran over there to pull them apart, but it was like being caught between two cats hissing and spitting mad. Roxanne was pretty bruised up, but Myers had deep claw marks down his face and throat. I didn't offer to tend either of them, figuring they both deserved it, Myers for opening his mouth and Roxanne for seeking him out."

"Myers should be more careful if he plans

to live to a ripe, old age," Gage remarked. "Courting disaster with the wrong person can make a man seriously regret his foolishness."

"Diplomacy has never been one of Myers's strong points, as you and I both know, but I doubt he can malign us too badly when we have truth on our side. Because of you, Annie is safe from his abuse and has become close friends with Calley. Annie's life has changed for the better, and if she's willing, we can start our own family. Perhaps someday she'll be able to forget the child that was taken from her. If you're in agreement, I'm prepared to repay you the money you expended in her behalf."

"I'm in total agreement," Gage replied, and lifted a brow in a lopsided query despite the ache in his head. "Will you invite us to your wedding?"

Colby chuckled. "If Annie will have me."

"She will."

The doctor laid a leather pouch filled with coins on the bedside table and then quietly left the room. In the stillness that ensued, Gage felt the hand resting on his chest begin to move in a leisurely caress, and he glanced down to find his wife smiling up at him.

"Have I ever told you, Mr. Thornton," Shemaine whispered sleepily, "how very, very precious you are to me?"

His heart swelled with joy. "Does that mean you love me, Shemaine?"

"Aye, Mr. Thornton. That means I love you very, very much."

Gage gathered the slender fingers in his hand and brought them to his lips for a gentle kiss. "And I love you, madam, very, very much."

CHAPTER 19

William and Gage Thornton resembled each other in more ways than just looks, Shemaine decided after trying to keep them both abed for more than a day. Though Gage was still suffering from a throbbing headache the next morning, he completed his regular chores and then went back to work in the cabinet shop. That same afternoon, while Shemaine was out in front of the cabin washing clothes in the stream, his father attempted to make his way from the loft to the privy outside, even though a chamber pot had been placed conveniently at hand. After descending most of the stairs, he became faint, lost his balance, and toppled down the remaining steps, ripping open a goodly number of stitches and, in the process, starting the blood flowing again. Andrew witnessed the event from the back corridor and, wide-eyed with fear, ran out to the front porch to yell for Shemaine to come back quickly and help his grandfather.

The clothes went flying helter-skelter, and by the time she arrived, William had pushed the tail of his nightshirt down over his naked loins, restoring his modesty to some degree, and pulled himself to a sitting position against the wall at the bottom of the stairs. The grimace on his face conveyed the pain he was suffering. Still, he uttered no more than a choked-off moan when Shemaine tried to haul him to his feet. William was too weak to lend her much assistance and too heavy for her to lift alone, as much as Andrew tried to help her.

"Andy, go get your father at the cabinet shop," she bade. "And hurry!"

Gage returned in short order with Sly Tucker, and between the two of them, they carried William back to his bed. His lordship, anxious to preserve propriety with a lady present in the room, dragged the sheet up over his waist before he would allow them to strip off the bloodstained nightshirt. It was Shemaine who gently swabbed his back clean while Gage pressed a towel firmly against the rent in an effort to stem the fresh flow of blood.

"Is Gran'pa goin' to be all right?" Andrew asked worriedly, reluctant to come any closer than the top of the stairs, for the sight of so much gore had frightened the boy.

Shemaine offered a smile of encouragement. "Your grandfather is going to be just fine, Andy. He's too ornery to allow a little mishap like this to trouble him."

Flushing red with chagrin, William shot a glance toward the girl and promptly became the recipient of a pointedly eloquent stare. Shemaine had no need to chide him for what he had done; he knew he deserved it only too well. Frightening the boy was only a small part of it.

Colby was already making the rounds and arrived soon after they had managed to stem the bleeding. He was furious that the elder had tried to get out of bed so soon after suffering such a serious wound.

"You leave this bed one more time and rip open any more stitches, and I'll have no recourse but to lay a red-hot iron to close up the wound! Do you understand what I'm saying? I didn't patch you up just so you could kill yourself going to the privy." In a vivid display of outrage, he jabbed a thumb over his shoulder to indicate the necessary item. "The pot's right there, just waiting to be used! So save me a few trips out here to mend you up and do so!"

Having bravely crept forward, Andrew now sank behind the head of the cot until his nose rested on the feather ticking. He wasn't at all certain he liked the man scolding his grandfather. If ever he got sick or injured, he just hoped the doctor wouldn't have to be fetched for him.

Colby Ferris didn't limit his criticism to his lordship, but turned a glare upon Gage, who was standing at the basin washing his father's blood off his forearms. "And what are you doing out of bed? Didn't I tell you to stay there for a while?"

"I did. . . . for a while," Gage retorted with a grin. "But I had work to do."

" 'Tis evident the both of you are close kin!" Colby grumbled, and eyed Shemaine as a possible source of help. "Perhaps you can do something to convince these two to heed my advice."

Shemaine smiled and began laying out clean linens for the bed and fresh swabs for the doctor to use while he restitched the wound. Remembering one of James Harper's favorite sayings, she turned it into a question. "Have you ever seen the sun setting in the east, Dr. Ferris?"

Flicking a glance from father to son, Colby set his lips awry in perturbation. The two showed no remorse and would obviously do what they wanted. "I see what you mean."

"Still, they might set a better example for the boy if they were more attentive to your instructions," Shemaine added, smiling up at Gage as she handed him a towel. "I'm sure they would expect Andrew to do what you say, Doctor, just as my husband expects his men to glean guidance from his expertise."

Colby smiled, realizing the lady was effectively getting her point across with gentle reasoning far better than he had with his ranting. Seeming suddenly abashed by the poor example they had set for the boy, Gage and William looked toward Andrew. It was William who twisted slightly to take his grandson's hand and pull him around to the side of the bed.

"Do you understand that I brought this new trouble on myself by not listening to the doctor?" The child stared at the elder with widened eyes as he continued. "I should have had more consideration for your mother and the trouble I made bloodying the sheets and the stairs. I know what I did frightened you, and I'm sorry for that. I should have stayed here in the loft and not tried to go downstairs. Had I done so, I wouldn't be needing more stitches now. Do you understand?"

The boy nodded, and William ruffled his dark hair, winning a grin from the youngster.

Wiping his hands on the towel, Gage gave his wife a smile as he ceded to her gentle arguments. "All right, my love, I'll go tell my men to work the rest of the day without me. Does that please you?"

" 'Twill relieve my worries knowing you will rest." Shemaine reached up and, lightly combing her fingers through his hair, gently felt the swelling that was still there beneath the neatly closed gash. "I don't want anything to happen to you now that we've found each other."

*   *   *

It was rumored that Gertrude Turnbull Fitch had caused such a row in Newportes Newes after the death of her father that officials of the hamlet had started making inquiries about her possible involvement in the plot to blow up Gage Thornton's ship. To assure himself of some avenue into the Turnbull wealth, Captain Fitch forcibly hauled his wife aboard the *London Pride* and set sail for England before anyone actually decided to arrest her. She hissed like a viper, laying a severe tongue-lashing upon him, but Everette only smiled, for her threats carried little weight now that J. Horace Turnbull was dead. He promised himself that it would be Gertrude's last voyage on the *London Pride*, for she had cost them more in lives lost than he had ever managed to pilfer from the coffers. James Harper and the crew guessed their captain's intentions, but they didn't dare let out sighs of relief. After the shores of England were reached and they had seen the last of the shrew, then there would be a celebration the likes of which they had heretofore only dreamed about.

At first, Shemaine and Gage were both hopeful that Potts had been aboard the vessel when it embarked upon the return voyage, but they soon learned that he had jumped ship and was still in the territory. Some said he was keeping company with Morrisa again, and if that was the case, it was not hard to surmise that with Freida closely watching over her girls and their accounting of customers, Potts was having to pay through the nose for any favors he might be receiving from Morrisa. A tar's wages could not last long with such prurient indulgences, and it was supposed that one day soon he would have to find work or resort to drastic measures to gain the coins he would need to merely exist.

Potts's welfare was of little consequence to Shemaine and Gage. They were far more concerned with the threats he had made in the past and feared the day was swiftly approaching when he would again be seeking his revenge. Not an hour went by that they didn't wonder if he was in the woods again, watching for an opportunity to kill one of them.

Soon after the departure of the *London Pride*, Calley gave birth to a little girl, and her joy was complete. Annie stayed for another week, just long enough for the woman to get back into the routine of running her household again. In the ensuing days a small wedding was planned for Annie and Dr. Colby Ferris at a church in the hamlet. Only a few close friends would attend the ceremony, but everyone else was invited to a large feast at the tavern, which served the best food in town. For that particular afternoon at least, the owner had promised to keep Freida and her girls from plying their trade on the premises, a situation that did not necessarily please the madam.

Mary Margaret kindly offered to come out and sit with Andrew and William while Gage and Shemaine attended the ceremony and festivities. Since it promised to be a late hour before they returned, the couple had invited Mrs. McGee to spend the night with them so she wouldn't have to make the trip back at a late hour. The woman readily accepted. But William was not at all keen about the idea. His hackles rose at the thought of having an Irish nursemaid looking after him, but being for the most part restricted to his narrow bed by firm orders from the doctor, he could find no avenue of escape.

Gage showed no sympathy toward William's grumbling complaints. "I've seen old boars with better temperaments than you have," he accused, having grown exasperated with his father's continual harping about Mrs. McGee coming out to watch over them. "You've complained about the discomfort of your bed, the lowness of the ceiling, the inconvenience of peeing in a pot, and a long list of other things, not the least of which is the fact that you and Andrew will be left in the care of Mrs. McGee, a perfectly capable, kindly old woman—"

"Old woman . . . humph!" William snorted, jamming his pillow more firmly beneath his head with a balled-up fist. "Old shrew, more likely! What is she going to do, run and fetch the pot when I've got to go? By George, I'll rot in hell first!" It was positively absurd to imagine himself being attended by some harpy who'd think of him as an invalid and, in her zeal to be helpful, try to lift the tail of his nightshirt as he staggered weak-kneed toward the chamber chair. He had been imprisoned in this damned loft far too long and certainly needed no decrepit ancient assisting him! "Blast it all, Gage! I don't need any nosy-posy tending me!"

Gage struggled valiantly not to laugh. He

could understand his sire growing petulant now that he couldn't move about with his customary agility and energy, but the wound had been serious and would take time to heal, definitely much longer than his father seemed willing to consider or, for that fact, had the patience for.

"Mrs. McGee will be coming here mainly for Andrew's benefit," Gage stated slowly, as if to help his parent understand the necessity of the woman's presence. "And if, in the process of looking after him, she may consent to serve you a meal or do you some small service, then I would urge you not to resist unduly. Mrs. McGee is not so old that she can't give you a proper tongue-lashing."

"Just how old is the biddy, anyway?" William barked. "Doddering and dowdy, I presume!"

"Actually, Mary Margaret is quite a handsome woman." Gage's lips began to twitch with amusement as he realized his sire seemed far more concerned about the woman's age than with anything else. "I suppose we could have found a younger woman to sit with you, but she might not have been nearly as comely."

William squinted suspiciously at his son

as he pressed the point. "How old did you say she was?"

Gage shrugged. "Actually, I didn't. I don't have any idea how old she is. I never felt inclined to ask, but it can't be too much older than you, if at all. What are you, sixty-five? She's got to be around that age, plus or minus."

Andrew came thumping up the stairs with an armful of books and, upon reaching the loft, immediately scurried to the cot, where he dropped his burden beside the elder.

"Mommee Sheeaim said you can read to me if'n ye want, Gran'pa, 'cause she's gettin' dressed and can't take time right now." Propping his elbows on the edge of the cot, the youngster settled his chin in his hands and peered at his grandfather cajolingly. "Will you, huh, Gran'pa?"

William could not resist his grandson's heartwarming entreaty. Clearing his throat, he assumed a more benevolent demeanor for the child, but his cheeks took on a ruddy hue as he flicked his gaze toward Gage and gestured lamely toward his leather trunk. "You'll find a pair of spectacles in the top receptacle. Will you fetch them for me?"

"I'll get 'em, Gran'pa!" Andrew cried eagerly, and ran to the chest as his father lifted the lid and folded back the cover of the first compartment. Receiving the eyeglasses with an admonition to be careful, the boy returned to his grandfather and watched curiously as the elder put them on. William glanced askance at the child, who, greatly intrigued by his own reflection in the lenses, leaned close in front of the elder's face.

"Do you see a little squirrel?" William queried fondly.

"I see Andee!"

"I think that's a little squirrel you see," William teased as a grin was wrenched from his lips.

"Oh, no, Gran'pa!" Andrew curled a finger inwardly and jabbed at his own chest. "That's me! Mommee Sheeaim show me in the water when we go down by the pond! That's Andee!"

"I see a little squirrel from this side of the eyeglasses."

"Can I see?" Andrew could hardly restrain himself as he pressed his face alongside his grandfather's and tried to look through the lenses from the older viewer's direction.

William's grin broadened as he cut his eyes askance. "See anything?"

Closing one eye, Andrew squinted more intently. "Huh-uh."

"Then perhaps you should wear them yourself for a better view."

Andrew willingly allowed the wires to be affixed behind his ears, but when he tried to look through the spectacles, his eyes soon crossed. Turning his head this way and that, he tried to right his vision. "Gran'pa! I can't see nothin'!"

Gage pressed a lean knuckle across his lips to forestall his laughter. From his point of view, the strong lenses made his son look more than a little bug-eyed. He tiptoed across the room to the stairs and paused there to glance back as his father scooped up a sketch of a squirrel he had drawn earlier that day.

William held it in front of the boy and urged, "Now take the glasses off."

Andrew obeyed, and his expression changed to one of elation as he saw the life-like sketch. "Oh, Gran'pa! You draw squirrel good like Daddee draw ship!"

Gage descended the stairs with the same care with which he had crossed the room, for he was unwilling to disturb the two, who were completely engrossed with each other.

It had warmed his heart immensely to see his father playing with Andrew, for it was a cold fact that he had never thought his sire would ever care for his grandchildren. Now he was seeing the elder in a different light, one that had been illumined by the natural inquisitiveness of a child.

Shemaine looked up as Gage came into their bedroom and immediately turned around to show him the laces that had become ensnared at the back of her bodice. "I must be getting fat! Or Victoria was as thin as a reed when she wore this gown! I had to let out the laces so I could breathe, and look what I've done trying to get them adjusted!"

Coming up close behind his wife, Gage slipped his arms around her and assumed a thoughtful expression as he cupped her breasts within his hands. "Aye, there's more than a handful now." He leaned over her shoulder and, plucking the neckline away from her bosom, peered down into the garment to admire the swelling fullness that rose tantalizingly above the lace-trimmed chemise. "Two ripe melons ready to be devoured. I can hardly wait 'til we return tonight."

Shemaine thrust an elbow backward, playfully jabbing him in the ribs, and tossed a smile over her shoulder as she coyly scolded, "Behave, sir!"

"With every woman but you, my love," her husband assured her huskily, spreading kisses upward along her throat. "You're my solitary source for carnal pleasures."

"I'm glad." Shemaine sighed, leaning her head back upon his shoulder as she stroked the lean hands that had returned to caress her breasts. "I could not bear to share you with another woman. I'm like Roxanne in that respect."

"Aye, madam, but I'm your possession, not hers. You have a right to feel that way."

A light knock on the front door interrupted, announcing the arrival of their guest. With the summons, Gage remembered that Andrew would have company in his bedroom that night and that the walls were not thick enough to keep the squeak of a bed from being heard.

"We'll have to try out the bear rug tonight," Gage mused aloud, slipping a hand inside his wife's chemise to fondle a round breast. "Or Mary Margaret will wonder about our inability to leave each other alone."

"I aired the rug outside yesterday," Shemaine informed him, lifting smiling eyes upward to meet his warmly glowing gaze. "Knowing your insatiable appetite, I considered our options with Mrs. McGee in the next room."

" 'Twas shrewd of you, my dear, to think ahead," Gage murmured, dropping a loving kiss upon her brow. Brushing his fingers with slow deliberation over a pliant peak, he withdrew his hand and let out a halting breath as he moved back a step, but his attempt to curb his excitement was greatly impeded when his wife reached behind her for a quick, exploring stroke of her hand, sending a thunderbolt jolting through his loins. Then, with a gleaming smile of appreciation, she cast a triumphant glance toward him, wrenching a grin from him. "Aye, I can't be around you without being affected. If not for Mary Margaret waiting outside our front door, I'd make time for us this very moment."

"The invitation is open anytime, my love," Shemaine breathed with a sultry smile.

"I'll collect upon your promise later," Gage assured her with a meaningful wink, moving toward the door.

Stepping into the parlor, Gage directed his thoughts to something far less pleasurable than his beautiful wife and had regained control of his appetites by the time he got to the door. As he opened the front portal, Mary Margaret greeted him with a smile and then turned to wave farewell to Gillian, who had brought her upriver in his father's boat.

"I'll see ye tomorrow," she called to the young man.

Facing her host again, Mary Margaret looked him over from head to toe and nodded her approval of his gentlemanly attire. His frock coat, breeches, waistcoat and stockings were of deep blue silk, nicely accentuated by a crisp, white shirt, jabot and stock.

Sweeping a hand to invite her in, Gage showed a leg in a gentlemanly bow and smiled. "Welcome to our home, my lady."

Mary Margaret complied with a grin. "Well, ye handsome rogue, I see ye've lost none o' yer looks since I last saw ye. Ye've garbed yerself a lot fancier, I vow."

"Something my father gave me," Gage admitted, smoothing the costly coat. He had almost forgotten the rich, sumptuous feel of silk. "He said his girth had expanded well beyond the fit of the garments, but that's not likely, considering he's the same size I've always known him to be."

"Then think of the garments as a gift from a dotin' parent," the woman recommended kindly.

A contemplative smile traced Gage's lips. "I never thought of my father as a doting parent before, but I suppose I'll have to change my mind, considering he took the lance that was meant for me."

The Irish blue eyes twinkled teasingly as Mary Margaret tilted her head at a coy angle. "Have ye missed me?"

"Immensely!" Gage replied with a chuckle, and brought in her small case from the front porch as she leaned on her cane and glanced about her.

"Where's yer pretty wife? An' Andrew, where is he?"

Gage swept a hand casually toward the loft. "Andrew's upstairs with his grandfather. You may go up and introduce yourself if you so desire. Shemaine isn't ready yet and has need of my services before she can be presented." He held up the satchel to gain the elder's attention as he stepped toward the bedroom door. "I'll put this in Andrew's room in case you should have need of it. I've already pulled out the trundle bed, so I'll leave the case beside the one you'll be sleeping in tonight. The taller bed will be more suited for you."

Mary Margaret elevated her gaze as she heard the low murmur of a deep voice drifting down from the upper story. It had a nice sound to it, she thought, but promptly faced Gage with one of her concerns. "Ye sure I won't be disturbin' Andrew sleepin' in his room tonight?"

"He'll enjoy your company," Gage reassured her. "He's been a bit lonesome in there since we put up the wall between our bedrooms."

"The wee tyke will no doubt be havin' a new brother or sister before too long," Mary Margaret ruminated aloud, cutting her eyes back toward Gage. "That will help ease his lonely plight, ta be sure."

Gage grinned and cocked a querying brow at her. "Now look who's watching for Shemaine's belly to grow," he teased, and lifted his shoulders in a casual shrug. "You'll have to give us time, Mary Margaret."

"As if I've not given ye enough as it is, ye

rogue!" she rebuked with a chortle. "Just how much time do ye need?"

"Give or take a month or two... or maybe more."

Mary Margaret flung up a hand as if to pooh-pooh his argument. "Ye've been wastin' time, else ye'd be knowin' whether or not yer wife has been caught." Growing suspicious, the elder eyed him closely. "But then, ye've always been a bit closemouthed, Gage Thornton, an' I'm thinkin' ye wouldn't be tellin' 'til the rest of us can see it for ourselves."

"Now, would I keep such an important secret from you?" Gage inquired in an affectionate tone.

Mary Margaret responded with an exaggerated snort. "Bet yer infernal hide, ye would!"

Curbing a smile as her host chuckled, the woman progressed several steps toward the back corridor and then, upon recalling a matter of grave importance, turned back to reclaim Gage's attention just as he reached the bedroom door. She was reluctant to bring tales of woe into the Thornton home so soon after their altercation with Horace Turnbull and his men, but she thought her friends needed to be told. "I assume ye've not heard that Samuel Myers went missin' for a pair o' days. . . ."

Gage looked at her, perplexed. "You mean he left Newportes Newes?"

"In spirit only."

Gage's brows drew together. "What do you mean?"

"They found Mr. Myers in his well this morn'n. His neck had been broken." She sighed pensively. "He might ne'er been discovered except, on the way down, his foot got tangled in the pulley rope on the bucket."

Gage set his jaw at a reflective angle. "I presume he didn't break his neck just falling in."

"Dropped, more'n likely. Alma Pettycomb said she came 'round ta see Mr. Myers the other day an' found him squabblin' with his neighbor, Dr. Ferris. 'Twould seem they were arguin' over Annie. Myers claimed ye had cheated him, an' Colby called him a bloody blackguard an' a liar ta his face."

Gage's lips twisted grimly. "So Mrs. Pettycomb is now pointing a finger at Colby as the murderer."

Mary Margaret dipped her head in the affirmative. "She's become quite taken with the fact that yer father is a lord and, for the time bein', has given ye a reprieve from her criticism. Otherwise, she'd be layin' the blame on ye, too."

"How kind of her," Gage jeered caustically.

"Not really."

He looked at the woman, sensing that something more was coming.

"Alma is now sayin' Shemaine's not fit ta be yer wife, what with her bein' a convict an' all."

"Too bad someone didn't drop Mrs. Pettycomb down a well!" Gage growled in vexation.

"Aye, someone might be tempted to do the deed one o' these days, but I'd rather it not be any o' me friends." Mary Margaret eyed the man closely until the full weight of her statement penetrated his awareness, then Gage laughed and reassured her with a shake of his head.

"Don't worry, Mary Margaret, I won't ruin my life killing that old crow. She doesn't bother me *that* much."

"That's good." Mary Margaret smiled in relief and, lifting her cane, pointed toward the corridor. "Yer father *is* decent, is he not?"

"Not really," Gage quipped, lending a whole different meaning to her question. "Right now, he could probably take on Potts and come out the better. Just be warned."

Mary Margaret's smile never wavered as she tossed a glance toward the stairs. "I think I can take care o' meself."

"I never suffered any doubts, madam."

With a chortle the Irishwoman waved him toward the bedroom with a flourish of a slender hand and continued toward the loft. Upon nearing the last step in her ascent, she rapped the tip of her cane against the floor to announce her presence.

" 'Tis Mary Margaret McGee comin' ta see the gentlemen in this upper room."

"Miz McGee!" Andrew cried, scooting off his grandfather's bed. The boy ran to meet her and, taking her hand, led her back toward the cot.

William hurriedly jerked off his eyeglasses, tucked them in a breast pocket of his nightshirt and pulled the sheet nigh to his chin before he glanced around with a scowl. The prospect of having a harping ol' biddy at his beck and call had put him in a sour mood, but upon laying eyes on the small, trim, winsome woman, he immediately had second thoughts. He sought to lift himself upright from his pillow, but an excruciating pain shot from his back through to the front of his chest, and he fell upon the bed with a sharp grimace.

"Your pardon, madam," William apologized in some embarrassment as she stepped near. "I have not the strength to rise and meet you with courteous attention. Lying in this cot without reprieve for so long has taken its toll upon me."

"No need ta bother yerself, me lord," Mary Margaret assured him with a sweet smile. "I'm well acquainted with yer infirmity an' do not hold it against ye." She swept her eyes casually along the length of him and, for once in her life, had to agree with Mrs. Pettycomb. He *was* an admirable specimen, even for an English lord. But then, she had always considered Gage Thornton an exceptionally handsome man, and there was definitely a striking resemblance between father and son.

"I was just reading to my grandson," William explained, gathering up some of the books that Andrew had brought to his bedside.

"Please continue," she urged, laying a hand upon the boy's shoulder. "I'm sure Andrew would love it. While ye're doin' so, I'll go down an' make us some tea. If I know Shemaine, she'll be havin' some wee cakes or crumpets made for servin' with tea." With a light, affectionate pat on Andrew's shoulder, she moved toward the stairs.

"Mrs. McGee . . . ?" William was amazed at the urgency in his tone and rebuked himself for having grown so awkward around women. Perhaps he had been too long a widower and too ambitious in his shipbuilding endeavors, for he had lost most of the social graces that women found attractive in men. In the years following his wife's death, he had grown hard, unpolished, and irascible. No wonder he found it difficult to talk to the fairer gender.

Mary Margaret returned to the cot and looked down at him inquiringly. "Would ye be wantin' somethin', me lord?"

He flicked a quick, hesitant glance upward, but upon meeting eyes that were a truer blue than the sky, he dared to hold her gaze. "I was wondering how skilled you are with cards. . . ."

The blue eyes twinkled as Mary Margaret raised her small, pointed chin and challenged him. "Skilled enough ta give yer lordship a run, ta be sure."

William grinned with the same cajoling charm his grandchild had mastered. " 'Tis boring up here all alone. Perhaps after Andrew has been put to bed, you'd consider a game or two. . . ."

Mary Margaret inclined her elegant white head ever so slightly, but the shine in her eyes was dazzling. "A game or two . . . or mayhap even three. . . ."

Shemaine and Gage were just coming out of their bedroom when Mary Margaret stepped from the back corridor into the kitchen. The elder paused to admire the young beauty who now wore a deep turquoise silk that had once been Victoria's most enchanting gown. The woman clearly remembered how comely the previous owner had looked wearing it, but not nearly as much as the present one. A narrow turquoise ribbon adorned Shemaine's slender throat, and from her earlobes hung pearl droplets, a recent gift Gage had bestowed upon his bride. Her fiery red hair had been swept atop her head beneath a white lace cap. Wispy curls had escaped around her face, lending an enchanting softness to the coiffure. A matching lace shawl draped her slender shoulders.

"Ye're a good-lookin' couple," Mary Margaret declared with exuberance. "The best I've ever seen!"

Shemaine sank into a shallow curtsy. "You're as kind as always, Mrs. McGee."

The Irishwoman softly hooted. "Don't ye be thinkin' I'd fill yer heads with lies 'cause I've nothin' better ta say, dearie. 'Tis truthful I be, an' don't ye be forgettin' it."

With a laugh Shemaine sank into a deeper curtsy. "I won't, Mrs. McGee, and thank you."

Leaving her, Shemaine hurried up the stairs to see if there was anything William needed before she and Gage left. As she came in view of his lordship, he swept off his eyeglasses and looked her over in avid appreciation.

"I wonder if Maurice du Mercer realizes yet what is missing from his life," his lordship pondered aloud as she began fluffing his pillows.

"I'm sure by now Maurice is being relentlessly bombarded with invitations from parents eager to make a good match for their daughters. In fact, he has probably chosen another young lady as his betrothed."

"I find it hard to believe that Maurice could forget you so easily, my dear, but his ill fortune has been turned to my son's gain."

Shemaine did not feel inclined to talk about her former fiancé when her husband was waiting. "Do you mind so much that we're leaving you with Mrs. McGee? She's really a very delightful woman."

At present, William was as reluctant to discuss his change of attitude toward the widow as Shemaine was to speak of the Marquess. "Don't worry about me. Andrew and I will manage."

Shemaine wasn't satisfied with his answer, but on impulse, she leaned down and placed an indulgent kiss upon his forehead, causing his brows to fly sharply upward in surprise.

"We'll be back as soon as we can," she murmured, and patted his hand before she turned to give Andrew a kiss and a hug. At the landing, she grinned back at them. "You both be good now, or Mrs. McGee will tell on you."

Andrew giggled at the idea that his grandfather was being admonished to behave. William winked at him and, resettling his eyeglasses upon his nose, picked up another book, drawing the youngster back to his side as he began to read.

CHAPTER 20

The wedding ceremony joining Annie Carver and Dr. Colby Ferris was a joyous occasion. Shemaine had never seen her friend looking so fetching. The pale blue gown, which Colby had hired seamstresses to make for his bride, suited Annie's coloring well, lending a vibrant glow to her light olive skin and gray eyes. Her lank, brown hair had been braided with blue ribbons and artfully swept on top her head. Miles Becker, a close friend of the doctor, had made her a pair of fashionable slippers and presented them as an early wedding present.

Colby Ferris had gone through a transformation as well. The stubble of whiskers that usually accentuated his gaunt features had been shaved away, and his gray hair had been neatly clipped and tied in a queue with black ribbon. Tailored garments of a somber gray lent a more dignified appearance to his tall, gangling form.

The vows were spoken in low, murmuring voices, and then, after sealing the pledges with a ring and a hesitant kiss, Annie and Colby knelt to receive the blessings of the priest. United in holy matrimony, they rose and turned to be presented to their friends.

"Ladies and gentlemen, may I present Dr. and Mrs. Ferris."

The guests responded with spirited applause, while chants of *"Hear! Hear!"* echoed throughout the church. Gage and Shemaine joined Calley and Ramsey in extending their congratulations to the newly wedded pair. With tears of joy filling her eyes, Annie threw her arms around Shemaine and held her close.

"Did ye ever think we could be so happy in this here land, m'liedy?"

"No, Annie," Shemaine murmured, laughing as she hugged her in return. "I never dared believe such happiness could come from my arrest until Gage bought me and took me home with him. Then my life began anew." Stepping back, she smiled at her tiny friend. "I wish you and Colby all the happiness in the world, Annie . . . and may you have *many* beautiful children."

Casting a timid glance toward Colby, Annie blushed. "Ye may think this strange, m'liedy, seein's as how I got a babe from it, but I've ne'er been with a man but once in me life. Ta be sure, I'm as nervous as an untainted virgin."

Shemaine smiled. "I'm sure Colby will be gentle with you, Annie . . . just as he was with Calley when he brought her babe into the world. You saw how careful he was. Can you imagine him being brutish with you?"

Annie shook her head. "Nay, m'liedy."

"Then don't worry."

Stepping back to allow others to talk with Annie, Shemaine slipped an arm through her husband's and smiled into his warmly glowing eyes. "Annie makes me realize just how fortunate I am."

"No regrets about leaving England, my sweet?" Gage inquired tenderly, laying a hand over the one she rested upon his sleeve.

Her fiery head tilted forward as she tried to swallow the sudden lump in her throat. "Only that I miss my parents very, very much."

"Perhaps after I sell the ship we can visit them there," he suggested. "Would you like that?"

Shemaine nodded eagerly, and then fanned herself with a handkerchief, feeling rather faint. "It seems terribly stuffy in here, Gage, don't you think?"

Gage gently stroked a finger along the side of her face. "Your cheeks are flushed."

"You do that to me," she murmured with a smile as her gaze delved into the warmth of his.

"Would you like to go outside and get some fresh air?"

"I can hardly wait."

It was only later, after blessings and good wishes had been bestowed upon the couple, that Annie again sought out Shemaine in the churchyard. Heretofore Annie had avoided talking in detail about the events that had led to her arrest, for she had deemed the memories far too painful to recall, but she seemed more relaxed about her past now.

"This land an' some o' its people have

given me a new beginnin', m'liedy. Here I be, married at last, an' with some hope for the future." Admiring her new gown, the petite woman smoothed her work-roughened hands over the sleeves. "I'd ne'er have been able to own anythin' this fine in England, m'liedy. We hadn't a farthin' ta our name after me ma started ailin'. I begged a man what worked at the apothecary's shop ta give me the herbs me ma needed 'cause she was really bad off sick. He said he'd do it if'n I'd let him have his way with me. He was so rough I started sobbin' afore he finished with me. He got real angry an' slapped me so's I'd be quiet. Afterwards, he called me a li'l slut for sellin' me virginity for a handful o' herbs. Then he booted me out without so much as a sprig, sayin' as how I didn't deserve anythin' 'cause I'd gone an' disturbed him whilst he was havin' his fun. I started poundin' me fist on the door, pleadin' with him ta give the herbs ta me, but he wouldn't answer. Later, I found meself carryin' his babe. I was nearin' the time for it ta be born when I went back ta plead with him 'cause me ma had gotten so much worse. He laughed at me an' said the brat was me own concern, not his. He made me so angry, I hit him over the head with a heavy vial an' stole the herbs. By the time I got back ta me ma, she was already dead. I gave birth ta me son that very same night. I hid out for a time, not knowin' where ta go, but the babe's father seen me beggin' on a street a short time later an' had me arrested."

Shemaine hurriedly blinked against the tears that had welled up in her eyes and, slipping her arms around her friend, enfolded her in a long, soothing embrace. "Did you tell Colby what happened to you?"

Annie nodded and sniffed. "I had ta, m'liedy. I couldn't wed him without layin' it all bare afore him. He said he loved me just the same an' we'd make a new beginnin' for each other. We'd start a family an' grow ol' together."

Shemaine smiled gently. " 'Twould seem you've been favored with a loving, caring husband, Annie."

Joining them, Colby slipped an arm around his bride's shoulders. "Our guests are heading to the tavern, Annie. We'd better go on ahead so we'll be there to greet them."

As they left, Shemaine glanced around for

Gage, then smiled as she felt a presence stepping up close behind her and blue-clad arms slipping around her.

"Are you looking for me, madam?" her husband whispered, bending near her ear.

Her answer came in a blissful sigh. "Only if you're the man of my dreams."

"Tell me, madam, what does the man of your dreams look like?"

"Tall, black-haired, amber-brown eyes . . . far too handsome for me to resist."

"Do you want to resist him?"

"Nay, never. I yearn for his touch even when I'm with others."

Gage swept his hands in a leisured caress of her arms. "Will my touch suffice, madam?"

"Only until we can get back to our bed and I can hold the man of my dreams in my arms again."

"We can leave now, my love," Gage suggested, intrigued by the idea. "There's nothing I foresee happening here that would be as enticing as what you speak of."

"If we were to leave now, your father and Mrs. McGee would still be up," Shemaine pointed out. "They'd wonder what brought us home so early and, no doubt, would want to talk. We'd face a delay either here or there. Besides, Annie will expect us to stay and share in her happiness."

Gage graciously yielded the decision to his wife. "As you wish, my lady. Shall we walk to the tavern or should I bring the chaise around?"

"We can walk, I think," Shemaine replied, and tossed a coquettish smile over her shoulder. " 'Tis not often I'm able to stroll along the boardwalk at a leisurely pace and watch all the women stare agog at you."

"That's because I'm anxious to keep you a secret from all the men in the hamlet," Gage countered. "They ogle you and make my temper soar."

"It needn't, my love, because my eyes are only for you."

Gallantly Gage presented an arm and led her toward the tavern. They were intent upon each other and barely noticed Alma Pettycomb approaching until they were almost upon her and the man who walked along beside her. For once the matron seemed far more engrossed in her own affairs than in the affairs of others. She grumbled and twitched in irritation beside her stoic-faced husband, who seemed oblivious to her muttered ranting.

"I told you, Sidney! I want to go to the docks to see that new ship that came into port!" Receiving no answer, she jerked testily upon his coat sleeve. "Did you hear me, Sidney?"

"Who cannot?" he asked curtly.

"Well?"

"I want my supper, woman! And that's final! I'm tired of you gallivanting all over creation, poking your long nose into everybody's business. I've decided henceforth there'll be some changes made in the way you conduct yourself, or you will answer to me. Colby Ferris is a friend of mine, and I was greatly shamed that you took it upon yourself to exaggerate a pettish argument he had with that toad, Samuel Myers. Because of you, I could not bring myself to attend his wedding until I've made some effort to put my own house in order. I'm a God-fearing man, madam, but I'll tell you truly there'll be some mayhem done if you don't keep your mouth closed from now on. And if you think I'm fooling, then I just might decide to take a thin switch to your arse to show you that I'm serious."

Alma gasped in outrage. "You wouldn't dare!"

Turning his head slightly, Sidney Pettycomb raised a brow sharply as he stared at her. "I'm a man of my word, madam. You'll pay the consequences if I hear one more rumor about you viciously defaming another person."

Nearing the younger couple, Sidney politely tipped his hat as he gave a nod of greeting first to Gage and then to Shemaine. The younger couple were totally amazed by what they had just overheard and became even more hopeful when Sidney spoke to them. "Give my regards to Colby for me, will you, Gage? I've sent a gift, but my best wedding present is in the making."

Subduing the urge to grin, Gage inclined his head briefly, committing himself to carrying the man's message and conveying his own interpretation of Sidney's *other* present, which Gage could only guess would benefit them all.

Musicians had been hired to lend a musical flair to the celebration, and a broad assortment of loyal patients, friends, and acquaintances came for the feasting. Gage was rather astonished that so many people were living in the area, but it was readily apparent by the vast collection of well-wishers that Colby Ferris was not without his supporters and a substantial number of friends. Ramsey and Calley Tate, toting their newborn in a padded basket, had arrived from the church to join in the festivities. Upon spying the Tates and the Thorntons, Colby beckoned the two couples to sit with them, allowing Annie the nurturing comfort of being surrounded by close friends.

The food was plentiful and delicious, but Shemaine found her appetite decreasing as the stagnant air in the tavern grew heavy with a mélange of odors: the foul stench of sweaty men, horse manure tracked in on the wooden floor, various aromas from the food laid out on the long tables, and the overpowering essence of toilet water with which an older matron had liberally doused herself. Whiffs of smoke from the hearth, where another suckling pig was roasting, made it difficult for Shemaine to breathe. Feeling nauseous, she dabbed a freshly scented handkerchief to her clammy cheeks, then pressed it beneath her nose. The delicate barrier sufficed for a few moments until her chair and her arm were haphazardly jostled by a backwoodsman, making her drop the filtering handkerchief in her lap. One whiff of the man as he leaned over her to apologize almost saw her undone, for he reeked of nearly everything she had been trying to avoid smelling. The man stepped away, and in something of a panic, Shemaine leaned forward to beg leave of her companions.

"If you'll excuse me, I need some air," she gasped out. Carefully averting her gaze from their plates, she rose to her feet, but when she turned stiltedly to Gage, he was already standing. She laid a trembling hand upon his chest and pleaded softly, "Stay and finish your meal. I won't be long."

He took her hand in his. "Madam, I would hate for the newly arrived sailors and passengers to mistake you for one of the harlots who frequent this place."

Seeing the wisdom in his concern, Shemaine acquiesced and allowed him to draw her back to the boardwalk. Inhaling several deep breaths of the late afternoon air, she promptly obtained some relief and actually started feeling better as she strolled along beside her husband. As he wandered casually toward the end of town, she looked into the windows of the shops they passed, now and then drawing his attention to something she espied. She enjoyed their leisurely walk together and felt a great measure of pride to be on his arm.

Passengers from the newly docked ship were already beginning to make their way from the wharf. A few of them seemed in a great hurry to reach the main part of the hamlet. A tall, dark-haired, well-garbed gentleman strode far ahead of them all. His long legs had served him well in that respect. Indeed, the silver-tipped cane he carried was obviously more of a swagger stick than an aid for walking. His strides were long and sure, and with his head held at a lofty angle, he glanced about, as if searching for something or someone. When he espied the Thorntons from a distance, he paused suddenly and cocked his head at a contemplative angle, staring intently toward Shemaine. Seeming somewhat confused, he resumed walking, but his pace was slower, a bit more hesitant.

Gage came to the end of the boardwalk and turned, drawing Shemaine's hand within the bend of his arm. "Are you feeling better, my sweet?"

"Aye."

"Need more air?"

"If you don't mind."

"Anything for you, love," he replied, slanting a grin toward her.

Gage caught the sound of running feet behind him and peered over his shoulder to see the richly garbed gentleman approaching them in haste. There was no mistaking it. The man's eyes were riveted on Shemaine.

A low growl issued from Gage's throat at the man's audacity. "What's this? A recent arrival already taken with you?"

Her husband's muttered question drew Shemaine's gaze back along the boardwalk, allowing the advancing swain to see her profile.

"Shemaine! Shemaine! By heavens, it is you!"

"Maurice?" Recognizing the voice, she turned in confusion, and suddenly her former betrothed was there, throwing aside his cane and sweeping her up in his embrace. Whirling her around in an ecstatic circle, he swung her completely off her feet.

"Shemaine, we thought we'd never find you!" he cried, continuing his whirling dance. " 'Twas only by chance your mother spied a woman wearing your boots and bribed her to tell her where she had gotten them!"

"Do you mind?" Gage barked. He had recognized the name and, upon espying the man's handsome and aristocratic features, considered himself in serious jeopardy of losing his wife's heart back to her former fiancé.

"Maurice, put me down! For heaven's sakes, put me down *now!*" Shemaine gasped, clasping the handkerchief over her mouth as her world reeled crazily awry.

The Marquess complied and stood in some befuddlement as Shemaine stumbled away to the edge of the boardwalk. Taking in large gulps of air, she struggled valiantly to subdue her rising gorge, but the town still seemed to tilt at a sharp slant around her. Her stomach heaved in rebellion, and feebly she extended a hand behind her, bringing Gage swiftly to her side.

Maurice watched in helpless, resentful confusion as the stranger slipped an arm around the narrow waist that he himself had once possessively embraced and laid a hand on the same smooth brow he had lovingly kissed. The casual handling of his betrothed aroused his ire to no small degree, and he almost stepped forward to protest, but the plight of his fiancée finally dawned on him as she tried to subdue a gag behind a lace handkerchief.

Spurred to action, Maurice raced back to the horse trough, wet his handkerchief and returned to offer it to her. Meekly Shemaine nodded her gratitude and wiped her face as she leaned against Gage. Brushing a strand of hair from her flushed face, he laid an arm around her waist as she rested her head against the solid bulwark of his chest.

The intimacy of Gage's embrace invited a dark-eyed glower from her former beau, but that was not all, by any means.

"What the bloody hell is goin' on here?" another voice demanded from the thoroughfare, snatching the very words from Maurice's mouth.

"Papa?" Shemaine lifted her head and glanced around in search of the beloved face. She could not have mistaken the voice, and when her eyes lit on the short, wiry, nattily garbed man standing with arms akimbo and legs splayed in the middle of the road, she could not mistake her own sire. "Papa! Oh, Papa!"

Nearly dancing along the edge of the boardwalk, Shemaine eagerly motioned him forward, and within four long strides Shemus O'Hearn was there, sweeping his daughter within his embrace. Gage's brows flicked upward in a lopsided angle as he stepped back a respectful distance, allowing the two to have this moment together.

"Just who the bloody hell are you, anyway?" Maurice du Mercer demanded as he stepped before Gage, but he gave the colonial no time to answer as he crisply explained, "When we started making inquiries at Newgate shortly after her boots were found, we were told that Shemaine had shipped out on the *London Pride*. We had the good fortune of catching sight of the *Pride*'s sails while we were steering a course here, and we had our captain bring our ship about to intercept the vessel. When we boarded her, Captain Fitch told us that Shemaine had been sold as an indentured servant to a colonial named Gage Thornton here in Newportes Newes. Are you that man?"

"Aye, I'm that man."

Maurice's face tightened with vexation. "The bosun on the *Pride* also informed us that he had heard rumors about town that the colonial who had bought Shemaine had killed his first wife."

"It was rumored," Gage acknowledged sharply. "But it could never be proven because I didn't killed her!"

Maurice tossed his head in jeering disdain. "Why is it that I don't believe you?"

"Perhaps because you don't wish to," Gage retorted.

"You're right. I don't wish to. What I really want to do is to lay you out with my fist!"

Gage's eyes grew noticeably less warm as he returned the Marquess's glare. "I give you leave to try."

"Shemaine!" A feminine voice cried, drawing their attention to a small, slender woman with pale blond hair who was hurrying across the thoroughfare toward Shemaine and her father. On either side of her were two women garbed in servants' attire who were hastening to keep up, one an older, plumpish woman with gray hair, and the other a maid of an age about a score and ten.

"Mama!" Shemaine cried, and was immediately swept to the thoroughfare by her father. Sidestepping to avoid an oncoming wagon and team, she waved to her mother, and then, as soon as the conveyance had passed, the two came together with a cry of glee. With arms wrapped tightly about each other, they stood in the middle of the road, not caring that riders and wagons were passing in front and behind them. The fierce embrace eased to some degree, allowing them to touch and gaze at each other as if they tried to comprehend that they were actually together again.

The older servant was weeping, anxiously awaiting her turn, and when she blew her nose loudly in a handkerchief, it finally dawned on Shemaine that their old cook was there also. Facing the elder, Shemaine hugged her jubilantly. "Oh, Bess! How wonderful it is to see you! All of you!" With a gay laugh, Shemaine stepped away and embraced the younger servant, who had come forward to claim her attention. "Nola! For heaven's sakes, what are you doing here?"

Her mother readily explained. "I've been using Nola's services in your absence, Shemaine, because my old Sophy began ailing. But Nola will be yours again once we get you back to England."

Shemaine looked around and, extending

her hand toward Gage again, invited him to join her. Her father and Maurice followed closely on his heels, having immediately taken a fierce dislike to the colonial. It was his familiar handling of the woman they held dear as a daughter and fiancée that they couldn't abide.

"Mama . . . Papa . . . Maurice . . ." Shemaine briefly settled a glance on each before she deliberately slipped an arm through Gage's, drawing him to her. "This is my husband, Gage Thornton."

"Your husband!" Maurice barked. "But you were betrothed to me!"

Catching Gage's shoulder, Shemus spun him about until they stood toe to toe. It didn't matter that the colonial stood a whole head taller. The elder seized his lapel and glared up at him with all the fury of an outraged father. Even his frizzled red hair, which had paled over the years with whitening strands, seemed to stand on end with his wrath. "What do you mean, marrying my daughter without my consent?"

Shemaine clamped a trembling hand to her throat. "Papa, don't!"

"I didn't need your consent," Gage answered tersely. Gripping the smaller man's wrist, he dragged the white-knuckled hand away from his coat. "Shemaine was already mine."

Maurice stepped near the two whose glares dueled like glinting sabers and informed Shemus bluntly, "He's the one who bought her papers . . . the one Captain Fitch told us about. The wife-murderer, so the bosun says. Obviously this colonial forced Shemaine to marry him!"

"No!" Shemaine pressed her hands to her face in dismay, for the world, which had seemed like heaven only a moment earlier, was now closing in around her again. Facing her mother, she pleaded for help. "He's not a wife-murderer, Mama! He asked me to marry him, and I accepted! Because I wanted to!"

Camille was as bemused as her husband, but she moved forward and laid a gentle hand upon Shemus's arm. "The middle of the road is no place for us to conduct inquiries into this matter, my dear. We must seek a private room; perhaps one at an inn will suffice."

"Your pardon, madam," Gage offered stiffly. "There's been an influx of ships docking here recently, and with only one inn in the hamlet, I rather doubt you'll find space for even one of you there."

"But where are we to go?" This time it was the mother who turned to the daughter for help. "There are so many of us. And we've come so far. What are we to do?"

Shemaine went to her husband and asked in a subdued tone. "Do you suppose Mrs. McGee would consent to putting them up?"

Gage would have gladly consigned them to sleep in the street if not for his wife. "Possibly tomorrow, but what about tonight, Shemaine? 'Twould be a late hour before we could get back home. We can't rout our guest out of bed and burden her with the task of returning to the hamlet and opening her home to people who are strangers to her. 'Twould be too much to expect of the old woman."

"Is there some way they can stay with us tonight?" Shemaine cajoled softly. "Perhaps you and I can sleep on the floor. . . ."

"We wouldn't think of putting you out of your own bed," Camille interjected, though she could hardly approve of their little girl being married to this stranger. She was so young, and he . . . so, so . . . Camille could find no adequate word to describe her feelings toward the man, except that she was sure he was nothing less than a scoundrel who had taken advantage of her daughter.

"I'd like to see the blackguard put out of my daughter's bed!" Shemus growled.

"I'd like to suggest an annulment," Maurice offered boldly. "The beast has no doubt imposed himself upon her. Whether Shemaine admits it or not, I'm sure she was under great duress when she accepted."

Shemus was not so civilized with his recommendations. "I'd like to see the man gelded!"

Shemaine clapped a trembling hand over her mouth and moaned, "I think I'm going to be sick!"

"Good heavens, child!" Camille cried, looking aghast. "Don't tell me you're . . . you're . . ."

"You're what?" Shemus implored, looking stricken. If his wife was upset, then it was damned certain he would be infuriated by whatever she was thinking.

Camille waved a hand weakly, hoping against hope it wasn't true. "With child . . ."

Shemaine closed her eyes and shuddered squeamishly as her father let out a horrendous bellow of rage.

"Where's a knife? I'll cut the bloody beggar's pebbles out right now!"

Shemaine spun around in a panic and bent forward to heave up her previous meal. Gage slipped an arm about her shoulders, lending her support as Nola ran to wet a cloth in the watering trough and Bess stepped forward to wave a vial of smelling salts beneath Shemaine's nose.

"There now, darlin', take a deep breath," the old cook coaxed.

Gage heard a familiar voice cautiously greeting the strangers and glanced around in some relief to find Ramsey approaching him apprehensively. "Calley wanted me ta come out an' see 'bout ye an' Shemaine afore we left for home," he informed Gage. "Soon as I come out of the tavern, I figgered ye were in some kind o' tiff with these here people. Do ye need any help?"

"Not unless you can supply these good people with beds for the night." Gage muttered none too happily.

Ramsey was clearly taken aback by the suggestion. "Ye mean ye want me ta be nice ta these here folks? But they were 'bout ta bash in yer bloomin' head!"

"Aye, an' I still might!" Shemus threatened, shaking a fist at Gage. "So ye needn't worry yerself about doin' any favors for me family!"

Casually ignoring the intimidation, Gage slipped an arm beneath Shemaine's knees and lifted her in his arms. She had not the strength to raise her head from his shoulder as he faced her father. "If you come home with me, sir, you'll either be sleeping on the floor or on the settee in the parlor, because your daughter is in no condition to give up her bed."

"Daughter?" Some enlightenment began to dawn as Ramsey glanced between his employer and the elder gentleman.

Gage ignored the interruption as he reluctantly offered to provide lodging for the O'Hearn family, improvising as he went. "Shemaine's mother can have the other half of the trundle bed, providing Mrs. McGee doesn't mind sharing my son's bedroom with her. My son will either have to sleep in bed with us or on the floor." His amber-brown eyes fixed the Marquess with an icy stare. "If Mr. Tate, here, will grant you a room at his home, then you may pass the night in reasonable comfort. Otherwise, there's a roughed-in bunk and a well-used feather tick

aboard the ship I'm building. The old shipwright who works for me uses it for short
naps after he's eaten at noon. 'Tis yours as
long as you don't interfere with his sched-
ule."

"And where is this ship located?" Maurice
asked crisply.

"On the river about a hundred or so paces
beyond my cabin, where the rest of us will
be."

"And is there water other than the river,
and a place to bathe?"

"In the stream in front of the cabin." Gage
waited, fully expecting the Marquess to reject the idea for want of something better.
The man was apparently well acquainted
with luxury, but he would find little of it in the
wilderness.

"Is this stream inhabited by snakes and
such, or have you bathed in it before?"

Gage gave him a slow nod and verbally
twisted the knife in the man's heart. "Shemaine and I have both bathed in it."

Maurice's dark eyes held his in a cold,
level stare. "Then perhaps Shemaine and I
will consider enjoying it together one day . . .
after they hang you for your wife's murder."

Ramsey gasped sharply and sought guidance from Gage. "Seein' as how ye're busy holdin' yer wife, ye want me ta slap his face or somethin'?"

Though they never wavered from Gage, Maurice's eyes gleamed in eager invitation, as if he anticipated such an altercation. "Is your friend suggesting that you might desire recompense for the insult by way of a duel?"

"No duel!" Shemaine cried weakly, lifting her head from Gage's shoulder. She knew only too well that Maurice was an accomplished marksman with dueling pistols. In fact, there were many things Maurice was adept at, not the least of which was his skill at verbally baiting men who antagonized him. He was at his best arguing against the ludicrous suggestions of pompous lords at court. He could flay an adversary with innuendos, and a foe would never know the death blow had been struck until he heard the loud roar of laughter filling a hall.

"As much as I'd like to accommodate you," Gage lightly sneered, "I see no need to confront you over Shemaine. She is my wife, and I don't intend to let you kill me so you can claim her as yours."

Maurice hissed in contempt. "You're a coward and a sniveling lout."

Realizing the man was trying to goad him into doing something foolish, Gage slowly responded with a facial shrug. "Think whatever you will, but I have a wife, a son at home and another child on the way. . . ."

With a growl Maurice stepped forward to challenge the colonial for possession of his betrothed, but he felt the wind being snatched from his sails as Shemaine, heedless of his proximity, lifted her head from her husband's shoulder and, with a finger, gently turned that one's face toward hers. Maurice felt forgotten and betrayed by this young woman whose disappearance had left him mourning and fretting in deep discontent.

Shemaine searched Gage's lean, handsome visage, and his responding smile assured her that what she had been trying to keep secret from him for at least a little while longer was something that he had already begun to suspect. He had not needed her mother blurting it out to be apprised of her condition.

Shemaine's lips mouthed a silent question, *How?*

Gage pressed his lips near her ear and spoke in a hushed whisper. "No interruptions in our nightly pleasures since we married, my love. From experience, a widower knows about monthly cycles and such. Either you were incapable of having them or had gotten with child soon after we wed. It was when I started noticing a change in your breasts that I knew for sure, but I bided my time until you were ready to tell me."

With a soft, contented sigh Shemaine nestled her head to his shoulder, and Gage continued with the business at hand.

"Your servants are welcome to bed down in some corner of my house," he told Camille. "Shemaine has been making some new feather mattresses for us. They're not finished, but they're still serviceable."

"Ye gonna be packed in tighter'n trees in a forest," Ramsey observed dryly. "An' ye know somethin' else? Ye ain't gonna be able ta sneeze without needin' someone else ta hold yer handkerchief."

Gage didn't need his friend to explain in greater detail, for Ramsey had a way of getting directly to the heart of what could eat at a man. Simply put, making love to Shemaine would be nigh impossible without their visitors overhearing.

Shemus brushed his frock coat aside and settled his fists on his lean waist as he stepped up to Gage. "If yer house is so sparse on bedrooms, just where in the hell did my daughter bed down when she wasn't hitched ta ye?"

"Papa, please," Shemaine begged, lifting her head and giving her parent a pleading look over her shoulder. "Can't we wait until we get home to discuss all of this instead of having it out right here in the middle of town?" Her eyes flicked toward the people who had stopped along the boardwalk to gawk at them. "We've become a bigger attraction than the bride and groom at the wedding feast."

"Just tell me!" Shemus insisted irately, fixing Gage with a persistent stare.

"Your daughter slept in the loft until we were married, Mr. O'Hearn," Gage replied. "But my father is presently ensconced there recuperating from a serious wound. We also have another guest, with whom your wife will be sharing my son's bedroom."

"Why can't she sleep with my daughter?" Shemus demanded.

Gage met his gaze directly and explained as if he were speaking to a simpleton. "Because *I'm* sleeping with your daughter, and *I* don't care to sleep with your wife!"

Hooting in glee, Ramsey clapped his friend on the back in a show of support, but upon finding himself the recipient of a green-eyed glower from Shemus, he brushed a hand down his bushy mustache in a lame attempt to wipe the grin off his face. He coughed behind a hand, managing to curb an unruly twitching at the corners of his mouth, and was reasonably sober when he faced Gage. "Will ye be needin' ta send yer wife's kin ta me house now that ye've committed yerself ta loadin' 'em all in yer cabin?"

Gage raised a querying brow at Shemus. "My friend here has some extra bedrooms available now while his sons are working at Williamsburg. If you'd care to pass the night in more comfort and privacy than I'm able to offer you, then I seriously suggest you consider his willingness to put you up. I'm sure your funds are adequate enough that you could ease the inconvenience of having the lot of you in his home. Mr. Tate arrives at my place just after sunrise, if you'd care to come out in the morning and discuss my marriage to your daughter."

"Perhaps it would be best, Shemus," Camille suggested, taking her husband's arm. "We're all upset, and if we're crowded together and can't sleep, we'll be snapping at each other like a pack of wild dogs."

Shemus reluctantly conceded to her wisdom. "As you wish, my dear, but I would have this thing out ere long."

"I know, dear," she replied sweetly, patting his arm. "We'll talk about it tomorrow."

Facing Ramsey, Camille bestowed a gracious smile upon him. "If you would allow us to be guests in your home, sir, we'll be more than grateful for your kindness and hospitality."

Ramsey gave her a generous display of his best manners as he swept an arm before him in a flamboyant bow, amazing Gage, who cocked a wry brow at his friend. "Yer ladyship, 'twill be me very good pleasure ta take ye home with me an' me wife."

Shemus raised a brow in sharp suspicion, noticing the man hadn't included him in his statement. "Do ye welcome the rest of us with as much eagerness?"

Ramsey never minced words when he was firmly set on a matter. "As long as ye don't slander Mr. Thornton's good name in me home or in me presence, then I'll welcome the lot of ye. Otherwise, ye can be findin' yer own lodgin' for the night."

Camille waited for her husband's response. The appeal in her gentle blue eyes told him that she, too, desired a truce for the night. In consideration of her wishes, he reluctantly nodded, yielding to the conditions bluntly stated by Ramsey.

"Blast, you evil woman!"
The outcry greeted Gage and Shemaine as soon as they stepped through their cabin door, causing them to look at each other in sudden consternation. They could only wonder what mayhem William yearned to commit on Mary Margaret McGee.

Gage bolted toward the back corridor, hoping he could mollify his father before anything more disastrous could be said. Shemaine hastened in his wake, for she could only foresee the Irishwoman needing some gentle soothing after suffering such slanderous abuse.

"You deliberately sacrificed your knave to draw out my king," William continued accusingly with a chortle. "And now I have nothing better to beat your queen. You take the last hand and the kitty."

Mary Margaret's jovial laughter drew Gage and Shemaine to a stumbling halt near the stairs. Weak with relief, they came together in a thankful embrace as the conversation continued to drift down from the upper story.

"Would ye care for another game, me lord?" Mary Margaret sweetly inquired.

"What, and let you beat me again?" His light-hearted scoffing laughter denied the possibility. " 'Tis certain I would have no manly pride left after such a thrashing!"

"I haven't a ken why ye'd be thinkin' that, me lord," the Irishwoman trilled in charming tones. "There is much ye have ta be proud o'. Why 'tis sure I've ne'er seen an Englishman better lookin' than yerself, sir . . . that is, except for yer son, but I'd swear he's the very image o' ye. And, of course, there be wee Andrew, who's claimed the best o' both o' ye."

"Aye, he is a handsome boy, isn't he?" William heartily agreed. "He brings back memories of Gage when he was no older than Andrew."

Only a brief pause ensued before the wily matchmaker queried amiably, "Where is yer wife now, yer lordship?"

"Oh, Elizabeth died when Gage was twelve. She caught a chill and became feverish. I was not prepared for the suddenness of her death. It made me terribly angry. I found myself ill prepared to nurture my son with the gentleness she had always displayed. I'm afraid I was gruff and demanding."

"An' ye ne'er remarried?" A note of surprise had crept into Mary Margaret's tone.

"Never wanted to. I was too busy most of the time, what with the challenge of building bigger and better ships. Then, too, I found myself at odds with women . . . I suppose in much the same way I was with my son. I'm sure those with whom I came in contact thought I was a crusty old man."

"I find that hard ta believe, yer lordship," Mary Margaret murmured warmly. "For ye seem quite pleasin' ta be with. Indeed, ye have a way 'bout ye that reminds me o' me own dear, departed husband."

"How is that, Mrs. McGee?" William asked curiously.

"Me name is Mary Margaret, me lord, an' I'd be honored if ye were not so formal in addressin' me."

"Thank you, Mary Margaret. And if you're of such a mind, my name is William."

"Aye, resolute protector." Mary Margaret sighed thoughtfully.

"I beg your pardon?" His lordship's tone conveyed his confusion.

"William . . . means 'resolute protector,'" Mary Margaret replied. "The name does ye service. Ye were a resolute protector o' yer son, were ye not?"

"I suppose I was. In truth, I couldn't bear to think of losing him after I had searched for him so long."

"Ye must love him very much."

"Aye, I do, but it has always been rather hard for me to tell him that."

"Well, ye needn't worry yerself 'bout it anymore, William. Ye proved yer love far better with yer actions."

Downstairs in the corridor, Gage pressed a finger to his smiling lips as he looked down at Shemaine. Taking her hand, he led her stealthily from the corridor and across the parlor. Upon entering their bedroom, he gently closed the door behind them. With the same noiseless gait, Gage stepped into the adjoining bedroom to look in on his son. The angelic face was too irresistible not to kiss, and after straightening, Gage found Shemaine slipping to her knees beside the trundle bed. Stroking the boy's brow lovingly, she sang a lullaby in a voice that was nearly as soft as the gentle brush of her breath. A smile drifted fleetingly across the small, rosy lips before Andrew heaved a sigh and rolled over to cuddle against his cloth rabbit. Gage offered his hand as Shemaine rose to her feet and together they retreated to the adjoining room. Very quietly the bolt was pushed closed.

"I think we should have a boy so Andrew can have a playmate," Shemaine suggested with a smile.

Gage stepped to her side and slipped his arms about her, drawing her close against him. As she leaned her head upon his chest, he lowered his chin to her capped coiffure and moved his hand in a gentle caress over her stomach. It seemed as flat as it had always been. "Whether boy or girl, my love, it makes no difference what the coffer holds. I only pray that it may go well with you. My heart would stop if I were to lose you."

Shemaine laughed as she snuggled against him. "Fear not, my love. My father's mother whelped six with no difficulty, and she was smaller than I. A very feisty woman, she was."

"Your father must have gotten it from her," Gage remarked with a fleeting grin. "But watch the fur fly when William Thornton and Shemus O'Hearn meet toe to toe. I'm sure each could give lessons to the meanest shrew in the area."

"Aye, but we were also afraid that your father and Mrs. McGee would get into a fray, and look what happened," Shemaine reminded her husband.

Gage's thoughts drifted back to what had been said upstairs, and he had to chuckle at his father's change of attitude toward the Irishwoman. "I gather from Mary Margaret's gentle inquisition that she has set her sights on making another match."

Shemaine smiled and rubbed a hand down the front of his waistcoat. "Don't be too surprised, my love, if it turns out to be a match for Mrs. McGee, as well."

With a grin Gage plucked the lace cap from his wife's head and began to loosen the satin tresses. "They *do* seem to be getting along famously together. Who knows? They might be good for each other."

A heavy sigh wafted from Shemaine's lips as she remembered her father's explosion.

"I wish my parents could be as understanding about us."

"Perhaps, with time, they'll come to think of me as less of an ogre," Gage mused aloud.

"My father has a terrible temper, Gage, so *please* try not to upset him unduly when they come tomorrow," Shemaine pleaded.

Her husband settled a reassuring kiss upon her brow. "I'll try to imagine the way I would feel if some blackguard took advantage of one of our daughters. I would probably be just as furious, especially if I had heard stories about the man being a wife-murderer."

"You must be very careful of Maurice, too," Shemaine cautioned. "Don't let him provoke you into doing anything foolish."

"I rather sensed that the Marquess is willing to reclaim you whatever the cost." Gage could not find it in himself to fault the man too harshly for desiring such a thing, for he knew he'd be just as adamant about winning her back if the roles were reversed. "But I will take care, my sweet."

"Maurice may look pampered, but don't be fooled. He's as talented with a sword as he is with a pistol. Thus far, he has only wounded his adversaries when they've challenged him to duels, but he may prove to be of a different bent with you."

"No doubt, no doubt," Gage replied, shrugging out of his frock coat. "If he can kill me, then he would have a clear path to you, and—"

"Or so he may think," Shemaine interrupted. "But if he kills you, then he'll win my undying hatred."

Gage doffed his waistcoat, hung it over a chair with the coat, and then rid himself of his stock and shirt before returning to loosen his wife's laces. "Mary Margaret will likely be upstairs for a while, talking with my father. With her delay in going to bed, perhaps we may dally in ours for a while just to see what arises."

"And would you be doubting such an event, Mr. Thornton?" Shemaine asked through the cloth of her gown as her husband lifted it over her head and swept it free from her uplifted arms.

"Not when the woman I'm dallying with is you, my love," he assured her with a chuckle, stepping away to lay the garment over the trunk.

When he turned back to admire the vision

of her garbed in nothing more than a lacy chemise, she threaded her slender fingers through her hair and lifted the curling tresses high above her head. As if reluctant to come too close, she moved cautiously in a half circle around him, commanding his full attention with a sweetly wicked smile and glowing green eyes. "Where I a sorceress, Mr. Thornton, I would keep you a prisoner in my den, where you would serve my pleasures both night and day. You would languish from my incessant demands until you had not strength enough to rouse from your couch, and then I would summon forth strange magic to make you pant in lust for me once more."

A lopsided grin widened her husband's lips as he taunted her with a devouring perusal. "I do that now, madam." Catching an arm around her waist, he drew her between the spread of his legs as he sat back upon the bed. His fingers plucked at the ribbons closing the bodice of her chemise and then moved the slackening cloth aside until the swelling roundness was brazenly displayed. The lustrous orbs thrust outward eagerly, tempting him to taste and devour as they gleamed warmly in the candlelight. He readily complied, evoking a wondrous enchantment as his mouth feasted greedily upon the voluptuous softness.

Shemaine's voice came in a whisper as she lowered her lips to his dark head. " 'Tis only when the handsome prince of my dreams becomes real in my arms that this sorceress yields up all of her devices and incantations and follows submissively wherever he leads. And then nothing can keep me from him."

Gage lifted his head and searched her smiling eyes. "Nothing, my love?"

"Absolutely nothing, my darling." Her lips parted as they approached his, and if any doubt remained, she snuffed it out with a long, lingering kiss.

CHAPTER 21

Gage had hurried across the porch shortly after the O'Hearns' hired livery pulled to a halt near the cabin the next morning. His guests were much earlier than he had expected, for he had been told by Ramsey that the Marquess and the O'Hearns had just begun to stir when he left for work. Gage begged their indulgence for a few moments more while he and Shemaine completed several chores which they were in the midst of. At present, he was helping his father bathe, and while the elder was occupied downstairs, Shemaine had set about cleaning his room and changing his bed linens so she wouldn't have to disturb him later. Although the visitors seemed apprehensive about the kind of reception they were receiving, Gage politely assured them that it would only be a few moments before he and his wife could join them. Until then, if they didn't mind, Ramsey would see to their needs.

In the absence of his employer, Ramsey took it upon himself to show them around the cabinet shop as Sly Tucker and the two apprentices worked at their separate tasks. With a great deal of pride and satisfaction, Ramsey skimmed over the painstaking process of making quality furniture, beginning his discourse by exhibiting his employer's drawings and designs, which readily evinced Gage's incredible talent with quill and ink. Ramsey went on to show them the difference in the grains of wood they used. Whether it was cypress, cherry, maple, oak, or some other, the unusual characteristics of each could make a piece of furniture unique. Upon concluding his talk, Ramsey led them back to where Sly Tucker was polishing a recently finished sideboard and eagerly urged the O'Hearns, their servants, and the Marquess to run their hands over the top of the piece to feel the smoothness of the hand-rubbed finish.

Camille seemed most enthralled by the merits of the buffet, for it was she who, during the length of her marriage, had selected the furnishings for their homes, a task which Shemus had willingly left to her discretion. He had realized long ago that his wife had a natural ability for turning the simplest dwelling into a comfortable, tastefully appointed haven, and he had never been one to intrude and possibly hinder perfection in the making. Over the years, Camille had acquired a keen eye for recognizing a worthy piece when she saw one, and though the lines of the sideboard were fairly simple, the tiger's-eye grains and burled woods from which it had been constructed made it distinctive and beautiful. Stressing the fact that it was among the finest she had ever seen, Camille implored her husband to examine it more closely, wanting him to understand the skill and dedication required to produce such an outstanding piece.

Outwardly Ramsey seemed inattentive to the couple's muted discussion, but his ears were closely attuned to their exchange. While helping Sly for a moment, he also had a chance to study Maurice, albeit surreptitiously. His lordship remained coolly indifferent to Camille's enthusiasm as he glanced casually about the shop. His reserved dignity seemed imperturbable, and when the tour continued, Ramsey tested the precise depth of that unflappable mien by purposely rubbing a bit of salt in the Marquess's wounds.

"Ain't no doubt 'bout it. Mr. Thornton gots ta be the most skillful woodwright in this here area. Why, he not only draws up pieces like this here furniture from his imagination"—Ramsey emphasized his point by tapping a finger against his own temple—"he's prosperous enough ta support several families, to boot. He's a fair man with his wages, he is, an' none o' us would be as well off today workin' for 'nother carpenter."

After motioning them to the window, he hurriedly wiped away some of the sawdust until they could view the unfinished brigantine that rested in bracing stocks near the river's edge. "Ye see that?" He glanced around to assure himself that he had gained their undivided attention and briefly noted the stoic detachment that his lordship still conveyed. "Mr. Thornton dreamed 'at there vessel up in his noggin, too. If'n 'tweren't for his love o' designin' ships an' buildin' 'em, he'd likely be the richest man in these here parts by now, just by what he earns makin' furniture. But ye wait, give or take a year or two more, maybe even three, he'll be provin' his worth as a master shipbuilder an' then people'll be takin' careful notice!"

Maurice allowed a pensive sigh to escape his lips as he turned away from the window. He had little tolerance for praise that was liberally heaped upon an unprincipled knave. If it were left up to him, he'd call Gage Thornton out right then and there and rid the world of a worthless scoundrel.

Ramsey flicked a glance toward the tall, well-garbed man. The brooding hostility now roiling perceptibly behind those noble features evidenced his success in baiting his lordship. He now deemed a tour of the brigantine to be in order to set the barb more firmly, just to let the Marquess know that it was no common man he had defamed the night before.

Bidding them to accompany him, Ramsey led the small entourage down the path to the riverside edifice and introduced them to Flannery Morgan. There he allowed the grizzled shipwright the honor of explaining the merits of Gage's design, for none could do it with more enthusiasm.

"When she's finished, this here'll be what ye'd call a two-masted brig'ntine," the old man informed them. "She's low in the hull an' sleek in lines. If'n ye be acquainted with ships at all, m'lords an' ladies, ye'll see that in this vessel, the beam is well nigh the bow. 'Twill give her good stability in the water, all right, but I'll warrant her best feature'll be her speed. Why, she'll skim through the sea like a mermaid lookin' for a mate ta sport with."

Camille pinkened lightly at his comparison, but the old salt failed to notice her unease as he encouraged them to follow him down the companionway. Gesturing here and there to draw their attention to several points of interest in the workmanship, he showed them around the lower levels, all the while extolling his employer's extraordinary vision and talents. At last, he brought them up to the main deck again.

Leaving the others behind, Shemus O'Hearn went to the far end of the ship and looked back upon it, wanting to consider everything he had been shown. He had taken in the comments with an attentive ear, trying to glean some insight into the individual, Gage Thornton. What he had been most surprised about were the employees. Shemus had hired many men in his lifetime, but he was not at all sure any of them had ever been as dedicated or had taken as much pleasure in their work and accomplishments as Ramsey, Sly Tucker, Flannery and the others seemed to. In the face of their loyalty and enthusiasm, he had to wonder how a rogue could have inspired such qualities.

Shemus Patrick O'Hearn had made his own way in life, starting with little and working his way up to much. It was not at all surprising that he began to feel a grudging respect for the colonial as he became cognizant of the many achievements and diligent ambitions of the man who had married his daughter. When he recalled his own beginnings and the misgivings that Camille's parents had once expressed about the Irish upstart who had thought himself good enough to court their daughter, he had to wonder if he was being too biased and harsh-minded when it came to the cabinet-maker. Over the years, he had won a place for himself in the hearts of Camille's family, and they were now among the first to declare that he was a member of their family. Would the day ever come when he, too, could esteem his new son-in-law?

The question of Gage's involvement in the death of his first wife, however, remained his primary concern. It was a matter that had to be reckoned with or it would remain a sharp wedge between them, dividing one from the other. Shemus knew in his heart that he'd have to be totally convinced of Gage's innocence before he could ever feel comfortable about Shemaine's marriage, no matter how industrious the colonial was. Yet when questions still persisted in the hamlet after the passage of more than a year, Shemus seriously doubted the probability of such an occurrence. And even if he had to drag Shemaine aboard a ship bound for England, Shemus knew he would never leave his daughter in the care of a suspected murderer.

Throughout the tour of the ship, Maurice du Mercer had maintained a phlegmatic silence. He still felt a fierce enmity against the man who had stolen his betrothed, and he'd have choked before disclosing the tiniest bit of interest or admiration for his rival's achievements. It could not be said, however, that he wasn't impressed, despite the ill will he bore the man. He had no doubt that Gage Thornton had a good eye for quality and beauty. Shemaine was certainly proof of that. Still, had he been able to dictate circumstances in his favor, Maurice could have easily wished the colonial had gone blind before laying eyes on the dazzling beauty to whom he had offered his own heart.

The clouds that had seemed to hang in a perpetual gloomy gray over Maurice's life since their arrival that morning vanished as soon as Shemaine joined them on the ship. She was wearing a fetching pale blue gown, a white lace-trimmed cap, and a white apron tied about her slender waist. In all, she looked very much like a colonial wife. Utterly delicious, Maurice mused, feeding on her beauty as she hugged her parents. Indeed, he was so moved by her presence, he became convinced that he would have given his entire wealth just to be the man who now claimed her.

"I'm sorry Gage and I couldn't come greet you properly as soon as you arrived," Shemaine apologized graciously. "His lordship still hasn't fully regained his strength, but he was greatly desirous of dispensing with basin baths and having a good soak in a tub. For that, he needed Gage's assistance. It seemed a good chance for me to clean his room. I hope you don't mind."

"His lordship?" Maurice had caught the significance of the address and was most curious.

Any doubts about the Marquess being equal in height to her husband were put to final rest as Shemaine leaned her head back to meet his gaze. It was a similar necessity when looking up into the amber-brown eyes. "Gage's father is Lord William Thornton, Earl of Thornhedge."

A look of wonderment passed across Maurice's face. Lord Thornton had been his advocate on many bills before Parliament which had been intended to define the rights of individuals under English law, including one that would have forbidden the shipping of prisoners to far-off ports, especially for the purpose of spilling out the refuse of English gaols onto their colonies.

"Do you know him, your lordship?" Shemaine queried.

Maurice cocked his head and looked at her curiously, deepening the color in her cheeks. His dark eyes glowed with luminous warmth as a poignant smile curved his handsome lips. "What is that which you called me, Shemaine? I thought we had progressed far beyond titles and formal addresses."

Shemaine was sure the apparent ease with which Maurice now seemed able to disconcert her was primarily due to the prodding of her conscience. In her eagerness to accept her husband's proposal, she had given little heed to how Maurice might be hurt by her decision. She had basically taken it for granted that with so many winsome admirers among the nobility, her former fiancé would have casually directed his attention elsewhere after her disappearance.

"We're no longer betrothed, my lord," she reminded him in muted tones, uncomfortable beneath the fervid intensity of those dark orbs. "And I do not think it proper to address you by your given name any longer."

"I give you leave to do so, Shemaine," Maurice murmured, moving closer. "You shall always have a place in my heart, even if I cannot win you back."

Where once she had been at ease with

Maurice, Shemaine now found herself on pins and needles. She was convinced that his nearness would bring about another confrontation after her husband joined them, and she was bemused by it. Was it some deliberate strategy on his part to rile Gage, or did he hope his proximity would play upon her emotions, perhaps making her regret her marriage to another? Whatever his reasons, Shemaine would have preferred him at a safer distance. Any moment now Gage would be coming up the building slip, and if there was one thing she had noticed since last night in Newportes Newes, it was the fact that her husband now seemed quite possessive of her, as if he feared losing her to her former betrothed.

In the awkward silence that followed, Camille stepped forward and placed a doting kiss upon her daughter's brow. "My dear, you look lovely." She had seized upon a portion of Shemaine's earlier statement and greatly desired to know more. "But tell me, dear, do you not have servants to clean for you?"

Shemaine laughed blithely, thankful for the interruption. "No, Mama, I do all the cooking and cleaning myself."

"The cookin'?" Bess repeated, staring agog at her former student. "Ye mean all of it?"

The cook's rampant astonishment drew an amused chuckle from Shemaine. "You'd be amazed by what I've been able to remember from your instructions, Bess. In fact, Gage has said that I'm the best cook in the area."

Bess was flabbergasted. "My goodness, darlin', an' here I was thinkin' I had failed ta teach ye even the basics."

Camille had been the one to insist that Shemaine learn such wifely duties, but she was certainly no different from other doting mothers who preferred to pamper her only offspring, at least for as long as they were near. Camille had wanted the servants to accompany them to ease their own adjustment to the untamed wilderness, and she now saw even more advantage in their presence. "Perhaps while we're here, Shemaine, you might enjoy having Bess and Nola take over those duties so we can visit together. Would you mind terribly?"

Shemaine wrapped her arms around her mother and hugged her close. "No, of course not, Mama. I've been missing Bess's cooking so much lately, my mouth waters just thinking about it."

"And Gage? Would he think us presumptuous if we took over his household?" Camille asked hesitantly.

Espying her husband coming up the building slip, Shemaine hurried to meet him. Noticing the frigid scowl that he bestowed upon the Marquess, she slipped an arm through his and gave it a reassuring squeeze as she whispered, "I love you."

A lean hand caressed hers as he breathed, "You make my heart sing even in the midst of anger, my sweet. You're my love . . . my heart's desire."

Beneath his warm smile, Shemaine could feel her own heart swelling with the joy of her devotion. Drawing him back to her mother, she presented the matter which she and her parent had been discussing. "Gage, Mama would like to know if you would mind Bess and Nola doing the cooking and the chores while they're here."

Gazing at Camille Thornton, Gage realized his wife had been bequeathed her mother's regal beauty. Shemaine might have inherited her coloring from her father, but she had definitely inherited the delicate features of her mother. "If Bess taught my wife, Mrs. O'Hearn, I have no doubt that she's an exceptional cook. I'm sure Shemaine will enjoy some leisured moments to spend with you."

Shemaine squeezed her mother's hand. "You see, Mama. He's not an ogre."

Camille reddened and was immediately reluctant to meet the smiling amber-brown eyes that rested on her. "I fear my daughter exaggerates, sir. I never thought you an ogre."

" 'Tis good to know that, madam," Gage replied easily, though he was just as certain she still believed him a murderer.

Gage moved away slightly, facing his rival, and silently presented a challenge with a cold-eyed stare. As handsome as the Marquess was, it was understandable that he had suffered pangs of jealousy when he had noticed the man hovering near his wife. Though the nobleman had doffed his tricorn after leaving the carriage, he was nevertheless meticulously garbed, wearing a royal blue frock coat with narrow breeches, waistcoat, stockings and costly shoes, all of a rich creamy hue. In the bright sunlight the much lighter creaminess of his shirt and stock nearly bedazzled the eye. His black hair was neatly tied in a queue at his nape, and his skin had taken on a deep, rich hue from his recent sea passage. Gage could now understand why Shemaine had been so sure that Maurice would find another. He was good-looking enough to attract women in droves.

"You seem quite rested, my lord," Gage commented with an absence of warmth. "Should I assume the accommodations were adequate?"

Maurice's eyes glinted with icy shards above a cool smile. "The hospitality of the Tates could not have been warmer, but I'm sure you can imagine that I had much on my mind."

"Shemaine, you mean," Gage prodded.

"Aye, Shemaine," Maurice murmured softly, as if the name soothed his very spirit. "She is like gentle springtime after a hard winter."

"Aye!" Gage agreed. "But she is mine!"

Maurice gave him a lame shrug. "For a time, at least."

Flannery drew Gage's attention as he approached from the companionway. "Cap'n, may I have a word with ye?"

"Of course, Flannery." Gage felt a bit frustrated with the intrusion, but he excused himself from his guests and followed the shipwright to the rail.

Flannery squinted up at him with an unbridled grin. "I know ye've got company, Cap'n, but I'm thinkin' ye'll be likin' what I have ta tell ye . . . considerin' it's 'bout some people what are wantin' ta have a look 'bout this here vessel today. Ta be sure, sir, they may have a mind ta buyin' her."

They spoke quietly together for a moment and then, battling the same contagious grin that had infected the old shipwright, Gage came back to Shemaine and, begging their guests' apology once more, drew her aside. "Flannery has just told me some great news, my love, and I wanted to share it with you so you can give me counsel. It seems there's a sea captain in the area whose family is in the shipping business. He made the trip downriver yesterday from Richmond, and last night he sought out Flannery in Newportes Newes. He's bound for New York with other members of his family later today, but before he leaves, he would like to come out and look over the ship. Flannery has sailed under him before and has assured me that he has the money to buy the ship if it meets his requirements."

"Oh, Gage, that would be wonderful!" Shemaine exclaimed, immediately mindful of the fact that her parents would be less likely to get into a verbal altercation with her husband while there were strangers present. It was a confrontation she desperately wished to avoid, and her heart was filled with hope that they might yet escape such an event.

Peering down at her rather dubiously, Gage queried, "Won't your parents be offended if I devote the greater part of my attention to these other people while they're here today? I cannot hope for acceptance while they continue to believe I'm a murderer, but if they become convinced that I'm deliberately avoiding the issue, they might try whisking you away without giving me a hearing."

"I would be furious with them if they did," Shemaine stated with firm conviction, but she soon smiled. "Oh, Gage, I'm sure my father understands the importance of conducting business when the moment is ripe. And I would not see you miss this opportunity for all the world. You've dreamed of selling the ship from the very beginning. Besides, 'twill give my parents more time to get used to the idea of us being married. It was rather a shock for them to arrive here hoping to rescue their virginal daughter from bondage only to find that I had not only been wed during my separation from England but had also conceived."

"Aye, they probably still consider you their little girl."

Shemaine laughed softly and spoke for his ears alone. "If they only knew how lustful I've become, my love. Why, they'd never believe I haven't been bewitched."

A grin teased Gage's lips. "What kind of bribe may I expect for keeping your secrets, my sweet?"

Shemaine pondered his inquiry with smiling sultry eyes, but she played the poor maid, constrained by circumstances. "Anything you wish, fine sir. 'Twould seem you have me at a disadvantage, for if I do not comply with your desires, you will surely defame my good name."

"Anything?" Gage's own eyes glowed.

"I'm at your mercy, sir. Whatever your will may be," she answered, lowering her gaze submissively as she tried to curb a threatening grin. "I only pray that you'll not treat me too harshly."

"Ah, nay, never harshly, my sweet," Gage promised. "Otherwise, I would spoil the treasures I heartily seek."

Shemaine yearned to know more. "What treasures are those, my lord?"

"Your love . . . and your eager response to my slightest touch."

"Is it so noticeable?"

Gage plumbed the wide, translucent depths of smiling green. "Aye, but I would have it no other way, my sweet."

"Nor would I," she breathed, her whole being brimming with love. "As you have correctly surmised, I tremble with desire at the lightest stroke of your hand. You have truly made me your slave, sir."

"Eh, no slave," he assured her, "but a wife warm and willing. I cherish our moments alone together, when we are of one mind and body."

Shemaine wanted to slip into his arms, but she realized that Maurice was watching them closely and felt a need to turn the subject to something far less stimulating. "Tell me, Gage, what time is this sea captain supposed to arrive?"

Gage glanced around, wondering what had caused her abrupt change in topics. When his searching gaze met the cold, penetrating glare of the Marquess, he understood completely. For a moment their eyes dueled in chilling combat. Then, pointedly turning his back upon the other man, Gage faced his young wife again. "Flannery thought they should be here before the noon hour, my pet."

"Then I will instruct Bess to cook up a feast for our guests," Shemaine declared, her enthusiasm beginning to soar.

"On such short notice?" Gage queried in amazement.

"Of course, my darling. Bess can work miracles in no more than an hour's time."

Gage was not at all sure it was fair to require a banquet from the cook when she was in a strange kitchen and there was so little time left to prepare it. "Perhaps you should talk it over with Bess first, Shemaine, and allow her to say whether or not she can manage such a feat."

"Bess enjoys proving her abilities," Shemaine averred. "So don't worry that she'll be provoked by my demands. But if you wish, I shall discuss it with her and let her decide."

"I would prefer that you do, my sweet."

Shemaine smiled up at him tenderly. "Whoever said you were an ornery beast really didn't know you very well, Gage Thornton. When you concern yourself about putting a servant to more trouble than she might normally expect, then 'tis plain to me you're a very caring individual. 'Tis but one of the reasons why I love you so much."

The amber-brown eyes glowed into hers. "You always make my heart soar with those reassurances, my sweet."

"Do you need any?" Shemaine asked, her lips curving. No matter who watched them, she found it incredibly easy to respond to her husband with all the tenderness and gratification of a wife who was loved and *in love*. It was strange, but she never felt so much a woman as she did in those moments when she was with Gage. "Haven't I always given you the best I've had to offer? My heart, my body, the very essence of my gender are thoroughly pliable to you alone. Or does perchance the presence of my former betrothed strip away your confidence?"

"The Marquess is a handsome man, madam," Gage admitted without answering her question directly.

"Aye, but so are you, my darling ... and *you* are the one I love."

Gage inclined his head briefly in acceptance of her affirmation as his eyes continued to gleam, this time above a roguish grin. "I need as many assurances as you're willing to give, madam. Once we've gained the privacy of our bedroom this evening, I'll require far more to assuage my heart. And, of course, I'd like to delve more thoroughly into the matter we were discussing earlier. *Anything* encompasses a lot of possibilities, madam."

Her white teeth tugged at a bottom lip as Shemaine tried to subdue a grin. "I shall accept that as an invitation, sir."

Gage's eyes glittered with the luster of yellow diamonds. "Then you've been advised, madam."

Shemaine acknowledged his warning with eager delight. "I shall look forward to the occasion."

"No less than I."

Shemaine glanced beyond Gage and noticed that Maurice was now scowling sharply, as if resentful of the fact that she had been flirting with her own husband. Shemaine sought to defuse his ire by assuming a more serious mien for the protection of the one whom she held most dear. She knew Maurice's abilities, and she dared not test his ire. "If this captain likes your ship, Gage, would he actually consider buying it before it's finished?"

"If what he sees and hears meets with his approval, then it's completely possible. With my guarantee that it will be finished as planned, he can be assured that no one else will buy it in his absence."

"But what if he wants to make changes? Is that permissible once you've agreed on a sum?"

"As long as such changes don't hinder her design, then they're completely acceptable. I'll just have to figure the cost of any additional work before we agree on a price, and then hopefully we can strike a bargain. A portion of her cost will have to be left as security, but once the ship is finished and meets all the requirements of my guarantees, then the man can return, pay the remainder of what he owes me, and take immediate possession."

Shemaine grew troubled. "There's no way he can cheat you like Horace Turnbull tried to do, is there?"

Gage laughed, easing her concern. "Flannery says the captain's word is like gold in a purse. If I deliver what he expects, then he will do the same. He's looking for a ship that's as swift as some of those the French are now sailing. I would not want to boast, but I believe this one will put the French crafts to shame."

Shemaine sighed with contentment. " 'Twould be nice to sail on the vessel for a few moments before she's gone forever from our sight."

"I'm sure that can be arranged, my sweet. The man will want to try her out before taking full possession, and at that time I'll ask him if he might allow other passengers to accompany us for a short jaunt along the coast."

"I'd love that!"

Camille joined them and laid a hand upon Shemaine's arm to draw her attention toward the path in front of the cabin, where Erich Wernher and Tom Whittaker were toting a pair of large trunks toward the cabin. "Dear, we've brought some of your clothes from England. Where would you like them taken?"

"My clothes!" Shemaine gasped in ecstatic delight. With cheeks rosy and green eyes sparkling with excitement, she faced her husband and gave him a dazzling smile. "Oh, Gage, I must go see!"

"Then run along, my sweet," he urged with a chuckle. "And don't forget to talk to Bess about our additional guests. There will be five coming, three women and two men. And if she's agreeable to cooking for so many, Erich and Tom can set up some planks on carpenter's benches to make a table on the front porch. We can all eat out there."

Shemaine nodded and, half turning, lifted a hand to her sire, bidding him to accompany her mother to the cabin. Pausing briefly, she faced her husband with another question. "Will your father be up to joining us?"

Gage responded with a slow grin. "I'm sure he'll make the effort with Mary Margaret here."

"Then I'll have a place set for him," Shemaine said, walking backward several steps. "Be sure and let me know as soon as our guests arrive. In the meantime, I'll be trying on my gowns to see which of them still fits."

Her husband gave her a doubtful stare. "You don't imagine that you've grown more than a mite, do you, madam?"

Furtively Shemaine passed a hand down the front of her bodice, denoting the area she worried about most. "In some places perhaps."

Gage's laughter accompanied her descent, but when he turned and found Maurice glowering at him, his mirth ceased abruptly. "Are you still here, your lordship?" he challenged, vexed with the man for having eyed them like a hawk. "I thought you'd have taken the hint by now that Shemaine is content to be my wife and left of your own accord. Or do you still see some advantage in drooling over her like some lapdog?"

Maurice was hardly in the mood to apologize. For too long, he had observed the couple talking together, and their obvious affection for one another had provoked his jealousy. If not for cruel fate, it might have been him for whom Shemaine had sparkled.

Folding his hands behind his narrow hips, Maurice approached Gage with a measured tread, thankful for this opportunity to be alone with the man. He was anxious to make certain truths known to the rascal and, for that, he needed privacy. His statement was as clear and to the point as he could make it. "I won't be departing the colonies, Mr. Thornton, until I'm able to leave with the woman I hold dear."

Gage's eyes chilled. "To do that, my lord, you'll have to kill me."

An indolent shrug accompanied the Marquess's reply. "I expected as much."

"Perhaps you should consider that Shemaine might prefer me over you."

Maurice's black eyes lightly skimmed downward from the bronzed features of his adversary to the broad shoulders clothed in a white, full-sleeved shirt and the taut, narrow hips garbed in tan breeches. He casually took note of the square-toed black shoes before he met Gage's mildly amused stare once more. "I'll allow that Shemaine may have cause to be infatuated with a man of your stature and good looks, sir, but I'm sure in time she'll forget you."

Gage's riposte nearly drew blood. "Like she did you?"

The black eyes smoldered with suppressed rage. "I'm sure 'twas only the circumstances in which Shemaine found herself that compelled her to agree to your proposal of marriage, Mr. Thornton. Had she known we were sailing here to rescue her, I have no doubt she would have rejected your offer."

"Perhaps," Gage admitted, "but only because she would have felt obliged to honor your betrothal." He looked contemplatively at the Marquess. "But tell me this, if you would. If you were to kill me, how could you ignore the child now growing within her?"

Maurice disliked the sharp prodding of his memory on that matter. "Because the babe will be a part of Shemaine, I will endeavor to give him every benefit that I would afford my own offspring."

Gage scoffed. "Every benefit?"

"Not my title, of course, but I will see that he . . . or she . . . lacks for nothing."

"Except his true father."

"That can't be helped, unfortunately," Maurice retorted blandly. "You see, I cannot leave Shemaine here alone with you, knowing there could come a time when you might kill her as you did your first wife. I would never forgive myself if something happened to her which I could have taken measures to avert."

"So you've judged me guilty to placate any qualms you might suffer when you attempt to kill me—"

"Attempt?" The Marquess laughed caustically at Gage's choice of words. "My good man, if I make up my mind to kill you, then be assured I shall do just that. I will not merely make an attempt!"

Somewhat incredulously, Gage inquired, "Are you so sure you can kill me?"

"Unquestionably."

Gage paused a thoughtful moment as he assessed the Marquess's confidence. His statement had not been conveyed with despicable arrogance but with an unwavering conviction. "Shemaine warned me about your talents with dueling pistols and a sword, but she also said that thus far you've only wounded your opponents."

"I shall take special pains to serve you a death sentence, sir."

Gage cocked his head at a contemplative angle. "If you're so skilled at dueling, my lord, would it not be the same as committing murder to fight with another who has never dueled in his life?"

Maurice's mouth twitched with sardonic terseness. "Hopefully, I shall be serving justice her due and saving Shemaine from the fate of an early death."

"And will nothing deter you from the path you've chosen?"

Maurice paused a moment to ponder Gage's question and finally responded with a brief, affirmative nod. "If you were to be completely exonerated of killing your first wife, then I must allow that you might be a fit husband to Shemaine. At least, with that assurance, I would be confident about leaving her in your care."

Gage returned the Marquess's steadfast stare, understanding the man completely. He would do nothing less himself. "Then I shall endeavor to hope for my family's sake, my lord, that your hand is stayed by such a miracle."

Maurice grew reflective as he appraised the other man. "I perceive you are no coward, Mr. Thornton."

Gage inclined his head imperceptibly as he returned the tribute. "Nay, nor are you, your lordship."

William Thornton made a valiant attempt to rise to his feet as Camille and Shemus O'Hearn entered the parlor, but Shemaine laid a gentle hand upon his shoulder, urging him back into his chair.

"Do not stress yourself, my lord," she begged softly. "My mother understands that you are recovering from a serious wound and cannot grace us with your sterling manners."

"I told his lordship as much meself, but he wouldn't listen ta me advice," Mary Margaret volunteered from the settee, setting aside the playing cards she had been holding in her hand.

Andrew scooted off the settee and ran to Shemaine. When Bess and Nola had entered the kitchen, he had sought solace in the familiarity of Mrs. McGee as a close friend, but now that Shemaine had returned, he felt at ease again. Shemaine introduced the elders to each other and then presented the boy to her parents.

"And this is my son, Andrew," she proudly declared, hugging him affectionately. "He's two years old, can count to ten and can even spell his first name."

"Oh, what a fine, handsome boy you are," Camille praised admiringly. "And so smart!"

"Mommee Sheeaim taught me," he said with a rather shy but captivating grin.

"Andrew, this is my mother and father. . . ."

He looked up at Shemaine wonderingly. "Your mommee and daddee?"

She answered with an effervescent smile. "Aye, they've come all the way from England to see us."

"My daddee, too?"

She responded with an affirmative nod. "They've only known about your daddy since yesterday, but they came out today to see him."

"That's my gran'pa!" Andrew proudly announced, motioning with a curled finger toward William.

The Earl of Thornhedge grinned back at the O'Hearns. "I say, we do need a foursome to play whisk. Might the two of you be interested?"

"My father is a wicked cardplayer," Shemaine warned with a twinkling smile.

Shemus snorted in amusement. "Yer mother may look like an angel, me girl, but she's done me in, in more ways than I'd care to count."

Camille patted her husband's arm dotingly. " 'Tis only because you let me win, dear."

"Ha!" Shemus scoffed at the absurdity of such a notion. Facing William, he swept a hand toward his wife. "The truth is, me lord, *she* lets *me* win."

William chortled and then winced slightly as he was reminded of his healing wound. A bit more soberly he asked, "Does that mean we'll have a foursome?"

"I would visit with my daughter in her bedroom first, then I'll be delighted to join you and your lovely companion in a game," Camille replied graciously.

Bess came from the kitchen into the parlor bearing a small platter of crumpets. She had cut the bread into small, bite-sized pieces and now offered them to her mistress. "Ye'll be wantin' ta try a wee taste of this first, mum."

Sweeping her eyes over the contents of the plate, Camille grew puzzled. "Whatever for, Bess? I've tasted your crumpets before. Are these any different?"

"Aye, mum. They're what your pretty darlin' made."

"Oh." Camille wasn't at all sure she wanted to subject herself to such a questionable task just yet. Through years of arduous disasters in the kitchen, she had been well educated to the faults of her daughter's cooking. She did not necessarily want another sampling now, something that she would indubitably taste the whole day long and come to regret upon retiring to bed later that evening.

"It's all right, mum. Taste 'em," Bess encouraged.

Gingerly Camille picked up a tiny piece and sampled it. By slow degrees the expression on her face was transformed from careful reserve to glowing radiance. She conveyed her approval with an exuberant smile. "Why, they're delicious!"

Bess nodded eagerly. "We did it, mum. We taught our li'l darlin' ta cook!"

William sought to squelch his amusement before he was again tormented by the consequences, but the more he tried, the more he was inclined to chuckle. Clasping a pillow to his chest to subdue the pain, he peered at Shemaine. " 'Twould seem, my dear, they've been entertaining doubts about your cooking skills for some time."

"Believe me, my lord, their distrust was well earned," Shemaine rejoined with amusement.

"Not anymore, though, I'll warrant," Mary

Margaret chimed in. "His lordship and I've been wonderin' if'n yer Bess can now cook as well as yer pretty self, Shemaine Thornton."

"Maybe not," Bess pondered aloud, then she heaved her plump shoulders upward in a good-natured shrug. "An' if not, then I'd be a-thinkin' I've outdone meself teachin' her."

"The acclaim belongs entirely to you, Bess," William responded jovially. "You've made all of our lives more enjoyable by your efforts."

"Thank ye, yer lordship." Bess bobbed a curtsy and bustled into the kitchen, tossing back a pleased grin.

Shemaine followed the cook into the kitchen, where she spoke to her privately for a few moments, informing her that there would be more guests arriving soon. Bess promptly reassured her there would be no difficulty in laying out a feast for everyone to enjoy. It would not be the most elaborate, the cook warned, but there would be plenty for all. It was what Shemaine had expected, and she gave the woman an affectionate hug. "I thought you could do it, Bess, but my husband didn't want me to upset you with more work than you could handle."

Bess grinned back at her. "Tell yer mister I'm appreciative o' his kindly concern, darlin'." Then she leaned forward to whisper. "He's a right fine gent, if'n ye ask me."

"He is, truly," Shemaine agreed in an equally quiet tone.

Shemaine quickly directed Erich and Tom where they were to erect the table, and when she returned to the parlor, Camille swept her hand toward the master bedroom, drawing her daughter's attention to the two O'Hearn trunks that stood near the end of the bed. "Shall we go in and have a look at what Nola packed inside the chests?"

"I can hardly wait!" Shemaine caught her mother's hand and pulled her along behind her as she ran into the room.

Shortly after being closeted with her parent in the master bedroom, Shemaine shook out a pale aqua gown of silk floral brocade fashioned with a square neckline and three-quarter-length sleeves. After Nola gave the gown a careful pressing, Shemaine swept it over her head. The garment seemed to settle in place with the eagerness of an old friend yearning to revive a close acquaintance. Camille stepped behind her daughter to tighten the laces at the back of the bodice, tied a narrow ribbon with a jeweled pendant about Shemaine's neck, and then called upon Nola's talents to create a suitable coiffure. The maid was teary-eyed with joy at the opportunity to brush and comb Shemaine's hair once again. Not so long ago, she had grieved for her young mistress, believing her dead, and was deeply thankful the O'Hearns' search had not ended with a morbid discovery. She considered it a celebration of sorts to be able to sweep the tresses into a charming coiffure on top of her charge's head and arrange a trio of ringlets that hung down coyly from behind a dainty ear.

A hand mirror was brought out from one of the trunks, and Nola held it while her young mistress admired the results. Camille looked on in approval and smiled as she counted their good fortune in finding their daughter again.

"Oh, Nola, I feel much like my old self again!" Shemaine exclaimed. "Thank you!"

"Ye're prettier than ever, mum," Nola replied, squeezing her mistress close to her in a fond embrace. Then, with a smile, the maid took her leave.

"You do look just as beautiful as ever, my dear," Camille said, blinking back the wetness that threatened to blur her vision as she gazed at her daughter. "Just wait until Maurice sees you."

Shemaine stiffened slightly, and when she turned to face her mother, she probed the teary blue eyes that seemed to plead with her. "Mother, I'm not married to Maurice. Gage is my husband. I would encourage you to remember that."

Camille's brows came together in a distressed frown. "Will he ever be able to give you what Maurice is capable of?"

Shemaine detected the slight quaver in the other's voice and recognized the hurt and anguish in the delicate visage. As much as she loved her mother, she would never allow herself to be coaxed away from Gage with beautiful clothes or promises of unending wealth. "Mama, I *love* my husband, and I will have no other. . . ."

"But there are many who say he killed his first wife—"

"Aye, and I have met several of those people who've dared say such things. If you were to meet them yourself, Mama, you would see through their ploys and their eagerness to spread tales that they've enlivened for their own purposes. Roxanne Corbin is a spinster who has wanted Gage for her own since he first came here to Virginia more than nine years ago, but he married Victoria instead. Roxanne could not tolerate that fact. Who knows? Roxanne may have even been the one who killed Victoria. She was certainly the one who discovered Victoria's body. After Gage and I were married, she came out here, intruded upon us while we were celebrating our love for each other, and vowed to tell everyone that he had killed Victoria. She's a spiteful woman, Mama, bent on having her way, and if not, then at the very least seeing Gage destroyed. Is this someone to whom you would listen? Would you entertain doubts about Papa if some envious fellow were to come to you and say that he was a thief?"

"No, of course not, Shemaine, but—"

"No buts!" Shemaine threw up a hand to halt her mother's arguments. "I will hear no more slander against my husband! And if you've brought these clothes to me today with the hope that you could somehow persuade me to leave Gage, then take them back. I can do without them. But know this, Mama, I will have no other husband but Gage until one of us is laid in a grave!"

Camille pressed a trembling hand to her brow, trying not to yield to the anguish that was tearing her apart inside. "How can I leave you here with him, knowing there's a chance you might not be safe . . . that he might kill you, too?"

"Mama, please," Shemaine murmured cajolingly. "Don't worry about Gage. . . ."

"I can't help it, Shemaine," Camille moaned in abject misery. "You're our only child . . . our darling little girl. We could not bear it if you were slain! And you are so very young! You've not had much experience with men! Gage is so much older. . . ."

"He's no more than two years older than Maurice," Shemaine argued desperately. "Do those two years make such a difference in your mind?"

Camille's brows flicked upward briefly as she tried to find a suitable justification for her prejudice. "Gage *seems* much older."

"Perhaps because he's not had the world delivered to him on a silver tray, Mama. He's had to work hard for what he has achieved. Just like Papa had to do once."

"Your father was much younger when he and I married."

"Let this discussion be at a end," Shemaine urged. Her mother tried once more to speak, but her daughter shook her head passionately. "I'm going outside to show Gage my gown. When I return, I hope you will have settled it in your mind that I'm married to him and I will not let that fact be undone. You have a grandchild on the way, Mama, and I'd like to think that you are looking forward to that event as much as I am. Please, don't waste your time telling me how you abhor and distrust my husband, because it will only drive me away from you."

Camille shook her head sadly and sniffed as she wiped her nose on a dainty handkerchief. "I do not abhor Gage, Shemaine. Truly, if I could be assured the accusations against him are only lies, I'd be content and pleased that you love him so."

"Then I shall pray that something may come to light to ease your fears," Shemaine said softly. "Because I cannot bear to see you cry."

Shemaine gently kissed her mother and

then left, closing the bedroom door behind her. William was the first to notice her change of attire and artfully arranged coiffure, and offered praises equal to those of a courtly swain.

"I'd have sworn by the glow filling the room that the sun had risen for a second time today, but I can see for myself that it's only your beautiful radiance."

"You're most gallant, my lord," Shemaine responded with a gracious smile, dipping into a curtsy.

Stepping to the front door, she paused there to look back at Andrew, who had charmed his way onto his grandfather's lap. "I'm going outside to see your father, Andy. Want to come along?"

"Goin' ta see Daddee!" he informed William happily, and wriggled quickly to the floor.

Taking the child's small hand in hers, Shemaine met her father's worried stare and managed a fleeting smile before she took her leave.

Her return to the ship caused both Gage and Maurice to stop and stare in deep appreciation of her beauty, but as her husband slipped his arms about her and drew her close for a kiss, Maurice felt a torturous pang of envy wrench his vitals. The need to escape the couple's presence became needful and paramount. He had endured their marital courtship too much for one day. With hands clenched, spine rigid, he stalked across the deck and never looked back as he descended the building slip.

In the absence of his daughter, Shemus hurried into the bedroom to find his wife weeping silently in her handkerchief.

"Did ye have a chance ta talk with her?" he asked anxiously.

"Yes, but no good came of it, Shemus. Shemaine is determined to stay with Gage. She says she loves him and will have no other."

"Damn the Irish pigheadedness!"

"Shemus! For shame! She is our daughter."

"Aye, but 'tis me own stubborn self I see in her."

"Perhaps she's right, Shemus," Camille offered dolefully. "What right do we have to condemn the man when we know so little of the truth? Shemaine swears 'tis envy behind part of the gossip. A spinster who wanted Gage to marry her—"

"We'll see what Maurice can do," Shemus mumbled, hardly hearing his wife. "Perhaps he'll be able to talk her into coming back with us. She said she loved him once, and I know he loves her."

"I don't think Shemaine will come home with us, Shemus, not without her husband. And if we force her, she'll hate both of us forever."

"Have we lost her?"

"Aye, Shemus, 'tis what I now fear. We've lost our little darling. She's grown up into a woman, and she has a mind of her own."

CHAPTER 22

"They're comin' now," Flannery announced shortly after Gillian had taken Andrew out to scout the woods for small animals. Gage and Shemaine joined the shipwright at the rail as he pointed a gnarled finger toward a large dinghy nearing the loading dock. A tall man wearing a tricorn jumped out and secured the painter to a post while his male companion drew the oars into the craft.

The first gentleman escorted two of the young ladies up the building slip while the man who had been at the oars lent assistance to the third. Upon espying Shemaine, the two men swept off their tricorns in courteous manner. They were as tall as Gage, but the older one had a thick crop of dark auburn hair tied in a queue behind the high, stiff collar of his frock coat. His face was rather squarish and angular, his eyes brown. An unquenchable humor was evident in the tiny lines around his mouth, behind which gleamed a fine collection of white teeth.

Flannery introduced him as his former captain. "Cap'n Thornton," he said, turning to Gage. "This here be Cap'n Beauchamp. . . ."

"Nathanial Beauchamp," the stranger announced, extending a hand of greeting toward Gage. "Or Nathan, if you'd prefer. . . ."

The usual response came as promptly as expected by those who knew the man. "Everyone calls me Gage."

After Shemaine was introduced, Nathanial identified the women who were with him. "These are my twin sisters, Gabrielle and Garland," he said, indicating the younger two. Then he laid an arm about the brown-haired woman who stood beside him. "And this is my wife, Charlotte."

The twins had hair as black as the mane of the younger man, and it was he, rather than her twin, to whom Garland bore a striking resemblance. The pair had eyes as golden and translucent as polished amber.

"My younger brother, Ruark," Nathanial announced, clapping a large hand upon that one's shoulder.

"Your servant, Madam Thornton." Ruark flashed a dazzling display of white teeth in a wide grin before he swept a gallant bow before Shemaine. "Your beauty bears more than a wee trace of the Irish colleens I've seen on that verdant isle, madam."

The green eyes sparkled back at him. "And you, sir, must have been blessed with the Irish way for your tongue to be so glib."

Ruark threw back his head and laughed in pure delight. "I do have a fondness for the Irish, to be sure."

"Then I'll warrant you have excellent taste, sir," Shemaine rejoined, drawing amused chuckles from the men.

Gabrielle came forward with a teasing gleam in her eyes. "I think I'd better warn you about my brother, Mrs. Thornton. He seems resolved to remain unfettered despite his advancing years. Yet he treats every winsome maid that comes within proximity as if she were the only one who could steal his heart away. In truth, he'll steal your heart if he can."

"For shame, you little gosling," Ruark chided his sister with a chuckle. "You judge me freely enough, but may I point out that you've now reached a score of years and have not yet found a mate whom you deem suitable."

"No need for your warning, Mistress Beauchamp," Shemaine responded, slipping an arm around her husband's narrow waist as he pulled her close. "My heart has already been taken."

"You're safe then. That's good!" Gabrielle tossed a teasingly triumphant smirk toward her handsome brother, who, in good humor, lifted a finger of warning toward her as if silently threatening her with dire consequences. She tossed her head with coquettish disregard of his silent admonition and then gave a sudden squeal and danced away as he stepped forward menacingly. "I'll tell Mama if you hurt me *again*!"

Shaking her head as she observed her gamboling kin, Garland approached Shemaine. "As you've probably noticed, madam, I'm the only sane one in the family," she claimed, drawing dissenting hoots from her grinning brothers. Snubbing them, she lifted her fine, straight nose to a lofty angle, but her golden eyes were aglow with merriment as she turned back to Shemaine. "Please call me Garland, Mrs. Thornton, and I shall also give you leave to address my sister by her given name"—she tossed a teasing glance toward Gabrielle as if to shame her—"since she lacked the manners to do so herself."

"And I shall be honored if you'd call me Shemaine."

Strolling forward, Gabrielle shrugged her slender shoulders, totally unrepentant. "Garland thinks she's far more dignified and mentally astute than the rest of her family. True, she was more attentive to the lectures of our tutors than I was ever wont to be. But I have other names that suit her better . . . Boring, Conceited, Priggish. . . ."

A muted groan came from the one being defamed, and like her brother, Garland advanced upon her twin as if to take her revenge, drawing a soft cackle of glee from Gabrielle. Wagging her head like a child who took great delight in taunting her playmates, the impish sister danced lightly away.

"Girls, behave yourselves," Charlotte implored, throwing up her hands in disbelief. "What will these good people think of us? No good, I trow."

Gage chuckled, thoroughly entranced with the family. "On the contrary, madam. They make me realize what I've missed by being an only child."

"We're a rather undisciplined brood," Nathanial admitted drolly. "We also have another brother who hasn't reached a full score years yet. He had a friend visiting and preferred to stay at home and do all the things with him that lads his age are wont to do. When last I saw them, they were flirting with the neighbor's girls." Nathanial's eyes gleamed with enthusiasm as he allowed his gaze to flit around the deck. "I'm growing anxious to see this beauty of a ship you've built, sir."

Accepting his statement as her cue, Shemaine faced the three women. "Shall we go to the cabin, ladies? My husband and I have other guests I'd like you to meet."

They all heartily agreed.

Maurice du Mercer had earlier retreated to that particular haven, but when Shemaine entered, leading the other three ladies into the parlor, he rose from the chair where he had been watching the foursome play whist. He was certainly thankful to have a more enchanting diversion than the card game, but he had not expected it in multiple numbers. He was first introduced to Charlotte and then to Gabrielle, who asked him so many questions in a flurry of breathless haste that he found it difficult to answer her and stare at her sister at the same time. Garland had paused to admire the furnishings, but when Shemaine brought her forward to make them acquainted, he found himself staring into darkly lashed amber eyes.

"Garland, this is a family friend, the Marquess du Mercer," Shemaine said. "Your lordship, this is Mistress Garland Beauchamp—"

"Maurice will be sufficient," he said, sweeping Garland a courtly bow.

The young woman dipped into a shallow curtsy. "And if you would, my lord, my name is Garland." A smile flitted across her lips. "Mistress makes me sound so . . . so unbelievably spinsterish."

"A very young and beautiful spinster, to be sure," Maurice murmured warmly.

Gabrielle mentally sighed, realizing it would do her little good to monopolize the Marquess with witty conversation. A blind woman could see that he was taken with her twin. Long ago it had become evident to her that when the right people came together, it usually took something akin to an ax to drive them apart. It certainly seemed to be the case in this instance, although Garland graciously maintained a nice favorable reserve that bordered interestingly upon aloofness. Gabrielle promptly decided she needed to take close note of the lessons her sister was presently demonstrating, for she had never yet enchanted a suitor with her own gift for incessant gab.

A valiant loser, Gabrielle made one more inquiry for the benefit of her sibling. "And is there a Marchioness, your lordship?"

"Beyond a grandmother, I'm without wife, kith or kin," Maurice answered, glancing meaningfully toward Shemaine, whose resulting blush lent him a small measure of satisfaction.

Gabrielle set a finger aside her mouth and pondered his reply. "I wonder how I might fare as an only child. There's five siblings in the Beauchamp family, and with Garland as

my twin, we've had to share everything . . .
or else. . . ."

Maurice was careful to remain silent, for
he wasn't at all sure but what Gabrielle was
suggesting that they would have to share
him, too.

"Dear, we'll need more chairs," Camille
informed her daughter. "Do you have others
available?"

"Of course, Mama," Shemaine replied,
and would have bade Nola to fetch a pair
from upstairs, but the sight of Bess trying to
catch her eye from the kitchen made her excuse herself immediately and go to solve the
cook's dilemma over the kind of sauce that
she should make for the venison.

"I'll get the chairs," the Marquess offered
in gentlemanly manner, having seen several
on the front porch.

The cards had been put aside earlier, and
the ladies' hats were doffed as the chairs
were brought in. As he placed a chair behind
Garland, Maurice failed to notice that it was
rather wobbly, for he seemed incapable of
taking his eyes off the nape of her neck,
where the black hair was coiled in an intricate knot. Beneath the mass, her skin was
fair and lustrous.

Garland was just settling into the chair when the seat came free of the back and the whole of it collapsed, throwing her backward. Astonished gasps equaled gaping stares, but Maurice's reflexes had been fine-tuned to react spontaneously to whatever crisis demanded his attention. Dipping forward with arms extended, he caught the falling maiden and was instantly rewarded with a tantalizingly delicate essence, a sweet blend of lilac and soap that wafted upward through his head like spring wine. As her head hit his chest, he caught a glimpse of softly rounded breasts swathed in mauve fabric and cascading tiers of an ecru lace jabot tumbling from the collar of her fitted bodice before his arms encircled her narrow waist.

"Gracious!" Garland gasped, amazed by how wonderfully secure his arms felt around her.

Maurice lifted her to her feet again and leaned over her shoulder to solicitously inquire, "Are you all right?"

Garland glanced around to meet those shining black eyes and felt a sudden gush of excitement sweep through her. She had always considered her brother too handsome to have a serious challenger in the area of good looks, but she would now have to revise her thinking. "Oh, certainly, your lordship," she hastened to assure the Marquess nervously. "I was just startled, that's all."

"Maurice," he reminded her in a whisper.

The couple finally became cognizant of the fact that the other occupants of the room had fallen silent and were watching them. A vivid hue darkened Garland's cheeks, but Maurice was well acquainted with being closely observed and took their close attention in stride as he bent to pick up the chair.

"I say, Shemaine, for a cabinetmaker, your husband leaves much to be desired." It was a sharp prod he used, but Maurice wanted to make it vividly clear to his former betrothed that the man to whom she had given herself was not without flaws.

Shemaine bristled in swift defense of her husband. "The fault lies with me, your lordship," she replied stiltedly. "I should have paid more heed to the fact that the chair you brought in from the porch was one that had been left here for him to repair. It was not one Gage made, by any means." She swept her hand about to indicate the furnishings filling the rooms and proudly boasted, "This is the kind of furniture he makes."

Suddenly a frightened wail came from outside, startling Shemaine, who readily recognized Andrew's cry. Anxiously she brushed past Garland and Maurice and rushed out onto the porch. Andrew was running full tilt toward the cabin, having left Gillian some distance behind. Shemaine hastened down the steps and ran across the yard toward the boy, who threw himself up into her open arms as if a pack of vicious hounds were nipping at his heels. Sobbing as she lifted him up, he hid his face against her shoulder and refused to look elsewhere. Gillian finally reached them, clearly out of breath.

"What happened?" Shemaine demanded. "What frightened him?"

"Cain," Gillian gasped, panting. "The hunchback was hunkered down in a rotten tree trunk, an' so well hidden I ne'er saw him, but Andy did."

Shemaine remembered the pitiful creature whom she had befriended. She had considered Cain harmless and was alert to the fact that she might have been wrong. "Did Cain hurt him?"

"Nay, 'twas only fright what sent Andy flyin' back here."

Relieved, Shemaine clasped the shivering boy close to her. When she saw Gage racing toward them, she called out with a laugh, "It's all right. Andy was just frightened."

When Gage joined them, Gillian was forced to recount everything that he had said to Shemaine, but his employer made further inquiries. "Did you ask Cain what he was doing in the woods?"

Gillian nodded. "That's what delayed me. He's hard ta understand, ta be sure, Cap'n, but as far as I was able ta make out, he was watchin' over yer missus."

"Watching over Shemaine?" Gage frowned in bewilderment and exchanged a bemused glance with his wife before he looked back at the younger man. "Did Cain say why?"

"Aye, he said somethin' 'bout Potts an' others . . . wantin' ta do her harm."

"Others? Did you question him about them . . . who they might be?"

"I tried, Cap'n, but he refused ta answer. He just wiggled out o' his cubby, dragged his mule from hidin' an' left." Gillian paused, shaking his head in amazement. "Cap'n, ye should've seen what he'd gone an' built. I've no ken when he might've done it, but he made a paddock with stout sticks for his mule an' then piled some brush 'round the barrier so's the animal wouldn't be seen. It looked so natural, I ne'er gave it heed though I was standin' just a few paces away. The way it looked ta me, he meant ta stay out there for some time an' wasn't wantin' anybody who might've come inta the woods ta see him . . . includin' the lot o' us."

"I wonder if he's been the one we've been searching for all this time," Gage muttered half to himself.

"Don't know, Cap'n," Gillian answered. "But it were plain ta me that he had ta have been out there for some time ta do ev'erythin' he'd done."

Gage frowned in confusion. "But how would Cain have stopped Potts if he had shown up?"

Gillian readily supplied the answer. "I was fifty or so paces off when Andy started screamin', an' I ran back ta see what had scared him so. That's when I noticed Cain hunkered down in a hollowed-out ol' tree trunk. He'd pulled a green branch in front o' it an' was hidin' there as still as a mouse until he realized I'd seen him. When he pushed the branch aside, I noticed right off he had a rusty flintlock across his lap. It gave me a start, 'cause I didn't know whether or not he'd be o' a mind ta use it on us. Ta be sure, Cap'n, the pistol looked so old, it might've blown up in his face if he'd fired it. I'm thinkin' he was plannin' on usin' it on Potts."

Gage took his sniffling son from his wife. Shemaine had dried Andrew's eyes and wiped his nose, but Gage could still feel the boy quaking against him. The tiny arms crept around his neck and held on resolutely, at least until Shemaine rubbed a hand soothingly over the boy's back. Then Andrew lifted his head and peered at her with a quivering grin.

"You little rascal," she teased, ruffling his hair as she tried to ease his trauma. "You nearly frightened the wits out of me."

"I'll take him back to the ship with me," Gage murmured.

"Gil'an," Andy called, looking around for the young man.

Gillian stepped to where the boy could see him. "Right here, Andy."

"We goin' ta Daddee's ship now. You comin'?"

Gillian chuckled. "I guess I'd better. Pa'll be wonderin' where I lit ta."

Shemaine watched them until they began ascending the building slip, then she turned and, espying everybody who had been in the cabin now watching from the porch, she went to join them.

William was the most concerned, and questioned her as she drew near. "What happened, Shemaine?"

"Nothing serious, my lord. Andrew was just frightened, that's all. There's a badly deformed man living somewhere between here and Newportes Newes. Andy saw him in the woods, and you know how afraid he is of strangers. Well, he's absolutely terrified of Cain—"

"Cain?" her mother repeated. "What a strange name."

"I agree, Mama, but if you were to see the poor man, you'd be able to understand how appropriate the name is."

"Has he made himself a nuisance?" Maurice inquired.

"Nay, not at all," Shemaine replied, noticing that her former betrothed had elected to stand beside Garland at the edge of the porch. The two truly made a handsome couple, and she hoped that more would come from this, their first meeting, and that Edith du Mercer might come to consider the girl a fit mate for her grandson. "In fact, if Gillian understood him correctly, he was watching over me."

Camille was immediately apprehensive and clasped a shaking hand to her throat. "Why would he be doing such a thing? Does he suspect that you'll be harmed by someone?"

Shemaine knew whom her mother immediately considered the culprit and tried to seem unconcerned as she shrugged. "There was a sailor aboard the *London Pride* who threatened to kill me—"

"Is he still here?" Shemus interrupted, sharing his wife's disquiet.

"Yes, Papa. Jacob Potts seems rather adamant about keeping his vow."

"But why should Cain set himself up as your guardian?" Camille could only wonder what had transpired to compel the poor man to play paladin. What was her daughter *not* telling them?

Shemaine was reluctant to explain, for

she knew her mother would be greatly distressed if she knew the whole of it. "I just helped Cain one day—"

"In what way?" her father pressed.

She lifted her shoulders in another lamehearted gesture. "Potts was beating the man and I interfered. . . ."

"How?" Shemus was becoming increasingly alert. He knew his daughter well enough to sense when she was trying to hide something from them. "What did you do *exactly*?"

"I hit Potts," Shemaine answered in a fretful rush.

"Ye what?" Shemus barked loudly.

Camille was nearly swooning from shock. "I dare not hear anymore!"

Her husband was insistent. "Tell us everything!"

Shemaine heaved a sigh, fully expecting an explosion to be forthcoming from her parents. It was obvious her father would be content with nothing less than the whole tangled tale. " 'Tis simple really. Potts was giving Cain a thrashing, and I grabbed a stick and whacked the tar across the head a couple of times. That's all."

Camille groaned in abject misery. "Oh,

she wouldn't! Shemus, tell me she wouldn't!"

"Oh, she did, ta be sure!" Mary Margaret informed them gleefully, thoroughly amused by their interrogation. "I saw it all meself!"

Maurice nearly choked as he tried to subdue his laughter, but he failed badly in his attempt, for he began to guffaw in amusement, much to the delight of the twins and the distress of Camille. Finally, he managed to calm himself somewhat, but not before he winked at Shemaine and cheered her on. "That's my girl."

"How daring you are!" Gabrielle exclaimed with obvious enthusiasm. "I should like to be so brave."

"You squeal at first sight of a little mouse," her twin accused lightheartedly, effectively squelching the other's dreamy sigh.

Gabrielle tossed her fine head, dismissing her sister's chiding. "Well, that's better than trying to feed every little animal you see."

Shemus posed a wary conjecture. "I must assume this Potts is smaller than the average man."

His daughter ventured a smile, but it was frail and unconvincing.

"Good heavens!" Shemus blustered, fearing the worst. "The girl has taken leave of her senses!"

"Just how big is this Potts anyway?" Camille asked tremulously.

Shemaine chewed her bottom lip worriedly as she turned her eyes askance. It was terribly difficult to meet her mother's anxious gaze while she was trying to hedge on her reply. "Large, I think."

Shemus certainly didn't care for her cautious reply. "Just how large might this man be, daughter?"

"Were you able to meet Sly Tucker?" Shemaine queried tensely, fervently hoping they hadn't.

"Oh, noooo!" Camille moaned, clapping a quivering hand across her mouth.

A roar of rage came from Shemus. "Did it ever occur ta ye, daughter, that such a man might have killed ye on the spot?"

Having the time of her life, Mary Margaret answered in Shemaine's stead. "Oh, the big lummox tried, but his handsome self, Mr. Thornton, went chargin' ta her rescue. Kicked the mudsucker inta the street, he did!"

"I'm going inside," Camille declared faintly. "I've had more than I can abide for one day. And may I never have another like it."

Shemaine heaved a sigh, thankful the worst of her parents' grilling had passed.

"This bloody wilderness is ta blame!" Shemus muttered disagreeably as he followed his distressed wife. "She should come back home with us! On the first ship that sails to England!"

Their entrance into the cabin seemed to encourage a like response from the servants and elders, leaving the twins and the Marquess standing on the porch and Shemaine in front of the steps leading to it.

Maurice peered down at Shemaine, having been thoroughly delighted by her escapade. "I always thought you had it in you to turn a man on his ear, Shemaine. It gives me great satisfaction to know that I was right about you all along."

"I think she's wonderful!" Gabrielle chimed in, yet she was most inquisitive about the relationship between the Marquess and the colonial's wife, for she was wont to think that they had been more than mere acquaintances at some point in their lives. She decided to appease her curiosity. "Have you two been friends for long?"

Maurice's dark eyes gleamed with admiration as he stared at his former fiancée. He was not the least bit uncomfortable about claiming her as the woman he would have chosen to marry. "Shemaine was my betrothed before Mr. Thornton stole her away."

"Oh." Gabrielle's response was barely audible, but her curiosity got the better of her and her voice strengthened as she asked, "I thought when a couple is betrothed, that's nigh as good as being married."

Shemaine blushed furiously, not wishing to explain in detail. "Maurice and I were separated, and I had no reason to hope we would ever find each other again."

"How sad," Garland offered in sympathy.

"Not really," Shemaine said carefully. "You see, I love my husband very much."

"But you must have loved his lordship," Gabrielle interjected.

"Aye, but perhaps not as deeply as I once may have thought," Shemaine confessed haltingly, meeting the beautiful dark eyes that watched her closely. "Maurice and I were swept up in the excitement of being together. He's so handsome . . ." She paused briefly, wanting to be truthful yet sensitive to any hurt feelings that he might yet be harboring. "I was in all likelihood a bit overwhelmed and . . . flattered by his attention."

Gabrielle glanced from one to the other and understood Shemaine's statement completely. They would have made a fine pair, these two. But then, she was of a mind to think that Mr. Thornton was no paltry match for her hostess either. In truth, it would have been impossible for her to make a decision as to which man was more handsome. Since her sister would never dare ask the Marquess about his present circumstance, it was up to her to make the inquiry. "Is there another maid you're presently courting in England?"

Garland felt her jaw drop. Terribly abashed that her sister could be so forward, she hurried to advise the man, "You needn't answer that, your lordship. My sister has surely forgotten the good manners our mother has tried to teach her."

Maurice was hardly offended. He had held himself in check for a lengthy time in his desire for Shemaine, and having now lost her, he knew that finding another who was just as admirable would be the only way he could ever ease the ache that still weighed heavily upon his heart. If truth were told, he'd take Shemaine back in a thrice and never make her regret anything that had happened while they were parted. Garland was a winsome young woman, and her pert, quiet manner pleased him. Still, he could not predict what might come of their relationship, but he would not be unwilling to give her some attention while he bided his time, waiting to see what happened between Gage and Shemaine. "I must assume, Gabrielle, that with Shemaine married to Thornton I must begin searching for another in the near future."

The young woman's responding grin could have easily been the most calculating he had ever viewed. It made him wary of what would follow.

"Perhaps you'd like to visit our home upriver after we come back from New York," she suggested. "I've been trying to find a fit mate for my sister so I can have our bedroom all to myself—"

"Gabrielle!" Garland gasped, outraged. "How dare you suggest that the Marquess may have some interest in me! We've only just met."

Her twin continued on as if Garland had

never spoken. "As it is, we must share the room, and she's so persnickety! I'm forever harassed because she claims I'm untidy. The truth is that I like things a lot more comfortable than she does."

Maurice accepted the fact that if he seriously intended a formal courtship of her sister then he would have an ally in Gabrielle. "If you'll tell me when you'll be expecting to make your return, I'd be delighted to visit your lovely family."

"Good heavens!" Garland whispered breathlessly, taken aback. In a nervous dither, she smoothed her lacy jabot, wishing she had a fan to cool her burning face. The Marquess was the very vision of what she had dreamed of for a husband, but she had never expected to be wooed by him. She was terribly aghast at her twin's outrageous boldness . . . yet more than a little thankful for it, too.

Bess came out to the porch and began spreading tablecloths on the makeshift table that the apprentices had quickly erected. "Me darlin', do ye have enough dishes for everyone?"

"Aye, I'll be right with you to show you where, Bess," Shemaine replied. Mounting

the steps, she paused beside her former betrothed and laid a gentle hand on his arm.
"I'm glad to see there might be some benefit
in you coming so far from England, Maurice.
I shall hope that someday you'll be able to
forgive me for breaking my pledge to you by
marrying Gage."

"I'm not yet over the hurt, Shemaine," he
said forthrightly in a subdued whisper.
"Whether you loved me or not, I loved you
and wanted you for my wife. And there is
still a matter I must deal with before I will
consider leaving you in your husband's care.
'Tis your life and your welfare that concern
me . . . and, of course, your happiness."

"I'm happy, Maurice, please believe me,"
she pleaded.

"For the time being, you are, but I have a
care for the future, Shemaine, and will not
rest until I'm assured of that. If Gage is not
a fit mate for you, then I most certainly want
to be."

CHAPTER 23

Edith du Mercer had dispatched herself with haste from the shores of England only a few days after receiving word that her grandson had set sail for the colonies with the O'Hearns in a quest to find Shemaine O'Hearn. Though Edith had paid a considerable sum for a private cabin on the *Moonraker* and had come unescorted by either servant or attendant, she had found, upon boarding, that she would be required to share her accommodations with another woman of comparable wealth. It had been a thoroughly torturous voyage. Having her sleep relentlessly disturbed by loud, piercing snores that came nigh to shattering her nerves had been a test of endurance that she had not expected to encounter en route to the colonies. Even a mild-mannered lady would have grown understandably vexed, but Edith du Mercer had never known anything but wealth and power. Her imperious disposition had been carefully nurtured by a demanding grandfather who had instilled within her the importance of aristocratic breeding and their family's preeminent ranking above lesser nobles.

If she had been able to manipulate circumstances in her favor without arousing any suspicions, she would have bribed someone to throw the lady overboard. But she had tried not to think of her own comfort in this instance, only her ultimate goal, and that was to see her grandson married to a woman of prominence and nobility who, by her own credentials, could be effective in elevating him to a seat near the throne. No one could dispute that Maurice had character, charm, dignity and integrity, but if there was one thing her grandson lacked, it was an overriding ambition to become a close confidant of His Royal Highness, King

George II, and perhaps the sire of those who would one day rule England.

In his desire to have that Irish twit, Maurice had failed to imagine that he would be giving up all hope of attaining that goal in his zeal to claim her as his wife. Had he been satisfied just to have Shemaine as his mistress, he could have taken a titled wife and not thrown away his chances for a place of eminence. But he had been far too intrigued with Shemaine and too content to think of his own happiness rather than the high position he could attain as a marquess. No doubt he'd have been gratified to sire a brood of Irish-tainted whelps who would have done nothing but sully the Du Mercer name and, at best, could have risen only to nominal distinction and position. In Maurice's many arguments to convince her of Shemaine's merits, one thing had become clear to her, that her grandson could not be swayed from his choice. If his marriage to that creature was to be halted at all, Edith had realized that it would be up to her to arrange for an alternative by devious methods. In that endeavor she had succeeded, with Maurice none the wiser. He was far too honorable to imagine the limits to which a grandmother would go to insure that the Du Mercer heirs would come to fame and greatness.

Now here she was in this squalid little hamlet called Newportes Newes, trying to find a private room for herself. She had grown a bit irate at the innkeeper when he had told her there were absolutely no vacancies to be had in his establishment. When she had tried to persuade him by offering twice the normal rate, he had complained that he already had three sleeping to every bed and each of them had bribed him just to be given a place to sleep. He had even spread out extra mats on whatever space was available in the rooms and halls just to placate everyone, and if he did not adhere to what he had already agreed to, his guests would surely turn on him and rend him to shreds.

"Ye might try the tavern," the innkeeper suggested. "They've got rooms ta let if'n ye can find one what ain't being used by Freida's girls an' their customers. Nowadays the cooks at the tavern are servin' better food than we've got here. Other than that, there ain't much choice outside of a private family rentin' out a room, but ta me mind,

the tavern is yer best bet an' one worth in-
quirin' inta."

"Thank you, I will," Edith answered
crisply. Turning arrogantly away, she settled
a long, bony hand on the silver knob of her
walking stick and strode out of the dingy establishment. She was especially thankful
there was an alternative available, for she
hated dust and filth with a passion, and it
was obvious the inn needed a thorough
cleaning.

Edith paused to dab the perspiration from
her face with a lace handkerchief. Her black
silk gown seemed to collect the heat from
the sun, and though her costly bonnet
shaded her face, its black hue made the
heat nearly unbearable. Indeed, if she had
had her grandson anywhere within speaking
distance right at that moment, she'd have
given him a severe dressing-down for putting her to such bother, all for that winsome
miss she had attempted to get rid of.

Obviously the promise of great reward to
the one who could provide proof of the chit's
demise had gained her nothing more than
frustration. Countless appointments with her
barrister, clandestine carriage rides to Newgate in the dark of night, and veiled meet-

ings on the street outside the prison with that foul-smelling turnkey had proven utterly futile. Even after news of the convict ship's departure, she had continued to hope the man had been right about the prisoner whose aid he had enlisted after he had failed to strangle the Irish wench. But then came news that Maurice was voyaging off to Virginia, and Edith had realized how imperative it was for her to do the same. She just couldn't take the chance that her grandson would find his beloved alive and bring her back to England. All of her efforts would have been for naught!

It had served her purposes well that favorable winds had filled the sails of the *Moonraker*, bringing them into port a mere day after Maurice's ship had docked. Her timely arrival rallied her expectations that she could handle everything efficiently and on the sly before her grandson ever became aware of her presence.

After questioning a local inhabitant near the wharf, Edith had learned that Shemaine O'Hearn was not only alive but apparently in good health and living with some backwoods colonial who had raked up enough coins to buy her. But the woman who had given her this news had seemed to fluctuate drastically between eager spurts of information and, without warning, a nervous reticence, as if fearful of being watched and saying anything at all. Mrs. Pettycomb was certainly the oddest creature with whom she had ever come in contact. Most of her gibberish had been just that, utterly useless. Still, Edith had to remember this was a land inhabited by convicts and the residue of whatever country could put forth a ship to transport them to these climes, and she shouldn't expect too much of the inhabitants. She had never agreed with Maurice's efforts to stem the export of felons, for the wilderness seemed the best place to send the refuse of their society.

Ohhh, Edith moaned to herself, why couldn't the little slut have died and eased her fretful worry about Maurice's objectives and his future as a nobleman? Any true lady would have succumbed to the hardships of imprisonment and a sea voyage aboard a prison ship. It had to be that tainted Irish blood of hers that was too tenacious to succumb.

Edith mentally jeered. Maurice certainly had no idea what he had caused his only kin to suffer by bringing that creature into their ancestral home and announcing in no uncertain terms that they would be married. All that red hair should have warned him ere they met that she wasn't an aristocrat. But no! He had to prove himself magnanimous in his liberal impartiality. No good had come from his tolerance, to be sure, for he had forced his grandmother's hand until it was nigh bloody.

" 'Twill be yet," Edith vowed beneath her breath. "All I need do is find the tart and set the hounds to eating her foul carcass."

Pausing on the boardwalk, Edith surveyed the facade of the tavern with a distasteful grimace and shivered in disgust as she heard a roar of laughter coming from within. A bawdy comment from a hoarse-voiced woman chilled her to the bone. What in the world had her grandson reduced her to? she thought in a panic. First the bribery of a conniving barrister to arrange for Shemaine's arrest and sentencing, then a multitude of other crimes no fainthearted aristocratic lady would have dared soil her hands with. And now this latest affront to her pride! Inhabiting the den of drunkards and harlots like a mere commoner! Perhaps she had sought to kill the wrong person, she thought testily. Her distress and troubles would certainly have ended promptly upon Maurice's demise.

Heaving a sigh heavily imbued with revulsion, Edith pushed open the door of the tavern and stepped inside in her distinctive lofty manner. The loud din nearly made her recoil and certainly made her shudder inside, but in slow degrees it ebbed as every head turned to mark her entrance.

Morrisa Hatcher leaned an elbow on the planks of a nearby table and dropped her chin into her hand as she stared at the newcomer in awe. She had never seen such a rich sheen to a fabric before, and though the hue was as black as her own hair, it was certainly the richest, finest gown she had ever admired in her whole life.

"An' such an ol' biddy wearin' it, too," she mumbled in envy. Pushing to her feet, she winked down at the harlot sitting next to her. "Maybe the liedy's come ta service some o' the lads, eh?"

The other strumpet giggled behind a hand and encouraged her. "Why don't ye go an' ask her which one o' the beds she wants ta work in."

Morrisa caught the madam's attention and

jerked her thumb to indicate the one standing just inside the door. "Where'd ye get yer new girl from, Freida?"

Freida's red lips curled in an amused smirk. "Buckingham Palace. I've got a whole shipment o' 'em comin' in."

Sauntering casually toward the entrance, Morrisa made a wide circuit around the black-garbed lady, looking her up and down. There wasn't one stitch the woman wore that didn't look expensive. "Are ye lost, m'liedy?"

"My greatest fear is that I'm not," Edith quipped haughtily. She sniffed as she dabbed a lace handkerchief daintily to her nose. The tart had obviously bathed in fermented toilet water, for she reeked of the nauseous scent. "I assume this is the tavern, the one I've been directed to, to inquire about a private chamber?"

"Ho-ho!" Morrisa crowed at the elder's elegant diction. "Ain' ye the hoity-toity one."

Edith swept the raven-haired strumpet with a derisive stare. "Haven't you ever heard a lady speak before?"

"O' course," Morrisa answered readily. "I've heared 'em afore. I even seen 'em now an' then. But the ones here don't come in much unless they be with a man. Otherwise, they might be put ta work."

"To bed, you mean," Edith challenged dryly. If the harlot thought her a half-wit, then she was seriously mistaken. She had not acquired seventy-four years to her credit without learning a few things. "I'm sure I'm far too old to interest any of your friends, so I shall deem myself quite safe here. All I need is a private room where I might bide the night, a hot bath and a tolerable meal. Is that too much to ask?"

Morrisa was impressed with the elder's spunk. "Guess not, if'n ye can pay for it."

"You needn't concern yourself about that," Edith retorted blandly. "In fact, if you make the necessary arrangements and send someone to fetch my baggage from the *Moonraker*, I shall pay *you* for your time. Or would you rather entertain the men?"

The pointed question drew a light scoff from Morrisa. "I can do yer errands for ye, alright, but I gots ta get 'nough ta satisfy the madam."

"You'll get enough," Edith promised. "But I'll not suffer a delay. I haven't had a good night's sleep since I left England, and I want what I've asked for posthaste. Do you understand?"

Morrisa supposed it wasn't beneath her to serve as a maid for once in her life. Besides, she was curious. It was a rare thing indeed to find a wealthy lady traveling alone, and she could only wonder at the elder's purpose. What dire circumstances had compelled an old woman to suffer through an arduous voyage without benefit of servant or manly escort?

With a nod, Morrisa accepted the lady's conditions, but in return she asked for double her usual earnings, planning on keeping Freida in the dark about the extra. Receiving a fine leather purse, she bustled off to talk with the tavernkeeper and was back in a wink. "Ye can have the last room on the right upstairs. The tavern maids'll be bringin' ye up a bath whilst I send a fella ta fetch yer baggage from the ship. Though the cap'n probably'll ne'er mistake ye, ye'd better give me yer name so's he'll know for sure 'twas ye what sent the bloke o'er for yer things."

"Lady Edith du Mercer."

Morrisa set her head thoughtfully aslant. "I figgered ye had breedin' an' a title."

"I'm honored that you noticed," Edith rejoined loftily.

Morrisa opened her mouth to give a crisp retort but promptly decided against it. This old bird would not take kindly to a dressing-down, Morrisa perceived, and if she grew snippish, it would seriously reduce or even negate what she might otherwise gain by holding her tongue.

"And your name?" the lady inquired.

"Morrisa. Morrisa Hatcher."

"Is Hatcher your real name or one you've taken on over the years?"

Morrisa squirmed uncomfortably. Whoever this ancient biddy was, she was no one's fool. "Me ma gave birth ta me without gettin' hitched, if'n that's what ye're askin'. 'Twas a butler she claimed what done it ta her, but he wouldn't own up ta it. She got kicked out've the gran' house where she'd been workin' at, but he stayed on like he ne'er done nothin' ta nobody. After she had me, she said he was a real sly bird an' she done gone an' hatched his li'l chick. The name stuck."

"Well, Morrisa Hatcher, what about some food?"

"I'll fetch ye some vittles meself after

ye've taken yer bath," Morrisa said. "Would ye be carin' for some assistance in unpackin' yer clothes or gettin' undressed?"

Edith du Mercer was as shrewd as Morrisa had ever hoped to be and could sense the judicious reasoning going on behind those dark eyes that watched her so closely. "Whatever assistance you're willing to render will be rewarded, Morrisa, but only if I leave here with no fewer possessions than I've entered with."

Morrisa met Edith's unswerving stare and recognized the challenge that she would be undertaking in aiding the woman. "I'll ain't gonna steal nothin' from ye, if'n that's what you mean."

"You're very astute, my dear. We understand each other very well."

"I ain't no thief," Morrisa declared, bristling.

"No?" Edith permitted a small glimpse of a smile. Her tone conveyed some disbelief as she asked, "Do you actually get as much as you claimed a moment ago? Or are you just a liar?"

Morrisa chafed under the elder's goading. "A girl's gotta earn her keep one way or t'other."

"Of course, Morrisa," Edith agreed. "And as long as you remain honest while you're working for me, you could possibly earn far more than you would by bedding a man. But you must remember, I'll give up nothing more than what I'm willing to yield to you, and that by my own choice. Do you understand?"

"I hear ye," Morrisa acknowledged.

"Then you may lend whatever assistance is needed."

Motivated by curiosity, Morrisa escorted the lady to her room, directed the preparation of the bath herself and laid out a chemise and dressing gown, both of which were so rich and beautiful that she had trouble imagining their cost. In some awe, she ran a hand over the garments, wondering how she might look in them, but she quickly banished the idea of rifling through the elder's possessions behind her back. She could almost bet the old snake could draw blood with her tongue if she were vexed.

"I ain't ne'er seen clothes what's as fine as yers," the harlot admitted, glancing around.

Edith had been watching her and was satisfied that the younger woman had kept her wits about her and not tried to stuff something into her clothing. "Perhaps if you serve me well enough, Morrisa, I'll leave you some when I sail back to England. I have plenty enough as it is in my home."

"That'd be real kindly o' ye, m'liedy," Morrisa eagerly replied with a buoyant smile.

"Then come help me undress," Edith urged, "and we can talk more while I soak in a bath."

Edith's directive was carried out swiftly, and two sheets were hung from the low beams to enclose the tub, providing some privacy for the matron. As Morrisa waited on the other side, Edith began making her own inquiries.

"Have you ken of a young woman named Shemaine O'Hearn living in the area?"

Morrisa snorted in distaste. It seemed nowadays everybody arriving on the inbound ships was asking where the li'l bogtrotter might be. " 'Course, I do. We sailed here on the *London Pride* together."

"Did you become friends with her?"

The harlot jeered. "Enemies would be more like it."

"What made you hate her?"

Morrisa was wary but truthful. No one

could hang her for disliking a person. "Sh'maine was always puttin' her nose in where it didn't belong. I had a right good way o' handlin' the other women 'til she started talkin' ta 'em. Would've had 'em all bowin' and scrapin' ta me, if not for Sh'maine."

"So you resent her?"

"Aye, ye might say as much."

"I'm sure at times you must have been angry enough to even wish her dead." Edith voiced the conjecture carefully and anticipated the response.

"Not only wished it, had reason to see it done. . . . Not that I would have, mind ye," Morrisa interjected cautiously. "Ye see, there were others what wanted her dead too, an' were willin' ta pay for it. The turnkey in Newgate said someone in London was anxious ta pay for her death. He even said some real good things could be done for me if'n I'd snuff out her breath an' send back proof ta him. But with him bein' in England an' me here so far away, it didn't seem likely I'd ever collect me due if I sent the li'l bog-trotter ta the grave. I've even been thinkin' lately he was probably hopin' I'd do it an' then provide the proof so's he could collect all o' the reward. An' me be damned."

Edith had realized there had been flaws in her efforts to arrange for Shemaine's demise, but unfortunately they had been unavoidable. Her barrister had understood the importance of the nobility protecting its name and heritage, and although he had enticed the thieftaker to arrest the girl and the magistrate to work his wiles in sentencing the girl, he had refused to be personally involved in arranging the murder of a young woman from a wealthy family. Consequences would be too steep, he had argued, and in that matter at least, no amount of coin could persuade him to do otherwise. He had a serious aversion to hanging, he had explained, but he would, however, find her a name of one who'd be willing to do the deed and arrange for her to contact the man incognito. Several nights later he had reported that there was such a man, a turnkey at the prison who had killed for hire before. But as Edith had later found out, that one had failed her. Now she was looking for new possibilities.

Edith concluded her bath, donned a chemise and wrapped a dressing gown around her slender frame. Joining the harlot on the other side of the sheet, she seated herself on a bench and picked up the conversation as Morrisa began brushing out her long, heavily grayed black hair. "I was wondering, Morrisa, if anyone has ever tried to do away with Shemaine."

"Aye, but so far the bloke ain't done nothin' ta speak o'."

"Someone you know?"

"A tar from the *London Pride.* He's kinda mean-minded toward Sh'maine, says he owes her for her uppity ways. But Mr. Thornton came inta town a couple o' times ta warn me that he'll come lookin' for me an' Potts if'n Sh'maine's e'er hurt again or killed. Well, it didn't rightly seem fair, him blamin' me, but he vexed me so, I warned Potts ta hide out for a while, else he'd be gettin' us both inta an ugly stew."

"If you were able to go anywhere you wanted to, someplace where this Mr. Thornton couldn't find you, would you consider letting Potts have his revenge on her?"

" 'Twouldn't hurt me none ta see the bogtrotter buried, but I'd ne'er kill her meself, so's if'n ye're thinkin' ye're gonna catch me up in a hangin', ye ain't."

"You needn't fret yourself, Morrisa," Edith encouraged. "I've wanted Shemaine dead just as much as you, but that event has never come about."

Morrisa couldn't imagine a proper lady wanting to see harm done to another. But then, she had never been around aristocrats long enough to be able to grasp what any of them were likely to think. She was inquisitive nevertheless. "Why would a fancy liedy like yerself be wantin' Sh'maine dead? What she e'er done ta ye?"

"She stole my grandson's heart, and I abhor her for that."

A loud, unladylike snort accompanied Morrisa's reply. "His heart ain't the only one Sh'maine's done stolt. That Mr. Thornton's gone an' claimed her as his."

"Yes, I've heard that some colonial had bought her—"

"Not only bought her but bedded her!"

"You mean she's been sullied?" Edith was at first jubilant over the idea, but when she considered her grandson's determination to find Shemaine, it seemed doubtful that Maurice would ever blame the girl because she had been forced by her master. A laborious sigh slipped from Edith's lips as

she imagined Maurice making magnanimous offers of marriage to the girl despite
the likelihood of her being with child by another man.

"I'm afraid her lost virginity will change
nothing. My grandson has been thoroughly
bewitched. The little trollop has her claws on
his heart and will not let go."

"Well, I'm thinkin' Sh'maine'll be havin' ta
make a choice betwixt the two, 'cause Mr.
Thornton ain't gonna let any wife o' his go
traipsin' off with 'nother man without a fight.
He killed his first wife, so's I hear. If'n he
catches Sh'maine cavortin' with yer grandson, he just might kill her, too."

"Shemaine is married, then?" Edith
asked, receiving a pert nod when she
glanced around. "Perhaps that fact might
dissuade Maurice from involving himself."

"Humph. If'n yer grandson be the one
what faced Sh'maine an' Mr. Thornton right
out in front o' this here tavern last night, he
didn't seem too keen on givin' her up, even
knowin' she's hitched ta the colonial."

"How I've longed to see her dead." Edith
sighed wearily. "If I could only find the right
person to carry out such a deed, I'd give
them a fortune."

Morrisa chewed her fingertip thoughtfully for a moment, wondering if she could trust the woman. If the elder was seeking to entrap her, then she'd be a fool to suggest that she could arrange for something terrible to happen to Shemaine. Still, why would Edith du Mercer travel all the way from England just to lure a harlot into a trap? The idea was so farfetched it was ludicrous.

From the very first moment of their meeting downstairs, it had been evident to Morrisa that this grand lady was tenacious and had a direct purpose in mind. And the more they talked, the more she became convinced that this was no lily-white angel she was keeping company with. "Right off, I can tell ye that this here Potts is just itchin' ta slice Sh'maine's throat."

"If you can get him to do away with Shemaine, there'll be a substantial reward in it for you. If you came here on the *London Pride,* then I would assume your papers of indenture are being held . . ."

"By Freida . . . the madam."

"With the funds I'm willing to give you, Morrisa, you'd be able to buy your freedom and set up your own company of girls anywhere you have a desire to go. If you're

caught, of course, you must not say anything about me encouraging you to do the
deed. 'Tis doubtful that anyone would believe you, but if you were to incriminate me,
I'd certainly repay you in kind and send
someone to get rid of you. There would,
however, be an even greater reward for
keeping silent, and since you wouldn't be directly involved, I could probably arrange for
your freedom."

"I knows when ta hold me tongue, m'liedy.
Ye needn't worry 'bout me."

"The moment I saw you I thought we'd be
able to understand each other."

" 'Tain't hard ta get Potts ta kill Sh'maine
with just meself doin' the talkin'. He'll do
anythin' I ask him. He'll have ta kill Mr.
Thornton, though, ta protect both our skins
after he kills Sh'maine. Afterwards, Potts'll
be needin' some coins ta tide him over while
he hides out. His own is down ta nubbins."

"I'm willing to pay him, a little beforehand
to encourage him and a greater reward afterwards, if he does the deed."

"Just in case he don't, I'm thinkin' there's
'nother one what might do the deed for her
own pleasure. She ain't gots no idea o' what
I seen or what I figgered out 'bout her an' a

certain pipsqueak what gots hisself killed 'cause o' her. She's too high an' mighty ta talk ta me, but if'n ye're willin', m'liedy, she might be o' a mind ta talk ta ye. I'm also a-thinkin' she wants outa this here place real bad an' will be needin' a fat purse ta break free."

"Do you think we need to have Potts and this other woman trying to kill Shemaine at the same time?" Edith remembered how trim and petite the girl had seemed standing before her after rejecting an offer of wealth beyond the shores of England. It didn't seem likely that two assailants were needed.

Morrisa was of a different mind. "Potts bungled his attacks too many times for me likin' an' ain't gained nothin' from 'em 'ceptin' a hole in his side. Mr. Thornton'll likely shoot him on sight if'n Potts don't kill him first. That's the main one I'm skeered o' 'cause he'll chase me down clear ta the end o' the earth ta get his revenge for us killin' his darlin'. But even if Roxanne Corbin is seen, she could at least get close 'nough ta Sh'maine ta do her some real harm, an' I'm thinkin' she'd be happy ta have a chance ta get a weighty purse 'sides."

"And this Roxanne Corbin is the one to whom you wish me to speak?"

"Aye, she'd be wantin' ta do the deed, alright, seein's as how Sh'maine stole the man what she was plannin' on marryin'. From what I heared from that li'l pipsqueak after the two o' them got into a squabble, Roxanne was real taken on Mr. Thornton maybe as far back as ten years. Some say she was servicin' his needs, but ol' Sam said not, 'cause she's too ugly an' Mr. Thornton's gots an eye for the pretty ones. Right after Thornton married his first wife, Roxanne went sorta crazy. Then his missus was kilt, an' first thing ye know, she's a-keepin' the Thornton house an' a-makin' plans ta wed him.

"Then Sh'maine come along, an' this Thornton fella up an' marries the bogtrotter. That left Roxanne a-stewin' an' a-frettin' like she was 'bout ta bust open with envy. Right now she's tryin' ta tell everybody Thornton kilt his first missus. But I knows she wants him back. I can sees it in her eyes when he prances his handsome self down the street with that bold stride o' his. O' course, she don't knows I'm a-watchin' her. Roxanne's so anxious ta get him 'neath her petticoats, all he'd have ta do is snap his fingers an' she'd snatch 'em up high just ta speed their couplin'. Truth be, Mr. Thornton's so caught on Sh'maine, he ain't wantin' nothin' atall from ol' horse-face or nobody else. I even tried ta talk him inta comin' upstairs with me, but he wouldn't have any o' what I could've given him. Roxanne has ta know she ain't gots a mule's chance with Sh'maine a-livin' . . . so's 'twould seem ta me she'd be awfully willin' ta consider snuffin' out the bogtrotter's life. If'n she's o' a mind ta do the killin', a purse'd push her forward, 'cause then she could skedaddle from her pa."

"You seem to know a lot about the people of this town, Morrisa."

The harlot shrugged. "Some o' me customers are real talkative at times. But then, I sees a lot while tryin' ta drum up business."

"You said you saw something that Roxanne did to this pipsqueak, as you call him?"

"Aye, I was in his house the night he was killed. She caused it, all right. Not that she laid a hand ta him, ye understand, but she's guilty just the same."

"If she's not willing to murder Shemaine for a purse, perhaps I'll be able to convince her that it will be to her advantage to comply unless she wants to be arrested for a man's murder."

"Like I said, m'liedy. Roxanne didn't do it exactly," Morrisa maintained, stressing the point.

"Well, if she laid a snare for the man, she's just as guilty, isn't she?"

Morrisa set her jaw slightly askew as she debated the danger of threatening the smithy's daughter. "She'll set her hound ta chewin' me hide if'n ye mention me name, m'liedy. I'll be as good as dead if'n they catch me."

"Is that why you wish me to speak to her? Because you're afraid of her?"

"I ain't 'fraid o' many, m'liedy, but what I seen that night sure sceered me a-plenty."

"Very well, Morrisa. I'll try to convince Roxanne to do what I want without using any threats. I'll give you a missive to send over to her this very afternoon. If at all possible, I'd like to see this venture accomplished before dusk on the morrow. I would prefer it if my grandson remains incognizant of both my arrival and my departure. So the sooner Shemaine dies, the better my chances will be to make good my escape."

"Ye don't think word will get around, m'liedy? This be a mighty talkative town."

"I'm willing to take that chance. Besides, if I'm gone by the time the townspeople start chattering, I can always say that I was searching for Maurice and was told he had gone up north or some such tale."

Morrisa smirked. " 'Twould seem I ain't the only liar in this here room."

Edith raised a lofty brow.

CHAPTER 24

A contract for the sale of the brigantine had been drawn up between Gage Thornton and Nathanial Beauchamp, designating the latter as the future owner of the vessel upon its completion. It had been a fair and equitable agreement for both men, but now that Gage faced the difficult choice of closing down his cabinet shop and building ships full-time, he realized he would be terminating what had become a very lucrative enterprise. There was also the fact that Ramsey Tate, Sly Tucker, and the two younger apprentices depended on the furniture-making business for their livelihood. Unless he continued to supply them with his designs and his expertise at matching grains and seams, the men would be at a considerable disadvantage. They were hard workers and skilled at what they did, but not necessarily creative, certainly not enough to compensate for the lack of his close direction and talent.

Gage had never hidden his aspirations from his men, and after the Beauchamps' departure, he had gone down to the cabinet shop and, with understandable jubilation, announced that he had sold his ship. It soon became apparent from the forced smiles of the cabinetmakers that they had been dreading what was in the offing. Their subdued congratulations made him wonder if they hadn't recognized their own limitations and were reluctant to argue in their own behalf. Perhaps they had even thought it was futile to try to persuade him to give up his long-held dream of becoming a major shipbuilder. He had found it immensely enlightening to see their sudden elation when he informed them that, after further consideration, he had decided it would be foolish for him to cease the production of furniture. He would therefore confine his shipbuilding ambitions to what he had done for nearly the last decade, constructing a vessel slowly and surely one day at a time.

Shemaine was equally delighted at the news, for she could not imagine her husband giving up a craft at which he was so skilled and gifted. The two of them had stolen a private moment together in their bedroom while the elders continued to play cards in the parlor and Andrew napped in his own room. Maurice had begged passage to Newportes Newes with the Beauchamps, but had ruefully promised Gage that he would be back on the morrow, for he would not leave Shemaine until the matter between them had been put to rest one way or the other. Bess and Nola were in the kitchen cooking supper, and for the first time since her parents' arrival that morning, Gage and Shemaine were able to enjoy the pleasure of just being alone together.

"Besides, you can't stop making furniture now," his wife told him. "You'll be needing to build more beds and other things for our growing family. After visiting with the Beauchamps, I'm convinced that we've both missed out on the fun of having brothers and sisters and should seriously consider having a large family. Oh, Gage, think of how much enjoyment we could have bringing up a family and, when we're old and gray, having grandchildren visiting us and crawling up into our laps for a kiss or a story. 'Twould be a veritable wellspring of delight and an elixir of youth. Why, look at your father. He has gained new life just being with Andrew."

Her persuasive arguments drew a grin from Gage's lips. " 'Twould mean a lot of work for us, nurturing and teaching them good manners, but imagine the pleasure we can have making them." He smoothed the folds of her gown over her stomach and drew back for a pondering perusal. To allow him a better view, his wife twisted this way and that, but he shook his head, noting no change since the last time he had inspected her. "As slow as this one's growing, it won't be out of the coffer until early next year."

"You're teasing me," Shemaine accused with a soft giggle, and snuggled contentedly against him. "You know full well that's when the baby is due."

"Aye, but I was wondering if you had forgotten about the nine months it takes for a babe to hatch. With the number of children you're obviously wanting, madam, 'twould seem to me that you'd always be having one brewing and another nursing at your breast."

Shemaine could imagine the frenzy of having to cope with so many close to the same ages. "Well, perhaps it wouldn't be right to rush them too much. After all, we must give each of them time to reap the benefits of their infancy before booting them out of the crib."

Gage chuckled in full agreement. "And we'd have more time to relish precious moments with our children. 'Tis far more important to cherish a child and discipline him in a gentle, caring way so he feels loved and secure, knowing where his boundaries are within the family. Indeed, madam, 'twould not be considerate of us to raise a large brood of unruly hooligans that everyone else hates."

Shemaine smiled as she traced her fingers downward from his temple to the firm line of his jaw. "Your wisdom has already proven itself with Andrew, my love, and I shall endeavor to heed your advice after our baby is born, though I know I'll be tempted to pamper the sweetling unduly."

"And that would be good for you both, but let us not make the new baby the most important member in the family. After all, my love, your husband enjoys being nurtured at your breast, too."

"Oh, I would never give up that ecstasy, my dearest," Shemaine averred. "With just a simple reminder, my breasts tingle in anticipation." Her sparkling eyes nearly bedazzled her husband as she clasped his open palms over the swelling mounds. "You see what you do to me."

His thumbs brushed across the hardened peaks, drawing sighs of pleasure from her. "Did I tell you how beautiful you look in your own clothes?" Gage breathed, brushing his lips against her brow. "You've always been a delectable vision in Victoria's gowns, and I certainly didn't mind how tightly they adhered to your breasts, but your own suit you better."

"Now at least I can breathe," she replied, sucking in a deep breath and, in the process, expanding her bosom against his hands.

"Still, wearing your own clothes isn't quite as delectable as when you wear none at all," Gage whispered.

Shemaine lifted a warmly suggestive smile to meet his glowing eyes. "The same can be said of you, Mr. Thornton." She slipped her hands around behind his hips to stroke the taut muscles admiringly. "You have the handsomest backside I've ever had the pleasure of viewing. . . ."

"In all probability the only one you've chanced to view," he countered in amusement.

"True," Shemaine conceded, "but I can appreciate good lines when I see them."

"Maurice is tolerably good-looking. How do I compare?"

Drawing back within his embrace, she feigned a perplexed frown. "I don't know, Mr. Thornton. Maurice is quite a handsome specimen. . . ."

"Humph!"

Gage's derisive snort evoked delicious giggles from his wife. "Why, sir! I do believe you're jealous!"

"I was better off not knowing just how handsome your fiancé is," he commented dryly, folding his arms across his chest and lifting his gaze to the ceiling. He maintained a stoic stance for a moment until her laughter made him look down his noble nose at her. Then, rather incredulously, he queried,

"Is that all you appreciate about me, madam? My backside?"

Nestling close against him, Shemaine purred silkily. "Certainly not, sir. There are other areas I find much more intriguing, but you'd think me lewd for admitting that I suffer from a particular fixation."

Much placated, Gage slipped his arms around her again and was not at all surprised to find himself responding to her suggestive remark. His lips widened with amusement as he considered his own eagerness. "Haven't I always encouraged your boldness, madam? Perhaps we should explore your fetish further."

She sucked her breath in through her teeth, as if anticipating a delicious feast. "Don't tempt me now, sir. Tonight will be better. With so many visitors in the cabin, these walls are not thick enough to deafen my cries of delight."

"What? Are you afraid you may give your mother the wrong impression about her innocent little darling?" Gage teased, remembering her earlier comment.

"Aye!" Shemaine grinned enticingly as her hand moved downward between them, making him catch his breath. "I don't want her to know that I've become an insatiable wanton, always hungry for the pleasures you arouse. My mother would faint dead away if she were to learn about my obsession."

Her husband grinned down at her. "Do you actually suppose she's never touched your father the way you're touching me now?"

Shemaine tilted her head at a contemplative angle. " 'Tis hard for me to imagine my mother being so . . . so forward."

"Your parents love each other, Shemaine. Is it too much to suppose that your mother would be eager to please your father in the same way you please me? And do you really imagine that we're the only married couple in the world who make love without our clothes and a sheet between us? You're far more of an innocent than you might imagine, my love, if you believe that."

" 'Tis rather hard for me to envision my mother and father doing everything we do," Shemaine confessed.

Gage smiled as he caressed her breasts again. "They may not be as creative, my sweet, but please allow that they may have some imagination."

Shemaine heaved a disconcerted sigh and seemed suddenly shy about fondling him. "I'll not be able to look at them now without envisioning them together in bed."

Gage chuckled at the honesty of his young wife. "I'm sorry I've vexed you with such worries, my love."

She pouted prettily. "You should be, but I can understand that you might have been jealous of Maurice and were tempted to seek a bit of revenge."

"Him again!" Gage growled, and struggled hard to laugh away her suggestion. "How I wish I'd never seen his pretty face!"

"You needn't worry, my love." Shemaine sighed, nestling against him. "You'll always be far more handsome in my eyes than other men will ever be. But then, my vision is somewhat obscured by love."

"As long as I have that, madam, then I'll be deliriously happy. And as much as I desire to stay in here and play with you, I must go down to the ship before the Morgans leave and talk to Flannery about some things."

"And I'd better wake Andrew or he won't be able to sleep tonight," Shemaine said.

"Give me a kiss, then, to last me 'til we're

together again," Gage urged, pulling her close to him.

Eagerly rising up against him, she slipped her arms about his neck and gave him what he had demanded until all of his doubts about Maurice had been swept away.

There was something about having the brigantine sold that allowed Gage to see the vessel in a whole new light. Whereas before he had been intent upon the unfinished areas and blinded by the clutter of building supplies that was ever before him, his vision now seemed much clearer and more comprehensive. His workmen had gone home, and the O'Hearns, Nola, and Mary Margaret had left with them, the latter to be escorted to her home, while their other guests would stay with Ramsey. Only Bess and Gage's immediate family now occupied the cabin. His father had retired to the loft, Bess was in the kitchen preparing bread and victuals for the morrow, and Shemaine was giving Andrew a bath. For one last time before the day came to an end, he wanted to walk the deck again and see everything bathed in the rosy glow of early dusk. With that time approaching, he was feeling strangely elated and yet a bit torn and somber deep within himself.

In the coming months he would see the vessel sail away, and he likened it to losing an old friend that he had coddled and nurtured for the last eight or nine years. Beginning all over again would be a challenge, but having a ship of his own making and design sailing the seas would be like having the wind at his back. The refreshing zephyrs of success would push him ever onward toward greater challenges. Difficulties would not seem so impossible to surmount; coins would not be so hard to come by. People would not scoff at his ideas or be so quick to condemn him for a fool. His father might even come to seek his advice or join him in his efforts.

The elder had recently mentioned that he had been thinking of selling everything he owned in England and returning to the colonies to live in the surrounding area. After all, Gage's sire had informed him with a chuckle, Andrew needed a grandfather living within visiting distance, and now, with another grandchild on the way, his possessions in England didn't hold his heart as solidly as his family did. And then, of course, there was his new friend, Mary Margaret McGee, who, he now realized, was just as much of an avid cardplayer as he was.

William also predicted that the O'Hearns would eventually come around once their trepidations about Gage's character were put to rest. Gage was not entirely hopeful of that event coming to pass. After all, a whole year and more had gone by, and nothing new had come to light that would exonerate him of Victoria's murder in people's minds. Perhaps her death had been an accident after all, and there was no killer to be found. Over the years, would he cease to be plagued by the suspicions of the townspeople?

Doubtful, Gage mentally sighed. For years to come, visitors like Maurice du Mercer would hear lurid accounts of his "awful" temper and condemn him without a fair hearing. Perhaps Maurice would even come back on the morrow and demand satisfaction in a duel, having been spurred to action by some fabricated "proof" which Mrs. Pettycomb or one of her old cronies had concocted. The Marquess had said he would not rest until he found a definite answer to Gage's guilt or innocence. In the face of such a warning, Gage realized his own limitations with a pistol. He was an exceptionally good shot with a rifle or a smaller firearm, but he was considerably less experienced at turning and firing. It was highly feasible that he would be killed and all the aspirations he had dared to envision would never really come to fruition.

Gage locked his hands behind him and wandered leisurely toward the prow. No one had ever accepted the fact that he had loved Victoria. He had worked diligently to give her everything that a wife could want in a home, and she had always been so excited, so very grateful and pleased with his gifts, that he had labored that much harder to gratify her smallest desire. Mrs. Pettycomb and some of the other townspeople had wrongly interpreted his work habits as a selfish quest to fulfill his own ambitions. But they had been wrong.

Victoria's death had haunted him mercilessly in the months immediately following the event. He had often found himself waking in the middle of the night from frantic dreams in which he had seen himself reaching out desperately to catch her as she tumbled from the prow. But he had always failed. During the long, exhausting daylight hours of his bereavement, he had chided himself relentlessly for having left Victoria alone. For some inexplicable reason, he felt as if he had let her down. Yet that day had been no different from others, for they had often ventured out together to the partially finished deck of his ship and had shared dreams of how it would be once his vessel was sold. Neither of them had ever suspected that she wouldn't be with him when that day arrived. They had been too busy enjoying life and their love for one another.

In degrees of love, Gage had to admit that his feelings for Shemaine had transcended those which he had once felt for Victoria. It seemed impossible, and yet he was convinced it was true. As Victoria's husband, he had once been led to think that no other woman would be capable of taking her place in his heart. He had honestly, deeply, and truly loved her. And yet here he was, totally enamored with his young wife. Sometimes the joy of his love for Shemaine bubbled up within him until he was nigh giddy. Whenever they came together in the intimate rites of love, he felt as eager and excited as an untried youth with his first conquest. Each night when he lay in her arms, he marveled at the overwhelming tenderness and devotion that throbbed in his heart for her. What had happened to him since that fateful day of Victoria's death? Had his remembrance of his love for her only been befogged or diminished by the passage of time? Or was he now able to see himself in a whole different light, like the ship he had designed?

Did Shemaine really know how much he loved her and how his heart seemed to beat entirely for her? If Maurice managed to kill him, could she, in the weeks, months or even years to come, be deluded into thinking that he might have eventually killed her in a fit of temper, just as Roxanne had predicted?

Heaven forbid, not that! His mind groaned. *Just let her go on believing in me! If I must die, don't let her love die with me!*

An almost imperceptible creaking of timbers at the top of the building slip made Gage look around expectantly. Shemaine had told him that as soon as she finished bathing Andrew and took him upstairs for William to read him a story, she would come out and join him on the deck of his ship. But the hulking form that stood there was not his lovely Shemaine.

Jacob Potts leered at him as he aimed a pistol directly at Gage's chest. "Now I have ye," the sailor boasted. "Morrisa said I should kill ye first so's ye wouldn't come after us once I did away with Sh'maine. Makes me sorry I didn't think o' the idea meself afore ye shot a hole through me."

Gage realized he was utterly defenseless. He had no weapon. He wasn't even close enough to Potts to launch himself forward against the man and take him down. All he could hope to do was to gain time until circumstances could be turned in his favor. "You must be aware that my men and I have been searching the woods for you, so if you kill me . . . and Shemaine . . . my workmen will have a good idea who did the deed."

"I don't know no such thing," Potts snarled back. "I ain't been out here since that day ye shot me." He snorted derisively. "Morrisa made me stay 'way after ye paid her a visit an' threatened ta come for us if'n we hurt Sh'maine 'gain. I wasn't skeered o' ye, but she sure was. O' course, Freida tellin' her ye'd kilt yer first wife might've had somethin' ta do with that."

Gage passed his gaze contemptuously over the hulking man. "I can see that you've recovered well enough."

"Aye, but it took a while, blast ye! Too bad the li'l bogtrotter is so tough or I might've killed her that day. Her death would've given me somethin' ta soothe the hurt o' me wound."

"Shemaine has never done you any harm," Gage reasoned. "Why are you so intent on killing her?"

"For one thing, I owe it ta the li'l snip. I promised her, ye see. That day she left the *London Pride*, I swore ta have me revenge on her, an' I always keep me word ta me foes." Potts lifted his massive shoulders briefly. "Now at least there's a goodly reward in doin' 'way with her. Pays me for waitin', so ta speak."

"Who has offered such a reward?" Gage couldn't imagine Roxanne having enough coins to interest Potts or Morrisa. Even deducting what she had to give Freida, the harlot probably earned more in a week than Roxanne could put together in a whole year cleaning and cooking for her father.

"Don't know, but Morrisa does, an' she ain't sayin'."

"Perhaps Morrisa is lying and hoping you'll be shot and killed. I did say I would kill you the next time I saw you out here. She obviously doesn't care about that. So why should you believe her?"

Digging into his purse, Potts produced a smooth leather pouch of too fine a quality to be something the tar would purchase or make. Holding it aloft, he shook it until the contents jingled. " 'Cause for starters, Morrisa give me this here purse full o' coins. If'n she didn't think I'd be comin' back, she'd ne'er've given it ta me. She'd'ave only told me a purse would be waitin' for me."

Gage seemed to consider the man's rationale for a moment, but only to search out possible avenues of escape. A ruse might be effective in fooling the dullard.

Shifting his gaze past the man, Gage frowned sharply toward the top of the building slip and jerked his head to the side, as if cautioning an ally to take cover. But the tar had been warned by Morrisa not to let himself be duped by the wily colonial and was immediately wary of deception. Holding his pistol carefully aimed at Gage, Potts sidled cautiously around until he could take a quick glance toward the slip in relative safety. As he had expected, he found no one there.

"Ye're tryin' ta trick me," Potts accused, narrowing his pig eyes in a piercing glare.

"I'm sorry, I had to do something to save myself," Gage apologized blandly. With a casual shrug, he dismissed his attempt as something to be expected and paced forward with guarded tread, causing the sailor to stumble back with a growl.

"Ye stay where ye are, blast ye, or I'll kill ye right here an' now!"

Gage spread his hands in a gesture of pure innocence. "I'm unarmed, Potts. Why are you so worried?"

" 'Cause ye're full o' pranks, ye are! Like that day ye stepped aside an' booted me in the arse when I went rushin' after ye."

Gage smiled pleasantly, gratified that he had caused the man some embarrassment. "You must allow, Potts, that if the situation had been reversed, you might've done as much . . . *if* you had thought of it, of course." His insinuation that the tar was thick-witted was subtle, Gage had to admit, but even a simple oaf should have recognized the insult. He was rather disappointed that Potts remained oblivious to the slight, so Gage spelled it out for the tar. "Too bad you can't think that far ahead."

"Well, this time I ain't gonna let meself get taken in by none o' yer shenanigans," Potts declared gruffly.

Gage decided to test the man's intelligence even more. Glancing this way and that, he made it seem as if he had lost something. But what he was really contemplating was snatching up an iron maul that was braced against a bucket of sand, very close to his feet. Sending the makeshift weapon flying full force against the tar's noggin would certainly dull Potts's senses, even if it didn't kill him, which Gage sincerely hoped it would do. He was tired of living on the edge of fear, wondering if Potts was near or far or if a member of his family would be hurt or killed by him. At least now his adversary had come out of hiding.

"Now what're ye doin'?" Potts barked, exasperated. "Tryin' ta get yerself killed afore I've had me say?"

"I'm tired of your empty threats, Potts, so spare me your gloating comments. You're nothing but a clumsy mudsucker—"

With a roar of rage, Potts stretched out his right arm and leveled the pistol at his tormentor's head, but Gage ducked and reached for the maul. He only had one chance to stop the tar from killing Shemaine! He fully expected his own life would be forfeited in the process, for he could not hope to throw the heavy hammer toward the man and still remain unscathed by an exploding flintlock.

Even as he heard the faint rasping of a trigger being squeezed, Gage swung the maul upward in a rounded arc over his head. In the next instant an explosion rent the silence as he hurled the hammer forward toward the tar. Gage waited in agonizing suspense for the shot to strike him full in the chest and was amazed when Potts's huge body jerked forward in a convulsive shudder. The maul barely missed the tar's head as he tottered stiltedly on turning feet. A strange gurgling gasp came from Potts's throat, and then a heavy trickle of blood spilled down the corner of his mouth. He gaped at Gage, his astonishment supreme.

Gage was equally stunned as he watched the man. Potts painstakingly raised his arm and looked under it at the large blotch of red that was swiftly mushrooming beneath the sleeve of his white shirt. Through the large hole in the garment, he glimpsed a sticky, dark red rent in the wall of his chest and felt the burning path of the lead shot clear through to his lung. In slack-jawed wonder, Potts lifted his eyes to the slender form standing at the top of the building slip, toward which Gage had directed his gaze a moment earlier.

Shemaine lowered the still-smoking pistol to her side and allowed it to slip from her benumbed fingers as she glared through welling tears at Potts. "You sh-shouldn't have tried to k-kill my husband!"

Gritting her teeth together to keep them from chattering, Shemaine made a valiant attempt to bridle her violent shaking, but her composure was steadily collapsing. Very soon she would be sobbing with the torment of what she had been forced to do. It was the second time she had shot a man to save her husband's life. She liked it no better this time than she had the first.

Awkwardly Potts turned his pistol toward her, but Gage threw himself forward and, with an upward sweep of his hand, knocked the oaf's arm skyward. The deafening roar of the exploding weapon seemed to echo across the river, sending waterfowl flying upward in diverse directions from the far shore. Gage rammed a fist into the broad face of the sailor, catapulting Potts backward and sending him sliding across the planks, leaving a wide streak of glistening red to mark his passage. Potts tried to rise, but his efforts only hastened the flow of blood gushing from his chest. Carefully he laid his head back upon the deck, as if extremely exhausted, and stared up at the rose-colored sky as a flock of birds wheeled across his line of vision. Very slowly he closed his eyes and, with a pensive sigh, gave up his life.

A shout from the cabin drew Gage's attention, and he hurried to the far side of the ship to see William, Bess and Andrew standing on the porch. Gage waved his arm in a wide sweep above his head to assure his father that they were safe. Then the three returned to the cabin's interior.

Gage hurried to his troubled wife and took her in his arms, dropping a kiss on the top of her head as he tried to quell her trembling. "Whatever made you come up here with a pistol, my love?"

"I saw Potts from the front door of the cabin," Shemaine muttered miserably. She had been about to leave when she had seen the all-too-familiar broad shape flitting across the clearing toward the ship. "But how did you see me? I thought I was being so careful sneaking up the building slip."

Gage was totally bemused. "I never saw you."

"But you frowned and looked directly toward me while I was crouching on the building slip. I thought sure Potts would turn and see me."

Gage recalled his ploy to draw the tar's attention away from him so he could launch an assault and was immensely thankful that Potts had been too suspicious to look around immediately. The oaf could have killed Shemaine. "I never saw you . . . or even heard you. I was only trying to divert Potts's attention so I could try rushing him. I never once imagined that you'd be hiding there behind the rail. It frightens me to think what I might have caused trying to distract Potts."

Shemaine sniffed and wiped at her eyes. "I was ready for him. I would have shot him."

"I can't even allow myself to think otherwise." Gage groaned. His heart had already turned cold at the horrible prospect of her being killed.

Shemaine began to shiver uncontrollably as she stared fixedly at the dead man. "I d-doubt that Potts ever considered his h-hatred of us w-would cost h-him his life."

Gage rubbed his wife's arms vigorously to chase away the chill she was suffering. The shock was settling in, and he knew he'd have to get the man out of her sight soon. "I'll carry Potts's body down to the cabinet shop and put together a coffin for him."

"I'd b-better clean the b-blood off the d-deck while you're doing that," she stuttered, unable to stop her shaking. " 'Twill be dark soon, and I w-would hate for the blood t-to soak into the w-wood overnight."

Catching the sailor's arm, Gage drew him up across his shoulders and carried him toward the slip. "I'll come back and help you as soon as I've nailed Potts in a coffin."

Shemaine straightened her spine with willful resolve and, by slow degrees, took hold of herself. When she was calmer, she went to the cabin briefly, spoke privately to William and explained what had happened. She received his assurances that he would put Andrew to bed and the boy would be none the wiser as to what had happened on the ship. She squeezed William's hand, communicating her growing affection for him, and he surprised her by catching her fingers in his grasp and raising her hand to his lips. Nothing was said. There was no need. His fondness for her was becoming more apparent with each passing day. After all, it was the second time she had killed a man to save his son.

Shemaine returned to the deck of the ship with a bucket of soapy water, a bundle of rags, and a scrub brush. Having changed her attire for an older gown and an apron, she shuddered at the gruesome task ahead of her as she settled to her hands and knees on the deck and began scrubbing and cleaning up the gore. She had hoped to spend some time alone with her husband and to share in his elation over the sale of his ship, but at the moment she would have been relieved just to have him near, to have his stalwart presence comforting her. With darkness approaching, she wanted to enjoy the nourishing succor of being with her family and was anxious to return to the cabin. She felt uneasy about being alone. It was almost as if someone was watching her, and she could only surmise that the trauma of killing Potts was plaguing her peace of mind.

The impression of being spied upon finally became too strong for Shemaine to ignore any longer. She sat back on her heels and glanced around toward the companionway, from whence the feeling had first arisen. Immediately her heart lurched, for standing there was Roxanne Corbin with a cocked pistol in her hand and a sublime smirk on her face.

"It took you long enough to realize I was here," Roxanne jeered.

Shemaine could only imagine that the woman had slipped aboard while she was at the cabin and for the last few moments had been enjoying the sight of her rival hard at work.

"I see you've already had one visitor tonight," the woman remarked. "Potts was his name, wasn't it? Poor soul, he really wasn't very handy at killing you, was he, Shemaine? He's tried before, I've been told . . . and was so inept he gained a hole in his side for his attempt. I could have told him that Gage was a marksman, but of course Potts had no reason to seek my counsel. But I can assure you I won't be so careless."

Shemaine rose to her feet warily. "What do you intend?"

Roxanne simpered smugly as she strolled forward. "Are you so naive, chit? When one holds a loaded flintlock aimed at you, what would you normally expect? A simple tête-à-tête?" She scoffed with snide humor. "I've never been one to chat with other women much. I only visited Victoria and made her think I needed her friendship because I wanted to be near Gage. I really hated her, you see. From the very beginning, I wanted to see her die. I abhorred her sweetness and the little favors she did for me. But I never once felt beholden to her. She had stolen Gage away from me, and I never forgave her for that. The night she gave birth to Andrew, I was hoping she'd die before delivering him. Then I wouldn't have been reminded of her every time I looked at the little whelp. I wanted Gage all to myself and loathed sharing him with anyone, even Andrew. But the little brat gave me a reason to come out here, and I took advantage of every moment I had with Gage, hoping he'd relent and marry me."

Roxanne's mouth turned downward in distaste. "Then you came along, and I saw the end of it all. He'd marry you, just like he had Victoria."

The blonde tossed her head, as if shaking away the thought. "But I have no desire to delay your murder until Gage comes back. He might try to stop me, you see. He was that protective of Victoria, too, the fool. I mean to leave you dead so he'll be accused of your murder. Only this time, I won't come rushing in to save him. I'll let him hang from the highest gallows. He's turned me away too many times. After your death, I'm sure the townspeople will be more ready to believe he killed Victoria than they've been in the last weeks. In fact, they'll likely give Gage a swift trial for murdering you both."

Shemaine tried to argue against the cleverness of the woman's plan. "There are other people in the cabin, Roxanne. Your ploy won't work this time."

Roxanne sneered. "Gage was as close as the cabin when Victoria was thrown over the prow to the rocks below. I knew the two of them usually went to the ship together on the days when his men were not here. I hid my father's boat in the brush and watched until I saw Gage go back to the cabin with Andrew. He was so considerate of her, he usually took care of Andrew's needs like that when he could, allowing Victoria a day off, so to speak. He came running after he heard her scream, but it was too late. Victoria was already quite dead by the time he came out of the cabin, but the strange thing about it, she died before she ever hit the rocks. Her neck had been broken, you see, just like Samuel Myers's before he was thrown into the well."

Curiously Shemaine considered her opponent, wondering how Roxanne would have had the strength to accomplish such grisly feats, for the woman did not look abnormally strong. "How did you manage to break their necks?"

Roxanne smiled with amusement. "Actually, I'm not the one who killed them. All I did was convince my friend that Victoria was trying to kill me, sweet little angel that she was. I lured my friend out here by telling him that I needed him to watch over me so I could talk to her and see why she wanted to kill me. For his benefit, I pretended to struggle for my life after I caught hold of her. Naturally my friend couldn't bear to see me hurt. He came out of hiding and grabbed her from behind. Victoria was so fragile, the arm he slipped around her snapped her neck, and then I had him throw her over the prow to make it seem like an accident or a suicide. He killed Samuel Myers for me, too, after that little rat beat me up. But my friend was more intentional about breaking Myers's neck. After all, I had the bruises to prove how much I'd been hurt." Roxanne heaved a sigh as if saddened by some matter. "Usually it's so easy to get my friend to do what I want. All I have to do is pretend that I'm being harmed in some way and he comes running to my rescue. But he's become much too fond of you, Shemaine, and refuses to do you any harm. He even imagines that you're his friend."

"My friend?" Shemaine's brows drew together.

"Really, Shemaine, I don't have time to explain everything to you in detail. 'Twould take hours to tell you how carefully I've planned everything before now, and you're such a simpleton. You can't imagine who it can be, can you? I was terribly frustrated trying to get our friend to kill you. Then a proposal was presented to me this very afternoon, and considering the haste in which it had to be done, I came out to do the deed myself." Roxanne motioned with the pistol, directing Shemaine toward the prow. "I want this over with before Gage gets back here. Then I'm going to leave, fetch my reward and put Newportes Newes behind me forever."

"What reward?"

"I'm being paid to kill you, you dolt. Considering my friend's aversion to hurting you, I would have come around to killing you myself eventually. Being offered a sizeable purse influenced me to do it now. The money will provide me with many of the things I've always wanted. Perhaps I'll even travel to England or some other place. With such a substantial reward awaiting my success, I'll be able to go anywhere I want." Roxanne gestured with the pistol. "Now, hurry, and do as I say."

Shemaine shook her head, becoming quite obstinate. "If you think I'm going to climb up to the prow and let you push me off so you can blame my husband, then you're the one who's a simple dolt, Roxanne!"

"Get over there, I say!" Roxanne barked, tightening her grip on the butt of the flintlock.

"I know how to use this thing, so don't think I won't."

"Oh, I'm sure that you're able to, Roxanne," Shemaine replied. "You seem very cold-blooded about getting what *you* want out of life."

"Aye, I've had to be, living with my father," Roxanne jeered. "All I've heard since my mother left him was how horrible the bitch was to have deserted us. Well, he deserves to be left, and that's exactly what I'm going to do after I kill you—"

"You're proud of what you've done, aren't you?" Shemaine interrupted. "You actually boast when you talk of Victoria being killed and how you planned it all. But you're not as clever as you think, Roxanne. Truth has a way of coming out eventually."

The blonde smirked. "Except for Gage, no one has ever suspected me. I wondered if they would, but none did. I was even fearful of that day when it seemed my friend had hurt you. I was sure that people would begin to suspect me. After all, people knew I had befriended him. It would only take someone who was more canny than most to put it all together. But I had nothing to fear. 'Twas only that stupid mudsucker who had tried to kill you in front of everyone."

Roxanne raised the pistol threateningly, having run out of her short supply of patience. "Now get over there, Shemaine, or your life will end right this very moment."

An inhuman whimpering whine from the top of the building slip startled Roxanne, making her whirl about.

Shemaine smothered a moan of despair as she realized exactly who Roxanne's friend was. It was Cain, the hunchback. He scurried toward Roxanne with an odd, twisted gait and, halting before the blonde, swung his arms in wild gestures.

"Naw Shamawn! Naw Shamawn! Naw Shamawn!" he pleaded in a panic, and reached out to grab the pistol from Roxanne.

"Yes Shemaine!" Roxanne insisted, snatching her arm away from his grasp. Growing visibly incensed, she hissed at him. "She tried to kill me, Cain. Can't you see that? But you don't care about that, do you? All you're worried about is your precious little Shemaine."

"Naw Shamawn! Naw Shamawn!" he sobbed imploringly.

"Hush up, you ugly creep!" Roxanne snarled. "Or we'll have Mr. Thornton down upon us."

Turning to Shemaine again, the woman pointed toward the prow. "Get up there now, you bitch! Or I'll blow a hole through you where you stand!"

"You're going to have to shoot me, Roxanne. And if you kill me like that," Shemaine gritted out, "then 'twill be difficult for you to lay the blame on Gage. There'll be witnesses in the cabin who'll come running and will no doubt see him leave the cabinet shop on his way here. In fact, his father will likely come up here, too, to see what has happened. He's not as agile as Gage, so it may take him a little time to get here, but he'll come. Aye, I think 'tis much better if you kill me with the pistol, Roxanne, because I'll know then that you won't be able to fool the people into thinking that Gage killed me."

"Lift her up on the prow, Cain," Roxanne barked, tossing a glare toward the hunchback. "If you don't, I'm going to shoot your little darling right through the head right now!"

"Naw Shamawn!" he croaked, his face

twisting hideously with the agony that roiled within him. "Plawse naw Shamawn."

"Please! Please! Please!" Roxanne mimicked sneeringly. "Haven't I begged you to help me? And what have you done? Turned a deaf ear to my pleas, that's what! Well, I'm going to kill Shemaine, Cain, and nothing you can say or do will stop me. 'Twill either be a shot through the head or a fall from the prow, but either way, she'll be dead."

Roxanne stretched out her arm, aiming the bore of the pistol between Shemaine's eyes. Shemaine felt her stomach wrench with sickening dread, but she refused to move one step closer to the prow. Allowing herself to be shot was the only way she could save her husband from a hanging.

A bellow of rage came from Cain as he lumbered forward and knocked the pistol aside. It went off with a horrendous bark, echoing through the clearing and the glade.

In the cabinet shop, Gage had just finished nailing Potts's body in the newly constructed coffin when the sound brought him upright with a start. In the next instant he was racing toward the door.

In the cabin, William had just stepped from his sleeping grandson's room when the echoing shot brought him to a sudden halt. Exchanging an alarmed glance with Bess, he hastened toward the tall cabinet near the door, took out a pair of pistols and checked their loading. Ignoring the pain that still encumbered his movements, he stepped out onto the porch, cursing his lack of agility.

Each man ran toward the ship, albeit one more swiftly. While William still picked his way hurriedly down the path from the cabin, Gage was already sprinting up the building slip, frantically calling Shemaine's name. He had just reached the top of the slip when Cain swept an arm around Roxanne's waist and hauled her toward the prow.

"You fool! What are you doing?" Roxanne railed angrily. "Put me down! Put me down, I say!"

The hunchback tossed a glance over his shoulder as Gage ran toward him, but Cain had more strength in his arms and legs than one might have imagined. He hauled himself and his burden up to the prow, despite the woman's screeching and her wildly thrashing struggles to free herself. Holding Roxanne clutched in the crook of his arm, he looked back at Gage and stepped near the edge, bringing Gage to a skidding halt. It became immediately apparent to Gage that if he came one step closer, the hunchback would leap to his death and take Roxanne with him.

"Cain, put Roxanne down," Gage urged quietly.

"Naw! Naw!" Cain shook his misshapen head and waved his free arm in a sweeping gesture, motioning for Gage to retreat. That one had no other choice but to step back several paces.

Cain canted his head at an odd angle and looked down at Shemaine. Tears were flowing down his distorted face, barely visible in the deepening twilight.

"Shamawn maw frawn." He touched his heart briefly. "Cawn lawve Shamawn."

"And I love you, too, Cain," Shemaine answered him anxiously. "You've been a good friend to watch over me." Wiping at the streaming wetness flowing down her own cheeks, she began to beseech him. "Please, Cain, please don't hurt Roxanne. Just come down here where you both will be safe."

"Cawn mawst daw! Cawn kawled Vecta-wrea! Cawn mawst daw!"

Gage had been looking at Shemaine, but

his head snapped around when he realized what the hunchback had said.

"No, Cain, you needn't die," Shemaine argued desperately. "Roxanne made you think that Victoria was going to kill her, but you didn't mean to break her neck when you grabbed her. It was an accident. Then Roxanne told you to throw her off the ship so it would look like Victoria had fallen, but that had been her plan all along." Shemaine glanced at Gage, who was listening intently to every word she was saying. She knew her husband needed and wanted to know everything about Victoria's death, but she could not pause to explain now, not when she had to stop Cain from jumping off the ship to the rocks below. "You thought you were protecting Roxanne from Victoria, but Roxanne lied to you, Cain. Victoria would never have hurt her. She thought Roxanne was her friend."

"Cawn mawst daw! Rawxawne mawst daw!"

At his declaration, Roxanne renewed her frantic efforts to free herself and began to claw at the gruesome face, crying in frightened hysteria, *"Let me go, you buffoon! Let me go, do you hear! I don't want to die! I want to live!"*

"Gawdbawe, Shamawn."

With that muttered farewell, Cain swept his captive around and leapt from the prow of the ship. Roxanne's scream lasted no more than a second, then it was forever silenced. Shemaine and Gage ran to the prow, and by that time William had gained the bottom of the building slip. He made his way back to the two whose broken forms lay sprawled across the jagged rocks. Though it caused him some agony, he bent down to examine each carefully. Roxanne's neck had been broken by the fall; Cain was still alive, but just barely. He lay sprawled across the boulders, but one that was taller and sharper than the rest bulged upward beneath his back. Wheezing loudly, the hunchback tried to smile as he felt William's hand gently stroking his arm, but he coughed instead, spewing up some of the blood that was rapidly filling his lungs. There was a horrendous pain in his chest, as if a long knife had been plunged through him. Then Cain saw Shemaine leaning over the prow above him with tears flowing down her cheeks.

"Lawve Shamawn . . . maw frawn," he whispered. Then he closed his eyes, took a gurgling breath, and grew very still . . . and lifeless.

"Poor man," William muttered sadly.

Gage lifted Shemaine from the prow, and together they ran down to join his father.

" 'Twill be too late to take the bodies into Newportes Newes tonight," Gage said. "I'll have to leave them in the cabinet shop until morning. Ramsey and the rest of the men can help me load the coffins in the wagon for the trip into town."

"I'll help you build them," William offered.

"I'd rather you go in and see about Andy, Father," Gage said. "He might have heard the shots or the screams and may be wondering what has happened. He'll be frightened if he wakes to find only Bess there with him."

William understood his son's concern. "I'll go inside and sit with the boy."

"Thank you, Father." Gage realized how much discomfort it must have caused his father to come such a distance from the cabin. He stepped near to lend the older man assistance. "Here, let me help you back to the cabin."

William laid a hand upon his son's arm, forestalling him. "I'd rather you stay with Shemaine, son, and watch after her. She's carrying my grandchild, and after what she's been through, I'd like to see her resting in bed so there'll be no chance of her losing it. If she will consent to come back to the cabin with me, then I'd be able to watch after her while you're finishing up with the coffins."

Shemaine managed a shaky smile for the elder. "I'm all right, your lordship."

"Why don't you call me William or Father, Shemaine," William suggested. "Papa sounds much nicer, but I'm afraid, with your own father around, it would cause some confusion."

She went to him and rose up on tiptoes to brush a kiss against his leathery cheek. "Thank you, Papa William."

His lordship smiled and nodded. "It sounds nice, daughter."

When his wife came back to him, Gage slipped a comforting arm around her shoulders. "Papa's right, Shemaine," he murmured, revising his own address and, in so doing, bringing a start of happy tears to his sire's eyes. "Why don't you go in and rest? I don't need any help. And I'm sure by now

you must be feeling at wit's end with everyone coming out of the woods trying to kill
us."

"I've got almost all of the blood cleaned
up from the deck," Shemaine said unsteadily. "Yet I'd rather not go back up there all
alone again . . . at least not yet."

"Nor will I let you." Gage raised a hand to
indicate William, who was still waiting. "Why
don't you let Papa escort you back to the
cabin? I'll be in as soon as I'm finished with
my tasks."

"I'm worn out," Shemaine admitted. "But
I want to help. 'Twill keep my mind busy so
I won't be reliving everything over and over.
And Cain will need to be washed up before
he's laid in the coffin. I can do that while
you're making the coffins, then we can come
back to the ship together and finish cleaning
the deck."

"All right, my sweet, if that's what you'd
prefer."

"Then I'll leave you two," William said reluctantly. "But don't be too long. I'm going
to fret until I know you're both safe inside
the cabin."

With Shemaine there, Gage dared not tell
his father that he might have good cause to

be concerned while there were still others in the area willing to pay for Shemaine's death. His young wife had been through a lot, and if she hadn't overheard what Potts had told him, then it was just as well, at least for the time being.

Shemaine brought the subject to light herself. "Gage, Roxanne said that someone had paid her to kill me. . . ."

William paused to look back at them. He had become concerned about his son's young wife, and her statement assured him that he had good reason to be.

"Potts said the same thing," Gage acknowledged with a weary sigh. " 'Twould seem someone is very serious about wanting you dead, my love."

"But who would seek after my death besides Morrisa?" Shemaine asked, totally baffled. "Morrisa wouldn't waste her money trying to get Potts to kill me. He'd have done it for her willingly."

"I don't know who it could be, my love," Gage replied. "But I intend to find out. Potts said that Morrisa knows who it is. I'll be paying her another visit tomorrow, right after I take the coffins into Newportes Newes."

A troubled sigh slipped from Shemaine's

lips as she searched her mind, but she found no face to put to this unknown adversary, at least none here in the colonies. "I won't be able to sleep wondering who had enough money to pay them."

"Then let us be about our tasks, madam, so we can finish up everything and go to bed," Gage urged. He stepped across the rocks and lifted Roxanne. He was amazed at himself for thinking how much heavier the woman felt in his arms than his wife. But then, it was true. He wasn't being illogical, despite the trauma of having had three more lives snuffed out on his ship. After tonight, he would be hoping to see the last of the vessel before any further disasters solidified his niggling apprehensions.

William walked with them as far as the cabin and went inside as they made their way to the cabinet shop. Gage returned for Cain's body and laid the hunchback on a table near Roxanne. At Shemaine's insistence, Gage fetched her a pitcher of water and a basin, then observed her with growing concern as she began to wash the blood from Cain's face. Her hands were trembling, and soon her whole body was shaking. He tried to distract her with questions as he took the cloth from her and took over the task himself. "What was that about Cain killing Victoria? You said Roxanne had lied to him. . . ."

Unable to drag her gaze away, Shemaine stared fixedly at the gnarled face of the hunchback as she told her husband everything that Roxanne had told her.

" 'Twould seem that Cain was Roxanne's own private dupe, poor soul," Gage commented at the conclusion of her story.

"I really don't think he meant to harm Victoria," Shemaine murmured. "He just didn't know his own strength, but it served Roxanne's purposes well. I think, at the very last, Cain realized just how evil Roxanne really was. That's probably why he said Roxanne had to die."

"He obviously thought he deserved to die, too, for killing Victoria," Gage reflected. "He judged himself and decreed the sentence of death was fit and just for what he had done."

"Roxanne said Cain was more deliberate about breaking Samuel Myers's neck before he threw him down the well."

"Well, at least I'm better able to understand Myers's death than I could Victoria's," Gage said, heaving a sigh. "She was so kind to everyone, I just couldn't imagine why anyone would want to murder her, and yet I refused to think that she had jumped to her death. The only one I ever suspected was Roxanne, but I just couldn't figure out how she managed to lift Victoria over the prow and throw her down. Victoria may have been slender, but she was incredibly strong for her size. No doubt Roxanne realized beforehand that she would need an accomplice to kill Victoria and lured Cain into believing her lies."

The whys and wherefores of Roxanne's motives and Potts's vengeful bent had been rehashed several times before Gage and Shemaine finally returned to the cabin. For the first time since their wedding day they did not conclude the evening making love. Shemaine was visibly distressed, and it was some time before she calmed down enough to drift to sleep in her husband's encompassing arms. Gage was too afraid for his wife to even think of trying to relax, for he could find no release for his roiling thoughts.

Once the house was quiet and dark, Gage roamed the interior, peering out the windows into the ebon darkness beyond the glass panes, rechecking the bolts on the doors, and placing his rifles within easy reach of the front portal. But after he realized he was disturbing Bess, who had spread a feather-filled mat on the floor of the kitchen, he went back to the bedroom and closed the door. He rechecked the loading in his pistols and, placing one on his bedside table, slipped into bed beside his wife. Taking her in his arms again, he stared up at the ceiling, mulling over the possible culprits in his mind. He could name very few, and although Morrisa was at the head of that list, he could only think of one person with enough wealth to enlist others in her efforts to get rid of Shemaine. With Maurice du Mercer's presence in the colonies, there could be a serious connection, albeit a very slim one. Still, Gage promised himself that he would go to the docks on the morrow to make inquiries among the captains just to see if a titled elderly lady had bought passage from England aboard one of their vessels and had recently arrived in Newportes Newes.

Daylight finally came, and after a hearty breakfast that Bess laid out for him, Gage went down to the cabinet shop. By that time Ramsey and the other men had arrived and were looking rather apprehensively at all the newly made coffins. They could only wonder if their employer had gone into that particular business.

"Ye can just tell us if'n ye've decided ta stop makin' furniture," Ramsey offered drolly. "The lot o' us will leave an' ne'er hold it against ye. Better ta walk out o' here on our own accord than ta be shipped out in one o' those."

Gage could not help but chuckle at the unassailable humor of his chief cabinet-maker. "Those boxes seem a bit small for the likes of you and Sly."

Ramsey took exception to his comment and ran his hands down his own torso, which had become rather bulky around the middle lately. "Are ye sayin' we've gotten a bit broad and weighty?"

"A bit?" Gage scoffed with quick humor. His friend's wit had always been a good tonic for easing his woes. "Why, the way you've been filling out lately, I'm wondering if we won't have to widen the doors around here."

Sly chuckled good-naturedly as he joined them. "Aye, I was wonderin' meself if I should extend him the use o' me britches ta cover his backside. Every time he bends over now, he exposes more'n *I* can bear."

Gage broke out into hearty laughter as Ramsey turned a wickedly baleful glare upon his fellow cabinetmaker. Already his heart was feeling lighter.

About that time, Gillian came charging through the door, looking for Gage. At sight of the three coffins he halted abruptly with one foot still dangling in the air.

"Holy Mother o'—" he breathed as he slowly lowered his foot to the floor. The young Irishman stared agog at the pine boxes and, after a moment, faced Gage with a noticeable gulp. "Who did ye put in 'em, Cap'n?"

"Roxanne, Cain, and Potts," his employer answered simply.

The three men gaped at him in shocked surprise, and Sly shook his head sorrowfully. "I was hopin' they were empty."

The two apprentices hurried in from the back, curious to hear the story firsthand. All of them congregated around Gage.

"I gather they vexed ye a mite," Ramsey voiced the conjecture, eager to know more. "Ye shoot all three?"

"Nary a one," Gage responded with a

lame smile. "My wife shot Potts, who was trying to kill me. Cain killed himself and Roxanne by leaping off the prow of the ship."

"Ye ever think that there ship is jinxed?" Ramsey prodded.

Gillian would not allow time for that thought to take firm root in anyone's mind. "Why did Cain kill Roxanne, Cap'n?"

"She was one of those trying to kill Shemaine, and he didn't like that idea. 'Tis all rather complicated, so while you're helping me load the coffins in the wagon, I'll tell you as much as I know." He peered questioningly at Gillian, who had apparently forgotten why he had come to the shop. "Were you looking for me?"

"Aye." Gillian suddenly recalled his mission. "His lordship's wonderin' where ye might be, Cap'n."

"My father, you mean."

"Nay, the other one, the younger, black-haired one."

Gage might have known the Marquess would hold to his word. "You may tell him where I'm to be found."

"Aye, Cap'n."

Maurice du Mercer entered the cabinet shop a few moments later, and his reaction upon espying the coffins almost paralleled Gillian's. His foot came down a little sooner and his oath was different, but the look of surprise that registered on his face was quite similar.

"Good heavens! What has happened here? Who are those coffins for? Is Shemaine all right?"

Gage smiled ruefully at the man's rush of questions. "You needn't fear, your lordship. None of these boxes are for my wife. She's in the cabin. She's not feeling too sprightly after killing a man last night."

"Shemaine? My Shemaine?"

Gage felt his hackles rise, and he made a point of correcting the man. "No, your lordship, *my* Shemaine . . . as if there were another."

"What happened?" Maurice asked. "Who was the man, and why did she kill him?"

"To save my life. Someone paid Potts to come out here and kill Shemaine, but the sailor decided to put me in the grave before proceeding to her. Shemaine has become quite handy with a flintlock. A few more lessons and she might even rival your abilities."

Maurice gestured lamely toward the wooden boxes. "Then who else . . ."

"You wouldn't know them," Gage assured him. "A hunchback from town who killed my first wife by accident, and the woman who deceived him and led him into doing it. Someone offered to pay her for killing Shemaine, too."

"Killed your first wife, you say," Maurice repeated that portion dubiously. "Convenient for you, isn't it?"

Gage returned a level stare to the Marquess. "More convenient for me than for you, I would think. Now you won't have any excuse for challenging me to a duel and killing me in the guise of saving my wife from my murderous bent just so you can have her. If you doubt my word about any of this, I give you leave to question Shemaine. 'Twas what she was told by Roxanne and Cain, as much as that poor man was able to explain."

Maurice fished into the pocket of his rich, taupe frock coat and produced the smooth leather pouch that Potts had tauntingly waggled before Gage. "May I ask where you came by this? I found it on the deck of your ship when I went up to ask the Morgans where you were to be found."

Gage examined the bag of coins briefly and then handed it back. "Potts showed it to me when he was boasting about being hired to kill Shemaine. The purse may have belonged to Potts, but it seems too fancy for the likes of the tar. Perhaps it belonged to the person who hired him on as an assassin." Gage tilted his head thoughtfully as he considered the nobleman. Maurice's face had definitely taken on a chalky white pallor. "If it doesn't belong to Potts, would you happen to know whose it is?"

"I may," the Marquess answered in a muted tone. He turned abruptly and strode back to the door. Jerking it open, he paused and looked back at Gage with a wretched smile twisting his handsome lips. "If what you say is true, Mr. Thornton, then you have indeed won my betrothed for yourself. I wish you well, both of you."

"Are you leaving for good?" Gage asked in surprise. He couldn't imagine that the Marquess would give up so easily.

"Aye, I won't be back unless Shemaine is widowed by some other means than what I had intended."

"You will have a long wait ahead of you before you can claim her," Gage informed him. "I plan to live to a ripe old age."

"So be it."

"Shemaine and the O'Hearns will wonder where you've gone," Gage insisted. "What shall I tell them?"

Maurice grew thoughtful as he contemplated the question, then he smiled rather sadly. "Tell them I've gone to catch a mother rat."

With that, Maurice stepped beyond the door and closed it gently behind him.

"Mother rat?" Ramsey was plainly perplexed. "What did his lordship mean by that?"

Gage watched through the window as his rival hurried toward the river. "I think his lordship means to have a talk with the one who paid Potts to kill Shemaine."

"How would he be knowin' who that is?" his friend queried.

"The purse," Gage answered distractedly. "I believe he recognized it . . . or at least the type of purse used by someone he's kin to."

"I didn't think he had any kinfolk here."

" 'Twould seem that circumstance may have recently changed. At least since the Marquess's coming, I would imagine."

CHAPTER 25

No sooner had Maurice du Mercer strode through the doors of the tavern than a definite hush fell over the place. Every harlot who had managed to rouse herself out of bed by that early morning hour paused to gawk at him with jaw hanging a-slack. In comparison to the clientele they had been servicing in the local area, the Marquess looked as luscious and tempting as a plump worm in a chicken coop. Like a brood of cackling hens, they rushed toward him, shoving and yanking at each other in their eagerness to seize this enticing tidbit for their own. True to form, Morrisa managed to force her way to the fore of her companions.

"Can I be o' service ta ye, yer lordship?" she crooned and, as was her habit, moving her shoulder in a rounded motion to send her sleeve tumbling down her arm. Another shrug bared a goodly portion of her ample bosom as well.

"You may," Maurice answered with marked disinterest. "I understand from the innkeeper that my grandmother is staying here. Can you direct me to her room?"

"Well, I don't know, m'lord." Morrisa sidled back several steps, recognizing her blunder. This was the grandson Lady du Mercer had said was in love with Shemaine, and since neither Potts nor Roxanne had returned from the Thorntons' to collect their reward, there was no way of knowing what had happened out there or what this man was after. Whatever his mission, it seemed dire, for his black eyes were like steel sabers slicing through her. Still, her ladyship hadn't wanted it noised about that she was there and certainly not to her grandson.

"If you don't tell me, I can find her myself," Maurice informed her bluntly. "I may startle a few of your companions in the process of opening doors, but I doubt that I'll be unduly embarrassed by the sights I may find behind them. However, their customers might be a bit upset by the intrusion."

Morrisa promptly relented, imagining the dander that Freida would fly into if any of her customers began to complain about being disturbed. She didn't know how her ladyship would react to her grandson's visit, but she had confidence the lady could handle it with far more grace than any of them could abide Freida's raging or vengeful tactics. "The last room on the right upstairs. I just took her liedyship up some tea a li'l while ago, so she's awake an' havin' her vittles."

Maurice leapt up the steps three at a time, leaving several of the strumpets gaping after him. His pace along the balustrade was just as swift, just as sure, and with no more than a quick rap of lean knuckles on the planks of the door, he swung open the portal and stalked into the room, startling his grandmother, who had been sitting at a small table partaking of her morning meal. She half rose from her chair at this unforewarned entrance, fully expecting to see some dirty brigand with a pistol in his hand who would demand her money. When she recognized the familiar face, she slowly sank back into her seat and clasped a bony hand over her fluttering heart.

"Why, Maurice, you startled me," she chided.

"I meant to," he stated crisply.

A brief, nervous twitch at the corner of her lips was the best smile she could manage. She didn't need to be told that something was amiss. "Have you taken to playing pranks on your elders of late?"

"If I have, 'tis a far less disastrous trick than you have played on me."

The delicate fingers trembled slightly as Edith picked up a lace handkerchief and daintily dabbed at the corners of her mouth. "I'm not sure I understand what you mean, Maurice."

The Marquess was not fooled by her innocent masquerade. "You should know far better than I, Grandmother, what you've done. I was in love with Shemaine, and now I've lost her—"

"Is she dead?" Edith had been waiting in anticipation for such an announcement, but she had never dreamt it would be delivered by her grandson, of all people.

Maurice's dark eyes glittered with ill-suppressed rage. "Shemaine is alive, married to a colonial, and carries his child . . . and I would give my whole wealth to be where that man is in her heart today."

Edith's own heart sank at the news of Shemaine's continued existence, but she was as accomplished an actress as Morrisa. "Your whole wealth?" She forced herself to laugh at her grandson's exaggerated assertion and waved an elegant hand to banish his claims. "Really, Maurice, no man in his right mind would give up the like of your fortune for a little twit of a girl. . . ."

"Her name is Shemaine, Grandmother," he stated with sharp clarity. "Shemaine Thornton now. It should have been Lady Shemaine du Mercer. If not for you, it would have been."

"Come now, Maurice, you're overwrought and don't know what you're saying."

"I know exactly what I'm saying." Maurice slipped his hand into the pocket of his waistcoat and withdrew the silky-smooth leather pouch. With a flip of his wrist, he tossed it onto the table near her hand. It landed with a clink of coins. "Recognize it, Grandmother?" he questioned caustically. "You've always been rather proud of your simple but elegant tastes. I need not look inside to see your initials to know that it's yours. I wonder just how many of those fine leather pouches you've had made for yourself over the years? I've seen them all my life. You gave me several while I was growing up. You were trying to teach me the value of a coin, remember?"

Edith's face remained a stiff, careful mask that effectively hid the inner turmoil that was raging inside of her. Her grandson's tone revealed far more than his words had yet disclosed. She knew down deep inside that she had lost this murderous game she had set herself to because of some silly mistake of her own making. She had instructed Morrisa to give Potts a few coins and to promise him more to hasten his return. How could she have known that a tiny little pouch would be her undoing?

"How did you come by this purse?" Edith questioned carefully. "I thought I had lost it."

Maurice curtly denied the possibility. "You didn't lose it. You gave it to Potts when you sent him on a mission to kill Shemaine. But he failed you, Grandmother, and paid for it with his life. That little twit of a girl you can't abide shot him when he tried to kill her husband. You probably promised a sizeable reward to Roxanne Corbin, too, but she won't be back . . . except in the coffin Gage Thornton made for her. What I would like to know, Grandmother, is how you could have been so cruel to me . . . and my betrothed."

Edith du Mercer sat in dignified silence, refusing to answer as she stared unseeing across the room. Her bony hand clasped the silver handle of her walking stick, which she had braced upon the wood floor.

"Answer me!" Maurice barked, slamming his palm down upon the top of the table and startling a gasp from his grandmother. "Damn you for your cold bitch's heart!" he snarled. "I know now that you must have connived with sticky-fingered magistrates and ambitiously arranged for Shemaine's arrest in London and her banishment from England, probably all the while thinking you were doing me a good service . . . for my fame and future as a marquess. It grieves me to think of what Shemaine suffered because of you. After the O'Hearns discovered what had happened to her, I refused to allow myself to believe that you had any part of it. But her disappearance was too convenient, hardly a month after our engagement. You

were so calm in your assurances to me that Shemaine would be found. I saw more distress in your eyes when I announced my intention to marry her." He sneered at his only kin, feeling nothing but contempt for her. "You were probably hoping that news of Shemaine's death would reach you so you could skillfully arrange for the information to come to my attention."

A bitter smile curved his handsome lips. "I'm sure you could buy your way out of any English prison I tried to send you to, so I've chosen a more fitting punishment for you, Grandmother. From this day forward, you shall never see me again. If I go back to England at all, it will be to collect my possessions. But I shall be returning here posthaste to live out the rest of my life as an ordinary colonial gentleman, and you will *never, ever* be welcomed in the house that I will build for myself and my family, should I be fortunate enough to marry. Whatever offspring I produce, Grandmother, you will never see them, never hear them, and never be able to take pride in my children or their children . . . if you should live so long. And you will never be able to arrange their lives as you tried to do mine. This is good-bye forever, Grandmother. May you have a long and miserable life."

Turning crisply on a heel, Maurice crossed to the door and left, causing Edith to flinch with the loud, resounding closing of the portal.

In the aftermath of his passage, Edith du Mercer sat in silence, staring across the room yet seeing nothing. She felt numb inside. Perhaps she was already dead. Everything she had striven for, yearned for, grappled for, had fled from her life with the slamming of that door. She could not even feel a spark of hope or interest when a few moments later a rather frantic rapping came again upon the plank. It was only Morrisa, wondering what had happened.

"Potts and Roxanne are dead," Edith informed her dully. "You'd better leave as soon as you can. There's a pouch of coins in my satchel near the bed. Take that. There should be enough to get you to New York . . . or someplace far off."

"But what about Freida?" Morrisa asked fearfully. "If'n I leave without buyin' back me papers, she'll send someone after me . . . may e'en have me killed."

Edith picked up the pouch that Maurice

had just delivered back to her and handed it over. "Perhaps there's enough in this to buy your papers. In any case, you should leave. I would expect Mr. Thornton will be arriving some time this morning, perhaps to bring in the dead bodies or to search for you. I shall be taking the next coach north myself and then a ship back to England."

Thoughtfully Morrisa tossed the small pouch in her hand, knowing full well what it contained. There was more than enough in it to buy back her papers, but as far as the other purse, she had no idea what it held. She could only hope that it would last her for a time, but once the money was gone, what would she do? Ply her trade again? It was a terrible gamble to leave Freida without paying her back, but there seemed no other choice if she wanted a few coins to spend on herself after she got to wherever she was going. Gage Thornton would be arriving soon and he'd no doubt be looking for her. She couldn't wait around. She had to leave *now!*

Hugh Corbin limped out onto the front porch shortly after he saw Gage halting the wagon in the lane in front of his house. He was aware that Roxanne hadn't come home the previous night, and even before he caught sight of the boxes in the wagon bed, he had already begun to fret that something dreadful had happened to her.

Gage swept his hat off his head as he approached the older man. Hugh squinted up at him, as if wondering at his mission, and Gage halted in front of him. It was the first time in ages that Hugh met him without an insult. "Mr. Corbin, I'm very sorry to have to tell you this, but I'm afraid Roxanne is dead." Turning slightly, he gestured with his hat toward the coffins loaded in the conveyance. "Her body is in one of those pine boxes there. I carved her name in it so we'd know—"

"Ye bastard, why did ye have ta kill her?" Hugh snarled in agony. "Wasn't it enough that she chased after ye an' made a fool of herself ever since ye come here! But that weren't enough for ye, was it? Ye couldn't rest 'til ye took her last breath from her just like ye did Victoria."

"I didn't kill her, Mr. Corbin," Gage assured him quietly. "Cain did."

"Cain?" Hugh Corbin stared at Gage, momentarily convinced that he had taken leave of his senses. "Cain wouldna've killed her!"

"I'm sorry, Mr. Corbin. My wife and I both saw him do it."

"Why?" Hugh demanded. "Why in the hell would Cain do a thing like that to Roxanne?"

Gage heaved his shoulders upward slightly. "Because Roxanne wanted him to kill my wife, and he was unwilling to obey her. He killed Victoria for Roxanne, too, after she tricked him into doing it. When she threatened Shemaine, Cain swept Roxanne up in his arms and leapt off the prow of my ship with her. Roxanne didn't survive the fall. She died of a broken neck after hitting her head on one of the rocks."

Hugh Corbin gaped dully at Gage, hardly able to understand what the younger man was telling him. After a moment of strained silence, he wiped his trembling hands on his breeches and muttered half to himself, " 'Twill take me a while ta dig two graves. . . ."

Gage looked at the smithy, not sure he understood what the man had said. "I thought I'd try to find that old woman's cabin in the woods where Cain lived and bury him out there. If you know where it is, it would help me. . . ."

"I'll bury Cain beside Roxanne."

"Are you sure you want to do that, Mr. Corbin?" Gage asked in quiet sympathy. "After all, Cain did kill her. . . ."

"This was where Cain was born; this is where he'll be buried."

Gage wondered if the shock of Roxanne's death had addled the smithy. "As far as I can remember, the woman in the woods never said where Cain came from. Are you saying that Cain was born in Newportes Newes . . . or near here?"

"He was me son," Hugh answered in a gravely voice. "Me firstborn. He was born a couple o' weeks afore he was due, an' when I saw how grotesque the babe was, I told Leona ta pad her belly so's everybody would think she was still with child. Then I took the babe in the woods an' left him on the ol' woman's doorstep. Didn't seem right somehow ta kill me own son. After the hag found Cain an' spread the news around, I told some people that Leona was goin' inta labor with our own babe, but I wouldn't let anyone come inta the house. Later, I built a tiny coffin, weighted it down with a small bag o' grain an' told the townsfolk that the son what had been born ta me an' Leona had come inta the world dead. I didn't want ta own up ta that hideous li'l creature I'd taken in the woods, but Cain was the only son I e'er had."

"Did Roxanne know that Cain was her brother?"

"I never told a soul . . . 'til this moment . . . an' now it just don't seem ta matter anymore."

Gage left the man alone to deal with his sorrows as best as he could. The smithy had made his own way in life, and it had become obvious to Gage during the short time he was there that Hugh wanted no one to pity him. He would remain as stubborn and harshly stalwart as ever.

Gage helped the smithy unload the top two coffins, then he took the third and a statement of how Potts had met his death to the British authorities in the area. Gage then proceeded to the tavern and found Freida in a raging tizzy.

"I'd like to talk with Morrisa," he informed the madam. "Do you know where she is?"

"I wish I did," Freida snapped irritably. "She left here without lettin' any o' us know she was leavin', an' from what I hears, she caught a ride goin' north with the first fella what come along, a mountain man what's been visitin' her lately. 'Twould seem she ain't plannin' on comin' back any time soon."

"Then I take it Morrisa didn't bother to buy her freedom."

Freida snorted angrily, attesting to the accuracy of his conjecture. "Ye can bet when I catch up with her, she's gonna wish she had."

"I suppose Morrisa was more afraid of what I'd do to her than she was of you," Gage surmised.

Freida squinted a glance up at him. "Potts go out ta yer place 'gain?"

Gage responded with a nod. "This time he tried to kill me and said that Morrisa told him to do it. He meant to kill my wife after doing away with me."

The madam swept him with a lengthy perusal, seeing no visible wounds. "But ye're here an' Potts ain't."

"His coffin is down the street a ways."

Freida pursed her reddened lips in a wrinkled "Oh?" as she leaned back in her chair to stare at him. "So's ye're here lookin' for Morrisa an' maybe thinkin' ye'll do her in like ye promised, but ye're gonna have ta wait yer turn, 'cause I'm gonna find her first an' lay inta her so harsh she's gonna wish she done gone ta the grave."

"Be my guest. As long as she's out of the territory, I think I can forget about her being a danger to Shemaine."

"Oh, I'm gonna bring her back alright or kill her tryin'. I gots friends what keep me informed 'bout things. Until I finds out where she's gone, I'll be a-thinkin' up what'll be the best punishment I can give her for leavin' here without me knowin'. She ain't gonna be much use ta me all scarred up by a whip. The gents won't mind a finger or two missin' on a harlot as long as she's got enough ta get their attention. An' I knows some other stuff what'll make the bitch take notice. If'n Morrisa's smart, she'll behave herself from then on. Otherwise, she'll be regrettin' it 'til her dyin' day. That much I've promised her, an' I always keep me pledge."

Gage didn't know which posed a greater threat to Morrisa, being at the beck and call of a mountain man or being at the mercy of a vicious adversary like Freida. Whatever her fate, he seriously doubted that she would enjoy herself overmuch.

*   *   *

News of Edith du Mercer's hasty departure from Newportes Newes reached Gage
before he left the tavern, and he returned to
his family confident that Maurice du Mercer
had handled the situation in a way that he
had deemed fit. Later, when Shemus and
Camille arrived at the cabin after venturing
into the hamlet, they informed Shemaine
and Gage that Maurice had come to see
them and had explained his intentions. He
was giving some consideration to the idea
of eventually settling near Richmond and
paying court to Garland Beauchamp to see
what would come of that relationship. At the
moment, however, he was still in love with
Shemaine and had decided it was best to
put some distance between them for his
own peace of mind. He was planning on returning to England after an initial visit with
the Beauchamps, and in a year or so would
be returning to the colonies and traveling
upriver to Richmond. If, at that time, Shemaine had been widowed or left to her own
defenses, she was to leave word for him at
the inn in Newportes Newes. Since she was
apparently deeply in love with her husband,
he would leave her alone, but should she

want him ere he wed another, he would return to her stoop with all the eagerness of a smitten swain.

Gage bristled at the announcement, but he could hardly blame the man. In fact, if Shemaine were ever widowed, Gage could not imagine a better man than Maurice to replace him as her husband. Still, Gage hoped he would completely frustrate the Marquess's desires and live to an ancient age with her, for she was clearly the kind of wife a husband could treasure beyond all the ships, fame and fortune in the world.

Shemus blustered at the urging of his wife and cleared his throat as he faced his son-in-law. The fact that William sat nearby only added to his discomfiture. "Now that ye've been cleared o' the murder o' yer first wife, I suppose I must beg yer pardon for the things I said ta ye the first day we met."

"Only if you're sincere about it," Gage assured him cordially. "An apology isn't worth much unless you truly mean it."

Shemaine slipped an arm around her husband's waist and, leaning against his long muscular form, smiled at her parent as she encouraged him to make things right. "You don't really want to geld him now, do you,

Papa? After all, 'twould mean no more grandchildren after the one I'm carrying now is born."

Her father reddened in painful chagrin. "Yer mother an' I wanted a large family, but it was never meant ta be. Several grand-children would make up for all the years o' our yearnin'."

"Then say it, Papa!" Shemaine entreated eagerly.

Shemus cleared his throat and began his apology haltingly. "I'm sorry for what I said . . . for wantin' ta see ye cut, Gage, but . . . at the time . . . I could only imagine that ye'd taken advantage o' me daughter. Can ye forgive me?"

"I can understand that you were con-cerned for Shemaine. In fact, I might have said as much if it had been a daughter of mine." Gage extended a hand in friendship and smiled as it was readily grasped by the Irishman. "We have a common goal, sir, and that is the welfare of Shemaine. I will pledge my troth to you that I'll do everything within my power as her husband to make her happy."

Chortling in good humor, Shemus laid his free hand upon the ones that were still clasped together and shook them, bestowing his hearty approval upon the younger man. "I'm grateful Shemaine was bought by yerself, sir. Otherwise, it might have been a disastrous end ta her adventure."

Shemaine freely expounded upon her father's conjecture. "Before my arrest, Papa, I didn't have the wisdom to search beyond the realm of my own limited aspirations. Against my will, I was set to a different course in life than the one I had directed my sights toward, and yet, looking back, I can only believe a kinder hand must have been guiding me through my hardships, for 'tis boundless love and joy I feel in my heart today for my husband, for my son, and for the child to come . . . and for our families."

"Hear! Hear!" Gage cried, and a triumphant shout of agreement came simultaneously from William and Shemus. "Hear! Hear!"

The foaming waves curled away from the *Blue Falcon*'s cutwater as the vessel skimmed effortlessly away from the tidewater region into the open sea. Her white sails billowed out with the wind pushing at her heels, and beneath the clear blue sky, the gleaming shrouds almost bedazzled those who stood on the deck experiencing the wonder of her first flight. A feeling of awe was shared by all, the captain no less than any.

"She's a beauty!" Nathanial Beauchamp exclaimed, casting a brief glance toward the man who stood at his side. "And you, sir, have created a marvel!"

Gage likened the ecstatic racing of his heart to that special moment when Shemaine had accepted his proposal of marriage. Yet he could find no words to speak, for his heart was full.

William Thornton reached up a hand and laid it upon his son's shoulder, squeezing it in silent communication. The joy that welled up within him had brought tears to his eyes, and he could not trust himself to voice his own praise for fear the gathering thickness in his throat would convey the emotion he was presently trying hard to restrain.

"Daddee, look at the big fish!" Andrew cried, pointing toward the school of porpoise racing along the starboard side. The boy caught Gillian's hand and begged, "Lift me up high, Gil'an, so I can see 'em better."

Shemaine smiled as her husband joined

her. His right arm came around her shoulder, drawing her close as his left hand slipped underneath the large shawl that she had donned to mask her belly, which had just begun to protrude. Beneath the covering of the wrap, he fondly caressed the gentle roundness.

"I think Nathanial likes the *Blue Falcon*, my sweet," Gage murmured.

Shemaine looked up with loving eyes and dared to correct his statement. "I think Captain Beauchamp is mightily impressed with the *Blue Falcon*, Mr. Thornton. He's been grinning ever since we got under way."

"Aye, I've noticed."

"But then, so have you, my darling, almost as much as Flannery." Shemaine inclined her head to indicate the old shipwright, who stood in the middle of the deck, visibly exhilarating in the feel of a good ship beneath him. His wrinkled face was lit up with jubilant glee, and it could be said that his smile stretched from stem to stern, showing his sparse teeth.

Gage thought the old man vividly expressed what they were all feeling. "Nathanial selected the right name for her, my pet. The *Blue Falcon* suits the brigantine. She'll soar through these waters like a bird of prey."

Shemaine cocked her head aslant to gaze up at her husband with a curious grin. "I'm thankful you're not a ship's captain, sir. I fear I'd soon be taking second place to a wooden mistress."

"Eh, never that, my love," Gage murmured, resting his chin on top of her head. "You're my only mistress and my dearest love. I could no more sail away from you than my own heart."

"Aye, 'tis that way with me, too." Shemaine sighed. "I could never leave you. When we first came together in love, it was not only the merging of our bodies but our hearts as well. We've truly become one."

"Aye, love, and our child will be a token of our love, for our joy was complete when you conceived."

Shemaine nestled her head against his chest. "Aye, to be sure, Mr. Thornton. To be sure!"

Epilogue

The gangplank of the newly docked ship from England was lowered, and after the first few passengers disembarked, Gage shifted his one-year-old son in his arm and thrust out an arm to point toward the nattily garbed couple who were vying for a place near the rail. Following her husband's directions, Shemaine finally located her parents and began to dance sideways along the wharf in an effort to get their attention.

"Mama! Papa! Look this way!"

Camille recognized the familiar voice that reached their ears and promptly scanned the dock in search of her daughter. Upon espying Shemaine, she waved an arm. "We're coming, darling! We'll be down shortly."

In a moment Camille and Shemus O'Hearn, followed by a whole complement of servants, were hurrying down the gangplank and running with open arms toward their daughter. Shemaine hugged each fiercely as Gage and William waited behind her with the children. Andrew was clasping his grandfather's finger and was not at all desirous of being kissed and hugged by any of the strangers who came near. Then Shemaine eagerly drew her parents forward to meet their new grandson.

"Mama, Papa, this is Christopher Thornton."

The one-year-old raised an arm to push away the loving caress of the older woman and, turning his green eyes away from her, tucked his dark head beneath his father's chin, making that one chuckle and hug him close. "Christopher takes to strangers no better than his brother does," Gage informed the O'Hearns. "But once he gets to know you, he'll be walking over your toes in his eagerness to get into your laps. He especially enjoys being read to."

"At such a young age?" Camille queried proudly. "What a smart boy he is."

"He looks like his father," Shemus mumbled with some disappointment. He had hoped to see more of his own daughter in the lad.

"Aye, but there's no mistaking where his green eyes came from, dear," his wife said sweetly, patting his arm.

Shemaine could not restrain herself another moment. "Is it really true, Papa, that you've sold everything and intend to live in Williamsburg?"

The elder tucked his thumbs in the pocket of his waistcoat and grinned. "Maurice said there are great opportunities to be found there for an enterprising man. He's living there now with his wife, Garland, and thought I should look into starting a business in the city."

"Oh, Papa, that's wonderful! Now we'll live close enough to visit on a frequent basis."

Shemus glanced up at Gage with an inquiry. "Are you still building ships?"

"Aye, along with my father, who has put in with me," the younger man replied.

"We've hired a few more men, and the work is going a lot faster now."

"Oh, I hope you haven't given up making furniture," Camille interjected, suffering some dismay at the thought. "We sold all of our furnishings before leaving England, so we'll be needing some more as soon as we can find a home."

"The cabinet shop is bigger now," Shemaine informed her mother happily. "And Gage has had to hire several new apprentices to help keep up with the demands of all the people wanting his furniture. In fact, we've enlarged the cabin and have acquired a servant to help me clean and cook. You and Papa will be able to stay with us and have a guest bedroom all to yourselves whenever you visit. William still uses the loft when he comes."

"But what about Mary Margaret?" Camille asked her daughter in a muted tone. "I thought she and William were interested in each other."

"They've had a long friendship, to be sure," Shemaine confided quietly. "But I don't think they're too serious about getting married, certainly not at this time. For one who has the wiles of a matchmaker, Mary

Margaret is not at all sure she wants to give up her single life as a widow. The two of them play cards together quite often, but they're also seeing others. William has all the older women simply goggle-eyed over him, and they're chasing him as hard and fast as the younger ones ever did Gage."

"With good reason," Camille whispered behind a smile. "My dear, if your husband looks as good when he matures to a ripe age as his father does now, then you'll surely have to fight the women off in droves."

Shemaine laughed, unconcerned. "Gage reassures me quite often, Mama, that I'm the only love in his life."

Andrew tugged on his father's breeches. "Gran'pa wants to take Chris and me onto the ship, Daddy. Can we go?"

"Watch your brother carefully now," Gage urged, squatting down. He stood his youngest son on his feet, and immediately Christopher slipped his tiny hand into his brother's. Taking hold of his grandfather's finger, the toddler looked back at his father with a wide grin that was closely reminiscent of the one Andrew had mastered at an early age.

"Bah, Da-da."

Gage chuckled at his youngest son's attempt to talk. "Good-bye, Chris."

Shemus chortled as he took note of his grandson's winsome charm and, bustling behind the other three, followed them up the gangplank. It didn't take him long to win the toddler's confidence as he pointed out the seagulls that were swooping close overhead. Before they left the ship again, he was carrying Christopher in his arms and making him laugh in glee. Camille joined her husband, and together they reveled in the delightful antics of their grandchild.

Gage pulled his wife's hand through his arm and spoke proudly as he watched their family. "Did you ever imagine, Shemaine, that you would see our parents looking so utterly happy? 'Twould seem you've gifted them with new life by bringing Christopher into this world."

"I believe you had something to do with it, too, sir," his wife reminded him with a coy smile.

A smug grin came to Gage's lips as he nodded acknowledgment. "Aye, we both did well by our son, did we not, my sweet?"

"Aye, my love. Very well indeed."

Gage leered at her over his shoulder. "And there's a lot more from whence he came, madam."

Her eyes glowing with love, Shemaine hugged her husband's arm close to her breast and felt the steely muscles flex in warm response against the softness. "Aye, Mr. Thornton, of that I have no doubt."

1-98

Lyons Public Library
448 Cedar St.
P.O. Box 100
Lyons, OR 97358